LANCER

LANCER

GODSLAYERS BOOK 1

T. R. More

Podium

Cover design by Macarious

ISBN: 978-1-0394-7481-9

Published in 2025 by Podium Publishing
www.podiumentertainment.com

LANCER

CHAPTER ONE

Planetfall

I dreamed about the gods again as we broke the translation barrier.

It's so still, that place between worlds. Time and space melt away—the clean lines of the gunner console, the thunder of the seat against my back, the pressure of my clenching fists—into placid infinity. For a moment, for an eternity, it's you against the universe.

The dream was always the same. I dreamed it first when they carried me to Veles, staining the ether with my bleeding soul. I dreamed it again when I graduated from the Academy—when they sent us to some heterocausal battlefield to earn our immortality and I refused to die. I dreamed it here, in the tac room of the *Ragnar*, en route to my first recon deployment.

This much I remembered. The gods were ragged, weak. I saw a cunning fox with bloodied fur—a weary soldier with a broken sword—a debutante—a snake—a farmer—and above them all, a matriarch, august, proud, furious.

Then we spoke. I could never remember the words. The matriarch was furious, lightning flashing in her eyes, a storm of bitterness washing over me. I was calm, smug, utterly confident. I was a rock parting the storm, biding time until I delivered their ruin.

Then the cataclysm struck: a flash of energy, cracking heaven itself, shattering the gods. The apocalypse descended around me, but I felt no fear—only the burning, contemptuous sense of *triumph* welling endlessly from the depths of my soul. They blazed and broke, falling to earth like stars.

The gods died, and I laughed.

I came out of translation with a hungry sneer on my face.

"Damn, Lils, were you getting laid in there?" Markus said, laughing.

"What? No! Shut up!" I shouted over the crackle of ether backlash.

The big guy just laughed at me, punching the diagnostic console on his chair, making sure all of him made it out of the ether. I followed suit, glancing over at Val as he did the same. Val looked content and peaceful despite the jostling as we reentered realspace. He'd probably been strolling around an art museum or something, boring dweeb that he was. I had a stroke of inspiration.

"Everyone knows Val's the sex maniac around here," I added.

"I'll note your envy in the mission log," Val replied. My response was lost as a bolt of etheric energy thundered across the hull shielding.

The commander pinged us over our comms.

"*Stow the chatter,*" she said, voice fuzzing from interference. "*Strap in, we're breaching the planet's defenses in T-minus fifteen.*"

We were already as strapped as we were going to get, but that's the commander for you. The monitor displayed a wall of etheric energy growing closer. Unlike the turbulence of the realspace horizon, this barrier was divinely crafted.

They knew we were coming. It wouldn't be enough.

"Here we go!" Markus cheered. "They fall!"

"They die!" Val and I chorused.

The world *wrenched* as the ethership punched through the defense barrier. I felt myself forced against the straps as we corkscrewed through space. Markus was screaming—in the I'm-on-a-roller-coaster way, not the I'm-about-to-die way. Me, I clenched my jaw and gut muscles and strained against the g-forces. I swore I could feel my skeleton rattling in the ether turbulence. I felt no fear—the *Ragnar* would carry us through.

The commander got us righted soon enough. The *Ragnar* plunged through the inner workings of the barrier, shaking us like a dog with a chew toy, until the storm subsided. We were tumbling out of the etheric barrier, free-falling through space toward a sparkling planet of green and blue. Designation: Theria. Civilization level: preindustrial. Pantheon threat level: moderate. Moderate because they'd built defenses, which meant they'd seen us coming.

Good. I *wanted* them to see it coming. It was never enough. In the end, they'd realize the truth of the gods, hard-won by the Eifni Organization thousands of years ago:

They fall. And they die.

We hit atmosphere. The Eifni Organization had come to Theria.

Worldjumping is awesome, and I can prove it mathematically. Awesomeness—or call it grandeur, or gravitas, *thalas* in Velean; the name doesn't really matter—can be mathematically described as an etheric wave function. It turns out that when you take a matter construct like a ship, turn it into an idea, and then turn it back into *the same* matter in an alternate reality, you give off a whole lot of awesomeness waves in the process. I think that's beautiful—which I can also prove.

When I was a young edgelord, I used to go around saying there's no meaning in the universe. I was wrong. The ether is all around us, carrying meaning from events to observers. A beautiful waterfall really is beautiful: we can detect it, measure it, amplify it. My native Earth never made the jump to paraphysics, but on Veles the Eifni Organization reached into heaven and dragged it down under a microscope.

We've answered the old questions. True love *does* exist, but only under laboratory conditions. There's no statistical difference between hot and cold revenge. We've measured the moral arc of the universe: turns out it doesn't bend toward justice after all.

But that's okay because it also turns out that everyone's a hero once you adjust for confounding variables.

And souls are real. They're complex ether constructs that interface with brains. Very tasty, too, if you're one of the various parasitic creatures wandering etherspace. Most of them don't prey on humans directly, instead living off the ambient meaning that human civilization generates. You know that strain of moss they found in Chernobyl that lives on radioactivity? Like that, only instead of uranium it's stuff like betrayal or humor.

But the apex predators—gods—need a more substantial diet.

They're the ones that reach out and con people into worshipping them, shaping their souls to resonate with the right ether frequencies. A deceased human soul in a sanitized environment just floats around until it can attach itself to a newborn, but if you're tuned in to a god's channel? Lunchtime.

Me, I'm a humanist, and I'll be damned if I let us be a prey species. That's why I strapped in with an Eifni deicide team, en route to a strange new world.

The *Ragnar* scythed through Theria's atmosphere like it wasn't there—which it wasn't, not for us. Eifni Org's engineers had long mastered the exchange between physical and etheric reality, a process called translation. The translator engines conceptualized the gas molecules before they could cause drag, spewing them out as *emptiness* and *breath*. The breath we left in our wake, to fade into the background noise of the ether; the emptiness we funneled into the ship's cloaking device. Whatever the Therians saw of us, they'd know, on a spiritual level, there was nothing there.

Such as that strange-looking flying beast, which was—oh shit, it was heading right for us.

"Contact!" I yelled. "Five o'clock!"

(In Velean, the equivalent phrase is "north of the watchtower," but you don't have the cultural background to make any sense of that, so we'll pretend I used the English version.)

"*Confirm,*" said Abby. "*Val, assess. Markus, find me a place to engage.*"

"Scanning." Val began typing into his console.

"I'm reading humans up ahead," said Markus. "Recommend we make for the ocean."

"*Acknowledged,*" said Abby.

"Permission to activate secondary batteries?" I asked.

"*Negative. Contact is not gaining at this time. We will not engage.*"

"Awwwww."

"*Stow it, Lilith.*"

"We're dealing with an oracle," Val noted. "It's conceivable this encounter was planned."

"Oracles aren't that good," said Markus. "They know the region we're in at best."

"Could be a scout," I said hopefully, caressing the trigger on my console's joystick.

You could almost hear Abby considering. "*We'll act out of an abundance of caution. Permission granted but hold fire. I'm notifying the other teams of our situation.*"

"Yes'm," I said with a grin. I pulled the targeting console down from the ceiling and flicked the switch to activate the starboard guns.

The timbre of the engines shifted, and we tilted slightly, avoiding whatever settlement Markus had detected. We accelerated, and I watched the animal behind us. It was built like a *gvodim*—actually wait, you don't know what that is. Okay, uh, think like a large eagle, except the head's a bit more feline, and it's got this really slick fur instead of feathers, but it can still fly because it's got these huge leathery membranes on the wings. Got that? Okay, the thing chasing us looked like that, but way bigger, and also it had a serrated beak.

It was also keeping pace with us. I frowned. That shouldn't be happening.

"Commander, I'm reading a divine blessing," Val said.

"Acknowledged. We assume an ambush. Markus, you're on guns with Lilith. Val, scan for more contacts."

"Drinks on Lilith! Calling it now!" said Markus.

"Land the shot first, then we'll talk," I said. The adrenaline was racing through my arms and my neck. Their stupid barrier couldn't keep us out. Couple of empowered beasties? I wasn't worried.

"No human life in the ocean," said Val, which seemed obvious, but you need to check, just in case.

"Acknowledged," said the commander. *"We'll hit minimum safe distance from the settlement and engage. If they have additional forces, they're already en route, so let's finish this quickly."*

The *Ragnar* thundered over the ocean, keeping our profile high enough that the ether wash from our passing didn't pollute the waves too much—if there was a Therian sea god, they'd smell us like a shark smells blood in the water. The *gvodim*-like creature pursued us, apparently too weak-souled for the cloaking device to convince it we weren't here. Mistake on its part. I thumbed the controls and took aim.

"Ready to fire," I said.

"Commander," Val said sharply. "There's an island with a divine aura, dead ahead. It was cloaked."

"Taking evasive maneuvers. Hold fire."

The *Ragnar* swerved immediately. This was definitely an ambush.

"Multiple contacts to port!" said Markus. "Shit, it's some kind of swarm!"

I looked at the port monitor and swore. A dark cloud of *something* was rising into the air, seemingly out of a random spot on the ocean, and spreading across our field of view.

"Multiple contacts above. Blessings likely," said Val. "Permission to engage primary batteries?"

"The fuck is this? Where did they come from? The clouds?" I said.

"Granted," said the commander. *"Weapons free, everyone."*

When in doubt, attack. She hadn't finished the sentence before a vicious grin swept my face and I squeezed the trigger. In an instant, etheric energies carved a magnetic tunnel to our flying friend, guiding a coruscating blast of unstable plasma that blew a hole straight through it and dropped its flaming corpse into the waves. Anyone watching would be blinded from the light and radiation as the plasma decayed, assuming they weren't close enough to get flash fried by the air temperature. Inside the *Ragnar*, I suffered none of those consequences.

"First blood!" I cheered. "Drinks on Markus!"

"Bullshit! You fired early!"

The ship lurched left in a barrel roll, and I saw a dark shape plummet through where we'd been. We were moving too fast for me to make out details, but I popped off a desperate shot as we rolled. I missed the creature and hit the ocean. It was close enough to the impact that the steam cooked it alive.

Markus was firing frantically, pulling the trigger as fast as his guns could recharge, slashing holes in the swarm of what appeared to be ravens at this distance. Their claws and beaks glowed in my display, probably indicating some kind of blessing for sharpness. Every shot vaporized several of them and burned dozens more around the beam, but we were dealing with thousands. And we were being herded by the things that dropped out of the clouds, so we couldn't increase our distance from the swarm.

If the oracle had deployed those birds against us, it was a safe bet that those claws could cut the *Ragnar* open. And they were closing on us.

"New contacts are angels," said Val.

"Shit," said Markus, while I said something much less tame.

"Does *nothing* faze you?" I yelled at Val.

"I'm going to see if I can pick up their god," Val said, ignoring me. "Can you stall?"

"Negative, Val, we're too hot. Do what you can while we disengage."

I swore as a sodden, black-cloaked figure blasted out of the ocean toward us. The one I'd steamed. It didn't look much worse for wear, and the spear it was carrying was causing all sorts of warning lights on my console. My adrenaline surged. I snapped all three of my plasma lances on it and fired. Even with flash dampening, my screen went white for a half second that lasted an eternity. In retrospect, probably a little overkill, but you never knew. I held my breath.

The screen cleared. I didn't see the angel, target tracking didn't show it anywhere, but was it actually dead? Had it just dematerialized? Angels are bullshit, man.

"Switch to disruptors and take out the angels," ordered the commander. *"We can outrun the birds."*

"Yes'm," I said, sighing internally. I could have taken them with the lances. Besides, you can't set *anything* on fire with an ether disruptor.

Commander Abby continued making evasive maneuvers as the flight of angels almost hacked us open. Those weapons were godtouched for sure. We were about a thousand times bigger than an angel, and they had numbers on us, but we were faster, and that was enough for Commander Abby to keep them from carving through the sanctuary field. I cycled the weapons on my battery and took aim with the disruptor.

"Bye-bye!"

I pulled the trigger. The disruptor probably made a cool hum or something, but I couldn't hear it in here. All the feedback I got was a green smokelike effect as the sensors picked up the disruptor fire. An angel-slaying fart, if you will. In etherspace, I'd just caused a burst of B-phase noise that would degrade any etheric structures it hit, kinda like how cosmic radiation corrupts hard drives in outer space. The angel I'd targeted dropped dead from instant soul cancer, tumbling into the waves. The one next to him got caught in the disrupter corona and started twitching erratically. So it was effective, but it just didn't look as cool, you know?

I sighed, took aim, and prepared to kill more angels.

That was about when the sea monster hit us.

CHAPTER TWO

The Oracle

Imagine just the ugliest fucking lobster you've ever seen, except skyscraper sized, and with these giant squirmy tentacles covered in impractically large suckers. Like, you're grabbing whales with those things and not much else. It was covered in mottled blue-brown armor, fuzzy with millions of alien barnacles, as it rose from ocean waters that were really too shallow for something like this to be hanging around in.

And it was *angry*.

The only warning we got was what I can only describe as apocalyptic chittering before a claw the size of one of those London double-decker buses crashed into the side of our hull. The *Ragnar* was practically indestructible, its neutronium hull wreathed in multiple layers of shields. Pelas-class etherships are rated to withstand meteor strikes because there's always that one prissy weather god that won't just lie down and fucking die. So we could take a hit from an overgrown prawn any day of the week.

As an almighty crunch blew out my eardrums and my world turned sideways, I made a mental note to figure out what kind of screwy weeks they had around here. In retrospect, that was probably me going into shock.

Alarms blared —the oh-fuck kind, not that I could hear them, but they glared a deep emergency red tinged with etheric notes of urgency. The g-forces whipped us around in our seats, bashing me against the headrest and bruising up my arms. Might have fractured a rib despite the cushioning, I don't know, I was kind of occupied, okay? The *Ragnar* spun end over end, bouncing on the waves like a skipping stone, if a skipping stone could bruise you down to your internal organs every time it hit the ocean. Oh god I was so nauseous. And the inertial dampeners were almost certainly fucked. One particularly violent bounce left the *Ragnar* pirouetting in the air. I screamed with pain and rage, which helped with the disorientation a little.

We slammed into the ocean one last time—it slapped the wind right out of my lungs, abruptly cutting off my scream—before the commander managed to regain control of the ship, taking us on a spiraling path away from the water. The *Ragnar* was limping but still airborne. I gasped, trying to get my breath back, but vomited instead.

Markus was shouting at me. I watched him distantly. He was handsome by Earth standards. Pretty wide face, good jaw, bit of stubble. He normally looked confident, but right now his expression was one of frustration. Maybe because

I couldn't hear him over the high-pitched whine. He needed to talk louder. Wait. I couldn't hear him at all. That seemed like something I should handle. I should handle it. Markus gestured emphatically at me. I should—my comm. I forced my sluggish thoughts to send an activation command to my personal comm.

Eifni comms read the speaker's meaning straight from the ether. Normally they're used for universal translation, but it also comes in handy if your fragile human ears just broke.

"I'm back!" I wheezed. Opening my mouth was a mistake. I vomited again next to my chair.

"Shoot the *fucking* angels!" Markus shouted back.

"What about fucking Lobsterzilla?" I asked, but obeyed, training my disruptors— the two that were still responding to controls, anyway—on a group of three cloaky boys trying to flank through my firing arc. Last mistake they ever made.

"Primary batteries engaged," said Val. "Permission to fire?"

"*Granted.*"

"Fuck you, Lobsterzilla!" I screamed, wisping another angel.

Val opened up with the fusion cannons. I couldn't hear a thing, but the *thud-thud-thud-thud* that echoed through the hull rattled my already aching bones. My vision went blurry. The cabin temperature, insulation ruined with the gash in our hull, immediately jumped to uncomfortable levels.

And we hit Lobsterzilla with the goddamn sun.

Oh, it screamed. My comm helpfully translated for me, which made my brain hurt until I managed to mute that particular signal. The four fusion rounds blazed through the air—literally, *they set the air on fire*—straight through the sea monster, disintegrating armor and flesh like it wasn't even there to begin with. The growing wall of fire in their wake followed immediately after, charbroiling the poor bastard through its armor. Between the exit wounds and the general trauma, Lobsterzilla snapped in half, flaming chitin shrapnel shredding nearby birds before the firestorm roasted the rest. The top half exploded as it boiled from the inside, spraying meat everywhere. One blackened severed tentacle flopped lazily through the air, trailing ember-illuminated smoke.

Behind the burning, bubbling fountain of lobster meat, four searing lights plunged into the ocean depths, where they dumped enough thermal energy to vaporize a couple million gallons of seawater. The scalding fog plumed upward like a mushroom cloud, darkening the sun.

"Target neutralized," said Val, like he hadn't just personally called down humanity's best imitation of the wrath of God. Smug bastard.

"Woooooo!" said Markus, pumping a fist in the air. I smiled fiercely, but to preserve the contents of my stomach, I only cheered in my head. Get smited, you fucking prawn.

"Perhaps this kind of behavior is why Abby doesn't trust you with the big guns," Val mused.

Not trusting myself to open my mouth again, I weakly flipped him off. The bird isn't a Velean gesture, but I did it often enough that a smart guy like him would have picked it up by now.

The angels were running. I chuckled darkly. One by one, they vanished into the steam like they'd never been there, leaving us alone with the boiling fog and the lobster bits still raining from the sky. The ocean foamed red with gore. The alarms were still blaring, the *Ragnar* was limping, but the fist of the gods had come down and broken on our ship.

"Screens are clear. They've withdrawn. We need to move fast. Markus, take over piloting. Val, damage report. Lilith, you're on overwatch."

"Yes'm," Markus and I said in unison, leaving Val on his own with, "Acknowledged."

Markus looked questioningly at me. I stared him down. He quirked his lips in the Velean equivalent of an eye roll.

"Commander, one casualty. Lilith's ears are bleeding. Probably double rupture."

"Val, take a look when you're done."

"Acknowledged," he said. Bastard didn't even look up from his diagnostic console.

Markus unstrapped quickly and moved to the cabin door, carefully stepping around the puddles of vomit. The hallway outside the cabin was more brightly lit than usual—the gash in the hull came surprisingly close to us. I wondered if the oracle had been trying to kill us specifically. I flipped a switch on my targeting console to give myself control of the full range of the *Ragnar*'s arsenal—minus the primary guns, damn Val. I was *perfectly* trustworthy. And I only felt slightly drunk from the damage to my inner ears. You remember when you were a kid and you spun around in circles until the whole world started spinning, too? The world was spinning, and it wouldn't fucking *stop*.

I leaned over the armrest and emptied the rest of my stomach onto the floor. I was never going to take the seat next to the door again.

"Sanitize," said Val, still not looking up. A scrubber detached from the wall, attending to my mess.

"What the *fuck* was that?" I asked when I felt like I could safely open my mouth. My voice felt growly from the stomach acid, and presumably sounded that way, too. "They were waiting right at the insertion point!"

"Team, your analysis," said Abby.

"We guessed it was a scout," said Markus, now on comms, probably still making his way to the helm. *"Oracles aren't that good. There were probably more ambush parties waiting for us in other locations."*

"It was too precise," said Val. "That ambush was choreographed."

"We beat it," I growled. "It's good. Not good enough."

"That could be a deception it's trying to sell us," Val noted.

"Val," said Abby, *"what did you get off those angels?"*

"It's still processing. I need a moment," he said. "What's the damage?"

"Thousand one, thousand two," I coughed. Val raised an eyebrow at me. *That* gesture meant what it usually did.

"*The hull's been breached,*" said Abby. "*The deformation around the breach is consistent with a blessing. Pure physical trauma would have crumpled more of the surrounding area. This close to the passenger cabin, we're looking at subsystem damage, as well.*"

"It's considerable," said Val. "My console says multiple weapons systems offline. We're down to three out of five conceptual shields. We've lost backup power, but main's still online. Inertial dampeners are down."

Ha! Called it!

"Translation engines have warning lights but pass macrofunctionality checks. Recommend minimizing usage of them. Climate control is, obviously, troubled, given the hull breach—but the systems are operational."

"We're not spaceworthy," I said, feeling the horror dawning.

"Correct," said Val. "Commander, the etheric background noise means jumping from planetside was already a dubious proposition, and between the barrier and the engine damage, we should assume it's a nonoption. We are stranded here until we can make repairs."

"*And if the oracle knew we'd be here, it's probable they know our next move,*" said Abby. "*Markus, are you situated?*"

"*Ready to go, commander.*"

"*Get us moving. Random walk until we have a plan. Val, continue your report.*"

He did. There was a lurch as we accelerated. Right, the inertial dampeners were out. The passenger door opened, and Abby walked briskly to the empty seat in the middle. There was an obvious moment where she took in the sight of me and the scrubber as she passed, but she didn't pause. She pulled down her targeting console as she sat.

"Thank you, Val. Lilith, you're relieved. I have overwatch. Go clean yourself off."

"Yes'm," I said, returning my console to the ceiling. I unstrapped, peeled myself out of the chair, and promptly fell over.

"Fuck," I bit out. "I can't walk, ma'am."

"Her proprioception is damaged," said Val. "Allow me."

"I'll crawl."

"Help her to med bay," said Abby. Val made his way over to me and helped pull me up. I grumbled.

"We'll get you fixed up," he said reassuringly. Normally I'd suspect condescension behind the statement, but what I was currently "hearing" was ripped straight from the meaning of his words, and they'd apparently been delivered without connotative information at all—as if he'd just been stating a fact. I didn't dwell on it too long because I was distracted by the fact that I *couldn't fucking walk.*

"I know," I said, the world swinging crazily with each step. "I just hate this."

"Just to set your expectations," he said. "With the warnings on the translation engine diagnostics, it might not be safe to reset your ears."

"Fuck," I said.

"Of course, you could also flash to—"

"How long to heal naturally?" I cut him off.

He didn't react to being interrupted. "Three to eight weeks, if I recall correctly." He always did. "If we're unlucky, months. You'll need antibiotics until we can determine if the oracle can pick up medical translators."

I didn't respond, mostly because a wave of nausea hit me and I had to keep my mouth shut. I didn't know if I could take three weeks in bed.

"Commander," said Val, "I haven't finished analyzing the frequency transform of the angels, but we're dealing with a fertility goddess at least."

"Acknowledged. You think it's our oracle?"

"The harmonics work out. The oracular aspect could be a progression out of the fertility aspect."

"Strong progression," I said. "Maybe it's biphasic already." Biphasic, a god with two fully developed aspects. Stronger than monophasic or progressive monophasic, but easier to kill: rip it in half down the aspects, and neither half survives the process.

"No," said Val, holding me up as I stumbled again. "Signal strength was consistent with progressive monophase. The concern is that there's another match for the frequency: the defensive barrier at the realspace horizon."

The rest of the team was silent.

We'd punched through easily enough, true, but your run-of-the-mill pantheon can't muster the firepower to match an Eifni ethership. We hadn't considered that defense might not be its only purpose.

Oracles work by reading the distant echoes of future events in the ether. Most of them can't pick up anything stronger than "calamity will happen," or "a great conqueror will arise," or stuff like that with big effects. Bright stars are easier to see in the night sky. Oracles see us coming often enough because murdering all the gods is kind of like a supernova in this analogy. The smart ones can even triangulate our general location, but there are ways to mute those signals with tactics or extraneous etheric noise. Light pollution, if you will.

The barrier wasn't a wall. It was the Hubble Space Telescope. She could see *everything*.

The first emergency broadcast hit us, then the second, and third. All over the planet, godslayers were dying. Maybe their ships had saved them, jumping their soulboxes back to Veles. Or maybe the oracle had crippled them like the *Ragnar*, and immortal lives were ending in this very moment.

Then all was silence.

CHAPTER THREE

Wrath and Ruin

The commander had a plan: "Val, you're the oracle expert. Come up with a plan."

"One step ahead of you," he said. "First problem is that we're the only entities making decisions out here. We need to be maximally indecisive about our future actions. Markus, randomize our course. Whatever method you're using, it needs to be completely meaningless. It'll blind her. Don't use the computer, it uses etheric noise to generate random numbers."

"There's nothing else up here, man."

"My dice," I said. "They're in my personal bag. I can get to med bay by myself."

Val shot me a doubtful look and didn't let go.

"Seriously, we don't know how much time we have," I said, trying to shrug him off me. He let me go. I stumbled to the wall and leaned against it, trying to stay up.

"Good point. Markus, I'm on my way," he said, leaving me without a second glance.

"Side pocket, black bag," I called after him. I looked down the hall. Okay, I had, like, thirty feet to go. I could do this.

When I was fifteen, I went to driving school. They gave us these "drunk goggles" that screwed up your vision and simulated being too drunk to walk straight. The idea had been to convince us that you can't fool a cop when they ask you to walk in a straight line with your heels touching your toes. Everyone else had stumbled all over the place, but I'd wanted to win. What do you need balance for? Not falling. So screw with your balance and you stumble because you'll fall if you don't stop yourself.

I decided not to stop myself. If you're gonna fall, fall forward. I'd put on the goggles and just rushed to the other end of the line, letting my momentum keep me upright. The other teenagers were super impressed. The instructor said I still would have gotten caught because my feet weren't touching, but whatever, I still did it.

Anyway, I bet I could make it to the med bay. I fell forward, one hand on the wall for support, hurling my body away from my unstable footing. My stomach wasn't happy with me, but it could shut the hell up. Just had to make it to med bay and then I could wash the sick out of my mouth. And maybe do something about the tinnitus. I never thought constant high-pitched whining could be so annoying, although phrasing it like that makes me wonder why.

I'd almost made it when Markus called out, *"Brace for course correction!"* and yanked the floor to the side.

"Dude!" I groaned from the floor, interrupting Val's exposition on the oracle. "I'm injured here."

"Thanks for the dice, Lils," he said, and I could just hear the shit-eating grin on his stupid face.

"To summarize," said Val, irritation in his tone, *"the oracle understands the meaning of future events but none of the actual details of what will occur. The more unique we are, the easier it is for her to discriminate us from similar possibilities. We win by ensuring that whatever we do is existentially generic, and by ensuring that none of what we do is tied to a specific location—she'll see that and ambush us again."*

I pulled myself up into a sitting position against the wall.

"This bitch has a planet-sized crystal ball," I said. "We're in a spaceship. We can't be that generic."

"We can dampen our profile," Val argued. *"The ship can be hidden in a remote location. If we prevent or eliminate native observers, we should avoid anything too identifying."*

"All our equipment's here!" I said. "You want to try killing a god without amplifiers? Or are we dragging those through the wilderness, too?" Also, I couldn't really walk, but I wasn't going to bring that up.

"Lilith, stand down," said the commander.

Yes ma'am, butt's already grounded, ma'am. I grumbled and tried to stand up. It worked the second time.

"Thank you," said Val. *"The most compelling argument in favor of this course is that the oracle's angels have already witnessed the ship's ether signature and aren't currently attacking us. That implies she can't find us on that alone."*

"Val, convince Lilith on your own time," said the commander. *"I need next steps."*

"We'll need to perform repairs. We can keep flying randomly for part of that time, but the translation engines will need to be shut down before I can look at them. And Lilith's out of commission until that point." Screw you, too, Val. *"I can try to improvise some kind of obfuscation during that period. We can do sociological recon at the same time, then strike when the ship is ready."*

I reached the med bay. Score one for Lilith! Markus called out another course correction, and I hurriedly threw myself into one of the beds before he knocked me over again.

"Our strategic objective is to destroy or compromise the planetary barrier. It's possible that the oracle designed her first strike to compromise our ability to strike at the barrier, which gives us some information about our options."

"Yes, that's quite obvious," I said.

"I'll let you explain it, then."

"Oh no," I said hurriedly, "I'm injured."

Val was definitely smirking. *"It means she agrees that we win if we hit the barrier. And the fact that she's trying to stop that from happening means it's possible."*

"*Unless that's what she wants us to think,*" said Markus.

The med-bay door opened. Commander Abby entered briskly, not even pulling to a stop before slapping the console next to my bed.

"Diagnose," she said. "Val, your strategy is acceptable."

"Am I gonna live, doc?"

"I should flash you to backup, but we'll try bypassing your comm first," she said.

"Thanks," I said. She flicked an utterly blank look at me.

"We've discussed your cultural hang-ups. This is an emergency. Your designated transfer is a perfect match for your birth body. Adapt."

"I do not consent," I said precisely, looking away. Abby didn't argue further, even though she probably could have pointed out that Val and Markus weren't having eardrum problems right now. That was the commander, always picking her battles.

"Val, I need a wide-area sweep ready to go. We're looking for hiding places. Markus, maximum atmosphere speed. There's another continent a few minutes away. We'll get close for maximum coverage."

I heard the engines starting to thrum as Markus pushed us as fast as we could go. The distant thunder of the wind catching on the hull breach picked up as our velocity increased.

"Wait for my signal to fire the scan. I need enough sites to make a credibly random selection. Markus, be prepared for resistance. The oracle can definitely pick up the signature on the scan, but it's possible the dice are doing their job. We will not engage if possible."

"*Acknowledged,*" said Val.

"Strap in, Lilith. This procedure needs about an hour of data to simulate your proprioception."

"Better than three weeks," I said, bracing myself for what I was about to do. "Can you get me some water?"

"Here." She pulled the sink out of the wall, deftly snatching a disposable cup, filling it, and handing it to me. I took a gulp, gargled a bit, and clumsily rolled onto my side so I could spit it out. I collapsed onto my back.

"Fuck that lobster. Thanks, commander."

"Good luck." She left, presumably to man the guns. No point waiting. I thumbed a panel on the side of the bed. Clear plastic ribbons slipped over the parts of my body that would flop the most under turbulent conditions, just tight enough to prevent motion but not enough to be uncomfortable. For now. It was a good thing I wasn't claustrophobic. To distract myself, I tried to poke holes in Val's plan.

The TL;DR of oracles is that they can't see everything: they're just attuned to this one kind of signal modulation you get on etheric cause-effect dyads. That probably doesn't make any sense, so here's the explanation for normal people.

My mom used to love saying that everything happens for a reason. One time she was trying to mail a package, but the post office closed early that day. The next day she went back and ended up meeting a friend she hadn't spoken to in a decade. To my mom, the connection between those events was more than just coincidence. It was "part of God's plan."

The truth is, it's just a natural phenomenon that anyone with a noetic organ can pick up on. If something is important, everything touching it becomes important by association. The post office closure was just a weird happening until it resulted in a meaningful occurrence—then it retroactively took on extra significance. That connection is what we call dyadic entanglement, and it's the signal frequency that oracles feed on.

Humans are linear beings, so we have to see both events in a dyad to understand the connection. But there's no time in etherspace: everything happens at once. So if the oracle could locate one end of the connection, they could find us at the other end.

In short, we could be as meaningful as we wanted about the fact that we were hiding, but as soon as it became meaningful *where* we were hiding, those angels would be back on us like cockroaches on a Twinkie. Hence the dice: if they didn't mean anything, the course they generated for us also didn't mean anything. So assuming the dice were sympathetically neutral—

My eyes widened.

"Fuck! Markus, don't use the red d20!"

I looked around the room wildly, but there wasn't anything else I could do. Helpless, I pulled up the ship's feed on my comm so I could at least watch what was going on.

"*The sparkly one? It's fine, Lils, I'm not gonna lose it.*"

"Fucking lose it!" I screamed. "It's my lucky die!"

There was a pause as everyone processed.

"*Oh shit,*" said Markus.

"*We go now,*" said Abby. "*Val, fire the scan. Markus, evasive maneuvers.*"

"*Probing now,*" said Val. I felt the bed kick under me as we accelerated away from the ocean's surface. The screen showed the water dropping away as we aimed at the sky.

Theria was very pretty. Deep-blue ocean, luscious green vegetation in the distance, fluffy off-white clouds—it all looked lovely and inviting. Well, the clouds were just a bit too dark to be inviting; there was a bleakness there. Actually, I'm not sure why I thought they were white, those were definitely rain clouds. Hold on. No, they were getting darker. That wasn't a good sign.

"*Markus, there's a divine energy spike,*" said Val. "*Diverting engine power to shields.*"

"*I think they've got a weather god!*" Markus called.

"No shit!" I said.

Our warning was a sense of utter wrath that began to fill the air, bleeding through the *Ragnar*'s conceptual shields.

"*Contacts! All sides!*" called the commander. But even as the lancer fire flickered at the edges of my screen, I knew—we all knew—our new attackers weren't the threat here.

I can't describe the grandeur of it. The feeling of standing on the beach with a tidal wave drowning the sky. Of looking up at a mighty volcano, of watching it spew fire and death into the air, of knowing that you can't escape. Of the bug watching the human's foot descend. Except those calamities don't care—the god hates you. Anger and contempt so vast it seems wrong to use the same words as for human emotions, even if intellectually you know it's just a couple orders of magnitude.

The wrath of a god.

We were so small, in the end. I was incapacitated, immobile, helpless, and all I could do was scream. So, as the clouds crackled with rage, so did I.

"They fall!"

My team answered me. "*They die!*"

It smote us.

The light and the thunder hit us simultaneously, electricity crackling over our shields, whiting out my display. The thunder boomed around us, such a powerful sound that I could hear it through the vibrations of my skeleton even with my eardrums out of commission. But beyond that was pure rage, a storm of corrosive ether trying to inflict destruction by force of will alone, smothering our defiance.

But *Ragnar*'s shields held. Mostly.

When my screen came back, we were spiraling toward the ocean—looked like an evasive pattern, and the engines were still running, so I assumed it was on purpose. The world itself seemed to take a pause, as if in confusion that our ship had withstood the strike. Even the god's anger withdrew for a moment as he considered us.

"*The scan is complete,*" said Val.

"*Upward! Now!*" said the commander. The ship sharply jerked toward space.

"We're not spaceworthy!" I shouted.

"*We don't have a choice,*" said Abby. "*We can't fight this thing. Hang in there, Lilith.*"

The god's anger returned.

Below us, the water surged upright into the form of a great muscled man—miles tall, seawater endlessly cascading where his hair and beard would be. A divine avatar. Too big even for the fusion cannons to kill, if the god were actually a giant seawater Godzilla and not an etheric monster stretched out across the entire planet. It reached out to grab us. Lightning flew from its fingers, pummeling us, shaking the cabin.

"*Primary shields down,*" said Val.

"*Everything to engines!*" yelled the commander.

My body was straining hard against the straps as we approached escape velocity. If the bed had been rotated ninety degrees, all the blood would have gone to my head and probably given me an aneurysm or something. The *Ragnar* was vertical now. The seawater hand reached above us. The ship shuddered as a lightning blast tore through the shields and coruscated across our armor.

"*Woooooooooo!*" yelled Markus.

I could only watch as its fingers closed around us, blotting out the sun, dark like trench water. But Markus aimed true. We slipped between its fingers and punched into the stratosphere as it howled in fury.

The god spoke.

Woe be unto you, it thundered. *Misfortune upon misfortune, death and disaster, wrath and ruin!*

Just words, or so I told myself. It couldn't touch us out here, beyond the boundary of its domain. It watched, divinely impotent, as we escaped to space. Ahead of us, the stars gleamed, twinkling behind the oracle's shimmering barrier. Space was as inhospitable to gods as it was everything else.

"*Ha!*" said Markus. "*I am awesome!*"

"I can't believe we made it out of that clusterfuck!" I cheered. "We lived!"

There was a worrying silence from the others, then a single ping hit my comm. It was from Val, using the nonverbal system meant for the field.

It meant no.

"We're not spaceworthy," I murmured, stomach dropping despite the lessened gravity.

"*Shit,*" said Markus. "*I'm taking us down.*"

A text message showed up in my comm feed, this time from the commander: "*NO too late Markus in command careful of god planetfall **randomly**.*"

"Sorry, guys," I said. "See you on the other side."

Fifty feet away, my teammates were dying. If all went well, they'd wake up in their backup bodies, but our shields were damaged, and this was a world with active gods. Sometimes godslayers flashed and didn't come back. Who knew how many we'd already lost?

Markus and I didn't say anything as he turned us in a random direction and pointed the *Ragnar* back to Theria.

We fell. They died.

CHAPTER FOUR

The Crypt

I was panting from levering the cargo bay open as I went to fetch Val's moirascope. Practically speaking, the fact that we hadn't been ambushed by yet more bullshit was pretty good evidence the random walk had worked this time, but we needed to take measurements to be sure. I'd never had to do those measurements myself, of course—our paraphysicist was usually alive—so it was questionable whether I'd actually be able to read the results, but I'd probably muddle through.

The punch switch on the wall dropped the cargo ramp. I took my first breath of Therian air, not counting whatever had gotten inside through the hull breach. Yup. Smelled like air.

I stumbled outside, moirascope in one hand, disruptor pistol in the other. I still couldn't hear anything, but my comm was rigged to alert me if anything big enough got too close.

Some forests seem built for cinema: the ground is covered in leaves and moss, but nothing that might impede an actor's movement; the trees are spaced out, the leaves providing a picturesque sort of roof, with enough light shining through to make everything look like a painting.

This was not that kind of forest. This was the other kind, a foreboding playground for insects where there were coarse bushes and random thorns and the ground looked kinda slimy. It smelled like rotting plant corpses. In short, this was the kind of forest that reminded you that the animal kingdom doesn't recognize your passport.

Godslayers don't bother with passports. We'd raked the area with disruptor fire before setting down in the hopes of shredding any lesser etheric creatures that might report our location to the pantheon. *Theoretically* not a detection risk—disruptors should be too entropic to form dyadic entanglements—but that's what the moirascope was for.

I passed the still-breathing corpse of some kind of cougar-sized lizard as I tried to get the whole ship in the moirascope's frame. The forest really didn't want to work with me on that, but I pushed through anyway. Having reached a good distance, I kicked open the moirascope's tripod and set it down facing the ship.

And what a beautiful ship it was. In contrast to the gloom of where I was standing, the *Ragnar* shone proudly under the tropical sunlight, the radiation shielding giving it a matte iron color. In shape, it was somewhere between a tapered cone and a hundred-fifty-foot water bottle, with some aerodynamic lumps toward the rear to accommodate the engine. The port lancer batteries were still deployed, the equipment having jammed due to the ugly gash Lobsterzilla had rent diagonally down the side. The plasma lances themselves were basically slagged—we'd decided for multiple reasons not to tax the translation engines during reentry, and the friction had melted them.

My poor, sweet, innocent lancers. They didn't deserve this.

I sighed and activated the moirascope. The *Ragnar* blazed with dyadic entanglements, but that was normal for a deicide mission. It was also reassuring: it meant the ship would be involved in events down the road, implying we'd successfully get it up and running. Mind you, those events could be stuff like "angels descend on it and kill everyone inside." I didn't know the instrument well enough to figure that out. Right now, as long as things were gonna happen *later* and *elsewhere*, I didn't care.

We needed time to recover and do the sociological recon that was necessary for a successful deicide. If the careless hand of determinism brought us to another battle in the ocean, the oracle would muster her forces there, which meant they weren't *here*. We could handle anything she threw at us if we prepared.

It took me a couple minutes of messing with the filter settings to get the all clear.

"We're good," I reported. "Let's desecrate some corpses."

The crypt was lit only by pale-blue emergency lights, hidden in crevices in the walls. No direct light, just ethereal radiance. The glow seeped out reassuringly from behind the rows of iron-gray caskets tucked into sterile shelves in the walls. Forty-eight of them, electromagnetically clamped to the undersides of shelves four high on each wall, all the way to the end of the room. Forty-eight soulless bodies. Well, hopefully forty-six.

With the translation engines shut down for maintenance, the bodies would be kept fresh by intravenous nutrient feeds and chemical misting. Hidden in some of those iron coffins were bodies that looked exactly like us, while the others varied. Bodies with optimized musculature or variant neurotypes or just different looks and builds for social infiltration. Most of them with full suites of military augmentations: bone lacing, neural hardening, gland adjustments, ocular implants, and most importantly, comm sockets.

The caskets were opaque, but the sci-fi nerd in me insisted that there should be windows in all of them to show the faces inside. With the lights dimmed and the room cast in contrasts of blue and shadowy gray, it also insisted that those faces would open their eyes and follow me around the room.

Instead of eyes, rows of status lights stared back at me down the length of the room. Yellow meant ready. That was most of them. Blue meant active, meaning they were synced up with our comms, all set to vacuum up our souls when we died. Once they did, the light would turn green.

There were two green lights. Markus sighed with relief.

"Thank Darwin," I said. I paused for a moment, then realized Markus wouldn't call me out on the irony and moved on.

"Okay, let me get the gurney in here."

I stepped farther back into the room. Spaceships were much like submarines in that there was no wasted space. The walkway between the shelves was about the width of an airline aisle and made it just as impossible to squeeze past a wheeled cart.

The first green-lit casket was on the ground. We collapsed the gurney first, then Markus disengaged the safety on the casket and started the draining process. I fidgeted while it shut down. There was a slight risk of the body going into shock as the casket's various support mechanisms left it to fend for itself. But the casket drained without incident. We rolled the shelf out over the gurney, then disengaged the clamps.

I was closer to the casket's release lever, so I got to do the honors. The airtight environmental seals made a weirdly satisfying noise when we hauled the lid open, releasing humid, stinking air into the sterile confines of the crypt. Inside was Val, looking just like the corpse in the hallway, except instead of corpse pallor and the blood leaking from every orifice in his face—note to self, never die in space—he was damp with nutrient solution and stiff from reincarnation sickness. You win some, you lose some. He was also shirtless, which I'm sure Markus appreciated. He was in good shape—it's easy when you grow the body to specifications. The same specifications, every time. Val was basic like that.

He was also intubated. Markus pulled out a handful of IV needles while I got the tube out of Val's face. My hands and arms tingled whenever they crossed the boundary of the stasis field and it told them to chill out and go to sleep. With the invasive stuff removed, all we had to do was rip off the biomonitors taped to his rebirth-slimed chest. At last we were done; Val was a biologically independent organism again.

The last step is to start the brain. We flicked the last switch on the casket. The neural cradle on the back of Val's bald head crackled alarmingly, causing the body to convulse and cough.

In a fit of whimsy, I dipped a finger in a pool of nutrient solution that hadn't drained and flicked it on his forehead three times. Get it? Now he was born again.

"Rise and shine, Val," I said cheerfully. "I hope your new brain is nice and fast 'cause you've got a lot of thinking to do!"

Val kept his eyes closed, wrinkling his brand-new face for the first time. His hand, shaking slightly, pinched the bridge of his nose.

"Naturally," he rasped, each syllable an obvious effort. "You two won't."

"We love you, too," I said, beaming. "Let's go, Markus!"

We got him situated in the med bay. Bit of hydration, some calisthenics, he'd be back on his feet by dinnertime. Well, okay, dinnertime in a week. Then it was back to the crypt.

"Place creeps me the fuck out," I said conversationally to Markus on the way back.

"They're just bodies," he said. "Some of them are gonna be you one day."

"One of mine is male!" I protested. "It's not me!"

"Eh," Markus said. "Could be. Unless you're static."

"Val uses the same body every time, and none of you give *him* shit."

"Val."

"Whatever. You first, hold the door."

We got the commander's casket down. Markus pulled the lever this time. I braced myself. I'd never seen Val in another body. The commander, on the other hand, I'd never seen wear the same body twice.

Her new body was short but heavily muscled. With those abs, I'd peg her as a mountain climber or something if I didn't know she cheated. Female again this time. Soft face, not too pretty, might look better when her hair grew in. Her ocular implants glared green through her eyelids for one eerie moment before subsiding. She shifted weakly.

"Thanks" was all she said after the trauma of rebirth.

How many times had she woken up in one of these caskets? How many bodies had she taken for a spin and discarded? Your memories don't all transfer. Some of that information is only encoded in the brain and doesn't come with you. Just little episodic things, the stuff not important enough to leave an imprint on your soul. Veleans don't care about that stuff. To some degree they're objectively correct—if there's no sympathetic effect, then it categorically doesn't matter—but I wonder sometimes if it matters in the aggregate. A thousand meaningless experiences adding up to make you into you. Until your body dies and you become someone else.

I didn't know the answer. I had never flashed. But in my line of work, it was only a matter of time.

The corpses went into the newly vacated caskets. Their status lights glowed a dull red—spent. With unreliable translation engines, they'd stay that way.

Forty-six to go.

My melancholy didn't last long. I was overjoyed to have Val and Abby back, even if the latter was entirely different in looks and slightly different in behavior, which was the more distressing part. Markus and I helped them recover over the next few days while they adjusted.

"Ooh, this one's adrenal gland is *way* more active," Abby said, prancing back and forth on the sparring mat. "Oh, this is very good." She threw some lightning-fast punches at an invisible opponent. "Ha! Like I'm flying a Celerity. I should have been on stimulants my last life."

"Celerity's the super expensive one, right?" I asked, stretching.

"Top of the line, top of the sky," she recited in a kind of singsong voice. Marketing slogan, I guessed.

"Not much of a car girl myself," I said. "Might have been if Earth cars could fly. Alright, I'm good to go."

"I should show you all my garage when we get back from this mission." Abby took a stance. "I used to think I'd start my own line when I retired from the service."

"Oh yeah?" I said, starting to circle. She did the same. "What changed?"

"I don't think I'll ever retire." She stepped in, opening up with a kick. I met it with a knee block and tried a counteroffensive, but she slapped my fists away and stepped past me. I took an elbow to the side as she did. I'd like to blame it on my injury—despite

Abby's somewhat hacky fix, I still wasn't at 100 percent—but I'd probably never beat her in a fight. She had at least three hundred years' combat experience on me.

"Ow. Nice one," I said, bouncing a bit.

"You need to be faster on those blocks," she said, and suddenly the chatty woman had been replaced by the commander again. "Your weight was still on the left foot when I hit you. That's why you couldn't get out of the way."

"Yes'm," I said automatically.

She smiled. "Attagirl." I charged her. I feinted a right cross, then went for the gut punch. Abby pivoted so the blow glanced off her back, shoulder checking me. A leg hooked around my ankle as I stumbled backward, and I took a blow to the collarbone that dropped me on my ass, knocking the wind out of me. I signaled a pause by holding up a hand, as if my wheezing wasn't enough. She grabbed my hand and hauled me up. I coughed a couple of times.

"You hit harder now," I said.

"Adrenaline is a magical drug," she replied. "Come on, let's keep going."

"You like winning more, too," I said, narrowing my eyes playfully.

"Oh, I've always liked winning," she laughed.

"Pick on someone your own age, why don't you."

She didn't.

Twenty minutes later, thoroughly sore—at least, I was—we made it back to the common area, where Val was engaged with Markus in his own kind of sparring.

"Ah! Just in time. I believe that's the game," said Val, placing a white stone on the board. They'd raided my board game stash. Val preferred Go to chess, even though I kept telling him he was totally a chess guy.

"I'll take your word for it," said Markus.

"You are no longer able to defend this area," said Val, indicating an area of the board. "Play here and I capture that section; defend that section and my defense on the right becomes immortal. Either outcome results in a majority of the board under my control."

"Man, why can't you just do math problems to warm up?" Markus complained.

"Numbers," Val said, smiling viciously, "don't fight back."

I smiled, too. We were all alive.

CHAPTER FIVE

Reconnaissance

I'd been on two missions before this one—a probationary period while Eifni Org assessed my compatibility with the crew of the *Ragnar*. They'd been combat deployments, fast and chaotic, and we'd been in constant communication with the other teams as we tore through temples and cut angels out of the sky.

Recon missions were supposed to be slower, but that didn't mean *silent*. We'd locked the ship's comms down, just in case someone tried to send us a message and exposed us both. Any other surviving teams were probably doing the same. The casualties—well, hopefully their ships were functional enough to flash them all to soulboxes and send them back before the ship was destroyed. It was supposed to happen automatically when the team's last operative went down, but what if their engines were damaged first?

If we got killed, would we spend a mindless eternity in soulboxes, or would our unreliable engines smear us across etherspace?

Either way, we were on our own, and the mission wasn't over yet. Recon missions were an honor—one we'd been lucky to score, especially given my status as a newbie operative. Once we'd gathered all the information the secularization teams needed to do their slow, multigenerational work, we were permitted to take a stab at the pantheon ourselves. Less work for them, and eternal fame and glory for us—the coveted Red Dagger was only awarded for delivering the killing blow to a god.

So now that the immediate threat was gone, or at least delayed, we started planning our sociological recon. Val was needed at the ship to keep the repairs moving, and Abby was our best mechanic. A couple weeks of low-intensity repair work would help them adjust to their new bodies before they had to go into the field.

That left Markus and me, but with my hearing still impaired it was really just Markus. That wasn't a problem. Markus could handle himself. We'd just need to be careful that he didn't run into any fateful occurrences and get the oracle's eyes on us. For that reason, the commander ordered no-contact recon only.

Overreliance on etheric technology could be problematic on deicide missions. That was especially true now, given that we didn't know what the oracle could pick up. Markus suited up in good, old-fashioned camouflage, packed a couple of autonomous surveillance cameras, and started the hike to the nearest town. The commander and

I could ride piggyback in his head, courtesy of an experiential feed from his comm system. Val was inside the engines, trying to figure out what was actually malfunctioning so we could fix it.

We followed Markus down game trails for a good hour or so. The forest was thick, and it seemed civilization had been content to leave it unmolested for now. The disruptor strafing should have killed everything in the immediate vicinity—for now, anyway, the bodies would attract predators eventually—but once Markus got out into the wild there was a slight chance of painful, and embarrassing, death by ambush predator. If Theria had, like, flesh-eating turbo elephants or whatever, Markus's comm could warn him in time to defend himself. If he accidentally stepped on a venomous snake, the comm would be no help. We're not gonna talk about the time Abby got swarmed by acid prawns.

The greens in the plants were richer here than on my version of Earth, which probably implied something about the Therian sunlight and/or atmosphere, but I didn't remember my high school biology class that well. Val probably knew. It wasn't just a biology thing; you also had to think about heterocausality, which is the paraphysics word for "every universe is deterministic but all of them ended up different." Evolution took a slightly different path on every world known to Veles, and Darwin knew what had to have happened for this one to have rainforests around the Mediterranean.

There were a lot of vines around, despite the lack of sunlight filtering through the canopy. Animal life was much less in evidence, as tends to happen when humans blunder through a natural habitat. Comm readings found traces of etheric entities— apparently the disruptor barrage had been a good idea—but nothing got close enough to get picked up.

Markus's first encounter with a human came about an hour in. Probably a hunter. No-contact recon requires avoidance as a first resort. Markus immediately hit the ground when his comm read the human soul in range. Due to the claustrophobic environment of the forest, that was significantly larger than visual range, so we didn't get a clear look at the Therian. A lost opportunity, but not an important one. There would be more.

He traveled more carefully after that, however. Unless we'd landed in a culture with itinerant hunters, someone navigating the forest alone meant we were within spitting distance of a human settlement. The forest was starting to thin out at this point, too, the paths demonstrating evidence of human passage. People back home always said that terraforming Mars was a fool's errand, but why not? Terraforming is what humans do.

"*Looks like clear-cutting ahead,*" Markus said. "*Farming. Grain, maybe related to barley.*"

That was where he stopped—we didn't have enough information to blend in, and his clothing was all wrong besides.

"I'm not seeing any people," I said. "You?"

"*Negative,*" he replied. "*Best to be careful anyway. I'll skirt the boundary of the field.*"

"See if you can get a good vantage point to deploy the first camera," said Abby.

"There should be a structure nearby, right?" I asked.

"*I don't see one.*"

"If you can find one, that's a good location for a camera," said Abby. "Otherwise, we can work with footage of field labor."

"*There's a path to the east. If there's a structure or settlement nearby, that's our best lead.*"

He didn't move, though, waiting for the order to begin. I glanced at Abby, who was tapping her fingers on the armrest. That was another weird mannerism; Abby didn't fidget before.

"Go," she said eventually. "No-contact order is still in effect."

We watched Markus creep through the forest, glancing around for people. Nothing. It was getting dark, so stealthy movement should be easier.

"*I'm switching to night vision.*"

"I can't see shit," I said. "Go for it."

The commander pinged agreement. Moments later, the lenses in his eyes swapped out for a different set. I smiled; I'd spent *weeks* constantly swapping lenses for the hell of it after I'd gotten my artificial eyes.

Our patience—and Markus's effort—was rewarded about ten minutes later when Markus came into view of a fenced compound. A bonfire in the center illuminated men and women dancing in a complicated pattern, laughing and probably drunk. Markus was too busy checking for sentries and line of sight to really focus on it, so I nudged Abby and frowned. She nodded in agreement.

"This is a perfect spot for the first camera," she said. "Do you think you can get it up in the tree undetected?"

Markus grunted in affirmation. We watched him take one of the softball-sized canisters off a clasp on his belt, heft it for a moment, and toss it up at a nearby tree. There was a slight *splat*, unnoticed amid the echoing noise from the party occurring in the compound. The softball deformed, then hardened again. Inside, miniature motors rotated the camera's lens to focus on the bonfire as Abby worked the controls back here.

"Material culture?" asked Abby. The camera feed was blurry, but slowly clearing as compounds released by the impact reacted with the adhesive. It would cure by morning, becoming transparent—or close enough that adjusting the lens could compensate for it.

"*Some ironworking,*" said Markus. "*They're using some kind of cooking grill. I can't tell if it's machined from here, but from the surroundings my guess is not.*"

You could tell there was a pattern to the way they were dancing. It was jogging my memory, but I couldn't track the whole thing at once. Men and women alternated, skipping to the sides in human daisy chains, sometimes parting to allow other daisy chains to rush through, sometimes changing direction.

"They're orbits," I realized. "They're all on oval paths. But not crashing into each other."

"*The word is 'elliptical,' Lilith,*" Val's voice cut in.

"No one asked you," I said.

"And look where that got you," he said. Abby barked out a laugh. *"Commander, I popped in to say I'm going silent for the next few hours. I've found some issues that require concentration to analyze. No major risk of injury."*

"Acknowledged," said the commander. "Update me when you're done."

"Oval paths," I muttered resentfully to myself.

"What was that?" Abby said.

"Nothing."

"I think you're right, Lilith," said Abby. "This must all be choreographed. We'd see more collisions otherwise."

"Does that get us anything?" I asked. This was my first time on a recon team. I'd been through training and everything, I'd just never done this part, you know, for real.

"Not really," said Abby. "Dances like this are cultural customs. They occur at all levels of cultural development."

"You have to be, like, specially trained to do that kind of thing back home," I said.

Abby shrugged. "What we're seeing is normal."

We lapsed into silence as Markus crept to a new position. We got a better look at some of their garb. Men and women wore skirts of varying lengths. Instead of shirts, they wore some kind of wrap that went over the shoulders and covered the torso. Many of them—often older members of the community or those not participating in the dance—wore a shawl over that. The shawls also varied in length, and each was covered in unique designs. With the scene viewed through night vision, it was hard to make out the exact nature of the designs. We were at least able to determine that the patterns varied by individual.

"That's another mark against mass production, then," Markus noted.

"Unless there's a tradition of making them by hand," Abby said. "They could be sacred."

"So they're priests?" I asked.

"Or elders," Markus said. *"I'll try to scan them."*

"Be careful," said Abby.

"It's me, commander. Lilith's still on the boat."

"The fuck is that supposed to mean?"

"Quiet," Abby snapped. "Let him focus."

Markus crept along the far side of the road from the fence, putting distance between himself and the dance. This took him closer to a set of wooden structures that looked like dwellings. We briefly debated deploying another camera; eventually we decided the risk of detection was too high, particularly without knowing how inconspicuous it would be once the sun came out.

He crossed the road there, briefly visible as a burst of movement in the moonlight. The road looked muddy, but with the noise from the dance, no one would hear it. From there it was a twenty-minute belly crawl over fifty feet of ground to get into scanning range, moving in tiny increments, making sure not to draw anyone's attention. Back in the command center, we held our breath, as if the Therians would be able to hear if we made noise, too.

Comms are great at picking up surface impressions, but understanding the deeper etheric picture is kind of like a network search: the subject is associated with a bunch of other concepts, which are linked to a second-degree set of concepts, and so on. Traversing that web takes time and focus.

A ping from Markus told us he was ready to start a deep scan on the first target: an older man who might be the head of the community here, judging by the deferential body language in the people around him. He had long gray hair, tied into a ponytail, and a cane with intricate carvings. His shawl seemed a bit more ornate than the others, but it was hard to tell from this vantage point. Abby gave the order.

"*Time to play dead,*" Markus subvocalized. He did.

Markus was awfully close to the fence. I worried the firelight might shine on him between the human strands weaving their way around and through one another.

"Nothing," said Abby. "The shawls might not indicate clergy. Try his wife."

The wife was a bit more promising to my eyes, if only because she was leaning on a staff instead of a cane, and those seem more wizard like to me. Look, I may have zoned out during sociology training, but I've still got my instincts, alright?

"That's a hit," said Abby, typing into a console. "Frequency transform yields . . . two divine frequencies. One god, biphase. Signal strength is consistent with occasional rites, so it's not her occupation."

"So she's an elder," I said. "Village leader's wife does the religious stuff, at first guess."

"*Or she is their leader,*" said Markus. "*Watch how people interact with them. They talk to her first.*"

"Hell yes!" I said. "I get to be on the right end of sexism for once!"

"Calm down, nothing's confirmed," said Abby.

"*Val's going to hate this,*" said Markus. "*That's got to be it, look at the way the men don't make eye contact with her.*"

"Man's got a point," I said, leaning back with my arms folded behind my head. I shot a smug look at Abby, who pursed her lips and ignored me.

"Hit the other targets," said Abby. "Actually, the clergy hypothesis is looking weak. Just pick people who stand out. Shawls and no shawls."

"*Yes'm.*"

"I'm gonna go sit on benches and take up all the room I want," I said happily. "Then I'll explain things to people who already know them. Oh, and I'm going to start interrupting people all the time."

"*You do that already,*" said Markus, marking another target. She was standing apart from the others, her face unhealthily thin.

"I'm a natural," I said, beaming.

"We're very proud of you," said Abby. "Is this the one who looks sick, Markus? Didn't get anything off her."

"*I thought there might be a chance she follows a taboo god. Small chance.*"

"It was worth the try, I agree," said Abby. "Try the one who just left the dance. That ornamentation implies a status differential in the community."

"*On it.*"

"You see, Markus, we have to look for status differentials because it helps us map the community," I womansplained. "Then we can find out how religion plays into the map, and that tells us where to find the gods."

"Lilith, stand down before I revoke your bridge clearance."

"Don't do that, commander. I'm just a dumb man, sometimes I need to be reminded," said Markus.

Abby narrowed her eyes. "Really? You, too?"

"Gotta start practicing now, don't I? Otherwise we'll start infiltr—"

The last word cut off as Markus jerked and went completely still.

"Markus?" Abby said. "Markus, respond."

A single ping. *Holding position.* He was alive—he was just playing dead for some reason. That reason quickly revealed itself as two entwined, giggling teenagers staggered their way past Markus's location.

"Welp, at least we got a hint on their sexual mores," I said. "Markus, you good?"

"Yeah. They hopped the fence when no one was looking. Permission to extract?"

"Granted," said Abby. "Track the couple's movement first. I don't want you stumbling over them in the woods on the way out."

"What do you take me for?"

"It's a security risk," said Abby, exasperated.

I patted her shoulder. "Don't worry about him. He's a man, you know. He doesn't always pick everything up."

Markus twisted to look over his shoulder. We tracked the couple down the road, where they appeared to collapse into some bushes.

"A really *big* hint on their sexual mores," I said.

"See if you can just cross the road," said Abby. "They're too close to the route you took on the way in, even if they're occupied."

Markus gave the road a considering glance.

"I think I can make it."

He started slowly, making sure to check for more aspiring trysts in the making. So slowly, in fact, that he'd barely left his original position when Abby called out, "Markus! They're coming back!"

"What? That was barely any time at all!"

"That's what she said," I snickered.

"Lilith—"

"No, really, look at her face!"

"I don't— Markus, just get out of there!"

Markus looked over his shoulder just once. Was anyone in line of sight? Too late now, the teens were coming back, the shamefaced boy trying in vain to get the girl to look at or respond to him. Markus rolled himself across the road and stopped on the far side from the compound. For a moment it seemed like someone was about to call out, or raise the alarm, or *something.* But the night went on. The Therians continued enjoying one another's company.

We breathed a sigh of relief. We'd done it.

CHAPTER SIX

Initiative

We had a name.

The Therians rose before the sunlight, gathering for a communal blessing before the start of the workday. Those preparing for physical labor—a minority of the village, all of them male—weren't wearing their decorated shawls. The square that had last night been the site of a bonfire and dance now hosted the workers in a loose gathering. The village elder raised her hands over the assembled workers, intoning a short liturgy:

"Tireless Seindel," she said, "he who carries sun and moon, guide our hands this day. Grant unto us strength for our labor and peace in our days."

"Great Seindel, guide our hands," the workers replied.

"Mighty Horcutio, he who commands the wind and storm, forbear thy wrath."

Correction: we had *two* names. Sounded like this was the asshole who killed Val and Abby. I glanced over at them as the elder continued, but neither reacted to learning the name of the god that got them. I guess multiple centuries of this job took the novelty out of getting smote.

"Offerings we have given, that you might look mercifully upon us. Be merciful, therefore."

"Boundless Horcutio, spare our fields," said the workers.

"Bountiful Kives, she who turns the wheel of the stars, grant that these fields and these your children may grow in their season. For the fruit of our harvest shall be returned unto thee."

"Great Kives, protect the harvest," said the workers.

Three names, including the name of what was *probably* their fertility goddess and thus the oracle paining our asses. Now *that* was a windfall. Oh shit, she wasn't done. Were we gonna get the whole pantheon in one go?

"Torgaior, who sits at the feet of the gods, smile on your descendants. Grant us your favor, that we may carry your name forward."

"Honored Torgaior, favor us," said the workers.

And with that, it was done. A word and a smile from the elder, and the workers dispersed to their tasks.

Back in the command center, the four of us looked at one another. The hunt was on.

Growing up, there was a brief window—before my parents caught wise—where my brothers played a bunch of video games where the final boss was some kind of god. And the god was powerful, as befits a god, but ultimately you killed it the same way you'd been killing rats and minions and whatnot for the entire game up to that point. When I signed on with Eifni, I'd been surprised to learn it didn't work that way.

We are krill in the baleen of a god's mouth. The size differential is planetary. There *is* no weapon big enough to inflict significant damage to a god. If you're fighting a god, you're on its home turf: a civilization-sized ecosystem, deftly tuned over millennia to maximize the etheric energies that sustain and empower it. You can't fight a hurricane with a leaf blower.

Luckily for us—I mean that earnestly—initial scans of Theria told us we weren't just fighting one hurricane: we were fighting twelve. (And a lesser host of tropical storms, tornados, and . . . Well, I'm running out of wind-based metaphors here, but the point is there's a bunch of smaller critters we can ignore for now.) Two hurricanes rotating in opposite directions just cancel each other out. Etherspace is more complicated than just slamming clockwise and anticlockwise together, but the principle's the same: if you take one god's frequencies and divert them into a god that can't handle them, it'll die.

Hence the sociological research. We'd get a handle on how things worked around here, Val would do the math, and that would tell us how to set up the death blow. Technically that information was supposed to be for the secularization teams for use in creating slow, holistic, *boring* cultural changes, but we got dibs. While Eifni Org didn't necessarily expect us to pull it off, they would pay us a shitload of luxury credits if we did.

A recon team wasn't expected to spend decades on a single kill. Our methods were the quick-and-dirty kind: setting up big dramatic events, bolstered with etheric amplifiers, that struck right at the heart of a god's aspects. Those were the fun ones.

It works like this. Gods have levels to them. At the top, the main bulk of a god is wrapped up in their aspects—the concepts that define and empower them. Aspects are somewhere between engine and stomach, and the more the god has, the more energy they have to throw around.

If the aspect is a stomach, the persona is a mouth. Gods want to eat souls that line up exactly with their aspects, but souls have a lot of complicated nuance to them. So the gods pretend to be more complicated, too. If Zeus has kingship and lightning aspects but for some reason he also wants to pick up horny guys, he can encourage stories where he engages in that kind of behavior. Once that becomes part of his persona, the connection between the two ideas lets him mulch his food—never forget that's you, by the way—into a flavor he can digest. That's what paraphysicists call "conduit theory": if two concepts are associated, you can substitute one for the other, with some attenuation based on the conceptual distance.

But conduit theory opens up a vulnerability: personas can break if you put them in conflict with the aspects they're supposed to fuel. All that weight, all that carefully cultivated cultural inertia can be subverted into something poisonous. The god's own feeding mechanism will drive the stake through their heart. Sometimes all it takes is one moment, backed by the might of Eifni Org etheric amplifiers. Works better for some than others: you can seduce the love god's high priest into apostasy, but what are you going to do to the weather god? Dump water on people?

There's one other way for humans to kill a god, and if you're lucky you only have to do it once. It's risky. You have to take all that fancy mathematical analysis about the ecosystem and use it to make the god *stronger*. If you can get them all the way up to triphase, they'll collapse under their own power. It's been mathematically proven that stable triphase gods could exist, of course, but you'd need much more controlled conditions than what we do to them. Just to be safe, we try to leave a god with unstable aspects for last.

The *real* issue with the forced-empowerment kill is by the time you're going for it, you've got a pissed-off god with a dead family and you're deliberately powering it up.

But that was years away at best. For now, we began the slow but necessary work of trying to learn about a culture without actually interacting with it. And, as a secondary matter, trying to keep ourselves from dying of boredom.

Our first mission was so short we'd never had any downtime. The second had been so chaotic that we'd never had any downtime. I'd been translating for years—the linguistics kind, not the paraphysics kind—and now that we finally had an opportunity, I'd cajoled the rest of the team into humoring me.

"Okay, so the first thing you have to do is make characters," I said. "We gotta do attributes first. You roll four of these dice, drop the lowest result, and add the rest up."

"I wanna be a muscle guy," said Markus, a muscle guy. "Is that strength?"

"You need to roll high on strength and constitution for that," I said.

"I note," said Val, reading the rules document I'd translated into Velean, "that there's a section on an optional point-buy system. May we use that instead?"

"Sure, whatever," I said, distracted by Markus's character sheet. He'd drawn a ripped dude with a disruptor rifle instead of filling out any of the actual details on the sheet. Well, at least he was engaging, I guess. He struck me as one of those players that was mostly in it for the role-playing.

"You know there's no guns in this game, right?" I told him.

"Markus!" snapped Abby. "Not that die!"

We all froze. Markus breathed in through his teeth, gingerly sliding my lucky d20 away from the rest of the pile. We stared at it for a moment as if it was a bomb that might go off any moment.

"Val, check it with the moirascope," said the commander. "Lilith, we may need to incinerate it."

"I understand," I said miserably as Val left with the offending object. And I did. But I only had a few items with sentimental value from my old life, and it wasn't like Eifni Org allowed worldjump tourism. Earth was still in its quarantine period.

"Lilith?" she said. I looked up. "I'm sorry, I know it's important to you. I've got a contact in etheric research. If we do end up incinerating your lucky die, I'll call him up and we'll make you a replacement. We can make it as lucky as you want."

"That's . . . very kind, commander," I said. "It's my fault for bringing it. We'll do what we have to. What are you thinking for your character?"

"I will be a barbarian," said Abby. "And when our enemies assume that my lack of civilized manners imply a lack of tactical ability, I will reveal that I am actually quite cultured."

"While smashing them in the face with your war hammer?" I asked.

"While smashing them in the face with my war hammer," she agreed, smiling. The smile instantly died. "*Godfire*, Lilith, what is this?"

"What?" I said, taken aback. "Godfire" was the most aggressive curse word in the Velean lexicon, which was weird to me as a native of a culture that didn't find religion taboo at all, but Veles wasn't Earth. She was pointing to . . . the line for the character's deity. I'd copied it over without thinking. "Oh shit, I didn't think . . . Yeah."

Abby looked particularly unimpressed.

"We can cross it out," I said in a small voice. "It's not important to the game."

"My character will be named Slinky," Markus declared. "He's the sneakiest rogue this side of the peninsula. He turned to a life of crime so he could afford to keep his muscles oiled at all times."

His timing was perfect; Abby and I couldn't help but laugh. That broke the tension a little. Abby returned to her character sheet in a nonverbal gesture of truce.

We blotted out the field for deities, though.

"I don't think F-36 is actually married to M-10," I said, holding pictures of the aforementioned individuals side by side. "They look too similar. They gotta be related. They don't do any PDA, either. All the married couples kiss in public."

"Siblings sharing a house, then?" asked the commander. "It's possible. They're noticeably older than the nonmarried individuals, though."

We were in the command center. It was my observation shift, but the commander had dropped in to process some old footage. We had four camera feeds now, courtesy of a couple of flawless midnight excursions by yours truly. We'd kept Markus back after learning the village had its own ancestor god; my soul's partly prosthetic, courtesy of the godseed that found me on Earth, and Eifni's pneumatologists had set me up with military-grade etheric cloaking.

"Maybe they're a priestly lineage?" I asked. "Have we seen anything ceremonial happen yet?"

"Outside the daily blessing, no. The new cameras don't have line of sight inside the possible worship location."

"I could try for it tonight," I said.

"We should take readings first," said the commander. "Their ancestor might notice you slipping a camera in the ceiling."

"We could kill it," I said. "You said we'd probably have to do it eventually for OPSEC reasons."

The commander breathed deeply, her eyes fixed on the cameras but too distant to actually be paying attention.

"Do you know how to kill an ancestor god, Lilith?" she asked, a little too casually.

"It's just a conglomeration of human souls from a single lineage, right?" I asked. "If we're looking at a dozen generations or so, disruptors should do it."

"If you can get it to concentrate in one location, yes," said Abby. "But you won't hit all of it, and the rest can go running off to Kives. No, standard protocol is to deploy amplifiers and then deliver an etheric shock down the lineage. Which, let me be clear, will likely require a murder. And as you're the only person who can safely enter the target area, you'll have to be the one to pull the trigger."

I took a moment to absorb.

"It's not my first kill," I said eventually, hunching in on myself a little.

"I know," said the commander, giving me her full, knowing attention. "It's still not something to be done lightly."

I looked at F-36 and M-10. If they *were* a priestly lineage, would that make them the ones I'd need to kill?

"Oh," I said. "F-36 is a widow, I'd bet. Brother took her in."

"Or the other way around," said Abby. "It's a matriarchal culture. But it's a good explanation." She paused. "Let me know if you need to talk about it."

"No, I'm pretty confident in this theory."

"Lilith."

I sighed. "I'll let you know."

"Okay, so the paladin goes up to negotiate with the goblins, but you can see that it's not going well. The group behind their leader raises their crossbows and aims them at Val."

"*What?*" said Val.

"Must be those fancy clothes you're wearing," I said smugly.

"I told you I was switching back to traveling clothes before we left the city," said Val. He didn't exactly raise his voice, but his tone was certainly more intense than usual.

"He did, Lilith," said Markus.

"I draw my battle-ax and threaten them in their language," said Abby.

"Wait, you know Goblin?" I asked.

"Of course." Abby looked at me quizzically. "You told us we'd be fighting the Goblin people. Were you expecting us to do a commando mission without learning the local language?"

I blinked at her. "Okay, whatever, it's not your turn yet. Anyway, Val, they're aiming at you."

He sighed. "I'm sure this has nothing to do with the fact that I happened to remember Markus got a save when you were trying to get his character arrested. Fine, you've forced my hand. I'll move up eight spaces and attack all of them at once."

"You can't do that," I said. "It's one action per attack."

"Cleave feat," he said, indicating his character sheet.

"You need two actions for that, and you used one to move," I said.

"I have the Quick Step feat," said Val. "And before you object to the target selection, my weapon has plus-five range."

I stared forlornly at him. "Fine, you dick. Roll it."

He rolled a twenty, looking way too fucking pleased with himself. "I can roll for damage," he said, "but the minimum on a critical with my attribute bonuses is eight damage, which I believe is the hit-point total on these particular enemies."

"*Ugh*. Fine, you kill all the crossbow goblins. Way to ruin my encounter. Their leader is furious, and he's gonna fucking stab you to death on his next turn. Markus, you're up next."

Markus gave the board a considering look.

"I roll to seduce the paladin."

After months of surveillance, the back wall of the command center was a tangle of pictures and string representing the vast spectrum of human relationships. Family, rivalry, respect, love, lust, ambition—it was all noted on the wall in one of four examples of handwriting. We'd picked up body language and gestures, family structures, even a marriage ceremony. What was the line from *War of the Worlds*? Something about going about their daily concerns while a greater intelligence scrutinized them like microbes under a microscope? In the space of a couple months, they'd gone from a run-of-the-mill community to lab specimens without ever realizing it.

We'd all packed into the command center to stare at our handiwork. I was proud of us.

"Commander?" I asked. "Are we ready for first contact?"

"Just about," she said. "Val's got the engines functional again, so we can make a quick getaway if we have to. I'd like to get more speech samples before we start live-contact exercises. It's a shame we had to put the cameras so far out."

"Perhaps now is our opportunity to kill the ancestor," said Val. "It would not be prudent to move in closer before that point."

The commander's eyes flicked my direction. "Lilith?"

I breathed in, out. "I can do it, commander."

"I'll prep an amplifier," said Val. "Hemispheric, do you think?"

The commander nodded. "Keeping things contained is good. I'll need you on standby with the moirascope in case we alert Kives. In your analysis, what's our best target for the etheric shock?"

Val studied the web of human interconnection.

"Three possibilities," he said after a moment of contemplation. "One, they're all valid descendants. Two, there's a distinct family descent. Three, there was a distinct descent and they're all dead now. Given the lack of an honored family other than the village elder's in the sociogram, we should assume that any such descent passes through the elder. If there is no distinct descent, she's the best indirect link due to her role and its association with the village. That makes her our best target irrespective of case."

I looked at the pictures of the elder and her husband. Both were smiling. She'd done nothing to deserve it; it was just an accident of birth. Killing her would deeply wound the community for certain. But there was a predator lurking just on the other side of realspace, a thing that had once been human and was now eating its descendants. A monster that had ended countless existences and might have ended countless more if it hadn't come to stand in our way.

"Okay," I said. "I'm ready. Let's do it tonight."

One eternity against many. Sometimes you just had to shut up and do the math.

CHAPTER SEVEN

Knife

The stars were bright in the midnight sky. They shone inconsistently through the canopy of the forest as I hiked to kill someone.

I didn't dwell on it too much. It wasn't a very comfortable thought. Instead, I focused on pushing my way through the dense undergrowth, holding branches aside for Val, who was carrying the main bulk of the amplifier on his back.

The resonator was vaguely torpedo-shaped, though more of a box with a rounded top than a tube. At four feet tall, with the straps positioned as they were, it extended over his head, which made navigating the forest difficult. Smooth, gray-white plastic encased the device's inner workings, a series of circuits designed to produce sympathetic effects that would read etheric ripples and pump them full of additional power. The resonator was only part of the amplifier; there were also seven collapsible nodes, to be set up at the village boundaries, that would reflect the wave back to the resonator rather than let it dissipate into the ether.

You know how dropping a grenade in an enclosed space turns everyone inside into chunky salsa? Same principle.

We were in camo. I had a shimmering white dress packed into my duffel for the mission proper. We were all armed with disruptor pistols and pulsers for the nonlethal option; Markus also had a duffel full of tricks and a rifle slung over his shoulder in case things really went to shit. Each of us carried a hand amplifier—basically a peashooter compared to the thing on Val's back, but useful against minor etheric beings. I had a knife in an arm sheath, but I wasn't thinking about that right now.

In the altered monochrome world of night vision, Markus and Val had glowing eyes, thanks to their ocular implants. My eyes would have looked the same to them, ocular implants being one of the few augments it was possible to do on Veles without building them into the body from the start. Funny how moving to fancy reincarnation technology slows down surgical advances.

"*You guys have been at this awhile,*" I subvocalized. "*You ever regret the stuff you've done?*"

"*No,*" Val replied. "*Perhaps when I was younger. But I've seen what gods do to a civilization. The division, the subjugation, the war. This is justified.*"

"*She's just an old lady,*" I said. "*She didn't do anything.*"

"*She doesn't know she's done anything,*" said Markus gently. "*But she prays every day for that ancestor to protect the village.*"

"*She is perpetuating a massacre,*" said Val. "*And by her death, she can end it.*"

"*For this Torgy fucker,*" I said. "*The pantheon's still out there. They're still going to get eaten.*"

"*And we will be free to act against them,*" said Val. "*We can sweep the gods from this world and hand it over to Eifni for uplifting. When the Therians can reincarnate without fear, they'll be able to truly self-actualize.*"

And that was the goal. Eternal life, eternal freedom. I centered myself, took a deep breath, looked ahead. The trees were thinning. We'd be there soon.

"*Are you ready?*" asked Markus.

I nodded, determined. "*Thanks, guys. Let's kill an ancestor.*"

The village was reasonably sized for a preindustrial farming community, less than a hundred people, all told. Seeing it in person was a strange experience, like visiting a location you'd only seen in photographs. Well, I guess that was basically what was happening here, I'd been staring at this place through cameras for months.

I got the shimmering dress out of my duffel and threw it over my camo. We'd not seen evidence of more advanced materials science in the surveillance period, so impressive-looking fabric like this should sell the ruse I was a divine agent. We'd argued back and forth over whether I needed a shawl like the villagers wore, but the dress clearly hadn't been tailored to work with one. The bride at the wedding we'd seen hadn't worn one, either, so we bet that it wouldn't raise too many eyebrows. The dress itself was billowy but left me a deceptive amount of mobility. The things you have to consider when designing a formal dress for combat.

The pulser went up my voluminous sleeve. My disruptor pistol stayed in its holster, disguised by folds in the fabric, which also disguised the slit that would allow me to grab it without hiking up the dress. Markus set off with the barrier poles, guided by directions from the commander, who was watching from the command center. Val planted the resonator in the ground, lining it up with the building we'd determined was their religious center.

"*The knife,*" he subvocalized.

I drew it without much hesitation and laid the blade against the dome of the resonator. Thousands of years of technological development and Eifni still made their combat knives out of steel. Val typed some commands.

"*Linking,*" he said. "*Hold it still.*"

I did. The resonator hummed softly as it created an etheric entanglement with the knife. We were silent otherwise, the night interrupted occasionally by soft conversation between Markus and the commander. Thirty seconds later, it was done: whatever happened with the knife would get channeled directly to the resonator. Val released a catch and flipped a small shelf down on the side. I put the knife on the shelf.

"*Starting attunement . . . now,*" he said.

This part always fascinated me. I'd made a habit in my pre-Eifni days of, whenever I noticed myself making associations with something, stripping those associations away and looking just at the object. The knife wasn't a murder weapon, it was just a sharp piece of steel.

But as the attunement process commenced, it became impossible to see it as anything but a murder weapon. I couldn't point to anything specific about it—because it wasn't actually physical, it was a conduit for etheric energies—but the angles seemed more wicked, the edge sharper, the shape insidious. And yet the process continued. It went beyond pure murder: it was the end of a lineage. The destruction of a people and every tradition they held.

Slaying the past by preventing the future. The exact calibrated frequency to kill an ancestor god.

It was also quite evil. It made me uncomfortable just to stand near it. But evil, as every godslayer learns, is ultimately a sociological concept. This, more than anything, demonstrates the insidious nature of gods. All cultures want to flourish and grow; all cultures want their pasts to be remembered. These things are good. And if a god, even a minor one, sets up shop inside that stream of goodness, then a community doing *exactly what communities should do* will, by no fault of their own, become fodder. The mathematical inverse of good is evil, and both are ultimately just wave functions in etherspace. Our preference for one over the other doesn't change the math.

It was done.

"*Your turn*," said Val.

I placed my hands on the dome of the resonator. We weren't going to link me up like we did the knife; this was just about etheric camouflage.

"*Starting now*," said Val.

Warmth spread through me then: trust, beneficence, hope for the future—that last frequency not much different than Kives's progressive aspect, perhaps. Subtones of awe, transcendence, beauty. It would make for a good first impression, but more importantly it would mask the aura of the vile knife hidden up my sleeve.

"*How does it feel to be an angel?*" Val asked.

"*Floaty*," I said. "*Be right back, gonna visit plague unto the enemies of the Lord.*"

He smirked. "*Commander, we're set.*"

"Good. Markus has four poles to go. Lilith, you're cleared to begin."

And lo, the angel Lilith descended upon the unsuspecting village of what's its name on a mission of woe.

I really did like the dress, but I somehow managed the discipline to avoid swishing it around unnecessarily. It wouldn't do for some farmer out for a midnight piss to see me twirling around in the moonlight like I was six again. Not very angelic. Instead I adopted more of a floaty, swaying motion as I walked to get the dress to billow around me. It wasn't my uniform, with the awesome Velean long coat, but it would do.

It was time to cloak myself. I reached through my comm and flicked a metaphysical switch. Inside my soul, something—shifted. I became smaller, more distant.

Less . . . real, I guess? Even to myself. The world faded a little, and everything took on a dreamlike quality. And I was a dream, too, the half-remembered thought of someone else, to be forgotten on waking, like I was never here. And by the transitive property I wasn't here now, either.

The villagers hadn't set a guard. With the pulser up my sleeve, it wouldn't have been a problem if they had, but it was still one less potential complication. I swayed through the gate unchallenged. A threshold, breached. I tried to focus myself, to keep my wits sharp.

In this alt-Mediterranean climate, the ground would never be completely dry. The villagers had dealt with that problem by tossing chaff from their grain over the paths, which over time seemed to have hardened into a fairly solid road. My combat boots rolled right off the path with none of the gross suction that came with mud. They were visible beneath the hem of my dress; between my newly acquired aura and the darkness, I was really hoping they went overlooked. Angel in Combat Boots sounds like a good name for a band, am I right?

The road was almost a little bouncy, even. My socio instructor always told us cadets that all cultures were highly adapted to their environments, and I could see why. Whatever the technology level, people found solutions to their problems. Problem solvers everywhere. I nodded to myself through the haze.

I observed their buildings as I passed through them like a ghost, shimmering pearlescent fabric sweeping behind me. Wooden structures, treated with some kind of tar to keep out the rot. The rot was metaphysical, I mused. Rot all around. I was here to cut it out.

I was here for the first time, only I wasn't here, so did it count? No, I was here. I tried to force myself awake, remember my meditation skills. Needed to focus on the mission, couldn't get too drifty, like this lovely, lovely dress. Maybe a quick spin? No one was here.

No. Needed to focus.

I walked down the path, light, just a wisp of death. Death to gods. They fall, they die. I didn't sneak; I *was* a god, or at least the agent of one, or at least I was supposed to be. I had every right to walk down this path in the starlight. I was supposed to be here: that's what they teach you in infiltration school. Act natural. Or supernatural. I smirked. Let them make the excuses for you. Don't give them anything to doubt. Like that young man over there. He was going to see me, I knew with that strange dream logic. And it was okay. I wasn't here, I won't have been here. I was just a dream.

He saw me, shimmering in the starlight, my eyes glowing a soft violet.

"My— Milady?" he asked in a language I'd never heard before. He seemed to remember something and quickly looked away. No eye contact, right. As befit a woman above his station.

I smiled. Just a dream. There was nothing to fear.

"Come," I said, holding out my hand.

He did, after hesitating. Who knows how long? I didn't. Time was just an illusion in the dream world. "Who are you? Have you come for me?"

"Yes," I said distantly. "I am a messenger of the gods. Close your eyes."

He did. My pulser was in my hand now. I pressed a chaste, angelic kiss to his forehead, then pulsed him. A targeted ether burst hit him right in the mind-body connection. He collapsed in the dirt. Now he was dreaming, too.

I floated gently over his prone body. The clouds parted, revealing the full moon. I liked the way it made my dress shimmer. The elder's house was ahead, full of people who weren't her. They didn't do the whole nuclear family thing here. Extended families, many people to pulse. Can you put sleeping people to sleep? I was going to find out.

"*I'm at the target's house,*" I told the team. I opened the door to the elder's house. In the main room, a family huddled together on mats, deep in sleep. Mom, dad, some children. One of them stirred.

"Sweet dreams," I told him softly. I raised the pulser and sent him back to sleep. Six more to go.

The pulser was a neat little tool, perfectly shaped to fit in my palm. Reminded me of Star Trek phasers, a thought that nearly made me giggle as I worked my way through the family. When fired it didn't make any visual effects, just a nice warmth while the trigger was depressed. *Click. Click.* Night night, Mom. Night night, Dad.

It wasn't really sleep, was it? More like interruption of consciousness. I was turning people off for a bit. Isn't that sleep, though?

I needed to come back. You could get lost in the cloak fugue. I had something important to do. The elder, right. Next room. Pulse the husband. Okay, pull it together, Lilith. Time to perform. I turned up the glow on my eyes.

A hand on the elder's shoulder woke her up.

"Do not be afraid," I said, channeling my memories of Sunday school. "I come with good tidings."

I wondered what she thought of me, with the moonlight streaming through the window behind me, wearing a dress unlike anything she'd even seen, eyes glowing violet. Keep your head in the game, Lilith.

"Who are you?" she asked.

"My name is . . . Arwin," I said beatifically. "I bear a message from the gods."

"Is this a dream?" she asked.

"Yes and no." I smiled. Mysterious angel. Remember that. "What is your name?"

"Arguel," said the elder, sitting up. She turned to her husband, shaking his shoulder. "Nima! Nima! Wake up!"

"He won't wake," I said. "This message is for you alone."

At that she seemed to sharpen. A light sleeper. I hoped she wouldn't wake up afterward and ruin the mission. Wait, no, that's not how being dead works. Stay sharp, Lilith.

"Then it's time?" she asked, touching two fingers to the bridge of her nose. "Gods preserve us."

I was about to say something else, but that threw me for a fucking loop. Had Kives set us up? No, I wasn't getting annihilated by an angel right now. A real one, I mean.

But this was weird. Sometimes you ran into zealots who treated this maneuver like an answer to prayer, but I'd never heard of them acting like your office had called them last week to confirm the appointment.

"Oh, uh, no," I said, wondering what the hell she was talking about. "Different message. Than that one. Come with me to the chapel and all will be revealed."

Arguel smiled at me.

"You're so young," she said wistfully. "Like my Giri. Does she serve the gods as you do?"

Giri must be dead, I realized. "I am but a messenger. There is much I cannot reveal," I said. Things were sliding off the rails. That was something that happened in dreams, too. "Come with me."

"Oh, you poor thing," said Arguel, taking my hand and climbing strenuously to her feet. "Don't be nervous on my account."

"I don't feel nervous," I said. I didn't. I felt distant. I felt ethereal.

"*Lilith!*" came the commander's voice. "*What the hell is going on?*"

"Don't lie to a grandmother, girl," said Arguel with a chuckle. "You look like a bachelorette before Stormbreak. Here, help an old woman keep upright."

I took her arm, mentally signaling the commander that all was okay. We left by the main room. The deception had unraveled, but all was okay anyway. That's how dreams worked. Things just continued.

"That's my Yani, and her Gurid," said Arguel as we passed her descendants. "And the tots, Yis, Vensla, Guryen, Kell, and little Fenra. He's such a light sleeper, he'll be so upset when I tell him an angel visited in his sleep."

"He's very cute," I said. Was that something an angel would say? Never mind. I was an angel, and I'd said it. Act supernatural.

"I'll tell him you said that." Arguel laughed again. "An angel of Kives. She does love the little ones."

"They are precious in her sight," I agreed, grasping at straws. Interesting that she'd pegged me as one of Kives's. Must be my supernatural perfume. "We go in silence now. Come, dawn approaches."

In, like, five hours. But it was the kind of thing angels said. Well, more like the kind of things *Lord of the Rings* characters said, but if you didn't grow up on Earth you basically can't tell the difference. We walked through the village together. I was unhurried because I knew—again, with that strange dream logic—we'd reach our destination without trouble.

The chapel was built more cylindrically the other buildings. The doors were larger than the ones I'd seen in the domiciles of the village. I opened one for Arguel.

"Someone needs to teach you some pride," she laughed, but walked inside. Did anyone hear? They did, or they didn't. Things would happen. That was the world of the dream. I followed and closed the door. I flared my eyes, taking in all the details. Frescos, wooden carvings, a firepit in the middle of the room. For burnt offerings, maybe?

"So what's all this about, girl?" asked Arguel. "You said it's not about the Calamity."

"It is, in a way," I said, with a distant sinking sensation as I began to suspect what—who—the Calamity must be. "The goddess is mustering all available forces. She asks that your honored ancestor take up arms in defense of her children."

Arguel touched the bridge of her nose again in that gesture of piety.

"By her will," she said. "What must I do?"

"Call him," I said. "Ask him to appear."

Arguel nodded. "Honored Torgaior! I, your descendant, call upon your name!" She moved to the altar, placing both hands on it. I glided behind her as she repeated the invocation twice more. She continued: "Hear me in this hour of desperation! Our gods call on us to muster against the end of all things! I pray thee listen and appear before me, your honored descendant, in the name of Kives!"

It was done. My comm read a slight uptick in divine energy in the chapel. Torgaior was preparing to appear.

"Your faith has been rewarded," I said. "He comes."

Arguel made that pious gesture again. "That this would happen in my time," she said. She turned to me. "Please," she said, clutching my arm. "Angel of Kives, I beg you. Fight the Calamity. I've had my time. Let my grandchildren grow up in peace."

"That is all I want," I said, which was perhaps the most honest thing I'd told her all night.

As my comm shouted warnings that a divine manifestation was imminent, I drew my knife and slit her throat.

CHAPTER EIGHT

Doom

The blood sprayed out between Arguel's wrinkled fingers as she grabbed at her ruined throat and choked. It ran down the topography of her sun-beaten skin, soaking into intricately woven nightclothes. Her pale-blue eyes widened; shock, pain, betrayal, and horror played across her face.

She collapsed onto the floor of the chapel, voiceless, her heart driving the blood out of her into a growing pool below her neck.

Her eyes never left my face as she died. I wondered what she saw there in her final moments.

My grip tightened on my knife. I'd killed people before, but from a distance. Somewhere beyond the cloak fugue, an almost dysphoric sense of revulsion wrenched at me. But for now I was safe. It couldn't find me because I wasn't here. I was just a dream. This was all a dream. The dreamer would wake, and Arguel would be gone.

A sense of solemnity filled the air as Torgaior manifested. Dark-brown hair, rounded face—kind of Asian looking, to an Earth native, but the eye color was wrong, and the facial structure wasn't quite the same—sharp chin. His eyes passed blankly over me and found the body on the floor.

"Who?!" he yelled. "Who would do such a thing?!"

The air was darkening, stained by the evil thing I'd done. The reverberations of the murder passed through the knife, its attunement filtering out exactly what was needed to slay the ancestor, passing through the resonator and rebounding across the village. Seven poles and a resonator, marking an octagonal boundary centered on the very building we stood in.

It burned him.

Torgaior arched in pain as the ether backlash hit him, fracturing his being along the ramshackle addition of souls. He screamed. A flicker of something hateful stirred in my gut.

"Go on, you piece of shit," I said. "Eat her soul. Choke on it and die."

He trembled as the corrupted frequency corroded his essence, the sympathetic effects crippling his avatar with pain.

"I hear you, murderer," he said through gritted teeth. "And I will end you."

"Murderer?" I scoffed. "How many *souls* have you eaten?"

"They are my progeny," he hissed. "They are *mine*."

"Fuck you," I said, taking a step closer. It would be okay. This was how the dream went. I could kill him before he died.

The dying godling tilted his head, sensing my intent if not my actual person, and clawed the air with his hand. The air screamed as his power rent the world. The wall behind me splintered, letting in the night air. I heard shouting outside. He slumped to his knees, looking blankly ahead. He hadn't been human in a long time, it seemed: he was ignoring the eyeballs on his avatar in favor of his etheric senses.

"You missed," I said, walking closer. Should I be afraid? No. He couldn't hit me because I wasn't here. "Arguel's never coming back because of you. And she was so sweet." I was in range. I lifted my knife. "She had *grandchildren*!"

My knife, still dripping with the blood of his descendant, punched straight into his heart. A scream ripped out of his throat, something too harsh to have been made with mere vocal cords. He fell to the ground, curling up.

"They fall," I spat. I kicked him in the gut. "They *die*."

"You—fool," the god gasped.

"What's that, granny eater?"

"No," he said, each word an obvious effort. "Didn't—her soul."

I paused. "What?"

"She goes now—to Kives. My life. For yours." A twisted smile worked its way across his face. "Calamity."

At last, he lay still.

Oh shit.

Oh *shit*.

"Everyone, we're compromised, get out!" I said.

"*Lilith, what's going on?*"

Right, I needed to update the team. I'd forgotten about them for a moment. The shouting outside had ended, but they meant they were probably going to be here soon. "Commander, I got the target, but he refused the elder's soul. And apparently the next-best match was Kives. She's going to know we're here any second now. Everyone needs to get out *right now*."

The commander responded instantly. "*Team, extract immediately. Val, grab the resonator and liquidate the rest. Lilith, do you need support to extract?*"

"I don't. They'll never find me," I said distantly.

"*Dammit, Lilith, you said you had a handle on this! Markus, get in there and extract her! Lilith, turn off the damn cloak!*"

"*On my way*," he replied.

I reached through my soul and turned off the cloak. All at once it hit me, the adrenaline, the fear, the disgust—oh god I could smell the blood—oh *god*, poor Arguel, had I really done that?—that *fucking* god, dead on the floor, the cause of all this, smirking in death. I gave him another kick, then retched. Didn't vomit, though, that was a plus.

It was *chilling* in here, where the etheric residue was thickest. In my newfound clarity of thought I realized the aura of concentrated evil was probably keeping the villagers away from this place. *I* certainly didn't want to be here, but for now it was keeping me safe, so I told my brain that we needed to stay in the horrible, creepy death environment.

"Markus, they're not approaching the chapel from what I can see," I said. "I might need a distraction if there's no window. I'll be recloaking when I exit."

"*I got you,*" he said.

"*Amplifier nodes successfully liquidated,*" said Val. "*I have the resonator. Extracting now.*"

"*Good job, Val. Lilith, you can use the cloak if you're surrounded, but if it's affecting your tactical judgment this much, I'm ordering you to leave it off. Now is not the time for mistakes.*"

"I'm handling it!" I said. "I killed the target, didn't I?"

"*Shut up and get out of there!*"

"I'm going, I'm going!"

The angel disguise had outlived its usefulness, and I had the etheric miasma all over me, so no one would buy it if I kept wearing the dress. I ripped it off, the light fabric tearing easily, and tossed it on the godling's corpse. My lighter came out of one of my newly accessible pockets. The dress, sadly, also burned well—couldn't leave evidence for the diviners to follow. I touched the lighter to a couple spots to make sure it caught. I snagged the knife while I was at it—it was entangled with the resonator, didn't want that pointing back to us.

"Scene is clear," I said. "Markus, I'm exiting north."

I drew my pulser and peeked out the chapel entrance—by which I mean the entrance that was supposed to be there, as opposed to their quisling ancestor's ad hoc remodel just now. The moon was full enough that people would see me if I ducked out. And there were people, huddled together. With my enhanced vision I could make out the expressions on their faces like it was day—they were scared to death. The amplifier had pumped the entire area full of doom, and it was strongest here. Some had crude weapons, others farming implements. Here and there people lit torches, which I appreciated because they were killing their night vision.

None approached. But there weren't any obvious openings, either.

"Markus," I said, "I'm gonna need that opening."

"*Copy that. I'm thinking demons.*"

"Shit, Markus, these kids are gonna have nightmares already."

He laughed. "*Repositioning to the east. Get ready to go.*"

"I might have to make a break for it," I said, eyeing a group of teenage boys who were obviously mustering the courage to investigate. "Possible incoming contacts."

"*You're authorized for disruptor rounds,*" said the commander. "*We can't let Kives get any more information.*"

I pursed my lips at that. I didn't want to kill anyone else tonight, especially with soul-shredding bullets. "I'll stick with my pulser if that's alright."

"*Twenty seconds,*" said Markus.

One of the kids had taken a few shaking steps toward the chapel. His fellows cheered him on. Emboldened by their praise, he set his shoulders and began walking, brandishing a stick. Some of the adults were taking notice. Good leadership potential, that one.

"I'm going now," I said. "Sorry, commander, I'll have to cloak. I'll do better this time."

"I mean it, Lilith. I'm not losing anyone today if I can help it."

"I know, I know," I said, trying to remember my training as I turned the cloak on again—to a lower setting, this time. The anesthetic haze returned like a warm pillow after you hit the snooze button for the last time, no, really. But even as I became less real, I tried to hold on to my willpower. I pushed through the doors and slipped away into the night, a shadow among shadows. Not invisible—irrelevant, illusory. I was pareidolia incarnate, the phantom movement in the corner of your vision, the shape that vanishes when you blink. I wasn't— I *was* there, unseen, and getting the hell out of dodge.

The would-be hero never saw me go. His prize would be discovering the bodies first. Sorry, kid.

The next hurdle was a smaller group—a family, by the looks of them—who were all looking to their matriarch for reassurance in the sinister fallout from the amplifier. Markus's timing was perfect: a horrifying roar spilled out through the streets. A noise like that would be a major concern for a precomputerized society with no conception of audio engineering. The children in front of me screamed, echoed all across the village. Their parents picked them up and started running away from the noise. Great parenting instincts, but they were heading straight for me. That was fine, I wasn't here. No, *focus*, Lilith, I *was* there, I had to get out of the fucking way.

I managed it, tucked into the shadow of a tree. Another roar shook the village. I ran toward the noise as fast as my legs would take me. I felt doomed. I knew exactly what caused it and why, but my stupid meat brain kept flicking back to the ancestor's final words. Was Kives tracking me even now? Fuck, I was carrying a knife that was entangled with something Val was taking back to the ship at this very moment. That was a little doom worthy, wasn't it? Surely all of this couldn't just be the horrible murder whose aura was still tied to my arm.

"Val, can you cut the entanglement?" I asked, breathing heavily. "I'm freaking out a little here."

"Lilith," the commander cut in, *"you're nearing Markus's position. It's a straight shot from there to the amplifier-effect boundary. Just hang in there."*

Val chimed in. *"Cutting the entanglement would require standing still, which currently seems unwise. I'm staying away from the ship for now."*

"Lilith, I don't see you," said Markus.

"I think I'm close," I said, barreling around a corner and nearly colliding with a cart. "Comm check."

I got a ping. Markus was close, like same-strip-mall kind of close.

"I'm in the field," he said. *"The corn-y plants."*

I barked out a breathless laugh—which probably confused the others, since that wasn't a pun in Velean. "Okay, I see you!"

"*I don't see you,*" he said. "*Tune me in.*"

I got another ping from Markus's comm. I fed it into the cloak, which would let anyone with that frequency see through its effect. With my night vision I saw him perk up and wave. I kept running straight at him until he caught me in a hug.

"Heya, big guy," I said, hugging him back. "Let's get the fuck out of here."

"Let me grab the duffel," he said, releasing me.

"Only if you give me the rifle," I said, flashing him a grin. "One of us should have it ready."

"Duffel's yours, then," he said.

I pouted but picked it up. "Oof, I'm gonna be sore in the morning. Which way out?"

Markus pointed. "I'll watch our backs. Commander, we're extracting. Route C, I've got a bad feeling about the others."

"Just the fallout, Markus," I tried, but the doom was clinging to me like my high school boyfriend when I realized I was ace.

"*Acknowledged. Val, what's your status?*"

"*Pretending to be a woodsman, commander.*"

"*See if you can circle back and provide overwatch in the case of pursuit.*"

"*Affirmative.*"

"We're out of the fallout area," Markus said. "Proceeding along route."

It was a breath of fresh air. We were making a good pace of it, but once we stepped out of the fallout, our breath came easier, our limbs moved just a bit more quickly. The sense of doom and calamity receded. Mostly. Some of it was still strapped to my arm.

"It feels like one of those nightmares where you're just being followed by something," I said as we jogged toward the forest. The dreaminess of the cloak was just making it worse. We left the clear-cut portion of the forest, following the path cut through by the villagers in past times.

"We are, if you think about it," said Markus. "We don't know how long it'll take before Kives sends her goons after us."

I shuddered for no logical reason. "Commander, I'm dropping the cloak."

"*Negative, Lilith. Just keep it manageable. It could be the only thing protecting you right now. Markus, if she fugues, snap her out of it.*"

Eugh, fine, I'd just live with the creeping sensation of horror for now. I was going to take *so many* showers after this.

Just before we hit the tree line, a shadow passed over the moon. We looked up and halted immediately. Our comms blared warnings. Almost invisible against the starry sky, a cloaked figure flew deeper into the forest.

"Commander, we owe you one," Markus whispered. "Angelic contact. Same as the ambush. Heading . . . east, by the looks of it."

I breathed a sigh of relief, or as much as I could while continuing to jog.

"*Ah. East, you say?*" asked Val. "*That may be a problem.*"

"Oh no," said Markus.

I checked my comm. The angel was heading straight for Val.

CHAPTER NINE

The Blessing of the Goddess

O*h* godfire," Val swore, followed by the sound of distant gunfire to the east.
        "*Val, report.*"

"*Busy—*"

More gunfire, suddenly stopping. Val yelled in pain over the comm. Three more shots.

"Val?!" I said. "What's going on?"

"*Die, you animal.*" Val was the angriest I'd ever heard him, voice strained with what had to be a significant wound. He fired one more time. "*Commander, I've been ambushed by dryads. I regret to inform you that they are combat effective. Disruptor lethality confirmed but multiple shots required.*"

"*How bad is the injury?*"

"*I—can't walk.*"

"Shit," Markus muttered.

"We'll circle around and pick you up," I said.

"*Ah, don't bother,*" said Val, grunting with some kind of exertion. "*My comm says more are coming. I have*"—another grunt here—"*insufficient ammunition.*"

"Fuck!" I yelled.

"Quiet!" Markus hissed.

"Whatever, I'm invisible," I said.

"*I've set the resonator to self-destruct,*" said Val. "*It'll cut the entanglement with the knife. Keep you safe. I'll try to hold them off until then.*"

"*Val, I'm deploying the ship to your location,*" said the commander. "*ETA—damn it! Val, you said the engines were fixed! It's not responding!*"

"*Error code?*" Val grunted. "*I have maybe ten seconds.*"

"*Nothing, it's just hanging.*"

"*Ah. Boot script must be glitched. I'll fix it when I get back. Or you could, if I don't.*" His vocal tone changed, confident, furious, only the slightest hint of pain behind them. "*Come and die, then! Your friends are dead! I can kill you just as easily!*"

"Is he trying to bluff *dryads*?" I asked. "They literally don't have brains."

"It's Val," said Markus. "He bluffed the high priest of a god of thieves once."

"How will you guard the forest lying dead in this clearing?"

"Wait, are they talking *back?*" I asked. "I thought they didn't do that."

"Commander?" asked Markus.

"Don't distract him."

"What does it matter if I'm wounded? My weapon works just fine. Walk away now. How many more corpses will suffice to demonstrate my point?"

"He didn't put *nearly* this much effort into role-playing his character," I said.

"You go to your doom, angel. My companions are even better armed. Your master spends you frivolously."

Angel? Markus and I looked at each other. Yep, Val was giving us a warning. There was no way we could make it to the ship before it found us, but we increased our speed as much as possible in the tangled undergrowth of the forest.

"Then die!" The muffled pops of Val's disruptor pistol sounded in the distance again. I hoped he made it. We had to worry about ourselves right now.

I was cloaked, but apparently the other end of the entanglement still pointed right at me. The angel came in low, flying between branches with supernatural agility. In the leaf-dappled moonlight I saw only a black cloak, not even a weapon.

It landed in front of us. Without the *Ragnar*'s shielding between us, I felt the full effect of its conceptual bleed: a sense of limitless, rushing time, the current of history, the endless cycle of ages. There was a deep gravity to it, as if this moment were eternal, infinitely recurrent.

I ignored all of that and opened fire.

It blinked to the side as the first few bullets passed through where it initially stood. One arm reached out and ripped a branch off a nearby tree, which began to warp and writhe in its grasp, lengthening into a staff. I fired a few more shots, tracking its center mass, but it stepped to the side, whirling under an automatic burst from Markus's rifle. I popped off what would have been a head shot had its head not bent unnaturally to the side as it came out of the whirl. Markus maintained trigger discipline, not spraying erratically like I probably would have, but it danced between the bullets. I emptied the rest of my magazine to similar effect. Its quarterstaff flicked the last bullet out of the air with a shower of sparks.

"Angels are *bullshit*," I said. "What is this, *The Matrix*?"

Surrender, it said, and its voice was the sound of rise and fall, the inescapable momentum of the past to the present to the future. Sexless, ageless, inevitable.

"Get out of here, Lilith," said Markus. "I'll distract it."

"The hell you will."

The Calamity may yet be minimized, it said. *You must surrender now, or the costs will be ruinous.*

Tactical mistake, all this chatting. It'd given us the time to reload.

"Oh no, oracle bullshit, we're so confused." My lips twisted in a snarl. "Guess what, asshole? *We did the math.* There's only one future. If there's a calamity coming, calamity is what you're going to get."

Its body language didn't shift, but a mixed sense of curiosity and disdain emanated from it. For our part, all that emanated were bullets. Markus in particular went for what the commander would probably frown on me for describing as "spray and pray."

We got its cloak, I think, but it didn't seem to care about the storm of bullets, blinking to the side again. Behind it, disruptor bullets slammed into tree trunks, leaving behind mere wood and leaves. The angel whirled its staff, knocking shots out of the air, then finished with a flick of the wrist. It must have done something to weight the staff unevenly because it spun through the air with the center of gravity near one end. The erratic-looking flight was impossible to dodge effectively, and it slapped the rifle out of Markus's hands.

The Calamity is foretold, this is true, it said. *The damage is not.*

Markus had drawn his pistol. The angel corkscrewed through the air at him, throwing off my aim as I unloaded on it, and pushed Markus's hand away as he tried to bring his pistol to bear. The angle of fire was too close; I'd risk hitting Markus, and even a glancing hit from disruptor ammo could disintegrate his soul. Markus turned the momentum from the push into a thrown elbow, which the angel casually blocked with one hand, but which left him able to fire at its feet. It jumped back.

"Markus! We have to coordinate!" I said, slamming another magazine into my pistol.

"How?!" he shouted.

I hear you but faintly, child, the angel said. Markus fired again, but it ducked and charged him. Two shots went over its head before it sprang up, its shoulder throwing off his arm and sending the third shot into the trees.

Wait, it couldn't see through the cloak? How was it dodging my bullets? If it was really just about speed, why not just take our guns?

Know that you cannot win, the angel said. *I am not slain today.*

"Still stabbable," I said to myself, drawing my knife, still hazy with doom. Markus threw a punch, but before it landed the angel put a palm on his chest and *pushed*. Markus yelled as he flew backward about twenty feet and rolled another ten. If he'd hit a tree at that speed, he'd have died instantly. I realized after a moment that it'd just invited me to empty the rest of my magazine, and it was only polite to fire six shots at its back as I closed the distance. The first two went wide as it swept to the side; it ducked the next, did some kind of weird floaty roll for the fourth, and righted itself with its staff to block the last two. But that put me near knife range—I lunged—

Crack! I felt my wrist bones shattering as the staff came down on my knife hand. I yelled and hadn't finished yelling before my wrist hit the ground and had to yell harder.

Frustration is a poor teacher, said the angel. It stalked toward Markus. *Control your passions. Examine the reason for your failure.*

"Eat shit," I said, struggling to reload my pistol with one hand. One last magazine. Twelve bullets against an oracle's soldier who—it'd seen them all coming, of course, I was an idiot. I just had to figure out a pattern of shots it was impossible to dodge. I levered myself onto the arm that still worked properly, getting onto my knees, raising my pistol to try to get this motherfucker. That coincided nicely with it picking Markus off the ground by the back of his shirt, using him as a meat shield.

"Just shoot me, Lil," he groaned. "I'll flash first."

I can catch your soul as it flees, human.

"I'm not risking that," I said. "Commander? Got anything for us?"

I'm still here, you know, said the angel, and for the first time that transcendent voice sounded annoyed. *Markus is not slain today, either. But perhaps I cripple him. Perhaps I bring his soul to my master as a gift.*

The commander's voice popped into my head. *"It tracked the knife here but missed you on the way in. The cloak can get you out of here if you stall until Val cuts the entanglement."*

"And what about Markus?" I subvocalized. I glared at the angel. "What do you want?" I asked.

You wear the blessing of Meris, yet she knows you not. You wield strange weapons, vicious in their way, bearing the touch of a strange god. Who is she? Why does she war with so few?

I smirked. Eifni tech was built to mimic divine signatures, but there was no way I'd ever give up that information. And we'd just gotten another god's name out of the deal.

"If I tell you, you'll let Markus go?" I asked. "Swear on your god."

Relinquish your cloak of secrets and I will.

"I'll have to think about it," I said.

Secrets or no, I can smell a lie.

"You got me," I said slowly, readying my pistol. There was no more gunfire from Val's fight; was everything okay? Would the entanglement actually end? Markus was hanging limply, but he winked at me, then glanced at my fallen knife. Did he have a plan? I'd trust him. "Alright, I'm decloaking now."

I slowly turned down the cloak's intensity. I couldn't see under the angel's edgy mysterious getup—which had somehow stayed on despite all the acrobatics, because *angels are bullshit*—but it seemed like its attention sharpened as I emerged from etheric stealth.

"Val, how's it coming?" I subvocalized.

"I'm alive," he said, his pain and exhaustion bleeding through the meaning of his words. *"Just a bit—ugh!—longer."*

The angel was just staring at me. I stared it down, not blinking. Just a bit, Val said. I could do this.

"You gonna swear?" I asked.

Thank you, said the angel. It threw Markus at me. I dropped my gun as I shifted to prevent the impact jostling my broken wrist, which partly worked. We fell to the ground, and I screamed.

"Sorry," wheezed Markus, pulling himself up. "Should have worked out less."

You will now accompany me to Kives, said the angel.

"Like hell," I moaned. "Val, what the fuck is taking so long?"

"Would you—ah!—would you believe dramatic timing?"

"If you can blow it, blow it!" I said.

The angel was walking toward us across the clearing. I was in so much pain I instinctively turned on the cloak to get some distance. It left me free to think. The angel kept walking—was it not enough cloak? Was it tracking Markus? It could see the future of my actions, at least when they involved bullets and knives, but couldn't see through the cloak. It had seemed to *react* to the uncloaking, not anticipate it.

The cloak was designed to countersignal the idea of me, not Markus. But if I loosened the idea of what "me" meant, maybe I could cover both of us. I worked fast, ignoring the warnings the cloak threw out.

"Markus, carry me and run," I said. "I'm going as deep as I can."

He looked at me, concerned, but picked me up. I hissed at the pain and embraced the feeling of the etheric cloak to escape. I was pushing it, I knew; I'd been skipping my meditations. This was dangerous. Markus's comm was tuned in to me, he wouldn't forget me, I could trust him to come pull me out of the dream. Or Val. Or Abby. Such good friends. The math said so. Friends for a hundred years, a thousand years. They'd be sad if Lilith was gone. I was going now. Poor, sad friends.

"*Detonation,*" said Val. "*You're clear, get out of there.*"

Lilith mumbled something to Markus but forgot what it was halfway through my sentence.

"Stay with me, Lilith," he said, limping away.

Do you think you are the first to use the blessing of Meris against me? the angel asked, looking around the clearing. *You are fools. You serve destruction but think yourselves its sole master.*

Lilith watched as the angel gently laid a hand on the nearest tree, which it somehow managed to do in the angriest possible manner. A pulse of power echoed through the forest and through her mind. Trees shook, leaves grew and fell. Her scalp itched as her hair grew half an inch in moments.

Be cowed, said the angel. *The blessing of the goddess.*

With a roar of power, the tree burst out of the ground, its trunk thickening, roots writhing through the loam. Other trees were uprooted, falling around Markus as his limp became a stumbling hop. The moonlight was snuffed as the tree's upper branches grew thicker and sprouted thousands of leaves. The trunk was the size of a school bus, stood on its end, but their real trouble was the roots, which grew ever thicker, and which were coming for them. Like a nightmare in which you couldn't run fast enough. The blessed monster tree had branches the size of the other trees now.

Then the roots caught up, and Markus tripped. Markus and Lilith fell onto the mass of wooden tendrils as they reached outward, frantically trying to keep their limbs from getting caught—well, Markus was, Lilith was just sitting there, which was kind of a silly way to react, didn't she know better? Markus yanked her back from a crevice before she lost an arm. In the chaos, they fell apart. The tree stopped immediately. Markus scrambled back to Lilith, picking her up.

Just in time: in the darkness of the titanic canopy, the angel of Kives swept overhead, looking in vain for its prey.

Markus gave the massive tree a lingering look, then began the long hike home.

CHAPTER TEN

Absent

I don't know if you can hear me in there, but Val's gonna be okay," said Markus. "Commander patched him up alright. We can replace the leg if we get the engines running, too."

Lilith lay listlessly in the medical bed, staring up at the ceiling. Markus turned her head to look at the bed next to her, where Val was unconscious, an improvised tourniquet still tied over the stump of his right leg. She stared blankly at it.

"Apparently he cauterized the stump by ripping the power source out of the resonator," Markus told her. "Then he had to get it plugged back in because we needed him to make it self-destruct. We all thought the dryads got him, but when the commander found him, he was lying in this pile of bodies. He held them long enough for the resonator to take out the rest when it blew. Totally out of bullets. There's no way the commander doesn't note him for a commendation after that, eh?"

Lilith continued staring at Val. Occasionally she blinked.

"It's, uh," Markus said. "I'm glad we got out of there. It's too bad about all of this. Normally they don't do soul augments on people under fifty, you know? Not really enough time for your self-concept to really develop. I worried a bit, when I heard you had a cloak. Like, shit, soul augments are pretty iffy to begin with, but cloaking? It's too much. Sometimes you end up with"—he gestured vaguely—"vegetables. Can you hear me in there?"

When she didn't make any indication of hearing him, Markus turned her head back and propped her up a bit on the pillow. That left her staring at the wall behind him. She should probably respond.

Markus watched her for a while.

"Alright," he said. "Well, if you can hear me, let us know when you wake up. Between you and me, the commander's worried out of her mind about you. She's trying not to show it, but you run around with someone for half a century, you pick stuff up, you know? She's way more expressive than on her last body, too, it's much easier to figure out. What I'm saying is, she'll be too happy to chew you out . . . Well, much. So don't let that stop you coming back."

He patted her knee and stood up.

"Hope you're alright, Lilith. I'm going to go chat with Abby about our next steps."

Lilith didn't watch him go.

"That's the issue, commander: as a technical matter, I *can't* get to her comm. The cloak is too complete," Val said wearily, looking at Lilith's bed. She wasn't there. "I can try to spoof us into Markus's frequency, but it's an imperfect solution, and a security concern besides."

"I think you've earned that trust," said Markus.

"Possession, indoctrination, mind control, consumed by a god," said Val, ticking them off on his fingers. "It's not an issue of trust, Markus, although I appreciate the gesture."

"Could we penetrate the cloak with a scan?" asked Abby.

"Presumably," said Val. "What would that accomplish? It's not an issue of communicating with her—there's no *her* to communicate with. Her self-concept is entirely collapsed."

"We could see her, at least," Abby said.

"Ah," said Val. "I'll rig up an optical camera with an etheric scrubber. Kriamin's lab managed to bypass etheric cloaking two years ago by pointing to the idea of the subject rather than the subject themselves. I can take a look over his research notes."

"You've got Dr. Kriamin's research notes? I thought he hated you."

"Abby," Val said chidingly.

"Ah," she said.

Lilith continued staring into space. Her body blinked when it needed to. It needed food. Lilith's friends would take care of that eventually.

"I'd like to hear your thoughts on the strategic situation," said the commander. "This location *was* innocuous enough, but with that obviously divine tree poking into the atmosphere, we'll have pilgrims blundering through within the month."

"I agree that we should move," said Markus. "It might be worth sticking around to watch their crisis response."

"We have the cameras in place," Val said. "If we stay in signal range, we don't need to be local. If we deploy a couple of low-orbit transmitters, we can extend our operational range even farther. It would be an investment of resources."

"We're in a critical window for establishing a foothold here," said the commander. The others nodded; she had centuries of experience on them. "Conservation wouldn't be as much a concern if the translation engines were passing precision checks—by the way, Val, you still need to give me a technical breakdown on that. I need you walking again. As it stands, we have six transmitters ready to deploy, and our future requirements are difficult to predict. The nearest town is thirty miles away. If we touch down there, one transmitter will be more than enough. We can attempt to retrieve it after concluding operations in this locality."

"As technical officer, I should point out that the angel recognized the etheric-cloaking technique," said Val. "The transmitter uses the same technique; we might lose it depending on their available countermeasures."

"I don't think so," said Markus. "Tall, dark, and handsy's best idea was to hit everything in the combat area, and he didn't even get us. It'll be even less effective in space."

"If they do have a viable countermeasure, we gain valuable tactical information," said the commander. "We'll take the chance. But since you bring it up, Val, were you able to derive the etheric signature of this Meris deity?"

"I've, ah, been occupied," he said.

She grimaced. "When you have a moment, then. How many more signatures do you need to crack the pantheon?"

"Two or three more to get the complete picture, I think," said Val.

The commander nodded. "Markus, get me a landing zone."

"Yes'm," he said, rising to leave. "Hang in there, Lilith."

Lilith didn't respond. The commander looked at the bed, glancing past the body under the sheets. She seemed to strain for a moment, but the effort receded.

"A friend of a friend went through this once," said Abby. "I hope this one doesn't go that way."

"How did it resolve?" Val asked, pulling his bedside console onto what was left of his lap. He began typing.

"He came back eventually," said Abby. "It was a worse case than this; he'd taken some kind of spiritual attack and used the cloak to protect his consciousness."

"Oops," said Val.

"All the trainings say never to do it, and everyone I've talked to with a cloak says they do it anyway," said Abby. "On deicide missions, the moments you tend to take crippling injuries are the moments you can't be distracted by the pain."

"That follows, I suppose," said Val. "You said he came back. Were there lasting effects?"

"It took seventy years," said Abby. "He retired afterward."

"Ah." Val continued typing.

Abby looked at the bed. "When can you get that camera set up?"

"If you can get me the supplies from the armory, I can do it from here," said Val. "Personally, I just had my comm overlay an image of Lilith on the bed."

"We can't actually see her that way," said Abby.

"You can't see her through the camera, either." Val looked up at her. "You'll see a digital representation of the physical matter of her body, coupled with the idea of her."

"Reductionist," Abby accused him.

"Structuralist," he accused her. They traded adversarial smiles. Val got back to work. Abby turned to the bed, where Lilith's body was currently hiding from her perception.

"Hey, Lilith," Abby said. "We're gonna get you out of this. Whatever it takes. Your survival is my responsibility. I'll figure out a way to bring you back."

"She doesn't want to come back, or she'd be back already," said Val. "There is no she. There is no volition. It's just a soul."

"Val!" said Abby, scowling at him. "What are you saying?"

Yeah, that was pretty rude. Lilith might be upset if she were responding to anything right now. But in the depths of the fugue, she just lay there as if dead.

"I'm saying," Val said, "that right now she's fighting nonexistence, and she's losing. She wouldn't be here in the first place if she'd sharpened her willpower to persist under the cloak. This is a failure."

Lilith might have breathed a little faster. But they couldn't see her under the cloak. They'd never wake her up without feedback.

"Val," said Abby warningly.

He looked at her, tilting his head. Something unspoken passed between them. The anger on her face slipped away, replaced by blankness.

"No," she said. "I don't want to risk driving her away. Good thought, though. Next time run it by me before taking an action like that. Markus should have been informed, as well."

"I suppose it was too much to hope that insulting her would provoke a response," he said. "It does when she's awake."

"I said stop," said Abby.

"Commander?" he asked innocently.

"One hundred and twenty-three years, Val. You're not as smooth as you think." She stood up, clapping him on the shoulder as she exited. "If you continue trying to annoy Lilith out of her coma, I will hang you from Kives's new holy site and let the angels take your other limbs. Are we clear?"

"Exceedingly."

"Good." The commander smiled. "I'll be back with the materials for your camera."

They'd lifted off and relocated to the nearby town, which they'd learned from their initial surveillance period was called Elsinat. Ironically, they'd never learned the name of Torgaior's village, its inhabitants having never used it in conversation while under observation. From what Markus said, it sounded like it was harder to find a landing spot, and the ship had circled for nearly a day while they did scans with the moira-scope. Eventually they'd landed in the sea, far enough from shore that the ship could fully submerge. That was when the translation engines had their first real stress test since the team's arrival.

They'd scanned the surrounding area, Markus told Lilith, and had the ship create a tunnel straight through the ground. Dirt and stone could be translated to *firmament*, which they'd sunk into the walls, ceiling, and floor of the tunnel to keep them stable. The tunnel had been reinforced with steel and ended with a vertical shaft. The translator engines had struggled with output precision, so after several failed attempts they'd just gotten an extendable ladder out of the cargo bay and secured it to the wall.

Then the commander ordered Val to stand on top of the ladder and learn some important lessons about the meaning of friendship so the growth energy could be translated into a crude wooden cottage, which was a much better cover than a spaceship.

Markus somehow managed to keep a straight face for that whole part of the explanation.

"There were trees nearby," said Val. "We used those."

"Spoken like a man who needs to learn some important lessons about friendship!" said Markus.

The commander entered the room, meaning the meeting could begin.

"I had a thought," said Markus. "I'm sure she can hear us. Right, Lilith?"

Lilith might have been grateful for that, if she'd been cognizant of it.

"She's trying to rebuild her self-concept, so we can remind her of who she is. Maybe we all take turns telling her what we think of her. Could give her a road back."

"It's worth a try," said Abby. "I could start now."

"What a facile solution," said Val.

"You're just jealous you didn't think of it first," said Markus. Lilith would have said it before him if she'd been there.

"Will you give it a sincere attempt?" asked Abby.

"Naturally," said Val.

"I'll start," said Markus. "The Lilith I know is energetic, driven, and a great shot with a plasma lance. You're so fierce, too. Always give me a run for my money when we spar. When we fought that angel, I thought you were actually going to pull off a kill. I'm proud of you, Lils. I know you'll pull through this."

Lilith stared at the wall behind them. It was nice that Markus liked his friend so much.

"The Lilith I know," said Abby, "is irrepressible. You're young, but you're bright and capable, and you grow so fast. You've been on the team for two years, and you act like a veteran of five. You face things that would scare the shit out of most people and spit in their eyes. I'm looking forward to the rest of your career, so I hope you can come back and resume it."

Scaring the shit out of others. Lilith had never thought of it that way. If you're going to fall, fall forward. Go down swinging. Struggle until you run out of breath.

Lilith was breathing just fine right now.

"The Lilith I know," said Val, "is drowning."

"Val!" said Abby and Markus simultaneously.

"You think she thinks of herself as just the bubbly parts?" he challenged them. "She's angry. Five years ago, something unthinkable ate part of her soul, and she's still taking a swing at everything in reach to prove it won't happen again."

Lilith didn't respond, but those were cutting words. It hurt to hear. The pain, the fear, wanting so badly to just hit something. To kill it so dead it couldn't hurt me again.

"He's got a point," said Markus, looking at Abby. "Lil's got her petty moments. Like when she said I got arrested for stealing muscle oil from the king's palace."

Hey! That was completely justified.

"The Lilith I know . . ." said Abby. She sighed, relented. ". . . is far too excited to play with dangerous firearms. And often insubordinate, besides."

"You're right that she's clever, in her own way," said Val. Couldn't find a nonback-handed way to phrase it, huh? "Ambitious. But it gets her in over her head sometimes."

"Oh man, remember that one time with the plague god?" asked Markus. "And she got herself backed into the altar with just a hand amplifier and that bottle of soap from her home?"

Abby laughed. "And she called out, 'Watch out, this kills ninety-nine percent of germs!'"

They all laughed at that. Lilith's cheeks reddened. Just a little. But it was a reaction.

"But we love her anyway," said Abby. Silence fell.

It felt right. The positive stuff had been a little stilted. But—they knew her. It was a road back. Back to—what? To me? I tried to reach back.

"Is she reacting, Markus?" asked Abby. "The camera's not showing a difference."

"Maybe a little?" he said. "I'm sorry, the idea sounded good."

No, no, they couldn't leave me. They wouldn't. They were Lilith's friends.

"We could try it again," said Abby. "Once a day or so. It's not a burden."

I need you now! I wanted to yell.

Val shifted slightly, narrowing his eyes.

"They fall," he said softly.

"They die," I croaked.

I feebly turned off the cloak and was immediately buried in hugs.

CHAPTER ELEVEN

Role Conformance

The second stage of our sociological recon began with the sound of a well-dressed lady striking our social officer.

"Ow," yelled Markus, looking at her in surprise. "What did I do?"

She was dressed differently than the people in Torgaior's village: shawls among the farmers had been single pieces of fabric, with complicated decorations we'd still not figured out, but which we were betting had something to do with the individual's identity in the village. This lady still wore a shawl, but instead of the designs it had strips in various shades of red and pink sown into it. Some looped over her shoulders, reminding me humorously of an eighteenth-century cavalry officer's epaulets. Salute for Major Valentine! Her skirt was white and reached nearly to the ground, the longest we'd seen in our surveillance period.

Obviously high-class; you didn't get hair that crazy without support staff. That staff might have been the two young women behind her, dressed in more subdued versions of the style she was wearing, but probably not. Their hair was crazy, too. They must have had, like, wire in there to support it because I don't know how else they would have gotten freestanding loops on top of their heads.

She didn't answer Markus's question—too bad, it did work sometimes—instead saying, "Kola."

"Kola?" asked Markus.

A tall, broad-shouldered man stepped out of her entourage. He had a ponytail of thick black hair, glittering with beads, and a beard that was styled into, like, claws or something? There were like five or six curved spikes coming off his chin made of equal parts beard hair and wax, judging by the sheen. Weirdest shit. He was also completely shirtless, and let's just say he would have given Slinky the Rogue a run for his money.

"Ah," said Markus. "Kola."

Kola slapped him. Markus fell to the ground, strategically getting out of their way. Could he have blocked it? Probably, but after decades of field experience he knew better than to start a brawl with a noble's—bodyguard? Husband?—anyway, he let Mrs. Kola win. Mrs. Kola walked on, not even looking back. The two young women trailed behind her, followed in turn by more shirtless men, with Kola at their head.

Kola did look back, and rather than the growly snarl I'd expect from someone with that hairstyle, he shook his head disappointedly at Markus.

Across the street, disguised as a beggar, I tried not to laugh at him. I failed.

"I wonder if this is role-conformant here," said Markus as he applied more makeup. Between translation and reincarnation technology it was possible to straight-up give yourself a different face, but makeup was still cheaper. Plus, after seeing what the translator engines had spit out while trying to make a ladder underneath our little cottage, none of us were very eager to point it at our faces.

I was applying makeup, too, trying to make it look like I had cheekbones. I'd never been that good with it—I'd mostly just slapped on concealer under my eyes and called it a day—but Markus had given me pointers when I'd joined the team.

"Was Kola wearing makeup when he slapped you?" I asked.

"Am I ever going to live that down?" he asked.

"Nope!" I said cheerfully. "Up until the next burly man lays hands on you."

"*Reviewing the footage, it seems he was wearing eye shadow,*" said Val.

"You, too?" asked Markus.

"*It's mission-relevant information,*" said Val. "*Whatever you're insinuating is certainly false. Lilith, I have your dress nearly completed.*"

Dresses were a thing here. We were still working on figuring out the connotations of the different clothing options, but dresses weren't so uncommon that I couldn't go out and see how people reacted. Dresses also came with sleeves, which would hide the fact that my wrist was still in a splint from the angel fight. Constant risk, danger of crippling injury, and a life of lies, science, and victory: I never wanted to do another job.

"On my way," I said.

Abby met me at the door, wearing a cute brown dress with various wraps piled on top of it. They loved their wraps here. It looked weird to my sensibilities: the base kind of looked like a sundress from an Earth perspective, but you don't cover them with weird rectangular scarves, and they don't have long sleeves, besides. The other thing that was tripping me up was that new Abby was shorter than me, which I kept forgetting for some reason.

"Godsmile, Lilith," she said aristocratically, somehow managing to look down on me from two inches below eye level.

"Naw, you can't," I said. "We've only seen that outer wrap on the merchant class."

Abby blinked, then altered her posture, radiating an almost motherly warmth. "Godsmile," she said again. "Are you ready for a day at the market?"

"You know, Markus is Markus, whatever he's doing," I said. "You? You scare me."

Abby laughed and gave me a hug, mindful of my wrist. She took my arm, and we strolled. I had my comm route video models to my eyes, mostly footage we'd taken of family members on the street. Abby and I didn't look related, but neither did a lot of families. We were pretty sure adoption was a big thing here. I tried to mimic the posture I was seeing: Therian women tended to project a kind of confidence, but it was less guarded than the confidence I was used to seeing on Earth. The muscle memory wasn't really with me.

"I won't say I used all of my life effectively," said Abby, "but five centuries is too much to waste. You can't help getting good at things. Today's the day, Lilith."

"The day?" I asked.

"I'm getting laid for sure this time," she said.

"Eugh, you don't have to come out and *say* it," I said.

"That lean fellow with the biceps scarring was definitely willing," said Abby. "If we hadn't misjudged the class distance, I'd have had him for sure."

"Gross," I said. "I bet he doesn't brush his teeth. I bet they don't do that here. Just think about all those sexy, sexy cavities."

"Every culture has mouth hygiene," Abby said. "With the matriarchal culture, I bet this one *especially*."

"Wait, what?" I asked. "Why?"

Abby jerked her head to the side mischievously, a Velean gesture whose closest analogue in American body language is a wink, but with a much smaller semantic range—usually just "Ha! I got something past you!"

"I don't— Ew, *gross*!" I said.

We grabbed my dress from Val, who'd shaken every one of my expectations when it turned out that he could sew. We'd set him up in the *Ragnar*'s costume area, where he was able to use his remaining leg to roll around in a big swivel chair. Some inventions are truly so good that every culture invents them.

I threw the dress on, then a half shawl, then this weird decorative garment that didn't really cover anything but left beaded strings hanging down all over me. The dress was a nice green color, and we'd come up with some bright arm bangles that went well with it. They were big into bangles here, probably because their fashions so often left their arms and lower legs bare. That was a bit of an annoyance for me—I'd gotten sunburned my first day at this—but nearly everyone we'd seen around here had a darker skin tone than me. I guess the shawls were enough to prevent burns. We'd since applied a combined skin pigment/sunscreen to my skin to minimize the foreigner-walks-into-town vibes. Kives might be looking for that.

Hair-wise we were careful only to emulate styles we'd seen in use—our knowledge of their aesthetics was still a work in progress, but in the worst case we could start a local trend. Kives would *definitely* be looking for that. Even women of the lower class had hairstyles I considered elaborate, though. Abby's hair was still pretty short since her reincarnation, so we'd put her in a wig, which we'd then manipulated so that it swooped back in two fins. I joked that her head looked like a fighter jet, which had confused her until I got my laptop to show her pictures of US military F-15s on my local copy of Wikipedia. We'd wound ribbons through it to make it less obvious that the hair was synthetic. As for me, I'd picked something that looked kind of like a mohawk, except the extra length of hair all got tied up into a ponytail at the top back. Looked like a weird mix of cyberpunk and Victorian.

Val was apparently quite detail oriented, and our costumes differed from the real things only in a few respects: the material was more advanced, and there were subtle access points all over where we could hide weapons.

We joined Markus, whose posture had shifted to make himself look smaller, and whose face had taken on a dour cast.

"How long until Markus gets slapped again?" I asked, shifting my eye color to match my dress.

"I don't know what I'm doing wrong!" he said.

"I still think it's the eye contact," said Abby.

"We've seen eye contact within social classes," I said. "He's not eyeballing VIPs after"—here I adopted a more singsong tone—"*Kooola*. It can't be eye contact."

If this were Earth, I would also have winked at Markus, but after a few *very* awkward encounters I'd learned that, in Velean culture, winking was an explicit sexual invitation. So I just smugged at him.

"There was also that one servant," said Markus. "But I was with Abby that time, maybe that affects things."

"We could test it," I said.

"Don't we have better things to do?" asked Markus.

"Negative," Abby said with a smirk. "We have to be culturally fluent, Markus. This is a cultural barrier that must be studied."

"I need a helmet or something," he muttered. Funny thing about comms? Muttering's really easy to hear.

The commander almost managed a hookup, but ditched him when her comm picked up etheric signs of an STI. Rather than risk the guy causing trouble, she left Markus and me at the inn to explore the eastern side of town, near the docks. We were staying out of the inner city for now; that was where all the temples were, and Kives had almost certainly warned them we were in the area.

We had a little money from my stint as a beggar, which Markus had used to hustle some hustlers at dice. They used the same trick you saw in Earth movies where you let the newbie win a game or two, then fleece them. Markus was their ideal mark, except for the part where Elfnl comms can pick up intent to cheat. He'd get up for a drink right when they were about to get serious. It was probably going to get us jumped in an alley at some point, but hey, all part of the fun!

For my part, I tried to make a friend. She was tall, brunette, with very dark irises. Her hair was all coiled up, and she was dressed in what we'd started calling the traditional style, the shawl/wrap/skirt combo they'd all worn back at the village.

"Godsmile," I said, placing my drink at her table. "Can we sit here?"

Markus smiled in a friendly way.

Fury flashed over her face, but it was replaced by an expression that looked like uncertainty as she looked back at me.

"Something wrong?" asked Markus. Judging by her face, that just made her angry again.

I had a stroke of genius inspiration.

"Tesla!" I snapped imperially at him. He looked at me in surprise, and I slapped him. "Ow!"

"Go wait outside," I told him. "You're embarrassing me."

I sat down at the table before the Therian woman could react.

"Sorry about him," I said. I reached desperately for an angle and decided on the universal human experience of disdaining other cultures. "He's from the far-off land of, uh, Krypton. They have weird ideas about"—I prayed to Dawkins that Abby was on the money here—"looking women in the eyes there."

"Disgraceful," said the woman, who was looking a little less tense. "Why do you keep him around?"

I did my best suggestive voice. "Why do you think?" I winked. Revulsion crossed the woman's face. Fuck, was winking a sexual thing here, too? I missed winking.

"Okay, uh, hold on, can you tell me what I just implied?" I asked.

"I do not know where you come from," said the woman, standing up, "but I will not lay with you, I will not lay with your husband, and I am leaving. *Pervert.*"

I sighed and leaned back.

"Hey, guys," I subvocalized. *"I just found out winking's a sex thing here."*

"I have, as well," said Abby. *"Occupied, will debrief later."*

I nodded absently. Then I blinked as I connected the dots.

"Fucking *gross!*"

CHAPTER TWELVE

Don't Mind Me

Val and Abby were arguing about something called an emitter when I strolled into the engine room. Ours were broken, apparently. Something about the etherspace part of the translator engines taking some damage when that weather god hit us. Guess they'd figured out why the translator engine's precision was so screwy, then.

The engines themselves—well, the part in realspace, anyway—were bulky monstrosities taking up the back quarter of the ship. I had no idea what all the different parts did, you'd have to ask Val or Abby for that. But I knew the general theory of how they worked. Meaning goes in, stuff comes out. Or sometimes the other way around. I knew the matter-to-ether process involved creating a specific kind of conduit effect and . . . making both planes the same somehow? Okay, you know what? I don't know anything about this, I'm gonna stop talking.

Val's head was buried in a small-scale etheric manipulator, the device we use for building etheric constructs on the other side of the sidereal boundary. The rest of him was reclining on a chair that looked like it belonged next to a pool. Every so often his new prosthetic leg would twitch. It was controlled remotely from his comm. Still not acclimated yet, probably. Abby was following along on a console, pulled out of the wall next to the door.

"Don't you dare ask me for a miracle," Val said, eliciting a frown from Abby. "You can see the damage to the rear pylons yourself. Our stored C-phase ether is *likely* sufficient to cover those repairs, but then how do we patch the conduit? Frankly, it's surprising that Kives hasn't tracked us by the leakage alone."

"We're not in the woods anymore," Abby said. "Three operatives won't cut it if we have to hit a temple. I need you back on two feet—*real* feet, don't even think about saying it—and I don't want to burn another body for it."

"What do we sacrifice, then?" asked Val. "The Bulgurov shielding? That could do the job, until another god smites us. Then maybe we don't have engines at all. We simply need more raw material, commander."

"I'm not picking a fight with another angel," said Abby. "The last one is half the reason we're in this mess."

"Obviously," said Val. "Angels aren't the only possibilities."

"Could we steal some from a temple?" I interjected. "That fucking mold god last mission turned his main temple into a total hardpoint. Should be a ton of raw material."

Abby looked over her shoulder. "Oh, hey, Lilith. I didn't see you there. Did you need something?"

"Nah," I said, entering the engine room proper and sitting on the end of Val's lounge chair. "Just bored."

"And you decided the engine room would solve your problem," Val said, with just a hint of skepticism leaking into his tone. Abby gave him a warning look, which he didn't see because he was still looking at the representation of the ether.

"I'd say, 'Fuck you,' but I don't want to make the engines jealous," I said happily. I was proud of that comeback; I'd come up with it on the way over here.

"Of me, surely," Val replied. "Technically speaking, you're the only one they haven't been inside of."

"I— That's—" I spluttered.

"Enough is what it is," said Abby. "Lilith, it's a good idea, but I already told you I'm not assaulting a temple with three operatives. There will be too much resistance in on both sides of the sidereal boundary, especially at this early stage."

"Temple's gonna have guards, right?" I asked. "Maybe we get them to chase us? The etheric ones, I mean. It'd be a much simpler operation."

Abby looked unconvinced. "Simpler, I'll grant you. But it sounds like the kind of operation that blows up in your face before you clear the second step of the plan."

"Guess we just have to catch fairies in a butterfly net, then," I said with a sigh. "Wait, are fairies a real thing?"

"I have no idea what you're talking about," said Abby.

"Shit. I always wanted to do the whole bargaining-for-boons thing. Oh well, my life is still plenty exciting."

"Except right now, apparently," said Val. I stuck out my tongue at him. He carried on, oblivious. "My advice, should you ever find yourself bargaining with an etheric creature, is to shoot it."

"Tried that," I said, remembering the angel. "It didn't take." I hopped off his chair. "I'm going to take a walk or something. I'll call you if I catch any fairies."

"Team meeting when Markus is done with his nap," said Abby. "I'll defer to our paraphysicist and say we have to catch something. We should think about directing our efforts in a more theological direction."

I didn't respond verbally, just nodded and threw a peace sign over my head as I walked out the door. Wait, shit, was that a rude gesture? No, it wasn't. I was just paranoid after a couple weeks of intentionally violating weird social norms to see how they worked.

Back in college, my intro psych professor gave us a homework assignment where we had to break a social norm on purpose, like standing too close to people or eating with your hands at the dining hall. I wonder what she'd say if I came back and told her I did it for a living now.

Repairing the engines was a priority. Injuries aside—my wrist was healing nicely, and Val was mobile if not combat ready—we had no way to replenish our stock of backup bodies without atomic-scale output precision. Bodies are full of tiny, finicky bits. A deicide team can take on repeated suicide missions as long as they have spare bodies to come back to, but we were working with a limited supply of extra lives right now.

So the solution was to capture some kind of etheric creature and dissect its soul for raw materials. An angel would work, but if they all made us look like fucking Stormtroopers like the last one, there was no chance in hell we'd manage to catch one. That left lesser paranatural beings like the dryads. The problem with dryads was that the forest we'd landed in was quickly becoming holy ground, and the whole point was to *avoid* Kives's angels. We didn't know what else was out there, but a good place to start was local mythology.

Normally you can just find some religious teacher to tell you this stuff, but after the fiasco with Arguel, we had to assume they were all compromised. We came up with this whole convoluted, multistage plan to get access to the city archives, con our way in, then grab a bunch of texts and try to decipher them and hope they had the right content. It was tenuous and risky, and it was lucky we didn't need it: the answers came to us.

Markus spotted her while on recon: wearing the robes of a scribe but eating at an inn that usually catered to a clientele of lower station than hers. You could tell by the skirt length, we'd realized a bit ago. Longer hems implied you didn't need to do physical labor, so your lower class had skirts above the knees and your upper class got to cover their ankles. The scribe's robes cut off just above her ankles, but everyone else there was at about knee level. She wasn't drawing that much extra attention, though. Either she didn't know where the better inns were, or she couldn't afford one.

Markus was already posing as someone too low status to approach her, so the commander sent Val and me to introduce ourselves. We frizzed up my hair and wound flowers into it, selecting a set of clothing that was—we knew from experience— slightly classier than what you'd usually find in that inn, but not so much that it'd look out of place. We still weren't sure where scribes as a profession fell on the social ladder, but we'd learned through painful experience—on Markus's part, at least— that it was better to aim high. The culture around Elsinat had a high power distance, it seemed.

We hid Val's prosthetic under a layer of fake skin and made sure he got a long enough skirt that the knee joint—which didn't really look natural, at least up close—was fully covered. Then we'd had to go back and make sure mine wasn't shorter than his, and at the end of the process we were edging toward out-of- placeness, but better that than an advanced prosthetic we couldn't explain. Val still walked with a bit of a limp, so we decided he'd pretend to be an ex-soldier. Me, I was a messenger. I'd wanted to be a traveling storyteller, but when I floated the idea I'd ended up letting slip that I'd been using fictional characters from Earth as cover identities. The commander chewed me out *hard* over that. So now I was a messenger, *and* I had to go by an actual Therian name instead of Lara Croft like I was planning.

Our mark was dressed in white robes, with accents of black and mahogany. The textiles here were more advanced than I'd expect from medieval Earth cultures; maybe there were technical advances in the more urbanized areas? She had brown hair, which she'd roped into a complicated mess all across her shoulders and back. Hastily, if I was any judge—the braids were chaotic, strands of hair escaping the order she'd attempted to impose. Chronically pressed for time, then. Her eyes were brown and intelligent, but currently glazing over as she stared at the mass of paperwork at her table. She reminded me of my college roommate, back before she dropped out of prelaw.

"Lady scribe," I addressed her. My tone was maybe a bit too casual, but we can't all be Abby. Val waited; men were introduced after the women had all had their turn. "Godsmile on you. You look like you need a break."

She looked up at us, blinking. Val was standing the proper distance away to signal that we weren't romantically involved—something else Markus's poor face had bought us. "I'm not licensed. You'll have to speak with my master if you want a contract drawn up."

"Not at all," I said, taking a seat. I didn't ask, like with the pervert lady a couple of weeks ago. Here, requests were made implicitly. Socially, anyway—people got blunter when trade came into the picture. "I'm Tain." There, proper Therian name. The commander better be happy about this.

The scribe's eyes flicked left, as though trying to place the name. "Godsmile, Tain. Ell."

"Ell," I said, smiling. People like happy people, and they like feeling that they make other people happy. Smiles make friends. "Ell, Hama. My traveling companion."

"Godsmile," she said. "You were right, I do need a break. My eyes hurt."

"I suppose it's no use asking what you're working on," said Val.

"You could guess," she said impishly, gathering the pages into a pile and turning them over.

Val smirked at that. "And would you tell me if I guessed right?"

Ell smirked back.

I gave the paperwork an appraising look. The sheets were larger and raspier than I expected paper to be, which probably had something to do with the lack of industrial paper mills on Theria.

"Uh, you're studying for your license?" I asked.

Ell raised her eyebrows at me but said nothing.

"No," said Val, looking intently at her. "You're not from Elsinat. You're here on assignment, but you're not licensed. But you won't tell us what the assignment is, so it's important. Too important for an unlicensed scribe, despite whatever pressure is pushing you to study until your eyes dry out."

"Maybe I'm just very thorough," said Ell, tilting her head and meeting his gaze.

"You must be," Val said. "Otherwise your master, who I deduce has traveled here with you, wouldn't have sent you off alone to do her research for her while she drinks with the rich."

A scandalized laugh escaped her lips. "Poor me. If you're right, that is."

Val leaned back with a satisfied smile.

"I'll buy us all some drinks," I said, standing up. "We're not rich, but I like to think we're better company."

Conning hustlers didn't pay all that well, but our cost of living was pretty low thanks to supplies on the ship. We could spend a little on making some friends. Couldn't topple a pantheon all by ourselves, after all.

"Just one," said Ell. "I'll need to get back to work at some point."

"I've heard contract work is easier when you're drunk," I heard Val say as I went to find the inn's owner. I didn't get her response, but his answering laugh came through over the comm. I pouted. He never laughed at *my* jokes.

I passed a man in the shortest skirt I'd yet seen, coming down about midthigh, whose torso wrap was done in a nonstandard fashion that emphasized his pectorals. He looked away when we made eye contact. I just watched, curious what he'd do next. He looked back at me a couple of times, briefly, meeting my gaze a little longer each time. On the fourth or fifth time, he stopped looking away and gave me a hesitant smile.

Man, the gender relations around here were pretty messed up, but it parsed as shyness, and that was definitely kind of endearing. I returned the smile. "Have a nice day!" I said and kept looking for the innkeeper. Eventually I was on the way back with some beer made from *sengua*, the grain they seemed to rely on around here.

"*Hey, heads up,*" said Markus. "*There's some dice hustlers here.*"

"*Good, I just spent some cash to lubricate this scribe contact,*" I subvocalized.

"*No, I mean they recognized me,*" said Markus. "*I'm exfiltrating, but they all just got up.*"

"*Shit,*" I said. "*Val, you're on your own, I'm gonna back Markus up.*"

The commander cut in. "*Good plan. I'm monitoring the situation.*"

I still had the beers, dammit. I hurried through the inn and set them down on the table.

"Sorry to leave you," I told them. "Just met a friend, I have to go handle something. Nice to meet you, Ell."

"Thanks for the drinks," said Ell, toasting me with her clay mug. "I'll buy you a round someday. May we meet again."

"Farewell!" I saluted her with an invisible mug of my own, then made for the door. "*Markus, location.*"

"*The street with the giant naked statue.*"

"*Of course,*" I said. "*No ulterior motives, I'm sure.*"

"*He's got a really attractive face, okay? Watch out, I only see two of them.*"

I palmed my pulser. "*Watch out for what? They don't know I'm with you.*"

"*Why, good evening, gentlemen!*" said Markus. They must have found him. I had to hurry. A ping from his comm put him in an alley about two streets away, so I stepped it up.

"*I'm sure we can all be reasonable about this,*" Markus said.

I slowed my run to a stealthier pace. I was nearly there. It was getting dark, but not enough that night vision would be that useful. I rounded the corner: Markus was surrounded, two at his front, one at his back.

"Smooth character like you," one of them—the only one with a shawl—was saying, "I figure you've got quite a purse. Now, we tried to cheat you, you cheated us, fair's fair. But I reckon some of that's ours now, ain't it, lads?"

There were nods and declarations of "yeah, yeah" from the other two.

"*Engaging*," I subvocalized. I was behind Markus with the lone guy, whose hair wasn't in a ponytail. I put on my most innocent face and walked forward.

"Ey, who's she?" said one of the hustlers on Markus's far side. The guy in front of me turned around, instinctively looking away from me. Heh. Matriarchy was fun.

"What's all this about?" I asked, like I didn't know already. I'd seen this all the time in movies. Things were going to erupt into a brawl at any moment now. Markus could probably hold off the other two while I handled the guy in front of me.

"Just collecting a debt between men, ma'am," said the guy who'd been doing the talking so far. "It's beneath your notice, I'm sure."

"Cool," I said. "Don't mind me, I'm just watching."

There was an awkward pause as everyone digested that. Any moment now. The guy closest to me would come at me punching, I predicted. I could duck and go for the genitals, that might put him down long enough to make it look natural when I pulsed him.

"We don't want trouble," he said instead.

I nodded, like it was the most obvious thing in the world. They must be biding their time.

"This man's a thief," tried the guy with the green wrap.

"Yeah yeah yeah," I said. "Skip the spiel, I know how this goes. I said not to mind me, didn't I? Go on, do your thing."

Shawl Guy looked uncertainly at Markus, then at his goons, then back at me. "Wait, I saw you at the Thresher's Landing. You were talking with that Oathkeeper!"

"Might have been," I said. "Is that a problem? What was all that about a debt?"

"I don't like this," he said. "Come on, boys, let's get out of here."

Markus and I watched them leave. Once it was just us, he gave me a high five.

"That was great!" he said. "Man, I thought we were going to have to fight them!"

I sighed. "Me, too."

"*Is the situation resolved?*" asked the commander.

"In spite of Lilith's best efforts," Markus laughed, patting me on the shoulder. Probably a dumb idea given that we were still in public, but I didn't see anyone with direct line of sight into the alley. I punched him good-naturedly in the biceps.

"Val, are you good?" I asked.

"*We may not need to use the archive plan,*" he said. "*Ell is quite knowledgeable. I told her I'm staying at this inn in order to prolong the conversation, so I'll report on my findings tomorrow. In summary, we're going fishing.*"

I smiled and cracked my knuckles. Fishing sounded like a great idea.

I had unfinished business with lobsterkind.

CHAPTER THIRTEEN

Friend of Heaven

I had breakfast with Abby in the lounge after morning PT. Markus exercised twice as long as the rest of us, so he usually joined us later. Velean cuisine emphasized strong flavors in a way that still tasted weird to me, but their breakfast foods tended to be sweet, so I always looked forward to it. We weren't in a hurry. Val had reported the all clear, saying that he was on his way back. We didn't get much out of him over the comm. Just that he needed to cross-check some information. We let him be: he got tunnel vision sometimes when he really sank his teeth into a problem.

Markus had just sat down with us when Val burst into the lounge.

"Morning, Val," I said.

"Hey," said Abby. "What have you got for us?"

"Everything," Val said, apparently in too much of a hurry to stop. "I'm going to run some numbers. Don't disturb me."

He swept out the door, presumably on the way to his terminal in the engine room.

"Damn," I said. "Must have been some sweet info."

It was. Four hours later, he pinged everyone and said he was ready to present his findings. We were all on hand—the commander had suspended operations for the day—so we gathered back in the lounge.

"I have names and aspects for every god in the pantheon," said Val, activating the main lounge screen. "Check your consoles."

"*Shit*, man," said Markus. "Nice work!"

"First, Ell works as an Oathkeeper," said Val. "They're sworn to Javei, who I've determined is a biphase god with a socially oriented truth aspect. The Oathkeepers function as the justice system here. That lends itself to Javei's other aspect, which could fall under either revelation or discovery. My error bars are too wide to determine which."

"That Oathkeeper status could be an issue," said the commander. "Are you aware of any connection between Ell and Kives?"

"A basic comm scan revealed no divine signature," said Val. "We'd have to get her in front of a moirascope to check for entanglements."

"Acceptable for now," said the commander. "Continue."

"Second," Val said, "when I mentioned I couldn't read, Ell suggested I visit a temple of Lorana. Worship of Lorana reportedly entails deliberately training a skill or ability. We should look into that once Kives is dealt with, by the way. I had the computer set up a twelve-dimensional matrix for the pantheon, using our three known gods as constants."

That would be Kives, recorded during our first battle; Horcutio, recorded during the second; and Seindel, who we'd gotten from Arguel.

"I took a comm reading of Ell to get a rough signature for Javei, then used the signature of Lilith's cloak as a proxy for Meris. Lorana took multiple tries. Growth was the obvious choice, but it was too close to Kives to be solvable. Nothing within a standard deviation of learning or training worked. Then I had a breakthrough: Lorana is the goddess of *mastery*. Progressive monophase; the progressive aspect seems to be something personality-based, which I've tentatively marked as 'wisdom.' And that," Val said triumphantly, "solved the matrix. I cross-checked with our compiled theological intelligence, and everything is within parameters. We now have signature information for every ascendant god on Theria."

He smiled a predator's smile.

"And I know how to kill every one of them."

Varas was queen of the gods: her domains were both of rule, one by the sword and the other by coin. But the sword and the coin can be turned against each other. We could rip her in half.

Gamal was her consort, the god of community, with a progressive aspect of communication. As an American with a social media account, I didn't need to hear Val's explanation of how one could break the other. We'd need to get him to biphase first, though.

Kabiades was also her consort. His domain was manly prowess, progressing to competition. The available counterfrequencies were many, including foul play, laziness, and disease. Wrecking a few competitions on his holy days should do the trick.

Androdalma thrived with creation and could be ruined with destruction. Lorana's temples promoted wisdom; we knew the techniques to turn them into propaganda. Meris hoarded secrets, but with sufficient amplification, the truth of the gods proclaimed might slay her outright. But such a massive revelation would empower Javei, so first we'd need to hit him through the Oathkeepers.

Alcebios, the Stranger, was the only god in progressive biphase. She was lord of death and bringer of discord, progressing to battle. Val's calculations showed that she was already unstable. Forced empowerment would break her. Empowered, she might drag Seindel and his peace aspect down with her.

Rucks, the Dancer, matched the frequency of excess. The societal upheaval from killing the others might even take care of him/her/them without our intervention.

Kives was our primary target. Fertility gods are hard to kill: they live off an etheric frequency that's sympathetically generated whenever a thing moves toward its potential. *Any* thing. It would take slow, grinding work of indirect attacks on everything related to her before she crumbled. Starting with her husband: Horcutio, the asshole weather god.

The frequency that weather gods thrived on wasn't actually the weather. Weather had all sorts of etheric frequencies associated with it. No, it was the frequency generated when the weather *fucked you over*. From the lightning strike that set your home on fire, to the sudden storm that drenched you after you'd already dressed for sun, weather gods were—properly speaking—gods of vicissitude, of *bad luck*. And this one was mono-phase, so our fancier strategies wouldn't work on him.

Unfortunately for him, his relationship with Kives was—appropriately—tempestuous, and he'd left a bunch of demigods running around.

Val's plan was simple. We'd kill them in Kives's name. With luck, Horcutio would kill her himself.

"Which brings me to my last piece of information," said Val, "which is that there exists a creature sacred to Horcutio called a hippocampus, and the Oathkeepers have received reports of piracy by a group who ride them. They are led, it is claimed, by a man named Kulades who claims Horcutio as his father."

"Please tell me hippocampus is a kind of lobster," I said.

"It is not. I had originally anticipated striking at these pirates for their mounts alone, but with the pantheon solved, I propose we heap enemies on our spear"—the Velean equivalent of "kill two birds with one stone," which I'd always thought was much more metal. "We kill the pirates, dedicate the victory to Kives, and harvest the souls of the hippocampi to repair the translation engines."

"So no lobsters, then," I said. "Fuck."

"It would be good to know if Kives has more of those sea monsters to deploy," said Abby.

"Ecologically, it's hard to imagine she would," said Markus.

"She could just as easily sustain it etherically," said Abby. "If she knew it was needed, she'd front the cost."

"I've been thinking about that," I said. "That temple island we ran into? Might have been one of Horcutio's. Sea monster could have been his, too."

"I agree with that analysis," said Val. "That weakly implies we won't face another. If the pirates had a monstrous creature like that at their disposal, the Oathkeepers would have heard at least a rumor."

"Absence of evidence is not evidence of absence," I said out of habit.

"What?" said Val. "Of course it is. A world with an aggressive leviathan looks very different from a world without one. I'll grant that it is not *certain* that the existence of such a leviathan would imply that it coordinates with the pirates—Horcutio might normally leave them to their devices but deploy it when they're threatened, for example—but you will note that I said it was a *weak* implication."

"It really is too bad that Eifni never gets the chance to study hyperfauna," said Markus. "Like, imagine if we were just sitting here arguing about whether there are more, but they're all super territorial or something and that was never a real possibility."

"That's not quite true," said Abby. "There was a case study back in the 7600s. A deicide team killed a god of defensive warfare, who left behind their giant siege turtle. The locals loved it, and it wasn't aggressive, so we left it lying around. Seemed like it exemplified its creator's personality characteristics, which is consistent with the kind of deep blessing you need to make these things."

"Dang. What happened to it?" I asked.

Abby tapped her fingers on the armrest, a distant look on her face. "Well, you know how it goes before the uplift teams get there," she said. "After a century or two, they started to worship it. We had to put it down. I remember it caused a minor stir on Veles at the time."

Markus laughed. "I forget how old you are sometimes."

Val paced slowly. "So if we reason from the premise that the creature follows the character of its creator, do we expect a sea monster raised by Horcutio would tolerate the presence of another?"

We took a moment to remember our encounter with him.

"No," the rest of us answered in unison. He nodded in agreement.

"We plan for one, anyway," said the commander, sitting up. "But our first priority is planning for Kives. How do we dodge entanglement?"

Val continued pacing. "We can't, I think. This is our first true strike against the pantheon. An objectively momentous event, with significant downstream consequences. Kives could see this even without her wastefully oversize moirascope. She'll have forces in position."

We let him keep talking. Val was half the reason our team was on this mission. He'd done his dissertation—well, the Velean equivalent—on potential applications of game theory to oracle combat.

"Ultimately only one set of events will transpire, and the sympathetic resonance will reflect that outcome, and thus cause her deployment."

His actual sentence was crammed full of acronyms, which meant the comm translation shoved an unpleasantly dense stream of information into my head. I grimaced.

"Shouldn't it be the other way around?" I asked when I'd had a moment to process it. "She picks actions to cause the events that end up happening?"

He pinched the bridge of his nose. "Lilith, when we get back, I'm enrolling you in a seminar on multilinearity."

"That sounds like math. I'll pass," I said.

"It is so much math," said Markus.

"I need a moment," said Val, staring off into the distance. His eyes flicked erratically as he thought. I tried to think it through faster. Okay, so Kives would be there. Maybe we go in fast, hit the pirates before Kives can hit us, get back out? But no, there's no before with an oracle, they have all the time they need. Okay, we could hide? Apparently they had a god that used the same technique to hide that we did, though. And if Kives knew there was going to be a battle, that implied that we'd be found anyway. So that was out—

"*Ah*," said Val in a tone of immense satisfaction. "Aha. Hahaha! Oh, my friends," he said, turning to us, "she is going to *hate* this."

We wasted no time preparing.

The docks of Elsinat were well maintained, the Elsinati deriving much of their wealth from trade. That was probably what Ell's contract was about, come to think of it. Statues of Varas stood at each end of the harbor, hands outstretched in blessing over the commerce flowing between them.

The shipwrights here had discovered more or less the same kinds of shapes that Earth shipwrights had, as they followed from the physics of buoyancy, which itself derived from the properties of realspace. There were an assortment of smaller vessels—rafts, catamarans, etc.—meant for fishing in local waters, we suspected, but they were useless to us. We were looking for a trade ship, of which there were many.

I was dressed as a well-to-do lady, wearing the sort of getup we'd seen on successful merchants. The hairstyles of the wealthy, we had learned, were made by artisans. We didn't have the funds to hire one appropriate to my supposed station. Fortunately, our grasp of materials science let us fake it. Some optical captures, a bit of 3D modeling, and hair gel left my hair rippling in overlapping black waves—a genuine counterfeit Gemyrne original. Hopefully Gemyrne wasn't visiting the docks right this instant, but we were pretty sure she was on the other side of town right now.

Markus wore a simple skirt and a shawl with abstract designs. We *still* hadn't figured out the actual symbolic ones, but abstraction was in vogue in Elsinat, so we'd gone for that instead. We'd braided his fake ponytail with enough beads that he was a believable representative for my notional business. He was currently talking with a sailor while I looked on impatiently in the sailor's field of view. Markus pressed a *drobol* into the sailor's hand, thanked him, and walked back to me.

"He suggested a *sephni* for our purposes," said Markus. "*Praise of Clear Skies* over there is the only one here, but it's under contract, and the captain's known to be a hard-ass. If we really needed to, we could go down to a *tulim*. They don't have the second deck. That's one over there—*Wave Husband*, I think it was called. Also under contract. It'll be cramped."

"*Any rumors we can use about their contracts?*" asked the commander. She and Val were en route to the Oathkeepers, settling another part of the plan. They'd elected not to get a reference from Ell because getting her involved with this would definitely sink her career and possibly get her executed or worse. Poor thanks for giving us the tip in the first place.

"Not really," said Markus. "All the big contracts come with an oath to Meris not to reveal anything. Best I have for you is that *Clear Skies* has been in harbor awhile."

"*It'll have to do. Any ships out of work right now?*"

"Just the one that looks like it's about to rot," said Markus. "*Friend of Heaven*, I think he said. It's a *tulim*."

"And a piece of shit," I said.

"*That's the one*," said the commander. "*Get prepared, then you're cleared to begin.*"

I got to slap Markus again.

"Two thousand *drobol* you let slip through my fingers!" I shouted at him, chasing him down the wharf. "A measly fifty would have paid for a counsel! Who saves fifty by spending two thousand?"

"I'm sorry!" he said. "*You're enjoying this too much*," he added subvocally. I slapped him again.

"Sorry? *Sorry?!* I gave *my* word! A hundred faithful souls! Where will they go, Kanabades? We have no ship to take them! Will you carry them on your back across the sea?"

"*You're definitely enjoying this too much*," Val commented.

"We can hire another ship," Markus tried, "there's still time—"

He dodged the next slap.

"Do you see another *sephni* in this harbor?" I shouted. "Where will you find me a *sephni*, Kanabades? Between your ears? It's empty enough in there! Perhaps that is the cause of your confidence!"

"You'd wake up Varas herself with that racket," said a middle-aged woman near us. "I couldn't help hearing—and believe me, I tried—that you need a ship."

I turned to look at her. She was known as Erid, captain of the *Friend of Heaven*. By repute, a practical and disagreeable woman. She'd been taking a nap against the poles on the pier leading to her ship.

Speaking of which, I gave it an evaluating glance, letting skepticism show on my face. "I doubt you can help."

"You're new money," she said wearily. "Always have to have the biggest ship. *Friend of Heaven* does the job, lady merchant."

"Danou," I said, nodding in greeting.

"Erid," she said. "You promised passage to a hundred people?"

"Oh, Captain Erid, it's a wonder—the goddess has moved," I said. "A great and holy tree has arisen in the jungles to the south. It is glorious to see, and I wished to provide the opportunity to others."

"Heard about that," the captain said. "I also heard the temple was telling people they shouldn't go see it."

I froze for a moment. The commander immediately whispered a response through my comm.

"We will not tread upon that most sacred ground, of course," I said hastily. "Why, even just a glimpse would be powerful enough."

"It'd be hypocritical of me to fault you for trying to make money off idiots," said Erid. I narrowed my eyes while I tried to figure out whether she had just insulted me. It was becoming apparent why she was between contracts. "Alright, so a hundred pilgrims for a trip to Salaphi. They coming back?"

"W-we could charge an extra fee," I said. "But surely your vessel is too small."

"They're pilgrims," Erid said with a grunt. "Some shade above deck, cram 'em below when it storms. How about supplies? That's a lot of mouths to feed for two *thessim*." *Thessim* were twelve days long, one day for each major god.

"Purchased already," I said, scowling, "but already delivered to the *Praise of Clear Skies*." I turned to Markus again. "I told you we needed a counsel!"

"I know a gal," Erid said. "But you're covering it."

"We don't really have funds to spare," I said.

"Every rat and gull on this wharf heard you yell about your two thousand," Erid said. "I want half. Throw in another two hundred for my commission and we'll bring it to the Oathkeepers."

"That's *piracy*. And besides, there's no time to bring it to the Oathkeepers," I said. "They're gathering tomorrow."

"Then make it five hundred," said Erid. "Or we go to the Oathkeepers anyway, and I tell them you made empty promises to a hundred people."

We really did want the money, so the fury on my face wasn't entirely fake. But we had our ship.

Your move, Kives.

CHAPTER FOURTEEN

Recruitment

We had a ship, but now we needed pilgrims, and Kives was apparently doing her best to block us there. Fine. She could try. Information supremacy isn't everything.

As far as realspace is concerned, there are many possibilities but only one future. There is exactly one chain of causality that will happen, that was always going to happen. The future is the final result of everything you do to change it.

Kives could spend an eternity developing the perfect strategy to counter us, but at the end of the day, we were on the ground, and she wasn't. No strategy is truly perfect, and in this case it was more expensive for her to preempt us than for us to react to her. For example: she could get the port blockaded. Mission accomplished, right? Except then we could go to another city. Or maybe we don't—how long does Elsinat survive without trade? She could try to persuade the people who end up on the *Friend of Heaven* not to go on the ship, but why bother?

There's only one future. If she knows who they are, it's because she knows they made it onto the ship in spite of her efforts.

Let her do her worst.

After an evening of attempted pilgrim recruitment, I started wishing for an angel attack. But rather than, like, *fight* us, Kives had elected to be *fucking annoying*.

"All were warned against laying eyes on the Great Tree, for not all are worthy," said Abby, whose presence was downright ethereal despite not having a cloak augment herself. "But the goddess has chosen only a few to witness its mysteries."

"What must I do?" asked the mark.

"There is a ship at the wharf, which by the goddess's favor will leave with the tide tomorrow," said Abby. "There is scant time to search your heart, my child, but it must be destiny that we meet thus."

"I don't need any time," said the mark, eyes shining. "How could I refuse—"

The door burst open. An Oathkeeper in jangling armor covered with strips of white cloth stepped through, followed by—*seriously?*

"She's the one!" shouted master hairstylist Gemyrne, pointing straight at the back table where I was watching the con go down. "This *thief* was seen wearing my Seven Waves, and *I* certainly did not touch her *filthy* scalp."

"What the *fuck*, Gemyrne!" I asked. "How do you keep *finding* me? I don't even *look* the same!"

The Oathkeeper stepped forward, making the ritual gesture of closure for the third time today. "In the name of Javei, I shall now reveal that which was hidden. The criminal fled from us by disappearing into the market, yet upon the sacred questioning of witnesses it was observed that a cloaked figure made her way along an alley. Guided by He Who Makes Plain, I investigated the local inns, until the suspect was before me." She bowed her head. "Suspect, do you have a statement in your defense?"

"Yeah, sure," I said. "Fuck you, Gemyrne! *No one owns hair!*" There was a collective gasp from around the room at my rebellion against fashion.

The Oathkeeper tilted her head. "Was that statement supposed to exonerate you in any way?"

"Exonerate this," I said, and activated my cloak.

"*Lilith!*" the commander hissed subvocally as the room erupted into chaos.

"*I'm fine, I'm fine,*" I said, excepting her from the cloak effect. I started walking for the exit. Gemyrne was screeching like the fucking Karen she was. "*Meditations have been going great ever since you made Val babysit me. I'm not going overboard again.*"

"*Be. Careful.*"

"*Yeah, yeah,*" I said, ducking past Gemyrne as she gesticulated violently.

"On second thought, I think I might need more time to think about this," said the mark.

"Let the goddess guide your path. Perhaps the message was truly meant for someone in your acquaintance," Abby said serenely. "*Shit. Lilith, we may need to keep you back so this stops happening.*"

"*For fucks's sake, doesn't she have a job?*"

The commander didn't answer me. "*Markus, Val, how's it going?*"

"*I think we got two?*" Markus said. "*We were working on another group, but then one of them got engaged.*"

"*Like, while you were talking to them?*" I asked.

"*Yeah, it was a surprise for everyone involved,*" said Markus. "*They look really cute together. We're invited to the wedding, by the way.*"

"*That's such a fucking trap.*"

"*We are not going to the wedding,*" said the commander.

"*Figures,*" said Markus. "*You never take us anywhere nice.*"

"*Goddess of legacies my ass,*" I said. "*Goddess of stupid-ass consequences, more like. Val, you've been quiet.*"

"*He's fuming,*" said Markus.

"*And I quote,*" Val said in clipped, precise tones, "'*I think the goddess is trying to tell me that what I truly need is to follow my heart.*'"

"*You can't make this shit up,*" laughed Markus.

"*This bitch needs to die,*" I said.

"At this rate, we'll still have enough people to lean on Erid to make the trip, anyway," said the commander. *"Keep circulating."*

"Warden! The Greatmother bids you release any prisoners that wish to make pilgrimage to the Holy Tree!"

"No, she doesn't," said the warden, not looking up from her paperwork. "A priestess came in a half *thessim* ago, said you'd be in here saying that."

"Huh," I said. "And you're not arresting me or anything?"

"She said I wouldn't catch you," said the warden. "Bye now."

"Fair enough," I said, fading to invisibility.

". . . The sheer statistical improbability *of it! They were on separate* continents *at one point! And she wouldn't even have* known *she was abandoned if her estranged foster mother hadn't* also *happened to have been in the room right at that moment!"*

"Val, did you consider framing the pilgrimage as an opportunity for them to get to know each other?" asked the commander.

"Obviously," said Val. *"But her birth mother, in an act of pious desperation, had just donated her last few* drobol *to the poor."*

"Okay, she's just mocking us at this point," I said.

"You!" shouted Gemyrne again.

"Are you freaking kidding me," I said. "Hey, Gemyrne, I bet you're not important enough to have an invitation to the Holy Tree pilgrimage!"

"Oathkeepers!" she shouted, ignoring me. "Oathkeepers! The hair thief is right here!"

"You probably didn't want that to work, anyway," said Markus.

"You can't tell me you weren't a little curious if it would," I said.

"Shouldn't you be getting out of there?" prodded the commander.

"The way I see it," I said, *"if I stay near her, she can't pop up unexpectedly somewhere else."*

"Get out of there, Lilith."

"Yes'm."

The sun was reaching its peak as Markus and I staggered to the *Friend of Heaven*. We were all at the ends of our ropes. I was emotionally exhausted from looking over my shoulder all the time and kind of hazy from cloaking myself—not too much! I swear! It's just draining, that's all, I was totally fine. Val had stopped speaking to any of us except to deliver extremely to-the-point updates on his mission tasks. The commander's patience was running thin, and even irrepressible Markus was less than chipper.

Friend of Heaven was just as much a piece of shit as last time I'd laid eyes on it, but now it was bustling with activity. Sailing was mostly a male profession here, like back home. Burly men wearing what looked like actual, honest-to-god *shirts* were hauling crates of supplies onto the ship, and some of our pilgrims were already milling about.

Val was around here somewhere with a sniper rifle and a moirascope. Go ahead, assface, send someone to call off the expedition. We were done fucking around.

I tried to summon the persona of Danou and mostly succeeded. I kept subconsciously emulating Gemyrne, which pissed me off every time I noticed it happening. I was wearing her Seven Waves again as a general middle finger to, well, everything. At least she wasn't going to be a problem this time. I'd tracked her down and pulsed her right before coming here. Like I said, we were done fucking around.

We probably weren't getting our alternate revenue stream, either. Val and Abby had negotiated a bounty on the Sons of Horcutio, as our targets named themselves, but after the clusterfuck that this trip was becoming, it was doubtful we'd be able to show our faces again to collect it. Fucking Kives hadn't even done anything to stop us from doing that, either, she'd just let us waste our time.

"You look like shit," a voice interrupted my inner kvetching.

"Godsmile, captain," I said without turning my head from the woman whose coin I was collecting. "I see your friend came through."

"*My* words don't waste away over fine food," said Erid, stumping around to my right and watching the preparations on her ship. She moved stiffly. I guessed hip issues; I had an aunt who walked like that. Her hair was bushy and—shockingly for polite society—unstyled, dirty-blonde curls bouncing off a deep blue sailor's cloak as she moved.

I forgot myself for a moment. "Yeah, well, they're fuck-ugly words," I said, drawing a disapproving stare from an elderly woman who was making her way toward the gantry.

Erid turned and gave me a smile, revealing several missing teeth. "I knew there was fire in you, girl. It's why I took the job. Which reminds me, we're due another quarrel."

"Should have guessed," I said.

"You promised a hundred pilgrims," she said. "There's eighty here. That's not coming out of *my* cut."

"Let's not be so gauche as to negotiate in front of these faithful travelers," I said.

Erid snorted. "Have your man handle the coin. Let's talk in my cabin."

It was a beautiful day. Gulls called above the hubbub of people, near and far, shouting to one another or engaging in conversation. Waves rolled noisily under the docks. Above us, the sky was a bright blue, with fluffy, pristine clouds. I eyed them suspiciously. A gentle breeze blew the scent of salt and rotting fish inland.

Friend of Heaven was crowded now, pilgrims getting in the way of sailors preparing to catch the tide. I followed Erid belowdecks to a room that was much smaller than I'd been led to expect from a childhood of watching pirate movies with my brothers.

Once we were inside I drew my knife and slammed her against the wall. She was in good shape, but so was I, and I was a couple decades younger with the element of surprise.

"Alright, listen here, you pirate fuck," I said, laying the blade against her throat. "I have had *a day*, do you understand?"

Erid laughed. I felt a sharp point against my stomach.

"We'll both die, girl, but you'll die slow," she said, her missing teeth showing through her smile. "And you're too soft to watch me bleed out."

A vision of Arguel suddenly flashed in front of my eyes, and I suppressed a flinch. Something changed in her expression; she'd seen.

"The thousand's nonnegotiable," she said. "Pila won't accept less."

"Convince her," I said, increasing the pressure on the knife.

"Not a chance in Horcutio's fucking deeps, girl. My legs aren't shit, but they're the only ones I got." The pressure on my stomach increased. "I'd rather take you out here than die a cripple."

I made a face to concede the point. "Alright, then your stupid commission. We're down to six hundred after Pila gets her cut. Five hundred's ridiculous. We split it two ways, even."

"Maybe I'll just let you knife me. It'd be kinder than what the crew would do to me if I didn't pay 'em. Better prospects for revenge, too. Four hundred."

"Dying slow just means I could get treatment. Kanabades could find me."

Erid grinned crookedly. "How much you want to bet he finds you before my crew? After clearly knifing their captain?"

"What makes you think I'll be lying helplessly on the ground?" I said. "I'll fucking stab everyone who comes in this room. Three hundred."

"Deal," said Erid. "But only because you remind me of myself when I was younger." She pushed me off her, rubbing her throat. "Foolish girl. Anyone with sense tries not to get stabbed. Only an idiot draws a knife when there isn't need of one."

"This idiot's a hundred *drobol* richer," I said, fuming internally.

"My treat," said the captain. "Take an old woman's advice and spend it now because you won't last 'til thirty."

I didn't have a response to that, so I left, biting back the anger. All around me, people were settling into place for a voyage of almost a month. Within the hour, the anchor was up, and we left with the tide.

"*Ship is leaving the harbor,*" said Val. "*Last chance to abort. Moirascope readings confirm a violent encounter of some kind in the near future. Commander, I'll circle back to rendezvous.*"

"*Acknowledged,*" said Abby. "*I am confirming no mission abort. Repeat, no mission abort at this time. Good luck, Lilith, Markus.*"

"*They fall,*" I said.

"*They die,*" came the response.

The *Friend of Heaven* sailed off to its date with destiny.

Behind us, underneath the water, a dark shape followed.

CHAPTER FIFTEEN

Nutters, the Lot of You

This fog looks pretty unnatural," I said. "Might be there's pirates on the hunt."

"Sky and sea, Idiot," said Erid, leaning on the railing next to me. "What *is* it with you and pirates? You've talked about nothing else for three days."

Paradoxically, she seemed to like me more after I pulled a knife on her than when she'd thought I was just some spoiled merchant, but the price I paid was my new nickname, Idiot.

"They're a concern, okay?" I said. "They could pop out at any moment."

I turned and looked expectantly at the fog, as though the Sons of Horcutio might come splashing out of the water at any moment. They did not, however, oblige me.

"Lilith, could you try to be a little less subtle?" Markus subvocalized, giving me a look. *"This is incredibly suspicious."*

"And that's another thing," said Erid. "You keep looking off at the horizon every time you say something like that. Is this some kind of play for you? I've siding that needs maintenance if you've got the time for fantasies."

"Okay, she thinks it's a sexual fantasy," said the commander. *"Sell her on that and then stop bringing it up."*

"What?!" I said. "No!" I wasn't sure who I was responding to, but it was the same answer for all of them.

Erid cackled. "We've all been there, Idiot. But shut your trap, alright? It's bad luck to keep talking about it."

I couldn't help it. I looked off for the inevitable pirate attack.

"You really are one of Kives's lot," Erid said. "Nutters, the lot of you."

I bristled internally at the implication that I was religious before remembering I was playing a role here. I could inhabit a character flawlessly for short spurts, but never breaking character is way harder when it's a full-time job. It didn't help that the character of Danou had drifted toward something more like my natural behavior: it was easy to forget things when I wasn't focusing all the time. Fortunately, in this case, I had an entirely natural response.

"You've never seen her work," I said with a harrowed expression. "She could do *anything.*"

Erid patted me on the shoulder.

"Sounds like there's a story there," she said. "If that's the case, I'll thank you to *stop talking about pirates on my ship, ye daft gull*! Now get out of my sight, Idiot!"

"Godsmile," I said, rubbing my aching ear. "I'll just get belowdecks, then?"

Erid's glare followed me down.

That, of course, is when the pirates attacked.

Our first warning was a deafening bellow of some great sea creature that sounded like a cow who just figured out you stole his wallet. I pumped my fist with a quiet "yes!" and then ran back up the stairs to see what we were in for.

The yells were louder and closer when I surfaced as the pilgrims discovered why Kives had warned them all not to go on this journey in the first place. Sucks to suck. The fog had dispersed somewhat, allowing us a glimpse of a dark shape moving across the water. The affronted-cow noise echoed across the water again, only this time it was joined by a second. I glanced toward the rear of the ship but couldn't see anything.

Captain Erid was snapping orders as her sailors rushed about. Pilgrims, at least those fit for physical labor, were getting press-ganged to man the oars. A couple of men brought out spears from belowdecks; others were stringing bows. I saw one of them with a crossbow and immediately called it in to the team. Theria was definitely more advanced than we were giving it credit for, and that was worrying.

"*You!*" Erid snarled, grabbing my arm. It was the arm with access to my combat knife; she hadn't forgotten. Her knife was wavering furiously in front of my eye. "You knew about this! Are you working with them? The hell are you two planning?"

"Please don't stab me," I said. "I'm your only hope of getting out of here."

"That's impossible," said Erid, looking up at me. "Answer me or I'll slice your skull open like a coconut."

Wasn't that a pleasant image.

"We're here to kill the pirates," I said, staring at her evenly. "Your ship will be okay. You can pray to Kives if you need more assurances."

"*Idiot* girl," said Erid, violently sheathing her knife. "Why'd you have to get my ship involved in all this?"

"Time pressure, mostly," I said. "Our lead had a limited window of success."

"Fuck you to the depths of the ocean," she said. "If I didn't need every hand I could get to fight off these upstart, dick-waving thieves, I'd stick you now and feed you to the crabs."

"Not the sharks?" I asked.

"What the fuck is a shark?"

"That's actually really disappointing," I said. Suddenly pain overwhelmed the side of my face, and I fell to the deck.

"This isn't a play!" Erid yelled. "Now grab a weapon or man the oars, and if I see you again I'll disembowel you with a krilhook!"

I didn't ask her what a krilhook was as she stomped off. I have *some* preservation instincts.

"Lilith, you need to focus," said the commander. *"We've got a huge uptick of marine life heading for the* Friend of Heaven. *Our demigod might have inherited the ability to commune with sea creatures."*

"Oh, really?" said Markus. *"I thought they just wanted to join the party."*

"That's so dumb," I said. *"Weather gods don't even do that. Horcutio must have given him that blessing on purpose just so he'd be a bigger ass to everyone."*

"Val," said Markus, *"ETA on the angels?"*

"No sign of them," said Val. *"It's possible Kives is holding them back to mitigate the political fallout with the rest of the pantheon. She'll have to commit them, however. It's mathematically necessary given her profile."*

"Grabbing equipment," I said. *"Wait, what kind of sea creatures are we talking about?"*

"They appear to be mostly carnivorous," said Val. *"Some herbivores. The common denominator appears to be killing ability."*

"Of course," I said. *"Shit, this is going to mess with the plan."*

"You'll be fine," said the commander. *"It's Markus I'm worried about."*

"I'll be fine," said Markus. *"Not my first time wrestling with sharks."*

"They don't have sharks here," I said, pushing some frightened pilgrims out of the way. *"That's just wrong. You can't do a proper pirate bit without sharks."*

"You know none of us have the cultural reference to understand what you're talking about, right?" said Val.

"Come on, I made you all watch Pirates of the Caribbean," I said. Ah, here we go, this was the crate I needed. There were more people huddled in front of it. "Move, people! Kives won't protect you down here! Get the fuck out of the way!"

That scattered them. I heard footsteps approaching behind me, glanced back, ignored them. Markus walked up next to me. "Need a hand?"

"I'm good," I said, levering off the top with my knife. Markus watched me for a second, then kicked the top off with a massive splintering noise. Inside there was a black waterproof case five feet long and about three feet wide.

"Fuck, man!" I shouted. "My face was, like, right there!"

"We don't have time," said Markus. "Alright, change of clothes, transmitter, water jets, rebreathers—Lilith, did you really?"

"What?" I said, fixing a tricorn hat on my head.

"The commander specifically told you not to bring that hat," said Markus. *"Lilith, did you really?"*

"I had to," I said, giggling a little. "Because now we're . . . pirates of the *Theribbean.*"

Markus was unimpressed. "That was a lot of work for a bit *in the middle of a combat situation."*

"Whatever," I said. "It was awesome."

"Lilith, ditch the damn hat. I'm not asking you again."

Markus knocked it off my head. "Lilith, there are consequences to this sort of thing. Never forget that."

"Fiiiine," I said. "Alright, turn around, I'm not getting changed in front of you."

"Suit yourself," said Markus. I snorted at the pun, which wasn't actually a pun in Velean, so Markus looked confused for a moment before shrugging and starting to strip. I looked away, grabbing my own clothes.

I took off Danou's dress, quickly replacing it with an armored wet suit produced with state-of-the-art Eifni materials science and hoping like mad that no one came through the door. The clinging, rubbery fabric was warm against my skin, terminating at my ankles and wrists. The transmitter, attached to a sparkling synthetic necklace, got tucked inside. Next, I strapped on a waterproof pouch with my disruptor pistol.

Over that, I threw a skirt and a wrap, which we'd given hooks to keep them attached to preinstalled loops on the wet suit. The Therian clothing was more or less to preserve plausible deniability, and also to help hide the next part. Markus and I levered sleek black tubes out of the crate and strapped them to each other's backs. Finally, a shawl each mostly hid the water jets from view. Markus handed me a clear plastic mask.

"Ten minutes of air," he said. "We should need way less than that."

"Aye, aye, captain," I said. "Let's go."

We barreled through the ship's corridors, Markus with the supply case over his arm. We'd pitch it overboard the first chance we got—leave no evidence behind. "Move!" he bellowed as we went. People moved. We emerged into the fog-drenched noon sunlight, boggling at the dark shape emerging from the fog.

"*Commander, we have contact,*" said Markus. "*Damn, he's got style.*"

The shape in the fog resolved itself into a great ship, easily twice the size of the *Friend of Heaven*, on a direct collision course with us. Before it, two sinuous beshelled forms arced through the water, occasionally mooing or bellowing or whatever the fuck they were doing. They were yoked to the fucking ship. Kulades or whatever his name was had a friggin' sea chariot.

In the waters on either side of the ship I saw the Sons of Horcutio arranged on hippocampi, looking comically like cavalry who'd somehow taken a wrong turn and ended up in the middle of the ocean. The image was belied by the large horizontal tails flipping behind each of them. Each of them had a long spear whose butt was trailing in the water, leaving its own little wake. I presumed they'd go in for the stab if they had to do a charge; that seemed like the kind of thing that would throw off their mounts' steering.

Shouts of fear came up from the civilians on the deck, including those hastily conscripted against the imminent attack. One man panicked and jumped overboard. The sea thrashed with activity as creatures converged on his location; the water turned red shortly after. Man, this was going to suck.

"I said I didn't want to see you again," said Erid, brandishing a sword as she stomped towards us.

"You also said you needed us defending the ship, so it was a little ambiguous," I said, backing up toward the railing.

"Took the chance to change clothes, did you?" she snarled. "Couldn't find a better use of your time?"

The railing was getting awfully close.

"Why, captain," I said in my most theatrical tone. "This is the day you will *always* remember as the day—"

Markus picked me up and threw me screaming off the side of the ship. I barely had enough presence of mind to shove my rebreather onto my face before I hit the water. The seal wasn't perfect—the strap wasn't around the back of my head—so a bit of water leaked in before I got it tight. It was pinching my ear pretty bad. I didn't have time to worry about that, though, because there were an awful lot of claws and teeth heading at me.

"Val!" I screamed. "Start the fucking jet!"

The water jet on my back kicked, and suddenly I was corkscrewing through the water, dodging all sorts of sea gribblies as they came to eat me. I was screaming the whole time. One claw scraped my arm, but the wet suit held, and I didn't get more than a bruise.

"*If you could quiet down, I've almost got you there,*" said Val. "*This isn't as easy as it looks.*"

"All I'm looking at is sea monsters!" I screamed. "Fuck fuck fuck, get me out of here!"

"*Predictable,*" Val sighed. My momentum shifted, and I was going—deeper?! Fuck fuck fuck, no, Val, you idiot, the surface is the other way—

I swerved again, I was heading upward, toward freedom, building up speed, and *oh god* that was a lot of scaly, clawed, angry fish, and here we go—

I rocketed out of the water, screaming and flailing, arcing gracelessly until I collapsed on top of the rear deck. A second or two later, Markus fell next to me with a *clunk* as his jet collided with the deck.

"Never doing that again," I groaned. Markus made a nonverbal noise of agreement as I pulled off my rebreather and chucked it overboard. A tug on the release strap dropped my jet onto the deck. I levered it off into the ocean. Markus did the same. We looked at each other, nodded, and stumbled over to where some actual, real-life pirates had rushed to see what was making all the noise.

"Ladies and gentlemen," I said as they approached. "Greetings! We have been sent from the deeps by Lord Horcutio himself!"

I grinned.

"Need some help raiding the trade ship?"

CHAPTER SIXTEEN

Lord Kulades

Markus and I stood on the upper deck of the pirate ship, absolutely drenched from our underwater journey, dripping like we were covered in faucets someone forgot to turn all the way off. Facing us were four pirates, evenly mixed between the sexes, all of whom were holding spears or long hooks or equally vicious looking weaponry. They were dressed mostly in dirty rags, with splashes of color here and there—from what I could tell, newly looted fabrics distributed among the crew.

These people were outcasts from civil society, naturally suspicious of outsiders. They examined us closely, which reminded me that my wet clothes were stuck right to my figure. I resisted the urge to shrink with embarrassment. We had appeared here out of nowhere, with only our word to back us up. Our approach would require great care and subtlety.

"Take us to your leader!" I said, because I possessed neither of those.

"You are not armed," said a woman, larger and more muscular than the rest. Her tone was almost a question.

"We offer not arms but victory," said Markus. "If we might but speak with Kulades, all will be made plain."

"You come from Lord Horcutio?" asked another pirate. This one was male, bald, with dark skin and a salt-and-pepper beard. A nasty-looking throat wound had rendered his voice a rasp. He was wielding what looked like a harpoon made of some large crustacean's shell.

"We are," I said. "We bring counsel. Kulades can triumph this day, but he must follow our advice."

"Kulades does not need your *advice*," spat the tall woman, "to hunt a limping *tulim*."

"The *tulim*," I answered calmly, "is full of pilgrims on their way to worship at the Great Tree of Kives. You are imperiling a hundred souls who even now cry out to the goddess for aid."

"Let them pray," she snarled. "They will not be the first. Lord Horcutio rules these waters."

"He does," said Markus. "That is why he sent us. Will you waylay the messengers of your captain's father?"

That seemed to give them pause. Sensing an opening, I jumped in.

"Surely Kulades will know whether we speak the truth," I said. "And if we are lying, how did we get up here? The seas are yours, and the hull is smooth."

Captain Ahab nodded to She-Hulk, and they fell in around us as we were marched to the front of the ship.

"*Infiltration stage one is complete,*" Markus subvocalized.

It was time to meet a demigod.

"Would I be correct if I said effects follow causes?" Val had asked during the planning session.

Paraphysicists are twisty bastards, and you can't trust them to make anything simple.

"No," I guessed.

"In fact, I would," said Val, looking just a bit smug. "In realspace, we have cause first and then effect; they are all oriented in one direction, which we call time. Now, what would happen if cause and effect still applied, but they were oriented in multiple directions? Such that, for example, one effect could influence a cause that was part of its own causal chain?"

"Hey, that's what I meant when I said no," I complained.

"It just keeps changing?" asked Markus.

"Understandable deduction," said Val. "But that answer assumes these interactions happen sequentially, as they would in realspace. In etherspace, we find that the best models are those that have them executing simultaneously."

"Then how do etheric entities experience time?" I asked. "That seems . . . chaotic."

"Most etheric entities—including us, by the way; we're more soul than meat—have a foothold on both sides of the sidereal boundary," said Val. "Your body obviously experiences time. The soul represents the body, so your consciousness uses conduit theory to reflect your physical state."

"Okay, but we're talking about Kives. She doesn't have anything over here."

"Correct," said Val, nodding to me. "Godseeds work like we do, being housed in physical bodies, but a fully grown god and certainly an ascendant god does not possess consciousness as we experience it. This has tactical implications."

A slight sneer passed fleetingly over Val's face.

"Amateur moirologists often build plans around the idea of *planning* to take an action, then relenting once they've forced the oracle to act. This betrays a fundamental misunderstanding of our opponent. In the first place, counterfactual futures do not exist, and the oracle has no access to them. In the second place, oracles do not act *iteratively.* They are the quintessence of a concept given agency. They don't try different behaviors to see what changes because realspace does not change that way. Instead, an oracle reacts as their character dictates to the conditions of realspace, which they experience *simultaneously*—past, present, and future."

The commander was tapping her fingers again. "Val, we appreciate the explanation, but this is a lot of theory with no application."

"The application is simple," said Val. "We accept that Kives wins."

The mooing from Kulades's sea beasts was louder here as we picked up pace. We were a minute from contact at most. As we approached the front of the ship, Markus and I got our first glimpse of the demigod. He was easily seven feet tall, wearing a cloak of many-colored seashells that had to weigh far too much. His hair was black, and his arms were massive, sun dark, and seemingly covered in fish scales. In his right hand he had a huge spear, probably nine or ten feet long, and over his left shoulder he rested a *massive* freaking sword, made out of some kind of bone and studded with some kind of teeth. I'd guess shark teeth, but apparently they didn't have those here.

"Lord Kulades!" called the muscly woman who was guarding us. "These two appeared on the top deck! They claim to be messengers from Lord Horcutio!"

Kulades turned, and *man* were those some muscles. Buddy was only wearing a skirt, made from rich purple cloth and belted with gold. His face was pretty darn ugly. Looked like an Easter Island head. He glared suspiciously at us.

"What manner of messengers are these?" he growled in the lowest voice I've ever heard.

"We come from Lord Horcutio," said Markus. "We bring tidings about the coming battle."

"Speak, then," rumbled the giant pirate. "Then I will return you to him."

I surmised that meant he was going to dump us overboard, and from the glint in his eye, he expected that to end messily for us. Without the water jets, we'd be shark bait. Er, not that they have sharks here, dammit.

"Three boons he grants you," I said, stepping forward. I took off the necklace I was wearing and held it out to him. "First, this talisman of victory. While you wear it, the wiles of Kives shall do you no harm."

He stared down at it, considering.

"It looks like no other gift of my father's," he said at last.

"It was stolen from Kives," I said smoothly. "The second boon he grants you is a warning: the angels of Kives will descend. With this talisman, you may slay them, for your nature will be hidden from them."

Kulades grunted. He handed his spear to the nearest crewwoman—whose reliability he secured with a rumbling growl that had her paling—and snatched the necklace with a swipe of his long simian arm.

"I will wear it," he rumbled. The chain was too short for his neck, so he looped the sparkling chain around the throat of his cloak.

"*Val, how's the connection?*" Markus subvocalized.

"*Excellent,*" said Val. "*Ah, this is fortunate. Our friend here is broadcasting his will to all the marine life in the area. Stall him a bit longer.*"

"*Where the hell are those angels?*" asked Markus. "*Did the pilgrims forget how to pray or something?*"

"The third boon is a promise," I said, ignoring them. "When your crew board the trade ship, you personally must hold back but a moment. *Then* attack and Lord Horcutio will lend you his strength."

Kulades stared at me for a long time.

"When we board the ship?" he repeated.

The mood shifted.

"They are spies," rumbled the demigod. "Hold them."

Markus and I were both immediately seized by the crew around us. Kulades stepped closer to us. He reached up, grabbed the transmitter, and ripped it off, throwing it on the deck. He spat on it.

"Show them my glory," he ordered. "Then I will flay them."

He turned his back on us as rough hands held us down and forced us to look at the *Friend of Heaven*.

"Behold," bellowed Kulades, pointing his sword at the ship, "a delicious oyster, full of pearls! Brace for impact!"

With a titanic keening noise, the creatures pulling Kulades's ship submerged. We jerked forward. The front of the ship smashed into the *Friend of Heaven*, splitting it open. Its defenders tumbled to the deck, water rushing inside its guts. The hippocampi charged ahead, flanking the dying ship. The water below them churned with carnivorous mouths.

The angels hadn't come. I knelt, wide-eyed, looking at all the people we'd just gotten killed.

"Phase one of the plan is to enlist a ship full of pilgrims," said Val. "Anyone willing to give up their livelihood for a time to travel to Kives's new holy site will have a strong connection to her. A ship full of them will be a target she can't afford to ignore. That means our battle will involve four groups: the pirates, the pilgrims, Kives's angels, and us."

"That's just asking for chaos," said the commander.

"Not if we take a secondary role in the battle," said Val. "We're not here to kill all the pirates. Just the demigod who claims affiliation with Horcutio. We insert Markus and Lilith with the pilgrims, then have them infiltrate the pirates before the raid. Fighting with the pirates means the angels will show up, defend the pilgrims—who will be desperately praying for aid—and maybe even kill Kulades for us. In the meantime, we'll use the transmitter to collect the souls of the hippocampi killed in the battle."

"That's a lot of assumptions," said the commander. "How certain are we that Kives will deploy the angels?"

"I mentioned that amateurs plan to relent from an action," said Val. "We will not. Kives has been the ultimate target this whole time. If she will not defend her followers, we'll kill them ourselves during the boarding action. It will be a small wound, but it is from many such wounds that Kives will die."

"I'm not comfortable with this kind of wound," I said. "The whole point is to save people."

"It should not come to that," said Val. "If she fails to intervene, she is lessened. If she intervenes, it is Horcutio who is lessened. The rational decision is obvious."

They were all going to die, and it wasn't even our fault—etherically speaking. Kives had let them become martyrs instead. We'd failed.

"*Lilith, Markus, prepare to flash,*" said the commander. "*There's no point in letting him flay you alive.*"

"They're all going to die," I said, not bothering to subvocalize. "This bastard of a goddess isn't going to save them."

"*It is a noted behavioral tendency of the species,*" said Val.

"You fucker!" I yelled, drawing looks from those around me. "You said she would!"

"Spy," said Kulades, not turning away from the disaster unfolding before us. "Who do you speak to?"

"No one," I said.

"Pain," he commanded. The pirates holding me threw me to the deck as Markus shouted something. A foot impacted painfully with my ribs, rolling me over the deck. Something snagged on my hand—the transmitter.

"*Val,*" I groaned. "*Have transmitter. Help?*"

"*Get it on him,*" he said. "*I have a contingency for this.*"

Another kick rolled me on my back. Two pirates dragged me in front of Kulades, I guessed so he could question me without missing the show.

"Answer," he said simply.

"Take this," I groaned, holding up the transmitter. "You'll hear."

He stared down at me. In a sudden surge of violent motion, he snatched it up and threw it overboard. Fuck. Then he reached down and picked me up by my wrap like I weighed nothing.

"Answer," he said again, taking a step forward.

"O-okay," I said, gasping, pawing at my wrap. I found the hidden pocket. "Look, I'll tell you."

Kulades kept walking forward, toward the end of the ship. Markus was yelling.

"Please, just stop!" I yelled. "I'll tell you!"

He just looked at me darkly, expression like stone. My searching hand got the pouch open.

"In the name of Kives," I said, drawing my disruptor pistol, "die, you piece of shit."

I shot him in his stupid Easter Island face, and everything went to hell.

CHAPTER SEVENTEEN

Calamity

I nailed Kulades straight in his oversize forehead. At this range, the bullet punched straight out the other side with a pink mist. In etherspace, I knew, destructive energies were scouring the *concept* of him out of existence, shredding his soul, corrupting memories of him—even Horcutio himself might feel a small sting. Probably not—it'd be like if one of your intestinal bacteria tried to punch you in the kidney—but there would be an effect, minuscule as it might be.

Kulades had been many things in life—a warrior, a leader, a living scion of a god—but what hit the ground wasn't even a body. It was semiotically decimated. It was meat, nothing more.

His soul had been shredded to ribbons, never to return to Horcutio. The ultimate act of violence, done in Kives's name. May it poison them both.

I landed on my feet, brandishing my pistol at the other pirates, who were staring in horror at what had been Kulades. They might not know what a pistol was, but the demonstration was convincing enough.

"Throw down your *fucking* weapons," I shouted. "On your knees! Hands on your heads! I said get the fuck down, I'm not asking twice!"

The muscly lady who'd been the first to welcome us on board snarled and lifted her weapon, a cruel-looking hook, and started toward me. Pity, I liked her aesthetic. I fired again.

The bullet caught her in the arm, but that didn't matter with disruptor weapons. I saw the exact moment when the ether shock fired through her arm to her self-concept and into her soul. Another pile of meat slumped onto the deck, weapon clattering onto the wood.

"I said," I shouted, "get your knees on the ground or I will *fucking erase you.* Is that clear?"

There was a clattering noise as the holdouts embraced the better part of valor.

Markus had broken free of his captors and was training his gun on the assembled pirates as he made his way across the deck toward me.

"How's it looking?" he asked quietly. I peeked a glance. The *Friend of Heaven* was in two halves, rapidly sinking, and the waters around it were frothing red.

"Bad," I said. "Commander, we need exfil."

"*Just stay put,*" said Val. "*Need to retrieve the transmitter.*"

"Yeah, sorry," I said. "Aquatic Mad Max over here didn't like the cursed necklace."

"*I've nearly caught it with one of the water jets,*" said Val. "*There we go. Reprogramming. I'm going to try to spoof Kulades's signal.*"

"Calm them down so we can get out of here," I said.

"*No,*" said Val. "*Kulades brought an army of killers and made them hungry. We still have our objectives. We need to coordinate them.*"

"Oh, shit," said Markus. "They're all turning on one another."

I peeked again. Sure enough, the red waters weren't just around the *Friend of Heaven*, they were spreading out. And they were especially hectic around the hippocampi. Screams and squeals filled the air.

There was a *clunk* as a boarding hook landed right next to me.

"Markus," I said urgently. "We have boarders incoming."

"I love it when things go according to plan," he said brightly. "It's bound to happen one day." He turned. "Lilith! It's not just boarders!"

Another hook, another *clunk*. I turned. There were a lot of people down there throwing hooks. I didn't see anything else.

"What?" I asked.

"The ropes are tied to the ship!" said Markus. "They're dragging us down with them!"

"*What?*" I said. "Who's stupid enough to—"

I stopped. I knew.

"Change of plans, my good friends!" said Markus, turning to our hostages. "It's a beautiful day, the sea life is active, and *every one of us is going to die* unless we act quickly!"

"Put all the weight on the back of the ship!" I said. "They're trying to capsize us!"

They stared at us dumbly.

"*Move it!*" I screamed. "Go go go! The fish have all gone crazy! If the ship sinks, we're bait!"

That got them moving. I wondered how often they saw feedings happen for it to be that motivating. Some went belowdecks to try to shift the cargo; others started pushing crates across the top decks.

"Val," I said through gritted teeth, "we need an exit here."

"*If I don't handle this perfectly, we have to do the whole thing again,*" said Val. "*Frankly, the only reason we weren't forced to abort is because I managed to recalibrate the broadcast after you lost the transmitter.*"

"Yeah, yeah, you're really smart," I said. "Can you calm the fish down?"

"*Ah, not at present.*"

"*We're making them angrier,*" said the commander. "*We've secured one hippocampus soul already. The plan is working. Just hold on.*"

Holding on turned out to be literally what we needed to do, as the stern of the *Friend of Heaven* started to tug on the dozens of ropes securing it to the pirate ship. It was only a fraction of the size of Kulades's ship, but that was enough to make the deck tilt alarmingly.

"Climb the railing!" said Markus. "We need to get to the top deck!"

A screaming pirate fell off the side of the ship into the bloody ocean. He did not resurface.

"Try not to slip, I guess," I said, running for the side of the ship. The deck continued to tilt, and in bare feet I wasn't super happy about the rough texture on my soles, but adrenaline pushed me through. Markus and I leaped for the railing just as the ship keeled onto its side, dropping some of the pirates into the carnivorous frenzy below. From this vantage point I could see Captain Erid climbing the ropes, with dozens of pilgrims behind her. They were out for blood.

"This day gets better and better," I said as I hung over certain death. I'd always hated the monkey bars when I was a kid.

"Mm," Markus grunted in agreement as he levered himself on to the side of the railing—which, relative to gravity, had now become the top.

"*Just a few more minutes,*" said the commander. "*Can you handle it?*"

"We're hanging in there," I said.

Markus groaned, reached down, and hauled me up with one arm. "Please don't pun," he said, setting me down on the railing in front of him. "You know it messes with the comms."

"Or what, you'll punish me?" I said with a smirk.

He glared. "We'll put you on the notice," he said.

"Ow!" I said as my comm tried to shove multiple meanings into my brain at once. It was like being really itchy, except the itch was also a migraine and, uh, fluffy? But an unpleasant kind of fluffy. I can't describe it. "Fine, I'll stop!"

"*Observe the damn translator protocols,*" said the commander. "*You know better, Lilith. No non-Velean puns. Both of you make your way to the back of the ship, it'll give you more time.*"

"The pilgrims are getting pretty close," I said as we stepped carefully from rail to rail. "Man, they're a motley bunch, but my money's on them right now."

Mostly because they, unlike the pirates, still had their weapons. The first of them had climbed onto the pirate ship proper, and they'd bared swords and gone for the pirates. Captain Erid was leading the fray. After hacking a man's leg off, she looked up and happened to spot me. She pointed, shouted something.

"Aw fuck," I said. "I think they want to kill us, Markus."

"If only someone hadn't spent the last three days making cryptic comments about pirates," said Markus. Good thing Veleans thought on such long timescales, or they wouldn't put up with me nearly this much. We stepped it up; we were nearing the end of the ship.

"Commander?" I asked.

"*Almost there.*"

"That's what you said last time!"

"*It's not, but whatever keeps you on your toes.*"

"*Thirteen seconds,*" said Val. "*I've got the last one in the dragnet.*"

"Precise fucker," I muttered. "Oh fuck. They're cutting the ropes."

"Underneath," Markus said urgently. We both started to climb between the struts of the railing, just in time for the ship to lurch back toward the water. Markus and I both screamed—although in his case it was more of a roller-coaster kind of thing—as we came within snapping distance of the killer gore slushie the ocean had become, then rocketed back. The ship's motion stopped suddenly, tearing our grips off the railing and rolling us across the top deck.

"That wasn't normal physics," Markus groaned.

"Let's get the fuck out of here," I agreed. We hauled ourselves to our feet, just in time for the sun to darken for a moment.

The angels had arrived.

"*Ah, there we go,*" said Val. "*I knew I did the math correctly.*"

"*You are* not *helpful,*" I subvocalized.

Five of them touched down in formation, black cloaks fluttering as they descended. The cloaks weren't just black—they were the color of the midnight sky, an infinite empty void with what appeared to be true depth, like you could fall into them and find another universe, devoid of stars or planets or anything except endless time.

Captain Erid did not fall into the robes of the angel carrying her. Instead, it set her down as it landed. She flashed her remaining teeth at us as she drew a wickedly sharp-looking blade.

"Pray to Kives, eh?" she said, advancing on me. "Good advice, Idiot. Shame about the *drobol,* but what a lovely ship this is. Think I'll call it the *Fool's Errand.*"

"My treat," I said, backing up slowly. "I see you've found my hat. *Commander, get us the fuck out of here.*"

"Oh, this was yours?" she said, touching the brim of my tricorn hat, resting snugly atop her messy curls. "Think I'll keep it. Looks dashing on me, don't you think?"

"Quite," I said, eyeing the silent angels behind her. "Your new friends?"

"Saved us in our hour of need!" she chuckled. "Asked them to hold off until I got a piece of you."

"*Commander?*" I subvocalized.

Erid continued advancing on us.

"I really don't want to fight you," I said, holding up my hands. "I mean, this all turned out pretty well for you. And I think you're pretty cool for an old lady. There's also the part where I don't have a weapon. I'm not gonna pretend that's not a big part of my reasoning."

"Regrets, Idiot," Erid replied. "I pay my debts."

She stabbed; I rolled out of the way.

"Commander!" I shouted.

"Commander?" Erid asked, slashing at me while I frantically scrambled out of the way. "Your man over there? I'll skewer him if he interferes."

"*Hold tight, Lilith, we're coming.*"

There was a dull roar from beneath the sea. The water churned, then bulged. The sleek, matte-iron shape of the *Ragnar* rose out of the charnel deeps, like an ancient alien artifact the protagonists accidentally woke up in a Hollywood movie. Erid's jaw dropped. The angels did not draw their weapons—one moment their hands were empty, the next they were armed with silver blades that had my comm screaming in warning. The port-side disrupter batteries began to hum as someone—probably Val—trained them on the top deck.

Markus stepped into position in front of me.

"We're leaving," he told the angels. "You can face us another day. There are innocents on this ship. If we fight, there will be casualties."

You are the Calamity, said the one that had carried Erid here. *There will always be innocents. Always casualties.*

I couldn't see Markus's face, but I could imagine him frowning at that. I *could* see Erid's face, and she looked more scared than I thought was possible for her.

"But there don't have to be any more today," Markus said. "You'd know better than me."

The angels held perfectly still for a moment that seemed to last forever. I prepared to activate my cloak.

No more are slain today, it replied at last. *Go.*

"No more are slain today," Markus agreed.

Two harnesses dropped from the *Ragnar*, which Markus and I stepped into.

"Good to go, commander," said Markus.

I saw Erid looking at me. On her face I saw confusion, rage, fear, and—strangest of all—pity. I don't know what she saw on my face. I just felt tired. The adrenaline was fading.

I cracked half a rueful smile.

"Sorry," I said. "If it helps, there's a bounty on these fuckers back in Elsinat. Talk to the Oathkeepers."

Erid didn't seem to know how to respond to that.

Then we ascended. The harnesses jerked us back to the *Ragnar*, the shape of the *Fool's Errand* slowly shrinking beneath us as the commander took us away.

"No, no, take it more left," I said, a couple days later.

"There's nothing there," said Val. "We checked already."

"You checked, like, part of it," I said. "I'm telling you, it was over on the side."

Val took one hand off the controls to rub his forehead. "And then it was violently impacted and deluged in seawater."

"Couldn't have gone that far," I said, unconcerned. "Thing was superheavy, man."

"I see the mysteries of rotational geometry continue to elude you," said Val.

"That's just rude, you know?" I said. Not even Val's sniping could get me down right now. "Wait! Underneath the wardrobe!"

Val reoriented the remote minisubmarine, zooming the cameras in on the location I'd mentioned. "Is that the chest?"

"Hell yes! That's it! Six hundred *drobol*! And do you know what that means?"

Val sighed. "What does that mean?"

"I've officially found sunken treasure!" I cheered. "That's my whole pirate check-list!" I gave him a hug from behind.

He awkwardly patted my arm. "This is quite uncomfortable."

"I love you, too, Val," I said, releasing him. "I'm gonna go find Markus and watch a pirate movie. See you later."

"I suppose that means you won't be assisting with the process of actually extracting the chest?"

"Nah," I said. "I have pirate-y things to do. You weren't there, man. You wouldn't get it."

I skipped happily out of the room, humming "A Pirate's Life for Me."

CHAPTER EIGHTEEN

Interlude: Kaleidoscope

Are you ready?" asked the commander, bracing with her spear. It was a fine weapon, she thought—reinforced with titanium, monofilament edge. Most of the manufacturing techniques required to build it would elude Theria for centuries after their mission concluded. Once uplift began, it would be mere decades. The only comparable weapons on the planet were godtouched.

In her younger years, she'd felt like that was cheating. She knew better now. The gods have their strengths; godslayers have others.

Behind her, Markus and Lilith hefted their rifles. No disruptor rounds this time; the cramped hallways of the *Ragnar* increased the chance of a grazing hit to unacceptable levels. Centuries of combat experience told her that the physical trauma of gunshots would likely be enough for any foe they encountered here.

Abby took a centering breath, taking a ready stance with the spear.

"Go," she said. In front of her, courtesy of a remote command from Val, the sealed door opened.

She took one look at the combat environment and instantly understood how to win there.

The hallway smelled of the sea and of carnage. Blood and algae slimed the floor; Abby instinctively prepared to adjust her footing for the decreased traction. Chunks of flesh and chitin were scattered through the hallway, presenting a tripping hazard. Drop to a knee to receive a charge; use her squadmates to take out the rest. If that meant she killed nothing herself, it was no dishonor.

She was a warrior of Veles. Her true weapon was the mind.

Their first opponent was a long segmented creature with many sharp legs. It was distracted, chewing on a carcass.

"Gross," Lilith said, with her typical lack of dissemblance.

"Light it up," said the commander, dropping to a knee.

Markus and Lilith opened fire. Their precision was satisfactory, shots clustering in regions likely to contain critical neural functions. Abby nodded to herself, so slight it would have been imperceptible.

"Clear," she said. "Move up. Check the passenger cabin."

The environmental seals had held in most cases, but in the case of the tac room, the already damaged door had buckled under the water pressure. Abby made a mental note for her after-action report. Inside, they discovered a translucent creature, similar in form to a slug, that was digesting a human arm.

The tactical calculation flashed through her head with a speed that was ingrained on her soul. Her spear snapped up and delivered a single, perfect death blow, just as if she were practicing in the exercise room. It shuddered once and died. Out of ancient habit, she checked for the seven signs of false death, then nodded.

"All clear," she said. "Alright, Val, you're clear."

The environmental seal to the rear section of the ship slid open, revealing a haggard-looking Val. He was worrying her; his previous combat record had been flawless, but with Kives in particular he seemed to have developed something of a rivalry. She wouldn't intervene herself. She'd nudge Markus to talk to him.

His manner, at least, was decorously circumspect. It was something the children had shown little interest in modeling, likely because they behaviorally mirrored each other.

"Eyyy!" said Lilith. "He's alive!"

"Good to see you, buddy," said Markus. "How was the engine compartment?"

Val had been stuck there for three days while they exfiltrated beneath the waves, flights of angels sweeping the sky over their heads.

"The peace and quiet was nice," said Val, subtly adopting a set of the shoulders that communicated false aggression. Markus smiled. Lilith missed it as usual, shifting to more defensive body language. That defensiveness was a problem and could hinder her training as an infiltration specialist. Abby should get Markus to talk with her, too.

Val brushed past the two of them. "I also ran out of food, and I suspect that Kives is somehow to blame. If you'll excuse me, I am going to eat and daydream pleasantly of revenge."

His response was so very *Val* that the team looked at one another and laughed.

Mission complete. A minor victory, but victory all the same.

Val paced urgently through the corridor to shut up his body. Months after reincarnation, it was still resisting his efforts to condition its chemical balance to the fine precision of the last model. Part of that was the erratic conditions of active duty, but part of it was just novelty. He estimated another six months' effort would reduce unwelcome biofeedback to acceptable levels.

He was estimating other things, as well. Part of him was analyzing the most recent interaction with the team, updating his models of their positions relative to one another. There was a faint effect, he thought. Kives was putting stress on the team bonds. Dangerous over time, especially if she was beginning at this stage, but ultimately manageable. Emotional manipulation was an effective tactic, as any godslayer knew, but was easily countered when its effect was measured and isolated. Markus joked about learning "important lessons about friendship," but Eifni had learned lessons about friendship that the gods never would.

The thought made him smile.

The greater part of his thoughts considered the actions Kives had taken. They had made several incorrect assumptions while engaging her on the field, all centering on a central premise: that Kives would commit superior force to the engagement with the strategic objective of crippling their operations. As a premise it was, he decided, not unfounded. Their first encounter with the oracle's forces had been, ostensibly, a life-and-death fight.

He had reached the lounge and began efficiently preparing a meal. When he'd worked in research, he'd known types that used nutrient solutions to escape the demands of food preparation. They did this in the name of science and superior modes of living, but it was mere rationalization. The body is a tool. It requires stimulation, even if the costs of going without are nonobvious. What was done in the name of science was merely an excuse to reduce cognitive load. This, he found offensive. Therefore, Val expertly chopped carrots and yugris and slid them into the air fryer with a slice of ghen meat and a sprinkling of spices.

Val reconsidered his assumptions while he chewed. That Kives had not earnestly sought to destroy them after the first encounter was suspicious. She had not saved all the pilgrims, although a surprising amount of them had escaped both drowning and predation. She had certainly opposed the deicide team—the thought came with a certain amount of gut-searing anger—but she had deliberately avoided the killing blow. Why?

The angel that fought Markus and Lilith could easily have slain them, but instead left them with a few cryptic statements. The key would be the moment Lilith had come out of cloak—it was supposed to negotiate but merely thanked her instead before following up with the accelerated tree growth. What had it seen?

Val blinked. The tree had inspired him to make the pilgrimage plan—the plan that was supposed to provoke Kives to intervene by threatening consequences that Lilith and Erid had ultimately obviated.

Kives had set them up.

The flash of utter, star-fusion rage was predictable, so Val patiently set it aside. It had its place, like any part of the soul, and a duel with an oracle was not one of those places.

Go further, past the humiliation. Kives had set them up, then *failed to destroy them*. She'd blocked every attempt to strike at her but allowed them to repair the ship and allowed them to wound her husband. Was she using them to permanently settle a divine marital squabble?

Go further yet. The first angel had negotiated, and so Markus had tried to negotiate their escape with the later angels. She'd taught them that negotiation was possible and let them go. This wasn't about her objectives: She was *communicating*. Offering a truce, perhaps.

Curious. She should know better than to truce with Veleans.

He frowned. That would imply the actual offer was—

"I'm going to interrupt you for a minute," said Markus, sitting across from Val. Val refocused, coming back from wherever he was. "I want to chat about Lilith."

"Brazen," said Val. "Go on."

"I think," said Markus, and he didn't miss the little shift that communicated Val's play skepticism at the concept, "that you're redirecting your frustration with Kives onto her. It's stressing the relationship, and you know she sees you as a rival."

"Social officer," Val said. Acknowledgment, agreement, conceding a victory. It felt hollow to Markus, but a slight twist of effort covered for the dip in geniality that resulted.

"I understand that Lilith's been acting suboptimally," said Markus. "I know that gets to you. We're working on it with her. You can participate with us, but we need consistent reinforcement schema. She's lonely. Be a friend."

"Emotional regulation is a limited resource, Markus," said Val. "This body is ill-suited for sustained efforts at it, and I need my analytical ability at maximum to handle my duties as technical officer."

"I understand," said Markus. "Just like you understand that the team dynamic is the foundation of our success. There's only us four. If we don't work well together, it won't matter how well you handle your duties."

"I agree," said Val. "In fact, just before you arrived, I had decided to do better on that score."

"So this conversation was pointless, then," said Markus, setting his lips to convey exasperation while softening the message with a shift in posture.

"I wanted to see what you'd say," said Val with a smile. Translation: he wanted to see if he could win the argument. Typical.

"So what's your plan, then?" asked Markus.

"I intend," said Val, "to give her more hugs."

Only Val could say that like it was some diabolical plan. Markus laughed and knocked on the table twice. "You do that, man. I'm gonna check on Lilith."

She'd been a little quieter after the last mission. Her answers, when he'd asked, were evasive—not proper Velean misdirection, just the vagueness that came with not having articulated the truth to yourself. It'd been something about her interaction with Erid.

That really had been a disaster, and it was his fault for not giving more guidance. Lilith just really wanted to be friends with the trade captain, whom she kept calling a pirate despite any evidence of piracy. That sort of loneliness was dangerous on this job. The work was ultimately compassionate—in the final analysis, it was good for people to know the truth—but at the micro level it was sometimes necessary to sever those connections. That was something Lilith would have to learn. It took time; they had been, and would be, patient with her. But in the interim, there'd be moments like this, where Lilith mourned the loss of a connection she shouldn't have made in the first place.

Grief was a wound like any other, and the treatment was conversation and company. So Markus went to talk to her, wondering what Erid was up to now.

"Three thousand *drobol* for the destruction of the pirates known as the Sons of Horcutio, may he turn his gaze away," said the Oathkeeper. He presented the chest to a somewhat shell-shocked Erid, who had remained somewhat shell-shocked since the battle. She accepted it distantly.

"Thank you kindly, Oathkeeper," she said, staggering a bit under the weight as she turned around. "Well, boys, how's this for a profit?"

Her crew, dressed in their finest clothes (read: the ones with the fewest holes), cheered. There were missing faces there. Elera, mugging stupidly with his handsome face. Vektades would have stood solemnly. Woutna, brave, idiot Woutna, would have yelled like a drunkard and slapped his brothers on the back. They were alive, thanks to him. They were trying to smile.

She'd kill that girl, whose name was not Danou. Who'd been so excited for the carnage to start and so sad when it ended. Who'd apologized, like she hadn't known what would happen after she played her silly games with their lives.

Who'd escaped on a *flying* ship like nothing Erid had ever seen. Whom the angels had named Calamity before warning Erid to silence.

"Someone take this and spare an old woman's back," she called, to general laughter. Otoja and Retiades stepped forward and lifted the chest of coin out of her hands and over their heads. The crew cheered, and behind them so did the assembled pilgrims. Pilgrims no more—soldiers, the angels had named them. Called from every walk of life to see Kives's purpose done in Horcutio's sea. They had, to a woman, accepted the call.

Underneath her coat, Erid wore a sword-and-scales pendant. She'd asked why Kives would choose a devotee of Varas to captain her ship.

Are we not all servants of Varas? the angel had answered. Troubling, given the long-standing enmity between the two goddesses.

The ceremony continued. The Oathkeeper officiant rose, presenting a charter. The *Fool's Errand* was put on permanent retainer to guard the sea against the enemies of Varas, whatever god they might serve. It was mightier than even a *sephni*, and under the blessing of Varas, no ship would stand against it. Or so the officiant declared.

Erid thought of the dark-iron skyship, held aloft as though by the power of the gods themselves, and shuddered.

She signed the contract anyway.

Ell smiled wistfully as the caravan left Elsinat. They'd been hired at the last minute for some ceremony and would now need to make good time to make it back to Kreios on schedule. She craned her neck for one last look at the town but didn't see dark hair and sharp, vibrant green eyes. She had to accept it was a fool's hope.

"No sign of him?" Cet giggled to her right.

"Shut up," Ell laughed.

"Must have left an impression," Cet said, elbowing her. Ell elbowed her back. Around her, the other apprentices were laughing and gossiping, excited to be heading home.

"He was great," said Ell. "Funny, clever, attentive . . ." She trailed off, distracted by the sudden intrusion of memories from a dark room, fumbling with clothes, lovely, lovely hands . . .

"Thorough," she added.

Cet snorted at her. "There are other guys. You'll be okay."

"I know, I know," said Ell. "It wasn't anything serious. Just . . . felt like it could have been."

"You'll get over him," said Cet.

Ell nodded. Cet knew her. The feelings would disappear once she was back home, up to her nostrils in case precedent. In all probability their paths would never cross again.

But while the whimsy was still with her, she allowed herself to hope a little bit. And—why not?—Ell made a silent prayer to Kives that, one day, she would reunite them.

CHAPTER NINETEEN

Vitareas

S ay that again, Val, because I don't think I heard you right," I said.

"Lilith, we know your comm is on. This is obvious posturing," said Val.

It was our first strategy meeting since the pirate op. We'd all had a chance to rest and recover, and I'd convinced Markus to watch *Muppet Treasure Island* with me. Now it was back to business, but instead of planning revenge on Kives, Val had a different idea.

"I don't know, maybe Kives just manipulated my comm," I said. "I can't think of another reason I'd hear you'd suggest *giving the fuck up on her.*"

"We cannot win this campaign by charging directly at the nearest threat like a—"

"We have to charge at *something.* Did your fancy thesis tell you that, or did it just—"

"Shut up!" said the commander. "Lilith, you're out of line. I don't want to hear another interruption out of you. Val, explain yourself."

"Kives allowed us to win," said Val. "She did not have to. But she let us injure Horcutio."

"Kulades threw the transmitter overboard. We weren't able to connect the kill to the amplifier," said Markus. "That's a stretch."

"We—her enemy—killed her husband's child when she could have stopped us," said Val. "Whatever the effect, make no mistake—this outcome had her consent."

"Why?" asked the commander. "Your best guess, obviously."

"I believe she is offering us a détente," said Val. "Obviously, our effectiveness increases as the pantheon weakens. Kives may be gambling for time to increase her own strength—perhaps develop her progressive aspect."

"Or more," said the commander. "Do you have a triphase model for her?"

"Not at this time," said Val. "Fertility and legacy are close enough, harmonically speaking, that a hypothetical third aspect would be unbalanced. On another god I'd say there's no possibility, but Kives is the most effective oracle I've ever seen or heard of. We must also consider the barrier as a potential stabilizing factor."

"Understood. Run me a report," said the commander.

"I must refuse on grounds of operational security," said Val. "If we learn that information, there's a risk of it getting back to her. I can do a preliminary investigation and recommend a threat rating, if you'd prefer."

"Mm," said Abby. "Good point. This isn't convincing me we should change targets, however."

"We could attempt some exploratory strikes," said Val, "but I suspect they'll meet with the same outcome. We should let the secularization team handle her."

"I can't tell you how glad I am to hear you say that," said Abby. "You seemed emotionally invested."

"Of course I was," said Val. "It was a challenging problem. The mission objectives come first, however."

The commander nodded, and that was the end of it.

Markus, who had clearly been turning an idea over in his head, finally spoke up. "We didn't kill her husband's child."

Val raised an eyebrow. Abby turned to him. "Expand on that, Markus."

"To be specific," Markus said, leaning forward, "we killed her husband's *bastard*. Maybe that's all she wanted."

"Vengeance isn't part of her portfolio," said Val.

"Infidelity's bad for a relationship, though, right?" I asked. "Doesn't that go against the fertility side of things?"

Val glanced up at the corner of the room as he thought. "I'll have to run the math, but I think it's not impossible."

I beamed.

"Good point, Lilith," said the commander. "Then we need to discriminate between hypotheses. We'll hit another target first. Meris is a priority target, but we're blocked behind Javei before we can hit her. Val, what do you have on the Oathkeepers?"

"Most relevantly, we won't be able to pass the literacy requirements," said Val. "One option is attend one of Lorana's temple-universities."

"What if Kives fucks us up again?" I asked. "For all we know, we're being baited into screwing up our best shot at everyone else. We just need to do one mission to figure out how much of a truce she's giving us, right?"

"Lilith's on a roll," said Markus. "Yeah, I'm with her. Let's hit a simpler target. We can figure things out afterward."

"Dice," ordered the commander. My bag with the RPG stuff was over in the corner, so I got up and brought her some. "To summarize, we're removing Kives and Horcutio from the decision space, we're blocked on Meris and Javei, and we don't anticipate operations against Rucks, Seindel, or Alcebios. That leaves five."

She picked up a d6 and looked at me.

"Do you have any emotional attachment to this die?"

"No, ma'am," I said, avoiding her gaze.

"Was it involved in any noteworthy events you can remember?"

"No, ma'am," I said. "Look, I'm sorry I forgot, it won't happen again."

"Does it possess semiotic implications of any kind beyond those natural to its form and purpose?"

"It will if you keep grilling me on it," I muttered.

The commander paused.

"Good point," she said, putting it back in the pile and selecting an identical one. "Same questions, no grilling."

"No!" I said. "Just roll the damn thing!"

She rolled the damn thing. "Looks like we're going after Kabiades next," she said.

Markus whooped. "I call athlete!"

"Are you serious? They compete naked, dude," I said.

Markus gestured at his body. "Look at me, Lilith. I'm doing them a *favor*."

Sporting events were traditionally held on Renatha, the day of the *thessim* devoted to Kabiades. Splitting the year into sections of twelve days had left the Therians with five days left over, and Kabiades got one of them as his holiest day. It was a little over four months out—eleven *thessim* and a bit, if you wanna count along—and we wanted Markus competing in it to get our best shot at the big guy. Like, sure, you can ruin the Olympics by calling in a bomb threat. But can you imagine if some dude won a gold medal and *then* blew up the stadium? Total chad move.

We needed Markus to be that chad. That meant we had to start making a name for him as soon as possible.

Val and Abby talked a bunch about field equations and harmonic dissonance and stuff, which I didn't really follow, but the bottom line was that they were still working on the kill plan. We'd figure it out when we had more opportunities. Besides, maybe it would turn out that Kives was only willing to hold back if we went after Horcutio, in which case we'd have to abandon the whole thing, anyway.

Every population center of reasonable size had a temple of Kabiades. Or, put another way, Kabiades had no temples. Instead, the Therians built arenas, in which competitions were held and sacrifices were performed in the open air. Women weren't technically *forbidden* from setting foot inside the arena proper, but we'd get really weird looks if we tried. Therian women instead took to the elevated seating around the arena, and did I mention the competitors performed naked? It was kinda creepy.

We'd set the ship down outside a city called Vitareas, a tricky operation that had required pulsing all the guards on the south wall in the dead of night so we could translate a cavern underneath the main road. The commander didn't let me do the pulsing because I'd been "using your cloak as a crutch," which was total bullshit. She got the guards herself. The *Ragnar* was now nestled under the ground right outside the wall, where—if all went according to plan—it'd stay until Val repaired the emitters or whatever was broken. He'd be working on that while Abby, Markus, and I explored the arena.

We got up early the next morning, exiting the ship via another ladder that led right up to the roadside. Once the engines were repaired, we'd make a more sophisticated entrance inside the town itself, but the translator engines' output precision was nowhere near good enough for that at this point. We'd dressed in travelers' rags, each with a large backpack full of "trading goods"—mostly costume changes, with a tablet and a few weapons at the bottom of Abby's pack. The guards waved us through with a cursory explanation of how to find the temple of Varas, where we'd need to pay a fee before using the market. Abby thanked them for the directions but took us down a side alley once we left line of sight. Varas could wait for another day.

We found the arena easily enough: it was one of the most open parts of the town. By the look of things it'd been built outside the city walls, once upon a time, before the city had expanded and another set of walls enclosed it. The temple grounds themselves were open to traffic from any direction, but most people seemed to prefer entering via the freestanding arch down the street to our right. After a brief subvocal discussion, we headed down that way. When in Rome, etc. A brief comm scan didn't reveal anything too fancy about the arch, but the carved marble testicles hanging from its peak suggested some kind of cultural meaning. Maybe it was supposed to be a good luck blessing.

Having found our point of entry, we briefly retreated to a nearby inn to set up a forward base of operations, paid for with coin salvaged from the wreck of the *Friend of Heaven*. A quick change of clothes and Markus and I were back on recon, leaving Abby behind with the bags.

We passed under the balls. Nothing pinged the comms, so it wasn't a fertility blessing or anything. Not that it would have worked if so: Markus wouldn't experience any effect because Eifni had stopped producing reproductively viable bodies millennia ago, and I—you know what? That's private, let's move on.

Next to the arch with the balls, there was this really well-built dude in a long cloth-of-gold skirt and metal shoulder pads. Bronze, I think. Like, not even a wrap or anything, just the shoulder pads and some impressive pecs. He had a cart with fresh-cut vine wreaths, which some of the people trickling in were purchasing for a *drobol* each. It *looked* like it was just guys buying them, but our sample size was pretty slim— we'd only seen, like, ten people go in here, two of them women. I chose not to get one. Gender roles were pretty rigid, and we weren't here to make a scene with an avoidable faux pas. Markus did get one. We moved to a social distance that communicated friendship rather than a romantic relationship, just in case the wreath was another unintentional invitation to a threesome again.

Ahead of us, there were stalls along the path leading up to the arena. Some of these were already taken, all of them by men wearing wreaths. Maybe the wreaths were like stall-rental permits? Delicious smells were wafting from all but one of them: one of the guys on the left was weaving. The rest were cooking variations on Therian breakfast food: vegetables roasted in pepper vinegar, tubers and chicken gravy on flatbread, and one guy was doing what looked like a hibachi routine on a *shield* with a couple of sharp knives and a slab of red meat. Apparently the point was part cuisine and part exhibition—hibachi dude was definitely the most inventive about it, but they were all cooking with some degree of showmanship.

"Oh my god," I told Markus. "This is medieval Tinder."

"Tinder?" he asked.

"It's a dating app," I said. "You, like, make this advertisement about yourself for people to read, and they can say that they're interested in you. And if you say you're interested in them, then the app puts you in contact. Apparently it's mostly just horny guys who swipe right on everyone, but it's a solid idea in theory."

"Ha!" said Markus. "They must be children, right?"

"Nah," I said. "I've heard horror stories about forty-year-old creepers who think age gaps are totally fine."

Markus looked at me questioningly for a moment, then realization crossed his face. "Uh, 'children' was a poor term given the culture gap. I meant more that . . . they don't understand the experiences and goals of other people."

"Assholes," I suggested.

"Assholes," Markus agreed. "So you're saying that the stalls are advertisements. And given which god these grounds are dedicated to, the women show up and take their pick."

"I guess you're on the market," I said.

"I should take this off," said Markus. "These poor guys won't get any attention otherwise."

I laughed and went for the shoulder clap, which, given the height difference, ended up being more of a clap on the shoulder blade instead. "You're the best, Markus."

We made it to the arena. Vitareas was a town of moderate size, so the arena had a decent capacity. Spectators could sit on long wooden benches affixed to stone terraces, one on each side of the course. It reminded me of a high school football field, except more Greco-Roman. Renatha was a few days away, but there were a few men training on the course. Mercifully, everyone was wearing some kind of—I guess you could call it a thong, but that would imply it was supposed to be sexy. More like a keep-everything-out-of-the-way kind of garment. I was cringing with vicarious embarrassment for Markus, but he just seemed to think it was funny.

Most of the athletes were doing laps—probably warm-ups—but there was a pair wrestling over to the right. "I bet Markus could kick those guys' asses," I said. "That might be our way in."

"*It would depend on the local fighting styles,*" said Abby. "*If it's a recreational martial art, Markus might be at a disadvantage. We train for combat, not fitness.*"

"Competitions of this type tend to be indirect combat training," said Markus. "I'm probably competitive. I'll see if I can find out what rules there are."

"Let's keep scoping things out," I said. "Running, wrestling—they've gotta have more things than this."

"Oh, shit," Markus breathed. "Lilith, Abby, look at that."

He pointed. I looked, and therefore so did Abby—she was watching my feed. Down the field, something like a chariot was rolling toward the course. It was different from a chariot in that there was no horse pulling it. Instead, there was just a complicated assemblage of gears connected to realistic-looking horse legs that were too stiff to be anything but artificial imitations. One man stood in the normal place you'd expect someone to be in a chariot; another man was somehow slung inside the mechanical horse, heaving on a lever of some kind.

"Fuck me," I said. "Is that a fucking steampunk horse?"

"*They don't have mass production,*" said Abby. "*We're into the more densely populated area of the region, so we're more likely to run into things like this if they exist, but they're probably one-off creations by master craftsmen.*"

"Craftswomen," I corrected her. "We're a matriarchy here."

"*Lilith, did you switch your comm output to your native language again?*"

"No," I lied.

"*Lilith. The word 'ultho' is gender-neutral.*"

"Fiiiiine," I said. "You got me."

"Val, can you make me a mechanical horse?" asked Markus. "I wanna compete in *that* event."

"*Val's offline,*" Abby said. "*I don't think the repairs will be done in time for you to gain recognition.*"

"Then I guess I'm doing this the old-fashioned way," Markus said. He stretched, grinned, and cracked his back. "Time to get some of that underwear."

"Please tell me you'll wear clothing when you're not competing," I said.

"We're operatives of the Eifni Organization, Lils," said Markus, slapping me on the back. "I'll tell you anything you want to hear."

CHAPTER TWENTY

The Temple of Kabiades

With the arrival of the steampunk horse, everyone else started clearing off this side of the track. That meant the wrestling guys had to interrupt their match, so Markus went over to make some friends. I moved down to the bottom row of benches so I could join the conversation. I mean, I could do that over the comm, but it was just more social this way. Plus, this way I could hear what the other guys were saying.

Markus, charming social butterfly that he was, introduced himself. Within five minutes they were bros. Laughing, being loud, slapping one another on the back—that kind of thing. They were pretty nice about explaining things to the out-of-towner, especially given the general distrust of foreigners around here. Markus cleared off to go find a thong—Darwin help us all—and I asked if I could watch them practice. They looked at me a little weirdly for that, but the one wearing a wreath said yes.

Ah, right, Therians didn't open requests with direct questions. Gotta be more roundabout, Lilith.

I really, really wanted to watch the steampunk chariot go, but there was a camera on my head. I tried to keep from looking around too much so the commander could keep analyzing the wrestling style. From her commentary, Therian wrestling wasn't too aggressive of a martial art. Markus would need to pull a lot of punches. They weren't punching at all, actually. Bit of a useless kind of combat practice, in my opinion—your limbs are good at striking, you should use them in a fight. But we still had to figure out what other events there were.

Chariot racing was certainly one of those events. In heterocausal realities where horses—or another domesticable beast of burden—developed, chariots tended to pop up in early human history. The progression was more or less predictable: horses are awkwardly shaped to pile stuff on top, so at some point you attach a little rolling platform to them, and then later people try standing on it. And once you have that much, the natural human impulse is to put a *second* guy on a *second* chariot and see which one goes faster. Chariot races aren't quite a human universal, but they're awfully fucking common, all things considered. Alas, Markus had never handled a horse before. We'd basically need an in with the steampunk guys, and that wouldn't help us execute the mission. No chariot races for Markus, unfortunately.

As for other events, we were expecting some kind of running competition because that *was* a human universal and probably a bunch of events involving thrown objects of various shapes. General combat-preparation stuff.

"Godsmile, fair lady," boomed a voice off to my left. I turned my head—sorry, commander—and beheld a giant naked dude striding toward me and the wrestling guys. No godsmile for them, I guess.

Dude was even more ripped than Markus. You could grate cheese on those abs. His hair was dark and pulled back into a ponytail, as was appropriate, but the pattern of beads marked him as someone with wealth. He was only wearing the dumb little athletic thong and one of the wreaths that marked him as romantically available, which made it obvious that his pecs were covered in tattoos. I had no idea what they meant.

"Godsmile, stranger," I said. Good, start by emphasizing the distance between us. It was against decorum for him to initiate contact, and he'd held eye contact a little longer than was strictly proper. Back on Earth, this would be the part where I started worrying that his interest in me wasn't safe, and to be honest those reflexes were still active here. Dude was a little too confident about this interaction to be the type that took rejection politely. My adrenaline was starting to pick up. I sent a request ping to the commander: *observe and support*. She pinged back in the affirmative.

"Is this your first time in a temple of the Lancer?" he asked pleasantly. "I have not seen you here before." Again with the eye contact. Well, he *was* wearing the wreath, I *was* a woman in the arena of Kabiades, I guess the assumption was reasonable.

"He's a regular here," said the commander, her tone reassuring. *"Still wearing the wreath—he seems an impressive specimen, he should have an attachment by now. He's likely gaming the system for sex."*

"First time in this one," I said noncommittally, refusing the eye contact to watch the wrestlers again. The wrestler with the wreath perked up a little and fought a little harder against the other guy. Aw, that was adorable.

"If it's a worthy man you seek, your search has ended," said Asshole, turning to the dudes on the ground. "Gaedera! Challenge me when your match has ended."

"Of—of course, Cades," grunted the other wreath guy, who'd nearly put his opponent in a lock. The opponent conceded before it happened, though. "Gather your strength," he told Gaedera.

While Gaedera rested, Cades took the opportunity to tell me about his many victories in this very arena. I guess some chicks found that hot. Or maybe it was just Cades who did. The commander had me keep prompting him, as his braggadocio was inadvertently giving us a comprehensive list of competitive events.

"Why, it was only last year that I took the rostrum as the triumphant victor of the pentathlon," he told me. "It is not the true pentathlon, you understand. They don't swim here. The men in this region are too weak to run the full distance to the coast."

"Quadrathlon," I said, still not making eye contact.

"Ha!" he barked. "You have a keen wit."

"Someone gets it," I muttered. Shame it had to be the pushy, looming, hulky dude, but you know what? A win's a win.

"A mighty quadrathlon it was, too. In the contest of swordplay I, of course, had no equal—"

"Of course." I rolled my eyes.

"—but these fellows gave me some trouble in the distance-running event! They run well here, in Vitareas. Great speed over short distances, if you know what I mean! Had the competition been a true distance run, I would have shone brighter than Androdaima's lantern."

"A true distance run. Like to the coast," I said.

"Exactly!" shouted Cades, pointing a meaty finger in my direction. I glanced over quickly at the movement, then looked away in the face of that absolutely shameless eye contact. Be unaffected, be relaxed, minimize attention. But the commander wanted me to keep him talking, and it was hard to balance those objectives.

"You suffered in the javelin throw," said Gaedera's friend, bemused. "You neglected to mention that."

"It is far too long a story to trouble the lady," Cades fired back, seemingly unperturbed by the attempted deflation of his ego. "If you must know, fair one, my arms are too great, my form too much like Kabiades himself. In battle I wield lances with thick shafts and broad points; the flimsy spears of the pentathlon, no offense to the Striver, were unworthy of my arm."

"He means he messed up the throw." Gaedera laughed.

"So Cades has a lot of experience handling thick lances?" I asked, managing to keep a straight face. Normally, making a pun like that would have immediately caused comm feedback, but the spear-equals-penis joke actually appears in all known cultures, so it's one of the few jokes you can safely make over comm translation.

Cades seemed to sour at that. Apparently he could take it from the other guys but not from a woman. "There is one more event in the pentathlon," he said. "Shall we demonstrate my wrestling prowess?"

Gaedera bravely faced the giant muscleman and held out his arms like he was about to receive a charge from a sumo wrestler. Cades took the same stance, but it made him look more like a hungry bear.

"For the lady's favor," he said. "Let's show her the excellence of the men of Vitareas!"

"In the name of Kabiades!" Gaedera replied.

Not gonna lie: if I were in the market for a relationship, I probably wouldn't go with the big guy who went around picking fights with other dudes to look good in front of women. If anything, I was rooting for the other guy.

"Go for it," I said.

The muscle heads charged each other, grabbing each other's shoulders and trying to throw each other to the ground.

"*Superior footwork,*" noted the commander.

Poor Gaedera was fairly outmatched—forget what the movies tell you, a foot of height difference will settle a fight all by itself. Cades had longer arms, and in a combat style that apparently involved pushing on your opponent's shoulders, that gave him control of the fight. Gaedera practically skidded across the ground as Cades wrenched him in different directions, admirably refusing to go down.

Then Gaedera threw himself backward right as Cades tried to push him. Cades overextended himself right as Gaedera dropped, himself falling. Gaedera rolled out from under wannabe Hercules before he got crushed, which allowed him to sweep out one of Cades's legs and get him in a lock. I couldn't believe it had happened until Cades tapped out.

"Okay, that was seriously impressive," I said. I held out my arms and wiggled my fingers at them. "Whoooo. There you go, my favor."

Cades roared with laughter. "A fine fight!" he said. "Let me up, scoundrel, you've had your glory."

Gaedera helped him stand up, and they clasped arms.

"Time to wash off, I think," said Cades. "My lady, may you grace our lowly course again."

"Have a fun jog to the coast!" I said, feeling a lot better now that he was leaving. I got a laugh out of all three of them that time. Man, I missed my brothers.

Gaedera looked up at me as Cades left. I smiled at him, then at his friend whose name I still hadn't learned just so no one got any ideas.

"So," I said. "Now that he's not here to contradict you, which events *hasn't* Cades won in?"

"Shit, guys, they've got dancing," I said. "Can Markus do that?"

"*I* am *incredibly limber*," said Markus.

"*The time frame is too short*," said the commander. "*Offhand, I'd say the combat events are his best shot at distinction.*"

"These guys are *good*," I said.

"*All the more reason to pick a different event*," said the commander.

Gaedera's friend—Kada, I'd learned—had joined up with a group of four other men to pull off some kind of dance routine. Their movements were surprisingly graceful, especially in contrast to the abrupt, forceful motion I'd just seen demonstrated during the wrestling bouts. Pity Markus wasn't doing this; this was like free front-row seats to Broadway or something. I mean, I've never been to Broadway, so I don't really know if it was Broadway quality. Whatever. They were really good dancers, that's all I'm trying to say.

Markus showed up, grinning like a loon and practically buck naked.

"Fucking exhibitionist," I said.

"Hey," he said. "If you worked this hard on your body, you'd be wearing a thong too right now."

"Fuck no," I said, waving him off. "Go bump muscles with the other jocks. Gaedera's jogging over there, but he said he'd show you the ropes when he got back."

"Awesome," said Markus. "I hear you're courting him."

"Fuck off," I said.

"Lilith, you might need to at least fake romantic behavior before the mission is over. You are our infiltration specialist, after all."

"Can't I just hide?"

"I can and will recommend your augment's deactivation upon return."

"Fiiiine. You gonna force me to do this now?"

"Keep doing what you're doing, Lilith. This is a good recon. You're blending in, you're not drawing attention, you're gathering good information. We'll worry about that later."

"Roger," I said with relief, and not a small amount of pride. I mean, I know I'm awesome, but hearing it from the centuries-old veteran is something else. I laced my hands behind my head and leaned back, watching Markus pick up a padded sword and go through some practice routines. They were second nature to my eye, but the unfamiliarity of it seemed to have drawn some attention. A couple of men were heading over to him. Within a few minutes, a cheer rose up as a contender took up his blade and faced Markus, introducing himself as Jerevai.

Markus picked up social information faster than anyone I'd ever known. He mirrored his opponent's salute perfectly despite never having seen one of these bouts before. Then the match began, Markus stepping closer with his sword held at guard.

"Tell me," said Markus. "In Vitareas, is it foolish to charge, or cowardly to hold back?"

Jerevai laughed. "Do words make for sturdy shields where you come from?"

Markus grinned. "Let's find out." He stopped forward and struck, the other man pivoting to avoid the blow. Markus himself barely dodged the counterstrike, jerking his leg back to avoid what would have been a painful blow to the knee, padded or not. A cheer rose from the men surrounding them.

"Your friend's got a nice butt," said a woman's voice to my right. I looked over at her. Long hair, about as dark as mine, straight and unadorned. She had quick, observant eyes and a playful expression on her face. She wore a dress, dark, with a cloak over it despite the pleasant weather.

I raised an eyebrow, channeling my inner Val.

"I saw you walk in together," said the newcomer.

"I didn't see you," I replied.

"Naturally," she said breezily, fueling my growing annoyance with her. "You must be hurting for refined conversational partners."

"If you want to duel me, the swords are over there," I said. Newcomer laughed the way that attractive people laugh, which is to say, while implicitly gloating about being the center of attention. She sat down, which made me realize belatedly that the last observation was one of those passive-aggressive Therian indirect requests. She still hadn't introduced herself. I studiously returned to watching Markus's spar.

"You made an interesting pair," she said after a few moments' silence. "His clothes implied an honorable trade of some kind—mmm, when he was wearing them." She eyed him up and down, then glanced conspiratorially at me. I scowled. "Your shawl, on the other hand, tells me you break silver for a living, while your skirt claims you don't work at all."

I looked down at my outfit, immediately realizing I'd made a mistake when I caught the satisfied look in her eye. The commander nudged me to start a comm scan, which I did with a feeling of spiteful satisfaction.

"I'm waiting for the speech about Javei," I said, tossing out my best guess.

She smiled knowingly.

"Alright, that's enough smug for today," I said. "You gonna introduce yourself, or are you going to keep being cryptic? You're right, we're new in town, I can't keep up with whatever politics are happening here."

"Lirian," she said, with a look on her face that said we both knew she'd won a victory. "A truth of the eyes, of course."

"Of course," I said, like I had any idea what that meant. "Call me Ajarel."

Her lips quirked dubiously at that, but I stared her down. I was done with whatever this was. At that moment, the comm scan terminated. My eyes widened a little.

"*What'd you get on the scan, Lilith?*" the commander asked.

"*Nothing,*" I subvocalized. Lirian's eyes flicked down at my lips.

"*What do you mean nothing?*" demanded the commander.

"Do you intend to enroll your friend in the Renathion?" asked Lirian as I nonverbally pinged the commander that I needed to concentrate. "From his performance over there, his knowledge of the Forms is lacking—Vitareas might not be martially renowned, but he won't beat the warriors in Bulcephine with whatever tradition he's brought with him. He's built for strength, not grace, so the races are out. You have no dancing companions. Why, Ajarel—surely you don't intend to debut him as a masseur? I can't imagine you have the connections for it if the local politics are giving you such trouble."

"He'll do fine," I said, trying to figure out why political connections were necessary to win at massaging people. Or was he the one being massaged? Were they evaluating his muscles or something?

"Of course he will," Lirian said condescendingly. "You're . . . fond of him."

"Is this some kind of cold-reading bullshit?" I asked, exasperated. "Lady, get the fuck out of my business. We're done here, go bother someone else."

"Ah," she said. "Well, a word of warning before I go. It's why I decided to have this chat with you, actually. Don't enroll your, ah, friend in the Renathion. There are competitions and there are *competitions*, you know?"

"I don't," I said, turning to face her directly. "If you want to threaten us, say it straight."

"Hmm," she said, tapping a finger theatrically on her lips. "No. Best of luck, Ajarel."

She swept off, and the part that was most unfair was that *she* got to have a fluttery cloak, but when *I* wanted a fluttery cloak everyone was like, "You ask for this every time," and "Stop being dramatic, Lilith." Fuckers. And fuck Lirian, too, with her cryptic bullshit. I swore I was going to punch her in the face at some point.

"*Well, now that* that *train wreck is over,*" said the commander, "*tell me about the comm scan.*"

"Fucking cloak-and-dagger bullshit," I said. "And, commander, I fucking got nothing."

"*As in, you didn't pick up a divine signature?*"

"I got jack shit," I said. "Commander, the scan said she wasn't there."

"*Your ear mic picked up her words, so the physical vibrations in the air were real, at least,*" said the commander. "*We already know of something that dodges comm scans like that. I think you just met our first agent of Meris. And it looks like they don't want Markus competing in the festivities.*"

"I can shoot her, right?"

"*Tempting, but there are too many witnesses.*"

"I could *cloak* and shoot her."

"*Lilith.*"

I crossed my arms and pouted. In the distance, Lirian fluttered away, tragically devoid of bullet holes. If she noticed my death glare on her back, she gave no indication.

The moment was interrupted by Markus's voice coming over the comms. "*What's this I'm hearing about competitive massage?*"

CHAPTER TWENTY-ONE

Enrollment

I checked our theology archives," Markus said, pulling up a file of notes on the lounge console. "As far as I can tell, that phrase 'a truth of the eyes' is a reference to Merisite doctrine. It came up in one of Val's interviews during the recon phase. Basically, there are things that are perceived to be true and things that are true no matter what you perceive. Eyes is the first category. The second category is 'truth of the hand.' Val didn't get clarification on that term, so I don't know why it's called that."

"Come on, Val," I said. He didn't respond, as he was still working on the translation engines and had his comm set to emergency communication only. It was the safest time to make fun of him.

"Hand," Abby said slowly. "Semiotically interesting. Grasp, acquisition, manipulation. Maybe violence."

"That doesn't contradict anything in our notes, but keep in mind we don't have that much on the Merisites," said Markus. "The point is, Lirian told you she was a Merisite and that she was using a fake name."

"Kinda defeats the purpose," I said.

"Not if the goal was intimidation," said Abby. "I'd assume a normal person in your position would back down if the cult of Meris threatened them."

"Val's interview wasn't with a Merisite, so it's safe to say this is common knowledge," said Markus. "That is, as long as this guy wasn't a secret Merisite spreading his cult's doctrine around for some reason."

Abby drummed her fingers on her chair, thinking. "Okay," she said. "Let's proceed under the intimidation hypothesis. Lilith, next part."

I thumbed a control on the console, playing my perspective of the conversation as captured by my ocular implants. On-screen, Lirian explained why Markus couldn't possibly succeed in any of the events.

"Oh yeah," I said, pausing again. "Why the fuck does he need political connections to compete in massaging?"

"We'll need to ask around," said Abby. "As for the rest, I agree with her that the combat events might be tricky, at least without causing lasting bodily harm to the opposition. Her assessment for the footraces is less reliable, given Markus's augments. Markus, you're using Einvorak, right? The fifteen percent boost?"

"Yes'm," he said, knocking on his biceps. "I've got a body with twenties in the crypt, but the metabolism requirements are a pain in the ass."

"Even if we did it immediately, reincarnation sickness would keep you out of two competitions at minimum," said the commander. "Three in the worst case. Let's just race with your current body."

"I'll do my best," said Markus. "I'll try wrestling, too."

"We need to understand the significance of the pentathlon in all of this," said Abby. "And Lirian's comments about the massage event also require investigation. Meeting adjourned. I'll figure out what's going on with the massages. You two figure out how to get Markus into the competition in two days."

The senior priest of Kabiades was like the man we'd seen at the entrance to the arena grounds, dressed in a skirt with the same style of shoulder pads. There were markings on it, different from the other man's, whose significance we could not read, but which probably signified his importance. He was an old man—still in surprisingly good shape—and we'd been directed here after some inquiries on the arena grounds.

"And who sponsors you?" he asked Markus.

"Arguel of Salaphi," I said with just a moment of hesitation.

"Ah," said the priest. "A lady of great repute in Salaphi, I'm sure."

She was, I thought silently. An image of Arguel's body flashed before my eyes, throat bleeding where I'd cut her, and I barely suppressed a flinch.

The priest continued. "I regret that she is not known to the arena of Vitareas. Nor, were it so, would her word be as compelling as one of the honored ladies who have volunteered to judge the contest of massages. Theirs are the backs that shall grace his hands."

"Understandable," I said, looking at Markus, who looked untroubled by this turn of events. "If we can get a recommendation by tomorrow, can he still compete?"

"By the toll of evening's bell, I should think," the priest said neutrally. He looked appraisingly at us. "Should you, ah, fail to procure one, the pentathlon is of course open to all. In fact, it's customary for those without your connections to begin there."

"We'll try to have that recommendation by tomorrow, then," I said.

"Either way, if he intends to enroll as a contender for glory, do return at midday tomorrow," said the priest. "It is not necessary if he merely contends to honor the god. But he will need to be assessed to be slated among the contenders for glory, and tomorrow at midday is when the panel convenes."

"He needs to be a contender for glory to compete in the Kabidiad, right? The big event in Bulcephine?" I asked.

The priest cleared his throat disapprovingly. "The 'big event,' as you term it, requires a sight more. Thala must earn laurels in any two events, one of might and one of passion. No less than three pairs are required to pass the Pallastine Gates as a contender. Although, should you be excellent enough to stand the rostrum as the overall victor in an event, a matching set of laurels may be provided should you fail to earn it in the course of competition."

"So basically," I said, looking at Markus—well, technically Thala for the moment—"if he's good enough, he's only got to win one event in either passion or might?"

The priest frowned at me, then fixed Markus with a stern glare. "I hope you aspire to more than that. We are creatures of passion and strength. A man possessing passion alone is weak; whose arm shall maintain his home? A strong man lacking passion is aimless; whose spirit shall warm his family?"

During this whole impromptu sermon, Markus was nodding with the kind of obedient enthusiasm found only in interviewees and people who have been pulled over for speeding.

"Absolutely," said Markus. "I aim to prove my excellence in both areas."

"I am glad of it," said the priest. "You would be hard-pressed to succeed, otherwise. Most *thessim*, Cades puts forth a marvelous effort to establish a one-man colony on our rostrum. Without a sponsor for the private events, you would have to choose between dance or song." His gaze became analytical as he examined Markus's body. "No man's worth is known but through action, of course, but one hopes your singing voice is outstanding."

"You'll think you've heard an angel," Markus promised him.

"We'll get that recommendation," I said. "Put him down for singing either way."

"I shall," said the priest with a venerable smile. "Godsmile. I pray good fortune for you both."

I was halfway through thanking him before it dawned on me which goddess was probably being invoked there, but I didn't flub it too badly, I think. We walked out of the office with a clear objective: we had less than twenty-four hours to get Markus in bed with the local bigwigs.

The commander worked fast. Within a couple of hours, she'd gotten the names of the judges who would ultimately decide whether Markus would receive the laurels he needed to make it to the end of the tournament. There were five families of repute in the city, including House Jeneretes, whose matriarch currently served as the weirdly named mayor of Vitareas. "Visionary" or something. Elsinat had had a governor instead; I wasn't sure what the distinction was. Anyway, it turned out that while the contests of might were pretty straightforward to judge, the contests of passion were all super subjective, so there was enough wiggle room for the judges to support their favorite champions and punish the champions of their rivals.

"*The Kessim are Gamalites, so they're bound to be more traditional,*" the commander briefed us as we rushed back to the disguised entrance to the *Ragnar*'s cavern. "*We'll need to pick up some songs that will appeal to them.*"

"Do we even know what traditional formal wear looks like around here?" I asked, panting.

"*It's the pattern-J shawls,*" said the commander. "*The ones that go wide. I'll scout out a hairstylist.*"

"Please don't tell me we're stealing hair again," said Markus.

"*Who's stealing?*" laughed the commander. "*We've got a chest of* drobol *to burn.*"

I threw a thumbs-up at Markus, who reciprocated with a grin.

"*The Jeneretti own the copper mines. They're economically important to the city, which is probably how they got Kovius appointed as Visionary. Conservative, but not too much to alienate the other factions. We can expect their judge not to rock the boat. The Kessim will probably follow their lead during the Renathion. The Jeneretti will be a poor choice for Markus to approach; all the other brownnosers will have the same idea.*"

"I mean, we're talking about the who's who of Vitareas here," I said. "This ball is gonna be one giant human centipede of brownnosing."

"*I don't know what that is, and I forbid you from elaborating.*"

"Yes'm," I laughed. Markus and I rounded a corner, the city walls growing higher in our view.

"*One of the better-looking choices is the Vitaressi.*"

"City's named for them?" Markus asked.

"*Yes. Old family, hemorrhaging influence. All they've got left is the Treasurer appointment. Outside of that, they're absent from city politics except for a few token gestures—judging at the Renathion being a relevant example. Strong connection to the local temple of Androdaima. I've heard the woman judging is a bit of an experimenter.*"

"Hell yes, let's team up with mad-science lady," I said.

"*She's also a recluse. She won't be at the ball. You'll have to find her younger sister. The sister's name is Roel.*"

"Got it," said Markus. "I'll grab some magnets back at the ship or something to get her attention."

"*Good idea. Another possible option is the Voranetti. They're a highly ambitious family. They're sitting on a lot of local political appointments. The Jeneretti are most likely wary of them, so don't try to befriend both sides.*"

"Hold on, commander, we have to clear the area," said Markus. We'd pulled off into an alley near the gates. After the encounter with Lirian, we'd need to be cautious about being followed.

Markus started a comm scan, but apparently our comms weren't powerful enough to punch through Meris's blessing. Fair enough. The *Ragnar* would have no such problem. I pinged Val.

"Hey, nerd," I said. "Light 'em up!"

"*With pleasure,*" came the reply. "*Give me ten minutes to get this pylon sealed again.*"

"So you're telling us we should have given you more warning," said Markus.

"*That must be one of those lessons on friendship you keep telling me about,*" said Val.

I peeked around the corner and didn't see anyone suspicious. That was expected. I also didn't see anyone who was so unsuspicious it wrapped around to being suspicious again, which was less expected but still good. I absentmindedly reached for my cloak but stopped myself, metaphysical hand still on the metaphysical switch. I mean, I didn't need to, right? I was properly dressed. There wasn't really any reason to doubt my disguise. Just . . . it wasn't, like, perfect. There was a chance I'd mess things up. People might see through me.

I tried pulling the familiar meditative mindset over my thoughts before pulling the switch. I let myself fall into the clarity of it, like I used to do when I was a kid and thought I could learn magic by opening myself to the Force or whatever. Being aware of the world, but also being aware of my soul.

The cloak pulsed gently under my attention. Like a ticking clock, or a heartbeat. It was a part of me, but the beat belonged to the world. It was the wake I left in the ether—and the aura that the ether left on me. One tug and the augment would invert, presenting a perfect null, erasing me from the ether. Just a dream.

Wait, if I was a hole in the ether, wouldn't a blessed Merisite also be one? I scrutinized the heartbeat of the universe, looking, precisely, for nothing.

"Lilith? You good?" said Markus sometime later.

"I got nothing," I proudly announced.

"What?" asked Markus.

"I went looking for nothing, and I didn't find it," I said.

"You're gonna have to run that by me again," he said.

"We're not being watched," I said. "I inferred it from my cloak."

"That's . . . Okay, I think Val's ready to go, we'll talk about it later."

"*Scanning now*," came Val's voice. He'd been less on edge the past couple of days, which made it less stressful to be in the same room as him. "*You're clear. Welcome home. I'm going silent again.*"

"Thanks, Val," I said. Markus focused on the cobblestones in front of him, probably pinging the remote lock, and lifted them up with a grunt. I checked the street to see if anyone was watching. They weren't; the remote lock produced a field that radiated unimportance. *Not* a stealth field—we didn't want to attract Meris's angels with *eau de hidey place*. We descended the ladder to the cavern.

"Commander, we're good to go," said Markus.

"*Excellent work,*" said the commander. "*We've covered Kessim, Jeneretti, Vitaressi, Voranetti . . . Yes, the Henadim. They're more of a neutral family, but apparently they lean more toward the Voranetti. They're our best target, I think.*"

We rounded a corner and beheld the cavern that contained the *Ragnar*. In complete monochrome, of course—we'd strung up lighting that only worked under night vision. Something in me relaxed upon seeing it. We were home.

The commander continued the briefing.

"*Among the families, the Henadim are the most recent to power. Due, I'm told, to the efforts of a demigoddess, reportedly born of Androdaima. She moved the family here, as Vitareas is sacred to Androdaima. They should be more receptive to outsiders like us; the migration was several generations ago, so any performative xenophobia has had a chance to die down.*"

"Performative xenophobia?" I asked as we reached the ship's door.

"They would have faced opposition when they moved here," said Markus. "It's adaptive to turn around and project that opposition onto other individuals. Makes you look more like one of the in-group. Once you've been around in a community for a while, it's less useful."

"So we've got a shot with the xenophobes," I said, squinting as the door opened, bathing us with light.

"They're all xenophobes," said Markus. "It's pretty common. Might be our fault in this case."

I connected the dots in my head. "Kives tells everyone we're coming, they learn to distrust strangers as a rule?"

"*Humans don't need an oracle to distrust strangers,*" said Abby. "*Get dressed, both of you, we've got two hours to get you embedded.*"

Val took a break from engine maintenance to get us dressed in the fanciest clothing we'd been able to manufacture. I wore a full-length dress with the fancy wide shawl that extended a foot from either shoulder. The dress itself was unadorned. The shawl used abstract patterns, a fact that would probably not endear me to the Kessim, but we still didn't know enough about the shawl patterns to pass at a high-society ball.

Markus, on the other hand, went with a wrap and an abstract shawl of his own. Men's shawls got thinner the fancier they got, and in this case we also clasped a belt around his torso to define his muscles a bit more. It was a whole thing. His skirt was long enough to make him respectable without claiming parity with some of the people we'd be talking to. Male arrogance was expected but not respected in this culture.

We whipped up something for my hair that was high-class but clearly temporary. I had a hair appointment in an hour. About our persons, we each secreted a disruptor pistol, a pulser, and a hand amplifier.

That just left the ladder out of the cavern, and let me just say that I hope everyone who designed this outfit gets trapped in a ladder factory where the only exit is on the ceiling. So I can set it on fire.

Rather than look out of place in the neighborhood, we each donned a traveling cloak. Under my shawl, I thumbed my hand amplifier to the same frequency as the cavern exit—nonthreatening, unimportant. Markus did the same. We'd have to scrub it off as we entered the fancier part of town, but for now it would let us avoid attracting attention.

We'd yet to run into any stupid coincidences, so Kives was either biding her time or honoring the truce. I'd been suspicious that my run-in with Cades was a coincidence, but according to the gossip he spent all his time at the arena and hit on anything that moved and had boobs. Meris, on the other hand, was definitely taking an interest in us, and the fact that she'd warned us away from the hit probably meant that Kives had forewarned her. That made our truce with Kives look a little more like a cold war, which, honestly, it was.

We still weren't sure what to expect from Meris. She definitely had angels—it's kind of a given for ascendant gods, they start to take over anything that bumps into them—but stories about her messengers never had any account of supernatural abilities. She didn't have temples, at least publicly known, and her cult was secretive to the point that all their official representatives blatantly used fake names and showed up in disguises for official functions. But there *were* tales of people acting on her behalf, and they kinda read to me like all those Old Testament stories about the judges. God(dess) maneuvers the right person into the right situation, person stabs the tyrant or over- hears the plan or something, day is saved. Bit of a networker, our Meris.

At least she wasn't exploiting causality like *some* goddesses I could name.

We arrived at the place of a stylist named Oloren, a woman barely into her thirties with razor-sharp eyes, endless enthusiasm, and absolutely no patience. Her hair was streaked through with almost fluorescent-blue dye, which gave me pause for a moment because they should *not* have that level of materials science here with a preindustrial economy.

"You're not on the schedule," said Oloren, applying wax to a swirl of hair while combing it with the other hand. The woman in the seat had her eyes closed and was in a fancy-enough dress that I suspected we'd be seeing her again tonight.

"We're desperate, honored Oloren," I said. "We've nothing left but prayer now. My ward and I rode ahead in hopes of making it to the ball on time. We asked for the best stylist in Vitareas—"

"Hsst!" A finger waved at my face. Oloren dabbed a bit more wax onto the curve, holding it *just* so. The woman appeared to have a horn now. Satisfied, Oloren nodded to herself, moving to the other side. I stood there uncertainly.

"Please continue," said Oloren. "Something about the best stylist in Vitareas?"

"I'm willing to pay," I said.

"And Geremine of House Feres has already done so. If she cancels, it's yours."

"How should I know if she cancels?" I asked, calling up the commander's feed.

The charioteer lay motionless, the horses unchained. The commander looked around, checking the unconscious attendants for signs of movement, then met the terrified gaze of Geremine Ferades. She drew her knife as suddenly and as violently as she could manage, eliciting a flinch from the prone noblewoman.

She leaned in.

"I apologize for your rudeness," said the commander, "but you're staying home tonight." From her position on the ground, Geremine nodded frantically.

"I'm sure your prayers have been heard," said Oloren.

"Lady Ajarel, was it?" said the woman in the chair, not opening her eyes. "You may be in luck. Oloren is persnickety."

"And you're a bag of slugs," said Oloren fondly.

"One-wheeled chariot."

"Cheese sculpture."

"Cheese sculpture?" I asked.

"It would melt in the sunlight and look terrible," the stylist said defensively.

"I look stunning in the sunlight, thank you very much," said the woman. "Lady Obol Jeneretes, by the way. Godsmile on you."

"Godsmile," I said deferentially.

"What this corkscrew of a hairstylist should have told you is that if the lovely Geremine does not deign to grace us with her presence on time, her appointment is forfeit. Oloren will not brook disrespect."

"Except from you, apparently," I couldn't help saying.

Lady Obol merely smiled.

"She's a misshapen loaf, but she arrives on time," Oloren conceded.

"Unlike the Lady Geremine, who is usually so conscientious about arriving early, which surely has nothing to do with her habit of eavesdropping by the door," said Lady Obol. "You may be in luck, Lady Ajarel."

"My luck is usually pretty good," I said, pretending like any of this was news to me.

Halfway across the city, my luck finished exfiltrating from the Ferades estate and headed for the mission site.

I spent the next twenty minutes making friends with Lady Obol and her bizarre stylist. Most of it was my natural charm, of course, but I also tuned my hand amplifier to look more friendly, with a hint of mentorable. Lady Obol hung around after Geremine tragically missed her appointment, giving me all the gossip on the other families and sniping back and forth with Oloren.

By the time my hair was done, I had an invitation to accompany her to the ball. I guess my luck *was* pretty good. Unless it wasn't luck, in which case . . .

"*Commander,*" I subvocalized. "*We* might *have a problem.*"

CHAPTER TWENTY-TWO

Starlight Ball

We checked. No entanglements, no divine signatures, no cloaked figures jumping out of alleyways with knives. Markus and I remained unaccosted as we traveled alongside Lady Obol's palanquin, chattering amiably. Specifically, *she* was chatting amiably. Lady Obol was a fountain of gossip, it turned out, and Val was taking copious notes back on the ship. There was nothing left to do but listen, politely continue the conversation, and keep one eye out for sudden, oblique disaster.

In addition to ruining the lady Geremine's schedule for the evening, the commander's objectives had also included figuring out how the invitations worked. Surely we couldn't just walk in there, right? Right?

Actually, it turned out that we could. There was the small matter of the cover fee—and by "small" I mean "most of our remaining money," making it critical to get some kind of patron tonight—but otherwise it was a matter of showing up and acting like you belonged. All of us were formally trained in exactly that, so I wasn't too worried. The part I *was* worried about was the Right of Challenge, which was a custom whereby those "of grace" could challenge others on grounds of having "insufficient grace" and get them booted out of the ball. I was so going to pull that on Lirian if she showed her face.

"*You are not engaging Lirian,*" said the commander. "*Focus on getting Markus a patron.*"

"*Aye, aye, captain,*" I subvocalized in between empty polite responses to Lady Obol's monologue on the evils of the Voranetti. Apparently the Voranetti'd just finagled some kind of contract with a merchant that usually worked for the Jeneretti because the normal deal had fallen through, and now it was confusion and hurt feelings on all sides, a state of affairs that, in Lady Obol's opinion, was entirely the fault of the other family.

"You'd think the merchant would have more loyalty," Markus said.

"Loyalty does not pass the city gates, boy," said Lady Obol, though in appearance Markus was the same age as her. "They're all Phrecians out west now, not a drop of the old blood left. Clans, not families. Their duties to their elders come first."

Markus made an enlightened noise.

"And that's another thing," she said. "Give me an inheritance any day. I can trace my descent through my grandmother's grandmother to Seindel himself. We're a family of the land. We know it, the city knows it, even our enemies know it. The thrice-damned Voranetti know it, that's for certain. You know where you stand with an inheritance. But a clan? Where's their foundation?"

"I've never thought of it that way," I said, which was technically true because I'd never thought about it in any way.

"Anyone can join a clan!" said Lady Obol, throwing her hands in the air. "There's no *identity* to it, just a bunch of people out to make money!"

Before we could enjoy more of what was beginning to sound like a suspiciously racist account of Phrecian sociology, we arrived at the estate. In Lady Obol's case, "returned to the estate" might be a more appropriate phrase, as the event was taking place in one of the Jeneretti holdings. The structure was enormous compared to some of the smaller inns and workshops we'd had occasion to frequent during our cultural forays thus far, with walls rising two or three stories. We had to skirt around the side—no servants' entrance for us, thank you—eventually coming to an opening that was too wide to be intended for defense. Inside, we were treated to a fantastic display of colored fire.

The central courtyard of the compound had been covered, great woven mats thrown over temporary scaffolding to block the light of the moon and stars. From that scaffolding hung fake stars—what must have been *thousands* of brightly colored lanterns burning in a hundred hues. Below the artificial starlight, we saw flurries of movement in darkness, interwoven with colored lights from masks worn by the attendees. The lights somehow managed to raise the ambient light level just enough not to bump into anyone, but not enough to make out any details. And the masks, it seemed, were designed so that the light shining from them did not reflect on the wearer's face.

It took me back to those photos NASA had taken of other galaxies, the bright lights thrown about in chaotic patterns. Something grand, something mysterious. And unlike NASA's photos, these lights were swirling around in real time, and they were really that beautiful, not just X-ray spectrographs photoshopped into the visible spectrum and breaking my little college-freshman heart.

It was too breathtaking for the memory to really distract me. I stood transfixed for I don't know how long.

"Isn't it magnificent?" said Lady Obol. "Only the Vitaressi have a greater collection of ghostlights. The goddess has favored us greatly, and in return we guide her holy city."

She was, I could tell from the comm translation, referring to Androdaima.

"How are they made?" I asked, pulling myself together.

"Spoken like a child of traders!" Lady Obol laughed, not unfondly. "The secrets of the process are well guarded by her temple, but the color at least is derived from brightflowers. Every hue you see before you was blended with great care by the hand of our Mistress of Colors, or one of her predecessors."

I'd heard of brightflowers before but didn't remember what they were. They had the feel of a common knowledge thingy, so instead of drawing suspicion to myself, I made a mental note to look them up later. The comms being what they were, Val saw the mental note and grabbed the answer out of our recon database.

"*Brightflowers are unusually pigmented flowers associated with Androdaima,*" he said. "*The pigments are easily released with a simple mortar and pestle, making them important to many industries. They're likely the reason for the advanced textile colors we've encountered so far."*

"A daughter of this house now returns in the company of friends," Lady Obol said formally to the doorkeeper, who saluted and stepped aside. Lady Obol passed quickly, heading to a table that had been set out with an array of masks, each burning with ghostlight. Markus and I followed.

"Ah, my lady," said the doorkeeper to me, her eyes flicking uncertainly to Lady Obol.

"Forgive me, I forgot myself in the face of all this spectacle," I said quickly.

"Repeat after me," said the commander, who was probably nearby.

"A friend of this house seeks the threshold," I said as she prompted me.

"The right of hospitality is ours," replied the doorkeeper.

"We shall repay what is given," I said. "Thala?"

Markus stepped forward, bowing, and presented the doorkeeper with a bag filled with my hard-earned pirate treasure.

"Enter, friend," said the doorkeeper, bowing us in.

We joined Lady Obol, who fortunately had only looked bemused at the faux pas of forgetting the hospitality ritual.

"Thala!" she said, waving him over. "Blue for you, I think. As if those eyes are shining through! One gets the sense of an ocean from you."

"Your kindness is great," said Markus, accepting the mask. It was thin, dark cloth, with a glass cylinder on either side in the same hue of ghostfire. Two loops on the ends were apparently meant for the ears, which would have caused issues with my positively baroque hairstyle, except Oloren had apparently seen this coming and left space around my ears. Markus put it on, covering everything above his nostrils with shimmering black.

"No significant visibility impairment from the mask," he reported subvocally. *"Peripheral vision fine. Night vision unaffected."*

"You look gorgeous," said Lady Obol, merrily pinching his biceps. "And Lady Ajarel, it seems this is your first Starlight Ball."

I knew how to look for the little etheric flicker in the comm translation now—that was one of those indirect requests, but the usage here was weird. Normally you'd solicit a request for help by making an observation about the other person's needs, but that was for things that benefited you.

"It is," I conceded, stalling for time. What did she gain by helping me pick a color? Shit, were the colors meaningful? Comm said no, other than the faint trace of Androdaima's divine signature. Huh, weird, that wasn't an active blessing. Worry about that later.

"Once you've chosen a color that suits you, I can announce us to the company and we can begin our evening," she said with a polite smile. I couldn't read her face—doubly so, under dark cloth and deep maroon—but there was still that subtle etheric note.

It hit me like Markus. If she announced us together, I'd be associated with her family, and her enemies wouldn't be able to snatch me up as an independent. We were heading into a fancy, decorated war zone.

"I'd be honored if you would," I said.

I scanned the table full of flickering starlight, looking to see what stood out. I had my eye on this really cool fire-yellow one, but Lady Ajarel was supposed to be more subdued. Green? It wouldn't go with my dress, not that anyone could really tell under these lighting conditions. Best not to risk it—these were people of grace, they'd be highly class-conscious. They *would* find out somehow. Best not to pick anything too close to Lady Obol's color, but I also couldn't go for anything that clashed with her, or it'd be making a different statement.

Aha! I snatched up a mask with a nice burnt umber tone to it. Subdued firelight, the aura at the center of the candle. Dark like hers, but different in tone. Opposed to Markus's, too, which in retrospect may have been a deliberate test when she picked out that blue color.

Lady Obol literally radiated approval as I picked up the mask and put it on. Definitely a test, then, and it seemed I'd passed. She'd been nothing but talkative and genial in my short acquaintance with her, so this was a valuable reminder that beneath all of that was the kind of social cunning that elevated a family to the top of the city. She wouldn't be the only one.

"I arrive: Lady Obol Jeneretes," proclaimed the woman I'd almost written off as someone's gossipy aunt. "With me, Lady Ajarel of Salaphi and trusted companion."

I would say something like, "All of these people were sharks," but they didn't have those here. So all of these people were, like, some kind of really sneaky soulless predator. Like a mongoose or something.

I'd won Lady Obol's approval by listening to her chatter away and passing a few subtle evaluative tests, but the next problem was actually getting her to sponsor Markus. Which should have been easy, given that she definitely liked me—I have no idea how I survived without a comm to handle social ambiguity—but she just wouldn't. Stop. Talking.

"Now, the Seborae have only been here a generation—practically foreigners!— but their scion Iani is quite the up-and-comer! I considered bargaining my *eldest/male/ unwed/status/child* to her, but it wouldn't do, no, not at all."

That was the fifth time she'd used that word—all of them in this context, poor kid—and I wasn't quick enough to catch the literal word the last four times. This time I was ready. *Primora*, I thought at my comm. I felt a satisfying sense of something *giving*, like the noetic equivalent of snapping some kind of one-way plug into an IKEA desk.

"*That's an opening*," Abby said, patiently coaching me, as she had for the last hour. "*Jump in now*."

"I wonder if she'd take a look at this lunk," I said, gracefully shifting to indicate Markus at my side. Well, shifting, anyway. But my hand amplifier was set to make me seem graceful, so either way it worked out.

"*Pride, Lilith*," the commander reminded me. Right, less of a culture of humility around here.

"He may not have much of a name in Vitareas," I continued without pausing, "but when he competes for glory in the Renathion, that will change."

"Ah, wonderful!" said Lady Obol, favoring me with an encouraging smile. "He reminds me of my third husband—he's a feisty one, not that you'd know it to look at him. Why, back in the day—"

And just like that, I'd lost control of the conversation again. Did she ever pause for breath?

"*You can't keep letting her get in like that,*" said the commander. "*What are they teaching you kids in Social these days?*"

"*I, uh, didn't actually take Social,*" I subvocalized while nodding along politely. "*I took Theory of Social Roles instead, it counted toward the requirement.*"

"*Max is getting an earful for this when we get back,*" said Abby. "*They filled in the cracks with fancy etherware and thought that made you an infiltrator. Do they all have flash damage? Even Torres signed off on your credentials, and I know for a fact he's been out in the field!*"

"*This is people infiltration, it's Markus stuff,*" I complained.

"*I'm not blaming you, Lilith,*" she said. "*This is my fault, I should have trained you better.*"

"*You're doing good,*" said Markus. "*Stay positive. You're facing a difficult challenge, just keep at it.*"

I didn't respond. I was too busy double-checking that my composure didn't show my frustration, as Lady Obol had given me a bit of a searching glance. The hand amplifier should mask anything I didn't, but this was exactly the sort of situation where someone might notice the dissonance and get suspicious. I didn't pick up any suspicion from her, so I didn't know what that was. I got another opening when she paused for just a bit longer than usual.

"Oh, yes, I can't imagine how hard it is to make connections with visitors," I said, perhaps a bit too close to rudeness but afraid of missing the opportunity. "It seems like you really need to snatch up everyone with talent before someone else does."

"*Good,*" said Markus. "*A bit direct, but that's acceptable given the context.*"

"Oh, child, you'll do well here," said Lady Obol. "I am a hunter, in my way. Flitting from here to there—I dare say my prey don't even realize they've been snatched up!"

"You honor us," I said with a smile, putting the slightest emphasis on "us." She *knew* Markus needed a sponsor, what was she playing at? The comm only told me that she genuinely approved of me, almost in the sense of a teacher or mentor.

And then we were talking about chariot races or some shit. My smile became a little forced as I resisted the urge to punch something.

"*The fuck am I doing wrong?*" I asked. "*Fuck, does she ever breathe?*"

A pause on the other end.

"*Yes,*" said the commander, and I could feel her frown through the word. "*You're not noticing it because she does it in the middle of a thought.*"

"*It's fucking strategic?*" I asked. I wanted to scream, but that would torpedo me worse than whatever she was doing. "*The comm says she likes me!*"

"*Send me a sample,*" said the commander. Markus tapped his thigh to let me know he was on it. The commander rendered her conclusions quickly. "*She thinks she's doing you a favor. Teaching you something.*"

"*I don't need teaching.*" I managed not to let my pout show on my face.

"*She has to know what you want by now,*" said the commander. "*She's using your inability to initiate to prevent you from asking for a sponsor.*"

"*How is that doing me a favor?!*"

A pause. Apparently Lady Obol was also considering bargaining her *primora* off to the youngest Vitares daughter, but of course it wouldn't be proper with the political situation as it stood. I nodded attentively at the proper moments, unable to get actual words in.

"*She can't or won't sponsor Markus,*" the commander finally said. "*But she wants you to think there's a possibility, so she's not turning you down.*"

"*She doesn't want me to compete at all, I think,*" Markus said. "*We should have considered this. Perhaps there's a competitor they favor heavily.*"

"*This op was last-minute,*" said the commander. "*We didn't have time to get the list of sponsored athletes.*"

Val's voice reached us from the edge of the city. "*Should I retrieve it from the temple records?*"

"*Too risky,*" said the commander. "*Disengage, you two. There's still time to find a sponsor.*"

I'd gotten angry enough that it was almost a physical thing, a lump beneath my sternum and the sensation of my tongue against the roof of my mouth. When I smiled it felt sharp.

"If you'll excuse us, Lady Obol," I said politely. "I should eat, and as much as we've enjoyed your company, it would be good to meet others of your city."

"By all means," she smiled. "Refreshments are at the east wall; I'll show you there."

Shit, I thought. "I wouldn't like to waste your time," I said.

"It's no trouble," she said. "I am your host, after all."

"*You're tired,*" offered the commander.

"It's not just that," I said. "We have been traveling all day and need to sit down. We wouldn't wish to keep you from your other guests."

"If you insist," said Lady Obol with an expression of generosity. "Rest well, my friends, and I'll be sure to check up on you soon."

As we escaped from her overbearing social clutches, I realized the old bitch was actually proud of me. Maybe she thought we'd still be friends afterward, but I was gut punching her next chance I got.

"Come on," I told Markus. "Let's get you a sponsor before something else goes wrong."

We almost made it to the banquet table.

"I arrive!" bellowed a familiar, hateful voice from the direction of the entrance. "Lady Lirian of Silence!"

I buried my face in my hands.

CHAPTER TWENTY-THREE

Networking Sucks

We'd been expecting Lirian to hit the ball tonight, so this wasn't, like, a Kives-level inconvenience. It was pretty damned inconvenient, though, because I figured she was going to head directly for me and try to get me thrown out of the ball. We didn't have the funds—yet, anyway—to attend another one, and Markus wasn't getting anywhere without a sponsor.

"I think we split up," I said to Markus. "I'm seeing some unaccompanied males around here, and we gotta make up for all the time we lost to Granny Gab Gums over there."

"That should work," said Markus. "Commander, can you step in to back up Lilith?"

"*I'm going to run interference on Lirian,*" said the commander. "*Lilith, just do your best. Val, support.*"

"*Understood,*" said Val. "*Lilith, I'm focusing your feed.*"

"Thanks," I said. That was more me than Lady Ajarel, but breaking character for a moment helped me center myself. I pursed my lips as I slipped between groups of chatting people. "Any advice for me?"

"*Have confidence,*" he said. "*I imagine that you're feeling unarmed right now.*"

"A bit," I conceded. "I guess I'll adjust my posture or something."

"*It's in the mindset,*" said Val. "*Appropriate levels of confidence communicate that you understand the situation and judge yourself capable of succeeding. Excessive confidence communicates that you don't understand the situation.*"

I reached the banquet table and stared blankly at the food there. It was too fucking dark to make anything out. There were bowls all the way down the table filled with—beverages? Soup? I sighed. I'd wanted to eat something, but with my luck it'd probably turn out that I was drinking a dipping sauce or something.

"The problem is I don't," I said. "Understand, I mean."

"*You are at war, Lilith,*" he said. "*What does it matter if your spear is dull? Aim for the throat.*"

"Aim for the throat," I said, nodding to myself. "Alright, I can do that. Where's my target?"

"I don't know what they look like, either," said Val. *"Just circulate. You'll recognize a name sooner or later. View it as sparring practice."*

"Really leaning on the stabby metaphors today," I said. "Alright, let's try the gals over there."

The gals in question gave me a warm welcome—so warm, in fact, that I almost couldn't believe the intense contempt coming off all but one of them. The lone holdout was from the House Kess, I learned during introductions, but there was no way I was making headway in this group. I was pretty sure I flubbed something about my own introduction based on their reactions, but a high-class event like this was always going to be socialization hard mode. There were still fine details about Therian social interaction we hadn't nailed down. I had Val make a note on the Kess girl, then cut my losses and excused myself.

"Fuck," I subvocalized as I walked away. Wasn't about risk a challenge over uncouth language.

"It's no great loss," said Val. *"She was too young to have enough pull with the Kessim to sponsor Markus."*

"It never hurts to have connections," I said.

"The mission takes priority," said Val.

"Yeah, yeah," I said. "Markus, how's it going?"

"I'm having a blast!" he said. *"These people are so great at polite rejections! I'm taking notes for later."*

"The mission takes priority, Markus," I lectured him in my nerdiest voice.

"Ah, so you did hear me," said Val. *"One is never quite sure with you."*

"Cut the *Mean Girls* crap, I'm getting enough of that from these assholes," I said.

"As you wish," he replied. Judging by the lack of further comments, Val was either shockingly well-informed about Earth culture or too proud to ask what *Mean Girls* was. I knew where I'd put my money.

I decided to nonchalantly swing by the banquet table again and go for a one-on-one chat with some other person taking a breather. I scanned a couple of likely targets, then picked one lady in a complicated-looking dress—purely because I saw her dipping bread in one of the bowls and decided I owed her a favor.

"You've got great taste. I love this stuff," I said by way of introduction. She turned slowly to me, giving me the impression of a raised eyebrow despite the mask covering the top half of her face. "Godsmile. Lady Ajarel of Salaphi."

"Godsmile," replied the lady, eyeing the bread I'd just dunked in the bowl. Her voice was raspy, like old paper. "I see you've managed to shake off the honorable Lady Obol."

Shit, she remembered me from my entrance. Think like Val, say something snide!

"Apparently I'm great company!" I said, wincing on the inside. Not snide enough. The other woman chuckled politely.

"She has an affinity for lost songbirds," she said simply.

Her dress was a deep navy blue, fading to black under the thousand ghostlights that gave us bare minimum of vision. It gave her a slightly inhuman appearance, aided in part by the fact that she was freakishly tall and rather thin. Her cheekbones and jaw—illuminated by flickering pale-blue ghostfire—were sharp, giving her a somewhat sinister appearance. On my comm, I got the impression of distant interest, like a scientist poking at a bug to see what it'll do.

She leaned in slightly, somehow indicating the bread in my hand without gesturing to it.

"You love *dvoli*," she said. "I would hate to keep you from it."

I sensed a trap, but shoving that bread in my face was the only way to avoid losing face. Like, social face. Besides, I'd just seen her eat some bread with that sauce, so it was probably fine. Aim for the throat. Or the mouth, in this case.

"To your health," I said. I took a bite and immediately coughed as the burning hot sauce ignited my mucus membranes and about two-thirds of my sinuses. Oh god I was going to die. Oh fuck me that hurt.

"Love this stuff," I coughed, tears welling up in my eyes. "Food should fight back."

"Indeed," said the other lady, straightening as if satisfied with her examination. "Please convey to Lady Obol my compliments on her family's ball and inform her that she is not as subtle as she thinks."

"Wait, what?" I said, almost distracted from the bonfire that my oral cavity had become. "Hold on, can I get your name?"

Something in her demeanor turned cold at that. "Must we continue this farce? Lady Eloi Voranetes. Herself. There, child—we are introduced. You may report the failure of your mission."

I knew it was a dismissal, but fuck it, I'd immolated my face, and I wasn't going to let that be for nothing.

"Lady Eloi!" I said, then coughed again. Her face turned back to me, conveying rapidly thinning patience. "I'm not here for Lady Obol's sake. My friend needs a sponsor to compete for glory in the Renathion. Lady Obol stonewalled us so we wouldn't get a chance to ask anyone. I know I'm out of my depth here, but this is our only chance."

"*Indirect requests,*" Val said sharply in my ear, but it was too late.

"You are a fool, Lady Ajarel," said the tall, thin specter in front of me. "Begone."

I clenched the fist that didn't have bread in it to restrain myself from throwing the one that did. Lady Eloi peered through her ghostfire-illuminated mask with cold satisfaction, waiting for me to leave. I was aware enough to recognize this as a power move, but knowing that just made it worse. I turned around and forced myself to march forward, barely watching where I was going. At some point I snagged a cold drink and started trying to wash the spiciness out of my mouth.

"Commander, I fucked up," I said. "Do you know if Eloi Voranetes is important? Because she hates me now."

"*I don't know that name,*" said the commander.

"*I do,*" said Markus. "*She's sash bearer to Sael Voranetes, the family head. Most people give her a wide berth.*"

"I can see why," I said. "Fuck her."

"*She has too much clout to engage directly,*" said the commander. "*The Voranetti should be considered off-limits tonight. Focus on the other families.*"

"I'm sorry," I said.

"*The preparation for this mission was incomplete by necessity,*" said the commander. "*Mistakes are to be expected. We will adapt. Just keep doing your best.*"

"*I was wondering why Obol let you go so easily,*" said Val. "*For Eloi to react like that, Obol might have an established pattern of using independents to accomplish her objectives.*"

I resisted the urge to wave my hands in exasperation—Lady Ajarel was more refined than that. "She won't leave me alone even when she leaves me alone!"

"*We're running out of time,*" said the commander. "*The ball ends in two or three hours. I'm guessing it'll take about an hour once you find a good connection.*"

I pulled myself up with a grimace, setting my drink aside. My mouth still hurt, but it was down to more of a dull twinge after the absolute conflagration that had been my initial taste of the *dvoli*. Damn Eloi. In retrospect, she'd only put a little bit of the sauce on her bread. That was probably what outed me. The worst part was she hadn't even been that wrong about why I was there. She just didn't know who I was working for.

I was still gonna gut punch her, though. She could wait in line after Lady Obol and the jerks from earlier.

Go for the throat. I threw myself at another group of women, all my seniors. They tolerated me, but I was otherwise ignored. Frustration quickened my heartbeat, but I *would not* let it reach my posture and expressions. Clamp that shit down. I had a job to do. But not here, apparently. I made my excuses and stepped away.

No luck, either, on my next two conversations. I made a new friend in the next one, then I learned she was Voranetti and had to make the minimum polite niceties before bailing. Sorry, Alceoi, maybe next time.

I had to spend the next fifteen minutes avoiding Lirian—she was wearing the awesome yellow ghostflame mask, which I could only assume was because she somehow knew *I* wanted it—who had wandered over to this area and was *definitely* looking for me. After two close calls and an incident involving a near collision with a servant carrying a food platter, the commander managed to block her path and draw her into a conversation. I tuned in and realized with vindictive amusement that she was pulling a Lady Obol on our wannabe spy. I was overjoyed to learn that Lirian wasn't any better at dealing with it than I was.

Free once more and down more time than I would have liked, I got back to it. On a whim, I found a group of men who were all hanging out on the edge of the courtyard. I cringed a bit as I watched their postures shift—I was making them uncomfortable by intruding on their broment. Don't let it matter, Lilith. Go for the throat.

"Hey, lads," I said. "Beautiful night, am I right? Lady Ajarel."

"How can we help you, ma'am?" asked one of them. He was a well-built dude, with a wide shawl decorated in more of a traditional style. Ruffly brown hair poked out over his mask, illuminated by neon-orange fire.

"*Just build rapport,*" said Val.

"I'm just trying to take a breather," I said. "This is all pretty overwhelming for an out-of-towner. Who are you guys?"

"Sela," said the spokesdude, touching his chest gently with one hand. "Of the grace of the Kessim, by descent. These are Joissa, of the grace of the Kessim, by bond; Kalim, of the grace of the Jeneretti, by bond; and Hortasia and Gurana, of the grace of the gods."

"*That means they don't count in demigod genealogies,*" Val interpreted for me. "*Not relevant here.*"

"Pleased to meet you," I said, giving them enough of a smile to communicate friendliness but not so much that it broke decorum, given our ambiguous relative social status. "It's my first Starlight Ball, so I'm a bit out of my depth here. It's nice to meet some friendly faces."

"Where are you from?" asked the other Kessim with polite interest. Joissa, that was it.

"Salaphi," I said. "Things are picking up over there with the whole tree situation, but the political maneuvering isn't as complicated."

"Don't go to Bulcephine, then," laughed Kalim. "At least in Vitareas you know who all the players are."

A couple of the other men shot alert looks at him and then me, but when I didn't seem offended they relaxed a bit. Sela, I noticed, was one of them. I gave them a rueful grin.

"I might have to," I said, tilting my head to the side—the gesture communicated more or less what a shrug would have, back home. "I'm here to get my friend a sponsor for the Renathion."

"For your sake, I hope he has an excellent singing voice," said Kalim. "Only a child of the gods could best Cades in the pentathlon. People used to think he was one himself."

"I saw him lose a spar this morning," I said. "It can't be that hard."

"Well, naturally," one of them—Gurana?—spoke up. "He's . . ." Gurana looked around, then continued. "Well, it's different in the tournament, you see."

"Hortasia," Sela said warningly. Okay, fine, I was wrong. I held my hands up placatingly.

"Hey, don't worry about whatever that was. I've got too much going on to dig into Cades's secrets."

That was a lie. I was totally going to dig into his secrets. But they didn't need to know that.

"It's nothing that would affect you," said Sela amiably. "Just a matter best kept in confidence to allow him to focus on reaching the Kabidiad."

"A man's gotta have goals," I said.

"Is that your friend's goal, as well?" asked Kalim. "I also used to dream of marrying the empress as a boy, but I haven't Cades's blessings in the arena."

"You'll just have to settle for Lidiel," said Joissa, to general laughter. I guess she was attractive or something? Mostly I was just thankful that the mask covered my widening eyes at the bombshell they'd just dropped. Normally I'd assume that was a figure of speech or something, but over comm translation the meaning was unmistakable.

"*Urgent. The prize for winning the Kabidiad is marrying the empress,*" I subvocalized quickly.

"*Yes! Excellent job, Lilith,*" said the commander. "*That was worth the price of admission by itself.*"

"*I always thought I'd make a good trophy husband,*" said Markus. "*This contact's a bust, by the way.*"

I hadn't flubbed the conversation yet—the culture's inherent sexism was probably helping me there—so I tried to bring up the sponsor thing again, while it was still on topic. But I guess none of them were important enough, or had the ear of a woman who was, to get us the thumbs-up we needed here.

"*Dead end,*" I subvocalized.

"*They might have more leads,*" said Val. "*Contacts are good for more than one thing.*"

He had a point, so I gave it a shot. "Do you know who else would be willing to sponsor Thala?"

"Sight unseen?" asked Sela. "I'm afraid not. Lady Ajarel, you seem like someone receptive to frankness."

"Go for it."

"It can't be done," said Sela. "Or at least it would be extremely difficult. With the competition so fierce, the risk of investing in an unknown athlete is higher. You're not the only ones whose hearts are set on the Kabidiad and the influence to be gained there. It might be best to move on to a different city."

Reasonable, yet I got the impression that he wasn't telling me everything. More importantly, so did my comm.

"We don't really have the funds for that," I said, grimacing. "I guess we'll just keep trying."

"It might be better if you went home," said Sela, with compassion in his voice. "Sometimes fate has other plans."

"Why do you say that?" I asked, looking between him and the other guys. They didn't look as confused as me, so I assumed they were all in on it.

Sela considered for a moment, then leaned in slightly.

"It's Lady Lirian," he said. "She arrived a year ago and began targeting anyone who might outcompete Cades. You know Merisites. Nothing ever provable and so on. But last year, a handful of our city's best athletes were involved in scandal. Another was crippled. The worst case was Kela of Borovin—he has, to the best of my knowledge, vanished utterly."

"Shit," I said, causing some smiles on the dudes around me. Hell yeah! Look at me with the rapport building! "I guess I know why Lady Eloi called me a fool."

Sela's face—what I could see of it—immediately became blank.

"I would not presume to know the thoughts of milady," he said neutrally.

Okay, got it. It's not safe to talk about the White Witch even in friendly territory. Well, I probably wasn't a real friend yet.

"Oh, I didn't mean to imply—uh, just forget it, okay?" I said. "Trade you for the Cades stuff."

"A bargain well struck," said Sela with a deferential movement of the head.

"I should probably go," I said. "Stay safe, don't let the Merisites bite."

Sela turned a bit red at that, and Joissa nudged him while the other guys laughed.

"Did—did you—" I started. "You know what, I don't wanna know. Bye!"

I escaped to an out-of-the-way corner of the room, looking for a table. Val started talking with the rest of the team about the new wrinkle with Lirian and its implications, but I was suddenly exhausted, and I needed to sit down. All this effort for nothing. Frustratingly, it turned out that most of the tables had already been claimed, but I found one that was only occupied by a bored-looking teenager reading some kind of book. I guess they had nerds on Theria, too.

My table companion had pulled her mask up to see better but hadn't taken it off entirely. Probably so she could use the ghostlights, which were fairly bright, to read. Smart kid. I wish they'd had those at *my* school dances.

True to type, she didn't look up as I collapsed into a seat near her.

"Go away," she greeted me.

"I don't wanna be here either, kid," I said, putting my head on the table. It was probably shameful, and people would talk. Didn't matter. This town was a wash. Probably Kives's fault again.

She seemed to regard me for a few moments.

"You can stay if you're quiet," she conceded.

"How generous of you," I said.

"It is," she said self-assuredly. "You didn't even ask to sit down."

"I'm tired, okay?" I said. "Give me a break."

"I did. That's why it was generous."

I made a frustrated noise. "I—you know what? Whatever."

"You're not being very quiet," she observed.

"Why don't you let me?" I shot back, sitting up. She was looking at me now, wearing a defiant expression on her stupid little nerd face.

"You were wrong."

"I'm just wrong about everything today," I said. "Alright, fine, I'll leave."

She looked intently at me, then awkwardly reached out and patted me on the shoulder. "I'm sorry. Are you having a hard time? Kuril keeps saying I need to know when not to argue with people."

"Kid, did you just decide we're buddies or something?" I asked. "A minute ago you were telling me to go away."

"I thought you were like them!" she said, gesturing vaguely at the rest of the ball. "Everyone keeps interrupting me so they can lecture me on proper behavior. They just want me to marry their kids. I hate it."

"I hate it, too," I said. I caught a blip from Markus and stood up in a hurry. "Shit. Uh, nice meeting you, but I need to go, like, *right now*."

"Why?" asked my new buddy.

"Because she's about to get thrown out of the ball," said Markus, walking up to us. "Head for the banquet table, we'll try to stall her there. Don't run."

"Confirmed," I said. "See ya, kid."

"Who's challenging you?" she asked, standing up with us. "It's a challenge, right? I *knew* something was going on with you."

"Markus, keep her out of the way. I don't want her going down with me," I said. "*Commander, what's going on?*"

"*Lirian talked to Lady Eloi,*" said the commander. "*She's got the leverage she needs for the challenge. Get out now, it'll be a public relations disaster if they catch you.*"

"Got it," I said, hurrying—but *not* running—toward the table. "Where is she?"

"*She seems to expect you to head for the entrance,*" said the commander. "*I'll get you out the way I came in. Whatever you do, do not use the cloak.*"

I swore internally as I saw the freakishly tall shape of Lady Eloi moving through the crowd to my left. If anyone could find me, it'd be her. I ducked behind a group of chatting ladies to avoid her sight and continued onward.

"Ah, there you are!" said a voice in my blind spot. I whirled to see none other than Lady Obol blocking my way, beaming in a nurturing kind of way. Here to do me another "favor," no doubt. "I hear you've caused quite a stir without my guidance."

"I, uh—" I stammered.

"You don't belong here," Lirian said, approaching from the other direction.

"I'd rather leave than talk to you," I tried.

"That might be best, my dear," said Lady Obol. "It's best to avoid a scandal, and there's always—"

"I invoke the Right of Challenge!" yelled Lirian, pointing at me. "If you are of grace, let it be shown before all!"

Lady Obol cast a dark look at both of us before settling her composure again. "Are there any who bear witness to this challenge?"

"I do: the lady Eloi Voranetes," came a withered voice behind me. "The lady Ajarel behaved in a manner most unrefined before my eyes."

Lady Obol sighed. "And are there any who would attest to her grace?"

I looked pleadingly at her, but she only met my gaze with blank warmth. I was fucked.

"I do: the lady Roel Vitares." I turned, surprised—everyone was speaking up from outside of my field of vision and it was *pissing me off*—and saw my nerd friend, standing nonchalantly with her book under her arm. Behind her, Markus gave me an apologetic look.

"Then let the challenge commence," said Lady Obol. "Time shall be given to prepare, then your worth will be shown before all." She punctuated the statement with a message just for me—a glare that said, "You better not fuck this up."

I sighed. Get in line, Obol.

CHAPTER TWENTY-FOUR

The Right of Challenge

In the wake of Lirian's overly dramatic challenge, a space had cleared in the sea of stars in preparation for the event. Markus and Roel stepped out of the crowd of people to join me in the line of fire. I knew Markus had my back whatever came, but the kid really had a pair.

"Let's do this!" said Roel. "I'm so excited, I haven't seen one of these in real life before."

I stared at her. "You know there's no way I'm winning this, right?"

"There's a chance," Roel said, doing the head-shrug thing. "If I hadn't spoken up, they'd just kick you out. Way less exciting."

"But now if I lose, you're going down with me," I said.

"Right," she said. "Then I don't need to go to any more social events. I'm happy either way, really."

I—huh. Clever girl.

"I've, uh, never done one of these before," I said. "Or know anything about them, really."

"Ah," said Roel, considering. "Well, there we go."

"So *help me out*, you little punk," I said. "You might be fine with never doing another ball, but that won't work so great for me."

"Well, it's pretty simple," she said, clearly gearing up for lecture mode. "You're basically fighting over the Twelve Virtues. If you can prove you've got one of the good ones, you're safe. Otherwise you have to try to stick her with one of the bad ones, and that'll be hard because no one knows anything about Lady Lirian."

"Alright, prove I've got the good ones," I said. "That sounds doable. What's that look like?"

"Who's your line of descent?" she asked.

"Uh—" I said. Right, everyone here was descended from a demigod. Well, I did impersonate an angel once. "Kives."

"Got any kids?" asked Roel.

"What? No," I said.

"Didn't think so. Done anything important?"

"Obviously!" I said, looking affronted. "Lots of things."

"Anything I would have heard of?" Roel asked with a spark of curiosity that wasn't just procedural.

"Oh yeah, I was involved with the—" I said, then stopped. Shit. We'd been outed as the Calamity during the pirate mission. If I brought that up, I'd have bigger issues than getting blacklisted by the upper class of Vitareas. "Er, no, nothing."

Roel gave me a knowing look, but she was a little punk, so I ignored her.

"So no Kives, then," I said.

"Legacy," she immediately corrected me. "Wait, you don't know the Twelve Virtues?"

"Uh, kind of?" I said. "We use different names for them where I come from." And also there were more than twelve, if you looked at the spectrograph, but humans liked their symmetry. Plus, something told me that if I brought that up, Roel would keep asking questions until she broke something.

"Oh, I didn't realize the terms differed," said Roel. "Here, I made this rhyme a long time ago to remember them—our versions." She launched into a singsong tone: "Rulership and prowess and conflict, legacy and labor and instability. Subtlety and freedom and connection, revelation and creativity and strength."

I narrowed my eyes at her suspiciously and almost opened my mouth to object that that didn't rhyme at all. I was saved by a warning look from Markus. Right, comm translation. I latched on to the tail end of the butchered rhyme.

"Strength," I said. "I can do strength. I'll punch her right in her stupid face."

"They'll definitely throw you out if you do that," said Roel. "Also, it'll go better if you pick a more feminine virtue."

"But on the other hand, I would get to punch Lirian in the face," I pointed out.

Markus cleared his throat.

"Fine," I said. "What else have you got?"

"Too late, we're out of time," said Roel, nodding to where Lady Obol was standing up and walking toward the impromptu arena that'd formed around us. "We can improvise. Just avoid the bad virtues."

"Conflict and instability, right?" I asked. Alcebios and Horcutio had the worst reputation of the gods.

"And freedom," said Roel matter-of-factly.

"Freedom?!"

She looked at me like she'd discovered the answer to some ancient riddle, letting out a noise of enlightenment. Before I could question her further, Lady Obol had gotten everyone's attention.

Lady Obol looked around the room, then spoke in a formal cadence.

"It is known," she said, "that all grace flows from the gods."

"It is known," echoed everyone in the room except me.

"It is known," she said, "that we are of grace through our descent."

"It is known," echoed everyone in the room, including me this time. I felt proud of myself.

"A challenge has been issued," she said. "The lady Lirian alleges that the lady Ajarel is not of grace. If they are of grace, let them show it."

It was no longer possible to ignore the attention of everyone in the room. The masks softened the impact of all that skepticism and disdain, but unfortunately it was strong enough that my comm picked it up. I was objectively on trial here. I hadn't felt so much collective judgment since my mom sent me to my first day of public school in a shirt that said, "My Only Crush Is Jesus Christ." I felt myself shrinking inward under the scrutiny, despite my efforts to keep my posture confident.

"Any last-minute advice?" I muttered to Roel.

"Don't interrupt her," she whispered. "That's usually how they get you."

"Oh no, not your greatest weapon!" Markus subvocalized. I shot him a death glare over my shoulder, not that he could see it through my mask. He was saying he had my back, I realized. All of them did.

"Thank you," I told the team.

"Win or lose," said Abby, *"make it a worthy fight."*

"Go for the throat," said Val.

Lirian stepped forward with a swirl of her cloak, fucking showboat that she was. She was loving this, I could tell. In her eyes, I was just a motorcycle ramp to glory. Well, if she was going to ride over me, I was going to shove a branch in her tires.

Ready or not, it was showtime.

"My ladies," she began, sweeping an arm across the audience. "We all know the lady Ajarel—what *am* I saying? We do not know the lady Ajarel. She appeared in our wondrous city only this morning with no acquaintances, no relations, not even a messenger to announce her arrival."

Roel shook her head when I looked at her, so I managed not to burst out about the inherent irony of calling Vitareas "our city" when she'd only gotten here a year ago.

As if sensing my irritation, Lirian flashed me a sweet poison smile before continuing. "Well, lacking connection is no crime, she will assure you. But it is not a virtue. And no proof of this is required beyond the evidence you see yourselves. What, I ask you, transpired when she entered our halls? She made enemies the way Resha the Smith made shields until they rose over the walls of Elyrium."

I wanted to protest that I'd only made one very tall enemy, but I didn't need to look at Roel to know it wasn't time yet. I crossed my arms and glared as best I could through the mask. Lirian let me stew for just a bit longer than she had to before moving on.

"I reiterate that we know nothing about the alleged lady! Has she works of great skill or words of deep profundity? Has she deeds to her name? Salaphi has been an exciting place of late—surely one of such grace had the opportunity to participate? Of course," she said, her voice taking on a sinister tone, "I've heard dark rumors about what transpired at Salaphi. Perhaps the reason for her hasty arrival is merely cowardice. Or perhaps she had a hand in the curse that struck those lands? Is that your *legacy*, sister?"

Markus put a hand on my arm, probably to stop me from answering the question. I shook him off. I was going to stab her, I decided.

Lirian paced along the line of noblewomen, gesturing emphatically with one hand. "All partake of the nature of the gods. But I tell you, the virtues she partakes of are not ours! Let me tell you about the event that convinced me that 'Lady' Ajarel was not fit to stand among us, brought to me by a lady of great standing among us!"

She went on to describe, in excruciating and exaggerated detail, my unfortunate experience with *dvoli*.

"Subtlety is supposed to be Meris, right?" I whispered to the other two while she went on. "Because she's really not subtle."

"You won't convince them with that," Roel whispered. "She's been chosen as a daughter of Meris."

"Okay, uh, I'm good at rulership?" I tried.

Roel stared at me. "Salaphi must be very strange."

"I guess no rulership, then," I sighed to myself.

Lirian was still waxing eloquent about me choking on my own mucus or something, so I pinged the team for support. This sucked. I could tell that Lirian was winning the audience over, and I hadn't even gotten a chance to speak yet. When I even got the chance to speak, they would already think of me as some kind of pretender. Which, in the final analysis, I was, so on some level I didn't even have the will to protest.

"*Lilith, I know this is hard for you,*" said the commander. "*Humans aren't built to take this kind of social punishment. I need you to remember that no lasting harm will come to you. None of this means anything to us. You can walk away when you're done.*"

"And that!" Lirian concluded, throwing one hand in the air, "is the point! Ajarel over there has the curse of *freedom*. She is not bound to our manner, my ladies, she is not bound to our customs, she is not bound to decorum! Let her roam the wilds with the followers of Rucks, but let her not stand in these halls a moment longer than it takes to expose her deception!"

"*I guess I am from the land of the free,*" I subvocalized. The joke gave just a bit of distance, but damn if I wasn't just drowning in all this hatred.

Lirian turned to Lady Obol. "Lady Hostess," she said, "let us hear the words of the accused."

I stepped forward, looked around, and couldn't open my mouth. Public speaking is, according to researchers, scarier than death itself. And that's without etheric confirmation that your audience is, in fact, actively hostile to you.

"I—" I tried, and my voice faltered. Lirian was already celebrating her victory in her head, I could tell. I turned slowly and looked at Markus. He smiled, and I knew what I had to do.

In *The Road of Spears*—supposedly written by Eifni Voriksson himself after the destruction of the Velean pantheon—there was a passage describing how a warrior should fight a losing battle. Eifni's first piece of advice was: don't.

But, he continued, when there is more at stake than your life, when it is necessary that you hold the line, you will find yourself incapable of weakness. Do you fear death? You are dead already. Does exhaustion grip you? You will rest soon.

Is your spear dull? It is still a spear, and the enemy stands before you.

I—socially speaking, anyway—was already dead. And my spear was pretty damn dull. But it was still a spear. I slipped a hand into my gown and found my hand amplifier. I set it to martyrdom, then cranked the output to maximum.

"I claim revelation," I told the disdainful noblewomen. My voice wasn't as powerful as Lirian's, but it didn't matter anymore. I was incapable of weakness. "It won't be a big one because you already know it. But someone has to say it. Lirian, you're *really* not subtle."

"*Lady* Lirian," Lady Obol sharply interrupted me.

"Oh, don't give me that," I said, "you didn't interrupt when she forgot to call me a lady."

That didn't clearly win me any points with the crowd, but fuck 'em.

"Salaphi's a small place, my ladies," I said, pacing. Less for effect, like Lirian had done, but just to think better. "What we call connection looks, uh, pretty different from, uh, all this." I gestured vaguely at the thisness. "This is actually pretty weird, if you think about it. Which, uh, I'm sure you do. Anyway. Not here to talk about that. I want to talk about how this supposed Merisite is *really not subtle*. Like, come on, no one's *said* anything, but we all know why she's here. I was here for *one day*, and she came up to me and threatened me about this guy."

I pointed over to Markus.

"That's Thala, everyone. Wave to all the pretty people, Thala."

Markus waved sheepishly. Someone chuckled in the back.

"Hey, there we go. Yeah, Thala's great. Real faithful devotee of Kabiades, and he's been training for the Renathion. We came here because we heard Vitareas had some good competition, and he wanted to honor the god here. But guess what happens? We didn't make it an hour before Lady Cloak walks up to me and goes all, 'Don't put him in the Renathion or I'm gonna make bad stuff happen to you.' *Subtlety?* Really?"

So many disapproving stares, even through the masks. I could tell I was digging myself into a hole on the freedom charge, as this little impromptu speech probably bore no resemblance whatsoever to the way things were supposed to go. And god, it hurt on a deep emotional level. I was going to have nightmares about this, I could tell. But right now the hurt didn't matter.

"I guess this is supposed to be the bad stuff," I said. "Because, I'll say it again, she's really not subtle. You know who's subtle? Lady Eloi."

The silhouette of Lady Eloi almost twitched against the illumination of the hanging ghostlights as the mention of her name brought greater scrutiny on me.

"Like, alright, I didn't know she was eating *dvoli*, and I was obviously trying to flatter her. And knowing all that, she set me to humiliate myself. And let me tell you, I could tell that something bad was about to happen, but I had to go through with it, anyway, because we both knew I needed something. Well done, milady," I said, giving her a stage bow. "That was a good plan. Now, by contrast, Lirian's plan was, uh, this."

I gestured at the thisness again.

"Her *very clever plan* was to, uh, yell at me in front of a bunch of people so you'd tell me to go away. Which, uh, I see you still might."

No one laughed. I was really not winning anyone over here.

"Okay, tough crowd. Anyway, uh, sure, maybe Lirian's plan is going to work, but my point is she's still not subtle. And the result is *we all know what she wants.*"

I paced a bit, gathering my thoughts. As I made a circuit past Roel, she whispered, "I told you this wasn't going to work."

I shook my head at her, gesturing as if to say, "Wait."

"If Lirian's virtue isn't subtlety, what is it? Well, that's the revelation, ladies. *Conflict.*" I made a kind of stabbing motion with one hand. "Division. Turning us against one another. We're here to honor Kabiades, aren't we, Thala? Don't we all agree that the god should be honored? But here's Lady Swishy Cloak preventing that from happening! We all know what's going on, don't we? Throwing her weight around, preventing *your* champions from performing their best. You can stand up to this. You want to throw me out? Fine. We can find another city. *You* can't. This is your home, and she's squatting in it."

I looked around one more time—come on, would it kill any of you people to nod or something?—then addressed Lady Obol. "Uh, Lady Hostess, that's all I have to say."

"Then the questioning will commence," she said. "All who stand with Lady Lirian may stand at her side. Those with Lady Ajarel, on her side. When a quorum is reached, I shall end the challenge, and the loser shall depart immediately. Lady Lirian may speak first."

"What a lovely speech," drawled the spy. "Your rhetoric tutors must have taught you so well. Tell me, how long did you spend in their instruction?"

"What, for rhetoric?" I asked. Let's see, one ten-week academic quarter was seventy days, divided by twelve was . . . "Uh, five *thessim*? And a bit?"

"Five thessim!" Lirian said to the crowd, with an expression that clearly said, "You can laugh now." "And a bit!"

I chose to believe they were laughing *with* me. Never mind that many of them were already shifting to her end of the circle, rapidly thinning my end.

"Might as well ask," I said. "Do you think Thala should compete for glory in the Renathion?"

"Of course," she said smoothly. "The accusations in your defense were . . . *creative,* I'll grant you, but completely fictitious. I think all who are willing should compete. My turn. Who taught you how to prosecute a challenge?"

"No one," I said to general tittering. "There's, like, six of us in Salaphi, it'd be pointless. Okay, hold on just a second, I need to double-check something."

That caused more laughter, but it didn't really stop the slow trickle of people heading to Lirian's side. I walked over to Roel, who was staring at me and fidgeting.

"What are you doing?" she whispered frantically. "We're going to lose!"

"I thought you didn't care," I said.

"That was before I had everyone staring at me!"

"I can corner her," I said. "We can win. All you have to do is promise to sponsor Thala if we lose."

"That doesn't make any sense," she said.

"Lady Ajarel," snapped Lady Obol. "This is not allowed."

"Almost done!" I called, to more mocking laughter. This was going to end soon one way or another. "Just trust me. Nerd to nerd."

She looked at me strangely, then glanced at Markus. "Deal."

"Deal," I said, clapping her on the shoulder and standing up. "Lady Lirian, before we let this go further, you should know that the honorable Lady Roel has agreed to sponsor Thala in the Renathion—*if* I lose here. And as you seem to be so well-informed, I'm sure you also know that bad things have happened to virtuous athletes like Thala here. So, since I'm sure you have nothing to do with those horrible accidents, will you give your word that nothing befalls Thala if I concede here and now?"

The support bleed slowed, even stopped in some areas. The crowd was already pretty lopsided against me, and Lady Obol was definitely fudging things in my favor—to give me a chance not to embarrass her, I guess. But the sudden attention on Lirian told me people weren't buying her blatant denials.

"You should have finished your sixth *thessim* of rhetoric instruction," laughed Lirian. "Or even attended an seventh. Perhaps then you could assemble a coherent question."

I raised one arm triumphantly at the crowd.

"She's dodging the question!" I said. "She claims she's not involved, but she won't give her word!"

One person even walked back toward my side, which immediately made them my new best friend.

"Do you even realize how out of line you are?" Lirian said.

"Do you think *I* care if I lose?" I shot back. "They're the ones who have to deal with you!"

"Ladies!" said Lady Obol. I grinned at Lirian. She was expecting me to play her game, but Darwin help me, I was going to drag her down to my level and beat her with experience.

"This," Lirian proclaimed to the crowd, "is unforgivably free. I need no further questions to demonstrate her lack of grace."

"Lady or not," I told her, "I will fight you every step of the way."

"You have no idea what consequences you've called down on yourself," said Lirian with a smug smile.

Lady Obol stepped forward. "Then I am afraid I must—"

A woman's scream cut her off. We all looked for the source of the disturbance and saw a cloaked figure drawing a sword and charging out of the crowd—straight at Roel.

"No!" I screamed, leaping at the attacker. The figure whirled out of the way and knocked me right to the ground with the pommel of their sword. Roel didn't move, staring dumbly at the assassin in shock.

"Roel! Run!" I shouted. The assassin's sword flashed down—

Markus dashed in front of Roel, yelling in pain as he took the blow on his shoulder. Oh god that was a lot of blood. Roel seemed to wake up from her trance and backed away to the crowd, those *cowards* parting around her as she got close—

Markus was fighting the assassin now, grimacing in pain as he moved his injured arm with obvious trouble, taking more cuts as he tried to wrestle the weapon away—

Screams and shouts from those who were present, people were calling for the guards, but none were coming, none were close enough—

I stood up and charged at the assassin's back, one arm going for my knife, but the assassin must have heard me coming because they whipped around—*she* whipped around and disabled my arm with a jab to my armpit pressure point before hitting me in what felt like eight locations at once—

I regained consciousness on my knees, Markus sprawled on the ground and bleeding heavily, the assassin fighting five guards at once before tripping three of them into one another and killing a fourth to make her escape—

I crawled over to Markus. "No, no, no," I moaned. "You're gonna be alright, big guy. We'll get you back to base, it'll be fine, we just gotta get you back."

"Move!" said Roel, forcibly dragging an older woman behind her. "He saved my life. You save his, okay? Kuril will pay you back, just save him!"

"Y-yes, of course," said the woman. "I need some hot water and bandages. The cut looks bad, but it could have been worse."

"Did she get away?" Markus groaned as she started tending to him.

"Yes, damnit," I said. "I think I have a concussion. My head is *splitting*." I switched to subvocal. "*Commander, where the fuck are you?*"

"*Oh, you know,*" she said, sounding pleased with herself. "*The usual. Dodging a city's worth of pursuers in unfamiliar terrain.*"

I blinked in realization, looking at the chaos around me. Markus on the ground, grinning weakly up at me, occasionally wincing as the old woman washed his injuries. Roel, staring at the process with a mixture of worry, horror, and curiosity. Lady Obol, speaking deferentially to what I assumed were older members of the Jeneretti. The challenge over, Lirian conveniently missing.

I burst out laughing. That made me feel kind of lightheaded.

"Lady Ajarel? Are you okay?" asked Roel.

"She," I giggled, raising a finger, "was really good." I slumped over.

CHAPTER TWENTY-FIVE

Preparation

We were heroes now.

My near conviction on charges of freedom was instantly forgotten. As Hadalce—the woman with medical training that Roel had dragged over—treated our wounds, no less than eight women approached us, offering to sponsor Markus in the Renathion. I thanked them tiredly, a polite smile fixed on my face.

An hour ago these people had practically wanted to burn me at the stake, and they were not forgiven.

Lady Eloi's offer was my favorite. The *dvoli* story had magically transformed from a tale of utter humiliation to a testimonial about my bravery, which she expounded on at length. Everyone's masks were off by this point, the drama having unceremoniously put an end to the Starlight Ball, and when we made eye contact for the first time I saw glacial blue and utter indifference. The story, and the sponsorship offer that followed, weren't for my benefit.

There was an excruciating bruise along the left side of my head where the commander had slammed her elbow into my skull and rattled my brain around inside like a pachinko machine. My thoughts were kind of fuzzy as a result, so I was probably missing the subtleties here. When Eloi was finished, I just did the head-tilt shrug and gave her a rueful quirk of the lips.

"You're too kind," I said. "Maybe next time."

We turned them all down, of course, as Roel had apparently decided we were hers now and argued exhaustively with anyone who seemed like they were genuinely trying to poach us. Kid was ferocious. She had citations and everything. The rest of the offers were pro forma, an indirect way of telling everyone they were on the winning team now. I hated it, but the commander's actions had salvaged the mission out of nowhere, and I wasn't about to throw that away.

I got filled in on the details between brownnosers.

Apparently Abby hadn't had any trouble slipping into the ball on her own. She'd been an infiltration specialist like me before taking a command position, but I have no idea how she managed that without a cloak. Once inside, she'd posed as a random noble and avoided conversation while she staked out the area. But at some point during the challenge she'd changed costumes, taken out one of the estate guards, and gone after us with the guard's sword.

The plan wasn't just hers: Val and Markus had been on a private channel with her during my speech, not wanting to distract me. I was annoyed at being left out, but on the other hand I was barely coherent without distractions from the team, so they probably made the right call.

Abby had led her pursuers on a winding route in the opposite direction from the ship before slipping into a compound that looked like a noble family's estate. While the Jeneretes guards argued with the people securing that location, she'd hopped out a back window and escaped into the night.

We, on the other hand, got invited by Lady Obol to stay the night here, likely so she could regain some face after everything that went down tonight. That backfired spectacularly when Roel icily pointed out that she'd nearly been murdered right in this room less than an hour ago. The look on Obol's face was priceless. After that, no one challenged Roel when she said we'd be returning to the Vitares estate. As soon as Hadalce cleared us to move, we were loaded into a couple of palanquins and shipped off.

No one seemed to know where Lirian was.

The first thing I noticed about Roel's carriage was that it was pulled by a mechanical horse. The second thing was the armed guards—the Vitaressi were apparently taking no chances after the assassination attempt. Fair enough, I guess. I was gently shuffled into the carriage while Roel rapidly fired off every thought going through her head. Guess her adrenaline was still spiking. Markus made the proper responses at the proper moments. Or so I assumed; I was having trouble following the conversation. Eventually Roel ran out of steam, and we made the second half of the trip in exhausted silence.

Roel's sister, Kuril, was waiting for us when we reached the gates of the Vitares estate, the family's last foothold in the city. It looked the part—there were subtle signs of disrepair all along the walls. The architectural style was distinct from the outer parts of the city—three stories high, rooms resting upon arches over open-air courtyards full of half-finished gizmos.

Kuril herself wore a simple shawl with scorch marks and an expression of worry. I mentally put her in her late twenties, maybe ten years older than Roel. Might be a story there. Her hair was tied back in a ponytail, and she was wearing a sword.

When the carriage pulled in front of the estate, Roel staggered out, legs stiff from the ride, and ran straight for Kuril, who knelt and caught her in a hug. Within moments, she was bawling into her sister's shoulder. Guess everything was catching up to her.

Markus helped me out of the carriage. Turns out concussions make you lightheaded, but I managed not to fall over in front of our new contacts.

"Nice to meet you," I said after Markus nudged me.

"Roel, get up," Kuril whispered to Roel. After a moment, she did, and Kuril stood up, Roel standing sheepishly next to her and wiping away the rest of her tears. Kuril looked back and forth at Markus and me, her expression serious. "Godsmile, Lady Ajarel. And to you, as well, Thala. I owe you a debt too great to measure."

"I'm glad everything worked out," I said a little blurrily.

"Is she alright?" Kuril asked one of the guards.

"She took a head injury while defending Lady Roel," said Markus. "Nonlethal. It'll heal in time."

"Praise the godesses," she said. Though her words were relieved, her expression remained one of intense focus. "Inside, then."

Markus helped me up the steps to the front door, where I stopped and said, "A friend of this house seeks—"

"No," Kuril cut me off. "You owe us nothing. You will always be welcome here."

"That's the nicest thing anyone's ever said to me," I said airily.

Markus and Kuril looked at me with concern.

"Let's find her a place to lie down," said Kuril.

I spent most of the next day lying down in a dark room and trying not to throw up. Concussions: the gift that keeps on giving.

While I recovered, Roel took Markus to the temple of Kabiades to get him enrolled. I tried to follow along on Markus's feed, but after about an hour of that I felt worse and had to shut it off. Things worked out, though. Markus got enrolled without a hitch, although I did cringe a bit when they had him take off his clothes to compare him against a statue of Kabiades. He did well, although apparently he was a bit *too* bulky to be maximally attractive. They didn't do ratings out of ten here, there was just some complicated system of graces and subgraces that I'd tuned out when Roel explained them to Markus. The bottom line, however, was that he was officially pretty enough to compete. Mission accomplished!

It was weird for me that the Kabiadesians thought of physical appearance as being part of athleticism. Like, American culture is pretty superficial in a lot of ways, but we don't gate keep people out of sports competitions based on looks. Explicitly, anyway.

"*'Lying to yourself is doing the enemy's work,'*" Val quoted at me when I asked him. "*You say Markus is athletic because he's in good shape. If he were overweight, the thought would never occur to you.*"

"Okay," I said, "but, like, you could still be athletic even if you were overweight."

"*I assure you, the thought would surprise you in any other context. Cultures struggle to separate the appearance of a thing from the thing itself.*"

"Not necessarily," I insisted. Like, probably yes, but I had a concussion, so it wasn't a fair time to ask. It's bad to be prejudiced. "Anyway, my point is, looking athletic is etherically different than being athletic."

"*They are different, yes,*" said Val. "*Did they teach you about personas in Combat Theology? They must have. I suppose the operational question should be whether you remember it.*"

I did remember, as it happened. Val was saying that prettiness was part of Kabiades's persona, so according to conduit theory they'd be the same here. An ascendant god like Kabiades probably had other personas in other cultures, so maybe on the other side of the planet they believed in a god of athleticism who was more about fairness or showboating or something. But that's how it was here.

My plan was to repeat enough of that back to Val to make him stop thinking I sucked, but my brain hurt, so I settled for a more elegant play.

"Concussion," I whined.

"*Let her recover,*" said the commander. "*Hang in there, Lilith. Val's almost got the translation engines fixed. We'll have you recovered in a week at most.*"

I sighed and braced myself for the prospect of a week with nothing to do but think.

Turns out having nothing to do but think was exhausting because, while my thoughts are awesome, they are for other people to deal with. Fortunately for me, my period of mental torture was interrupted by the preparations for Markus's first Renathion.

Rather than admit we didn't know any of the local songs, they'd withdrawn him from the singing competition while putting him in massage. He was still in the pentathlon, but his arm wasn't moving right, and there was no way he was going to win. (Abby had cut a bit *too* deep. Markus kept giving her shit for it.)

In spite of what the old priest said, we were hoping Markus would do well enough at the massage competition that he could win laurels. Otherwise, we'd just have to hope that Val got the translation engines functional enough to patch him up before the next one.

Markus was actually a trained masseur—man, I was going to be so cool when *I* was eighty—but the massage competition wasn't just that part of it. While the contestant actually performed the massage, the judges grilled them on philosophy. And Markus didn't know any Therian philosophy, but Roel had spent the last day going over the major areas of contention with him. It was better than nothing.

We weren't just relying on Markus's ability to improvise, of course. Both Val and Abby had gone out and tracked down some local philosophers, who they were paying for private lessons around the time Markus was scheduled for the massage. We'd feed him answers over his comm on anything he wasn't ready to answer. The commander had snuck over and rigged him up with an arm sling that could conceal a hand amplifier. When he spoke, regardless of the actual content, his words would seem extremely profound.

The morning of the competition found us gathering at the Vitares' carriage, preparing to leave. Kuril was distant and not all that interactive—she'd been up late tinkering with one of the devices in their garage equivalent. Roel had decided to come along, something I understood was unusual for her, but her head was still buried in her book. A different one than she'd been reading at the ball, which raised several questions about their manufacturing capabilities I was too brain fogged to consider. Markus was his usual offensively chipper self, having shortened his morning PT to what I'd consider a normal amount of time "just to warm up for the competition."

And me? I was jumpy.

"Gee, I hope no one tries to kill us again on the way to the temple," I said.

"Don't tempt the goddesses," Kuril shot back. "They take issue with that kind of comment."

"I'm sure their angels are watching over us," said Roel.

Five blocks away, the commander was assembling a sniper rifle.

"Sure," I said. "Let's go with that."

CHAPTER TWENTY-SIX

The Renathion

The arena was stuffed with people when we arrived. They were mostly Estheni, the majority demographic in this region—lots of saturated brown hair, gray eyes, prominent cheekbones, larger builds, deeply tanned skin—but there was enough diversity that people wouldn't give us foreigners a second look. I say "us," but Markus had shifted his eyes from their usual brown to gray for the role of Thala. His cheekbones weren't all the way there, but makeup had helped with that.

We entered through the testicle archway—I almost asked Roel to explain its significance, but my head was too fuzzy to think about whether that was a good idea. People gave us a lot of room, either because of our expensive clothes or because the Vitares girls were recognizable.

I still wasn't feeling that great. Given that the baseball cap hadn't been invented on Theria, I'd asked House Vitares's private hairstylist to whip up something to shade my light-sensitive eyes. After she laughed me off I'd acquired a fan instead. My other arm was linked in Roel's in case I overbalanced or something. I'd tried to do that with Markus, but the girls had informed me that implied a romantic connection around here. Fucking microcultures, you can never get anything right.

As we walked to the arena, our little bubble in the crowd hit an antibubble, a bunch of people squishing in close. The source of attention was easy to spot because he stood head and shoulders above the crowd—Cades was standing there in all his scantily clad glory. His +1 Wreath of Sexual Availability draped over his overdeveloped pectorals, which faintly gleamed in the morning sunlight. You'd almost think his smile would gleam, too, but actually his teeth were kind of dull. No whitening treatments at this level of tech, I guess.

He caught sight of us and quickly began to make his excuses, moving through the crowd of fans. Kuril left us, citing judge responsibilities, but the rest of us didn't have an excuse to escape.

"Godsmile, my ladies! By the goddesses, Thala!" he said with a dismayed tone, his deep voice cutting effortlessly through the noise of the crowd. "You are injured!"

"I wanted to make it a fair competition," Markus shot back. Cades laughed.

"I saw you at the grounds when you arrived," said Cades. "You looked like a worthy challenger. I looked forward to today. But this won't do at all! How long will you be out of competition?"

"I'll face you today," said Markus, grinning. "Have you heard the tale of how I came by these injuries?"

"Who hasn't?" Cades gripped his uninjured shoulder. "I hear you saved these bright ladies from a craven assassin. Vitareas glows today, ladies, for you still shine upon it."

Oh, real fucking smooth. I checked my comm. Yup, attraction all over.

"I fought, too, muscle brain." I scowled at him. The attraction levels dropped as he looked at me in surprise. Good. Buzz off, creep.

"I thought you had the heart of a warrior," he told me in approving tones. "You make a mighty couple."

"It would help if you called off your guard spy," I said. "I don't wanna get knifed out here."

Cades's face grew uncertain at that, glancing at Markus. "The lady Lirian does not answer to me, Lady Ajarel. If these rumors are true about her, they are troubling. I had thought to approach her—but one does not lightly meddle in the affairs of goddesses."

"Well, she meddled pretty hard with us," I said. "Thala won't be able to compete at full strength now."

"Lady Ajarel," Markus interrupted. "Cades isn't to blame here."

I shot a look at him that meant something like, "Really? You're defending the creepy dudebro?" Markus didn't react to it.

"Plenty of Renathions before the Kabidiad," he told Cades. "I'm sure we'll learn each other's strength in time."

Cades nodded, looking a bit distracted. He looked up at Markus.

"I owe you a debt," he said simply, without the larger-than-life grandstanding I'd come to expect from him. "Already my name is tarnished by the accidents. Your courage is a boon to us all."

"Buy me a drink," said Markus, his face softening just a bit. "We'll call it even."

Cades looked searchingly at him for a moment, then effortlessly switched back to stage-performance mode. "A drink it is!" He laughed, clapping Markus's shoulder again. "But for now, the contest!"

Then he set off for the competitors' area. Markus said his goodbyes and followed.

"That was weird," I said.

"Do you think he's in on the conspiracy?" asked Roel.

I looked at her. "What? Conspiracy?"

She nodded seriously. "Yeah, the Cult of Silence's plan to use Cades as a distraction so they can secretly get another candidate into the empress's harem. Otherwise there's no reason for Lady Lirian to parade herself so openly. It's obvious if you think about what you're supposed to think is going on."

"Oh, that conspiracy," I said, trying to parse what she'd just said.

"I read the whole *Pelnassiad*. They usually design their operations to make you think something's going on when it's actually not. I bet Lady Lirian's actually just one of the other nobles in a disguise."

"Huh," I said.

"Yeah," said Roel, starting to warm up to the conversation. "Did you hear that Geremine Ferades never showed up to the ball? There's no way she'd have missed it if she weren't pretending to be someone else. And the guards say the assassin disappeared into the Jubios estate!"

"I have no idea what that means," I told her, which kind of took the wind out of her sails and made me feel like a bad person.

"They're allies," she said curtly.

"Oh," I said. We walked in silence for a little bit, heading for the administrative building. "Uh, sorry, Roel. I didn't mean to be rude. It's my damn brain injury."

She looked at me curiously. "Brain injuries make you rude?"

"Well, you know, you have less self-control," I said. "Also it hurts."

"That makes sense," she said. "I guess it means your blood doesn't get to your heart effectively."

I blinked. Fuck, I'd almost spilled medical knowledge I wasn't supposed to have. "Uh, yeah. Exactly."

She didn't press me further, which meant I hadn't just blown my cover and accidentally caused a medical revolution. Weird thing to celebrate, I guess, but that's the job. You had to triage. You can reincarnate after a deadly illness, but there's no coming back from the stomach of a god.

The opening blessing ceremony was long and pointless, but we confirmed that Kabiades's divine signature was present while the old priest rambled at the crowd. That meant that the arena would be active, worship wise, and whatever Markus achieved today would count toward his eventual installation as a stand-in for the big guy himself.

The plan had changed because the targets had changed. We'd immediately recognized the ceremonial marriage for what it was: a conduit event designed to allow Varas and Kabiades to stake a claim on the idea of marriage. If you graph Kabiades's persona, there's a part of him that says "husband of Varas," and she's got one that says "wife of Kabiades," and overlapping them with a religious ritual lets them pound that idea into the local culture.

With Markus standing in for Kabiades and the empress for Varas, they'd serve as icons—conduits passing mortal significance onto their respective gods.

So naturally Markus was gonna stab the empress.

Bam! Symbol of rulership killed by the person supposed to be most loyal to her! Bam! Perfect husband stabs his wife!

Val said it wouldn't quite be a kill shot on either of them, but that's where we get to the best part—with proper amplification and filtering, if Markus assassinated his royal bride while at the center of the conduit, it'd register to Varas like Kabiades had actually tried to stab *her*. She'd fucking tear him apart, and with the conduit active, she'd have an easy vector for her first strike. Best case, she ripped out one of his aspects and collapsed under the internal pressures of triphase. Unlikely, but hey—maybe we got lucky.

Just so we're clear, by the way, marital violence is bad, and I wholeheartedly condemn it. But let's not forget the stakes here—Kabiades *fucking eats people*. Varas, too. All the competitors here were basically slabs of spiritual meat being fattened up for the gods' table. Cades, Gaedera, Jerevai, Kada—one day they'd die, then they'd be god food, and that would be that.

We were here to *put those monsters down*. If you're a surgeon, you cut people's bodies to save their lives. If you're a godslayer, you cut people's cultures to save their souls. The damage was both necessary and temporary. We'd ruin their little premodern Olympics for a bit, but they'd have eternity to make something else. Something that was meaningful because *they* made it, not because a supernatural predator wanted to fatten them up.

Basically what I'm trying to say is I didn't pay attention to the opening ceremony.

The massage event was held privately, located inside the administrative building on the arena grounds. The five judges attended, along with a handful of other women who I assumed were important for some reason. I drew some looks when I walked in with Kuril and Roel, but the people looking seemed to recognize me. So they'd been at the ball the other night. Lovely.

There was a table covered in blankets, where I assumed the massages would be taking place soon. Rows of stone benches surrounded it in a semicircle, reminding me of a lecture hall. The first vulture was on me moments after I sat down on one, full of polite smiles and hints at some sort of request that I was too tired and fuzzy minded to unravel. Roel shooed her off after it became clear I wasn't going to, but then the next one approached. I started wondering if I could pretend to fall asleep or something before I realized it was Alceoi Voranetes, one of the people I'd talked to at the ball.

Alceoi was a pixie of a woman, thin like Eloi but short enough that she didn't look like the skeleton dude from *The Nightmare Before Christmas*. Same sharp features, though, and even though her eyes were green—my first time seeing them, come to think of it—I realized I was looking at a close relative of the spice queen herself. Fuck, I really did not have the mental capacity to deal with this. Next Voranetes I met, I was just gonna run away.

"You're alive," she said after we'd exchanged greetings. "I heard you were dying."

"We're all dying," I said grumpily. "Getting smacked in the head doesn't make it go any faster. Unless it does."

She laughed. "We'd miss you. All these gossips would have no one to bother."

I blinked, trying to figure out if she was asking me for something. Eh, fuck it, she'd been alright at the ball.

"Whatever, sit down if you want," I said. "Sorry in advance, I'm gonna be rude today."

"It's her brain injury," Roel interjected. Her book was out again; she hadn't even looked up.

"Don't make me challenge you," Alceoi mock threatened me. "Goddesses, can you imagine? Aunt Eloi would throw a fit."

I froze.

"Oh, come on," I said. "She told you to be here, didn't she."

"Wouldn't you?" asked Alceoi. "You were charming enough before that disaster with Lirian. Neither of us want Auntie's displeasure. It's dangerous to be lonely in this city."

"I'm not lonely. I've got friends," I said, giving Roel a side hug. She leaned into it but still didn't stop reading.

Alceoi peered at me. "Is that the head injury talking?"

"No, I'm just fed up with the—" I started. "Actually, you know what, let's go with the head injury."

Alceoi laughed like I'd said something witty, which I was 90 percent certain I hadn't. I would know—I was there. Fucking politics.

"So what did the lady Eloi ask you to do?" asked Roel. "Is she working with the Cult of Silence?"

Alceoi waved that off. "Oh, you know how it goes. Caught in the web of the Whisperer, as are we all, so on, so forth. Not a hint of her true thoughts to anyone, except maybe the lady Sael, and no one's even going to think of sticking their hand in a *priasor* trap."

I nodded in understanding.

"*The fuck is a* priasor *trap?*" I subvocalized to the team.

"*A moment,*" Val replied, relaying the question—minus the profanity, I assumed—to the philosophy tutor we'd paid for lessons.

"So here we are," said Alceoi. "Do the men of Salaphi train in massage?"

"I've heard the custom is different here," I said, dodging the question. "I'm looking forward to the Vitarean traditions."

"*Priasors* are moderately sized pest animals," said Val. "*Farmers put bait in a metal bucket with inwardly facing spikes. When the* priasor *attempts to extract the bait, the spikes dig into the limb.*"

"*Shit,*" I said while Alceoi small talked at me. "*Then what, it chews its paw off?*"

"*The spikes are smeared with poison,*" said Val.

Right then. No messing with Sael Voranetes. Must be nice to have everyone be so afraid of you. Hm, maybe I could be like a *priasor* trap. Then all the Lirians and Alceois of the world could just watch their step around me and let me hang out with actually cool people.

I nodded to myself. New life goal acquired.

CHAPTER TWENTY-SEVEN

Competitive Massage

With the judges seated, a middle-aged priest of Kabiades with a belted sword and a sour expression spoke a few words, and the massage contest began. One of the five judges stepped forward.

"The lady Gamourin, of the grace of the Voranetti," she announced.

"My esteemed cousin," Alceoi muttered to me. I looked back and forth between the two skeptically—Gamourin was at least a generation older than Alceoi, with a healthier skin tone and curlier hair—but Alceoi met my expression with a challenging one of her own.

"And whom do you sponsor?" the priest asked Gamourin.

"The honored cartwright Peloman, of the grace of the gods," she said.

"You may disrobe," said the priest. "Let the contender step forth."

I averted my eyes from the suddenly topless noble, a reflex from my conservative upbringing I should probably root out one of these days. The nudity taboos were, ah, much lighter here than in America. I found it much less uncomfortable to watch a man, whom I presumed to be Peloman, round the corner, and dammit he was naked, too, except for one of those stupid thongs they made the competitors wear.

I shot a sidelong glance at Alceoi, whose attention was so obviously not on me that she had definitely been watching my reaction just now. Roel, on the other hand, was unsuccessfully attempting to pretend she was still reading and not stealing glances at the naked guy. Eh, fuck it, might as well train out my dumb shame reflex. I looked back at Peloman, fighting the feeling that someone was about to catch me and lecture me about impure thoughts or something.

My mind stuttered to a halt as the priest drew his sword and held it out at neck height before Peloman could approach the table where Gamourin was now lying.

"These are the halls of the god himself," said the priest. "Your hands must be as his hands. Should those hands transgress, they shall be removed."

"Let it be so," said Peloman.

"Then pass," said the priest, lowering his blade.

"*Damn, that was metal,*" I subvocalized—out of habit, mostly, the comment not being directed to anyone in particular.

Watching someone else get massaged was surprisingly relaxing, even if it didn't make my headache go away. I tried to tune out the questions the judges were asking him and just watch his hands go. The technique he was using was probably different from the ones Earth masseurs used in some way, but I don't know how Earth massages work so I didn't really have a point of comparison. Gamourin was making appreciative noises every so often, so it was probably good. The sound of her voice annoyed me, though, because it kept reminding me that I wasn't the one getting massaged. I'd have to guilt a massage out of Abby after this op was done.

"How do you judge his hands?" asked the priest.

"There is great strength in them, fit to hold a shield and slay his foes," answered Gamourin. "Though with a gentleness well suited for carrying children."

"Well spoken and well soothed," said the priest. "You may surrender the dais."

Peloman sat down on the bench reserved for competitors as the women present all stomped their feet for him—the equivalent of applause, I was assuming. Peloman pressed a fist to his chest to accept the praise. Then it was time for the next overly muscled naked man. I blinked in surprise when I recognized him—it was Gaedera, the dude who'd won against Cades in that wrestling match on our first day at the course. The priest pulled a sword on him like before, which was *still* wigging me out, but soon he was working knots out of the Kess judge's back. I forced myself to watch the naked people touching one another in public, like seriously, who the hell thought this was a good idea?

Alceoi was still *definitely not looking* at me, and I inwardly cringed at the report I assumed was heading straight to Eloi after this. I probably looked super uncomfortable.

They were asking him the same questions as Peloman, so there was probably a list they'd all agreed on beforehand. I still wasn't paying that much attention. Val was looking in on my comm feed and taking notes to prep Markus before it was his turn. I, meanwhile, got to vicariously enjoy a couple more massages.

Cades had been among them, and his answers had been met with approving laughter. He'd been sponsored by the Jeneretti, which I probably should have thought to figure out before now—you know what? No. Concussion says not my problem—and Deline Jeneretes had pronounced his hands "like the caress of a mountain," which had gotten a collective titter from the audience.

I knew our turn had come when Kuril stood up, announced herself, and declared her sponsorship of Markus. He came around the corner, hand still in the sling, which caused the audience to whisper to one another. Unusual for a contender to show up with an injury, I guess. Kuril had said it'd be okay, so I was assuming nothing too bad was about to happen.

"Let the contender step forth," said the priest again, hand going to his sword.

Markus must have been forewarned about the hand-choppy thing because he didn't jump at all when the blade went to his throat. I was half expecting him to do some kind of Jason Bourne thing and disarm the priest, but I guess Markus wasn't the trigger-happy kind of badass.

"These are the halls of the god himself," the priest said, maybe a bit more pointedly than with the others? Did he know something? Markus was a new face, I conceded. "Your *hands* must be as his hands. Should those hands transgress, they shall be removed."

"Let it be so," Markus said solemnly, the strength of his belief evident through the clarity of his words.

Wait a second. Markus was a Velean. He didn't believe in—god dammit his hand amplifier must be running already.

"Then pass," said the priest, a bit more respectfully than he'd opened with. But his resting bitch face seemed to deepen a bit when he looked at Markus's wounded arm. Oh, our cover wasn't blown, it was just ableism. Wonderful.

"*Here we go,*" said Abby. "*Markus, we're standing by.*"

There was no way Markus was going to win the pentathlon, so we were counting on an outright victory here to secure the dual laurels we needed. Markus was at a disadvantage as far as training went, but no one else would have the advantages we could give him. The Therians were only human. Eifni Org, on the other hand, had stolen the fire of the gods.

Kuril had already taken off her shawl and wrap, allowing Markus to start rubbing the back of her neck. Oh man, that looked so relaxing. I was definitely getting him to practice on me for the next competition.

Lady Gamourin was the first to toss out a question.

"What is the grace of the body?" she barked at him.

I tried to remember what the other guys had answered. I looked over at the bench where they were all sitting, saw the confusion on their faces, and realized they hadn't been given this question at all.

"Is that allowed?" I asked the girls on my bench.

Alceoi tore her eyes away from Markus's chest and looked at me with nearly disguised irritation. "Of course, they can ask whatever they want."

I let her get back to ogling and watched Markus, who was deep in thought, nodding slowly as he considered. The room was silent except for the faint noise of the massage as he commanded our attention with just his contemplation.

(A mile away, Val and Abby listened as their philosophy tutors answered the question.)

"You ask me that question so I can speak of the Twelve Virtues," said Markus with a slight smile. He seemed so *wise*. "You would force me to say that this wounded arm of mine lacks grace. And perhaps it does. But it is the grace of men to stand between blades and the innocent, Lady Gamourin. If it happened again, I'd give the other arm and smile."

There was some pounding of feet at that answer, quickly silenced when Gamourin glared around the room.

Lady Heste was next, the judge for the Henadim family. This question, at least, had been asked before.

"What is the justice of the gods?" she asked.

Markus nodded thoughtfully, and we all got the sense that it was an important and worthy question and Lady Heste was wise for even thinking to ask it. The pause was purely for dramatic effect; as this was one of the repeat questions, he'd already worked out an answer with Val.

"That all things come in their time," Markus answered at last. "That those of grace are elevated, that the pious are given aid."

Actually pretty banal, as answers go, and some of the other competitors had said similar things. But they just didn't have Markus's augmented stage presence or the aura of deep wisdom clinging to their every word and movement.

"Is it abominable for a woman to direct her husbands to have sex with each other, as it would be if they had no wife?" asked Lady Deline.

I almost snapped "*What?!*" at the top of my lungs but settled for subvocalization instead. There were just—so many things wrong with that question.

"*Keep the line clear,*" said Abby, unfazed by the homophobia.

Fucking hell. Yeah, okay, I was shedding no tears over this op. I looked over at the other competitors and was slightly relieved to see they looked a bit uncomfortable, too. They were rooting for Markus, I realized, and from the tension in their body language this question was easy to mess up.

Markus let out a slow "hm" as he kneaded below one of Kuril's shoulder blades. Over the comms, I listened to our philosophers giving all sorts of caveats so they could avoid answering the question. Markus was on his own here.

"The temperament of man is fire, as the sages have spoken," he said, a piece of Kabiadesian theology we'd picked up yesterday. "Our wills are very strong, and to entangle them would be to have them burn twice as fast. That is why relationships between men are competitive, and a sexual relationship would be no different. A family must be cooperative instead, or it will crumble. For that, a man needs a woman to guide him."

He paused, switching over to Kuril's other shoulder blade.

"*I cannot believe I'm listening to this,*" I said.

"*Keep the line clear, Lilith,*" said Abby.

Markus began speaking again. "If, as you suggested, a woman bids her husbands to have sex with each other, then her influence is present as well as their fires. It is her wisdom that can temper the competitiveness that would inherently develop. But I could not tell you under what circumstances she might succeed or fail. That is women's wisdom."

I was completely aghast at the *stupid* things they believed here, while simultaneously impressed at how wise an answer that was, and how well he had navigated the details, and holy fucking Darwin was Markus an expert with that hand amplifier.

Everyone else, however, was stomping wildly, blind to the idiocy of their own culture. I suddenly felt very isolated. Alceoi was a bit more subdued about her reaction, maybe she didn't buy this shit? And Roel wasn't stomping, but was that because she hadn't bought into the homophobia or just because she hadn't been paying attention? What about the other men, surely about 10 percent of them should be feeling like crap right now, did they just hate themselves?

I felt like the time I went home for Easter and Uncle Richard started going on how women shouldn't get jobs because it means they're not submitting to their husbands and everyone just started *nodding* as if they didn't understand *you can't fucking say that*. But I was the only one in the room who agreed with me.

And, like, this was probably just me overreacting. I knew Markus couldn't mean any of this, I'd met his fucking boyfriend a couple years ago. Ylmir was like the chillest guy I've ever met! They split up because Markus was being deployed for this mission, not because of some kind of competitiveness thing! How did the Therians all *not* notice that people actually have different personalities?

"Lilith, your vitals are spiking," said the commander. *"I need you to meditate and calm down. You almost certainly have eyes on you."*

Repressing a grimace, I tried going back to my breathing exercises. I wasn't stomping, but I hadn't stomped for anything else—the plan was to blame my concussion if anyone brought attention to my behavior. Because, well, my head would actually hurt if I stomped.

"How do you judge his . . . hand?" asked the priest when Markus had concluded.

"His *hands* were wonderful," said Kuril, replacing her wrap and shawl.

"Lady Kuril," said Gamourin, smiling poisonously, "don't lie for the sake of a cripple."

"I felt one hand for a span," Kuril replied, ice in her tone. She gestured at Roel, who looked nervously around the room as she became the center of attention. "The other I will feel for the rest of my life."

Gamourin didn't have anything to say to that, possibly because I'd palmed *my* hand amplifier and absolutely smashed her with "what a good comeback"—I had it on speed dial. *Sic semper bigotus*, bitch. Markus stepped away from the dais, sitting down next to Cades. After a couple more guys, it was time for the judges to vote.

"Excellent work, team," said the commander. *"Markus, your performance was excellent."*

"Thanks, commander," he said. *"Hey Lilith, what's getting to you?"*

"These people are savages," I said. *"And we can't break them fast enough."*

I ignored the look of concern he gave me from across the room. Whatever, meathead, you can't corner me until we're back home.

The votes came in. Markus won laurels.

But Cades won first place.

Calmly, reasonably, I decided I was going to burn their world down.

CHAPTER TWENTY-EIGHT

Ambush

It was midmorning by the time I exited the building with Roel and Alceoi. The latter, to my annoyance, was ignoring all my subtler attempts to get her to go away, and I was too brain fogged to figure out if escalating further would be damagingly rude. The crowds had grown since this morning, and a lot of delicious smells were drifting over from the cooking stalls. It was overstimulating, and my head hurt.

The pentathlon wasn't starting just yet, so we had to kill some time. I was about to suggest turning around and killing it indoors when Roel spotted Markus, who was talking with Cades.

"I'll be alright," Markus said to Cades, patting him on the back.

"I didn't deserve this," Cades replied, fingering the laurels on his chest. "You spoke with such elegance."

"Next time," Markus promised him. "I'm sure your performance was worthy enough."

"Always," Cades said, a flicker of his boisterousness reappearing for a moment. "But hear me, Thala, that was nothing but disdain for an honorable wound. The people of Vitareas are too comfortable with peace."

"Yo, boys," I said, walking up with the girls.

"Godsmile, Lady Ajarel," said Markus just a bit pointedly. I pursed my lips at him. Gotta hand it to the Veleans—much more subtle than eye-rolling.

"Lady Ajarel!" said Cades. "You *must* agree with me."

"Sure," I said, trying to tamp down the burning sensation in my gut and mostly managing.

"Godsmile, Cades," Alceoi said with an edged tone. Cades's face turned wary at that. Shit, was *he* scared of her? Was I missing something?

"Forgive my rudeness, Lady Alceoi, Lady Roel," he said hurriedly. "I'm just caught up in the judges' decision—they've done Thala *such* an injustice—"

"Your emotions are running away with your heart," Alceoi interrupted him. "Center it."

"Whoa! Calm down," I said.

The look she gave me was *almost* disdainful, but she seemed to catch herself and reset her expression to blankness. Friggin' mongooses everywhere. "It's just the custom here, Lady Ajarel."

From the look on Cades's face, I doubted that was all that was going on, but I didn't know how to pursue it. I needed my brain back. Val couldn't finish those repairs fast enough.

"In any case," said Alceoi, turning to Cades, "the god has entrusted our honored judges with discerning the grace of the contenders who compete in his honor today. Don't forget it."

"I'm sure he gets it," I said. "We're good."

Alceoi looked at me searchingly, then shrugged with her head. "Then we're good." She frowned briefly, then messed with one of the trinkets in her hair. "I think I've dislodged something."

Roel and I chuckled politely.

"Welp, are we heading home?" I asked Markus.

"I'm competing," he said.

"You're competing!" said Cades in surprise.

"But there's no way you'll win," Roel said.

"Sometimes you try it anyway," said Markus with a smile.

"*Reputation building or something?*" I subvocalized to him.

"*Next competition I'm going to be* everyone's *favorite*," he shot back with an etheric laugh. I swear, the man was just irrepressible. The loss—or not getting first place, if you wanna be technical about it—wasn't affecting him at all. What a guy.

Then I realized I was being way too fond of him for my current state of grouchiness and did a comm scan. Hand amplifier. I fucking knew it.

We got premium seats for the start of the pentathlon since Kuril was one of the judges. Alceoi was off getting us food, probably so she could win back the points she'd lost with me for chewing Cades out. Speaking of which, Cades was warming up on the other side of the arena, near Markus. Markus was trying to warm up, but the sling was giving him some trouble, which I assumed was the cause of at least some of the deafening audience chatter making my headache worse.

"I'm going to need to lie down after this," I told the girls.

"You don't need to stay," said Kuril. "I'll have the servants bring the carriage around."

"I'm staying," I said. "We owe him that much."

Kuril nodded. "You're both so courageous. Thank you again."

"Thank you," Roel echoed softly.

"You're welcome, kid," I said, rubbing her shoulder. I would have gone for ruffling her hair, but it had, like, eighteen overlapping braids in it, and messing up someone's hair over here was like drizzling mustard on someone's tuxedo while you stared them dead in the eyes. Roel shifted her shoulder away from me with a pout.

"You're just calling me that to annoy me," she said.

"Absolutely," I said happily, leaning back in my chair.

"Well, stop," she said.

"Saved your life," I said. "I get unlimited annoyance privileges."

Kuril started laughing.

"If we're being precise, *Thala* saved my life," Roel countered. "You just stood there and got knocked silly."

"Hey!" I said. "No fair!"

"She did distract the assassin for a moment," said Kuril. "Doesn't that mean she can annoy you momentarily?"

"Yes," said Roel, thinking quickly, "but only a really brief one. The blink of an eye. So it's too short to do anything, and practically it means not at all."

"Sounds good to me," I said.

Roel looked at me suspiciously. I poked her.

"No!" she said. "You can't! That was much too slow!"

I laughed and poked her again. She poked me back. "Ow! Injured!"

"Roel!" Kuril said, giving me a glare that said she couldn't rebuke me directly but thought I deserved it. "Act like a lady!"

Roel and I apologized sheepishly, then made faces at each other. Alceoi chose that moment to return with the food—by which I mean she returned, and she also had three attendants, and *they* had the food—so we had to quickly shift back to our original positions and pretend like we hadn't been doing anything indecorous.

In Vitareas the local food culture involved a lot of pastries with random fillings—kinda like smaller piroshki, if I had to pick an Earth equivalent—so we ended up with a couple platters piled with them. Stadium food is stadium food anywhere in the multiverse, I guess. Alceoi had also found a jug of wine somewhere, which I probably shouldn't be drinking. My cup was already half-empty.

"These are delicious. How full was the cook's beard?" Kuril asked Alceoi.

"Exemplary," Alceoi drawled, to laughter from the other two. I joined in like I got the joke.

The opening words of another priestly blessing told us that it was time for the pentathlon to start. The competitors lined up at the edge of the course, body language full of anticipation. Then they were off with a shout. Markus, surprisingly, was out in front, with Cades close behind him.

Except the other contenders seemed like they weren't trying all that hard to catch up. The foremost were staying, like, one step behind Cades. And Cades was one step behind Markus.

"*No fucking way,*" I subvocalized. "*He did this with thirty minutes and a hand amplifier.*"

"*Incredible,*" said Val. "*Put him up for commendation when we return, commander.*"

"*I'm guessing Cades bears partial responsibility,*" said the commander. "*It'll be impossible to say he's colluding with Lirian now that he's publicly let Markus win.*"

"Are they . . ." Roel said, looking at me.

"Yes," said Alceoi, handing me a pastry. "Lady Ajarel, your friend's charisma is dangerous."

I nibbled at the pastry, dumbfounded, as the pack of naked, sweaty men ran out of our line of sight. But not before we heard a familiar voice's bellow echo across the arena: "Honooooooor!"

"Cades," I said. "What a guy." The other ladies made noises of agreement.

I had no idea if Markus could win at the other events, but it didn't matter. If he placed first here, he'd earn laurels. Against all odds, we'd done it.

I helped!

My cup of wine was empty now, which was unfortunate, so I signaled that I wanted a refill. That reminded me that I really needed to go to the bathroom, which I really didn't want to do because did I mention that they had public toilets here? I don't mean like restaurant bathrooms, I mean like literally a bench on the side of the road with a hole that drops into a pipe with running water. I can barely handle the bathroom at Starbucks, I had no idea how I was going to handle this. But I also couldn't hold it, so probably my best bet was to cloak and hope no one else needed to use it while I was there.

You'd think that absolute social terror would prevent your bladder from betraying you like this, but unfortunately intelligent design is a fucking lie, and bodies don't work the way they should.

I excused myself, waved off Kuril's offer of an attendant—that would raise *so many* awkward questions—and set off in search of one of those roadside-toilet thingies. But I didn't look too hard because if I found one I'd actually need to use it. Yes, I know that doesn't make sense, but how about *you* try taking a piss on a public street. See how motivated *you* are.

I ended up in a street that didn't seem like it had much traffic, which was great in terms of public decency and not so great in terms of the knife that was suddenly pressed against my throat.

"Be silent," said a familiar voice from behind me.

Fuck. It was Lirian.

Adrenaline jolted through me. I felt my whole body get ready to fight or run or something, which was counterproductive because if I moved the wrong way I was definitely getting my throat slit. I didn't speak. I didn't even subvocalize anything because I had no idea if she'd notice the micromovements in the region of my mouth and throat. I didn't dare cloak because if she forgot my throat was there she might cut it by accident.

The best I could do was a nonverbal emergency ping. Pretty sure she couldn't detect my soul activity.

"Good," the cloaky asshole said. "Hands find their way."

I had no idea what that meant, so I didn't say anything.

"Lilith, are you okay?" the commander said immediately.

Emergency, I pinged back.

"Val and I are en route to your location," she said.

"Hands find their way," Lirian said again.

"Where?" I asked.

She ignored me. "Why did the Vitaressi hire you?" she asked.

"They didn't," I said carefully. Couldn't press too hard or she'd go after them anyway.

"Unlikely. Try again."

"Do you have a truth-detection method?" I asked. "Use it."

"I am," she said, putting a little more pressure on the knife. "So you have a truth-detection method. Tell me about it."

"I don't," I lied.

"If your next answer isn't satisfactory, you'll bleed," she said. "What do the Vitaressi know?"

I racked my fuzzy brain for ideas. They all sucked. I decided I just needed to stall her until the cavalry arrived. I opened my mouth to speak, then was interrupted by a stomp to the back of my knee as Lirian quickly shifted her hands to my shoulders. I went down hard, the impact with the ground jostling my aching head, then she bodychecked me to the ground.

Then she grabbed my left wrist and jammed the knife right through the back of my hand and into the grounddirt. I screamed. Sharp, *sharp* pain, whiting out my thoughts for an eternal, excruciating moment.

"What do they know?" she said calmly. The smugness from our first meeting was gone, leaving only cold professionalism.

"I'm just a guest!" I shouted, then screamed as she twisted the knife.

"We can do this for as long as you like," she said. "We're shrouded by the Lady of Secrets. No one can hear you. No one can find you."

I pinged *emergency* frantically. I didn't get a response.

"I'll fucking kill you," I said.

"Interesting response," she said neutrally. "I'll give you a moment to spend your resistance. Then we'll go back to knife wounds when I don't like what you say."

Should I just flash? I didn't want to, but it had to be better than bleeding out from a bunch of stab wounds. Fuck, it hurt. I could cloak. Maybe she'd think I got away somehow. Except apparently my cloak looked like a blessing of Meris, and maybe she'd been trained in dealing with those.

Give her what she wants for now. Minimize stabbing. If I could make it back to the *Ragnar*, I'd be okay, Val could patch me up.

If he can find me.

"I'm just a girl from out of town," I tried. "You're paranoid."

"You're a terrible liar," said Lirian. "And you are *ruining* things." She grabbed my hair and yanked it painfully upward. I gritted my teeth and groaned as she yanked the bloody knife out of my hand and started hacking at my hair. It didn't cut cleanly. Every impact cut some hairs and tore others out of my scalp.

"Ow! Fuck! What's your *problem?*" I shouted. I tried pushing at her, but the angle was poor to have any effect.

"That's all you have to say? It's your *hair*," she said. "What backward barbarian city do you come from?"

"Your mom," I said through gritted teeth.

"Congratulations, you just lost your ability to walk," she said. She dropped my hair and pivoted her weight. Oh shit, she was going to fucking hamstring me. I tried kicking to stop her, but she slammed the knife handle right into the bruise the commander had left on my head. The pain made it too difficult to think for a moment, and a moment was all she needed.

I felt a searing line of pain across the back of my ankle and screamed into the dirt.

When she shifted her weight, she'd moved off the part of my dress where my pulser was stowed. I jerked my arm in that direction, but just as my hand closed on it, she slammed her other knee onto my arm. I struggled to gain any kind of leverage, *something* that would let me fight on even footing while she pried the pulser out of my hand.

"You treated this like a weapon," said Lirian. "You have more secrets than anyone I've ever met. This continues until you explain who you really are and why you're meddling."

Sudden, desperate inspiration struck me. I reached for my etheric cloak, slowly increasing its power to take the bite out of my various wounds. Once the pain was no longer affecting my behavior, I spoke.

"A truth of the eyes, of course. Congratulations, Lirian of Silence," I said, fading out of reality. "You've passed the test. We'll meet again."

Then I spiked the power, enough to disappear. Not overloaded like I'd done with Markus and the angel—I liked existing, thanks—but as high as I could manage in my adrenaline-fueled state. The pain of the knife wounds and the pressure of Lirian's knee on my back faded behind the dueling sensations of "you don't exist" from my cloak and "holy fuck you so definitely exist" from my adrenal glands.

No luck. Lirian immediately realized what had happened and began stabbing repeatedly near her knee. She got the ground a couple times. The other times, she got me. Arm, chin, shoulder blade. They didn't matter, the pain didn't exist. Lirian had my pulser, but I still had my hand amplifier. I reached down. Lirian couldn't see the movement this time, but I almost failed anyway due to her knee's awkward position next to my holster.

I grabbed the hand amplifier. No time to program it, every time the knife came down was a chance to hit an artery. I overclocked the hand amplifier's output and hoped whatever frequency was on there was intrusive enough to incapacitate her.

I barely reached her leg. The hand amp made contact—she immediately stopped stabbing, collapsing off me. The instant we were no longer in contact, I was alone.

I rolled painfully onto my back. There was no sign of whoever had attacked me. I kept the cloak up, quickly excepting the team from the cloak effect in case I disappeared again. Within moments Val and Abby were rushing around the corner.

"*Godfire, Lilith, what happened?*" asked Abby.

"I think I got stabbed," I said, struggling to stand up and failing. I looked down at my hand amplifier, which was in my hand. That made sense. "And then apparently I made a really devastating comeback."

Val immediately snapped his head up.

"Pulser!" he barked. "Check your comm shields!"

I didn't quite follow what happened—he snapped out a side kick, apparently at thin air, and bounced off as if he'd hit something.

"Attacker is cloaked," he said to the commander, scanning the ground near him for footprints.

The commander drew a telescoping baton from within her shawl. "*Get her to the ship,*" she said. Val immediately strode to my location and picked me up in a fireman's carry. I was starting to feel lightheaded. I reached deeper into the cloak to make it go away. No. Wait. That's not how it works. Don't do that, Lilith.

"Put that toy away," said the commander to the empty air. "You'll need more than that to kill me."

I could *see* something. Or—a *not* something. It was behind Abby—

I fainted before I could shout a warning.

CHAPTER TWENTY-NINE

Interlude: Sublimity

The perfect war begins and ends in the mind. You are the first and
the last of your foes.

—Eifni Voriksson, *The Road of Spears*

S he did not draw her gun.

The collapsable mace was cool in her hands, carbon fiber with a wooden grip
and contact filaments on the ball. Tungsten ball bearings distributed the weight of
the weapon for perfect balance just above the handle. The grip trigger was cleverly
positioned so that a slight change of angle was all you needed to start the electric
current on impact, whereas a different alignment would activate the kinetic-force
translator housed in the weapon's head. Adaptable, concealable, and lethal—it suited
her. And it would be sufficient for an opponent of this caliber.

The knife missed her because its wielder did not know how to cut. There was,
Abby knew, no one there. But *not existing* wasn't enough to prevent Eifni Organization
from preparing to fight you.

Abby stepped to the side and slammed the grip of her mace to where an assailant
might be if, hypothetically, one was trying to stab her. She felt the retort as the equal
and opposite reaction of an impact rippled through her body. There was no one there,
but that's what the kata was for. Abby fought nonexistent opponents every morning.

She swung twice—disengaging strikes, zoning off imaginary foes—stepping back
each time to pivot toward the threat's location. The fight slowed, the rhythm of the
surprise attack disrupted. She could not perceive an attacker. But the rhythm remained.
Now. She spoke the Challenge, the abbreviated version that had been cleared for use
in deployments.

"I am a warrior of the Old Ways," said Abby. "I give you this chance to surrender
the field. There will not be another."

Nothing answered her. Nothing had been warned.

Abby thumbed her hand amplifier to the preset for battle pride, a nuanced mixture of eagerness, ambition, and abhorrence of cowardice. In that moment she became
an etheric metaphor for unclaimed potential, the symbol of all that kept her opponent

from reaching the peak of who they were. Against all but the strongest of wills, there would be no retreat except in shame, a piece of their pride forever abandoned on this field.

It was no lie, no manipulation as the hand amplifiers were normally used. She was the gate. They would go through her, or they would die.

"Impressive first shot," said Lirian, lounging against a wall to her left. She was pretending not to be out of breath, pretending there was no bruise on her upper-left stomach, but there was too much muscle tension to hide. "But you won't stay lucky forever. Are you sure *you* don't want to surrender the field?"

Abby took in her posture, her words, her tone, her face. They told a story of pride, excitement, intelligence, power.

She was competitive, much like Lilith. The battle was over, then. All that remained was painting it.

"To the death," Abby replied, and stepped into threat range.

The opponent was gone immediately, but the battle was not, and Abby had known battle for nearly four hundred years. She closed her eyes and began fourth kata. Her favorite: elegant, smooth, versatile. A strike, a sweep, a step—she felt the air change, the absence of a blade striking for her neck—repositioned, transitioned smoothly into second kata—violent, punitive, unpredictable.

She knew the kick was coming because she'd seen it come in a thousand fights, so her mace was already swinging to meet it. She fired the kinetic trigger with an upward flick. It fired with a bass note and a thunderous crack, as it would if there had been an opponent to connect with. To the ground, then. Pattern ten, stomp kick into knee drop into falling hammer. Her kneepad broke a cobblestone, and the mace blasted shrapnel into the air (her face turned aside, perfectly timed with the kinetic discharge). A less-reactive opponent slain. Now imagine a faster one.

Sway to the side, duck, stand, step back. An opening in her guard inviting an underhand stab. There was no stab. She reversed the mace along her arm to twist the imagined knife out of its wielder's grip. Another flick of the mace and the *crack* of the kinetic translator shattered the air again.

A vase shattered on the other side of the street. If someone had been thrown into that, they would have broken ribs, maybe an arm, on top of the damage the mace itself could inflict.

The shards of the vase scattered, too energetic to have been pushed by something with broken ribs. Physical resilience beyond mere human. Abby's eyes were still closed. The shards had scattered closer to her. She turned her back to them, mace in salute position, counted to two, stepped to the side—the mace flicked out, electric contacts arcing, made no contact—into a feint pattern, then eighth kata, wide sweeps and quick foot movements. Deny the ground. She transitioned seamlessly to modified ninth kata, dodging and weaving amid her own strikes and a phantom knife seeking her throat.

"*We're safe,*" said Val. "*Lilith is stable. You can stop stalling.*"

Then strike home. Pattern twenty-seven, side parry into knee, elbow, stomp kick into bash into filament contact along the side of the neck. Maximum wattage, humming, crackling, spraying sparks and ozone into the air.

Which didn't happen. No discharge. She double-checked the weapon's battery to be certain.

Abby waited a moment for an attack from a new angle, but there was no rhythm. The fight was over.

"*Lirian is gone,*" she said. "*She vanished the moment I went for the kill.*"

"*The implications of that are concerning at best,*" said Val.

"*She might not have left,*" said Abby, before addressing the empty street: "Lirian! Remember that you chose to run."

Eifni had written: "In war, if you cannot strike at your enemy's life, strike at their pride. They will gladly give you their life instead."

Lirian had escaped today, but she had left her pride on this field. She would return for it.

Abby reflected on the battle, noting minor mistakes of form, re-creating her footwork. She asked herself: Was it beautiful?

She remembered the dance, the rhythm, the crispness, the decisive blows.

Yes, it was beautiful.

Was it true?

She thought about the battle pride, the kata and the patterns, the flow of the battle, leading up to a sparking mace smashing into empty air.

No, she decided. No, the story of the battle was false. It built to a killing blow, but when the killing blow landed, the enemy wasn't there. The rest, as Lilith sometimes said, was commentary.

She had been deceived. Lirian would not be the only one looking for a rematch.

CHAPTER THIRTY

Recovery

It was easier to lie in bed than stumble around the ship like a cripple. Which, if you want to be technical about it, I was. They had me on pain blockers, but not feeling the pain didn't change the fact that the fingers on my right hand wouldn't move. My left arm still moved, but not the way I wanted it to. Lirian's blind stabbing had caused muscular damage to my biceps and shoulder, and everything was horrifically inflamed. And let's not forget, of course, that if I wanted to go anywhere I had to hop on the leg that Lirian hadn't gotten to. It wasn't even my favorite leg.

Yeah, I could think her name again. Watch: stupid Lirian. Lirian's face is dumb. I hate Lirian. Lirian isn't even good at her job. Lirian thinks she's *soooo* much better than me just because *her* cloaking technology is *memetic* and not just etheric-signal obfuscation. Well, you know what? Divine blessings are just cheating. When you rely on divine substrate to perform miracles it's just wastefully overcomplex because gods don't need to care about efficiency. So really my cloak was better because it actually made good use of the power my soul generated.

I wouldn't need to suffer much longer, though, because Val had finally completed repairing the translation engines. No more lounging around in the med bay for me! Just as soon as Val finished replacing his leg. He *claimed* it was because he wanted to test the system on something less critical before addressing my concussion, but, like, you can get blood clots from your legs, so he was definitely making that up. He was totally just doing this because he wanted his leg back first. When I said that, though, he retorted that I'd need to flash to a backup body if the procedure scrambled my brain, so I didn't call his bluff. I was totally getting him back for this.

I watched from the neighboring bed as he extended the focusing relay from the wall and positioned it near the stump of his leg, now bare of the prosthetic he'd been wearing. The relay itself was a perfectly circular band of plastic, with multiple embedded channels to run both electric and etheric energy. Val typed a few final commands into his console and nodded.

"Commander, I'm set. Have you prepped the pig?"

You can build a leg from scratch with just the translation engines, but the energy costs are ruinously expensive. It's stupid to do that when you can just get the requisite etheric energy by translating something conceptually similar to your target.

In this case, an iron bracer, a set of dentures, and a freshly butchered pig.

"*One moment,*" grunted Markus. "*Wow, that got messy.*"

"Have you never slaughtered an animal before?" asked Val.

"*Not with a knife,*" said Markus. "*There was that war elephant on Juricha.*"

"*Boooo!*" said the commander. I started laughing—this was a familiar argument.

"For shame, Markus," said Val. "That was Abby's kill, and you know it."

"*I had him right in my sights!*" Markus protested. "*The bullet hit him right before she got him with the plasma cannon!*"

"*That thing was way too big to die to a single bullet, disruptor or not,*" said Abby. "*I'll give you credit for this pig, though.*"

"All hail Markus Swineslayer!" I said.

"Vanquisher of bacon!" Val added.

"*It's not funny, guys,*" said Markus, actually sounding a little hurt. The other two just laughed at him.

"Maybe we should back off," I said to Val. He considered me.

"Ah," he said after a moment. "You missed a cue. The slight upward inflection on 'guys' acknowledged the blow."

"So he was joking?" I asked.

"*It's more like a sparring match,*" Markus explained. "*I tried for a minor social victory, but they caught me out of position. So I demonstrated that they got me to reset the field.*"

"*It's the fact that he's done this more than once that makes it a joke,*" said Abby.

"*Sabotaging your team is treason,*" Markus replied.

"*Neglecting your training is dereliction,*" she countered.

"You're both sabotaging my leg and Lilith's totality," said Val. "Is the pig prepped?"

"Yeah!" I grinned. "What he said!"

"*Why yes, your majesty, it's been prepped this whole time,*" said Abby with an audible smirk. "*Did you need it for something?*"

"I'm owed some impatience, I think," said Val, looking annoyed. "You should have said something. Starting—now."

There was a faint hum, so low it was almost more tactile than audible, and the stump of Val's leg disintegrated before my eyes. He watched it dispassionately. There would be no pain—any experiences along that frequency would get filtered to abstract knowledge by the surgical equipment. Blood sprayed over the bed, dissolving as fast as it spurted—the engines were retranslating it back inside his spleen—then eventually stopping as his blood vessels knitted themselves closed.

The bone materialized first. But we were Eifni. We could do more. The *Ragnar* turned the bracer into the concepts it represented: protection and strength. What Theria had reified in wrought iron, we instantiated as carbon fiber lacing designed to maximize the bone's remaining calcium storage. There was still an effect on the body's calcium-retrieval capabilities, I knew, but Eifni's anatomists had compensated for that by inserting microfactories along the length of the shin and tibia. We used part of the denture energy to pay for that bit—they were modifications of the body.

Dual sterility fields, one encompassing the room and the other focusing on the bed, eliminated the risk of infection from any microbes that might try their luck piggybacking on the exposed surface of his new skeleton.

The reconstruction paused, and for a moment I took in the sight of Val just hanging out on the bed with one leg missing everything but weird, black-veined technobone. It looked like some weird kind of necromancy, the way the bed kept them all floating there. The bones gleamed with moisture trapped by the stasis field that was keeping them alive.

"Phase one is done," he said. "Precision is within tolerances."

The rest of us treated that with cheers. Val allowed himself a smug smile.

"Phase two," he said.

His previously stopped-up circulatory system grew out of his leg stump like some kind of weird vine that grows on air. Except the vines also branched into fuzzy red clouds that more or less outlined the shape of his leg. Look, I was concussed, I didn't have a better metaphor on hand, okay? It wasn't just the blood vessels, either, I also got to see his lymph nodes weirdly floating in the air. Presumably his nerves, too, but from across the room I couldn't make them out.

Phase three involved the slow weaving of muscle fibers and tendons around the vasculature that had been, so far, floating around the bone. The spaces between the bones filled in with spongy-looking connective tissue and tendons. The bones themselves were wrapped in dark-pink muscle tissue.

This was where the rest of the dentures came in. Interwoven in the fibers were occasional strings that looked like black threads—micropylons, the components of a system that would allow him to redirect muscle control from his nervous system to his comm. I'd heard of godslayers walking off broken spines with those.

Then a thin layer of fat sealed up the meat of his leg, capped off with skin. I'd expected the skin to come out nerd pale, but it was just as tanned as the rest of his skin.

"Nervous system functionality is passing safety checks," said Val. "This was the temperamental section. I'm happy to consider this the final test of the engines' functionality."

"Yes!" I cheered. "I get my brain back!"

"Was it gone?" Val asked. "I didn't notice."

"Shut up, bone boy."

"Bone boy," he repeated, deadpan.

"Shut *up*."

The operation was nearly finished. It concluded with a final sweep by the system, targeting anything conceptually tagged with "potential death" and translating it out of Val's body. Any blood clots, cancers, etc. vanished in an instant.

"Done," said Val. "I'm releasing sensation blockers."

"*Wait, wait, I want to see the look on your face when you do,*" said Markus. Val pursed his lips and swiped a control on his console. He immediately grimaced, hunching forward with a grunt.

"You okay?" I asked.

"Every sensation," he said through gritted teeth. "At once."

"Aw shit," I said. "Markus is gonna be here when it's my turn."

"*Did you start already?*" asked Markus, not sounding particularly disappointed.

"Swineslayer," Val grunted.

"*Wow, that's the best you could do?*" asked Abby.

"Yeah, that was one of mine," I gloated. The look he shot me promised vengeance. Don't taunt your doctor right before surgery, I guess. I blamed the concussion.

"I'm going to prep Lilith for her operation," said Val.

"Wait, what? No one told me about this," I said.

"It's a brain operation," said Val. "We'll have to put you in stasis."

"I'm like ninety percent sure you're—"

Val swiped something on his console and now I was on my back, staring at the ceiling.

"—making that up," I said.

"What's she talking about?" asked Markus, who was now standing in the corner of the room. He'd changed his shirt.

"He turned me off!" I said, but I was grinning too much for the complaint to have any bite. I was fixed!

"Lilith!" snapped Abby. "It's not important right now. We found something in your system."

"You were given a diuretic," said Val, looking serious.

"What's that do?" I asked.

"It induces your kidneys to release water," said Abby. "Basically, you left the contest to piss because you were drugged."

"I wish it'd been a fun drug," I said. "Alceoi?"

"You're suspicious of her because she's salient," said Val. "There were also three attendants and two cooks who had access to that food. Not to mention that Lirian could have been in that booth herself and you'd never have known."

"I hate it when other people have cloaks," I said. "Nerf, please."

They all paused a bit at that.

"Don't use that word while you're undercover," said Abby. "Velean doesn't have an equivalent term, so we just got hit with *competitive play adjustment* brushed with irony."

"Sure. Hey, my brain works now!" I said, wiggling my fingers and rolling out of the bed. "And my limbs! Thanks, Val!"

"Ah, yes, you should expect a sense of euphoria as—" he started, then was cut off as I glomped him.

"I love you, too," I told him happily.

"What about me?" Markus asked.

"You, too!" I said. "C'mere, you big cheater!"

"You surpassed expectations on that one," Abby told him as he crushed me in a bear hug. "Again, *excellent* job.

"The outcome was never in doubt," said Markus, releasing me. "I'm just too manly."

Abby got a hug, too. It was only fair.

"So what's the plan?" I asked her.

"You've got a trauma debrief with Markus," said Abby. "We'll debrief the op afterward. Then we need to plan your reinsertion with the Vitares family."

"They're not expecting us yet," said Markus. "I met with them briefly and organized a search for you. Right now, their concern is that the Cult of Silence vanished you."

I smiled. That hypothesis almost certainly came from Roel. Markus matched my smile and nodded at me, as if to say I was correct.

"Why don't you grab a board game?" said Markus. "Something simple for us to do while we chat. I'll meet you in the study."

"So the commander tells me you almost died today. Tell me about it."

I like to think I'm good at chess. I used to think I was bad at it because there's just too many pieces, and it's hard to figure out what needs to move where. Then I discovered that you can just keep forcing your opponent to take trades. Either you both lose a piece and the game's easier to think about, or they run away and you get an advantage.

Markus *almost* let me set up the thing where you fork the opponent's queen and rook with your knight, but he got his own knight into position to deny it right before I pulled the trigger. Suddenly my side of the board looked like a house of cards, and I'd have to actually think about how to get out of it. I sighed and answered the question.

"I was worried about the dumb bathroom thing, so I didn't notice she was about to jump me," I said. "I fucking hate that people just piss on the side of the street here."

"You've said before that the nudity taboo is stronger back home," said Markus. "We can work on that if you'd like."

"Ew, I'm not a pervert," I said.

"You know that's not how I mean it," he said with a smile. "Your move, by the way."

Eh, fuck it, threaten the knight to keep the house of cards going.

"Isn't there some kind of, like, etheric surgery we can do to get rid of it?" I asked. "Actually wait, culture's in the brain, right? If I switch bodies, does it just go away?"

"Culture is complicated. Sometimes it's better to handle things the natural way," he said. "And even if flashing was a viable solution, you'd have to be okay with it before it was a live option for you. Which brings us back to your near-death experience."

"It was totally unfair," I said. "I still did really good. Didn't say anything even though it hurt."

"You did a good job of showing why that style of torture doesn't work," said Markus. "Lirian made you look really cool for resisting it."

"Yeah," I said. "And I still got her before she killed me. So that was cool, too. It's still your move, right?"

"I think so." He took a pawn. "Did you consider flashing?"

"Yeah," I said. "Thought I could win."

"There's a trade-off here," said Markus. "If you flash too early, you might lose out on a winnable situation. If you flash too late, the pain can result in changes to your soul that carry over to your next body."

"Like what?" I asked.

"Trauma is one," said Markus. "Grief is another. Most grief isn't avoidable by flashing, but it's been demonstrated that a sufficient threshold of violence can cause existential damage as well as physical. The affected usually describe it as losing some kind of fundamental belief in the safety of the world."

My parents only watched and prayed to their god. I shouldn't have gone, but it was this or homelessness.

"In the name of Jesus, I cast out these demons of depression!" cried Pastor Barnes, placing both hands on my skull.

Nothing happened.

"Dig deep, Morgan! Feel the Spirit in your heart!" he yelled at me.

But I didn't. Instead, something tore inside me. I screamed at the deepest pain I'd ever felt.

Gunfire. Pastor Barnes's head snapped forward, splattering me with blood. My mom was screaming now, too.

"Target hit!" yelled a man, stepping out of nowhere. "Get the civilians out!"

The world blurred, people shouting, more gunfire, Pastor Barnes's body riddled with holes. My parents dropped to the ground.

The pastor growled.

"We can't!" shouted the first man. "Godfire! The girl's still alive!"

There was an otherworldly screech as the pastor's body lifted off the ground. I heard the office splintering. A woman screamed and dropped wetly to the floor. There was a sound like a massive gong, and Pastor Barnes was flung across the room. I was in someone's arms.

"Are you okay?" he asked me.

I realized with horror that I had forgotten how to speak.

"Oh, is that all?" I said to Markus. "No worries, man. That train left the station a long time ago."

CHAPTER THIRTY-ONE

Debrief

Before we debrief, I want to congratulate you all," said Abby. "The mission was a success, and we're one step closer to enrolling Markus in the Kabidiad. Markus, that maneuver at the end was outstanding. I think the rest of us had given up hope of a victory there."

We were hanging out in the lounge. Val was standing, probably to enjoy having his own leg again. Or as some kind of test to himself, I don't know. He was weird like that sometimes. The rest of us were ensconced in the extremely comfortable armchairs. I was fairly certain that they had built-in amplifiers designed to pump out the idea of comfort, actually.

"It wasn't me," said Markus with a smile. "Cades told the other guys what had happened. I'm a bit of a celebrity at the moment—none of the competitors are happy about the situation with Lirian. I was in the right place at the right time to serve as their protest candidate."

"Did Cades catch any flak for that?" I asked.

"Yeah, one of the Jeneretti came down and grilled him," said Markus. "It was pretty great. She asked if he was sure he couldn't run any faster, and he was like 'I could not have run more honorably.'"

"What a guy," I said.

"And a friend to wolves, too," said Abby, nudging Markus. It was an idiom on Veles—they mostly think of wolves as battlefield scavengers over there, so Abby was basically saying Cades could kill a lot of people if he felt like it. A lot of Velean compliments work that way, now that I think about it.

Markus laughed, a bit bashful. "I wouldn't mind a deep-cover assignment if it would help the operation."

That got a chuckle from the other two, while I tried to look like I knew what was going on.

"Really?" Val asked me.

"Shut up," I said. "Hey, we gotta move fast so Markus and I can reinsert with the Vitareas girls. Let's move."

Val smirked and inclined his head a degree or two.

"Self-critiques, everyone," said Abby. "Markus?"

"I am perfect," he declared, preening.

Abby snorted. "You shouldn't have thrown your whole shoulder in the way of the sword. You could have had an extra working arm for this whole operation."

"I am nearly perfect," he said, still preening.

Val chuckled. "That's the ideal, isn't it. For myself, I should have been monitoring Lilith when she left the stands. With proper overwatch, we might have eliminated Lirian when she attempted assassination."

"And I should have called for backup before leaving," I said.

"We need to get your social up, too," said Abby. "We'll work out a training regimen after this meeting. And my mistake was trusting Max to do dossier work for me. You could have had weeks of prep for this."

"She did well enough on her previous missions," said Val. "Personally I wouldn't have guessed."

"Thanks," I said.

Markus flashed a smile at me.

"Next item: we need to counter Lirian," said Abby. "Val, I know you did a sweep. Can you give us a confidence level that she's not on the ship?"

"High," said Val. "At progressive monophase, using weighted estimates for cult size, Meris can sustainably output around thirty *tetrons* per operative, and maybe up to fifty for her favorites. In her best case, the scanner needs about sixty *tetrons* to punch through the blessing."

His lips stretched into a thin smile.

"I gave it a hundred and twenty. She's not in range."

"What if it found her but the cloak stopped you from reading the results?" I asked.

"That would be proof of an enemy," said Val. "Cloaks can be intimidating to face at first, but eventually you learn that gods of secrecy don't understand information theory. Failure to read the results would give me exactly the information she would be attempting to obscure."

"I'm satisfied with that," said Abby. "We need to reassess her capabilities. As Lilith observed, she has not been subtle. That was apparently an act. Her hit on Lilith was executed professionally, and without our synchronous communication methods it might have worked. She also walked away after taking a hit from a force mace. From that, I'm inferring physical enhancement of some kind."

"A demigod?" asked Markus.

"Best explanation," said Abby. "A less-likely explanation is that she had some kind of blessed armor underneath her clothing."

"Roel said she'd been chosen by Meris," I said.

Abby nodded. "Demigod, then. Let's talk countermeasures."

At that, the mood in the room shifted. Val's attention sharpened, and Markus leaned forward in his seat. I felt a little warm at that. Lirian was kind of my enemy, but I wasn't facing her alone. She'd never know what hit her.

"We'll need to be more careful about our movements," said Markus. "MDOs should still work on her, right? The cloak seems to be countersignaling the idea of her rather than generating emptiness."

"Yes. As long as she continues blocking our comm scans, MDOs should work," said Val. "Lilith should probably work on absence meditations in addition to her presence meditations."

"What's with all the words?" I asked. "Someone explain the words please."

Markus cracked a grin, and Val huffed. The duality of man, I guess.

"MDO stands for mixed-detector overlay," said Markus. "We slap two or more sensors onto a processor, and it marks everything where their results don't match up."

"Infrared will likely be most effective," said Val.

"Got it. And absence meditations?"

"I'll go over it with you after the meeting," said Abby.

I gave her a thumbs-up and leaned forward in my chair. "She got my pulser. Can we track that?"

"No," said Val. "I've been trying at regular intervals. She's either not in range or her cloak is covering the signature. By conjecture, the cloak is active in her sleep, although it's possible she doesn't need to sleep."

"That's bullshit," I said. "Lirian is just bullshit in general."

"The war on the gods isn't *fair*, Lilith," said Abby. "This is about pitting our capabilities against the enemy's."

I sighed and let my head roll back into the armchair. "Yeah, yeah."

Abby started tapping her fingers on her armrest. "We should review Lilith's encounter with her. She repeated a code phrase twice—'hands find their way.' I assume that means she suspected Lilith of being another agent of Meris."

"Well, I blew that, so she doesn't anymore," I said.

"Don't be upset. That actually tells us a lot," said Markus. "If they have a recognition phrase, they must not know about one another's operations. That's exploitable."

"You also vanished," said Abby. "There's at least a measure of ambiguity there. The pulser will be the key. Her actions going forward will depend on what she makes of that."

"Androdaima," I said suddenly, sitting up. "It's a complicated device. The obvious conclusion is one of her worshippers made it. She's going to target the Vitares girls. We have to cover them *now*."

"Lilith!" said Abby. "Sit down. We need a plan first."

I sat. "Stab, stab, shoot," I said, bouncing my leg impatiently. "There, we've got a plan. I mean, come on, all we can do is wait for her to come after us."

"She'll observe first," said Abby. "She'll strike if we give her another opportunity. We can bait her."

"She's only gone after athletes so far," Markus told me reassuringly. "The girls will be fine."

"She knows I'm some kind of operative. Maybe she changes tactics."

Abby exchanged looks with the other two. "We can continue this meeting later. Val, can you rig up the MDOs? We should get those planted on the Vitares estate ASAP. Markus, escort him."

"Yes'm," they replied, scurrying off to the armory. I looked expectantly at Abby. There was something gentle in her expression.

"Spar with me," she said.

"Roel—"

"She'll be safe. Spar with me."

I took a deep breath, which sounded kinda shuddery because of the motion from my bouncing leg. I clenched my fist.

The practice sword slammed into Abby's foam-core armguard. She had two of them, a solid chunk of impact absorption strapped to each arm, and no weapon of her own. I still wasn't landing any hits.

"Good," she said. "I like your footwork. Controlled. You're favoring that overhand, switch it up a little."

I obliged, going for a lunge that she sidestepped and knocked away with her right arm. I swung from that side, the first just a feint for the follow-up strike at her head. She blocked them both, like I knew she would. The *wham* of the sword against the foam core echoed in the sparring room.

"You're telegraphing," she said. "I can see where you're going with all of those."

"You literally fought an invisible lady," I said.

"Then you can't afford sloppiness," she said, bringing her armguards together with a percussive slap. "Tighten your form."

I did. We squared off again, then I went for her legs. She danced backward, daring me to overextend. I took the bait, stepping in, sweeping the blade up from the side. Rather than take a hit to the thigh, she knelt, clasping her hands, and threw her forearm into the path of the blade with so much force it bounced away, jarring my hands. She lunged at me and before I could get back into guard position, she was pushing the blade aside with one arm and swinging with the other. I dropped on my back rather than take the right hook, trying to get the blade between us again. She backed off rather than push the attack, leaving me on my ass. I hated this.

"So is this supposed to be some dumb moral lesson about staying cool in the field?" I asked while I got up.

"Do you think that's a lesson you need to learn?" Abby asked, expression attentive but otherwise neutral.

"I'm not an idiot," I said. "I know what you're doing. It's just pissing me off."

"What do you think I'm doing?" asked Abby. We circled each other slowly, Abby content to let me initiate.

"Just, like, frustrating me," I said. I mimicked her tone of voice. "Do you think that's a lesson you need to learn, Lilith? Are you too angry to perform, Lilith? Aw look, the team baby forgot to learn her social skills!"

"Footwork," said Abby. "You're leaving openings right now."

"Everything's an opening to you!" I yelled. "You're a fucking ninja! I can't just close my—"

I stepped in and swung hard, right at her face, and I probably would have caved in her skull if she hadn't deflected the blow at an angle that missed her shoulder by half an inch. I swung back at her, once, twice, then shifted into a shoulder check when she shifted her stance to better take the sword hits. She pushed back at just the right angle to overbalance me, and I landed on my ass again.

"That's why you watch your footwork," she said. I yelled and swung at her feet, but she skipped out of range.

"Do you need to take a moment?" she asked. I bristled at the fucking condescension of it.

"Nah," I said through gritted teeth. "I'm fine."

"Okay," said Abby. There wasn't any skepticism in her tone, just professional neutrality. I knew she didn't fucking believe me, anyway. Whatever.

"Okay," I said sarcastically, doing a kip-up. "Come on, let's go!"

"I'm ready," said Abby, still judging me behind her whole neutrality thing.

"Just fucking stop, okay?" I said. "I get it, you're super controlled and everything. That's not why I'm losing the fucking spar!"

"I'm ready," Abby repeated. "If you don't need to take a moment, attack."

I yelled and went for the left shoulder, driving her back toward the wall. The blow made a solid impact on her armguards that she seemed to brace against. Some animalistic part of my brain registered that as a weakness.

"Fuck!" I yelled, striking the same spot again and again. "Fuck! Fuck this!"

"Lilith," Abby said.

I threw the fucking sword at her and rushed her with just my fists. Her arms went under my guard, but I got my right arm around hers, punching her repeatedly in the side with my left. She was wearing protective padding, but *dammit* I was going to make her feel this—

"Shhh," she said softly. I realized belatedly that her arms were around me because she was hugging me.

For a moment, I stood paralyzed by, just, everything. Then I buried my face in her shoulder and screamed. She hugged me tighter.

"Shhh," she said again. "It's okay."

"S'not okay."

One hand started stroking my hair. I hugged her back.

"You're going to be okay," she said.

"I can't do *shit*," I said. "I can't talk, I can't make friends, I can't fight, I can't—I can't—"

"Shhh," said Abby. "You're going to be okay."

She held me while I cried.

CHAPTER THIRTY-TWO

Absence Meditation

After the sparring/therapy/whatever that was, Abby sat me down in the conference room where I'd just met with Markus. I'd been dreading this debrief because I was pretty sure I'd done everything wrong. For example, the op ended with me almost getting stabbed to death.

In her previous body, Abby gave off this sense of absolute stillness. Now she was a bit more active. Her pale-green eyes never seemed to stay on any particular thing for too long, and her face quirked with slight emotions as she thought. Her posture was blade perfect as ever. The features of her face were informed by racial characteristics I had no context for, but they'd probably come from the area of Veles that corresponded to the Middle East on Earth. Brown skin, dark hair that she kept short. The guys were growing theirs out, along with their beards, but Abby followed an old code. Give the opponent nothing to use as leverage in a fight.

Give your subordinates nothing to use in a debriefing, either, I guess. She was waiting for me to start or something.

"So," I said eloquently.

"So," she echoed affectionately. "You seem tense."

"Uh, I'm not," I said.

"Shoulders," she said, nodding to them. "Fingers clasped. Jaw clenched. You're frowning."

I frowned harder, realized I was frowning, and tried to wipe my facial expression. I straightened my posture, too, something more formal like hers.

"Better," said the commander. "But you're still tense, and the effort you're putting in is making it more obvious. Will you entertain a critique?"

"I don't have a choice," I said.

"Of course you do," said Abby, leaning back into a more relaxed posture. "You can leave. You can talk over me. You can pretend to listen while arguing internally. You can tune me out and woolgather."

"None of those are the mature thing to do," I said. "This is a pressure tactic."

"Good," said Abby. "You don't want to be seen as immature, so I can use that to push you in certain directions. Watch out for that. Tell me, do you think you did a good job on this op?"

My stomach dropped as the sudden change of topic caught me off guard. I grimaced, feeling my pulse start to race. My chest muscles were clenching, too.

"No," I said in a small voice.

"You're wrong," said Abby. "Your mission objective was to locate and build rapport with a sponsor. Roel stood up for you during the ball because you made a connection with her. And you did it in the span of a single conversation."

"Not on purpose," I said. "And I flubbed everything else. You all had to cover for me."

Abby nodded. "That's exactly why you have a team, Lilith. But I need you to recognize what you did correctly so you can build on it for the next time. Don't focus on your mistakes. Contact with an alien culture involves too many variables to expect perfection, particularly from a trainee."

"I'm full status," I said, crossing my arms and looking away. "Besides, Val doesn't seem to think so."

"Watch that body language," said Abby. "Try again."

I blinked, reassessed how I was sitting. "How was I supposed to say that?"

"That depends," said Abby, her eyes crinkling softly. "What were you trying to achieve?"

"Complaining, I guess," I said. I was awkwardly aware of my body's positioning, and nothing I could think of made it seem more natural.

"To regulate your emotions, or to triangulate me against him?"

"What? No! I'm not trying to be toxic or anything," I said quickly.

"Try it," Abby said impassively.

"But—"

"Try it."

I blinked at her. No way this was good for team morale.

"Val's been harassing me about every little mistake," I tried.

"You didn't mean it that time," said Abby.

"It's hard to complain when you're ordering me to do it," I said. "Feels weird. You shouldn't want this in the first place, it would stress the team dynamic."

"I've let Val harass you, haven't I? Don't just complain. Be tactical. What do you need to present to turn me against him?"

"Not a complaint," I said slowly. "That's whiny, and you won't respect it."

Abby inclined her head, as if to say, "Go on."

"I feel like Val's expectations are unreasonable?" I tried. "Is that still a complaint?"

Abby raised an eyebrow. I was on my own for this, I guess. That probably meant the answer to my question was a yes.

"How about, you say that you don't have these expectations, but you let Val harass me all the time?"

"Would you ask a mark what will persuade them?" Abby said.

"How can you say that when you let Val nitpick everything I do?" I said, anger coming through in my voice. It wasn't faked.

Abby smiled at me. "Much better. But are you attacking me or Val? I believe the advice was 'Go for the throat.'"

I opened my mouth, closed it. "You two go back longer than I've been alive. What's my angle?"

"What do I care about?" Abby asked patiently, pale-green eyes not leaving my face.

"Team performance," I said immediately. Okay, be mature, be professional. "Commander, you say no one expects perfection from me, but Val constantly points out my mistakes. It's not constructive."

A look of obvious satisfaction spread across the commander's face. "That was excellent self-advocacy, Lilith. You invoked my duties without directly accusing me of neglect, which would create cognitive dissonance under normal circumstances."

"It took me like six tries to get it right," I sighed, putting my head in my hands. "And you're still not going to stop him. I can tell."

"Val is perhaps too traditional," said Abby. "On Veles, such probing attacks are considered friendly reminders to secure an exploitable weakness. In theory, you learn to deal with Val so that you're equipped to deal with Lirian."

"Why can't he just *explain* this stuff?" I asked.

"Spelling it out like that would be insulting," said Abby. "It means he thinks you can't figure it out for yourself."

"I didn't." I crossed my arms again.

"You would have, eventually," said Abby. "However, the custom is adaptive because it encourages self-directed development, and you don't trust yourself enough to commit to that. So we'll target your confidence first. Tell me what you did right with Roel and why."

My final appointment before I went back into the field was meditation practice with Val, who was back from securing the Vitares estate. There was no sign of Lirian; the girls were fine for now. I, apparently, was not fine, so I was sitting cross-legged with Val in the exercise room. He'd used the translation engines to grow his hair out all the way, along with a longish beard. Both the beard and his mane were braided, making him look kind of like an ancient Viking, but with beads in his hair appropriate to a Therian of middling social class.

"I gotta ask," I said. "Who braided your hair?"

"The braids were translated," he said. "I added the beads afterward."

"Okay, but you got the image from somewhere," I pressed.

He pursed his lips. "Markus and I made this recording about fifteen years ago."

"So you got to spend some quality time with Markus while he played with your hair?"

"You're being a child," he said. Abby's advice still fresh in my head, I smirked at him. Admit no weakness, convince both of us that I had come out on top. The set of his lips deepened, and I flicked my head to the side—the little Velean gotcha gesture.

"Almost," he said, face resetting to neutrality. "Commendable, however. Now, are you ready?"

I made a little frustrated sigh, and the gleam in his eye was a little too smug just to be a constructive attack. I tried to center myself. "I guess."

"In order to combat Lirian's cloak, you'll be learning absence meditation. Absence meditation is similar to what you do with your own cloak," said Val, closing his eyes, dexterous fingers steepled in his lap. "The fact that you are learning how to handle the cloak at the same time will make parts of this process easier and the rest more difficult. Expect to fail often at the beginning. But practice will build competence. The goal is to completely remove your soul from your awareness. Do you have an idea as to how that might be achieved?"

"Hold on," I said. "I thought people need presence meditations because they already don't notice their souls. How is absence meditation different from baseline?"

"Humans tend not to possess *conscious* awareness of their souls," Val corrected me. "It is, after all, the seat of their consciousness. But bracketing your *unconscious* awareness requires intentionality. For an absence meditation, you must first direct full attention to your consciousness, then banish it more completely than mere disregard can accomplish. This will allow you to function on sensory information alone, acting only as your body, which will render you immune to etheric trickery. But not, I should be clear, to etheric attack. A pit trap is less easily avoided in the dark."

"So, I have no idea how to do any of that," I said.

Val nodded. "It's good to be cautious of your limits when dealing with the soul."

I glared at him suspiciously. He didn't open his eyes but gave a little shake of the head. "It's serious time," he seemed to be saying. Whatever, Val.

After a pause, he spoke again. "Your consciousness is an illusion. Start there."

"Uh, no it's not," I said. "We can measure that shit."

"What is measured is just a substrate," said Val. "It is the stuff of you, but it is not you. Think on the difference."

"So what, I'm only imagining I exist?" I asked. "That's, like, Philosophy 101, man. I think, therefore I am."

He opened his eyes, fixed me with an empty look. "Is it you who does the thinking?" he asked. "If not, then what? Find it. Tease it apart."

His eyes closed again with a kind of finality that communicated that he wouldn't be answering more questions.

Okay. Find the thing that wasn't me that was thinking my thoughts. Well that was super fucking useful. I was the one thinking my thoughts, right? It was really easy to find myself. I was just—here. And my thoughts were here, too. Case closed, I guess.

Val was probably going to be annoying if I didn't give it an honest try, though. He was way too serious to do something like troll me over the right way to do this meditation. So there was probably something to it, at least. I closed my eyes and let myself relax. My soul was there, almost glowing in my awareness. My cloak was there, too. I could feel the activation trigger, almost tense under an etheric switch I just had to grip. I mean, hey, Val said it was similar, right? Maybe I could cheat. I started to slowly toggle the power—

"The cloak," said Val, "is an etheric effect, if you recall. I can feel you turning it on."

"I thought absence meditations made you blind to those effects," I accused him.

"I am performing both absence and presence meditation simultaneously," he said.

"Bullshit."

"Regretfully, you have no way of confirming that at this stage of mastery. Back to work. No cloak."

I shoved it off with ill grace and submerged myself in my soul again. There *had* to be some trick to this. What *wasn't* me that I could focus on? Because, like, again, *me* was right there, and that's where all the thoughts were coming from. It wasn't an illusion, which I could tell because *I was experiencing it*. Maybe it was like a meta thing? Like, maybe the thing experiencing my experience of myself was somehow different than the thing experiencing that thing? Fuck, I didn't even have words for these half-baked ideas, how was I going to organize them?

I decided to focus on the frustration to make it go away. That was something you could do in presence meditation. You focus on your soul, contextualize the emotion in the greater integrated picture, and let it run its course. The emotion wasn't my experience, it merely colored it. Which . . . I guessed meant that it wasn't identical to my experience, logically speaking. Maybe that was a good place to start. The frustration was not me, it was just acting on me. But it was also part of me. Part of and yet distinct. Ugh. I was getting nowhere with this.

A frustrated huff escaped my nostrils. Val didn't respond.

My thoughts cycled uselessly for some time.

"It's been fifteen minutes," said Val. "According to the research performed on this exercise, giving you time to explore on your own will increase your level of skill acquisition. Did you give up?"

"No," I said, trying not to sound defensive.

"Good job," Val said blandly. "The recommended next step is to induce cognitive dissonance. This will be unpleasant but effective. All selves have cracks which can be used to get at their inner workings. Do you consent?"

Don't show weakness to Val. Be confident. Be mature. "Sure," I said, outwardly unconcerned.

"Your relationship with Roel is a lie," he said.

"Nice try," I said, resisting the temptation to open my eyes.

"Don't fight stupid battles. Focus on the meditation," he said. "Examine the feelings that arise. Articulate them to yourself."

"I do like her! It's not a fucking lie," I protested.

"To yourself," he repeated firmly. "Recall that the life debt that she supposedly owes you was manufactured. The honor bestowed upon Markus is a lie—his wound was entirely for show and easily healed once it was convenient to do so."

I hated this. I clenched my fists. I wanted to argue, but I couldn't. I'd consented. I wasn't about to go back on that and prove him right about being weak.

"Cades threw that race over nothing," Val continued dispassionately. "You have acted as their friend, but you are taking advantage of them. They're worried about your safety right now, but you were never in ultimate danger, and you will never tell them."

I really did care about them. I swore that to myself. But nothing Val said was factually untrue.

"Is this hypocrisy the work of a unified self?" asked Val.

"People are complicated," I ground out between my teeth.

Val was relentless. "Complexity is the mark of a composite entity. Now find the seams in that entity."

Stop resisting. Fall forward. I wrenched my attention away from the pain and pointed it at the part of myself that wanted to give Roel a giant hug whenever I saw her. And at the part of myself that was impressed with Markus for cheating so well. They'd fought for him, not knowing we were here to destroy the entire institution. And I'd let that happen. I was a horrible person.

But if I didn't do this, one day they'd be eaten.

My conviction and my attachment strained at each other for a long, painful moment.

I caught myself turning on the cloak and stopped, redirected to the clash of self-concepts. Which one was me?

Both, the answer came. Neither. They were distinct from me, so they were not me.

"Your body language tells me you're making progress. What about the thing observing all of this?" asked Val. "Is that you?"

Yes, it was, except—that wasn't where I was located, was it?

"No," I realized. "It's just the observer."

"What do you feel?"

Fear. Grief. Confusion. Triumph. Tension. Anger. Elation. Freedom. Guilt. Exhaustion.

"I'm sitting," I said.

"Correct," said Val, and I knew I'd won.

CHAPTER THIRTY-THREE

Reunion

Val cut me up to facilitate my alibi for the Vitaressi. Etherically, not with an actual knife—we're not barbarians. These were definitely going to scar, which was cool on the one hand, but on the other hand I kinda wished I had some battle scars that weren't faked. The ones from Lirian were gone, courtesy of the translation engines.

I wanted so badly to see her face when she noticed that. Too bad she'd probably be invisible when it happened.

We'd replaced Lirian's more utilitarian stab wounds—mostly on my back, where no one would properly appreciate them—with a series of bloody frontal slices that were dramatic but mostly superficial. They stung. I'd nudged my cloak on *juuust* a bit to take the edge off. The commander kept looking at me like she wasn't quite sure if something was off, and Val hadn't made any comments, so I was pretty sure I was getting away with it.

I changed back into the bloodstained clothes I'd been wearing during the attack. The bloodstains didn't exactly match up to the wounds, but whatever—when they found me, no one was going to look that closely.

Abby walked with me to the exit of the artificial cavern where we were hiding the *Ragnar*. It looked like something out of an Indiana Jones movie—thick cables strung between lights spiked into the walls, illuminating a walkway of toothed metal. The ladder was gone—with the engines at full precision, we'd just put in an elevator that shot straight up into a hollow in the city walls.

Abby's hand paused before hitting the button to take us up.

"Tell me the rules of weapon safety," she said.

"Where is this going?" I asked.

She let her hand drop, leaning against the railing with a smirk. "It's a power play, obviously. Go on."

I rolled my eyes, recalling the list they'd taught me at the Academy. Same idea as the ones I'd learned on Earth, with minor variations. "Whatever. Rule one, weapons aren't safe even when you think they are. Rule two, pick your targets on purpose or not at all. Rule three, follow escalation procedure. Rule four, if I get killed by my own weapon then Instructor Hetle will track me down, resurrect me, and kill me twice."

Abby giggled. "You know that's not an empty threat, right?"

"No fucking way," I said.

"About a thousand years ago, a student got lethally disarmed during the final exam. Hetle was so mad, they pulled him out of the academy crypt and shot him again. Made him spend the lifestyle credits on both bodies, too. At first, rule four was just a joke among the other instructors, but Hetle decided to own it after a couple of years."

"Shit," I whistled.

"Anyway," said Abby. "You got angry during the Renathion. Any particular reason for that?"

"They were assholes," I said. "The real question is why none of you were angry."

"Val's an asshole. You're not constantly losing your cool with him."

"*I heard that.*"

"Back to the science mines, peon," Abby said, sharing a grin with me. "Well?"

"Look, it's just not right," I said.

"No disagreement there," said Abby. "We can demonstrate that etherically. Why were you angry?"

I gesticulated unintelligibly. "Because it's something you should get angry about! Are we done here?"

"Not if you don't understand this," said Abby. "Injustice is a waveform like any other, Lilith. As a godslayer, waveforms are *your* weapons. *You* decide who gets angry, who gets inspired, who feels entitled or threatened. But that means you have to follow rule two. When you get angry like that, you're shooting yourself."

"Not gonna lie, that's kind of fucked up," I said.

"Did you think this was some kind of vacation?" asked Abby. "We're not here to interface normally with this culture. We're here to tear it apart. You have to be above all of this."

"Yes'm," I said curtly. "As ordered, ma'am."

Abby considered me. Wordlessly, she pressed the elevator control.

They found me shivering in an abandoned building, bleeding from numerous knife wounds, bleary from induced exhaustion. The Vitaressi would never learn that Abby was the old woman who'd given them the tip, or that Markus had scouted the location during yesterday's searches.

I was bundled back—home?—in a flurry of activity, soothing words, worried faces. As I came in range of the walls, my comm overlaid sensor data on my vision, overlapping fields of vigilance against our invisible bullshit enemy. Lirian wasn't here. I dismissed the sensor data with a thought.

Kuril was present only briefly, patting my cheek with a glib comment about all the adventure in my life. Her words bled an etheric mix of relief and worry. The worry might be a problem—would she decide I was endangering the family and throw me out? What would happen to them if I left? For that matter, what would happen when we completed our mission and I had to go anyway? I didn't get a chance to probe—the Visionary had called a council, and Kuril was duty bound as the head of House Vitares to attend.

Roel didn't leave my side. She'd had a couple servants drag what appeared to be a lap desk into the corner of my room and spent most of that time sketching something she wouldn't let me see. When it was done, she promised. For all that she seemed terrified of letting me out of her sight, she ran out of conversation after about two hours of sporadic chatting. I ended up faking a nap while streaming a Velean romance novel from the ship's library. I'd had to pause this one right when it was getting good—Farkan had just betrayed the rest of his polycule to advance a couple ranks in the academic hierarchy, and Sevil was trying to convince the other two that it was all part of a larger plan because she might get audited if they deregistered at the same time.

I didn't see things going well for Sevil—she was kind of codependent, that gets punished in Velean stories—but maybe she'd catch a break.

When I got bored of that, I got them to bring me another lap desk so I could draw, too. Roel wasn't allowed to peek, I decided. Only if I got to see her sketch first. Hadn't really drawn since college; I'd taken an art class for elective credits and ended up being the one to draw character portraits for all the nerds in my RPG group. I'd also never used these tools to draw before. The charcoal stick wrapped in hard wax was at least theoretically similar to a pencil, but their paper wasn't the industrially emulsified wood pulp I was used to. The level of friction felt wrong. Therian paper was a lot thinner and texturally felt halfway between paper—Earth paper, I guess—and linen. I asked Roel what it was made of, but she just named a plant I didn't recognize, and the conversation stopped there.

Anyway, despite my various difficulties, I managed a pretty good sketch of a displacer beast. It's kinda like a panther, but with these giant tentacles that, like, teleport you if they touch you. Or something. I had to recreate most of the monster manual from memory, and not everything made it.

Kuril came back, looking very concerned, but she wouldn't tell me what was going on. She managed to pry Roel out of the room for long enough to explain whatever it was. Roel had to leave her sketches behind. She warned me not to peek. I nodded and promised her I wouldn't. She had a cool thing she wanted to keep secret. I could respect that.

About one minute later, I decided that as an honorary big sister it was my god-given right to peek, so I wormed my way out of the sheets, setting my lap desk aside, and stumbled over to her chair.

It wasn't art.

The centerpiece of her sheet was a series of drawings on a sketch of a human head and torso. In the first, the subject wore a complicated filigree headpiece halfway between a beekeeper's veil and the big straw hats that rice paddy farmers use to keep the sun off. The only clue that it wasn't just a fashion statement was a bulky box at the base of the neck containing some kind of spring. Roel apparently intended for it to be covered by the subject's hair.

In the second drawing, the spring had fired, and the headpiece had resolved into twelve independent mechanical arms swinging away from the head. In the third, the mechanical arms had extended to their full length, their tips retracting to reveal blades.

I wanted to dismiss it as some fanciful product of her imagination, but the pictures of the Head-Mounted Instant Lawn Mower were surrounded by some kind of script I didn't recognize. My heart sank. I couldn't read it, but even in another language I could identify what looked like equations.

Roel was designing a weapon. A stupid, impractical weapon whose only purpose was decapitating everyone in a three-foot radius around you. The kind of weapon you'd only think of building when you were in danger of getting stabbed by invisible people.

"Guys," I said. "Look at this."

"*Are those mathematical equations?*" said Val. "*This is an excellent sample, Lilith. Well done.*"

"Thanks," I said distantly. I was way too out of equilibrium to care about the praise. "But that's not why—uh, Roel drew this."

"*She's clearly inexperienced,*" said Abby. "*That much torque would sprain her neck.*"

"*You're worried,*" said Markus.

"That one," I said. "Okay, look, I know this sounds dumb, but—am I traumatizing my fake sister?"

"*This line of work can be emotionally taxing,*" said the commander. "*Normal humans aren't built for the level of deception we engage in, and it can be hard to accept the consequences that happen to the people we work with. If you'd like, I can have Val adjust the empathy on your next body.*"

I clenched my fist. "Do *not* pressure me right now."

Markus interrupted. "*Roel's just a kid, Lilith. This is probably just how she's dealing with your recent brushes with danger. It might help to think of it as Lirian's fault.*"

"I guess she did try to kill me twice," I said.

There was a pause.

"*Once, Lilith,*" said Abby. "*We faked the first one.*"

"Riiiiight," I said. "That happened." I was about to say something else to deflect the embarrassment—exactly *what* I had no idea—when the door opened and Roel came back in.

She looked at me standing over her drawings with an expression of surprise—which quickly flashed to hurt, then anger.

"Oh," I said. "Hi."

"You said you wouldn't look!" Roel yelled.

"Why is a teenager designing weapons?" I asked, gesturing at her drawings. "You're just going to get hurt."

"Excuse me, which of us is recovering from multiple stab wounds?" the little brat shot back, cocking a hip and glaring at me.

"It'd be both of us if you actually tried this thing on," I said. "There's way too much torque on this, you'll break your neck. And that's assuming you don't slice yourself to ribbons with a misfire."

She blinked at me, considering for a moment. Then her eyes shifted to my displacer-beast drawing.

"What's that?" she asked.

"Just some imaginary creature," I said.

"I heard Salaphi got attacked by a monstrous creature," Roel said, examining my face. "Did you see it? Is that what it looked like?"

"No, I just made it up," I said, waving a hand as if brushing away the tangent. "Look, Roel, weapons development isn't safe. You can't just do this unsupervised. Do I have to tell Kuril about this?"

"I just told her," said Roel. "Did you think I wouldn't? She just told me to have Peres supervise. I told you not to look because it was supposed to be a surprise. Now you're yelling at me in my own house!"

"I'm sorry," I said, sitting down on my bed. "I'm just worried. Lirian's not going to go after you, okay? It's me she hates."

"Her lackey attacked me during the ball," Roel said, stiffening. "She's still out there somewhere. I'm not you, okay? I can't fight. If she'd attacked me during the Renathion, *I would be dead*. I could have died two days ago!"

"Roel, I'm sorry, it's okay—"

"It's not okay!" Roel yelled, crying now. "Lirian's never attacked a lady of grace before. Now she has! And you won't tell me why!"

"Wait, me?"

"I'm not stupid," said Roel. "Thala and Kuril keep talking when they don't think I'm paying attention. And Alceoi, she kept making cryptic comments after you left. You can't keep hiding things from me after everything we've been through together!"

It'd been, like . . . a week?

"You mean, like, the ball and stuff?" I said.

She shrunk in on herself. "It was a line from *Mephele*. The sentiment felt appropriate."

"Do you want a hug?" I asked. She nodded. "Come here."

She nestled up against me as I held her close.

"I don't know what's going on," I said. "But we'll figure it out together. I'll help you, okay? You can teach me how the workshop works."

"It's a stupid project, anyway," said Roel. "I could tell Kuril didn't think it was going to work. The arms are too thin and I can't work out how to get thicker ones."

"I'm sorry." I wasn't sure what else to say.

"Did you mean it when you said we'd figure it out together?"

"I did," I said, because there wasn't really another answer.

"Do you promise? Not like when you promised not to look at my schematics. Do you *really* promise?"

"I promise," I said.

The lie felt like getting stabbed. Believe me, I would know.

CHAPTER THIRTY-FOUR

Fairness

Markus didn't win both laurels in the next Renathion. He placed in the pentathlon—Cades didn't hold back this time, which seemed to make them both happy—but in the massage competition the Jeneretes judge hit him with some kind of double bind on an obscure topic and we couldn't get a nuanced answer to him in time. It was a targeted strike. We weren't sure why the Jeneretti turned on us, but it was definitely political. Alceoi had deliberately avoided me, which was probably a good indicator of which way the wind was blowing.

Her expression betrayed nothing when she saw me, but she couldn't hide her surprise from my comm. She wasn't expecting me, which meant she knew something about the assassination attempt. At least she wasn't being blackmailed, I guess.

It was nine *thessim* until the Kabidiad, which meant eight opportunities left to qualify—seven, if we traveled by caravan to preserve his cover. We sat down with the girls to strategize about the situation and decided to try branching out for a competition or two. Kuril hired a local musician to teach Markus some traditional songs. He picked them up easily enough, but his execution was terrible. We'd have to stick with massage for the next Renathion at least.

"They're way too nasal over here," he told me. "It doesn't help that my imported muscle memory is all for soprano."

"You used to be a girl?" I asked.

"I learned to sing female." He patted me on the back. "I know you've had a lot of culture shock. It'll get easier. I went through it, too."

"Honestly, no, that's not the problem," I said. "I just can't imagine you without all the muscles."

"*Oh no, the muscles were there,*" Abby laughed.

Fortunately for us, the Estheni musical tradition valued expression within a certain set of technical constraints, so if Markus could hit a minimum level of competence, we could close the gap with ethertech and pretend the rest were artistic flourishes. Val was cooking something up for that. It was tempting to see all of this as unfair, and thus invalidating the hit on Kabiades—a couple weeks of training shouldn't put Markus on even footing with people who'd been doing this their whole lives—but it actually wasn't. I would know: I bugged Val until he walked me through the math.

"*Fine,*" he said. "*Why do you think cheating is unfair?*"

"Uh, it's unfair by definition?"

"*Almost. Fairness is a kind of justice. That's a simple permutation of the wave function. Cheating is unfair because it's unjust. And it's unjust because a fair competition is one in which contestants restrict themselves to a set of allowed actions while attempting to win.*"

"Right," I said. "So, Markus can't compete justly because he's got this advantage that the rules proscribe."

"*They don't, as it happens,*" Val said. "*The only precedent for competing with an etheric advantage are demigods, and the rules explicitly allow them to compete. But that would be arguing a technicality; you can infer noetically it's not enough to make it fair.*"

"Honestly, no," I said. "If I'm up against a demigod, I'm taking any advantage I can get."

Val paused.

"*Because if you did not?*"

I grimaced. "It . . . would be unfair."

"*Which is the point,*" he said. "*You would compete fairly against the demigod and unfairly against everyone else. And in practice that sort of competence discrepancy exists across multiple dimensions for every competitor. We can therefore posit a sort of background noise of unfairness, which does not meaningfully affect the fairness of the competition until a particularly meaningful intervention causes it to pass a threshold of significance.*"

"Aw crap, did I mess it up when I shut up that one judge with the hand amplifier?"

"*Possibly. It was, in fact, an intervention by a third party. But you can't say the rest of the audience was avoiding intervention, either.*"

"Yeah, that was bullshit."

"*Markus was injured, and much of that competition involved cultural knowledge he, through no fault of his own, did not possess. So mathematically he was actually at a disadvantage. So once we've demonstrated that, we execute a scope shift with Arnje's Equation.*"

I blinked. Arnje's Equation was the mathematical proof that godslaying was just.

"Wait just a fucking second—"

"*I will not,*" Val said fondly. "*You guessed correctly. Markus has to win to accomplish the ultimate goal of slaying Kabiades, which is just. We've already translated the cheating equation to justice. All that's left is to combine the two. Therefore, anything we do to ensure that Markus is competitive is just.*"

"Even, like, shooting everyone?" I asked. "Or disappearing them, like Lirian's doing?"

"*I said competitive. Removing the other competitors would invalidate the competition. Lirian's campaign is doing the same for whoever her chosen candidate is, but maintaining the competitiveness of the Renathion is presumably not one of her objectives. In fact, it's possible this represents Meris moving against Kabiades. Either way, as long as she's against Markus, we can just tally it with the rest of his disadvantages.*"

He walked me through them. I pointed out that Val hadn't included the part where Markus hadn't trained as much as the other athletes, but Val countered that they'd had much more opportunity to train than Markus. After adjusting for con-founders, Markus actually came out ahead on diligence. Which brought us back to cheating just enough to make things fair.

I love my job.

We got back to our respective jobs—mine a repetitive scribing task Kuril had assigned to me, Val's the endless work of updating the etheric profiles of the pantheon—before I had another question.

"Hey, Val," I said. "I just realized I never looked into sports competitions on Veles. Do they, like, measure fairness before games?"

Val chuckled. *"Why would we do something like that?"*

For my part, I was expecting the lifestyle of minor nobility to include more leisure time. I didn't get it. Alongside Markus's music coach, Kuril had discreetly hired an etiquette tutor for me. I knew she was probably right to do so, and Isseret was a gold mine for our sociological archives, but the sessions were, like, an hour long. It's not really the same feeling as when you're undercover and just trying specific things to figure out how the culture works. By the end of the first *thessim*, I came to dread her lessons.

I'd unwittingly revealed that I knew what torque was, so the sisters started dragging me into the workshop with them. "Workshop" was a misleading term for multiple project-laden rooms and an entire covered section of the estate's central courtyard. That was another source of stress, for reasons I really should have anticipated.

"Check this over for me," said Roel, plopping a starched folder on top of the pile. I was at the desk they'd had someone shove into the corner of the main construction room, which was a cluttered space that felt half its size due to all the shelving covering the walls and the display platform occupying most of the floor. I had to squeeze past a shelf just to get behind it, and sitting down was an athletic challenge of a level I'd not experienced since the Academy. Within an hour, I'd lost a third of its surface area to various tools, trappings, and two plates of wraps the staff had brought in for Roel and me while we worked. Roel's was untouched.

I'd not been initiated into the Sisterhood of the Wheel—the cult the Vitares sisters belonged to, one of many under Androdaima—so I wasn't allowed to actually help. Instead, they just had me learning the function of the workshop while I copied paperwork for Kuril. But I'd revealed I could read equations, so Roel was skirting the limits of what was allowed and having me double-check her math.

"Newton save my illiterate ass," I whimpered as Roel stared expectantly.

"I'm available if Newton isn't," said Val.

"I'll take it."

"Anything?" asked Roel. "I'm not sure about the last page. It feels like the spring should put out more force."

"The spring," I said blandly, spreading out the pages on my desk.

"Right, this bit here." Roel pointed at a part of the page I definitely would have picked out without her help.

I inwardly rejoiced that Roel was so thorough. In high school I'd lost so many points for not showing my work. Roel wouldn't have had that problem.

"The lines over those numbers might indicate negative quantities," said Val.

Grateful to run into familiar ground, I gave it a shot. "Maybe you have a sign error somewhere?"

"Sign error?" said Roel, brow furrowing.

Oh shit, oh shit. "Yeah," I said, trying outwardly to remain calm. "You know, where you've got a negative number, but you forget to put the little negative line on top."

"Oh," said Roel. Her expression relaxed into recognition. "That's a funny phrase for it. I know what you're talking about. Let me take another look."

She snatched up the papers and started poring over them.

"Thank Darwin," I breathed.

"You know she's only doing this because she wants to impress you, right?" asked Markus.

"That's fine, right?" I subvocalized. *"That's what we want."*

"It means she's handing those equations right back to you when she's done."

"Vaaaaaaaal! Help!"

Val continued to be my lifeline during those stints, and Abby told me later he was spending his free time trying to derive paraphysics equations with Therian numerals. What a nerd.

Masquerading as a literate engineer with legitimate expertise had one benefit: I learned a lot about the Vitares family business. They were an old family—their great-great-great-grandmother had literally founded the city—but they were constantly investing their wealth into new projects.

Only one of each, though. I grew up in a postindustrial service economy before emigrating to a culture I'd taken to describing as "fully automatic luxury space capitalism," so I found the whole thing kind of weird and inefficient. I didn't dare ask them about it. If I accidentally nudged them into inventing mass production, the commander might just shoot me.

Just when I was starting to get a handle on the math, I asked one too many intelligent questions about how the business side of things functioned. Kuril evidently decided I was smart enough to contribute and started making those little indirect offers to hire me as her secretary in her meetings. I'd managed to deflect so far by playing dumb, but Kuril had taken that as evidence that I needed further social refinement and scheduled more sessions with Isseret.

I could only dodge this so long before it got awkward—well, more awkward—so I was going to have to learn to read. The obvious move was to admit I was illiterate and ask them to hire another tutor, but I'd already bonded with Roel over reading, so that course of action would raise all sorts of inconvenient questions. I was reduced to sneaking into the house library after bedtime, cloak on, and streaming the contents of random books back to the ship. Between that and Kuril's paperwork, we had a good evidence base to work on. Abby took point on that, but it wasn't a fast process—especially considering none of us actually spoke Estheni. Our short-term plan was to try to get literacy tutoring for Markus and have me etherically piggyback on his feed, but there was still so much we didn't know about Therian social norms, and we couldn't risk offending our hosts. I hadn't made the request yet.

We were looking into finding a tutor on our own, but that route had a different problem—fucking Lirian.

She was following us. She never got close enough to the Vitares estate to trip the MDOs there, but we were all carrying shorter-ranged personal models. Whenever one of us left the estate grounds, we'd get little feather touches right at the outer range of the devices. Subtle enough that maybe you could mistake it for sensor noise, but our standard protocol now was to check in by thinking her name over the comm network. Apparently her bullshit extended to feeling out the range of our detection network, but she hadn't figured out that her antimemetic effect was giving us that information, anyway.

"Or that's what she *wants* us to think," Markus had said.

"Don't *say* that!" I'd yelled.

Of course, per *The Road of Spears*, any pattern of behavior is exploitable, faked or not. If she kept this up, we could finish her off. We knew so little about who her allies were or what her goals were. Our only lead was what I'd heard from Sela Kess at the ball.

So, after Markus failed to get laurels in passion at the third Renathion, we had him ask Cades out for drinks.

CHAPTER THIRTY-FIVE

Career Counseling

Isseret was dirt and stone—earthy brown hair graying to match her hard eyes. She had all the enthusiasm of dirt, as well. The colorful material culture of Vitareas had found little to no purchase in her fashion choices; all her shawls were brown, adorned in the traditional style with images and symbols rather than abstract designs. (I still didn't know what those meant.) The sole exception was a ruby earring worn on the left ear, indicating the second degree of mastery in her profession.

She was less than impressed with me. But that was okay because I had a plan.

See, Markus's working theory was that the judges weren't happy about Cades throwing that race back in the first competition. Punishing Cades would look like a strike against the Voranetti, and maybe invite Lirian to retaliate. After all, she'd gone after Roel! Markus, on the other hand, was a new face and an outsider. His only political connections were a dying house whose political presence was mostly notional at this point. He was a much less costly target.

Maybe we had a way out of this, maybe not. But this was finally an opportunity to pull my weight on the high-society end of things, and getting Isseret to help would win me some points with her at the same time. Theoretically, anyway.

"My mom always said it was a great joy to watch her students learn things," I told her. Importantly, I held eye contact to communicate that this was a request. But not so long as to imply familiarity. There's a subtlety to these things, you know. Isseret told me that a lot.

I'd learned a lot about the form of these requests in the past month. You were supposed to open with an observation about a perceived need of the other person, so that your request could be viewed as a trade rather than a favor. That functioned both as a face-saving mechanism and a way to honor Varas, Queen of the Goddesses and patron of commerce. I could personally do without the second part—like, c'mon, you can do reciprocity as an agnostic society—but those are the realities of the job. When you practice a culture, you worship its gods.

So in effect I'd opened by offering to learn something and make her happy. Now she had a few options. She could deflect, signaling that she wasn't interested or that I wasn't entitled to make a request. She could validate the offer (indicating that she was interested) or make a neutral statement (indicating she was waiting for more informa-tion). Or she could make a counteroffer.

"Let no one contradict her," said Isseret. "I hope to learn the truth of her words sooner rather than later."

"*Ouch*," said Markus over the comms.

"I've learned things!"

My tutor adopted a neutral expression rather than directly contradict a lady of grace. As if I couldn't remember her making that face, like, three days ago when she taught me that. A lot of these rules felt stupid and pointless, but every time I com-plained to the team about that, they laughed at me.

"Anyway," I said, choosing to interpret Isseret's words as validation, "I've been try-ing to follow your lessons while in public. I wasn't sure about how to act in this one situation, though."

Part of her expression softened at that. I guess it was harder to disapprove of me when I was actively trying to learn. I'd have her in my corner eventually.

"Such questions are within my duty as your tutor, Lady Ajarel," she said. "The formal request wasn't necessary."

"Aw," I said.

She threw me a bone. "You organized it correctly. I did notice."

I smiled. "So about this situation. I've got this, uh, friend? I think? Uh, Alceoi Voranetes. She sat with Roel and me at my first Renathion here, but now she won't talk to me. Or, like, make eye contact. I'm not sure what I did because she wasn't upset with me before I—before, uh—"

My mouth kinda just ground to a halt.

"Before you were attacked?" she replied, taking pity on me.

"That," I said, looking away.

"You are of grace," Isseret snapped. "Self-control is your first duty. Look at me."

I refused for a moment, clenching my jaw. Then I turned back and glared at her.

"If that decorum is what you showed the ladies at the Renathion, she might have wished to avoid embarrassing herself by association."

If this were any other situation, I'd have started unloading on her about what an ass she was being, but we were supposed to be using the top level of formality rules for these sessions. I didn't say anything.

"That wasn't an issue the first time," I said. "Let's say for the sake of argument that it was something on her end. What do I do? I'm worried she's throwing in with the Jeneretti to act against Thala and me."

"Perfect your behavior," Isseret said instantly. "Grace reflects the nature of the goddesses. If you embody it more fully, others will seek you out."

"That can't be all, can it?" I asked. "Like, they'll seek me out more if I'm wealthier."

Isseret stared at me. "Wealth reflects the grace of rulership."

Dammit. Okay, play it cool. "Oh, right. Okay, so, graces. How do I get those?"

"That is what we have been doing for two *thessim*."

I chuckled guiltily. Isseret continued not to be impressed.

"Can we focus on, uh, connection? I'm going to need it. What's my angle with the Jeneretti?"

"You're in no position to be asking such questions," she said. "I suppose Salaphi was too small to practice. First, recite the Wisdom of the City."

I hadn't memorized that particular litany—Gamalite, right? Yeah, sounds right—but I *did* have access to our theology archives.

"A city is composed of houses," I read from my comm stream. "A house of families, a family of women, a woman of body parts. Each has their faculties, their organs of perception, their limbs to accomplish their will. Therefore, as a woman's heart is the seat of her will, so does the city have a leader to direct its action. As she has a tongue, so does the city have emissaries. As she has hands, so does it have laborers."

Isseret's brow furrowed slightly, as it often did when I was supposed to be quoting something in Estheni. I'd primed her to think the problem was my accent. The probability that she figured it out was minimal, even if she obsessed over the problem: comm translations act on preconscious cognition, so by the time her brain presented the experience to her soul, it was too late to catch the etheric sleight of hand.

"Good," she said after too long of a pause. "What do *you* think you should do about the Jeneritti?"

"I guess they're supposed to be the heart of the city," I said. "That's not right, though. The Vitares family should be the heart."

"Is that an attitude that would endear you to the Jeneretti?"

"Yeah, yeah. Okay, so I gotta be a different body part. Like what, the liver?"

My tutor leaned back in her chair, rubbing a cheekbone with her thumb. "How you've managed to read so much without grasping any of it is beyond me. It's a metaphor, Lady Ajarel."

"The quote was very specific!"

"Toubos wasn't arguing that you can learn statecraft by studying anatomy," said Isseret. "The point is that we are all part of a body. To understand the function of a part, you need to understand its place in the whole. For the Jeneretti *and* for you."

"But I don't *have* a function in this city."

Isseret looked at me.

"Ah," I said.

Isseret looked at me.

"Fine! I'll find something to do!"

I thought about it while we set up for Markus's rendezvous with Cades.

The process was methodical. We'd had Markus take an indirect route to the op site, giving Lirian a chance to follow. I gossiped with him until we got the signal.

"I bet Lirian goes invisible whenever she tells a joke and no one laughs."

"I bet Lirian's never won a conduct award from the Cult of Silence because no one remembers what she did."

"I bet Lirian's mission actually ended a year ago, and no one remembered to tell her."

"*I, uh . . . Shoot, I lost it. I had a great joke.*"

"A joke about Lirian?"

"*Uh . . . Can you repeat that?*"

"Hey, team, we've got contact!"

The signal, of course, was Markus losing his train of thought. By gathering information so predictably, Lirian had allowed us to control her location. Markus's orders were to wander around the city and avoid the meeting point. That gave Val and Abby space to leave the ship without leading her back to it, allowing them to deploy MDOs.

They would be on-site, in disguise. Lirian had likely seen their faces when they came to rescue me. It probably wouldn't mean much in the end. Reviewing the footage of my, uh, attack, Lirian had claimed to be able to feel people's secrets, and all of us were probably carrying more secret knowledge than the rest of the city combined. But it would be stupid not to take an easy precaution because our enemy had possibly countered it.

In terms of equipment, we'd decided to leave the disruptor weapons home tonight to prevent the risk of Lirian stealing one. You can shield against a pulser, but if you take a disruptor shot, that's it, you're done. They both had knives, though. Local make, nothing from the armory that might raise questions about advanced manufacturing techniques. We'd used a resonator to etherically paint them with slowness and ineptitude. If it came to a knife fight, Lirian would hopefully underestimate how urgently she needed to dodge.

Then they were done, and it was just a matter of getting Markus over to the op site. Which meant I had time to do some fake career counseling.

"So about me picking a vocation in Vitareas."

"*Everyone was happy to court your favor when you looked like you were going to advance,*" said Abby. "*It seems we missed the window to take advantage of it. Lirian's assassination attempt might also have had a chilling effect.*"

"*With the translation engines at full capacity, we can start faking coinage,*" said Val. "*You could reasonably compete in any industry here. As long as you appear successful, you could gain support for Markus.*"

"I don't know how bribes work here," I said. "I could ask Isseret."

Abby pinged dissent over the comm. "*Worship of Varas emphasizes exchange of values. The Jeneretti will be mindful of that. This will have to be presented as an investment.*"

"Maybe I could go back to Lady Obol and offer her something. I have no idea what. But, you know, something."

"*I can inquire after her interests.*"

"The secretary job would really be the best," I said. "That way I'm elevating House Vitares at the same time. You know, demonstrating loyalty for the connection grace. Shame we're backed into a corner with the literacy stuff."

"Commander, what's your risk tolerance on either of us attending the sebekos*?"* asked Val, using the local name for the temple of Lorana.

"Lirian's already poking around the primary exit," said Abby. *"We cannot risk the ship."*

I shivered. "Yeah, okay, no. Markus is almost there, let's finish this later."

Lirian boarding the *Ragnar* would be catastrophically bad for numerous reasons, but the most important one was that we had to assume there were no more godslayer ships on this planet. If Veles lost contact with all of them, Theria's threat level would be escalated to "severe."

That is not just a bureaucratic category. It is Eifni Organization's best guess as to whether a pantheon is capable of producing a triphase god and ending us all. The risk of an omnipotent divinity overflowing its universe and overwriting reality with its essence cannot be tolerated.

They would burn Theria to glass.

I'd, uh, just have to go into carpentry or something.

CHAPTER THIRTY-SIX

Totally a Date

I'd told the girls I was turning in early. Kuril wasn't too happy about that—I could tell she'd been trying to get me alone for a day or two—but let me escape this time. I'd been conspicuously yawning as we all sat in the library, and I made a show of stumbling out like I was asleep on my feet.

Kuril was really angling for me to take that secretary job. I could probably push it another couple days, but then I was going to have to think fast if I didn't want to risk blowing my cover.

Alone in my room, I shuttered the ghostlights and pulled out the lockbox that allegedly contained my personal belongings. In reality it was just a combined transmitter and console. I didn't even open it, just felt it out with my comm and ordered it to connect. My world expanded as my noetic bandwidth grew exponentially. I felt like a fucking wizard, reaching out across astral space with the power of my mind.

"Ops is online," I told the team. "Syncing feeds."

My comm code unlocked four bright points of light in etherspace. I ignored mine and focused on the other three: one a shining pool of liquid stillness, one the inviting flicker of a crackling bonfire, and one the cutting precision of a laser.

I synced Abby first, leaning against a wall and chatting up some black-bearded dude in a sparse shawl. I could tell she was talking on autopilot as her eyes scanned the crowd. The dude probably didn't notice, since he wasn't making eye contact. Abby had full vantage of two streets, including partial visibility of the bar the guys would be frequenting tonight, but Abby's dude was big enough that she wasn't immediately visible to the street.

"Abby, check."

"*Copy.*"

Val's feed was next, from his vantage point in a shadowy corner of the room. Leave it to Val to pull a fucking Aragorn. I bet he'd have gone for a hood if that was fashion appropriate here. The bar had one wall exposed to the open air, and from the way his eyes were tracing the buildings across the street, I could tell he was thinking about enemy firing positions. There were a lot of fit dudes in here—we were close to the arena, it was a popular spot for the athletes to hang out—who Val was mostly ignoring. I got the sense he'd already performed a sweep and judged there was nothing more to learn. As I watched, he caught a new guy walking in, efficiently checking him over for concealed weapons.

"Val, check."

Val's field of view bobbed precisely as he nodded.

I reached for Markus. Elements of his experience came into view—an older woman with a sharp expression, a room lit by candles and the orange glow of a forge, a really nice-looking dagger. The fluttery pulse of excitement in his chest, the feathery itch of a presence somewhere behind him. Markus was haggling. He paid for the dagger, bowed to the forge mistress and her husband, and left. I felt his body shifting as he walked, the quiescent power of his augmented muscles propelling him along. The world felt smaller from his perspective. He was on his way.

"Markus, check."

He snapped his meaty fingers with a force that had me momentarily wondering if I'd bruised my own hand.

"All feeds synced," I said. "I'm loading diagnostics now."

"*You're doing great*," Markus subvocalized.

The praise made me smile. It was my first time on ops—normally senior team members are supposed to handle it, but the logistics worked out this way.

"Thanks, big guy." I called him that all the time, but *man* it was different being on the other end of things. Being taller than everyone else—if vicariously—was jarring in a good kind of way. I idly wondered if I could pilot one of Markus's spare bodies for a day or something. But then . . . I'd have to flash. So no. Not happening.

The feeds all ran through the ops console—that was way too much data for one mind to process, so the console took on some of the load for me. For each team member, biosensors relayed diagnostic information through their comm sockets, piping through the translation barrier to where their comm rested in etherspace. There it was interlaced with their experiences and transmitted to the ops console, where I received it as a holistic package. I felt Markus's heart beating and knew it was eighty-three beats per minute, and those were the same thing. I felt Abby's hand (muscle tension within parameters, pylons operational) near her pulser (100 percent charge) and the calm with which she was prepared to draw and fire it. I tasted the *unexceptional/4.26 percent grain alcohol/beer* in Val's mouth.

I couldn't feel my own body. I felt panic rising up—where? In my chest? It should be in my chest, *where was my chest?*

"Commander, I think something's wrong!"

"*It's overwhelming at first*," Abby said soothingly. "*You're safe. You can check your own feed if you need to.*"

Reluctantly, I regarded the guttering neon of my own comm signal. It couldn't seem to decide on shape or color, though the chaotic variance definitely gave off a sense of danger, so that was something at least.

It was pathetic. No wonder I didn't get any respect around here.

I didn't go for a full sync, just checked in to limit the feeling of dissociation. My vitals were good. Opening my eyes took a moment of clumsy maneuvering, but it was enough to confirm everything was alright. The panic subsided a little—I got to watch it happen, heart rate dropping, hormone levels stabilizing, spirit regaining equilibrium. Seeing myself calm down calmed me down faster.

"Lilith? Status."

"I'm good to go, commander. Let's kick some invisible ass."

Markus arrived early, or at least earlier than we thought Cades would show. He spotted Val immediately—really, brooding in a dark corner wasn't subtle—and swept his eyes over the crowd with an efficiency that felt like the result of decades of practice. I knew he'd probably just mapped out the social dynamic of the entire room—a reminder my teammates were *good* at what they did. In moments, he was ordering a round of drinks from a skinny little kid with a harried expression and not enough hands for all the stuff he was carrying.

"Thanks," he said, handing the kid a couple *drobol.* He was overpaying, which was another way to say he was buying goodwill. Markus's lips quirked just so, his attention on the kid's reaction. A feeling of satisfaction told me he'd accomplished whatever he was trying to accomplish there. Probably just trying to make sure the kid knew it was a tip and not overpaying out of ignorance, but Markus had a deeper understanding of the arcane art of friendship than I ever would. Having such intimate access to my teammates' experiences without knowing their thoughts was really weird.

Drinks secured, Markus barreled through a group of men that had earned his attention earlier. In moments, he was the most popular person there. My millennial ass was reeling from the sight of him just taking over a group of strangers like that. Markus was in his element, all right. The excitement was just pumping through all his signal channels. Every so often, his attention turned back to the presence outside the bar and that excitement would wane. I guess it was about hanging out with Cades tonight.

Lirian was playing it conservative. That was expected; we had the entire area covered by MDOs, and she really didn't like hanging out in detection range. After probing the edge of Markus's detector range, her presence faded out.

"Lost contact. Anyone getting anything from Lirian?" I asked, as if I didn't know the answer already.

Abby pinged negative, laughing convivially with her conversation partner.

"Lirian," said Val, and I felt a cold satisfaction, the resolution of a tactical question. "She's not in the bar."

She could have a confederate in here, of course, and that could be anyone, but over the past month she'd been the only one to trip the MDOs.

I sifted through the sensory data of three different people, looking for female faces, but the few I located belonged to people who had been here the whole time. I was suddenly distracted by a burst of attention from Markus.

Cades had arrived. And I had a front-row seat as Markus checked him out.

"Markus, what the fuck is going on with you?"

"Isn't he gorgeous?" Markus subvocalized. He focused on particular details: the shape of the face, the pectorals underneath a fine shawl, good, strong arms—Markus's muscles shifted as though preparing for a hug—his *posture*, the way he *walked*—

"Okay, okay! Enough!" I said. "Do you all feel like this all the time? How the fuck do you operate?"

Abby cut me off. "Stand down. Focus on the mission."

The feeling in Markus's throat was so *sharp*, like some kind of pleasant ache. I couldn't get any space from it because it wouldn't fucking *stop*. Every time some aspect of Cades caught his attention, his whole reward system shouted, "Yes please!" in clouds of dopamine and norepinephrine. It was just way too much. Libidos are stupid.

"Cades!" Markus bellowed, raising a mug.

"Thala!" Cades shouted back. "A joyous night!"

They met in a bear hug, which Markus really liked and I merely endured.

"I got you something," said Markus, untying his new knife from his belt. "In honor of your victory yesterday."

Guilt crossed Cades's face. "There was no need for this."

"I'm happy for you." Markus smiled. "That's need enough."

Markus offered his arm in a warrior's salute. Cades took it with a resigned smile. Their eyes met, and I realized Cades had it just as bad as Markus. This was totally a date. This had been a date the *whole time*. And I was gonna be stuck playing brain jockey like some kind of fucking creep all night.

"Someone shoot me now," I said.

Abby pinged vigilance, which usually meant, "Everyone needs to look out," but in this case probably also meant, "I'm watching you." Veleans like doing double meanings like that sometimes. I watched Markus hand the knife over to Cades—their fingers touched, blegh—and get everyone drinking to Cades's victory.

"We should figure out if Lirian's actually here," I said, mostly to distract myself from the hormone stew in Markus's brain. "Commander, do you think we should do a sweep?"

"Good call," she subvocalized. *"Give me a minute. Val, stay in range to support."*

Time for why we were *really* here. We were in a cold war with Lirian, and the first step of winning that war was from good old Sun Tzu: know the enemy and know yourself. Lirian had established some ground rules—staying out of detection range, following us whenever possible—so we were going to give her some openings and see what she did with them.

But first we had to find her.

Abby ditched her cover dude and ducked out of the busy street. She pulsed a possible witness so no one would see what came next. I felt a buzz of etheric activity in her legs as she activated the kinetic translators installed in her femurs. Then she *launched* into the air. I felt everything—the colossal force of the jump, the air streaming past her and the sudden wind chill, the moment of weightlessness at the apex of the jump, the gradual settling of her body weight as her feet practically floated onto the roof.

"In position. Roaming."

Below her, Val casually strolled down the street, subjecting every passerby to a comm scan. His feed supplied me with an endless deluge of etheric information—boredom, self-importance, worry, pride, excitement, bitterness—which I didn't have to *directly experience*, so that was fine. Markus was over there trying to talk Cades into a private sparring session, and I fucking hoped I was off ops duty by the time that happened. Fortunately for me, Cades was demurring because the Voranetti had made some unhappy noises about his friendship with Markus. He seemed to wish he could, though.

Abby continued circling the area, getting no hint of Lirian. I tried to take in as much of everyone's perspectives as possible, looking for that itchy feeling that indicated an MDO had found something.

"The MDO is set to trigger if the infrared finds a target, but the soul detector doesn't," Val said. "If she's evading the infrared, it won't pick her up."

"So we basically need line of sight to her," I said. "She wouldn't have spooked off just seeing us out in force, right? If we're pulling an operation, she needs to do recon."

"Cades, you're the best athlete I've ever seen," said Markus. "Anyone would be happy to sponsor you. Surely someone else would treat you better."

"Assuming no supernatural intelligence-gathering abilities, she should still be in observation range," said Abby. "We didn't pick anything up from the street or the bar. If she decloaked, we would have seen her. Lirian. Yeah, she's not here. One of our assumptions is wrong."

"I'm no mercenary," said Cades, which put Markus on edge.

"I *almost* feel something," I said. "I think she might still be here."

"She could be in a neighboring building, perhaps," said Val. "The compound over there has glass windows and line of sight. Lirian could read lips without tripping the infrared."

"At that range? How good are her fucking eyeballs?"

"I'm not saying that," Markus said. "None of us are, right, friends?"

"It might explain why Lilith is getting a faint signal. It's not on my end. Must be one of the emplaced detectors."

"I know. But I pride myself on my loyalty."

"I'll infiltrate just to be sure," the commander decided. "Val—flank left, get me an angle on those windows."

"Yes ma'am."

Markus changed the subject, but I could tell he wanted to keep arguing about Cades's career choices.

"Hey," I said, "do we know for sure that Lirian doesn't have collaborators?"

"We know Lirian followed Markus to the op site," said Val. "She would have had to hand off reconnaissance to a confederate."

"What do you mean, you've never done a chariot race! Cades, we should be a team!"

"The confederate probably doesn't go by Lirian is my point."

Val hummed. "It's worth considering."

"We know she was here earlier," said Abby. "If she's gone, we've learned something either way. Lilith, can you narrow down which detector is getting the signal?"

"I can't tell which one," I said, digging through the fire hose of sensory data to find it. "Fuck."

"Just focus on it," said Abby. "Let the console do the rest."

"It's *not working*," I said. "Console's doing fuck all! It's, like, distant."

My brain heard what I was saying. My stomach dropped in a horrible moment of cliff-plummeting epiphany.

"It's not on the console," I said. "It's my personal comm."

I unceremoniously cut the sync, waking up in the darkness of my room. My head was back to only housing one set of thoughts. There was an itch in the world up and to the left. That was the MDO signal.

I let out a stream of curses.

"*Lilith, status!*" The commander's voice echoed in my head.

"She's here," I said. "She's in the library."

CHAPTER THIRTY-SEVEN

Let's Talk

I'm going after her," I said, jumping out of bed.

"*Lilith, be careful,*" said Abby.

"I will," I said, lifting a sword off the wall. I tested the edge. Decorative. Whatever—it was still a five-pound chunk of metal, you can still kill someone with that.

"*Your priority is ensuring the girls' safety,*" said Abby. "*I'm on my way to your location. Stall her if you need to.*"

"Sure," I lied. I was not going to stall her. I was going to fucking gut her.

I checked my pulser. I was still in the clothes I'd worn today, minus the shawl, so it was easily accessible on my hip. Easily visible, too, but if someone saw we could fix it later. Dead people, not so much.

That was all the preparation I was willing to do. I ran for the library.

The Vitares compound was a giant rectangle, three stories of rooms surrounding an open-air courtyard the size of my high school's assembly room. My room was on the right side of the compound, and the library took up a large part of the back. There was an internal hallway that would take me to the spiral staircase at the corner. I dashed for it.

My bare feet slapped frantically on the lacquered concrete. I let the sword trail behind me—I'm sure Lirian would just *love* if I tripped and impaled myself—pumping with the other hand. Someone heard me barreling down the hall and peeked her head out. One of the workers, I recognized her.

"Trouble in the library!" I yelled at her before she could ask. "Get a doctor!"

I was around the corner before she could respond. Hopefully no one needed treatment, but better to have it available. Unless it was Lirian, in which case I was going to let her bleed out while the doctor watched.

I swung my momentum around on a railing post and took the stairs two at a time. Ghostlight-illuminated frescoes slid through my field of vision. I'd been meaning to spend a couple hours looking over everything, but there was always another priority. That was truer now than ever. Following the itching sensation that was the MDOs' representation of Lirian, I hit the top of the stairwell and sprinted for the library doors. Closed. Let that not mean anything, please let that not mean anything—

I threw my shoulder against the door—it wasn't locked—and came through swinging. I only hit air, but just in case I threw my weight against the door until it cracked against the wall. Entrance cleared with extreme prejudice.

The library was a large space, mostly full of couches and tables, with the shelving along the walls. Books were expensive on Theria, despite whatever printing process they used to make them, so there weren't enough in here to merit the parallel shelves I'd always associated with libraries. Good thing, too, one of the two stand-alone shelves had been knocked over, books scattered all over the floor. The top half of Kuril's body protruded from the pile.

She had better be breathing. I started a comm scan. My comm warned me that I'd just been hit with pulser fire. My lips twisted into a snarl.

"Hey, asshole!" I shouted. "You've got six seconds to tell me they're alive! Five! Four!"

Pulser fire hit my comm shields again.

"That's not going to work! Two! One!"

"Lilith, she's probing you."

"Time's up!" I said, ignoring Abby. "Fine, we're doing this the hard way."

I closed the door behind me and drew the heavy dead bolt back to lock it. I avoided turning my back to the room. After a moment, the scan concluded, telling me there was one soul in the room besides me. So Kuril was alive. Maybe Roel had gone to bed already. That was something she'd do, right? Then I didn't need to worry. I just had to think about killing . . . someone. My enemy. Who was standing north of my position, between me and the other exit to this room.

Shifting to a ready stance, I dashed sword first straight at the north doors.

"Die, motherfucker!" I yelled.

The presence hesitated for just a moment, then moved hastily to the side. I ran straight past it, reaching the doors in moments. The presence realized its mistake too late, starting for my location as I wrenched the dead bolt closed. It slowed to a stop.

"There is no running from this," I panted. "Your cloak won't help you. If you dive out the window, you'll hurt yourself, and I will follow the trail of blood until I cut your *fucking* legs off. So how about you come out before I decide to rip your lungs out through your stomach."

The presence stood still evidently thinking. It slowly moved—toward the window?—no, to a chair, which it pushed in my direction. I scoffed. It moved casually toward a second chair. Taking its time. My grip tightened on the sword handle. They wanted to talk? The second they decloaked I was going to run them through. My muscles tensed in anticipation.

Roel materialized in the chair, open-eyed but unresponsive. She'd been pulsed. Lirian was standing behind her, holding a knife to her throat.

"Let's talk," she said. And smiled.

All I could do was stare in impotent fury. My comm was reading three other souls now, so the girls were safe. *For now.* Lirian had shown that she was willing to use that knife on me, but unlike me, Roel wasn't coming back if she got stabbed to death.

"*Lilith, I need you to keep it together here,*" Abby said. "*Get them out alive. Anything else is recoverable.*"

I breathed in, out. Okay. Abby was on her way. I could stall. And I knew how to open.

"Hands find their way," I said.

Amusement rippled over Lirian's face. "Don't they ever. No, not today. That's not a code phrase, *Ajarel*. It's a promise, and I'm fulfilling it tonight. I have, in my *hands*— see how that works?—something you care about. So now, finally, you will answer my questions."

"You know I can say anything, right?" I said, turning slightly to hide my hand creeping for my pulser. "This is such a terrible way to get information."

"*This* is to get your volatile posterior in the chair," said Lirian with a huff. "Drop the weapon, please, I can move faster than you."

I dropped my sword as insultingly as I could manage.

"We both know that's not the weapon I was talking about," said Lirian.

"That's not a weapon," I said. "That's a party trick."

Lirian indicated Roel without taking her eyes off me. "A truth of the eyes. Drop the party trick and sit down. It's just us. No need for these games."

I slowly unclipped my pulser. For a moment, I calculated whether I could draw on her before she killed Roel. She saw, I know she did. She dropped the smile, just watched me, waiting to react. The calculations didn't come out in my favor. I dropped the pulser.

"But I'm not sitting down," I said.

"Now you're making it a power struggle," said Lirian. "Must we? I'm here for secrets, not lives. This is already distasteful."

"You fucking stabbed me," I said in disbelief.

"Did I?" asked Lirian. "The evidence of that has mysteriously vanished. Let's start there."

"I'm not fucking cooperating."

"It takes hours for people to come back after whatever your party trick does to them," said Lirian. "I've tried pain, of course, but perhaps I didn't use enough. There's another secret there. I'll take it if you don't trade me for another."

"Trade," I said slowly. "No. That's not trade, that's extortion. You want to trade? Give me one of yours."

Lirian tilted her head forward, an Estheni gesture roughly meaning, "Go on." "Your wounds."

"Your mission," I countered.

"I must have forgotten—which of us has the hostage, again?"

"Your mission, and I'll let you walk out of here when we're done." Abby would be here before then, of course.

Lirian sighed. "If you cannot take this seriously, I will slit her throat and leave." She punctuated the sentence with a sudden, vicious downward strike of the knife. I shouted and leaped for her, but she fixed me with an intent look and froze her strike before it met Roel's leg.

"Sit *down*, Lady Ajarel. That hand-truth is plain: you care for her."

I sat.

"Your wounds," said Lirian.

We had a cover story prepared. "I'm descended from Kives. Why are you going after Cades's competitors? He could win glory without it."

"For a promotion," said Lirian.

I nearly got out of the chair and strangled her right there. She shifted the knife against Roel's throat.

"You had better be lying," I said.

"That can be my next secret," said Lirian. "What's the provenance of your weapon? I see you acquired a replacement. Do all four of you have one?"

I was about to say something flippant, but she must have seen it on my face because she indicated the knife again.

"*Lilith, you cannot tell her,*" said Abby. "*I'm almost there. Just hold on for ten minutes.*"

"They're from my home," I said. "They're godtouched. That's why they don't work on us."

Lirian examined my face. "Interesting. And of course you're not from Salaphi, but both of us knew that."

"Of course," I said. "You've attacked the girls for this. Will you do that again?"

"You know I can say anything, right?" she said, mimicking my tone of voice. Well, kind of—the comm translation made it a little wonky.

"There's no way you'll be allowed in the city after this," I said. "The Cult of Silence would be hunted to extinction if they crossed lines like this all the time. Tell me if I need to make that happen."

Lirian smiled sadly. "I'm afraid if little Roel dies, the blame will fall on you."

"*What?!*" I screeched.

"You ran in here brandishing a sword and screaming about trouble you had no way of knowing about," said Lirian. "What do you think the city will conclude? Vitareas has been all abuzz with tales of your emotional outbursts and the way you and Thala have been manipulating the poor girl."

I opened my mouth and froze, looking at the knife. Roel could *die* here. She could *die* here, and I would be blamed. Kuril would blame me. My breath started to quicken.

"How are you locating me, by the way?" asked Lirian. "I felt eyes on me from atop the bookshelf, but I couldn't find them. Is it a ritual? Some form of sorcery?"

I couldn't answer. I knew I was breathing too fast. Roel was still staring off into space. The knife was right there at her throat. If Lirian just pulled, it would bite into the skin, sending the blood gushing out, over her clutching fingers, flowing over her skin, into her intricately woven nightclothes as she choked—

For a moment I was back in Salaphi, watching Arguel die.

"Lady Ajarel!"

Had I been screaming? My throat felt a bit sore. My eyes were tearing up. Lirian was watching me, unamused, unsympathetic.

"So this is the hand-truth of you," she said. It felt like a judge's conviction. I glared up at her through the tears, the humiliation of showing vulnerability to an enemy.

"And is this you?" I choked. "A monster threatening a kid?"

"I am nothing," Lirian said immediately, with the cadence of a habit. "Now, the eyes. Please cooperate, I still have the knife and so on."

I waited as long as I could manage, wiping my face while pinging Abby for her status. "Also from home."

"Almost there. Keep stalling her."

Lirian leaned in. "And where is home?"

"Don't I get a question?"

"By the goddesses, Ajarel, the *knife.*"

That was fine, just stall her more. I pretended to think about the question, taking a moment to compose myself. I sniffed.

"It's big," I said, slowly, seriously. "And really old. Kind of angry and unloving. And fat, so fat."

Lirian tilted her head again, the go-on gesture.

"It's . . . your mom." Something gave way in my chest, and I started giggling.

She blinked once. "I see. Well. It's been a trying night, I'm sure."

I couldn't help it. "That's what *your mom* said!"

Lirian sighed, reaching around Roel with her free hand. "Observe." She placed the blade against her palm, then sliced it open. I stiffened at the sight of the blood. "You see?"

"Fine, fine," I said, trying to pull myself together.

Lirian nodded, then spit on the now-bloody blade. "You see?"

"I mean, yes, but what does—"

She drove the knife down into Roel's leg. Roel started screaming. I jumped out of the chair, but Lirian was already gone, and I *couldn't go after her, I had to save Roel—*

Lirian was already gone. The south door was open, revealing a crowd of worried faces. Someone had actually gotten a doctor, thank god, I screamed at them to *come help her she's bleeding so bad—*

"Ajarel, help," Roel asked, her tear-stricken face screwing up.

"Lilith, status," said the commander.

"It's okay, Roel, I'm sorry, I'm so sorry, I let her get away, please come help," I babbled.

"I'm right here," said the doctor. Hadalce again. "You, bring the boiling water! Child, you should step away."

"Don't go," Roel pleaded. "It hurts."

"I'm on my way, Lilith," said the commander. *"Lirian's out of range. I'll come support."*

"I won't, I won't, I'm so sorry," I said, holding her hand. "I fucked up, I'm so sorry."

Hadalce nudged me to the side. "Roel, child, look at me. You have to stay awake, okay?"

Roel screamed in reply.

Val's voice cut in. "*Lilith, this is urgent. Get Lirian's blood. As much as you can.*"

The tone of command cut through the panic and the stress and Roel's screams, and I scrabbled after it for something to hold on to. Blood. I could get blood. I shifted my grip on Roel's hand—she gripped me desperately, her strength feeble now—and tore a strip off my wrap.

"I need to see the knife!" I half shouted, half cried. "Move!"

Shouting opened a space, and there was the knife, sticking out of Roel's leg. I felt faint for a moment but held on.

"I'm sorry, this is going to hurt a bit," I said, reaching for the knife.

"What are you doing?" demanded Hadalce. "You can't pull that out!"

"I'm not!" I said. "I just need to—"

I wrapped the torn cloth around the blade near the hilt, where I was sure the blood was just Lirian's. Roel screamed again as the process agitated the wound. Hadalce swore and yelled at me to get away from her.

"I'm done! I'm done!"

"Get out of here!" she shouted at me.

"Roel, it'll be okay," I said. "You're going to be okay, just remember that."

I suddenly found myself outside the circle of agitated people, Roel alternately begging me not to leave and asking for Kuril. I stood, completely drained, bloody rag clenched in one hand.

"I have the sample," I said.

"*Then we've won,*" said Val.

It didn't feel like a victory.

CHAPTER THIRTY-EIGHT

Blood

The library was full of worry and panic and Hadalce's shouted orders and Roel's cries of pain. Roel's sobbing intensified as Hadalce and several of the estate personnel lifted her out of her chair and onto a woven mat of some kind. The poor girl kept crying for her sister and, as the pain became more intense and her cries more incoherent, her mother. The girls never talked about her, and hearing it now made me feel like I was witnessing something I shouldn't. I wearily retrieved my pulser.

"Let me help," I said to Hadalce.

"You've done enough! Get out!"

I closed my eyes, took a deep breath, opened them.

"Roel," I said, ignoring Hadalce's death glare. "Close your eyes for me, okay? I'm going to make it better."

She looked up at me with hope, then shakily nodded and screwed her eyes shut. I pulsed her.

"What have you done?!" Hadalce screamed.

"She's asleep," I said, utterly exhausted. "Or close enough. You have three hours, give or take."

Abby's voice interrupted me. *"Lilith. You are jeopardizing your cover and the mission. Hide the pulser and don't say anything else."*

"Fine," I subvocalized, too tired to fight this. *"What do I do with the rag?"*

"I'll pick it up when I get there."

"Where's Kuril?" I shouted to the room.

"Here," a man called, but his voice was too full of grief for the news to be good. I trudged over.

Kuril's body was lying on the ground. They'd pulled her out of the pile of books and the downed shelf, but there was a bad-looking bruise on her head, and she was staring blankly at the ceiling. Weeping members of the staff surrounded her.

She was breathing. It was just a pulse fugue. Nothing they'd seen before, but nothing to worry about, either. I breathed a sigh of relief.

"She's alive," I said. "I can fix her. Move."

"Lilith," Abby said warningly.

"Cat's out of the bag," I subvocalized. *"Cover story has to adapt. I get points for waking her up this way. Permission to perform feedback therapy?"*

Abby barely even paused. *"Granted. This is your cover, you have the right to take initiative. I just wanted to be sure."*

I didn't respond, kneeling down to pick up Kuril's hand. After a moment, I found her pulse, nice and regular. A bit high for a resting heart rate, I thought. Maybe with the constant stress of managing the household she didn't have time to stay in shape. I'd barely had time for morning PT myself.

Stay focused, Lilith. The heartbeat is the foundation of the body. It's the clock in your hindbrain that ticks no matter what, the slow rippling of neural activity in the frequency of life. In etherspace, Kuril's soul was vibrating at the same frequency, connected along the pulse of that heartbeat. It's not a simple connection—in fact, it's one of the most complicated etheric structures in known paraphysics—but this was the pillar that kept her body and soul together.

Lirian had essentially jammed that pillar with the pulser, choked it with so much noise that the signal couldn't get through. Body and soul weren't speaking to each other anymore. Kuril was technically still conscious in etherspace, but with none of that information filtering back to her brain, it'd get overwritten by the next thing that happened in realspace. Same reason you forget your dreams. But eventually the communication patterns of the brain and soul would reestablish themselves.

Feedback therapy was a way to make that happen faster. And it started with the heartbeat. I took the pulse, internalized it, and started rubbing circles with my other thumb on the palm of her hand. Nice and slow. Give her something to latch on to.

"Hey, Pelain, I need your help," I said, addressing an older woman who usually attended Kuril. "I need you to sing a song that Kuril's familiar with. Something personal. It needs to be *exactly* this fast."

I tapped my foot to the beat of Kuril's heart. Pelain thought about it.

"There was a song her mother used to sing to her."

"Perfect," I said, bracing myself.

The human brain is highly attuned to rhythm. The human brain is also highly attuned to language. That's the reason (among a bunch of others, I guess) you get singing in every human culture. So godslayers will always hear the music of the cultures they deploy to, in something that sounds like their own language, but with the rhythm of the original language. It's a literal headache. But it'd wake Kuril up faster, so I just had to suck it up.

"There is a place where," Pelain sang, "the water is cool."

I clenched my jaw as my brain insisted a five-syllable phrase actually took eleven syllables. I didn't let it interfere with the rhythm of my thumb on Kuril's palm.

"Where the sun is pleasant," nine syllables, "and sorrow is no more."

Kuril shifted, which probably indicated reconnection was underway in the motor regions of her brain.

"In this place, all that you need will be at hand.

"And I will wait for you there."

Darwin, I hated it. "Lovely song," I said. "Is their mother . . . ?"

Pelain gave me a look and kept singing, which I realized too late was mutually exclusive with answering my question. I nodded at her to keep going.

Kuril made a soft noise.

"It's working," I said. "Keep going. Kuril, can you hear me?"

Kuril made another noise.

"You're doing great," I said. "Listen to Pelain. Can you move?"

Her hand gripped mine. I squeezed back.

"That's good. Are you hurt?"

"Hurt?" she croaked.

"Are you injured anywhere?" I asked. "Looks like Lirian dropped a bookshelf on you."

"I don't remember," said Kuril, pulling her hand out of mine. For a second I worried that she blamed me for this. Then she pulled herself up on her elbows, and I realized I was getting jumpy for nothing. Then I remembered Lirian's words and realized she *still* might blame me for everything. All the advice I'd heard for dealing with impostor syndrome didn't work as well when I was literally an impostor.

"I feel like I'm still dreaming," said Kuril.

"We need you to wake up," I said. "Please. There's been an attack. Roel's hurt."

Her eyes snapped to me as I said that. With obvious effort, she tried to pull herself to her feet. I helped her stand up, maneuvering my shoulders under her arm.

"She's over here," I said. "She's asleep. Lirian stabbed her in the leg."

"No!" Kuril shouted. She shoved me off and stumbled over to the group surrounding Roel's prone form.

"*Commander, we really need to get her some antibiotics,*" I subvocalized. "*Lirian made a point of contaminating the blade. It might also be poisoned. Fuck. Can we scan for that?*"

"*Threat of death, artificial,*" said Abby. "*You can filter by intent.*"

"*Got it.*" I started the scan.

"*You don't have the social capital to apply strange medicines to Roel's injury. Fix that first. I'll bring a med kit.*"

"*. . . Got it,*" I said.

Okay. I could do this.

I approached the patient, already steeling myself for Hadalce's displeasure. That was the first problem. Second problem was what Lirian had said about getting blamed for this. Third problem was that Kuril was probably about to kick me out of her house. She'd been too close to losing Roel, and it was my fault, so the rational thing to do was call it square on the life debt and wish us the best of luck on the road.

"Hey, Kuril," I started. I'd noticed an open window and come back? I'd fought her to a standstill? Fuck, I didn't know what to say.

Hadalce turned bright red. "Lady Kuril, this *trash*—"

She trailed off as Kuril threw her arms around me and squeezed me so hard I felt like a rib was going to pop out. My mind went completely blank. Then I hugged her back. I abandoned my half-assed cover story.

"I couldn't stop Lirian," I whispered, holding her tight. "I'm so sorry. I tried."

"She's alive," said Kuril. "For now."

The scan for poison had returned negative. I sighed and gave Kuril a squeeze. "I promise she'll be okay."

Kuril didn't respond, reciprocating the squeeze.

"We can find Lirian," I said. "I know a guy in the city. We'll stop this. I promise you."

"No!" Kuril said, releasing me, looking up with fierce eyes. "You're staying right here with Roel. Your duty is to the house, both of you. I'm going straight to the Visionary. The Oathkeepers will have her by sunrise. *Keep her safe*, Ajarel."

"Lady Kuril," Hadalce protested. "Ajarel hurt Roel!"

I had to shut that down fast. "Then who unlocked the library doors?" I shouted. "I was all the way over here!"

"Not that! You grabbed the knife in her leg!"

That one caught me off-balance. I checked Kuril's reaction, which was mostly confusion. I knew I had to say something.

"It needed to happen," I tried. "Kuril, please trust me."

From the expression on her face, that wasn't the right thing to say.

"I am exhausted and at my wit's end," said Kuril. "Ajarel, explain."

"I—"

"She wrapped a rag around it!" said Hadalce. "It's blood magic, Lady Kuril! Get her out of this house!"

Oh shit, that was a lot of stares. Really *suspicious* stares. My stomach sank as Kuril's face grew darker. My shoulders hunched defensively of their own accord.

"Lady Ajarel," she said dangerously. "Come with me."

Her grip on my hand didn't leave me much of a choice. We exited the library and took a turn out onto the courtyard balcony. The ghostlights out here were in shades of gray and blue, accentuating the moonlight rather than fighting it. Kuril released me.

"I need you to listen like you have *never* listened before. Do you understand?"

I nodded, wary.

"This house is *crumbling*," said Kuril. "Vitareas has all but forgotten us. Our mother died in battle against the Phrecians. I cannot handle our affairs alone. I am trying, but I cannot shout into Horcutio's breath. The Henadim abandoned three generations of friendship for rank opportunism, and the Voranetti's rapacity has *never* been more audacious. I know you have your secrets—*shut up and listen*, Ajarel! Of course I know! You're not as subtle as you think! I am telling you I *do not care*. I do not care what you left behind you in Salaphi. I do not care about the true nature of your relationship with Thala. But I cannot have even the rumor of blood magic in my house."

So that was it. The rejection felt like a knife in my sternum. I avoided her eyes, my gaze settling on her feet.

"I understand. I can leave."

She hit me. Right in the face, an unexpected, stinging impact that threw me off-balance. I threw my hands up defensively, looking at her in shock.

"Coward!" she shouted. "You *know* I can't handle this alone! Roel needs a sister!"

"I—what? I thought, uh." I must have looked very silly, frozen in a half-assed guard stance, but my body wasn't entirely sure how it was supposed to move right now.

The confusion on my face must have been contagious because it looked like Kuril got thrown for a loop, too. We stared at each other wordlessly while my arms slowly sank out of high guard. But underneath the confusion was a desperate bloom of hope.

"I, uh, thought you were throwing me out," I said. "Is that not what's happening?"

"You cannot possibly be this dense," she said. "No, you idiot! I want to adopt you!"

"Oh."

"But I can't do that if you're causing blood-magic scandals."

"Oh."

"So just give me the rag and we'll burn it. If you're addicted already, I'll pay for a priest of Gamal. They're discreet. We'll tell Hadalce you read it in a book and didn't realize what you were doing. And you *will* start working as my secretary. I know there's nothing for you back home. Stay here. Help me hold things together. *Please*, Ajarel."

I slumped against the railing. I was feeling a lot of very intense things, but damned if I could tell you what they were. "This is a lot," I said.

"Please." Kuril looked more desperate than I'd ever seen her. "That wasn't a clean wound. I've seen them before. Roel will need you more than before."

I wanted so much to say yes. I wanted it so much it hurt, coiling around the pain of rejection like a snake on a knife. But I couldn't give her that rag.

"I don't know any blood magic," I said instead of answering her. "The guy I mentioned? It's for him. If I get it to him, he can track down Lirian for us. We won't be safe until then. Please let me get it to him."

"The Oathkeepers will handle it," said Kuril. "Give me the rag."

"*Lilith, do not give her the rag*," said the commander.

"I need to do this," I pleaded with her. "I need to beat Lirian. I've failed twice."

"Is Lirian more important than Roel?"

"This *is* for Roel," I said. "She had a knife to her throat, Kuril! I can't do that again!"

"Let the Oathkeepers handle it!" shouted Kuril. "Are you too far gone already?"

"I don't know any fucking blood magic!" I yelled.

"But you know someone who does," Kruil said softly. "Maybe that's all it takes."

"Okay," I said. "Okay, maybe you're right. Call that priest, then. Preferably right now."

The balcony was about twenty-five feet off the ground, so if I stuck the landing just right—Kuril grabbed my hand, accidentally preventing my glorious plan to save the day.

"We can all get through this together," she said.

I took a deep breath, holding her hand. I didn't have a way out of this after all. But if you're going to fall, fall forward.

"Commander, you said I could use my initiative," I subvocalized. *"I'm securing the mission."*

I retrieved the rag from my wrap and handed it to Kuril. She gave me a weary smile and hugged me. There was a ghostlight on the railing not far from us. Kuril unlatched the top and dropped the rag in. It flared bloody red, decaying into ash with supernatural speed. Then both fire and rag were gone, leaving only glittering ash in the lantern basin.

"Huh," I said after a moment.

"What is it?"

"I guess Roel's my aunt now."

CHAPTER THIRTY-NINE

Tribunal

The lights in the conference room were dimmed, the consoles all dead except the one Abby was using to fill out the paperwork for the proceeding. Val sat to her right, twirling a stylus between his fingers. He didn't have a tablet.

I sat awkwardly on the other side of the table, shifting nervously in my seat. It was approaching midnight local time—the only window I could get away from the estate without drawing attention to myself. I ineffectually stifled a yawn, causing Abby to yawn, as well. Val gave me a sardonic look and kept his mouth resolutely shut. I was fairly certain you couldn't actually do that, but the yawn never came.

"What, are you performing presence and absence meditations simultaneously again?" I asked.

"Val, what are you teaching her down there?" Abby asked, not looking up from the paperwork. "That's ridiculous."

"I'll have you know my methods are peer reviewed," said Val.

"Now I really don't believe you," I said. "There's no way you think you have peers."

Val smiled. His teeth looked sharp.

"Let's get this over with and go to bed," said Abby, slapping the console with a sense of completion. "Lilith, before I initiate proceedings, do you have any questions?"

My hands found each other in my lap. "What happens if this goes bad?"

"In the worst *possible* case, we crypt you," said Val.

Abby smacked his shoulder. "I want to be clear that in order for that to happen, you would basically need to swear allegiance to the Therian pantheon while trying to assault both of us. The worst *nonoutlier* case is where we scrap the op and reevaluate what kind of mission roles are appropriate for you in the future."

"Okay." My voice felt very small.

Abby gave me a reassuring smile. "You did ask about what happens if things go poorly. They might not. They might even go well. I have full confidence in you."

"Obviously not," I said, indicating the room with a sweep of my eyes.

Val shook his head. "Deicide teams are by necessity a complicated system of overlapping relationships. This is protocol. Abby's feelings have nothing to do with it. If you continue clinging to that sense of defensiveness, your performance in the hearing will suffer."

"Thank you, Val, that will be enough," said Abby. "I am officially beginning this inquiry. Subject is mission behavior of Eifni operative M9-30-0671, self-designation Lilith, while on deep cover assignment. Presiding, Eifni operative C4-57-5824, self-designation Abby, commanding officer. Also present, as witness, Eifni operative C3-93-5748, self-designation Val, technical officer. I have called for an inquiry per the powers and responsibilities vested in me by the Eifni charter as commanding officer. If there are any objections before we proceed, state them now."

"Max," Val said with a smirk. "If you're watching, you owe me five hundred luxury credits."

Abby gave a resigned sigh. "That's an automatic demerit."

"How terrifying," said Val.

"Dare I ask what the bet was?"

"On the record? Please."

"We'll do your inquiry next."

My brow furrowed a bit as I stared at Val, trying to figure out what his game was. Blatantly ignoring protocol wasn't really his thing. Was he trying to get me in trouble somehow? If anything, it seemed like the opposite was true.

Shit, was Val taking a fall for me?

"*Hearing no objections,*" the commander said emphatically, disrupting my train of thought, "I will proceed. Lilith, the purpose of this inquiry is to address three decisions made in the field under crisis conditions. Your answers to these questions may affect eligibility for duty and may, in extremis, result in court-martial. Do you understand the scope of concern for this inquiry?"

"I understand," I said.

"First, records indicate you fired a pulser in view of civilians, representing a high-level breach of operational security. The fact of this event is corroborated by review of your personal comm feed, duly submitted as evidence for these proceedings. Do you have any defense of this action?"

I met Val's dispassionate gaze, trying to imagine what he'd say here. Something that made Abby look stupid for questioning him, I'm sure. I wasn't confident I could manage that.

"Uh, I do," I said instead. "Can we talk about Kuril first, though?"

"Very well. Let the record show I am granting Lilith's motion to table discussion of this decision. The second decision was the use of feedback therapy—also restricted for OPSEC reasons—in plain view of civilians, as well as recruiting a civilian to assist you in performing it. Do you have any defense of this action?"

"Okay, so first off," I said. "Lirian's got a pulser, and she's been using it on people. Everything I did is because of that."

"Lirian is an enemy agent of the goddess of secrecy, who has been engaged in psyops and targeted intimidation by use of an antimemetic blessing," Abby said to the console. "Continue."

I cleared my throat, gathering my thoughts.

"So, like, as long as she's out there, people in the Vitares household are going to get pulsed. And since we're one of her big targets, one option was to pressure them to kick Markus and me out of there. So when I demonstrated feedback therapy, I was stopping her from using the pulser as a terror weapon. And now everyone's going to be really happy I'm on their side because I know how to wake them up from the nap. Oh, actually! Uh, immediately after waking up, Kuril offered to adopt me. So I think my results speak for themselves."

"And do you have anything to say about the fact that you've damaged the effectiveness of a key Eifni technology in the long term?"

I gave her a look of betrayal, but she didn't react. Val just watched me. I was on my own here.

Val had said that these teams were a system of overlapping relationships. Abby wasn't pulling her punches here, which wasn't a good thing to do as my friend and mentor, but maybe that was what she had to do as team leader. That was the trouble with being so many things to one another—you couldn't be them all at once. You had to compartmentalize.

I let the betrayal fall off my face, smiled slightly, and nodded the way Val did.

Abby *beamed* at me. I had never seen her look so proud. Val nodded in approval. I realized that *this* was what he was trying to tell me with that stunt in the beginning. Pure, liquid happiness shot through me. I'd done it. I could do it. I was still figuring out what *it* was, but dammit I could do it!

Suddenly, I wasn't on trial anymore. I was playing a role for Maxwell and anyone else who was watching this. This was just another layer of my cover. I was *getting* it.

Alright, console people, you want to come after me? Watch out. I bite.

"No," I said. "I didn't damage *shit*. The other teams are dead or holed up like us. If there's a long term, it's either gonna be us or an invasion fleet, and the invasion fleet isn't going to be fucking around with nonlethal weapons. But if it's just us, and there's pulsers on both sides, I'm making sure my side can deal with them. I made the right call."

"Temporarily," said the commander. "Once that information leaks out, the playing field is even again."

"If we get Markus those laurels in the meantime, it doesn't matter," I said. "Eifni said the point of an advantage is to spend it to win. It doesn't matter how good your cards are if you don't play them."

"Thank you," said the commander. "Would you like to revisit your use of the pulser at this time?"

"Yes. Lirian had just stabbed Roel. She was in a lot of pain. The pulser helped alleviate it."

The commander tapped her fingers on the table. "That's not a tactical benefit."

"You wanna go there? Of course it is," I said. "Remember the whole adoption thing? The lady who made the offer just heard I saved her fifteen-year-old sister from unnecessary pain. Because guess what, if it turns out later I had one this whole time, questions are gonna get asked."

"Questions will be asked now," said the commander. "How are you planning to explain your possession of this device?"

I hadn't really thought that far ahead.

"I am still refining my strategy," I said, as if formality would make the lack of a good answer any better. "It has been four hours since the event, ma'am."

"Give me an idea of your thoughts."

"Lirian's got one. That makes it not weird for me to have one. Maybe I stole it from her?"

A moment passed, the commander's drumming fingers the only noise in the room.

"So you admit," she said slowly, "that you took action without having a prepared strategy in mind."

"As you said, ma'am, it was under crisis conditions. I trusted in myself and my team to design an appropriate strategy after the fact."

The commander regarded me.

"Tell me about your attachment to the Vitaressi. Particularly Roel."

"I like them, and they've been nice to us. Roel stuck up for me in a stressful situation the first time we met. Is there a point to this question?"

"The third decision involved a blood sample collected from Lirian," she said, ignoring me. "Technical officer, can you explain the use of such a sample?"

"The simplest use is setting up a direct line to her soul for surveillance purposes," said Val. "With some preparation, we might use it as a pointer to the idea of her, allowing us to subvert or erase her identity and suborn her for counterespionage. The physical DNA could be used to clone her body, allowing an operative to impersonate her. The list goes on. It's a versatile asset."

"Lilith, you made the decision to destroy that sample against direct orders," said the commander. "Replacing it will be difficult or impossible. Do you have any defense of this action?"

The look in her eyes was more than a little vicious. But not because she *was* being vicious, I reminded myself. She was *presenting* viciousness. Telling me what I needed to defend myself against. So I struck back with equal force.

"Apologies, commander, but those orders would have jeopardized the mission," I said. "Due to local superstitions, collecting the blood was socially untenable. My position in the family and thus Markus's sponsorship was at stake. Had I retained it, we would have lost our local support, and the mission would have failed. I'm sure you would have rescinded those orders yourself if you knew. Due to my decision, Lirian is still in play, but Markus still has a sponsor. Additionally, maintaining my cover allowed us to turn other elements of the city against Lirian. The Oathkeepers might take care of her for us."

"And you're certain this had nothing to do with your attachment to the family, whose adoption offer was contingent on sacrificing that asset?"

"I was prepared to turn her down," I said, the model of a perfect soldier. "The tactically advantageous decision was otherwise."

"What other assets are you willing to sacrifice to maintain your emotionally comfortable cover?"

This one. This one I knew the Val response for.

I smirked at her. "What a stupid question. Whatever it takes to see the mission through."

Val raised an eyebrow. Abby's face was blank.

"That will be all," she said. "This inquiry is concluded."

I slumped back in my seat. I almost asked how I did, but in the wake of the epiphany that'd been carrying me through the hearing, I wasn't sure if I was supposed to do that. I blinked sticky eyes and remembered that without all the adrenaline, my body really wanted to be asleep right now.

"You're growing up," Abby said softly.

"Aw, come on," I said. "I'm an adult where I came from."

But the protest was pro forma, and I was grinning like a maniac underneath it. Val stood up and walked for the door, pausing as he passed me.

"You did well," he said, offering his hand. I shook it.

"By the way, what did you bet Maxwell?" I asked. "Was there even a bet in the first place?"

"What a curious question," he said. Vivid-green eyes flashed with mirth. "Good night, ladies."

I turned to Abby. "I don't want to rain on anyone's parade here, but I, uh, don't really get how any of this works."

"Watch," she offered. "You'll pick it up. We all did."

She hugged me. Just for a little while, I let myself rest in her arms.

CHAPTER FORTY

Coma

Roel didn't wake up the first day.

When I got back from the inquiry, I checked in on her to make sure her vitals were stable. Eifni comms are etheric devices: they don't really have access to realspace the same way an MRI does. What they detect is significance, implication—not the MRI results, the stuff your doctor sees *in* the MRI results.

My comm told me Roel was gravely wounded, and that her condition was getting worse. I picked up the signal of an infection, despite the honey that had been slathered all over the wound, so I slipped back to my room, extracted my emergency med kit from the false floor underneath my belongings, and returned with antibiotics. It took some wrestling—thankfully Hadalce had gone home, or she'd have tried to kill me on the spot—but I managed to administer the medication orally. A week of this and she'd be good to go. Well, aside from the deleterious and probably permanent effects of the stab wound.

People walk off stab wounds in the movies all the time. And the human body is pretty durable, you're built to survive stab wounds. But physical trauma is physical trauma. You don't just bounce back to 100 percent. That's why Velean medicine is optimized for first aid; when your body takes a hit to efficiency, they assume you just flash to backup. For the poor souls without reincarnation technology, you're dealing with severed muscle fibers, long-term scarring, inflammation, and other stuff like that.

And it's not just the immediate area of the wound that's affected. Maybe you end up walking with a limp and it throws your back out. Maybe an infection overstresses your immune system and you get autoimmune problems. Maybe a blood clot makes its way into your vasculature and you have a stroke.

There was a medical translator in my kit, and I was going to sneak in here every night to prevent as many of those issues as I could, but this wasn't the med bay back on the *Ragnar*.

Kuril found me asleep in Roel's room the next morning.

"Make yourself presentable," she whispered, shaking me gently by the shoulder. "I've called for a priest of Gamal. We'll do the formalities when she wakes up this afternoon."

I felt anxious about leaving Roel—if something were to suddenly go wrong, I wanted to be on hand to react. Kuril picked up on that, telling me that Hadalce was going to be there, and everything would be okay. I realized too late that I probably wasn't making too great an impression there—she'd specifically said she wanted to adopt me to reduce her burden, and here I was, adding to it—so I put on a brave face and told her I'd handle myself. I even swallowed my middle-class discomfort and let the attending ladies do my hair.

I knew there was a problem when they called me in to wake Roel up. They should have known better.

"The fugue shouldn't have lasted this long," I said. "It should have worn off overnight. Are you sure she's not just asleep?"

"She won't wake," said Kuril. "Will you try, anyway?"

"Of course," I said, knowing it wouldn't make a difference.

It didn't. The comm now read, "Coma, terminal."

We sent the priest home.

Roel didn't wake up the second day.

I wasn't panicking—yet—about the coma. Ether signatures are timeless but contingent; the fact that she was in a terminal coma didn't mean that the coma wouldn't become nonterminal later. You can check that sort of thing with a moirascope if you're really curious, but after some testing Eifni operational doctrine restricts the use of moirascopes under most circumstances. Otherwise, you run the risk of introducing a self-fulfilling prophecy and screwing yourself over.

(Squad one assaults the west flank, wins the engagement. Future is contingent on proactive squad decision: observers' moirascope detects victory ahead of time. Squad two doesn't engage without go-ahead from the moirascope, shifting future contingency to the moirascope instead of their own decisions. Moirascope is reactive rather than proactive, does not detect successful engagement on the west flank. Squad two does not engage.)

What I *was* doing was spending a lot of time by Roel's bedside while Abby learned to read. Lirian was biding her time again, it seemed, and we'd taken advantage of the opportunity to hunt down a *sebek*—basically a tutor, with Loranan religious baggage— and buy her knowledge with translated coin. I pulled up Abby's feed, bracing myself for a headache. Learning the alphabet would be the easy part. The problem was I'd need to learn Estheni in order to make sense of what the alphabet was saying. And to do that I'd need to have my comm in dual-processing mode, which was migraine inducing if you kept it up too long. Technically I was supposed to have been doing this my whole insertion, but I'd, uh, been less than diligent. Sue me, it'd been a chaotic couple of weeks. I was going to get around to it eventually.

Abby pretended to be a foreigner to explain her weird accent and lack of literacy. Apparently the Estheni valued reading quite highly. The *sebek* took it in stride— Abby's pretended circumstance was common—which let them get right into it, leaving me to frantically try to parse the *sebek*'s Estheni.

Two brutal hours passed. Roel's attendants mostly ignored me, lurking in the corner of her room with a book I was struggling to read. Occasionally I threw phrases from the book back at Abby, like what the fuck does "*Ou eloi camereon*" mean, the *sebek* said the "*-eon*" ending is just for questions, and *it's not a fucking question*. Oh, great, it's sarcasm? Their *grammar* has *sarcasm*? Who designed this shit? By the end of the session my head was swimming with a mess of English and Velean and Estheni, declensions and conjugations and endings swirling around limping thoughts that blorched through the sludge of what was left of my brain at that point. *Haldou sebek-oui an uthena maresthe*: let all the *sebeks* trip on their robes and break something. Roughly. Don't fucking ask me if I got all the endings right.

The promised migraine had shown up by that point, my meatware footing the price for a month of learning accelerated a thousandfold. Fortunately, my eyes were artificial, so I was able to deal with the light-sensitivity part by cranking the signal intensity down. The augments giveth, and the augments taketh away.

Kuril had been putting on a brave face—the graced were supposed to be above things like fear or anxiety—but you could kind of tell her composure was slipping. The Vitares girls didn't check all the boxes they were supposed to, and Markus had speculated that had more to do with their decaying social position than what Kuril termed "rank opportunism." It was just little things, behaviors you could write off individually but that collectively told a story of immense emotional strain.

She was terse with people, and her smiles were brittle. The time she spent on paperwork doubled without external reason, and despite the fact that I should have been shadowing her, I was rarely invited. One time she handed me a document with a teardrop-sized spot of water damage. I didn't comment. Drawing attention to a lapse of control was what the Estheni did to their enemies.

Between Kuril's distance and the time camping out in Roel's room, I was left interacting with the other members of the household more than usual. I quickly realized I'd blundered with my insertion strategy. Dumb in retrospect. The house wasn't just the Vitares girls, obviously, it was also a bunch of staff sworn to the Vitaressi who managed the upkeep of the estate and various aspects of the family's business investments. They weren't exactly servants, and they weren't exactly employees, but they were certainly part of the house as far as the cultural norms were concerned. I'd been trying not to get in their way, but apparently that had come off as snootiness. The rumors about my manipulation of Kuril and Roel weren't a Voranetti maneuver—they had started here.

They loved Markus, though, which was probably the only reason they weren't openly siding with Hadalce's accusations. But I needed to get control of the situation. My first idea was to ask Kuril if we could have the priest cleanse me of blood magic just to kill the rumors, but after an *uncomfortably* long blank stare she informed me that I might as well hold individual meetings with the entire household and confess to everyone one at a time. I didn't ask any more questions, especially about why her eyes were red.

I spent some time jumped into Val's feed that evening. He was prepping for the Renathion tomorrow, assembling the instrument he'd brought among his personal effects. The notion organ was a typically Velean approach to music, in that they'd skipped the actual music part and had just built a device that would shove the experience of music straight into your noetic faculties.

"I admit I would prefer a more efficient storage solution," he said while adjusting a bolt. "I've spoken with some deicide operatives who use Kiri instruments while on deployment. They're designed to be portable. Setting up the Benivok will take all night. I could have had a Kiri operational by now."

"Why'd you bring it, then?" I asked. I felt the practiced surety of his hands on the inner workings of the machine as he slotted each part into place. It was meditative, a relaxing separation from the stress of the last couple days. It was weird experiencing that kind of skill firsthand, though—I didn't have any fine muscle movements trained to this degree.

"I was displeased with the semantic range on the Kiri," he said. "And there are technical limitations with the axis controls—here."

He gestured at—and very carefully did not touch—an intricate series of interwoven rings, each similar in design to the emitter in the med bay. It was like one of those old desk globes, only instead of a sphere inside the rings, there were just more rings. Thin, flexible spindles ran from the rings to the pipes and levers that made up the rest of the notion organ's guts.

"I have sixteen channels on here—which is absurd, I'll be the first to admit; even Setsiko's *Implosion* only uses thirteen—whereas the Kiri models are limited to three so they can fold in on themselves."

"It can't just align the rings in one direction?"

Val's attention moved to one of the fine spindles coming out of the axis controls. "Those threads have ethertech complements. If they get tangled, the wires cross in etherspace, and the instrument requires serious repair. On a purely physical instrument, we'd already have solved the problem, but with bi-ontological engineering the complexity jumps by an order of magnitude."

The usual bite in his comments was completely gone. He hadn't snarked all evening, even when I professed ignorance about something. Granted, we were mostly talking about his hobby, so maybe that was it. But the interaction just felt different somehow. Ever since I'd taken my first baby steps in the weird Velean role-playing thing, the vibe had changed. I didn't think anyone had lectured me at all since the inquiry. Judging from Abby's comments, I was supposed to figure this out without asking for help, so I wasn't. It felt like it'd be a step backward in some indefinable way.

"I should play 'Road to Nowhere' for you," said Val. "It's an old favorite. It's about two lives ruined by separate betrayals and the alliance they build to start again. You can't do it justice on fewer than five channels, of course, which is another reason to use the better instrument."

"You never struck me as sentimental," I said—teasing him a little bit, a risky decision last week and maybe still risky now.

He smiled. "What would I gain from that?"

The lack of the expected clapback was such a pleasant surprise that I laughed. It was now or never, I guessed.

"I wanted some advice," I said.

I felt the set of his face shift minutely. His posture, too. He'd opened up a bit, I realized, and now I was losing that. After a beat I could tell he was about to tell me to go on, and when that happened I'd lose whatever weird peer respect he was giving me now. I barreled ahead.

"I've decided," I said, relishing that little bit of agency, "to adapt my insertion strategy. I need more social capital with the house staff."

"Before the Roel situation resolves?" Val asked, aligning two pipes for some reason. They weren't connected as far as I could tell.

I bristled at the implicit questioning of my judgment. Was this more role-playing stuff? Some kind of social move made for structural reasons rather than sincere intent?

"This is part of the Roel situation," I said. I could tell immediately that I was being too defensive. He didn't say anything explicitly, though. "My usefulness to Kuril is limited if I don't have staff support. I need to win hearts and minds here."

"So, naturally, you went to the technical officer."

I tried to project as much casualness into my voice as I could. "You're the strategist."

Val barked out a sharp laugh. "Well played. You're coming along."

It was so tempting to accept the praise, and if I wasn't currently sharing his experience I probably would have. But something about his posture kept me on edge. That smile was a little too close to a smirk. And no one had been explicitly acknowledging this stuff since I started.

I realized after too long what I should have expected from the beginning. It was a power play. If I let him have this, I was letting him paint me as the junior team member whose progress he got to judge.

The moment had already passed, but I tried, anyway. "That's not what I asked, technical officer."

He gave it to me. This time the smile was genuine, and when he nodded I wanted to pump my fist.

"It seems to me," said Val, "that if this is part of the Roel situation, the solution must involve Roel."

"I know Lirian did something to her," I said. Val's head tilted slightly, *go on*. "But the comm scan didn't find anything. Wait, can she do a stealth poison? Is that why we didn't find anything?"

"I could arrange for more powerful scanning equipment," Val said neutrally.

Bastards. He'd known. They'd all known. They were just waiting for me to ask.

"I think that would be a good idea," I said. "How soon can you get it here?"

On the third day, I rushed into Kuril's room.

"I can wake her up," I said.

She started to cry.

CHAPTER FORTY-ONE

The Ritual

Of all the roles I expected to play as a deicide operative, wizard was not high on the list, but here we were. Roel was already cured; I'd extracted the poison with the medical translator as soon as we'd gotten its signature. But of course my social obstacles were based on the *perception* of her sickness and my supposed complicity in that. So now I was also going to pretend to cure her.

In service of my plan—which I was going to continue claiming ownership of, despite the occasional assist from the rest of the team—I had set the translator to vent the translated poison all over Roel's room. Val had to help me with some of the math, but I managed to split it into *intentional harm* and *illness*. The translator wasn't optimized to handle Meris's blessing of stealth with any kind of efficiency, so after some discussion we left it in Roel's system. The poison it was supposed to hide was gone, so it would naturally fade into the etheric noise over time. Roel might have lessened stage presence or something for a couple months, but those are the kind of trade-offs you make when you're doing medicine in the field.

Now that Roel was ready to wake up, I set my pulser to maximum and made sure she wouldn't.

"Sorry, kid," I told her prone body. "Gonna need you to sit tight for a bit."

I'm pretty sure she'd have volunteered for it if she knew all the crap I was going through, so I didn't feel too bad about it.

The end result was that Roel was perfectly fine, but now the sense of her impending death by poison was palpable when you walked in her room. Perfect for what I needed to do, which was get people freaking out.

Step two, I told Kuril that I was going to ask around to see if anyone had information on the weird blood-and-spit thing Lirian had done before stabbing Roel.

"I don't want to miss something important," I said. "That's the problem with the fucking Cult of Silence, there's one more piece of bullshit you didn't expect."

"You sound familiar with them," said Kuril.

"Let's focus on Roel," I said. Something in her expression told me her patience for my mysterious past wasn't unlimited, but I just had to dig myself out of this hole right now. I could worry about the cracks in my cover afterward. I had a month or so before this all came to a head, maybe more if Lirian went away and all this crap stopped being so salient.

"I'll send a message to the Oathkeepers," said Kuril. "If Lirian's done something like this before, they would know." I'd never been too conscientious about remembering to put "Lady" in front of Lirian's name, whereas Kuril was usually the very soul of conscientiousness. That had ended as soon as Roel had gone into the coma.

"Okay," I said. "I'll talk to the staff."

"I'm sure they would have come to me if they knew anything," said Kuril. "It's been three days."

"Uh, yeah, about that," I said. "They've, uh. We've been giving you space."

Kuril's expression stiffened, anger widening her eyes. "And why have you been doing that?"

I drew in a breath as I realized I'd just told her that everyone had noticed her humiliating lapse of composure over the last couple of days. "Uh, out of respect?" I tried. That didn't improve her disposition. "Uh . . . Sorry, Kuril. I didn't think. It's been hitting all of us pretty hard."

She sat in rigid silence for a few uncomfortable moments.

"Some of us more than others," she said at last. There was an unspoken accusation behind her words that had my heart sinking and my bile rising.

"Okay, that does it," I spat. "Where the fuck is Hadalce? I need to beat all the slander out of her. I'm literally trying to fix Roel right now, how is this supposed to be manipulative?"

"The city of Sargaos fell to thirty doctors," said Kuril. "The Stranger's claws are ever welcome, as they say."

I'd never heard that story, and I couldn't really follow the aphorism, so I wasn't sure how to respond. Also I was reeling a bit from the realization that Kuril was suspicious of me, but that was completely beside the point, thank you. I breathed out sharply and dropped back against the couch.

"So what, am I on trial now?" I said. "I thought you were going to adopt me. What happened?"

"I told you not to cause any blood-magic scandals," Kuril said.

"That's a rug pull," I muttered. "Okay, forget about the adoption. Roel. If you *don't trust me* after everything I've done, then hire a fucking priestess. I'll tell them about the method I know, and they can do it if theirs doesn't work."

Kuril bit her lip. I tried to press my advantage.

"Look," I said. "Let's get something straight. I saved *both* your lives."

"You did," she admitted. "I'm sorry, Ajarel. It's hard to know what to think right now. I never should have read Roel's whisper stories. They're full of things like two whispers pretending to feud so one of them can insinuate into the victim's home. You need to build relationships with the rest of the house to stop these rumors from festering."

"Uh, yeah," I said, trying to pretend like I wasn't suddenly full of adrenal lightning. "Look, I know things look kind of bad right now, but I'm going to try to claw my way back into everyone's esteem. And we don't have to do the adoption until then, if you think that would be better. Let me ask around about the knife thing. I think it'll help."

"No, no," said Kuril. "The seemingness of the process is less important than the process itself. The sooner you're part of the house, the sooner you can take on more responsibilities."

"With respect," I said, "have you also been disregarding optics in your dealings with the other houses?"

Kuril hummed in thought, slowly tapping a charcoal stick against her desk. "I confess, your dull manner makes me forget you're this sharp."

"Ouch," I said.

"You cut deeper," she countered, but with the comm translation I could tell that what she meant was "I forgive you."

"I'm sorry about that."

"It was the truth," said Kuril. "Allowances must be made—something the other houses would do better to respect. Go talk to the house, Ajarel. But promise me you'll wake Roel."

"I will," I said. "If I seem like I'm not concerned about her, it's because I'm confident this will work. I just want to do due diligence first."

The engineering terminology seemed to win me some points. Kuril gave me a weary smile in dismissal.

Delain knew of a Merisite ritual involving stabbing someone with your bodily fluids. She'd been there the night of the attack and had seen me wake up Kuril, so there wasn't any doubt in her mind who was at fault here. In her mind, the mingling of blood was supposed to exert mental control over Roel, and Roel was still asleep because she was fighting it. I asked her to ask around, see what she could find from the other attendants. She said she would.

Peres, the forge mistress, knew me from my time helping Roel in the workshop. She was a little more standoffish than Delain, since we hadn't interacted *at all* outside of workshop stuff, but she was willing to hear me out. Weathered, observant, hair bound in a Sisterhood-approved wrap, she patiently listened but didn't have anything for me. She thanked me for trying to help Roel. I asked her to let me know if she found anything out.

I wasn't expecting anything useful, mind you. If I picked up more intel that'd be great, but the important thing was to be seen asking questions, reaching out. Working on getting her better. I had some occult clout after the whole pulser thing, so I could be trusted—for those willing to trust me, which wasn't everyone.

Hadalce wouldn't speak to me. Hopefully I didn't get stabbed again; I got the impression she was just waiting for an opportunity to do some malpractice. She wasn't the only one, and I later found out one of the others—Belainel, who was apparently in charge of cleaning my room while I was out—was one of the main vectors of rumor against me. I'd have to do something about that later.

But the real problem was the ones who were trying too hard on my side.

"Can you teach me blood magic?" asked Alouren, one of the cooks, when I pulled her aside.

"What?!" I asked. "Fuck no. First off, I don't know any."

"Right, of course," she said, nodding rapidly.

"I'm going to pretend you meant that. Second, that shit's addictive. You're, like, seventeen, you'll fuck up your whole life."

"I can handle it!" Alouren insisted.

"Like hell. If they have to bring a priest to clean you up afterward, that means it's messing with your soul. If you want to mess with soul stuff, you need to wait ten more years, minimum. Hopefully by that point you'll be smart enough *not to mess with soul stuff.*"

Her eyes narrowed thoughtfully. "You're younger than twenty-seven."

"Yes, and that's fine because *I'm not doing blood magic.*"

She considered me with what I assume was supposed to be a piercing gaze.

"Look, kid," I said. "They told me you were really into the occult. Do you know anything that might be useful for counteracting what Lirian did to Roel? I can't bring her back unless we all work together."

"You think Lirian was doing blood magic?" Alouren asked, leaning in conspiratorially. "Maybe she serves Meris *and* Alcebios!"

I belatedly made a circle with my thumb and pointer finger and pressed it over my heart. It was a superstitious warding gesture meant to protect against the madness of Alcebios. As a pretend Estheni my reaction wasn't truly reflexive, which Alouren took as hesitation.

"Don't worry, your secret's safe with me," she said.

"Your lack of survival instinct is kinda just impressive at this point," I said. "Alright, kid, you wanna know a secret?"

"You can trust me!"

"In that case . . ." I said. I leaned closer, pulling an amulet out of my shawl—a tree, the symbol of Kives worship, as would befit a graced claiming descent from her. "Get wrecked, squirt."

Alouren's face fell. "I have to get back to work."

"Tell me if you hear anything useful!" I called after her retreating back.

A passing attendant paused to give both of us a look.

"Kives!" I said, waving the tree at him. "Not Alcebios! People need to stop spreading dumb rumors!"

He pressed thumb and forefinger to his heart.

"It is as my lady says," he said, and scurried away.

All cultures have a tradition of magic and ritual. The world is complex, which is another way of saying it's chaotic, but you can project patterns onto the chaos to make it feel more navigable. We're hardwired to find those patterns so we can function. They help us predict what the world will throw at us next, allowing us to have some control over our lives. That's why Earth invented science, with all the magic of replicating results and well-tested theories. Without control over your world, you die hungry and unhappy. Science lets us be something more than savages dying of preventable disease.

But of course science is only the perfected form of the human tendency to pattern match. If you don't have access to science, you use its imperfect form, superstition. Little behaviors or categories that worked for someone once and persisted for generations because no one bothered to try replicating them. The important thing about superstition is the placebo effect, the verisimilitude that convinces everyone that there's real weight behind it.

So I started with props. We moved Roel to the middle of the room, placing twelve candles around her. They helped me hang my tree amulet from the ceiling over her head. At each corner of the room I had them place a bundle of the barley-like grain they used here—representing life and growth. I wore the wispiest clothing at my disposal and had them do my hair in braids like a priestess of Kives.

Next, I used my hand amplifier to project an aura of hope, mystery, and power. I incremented the output by degrees as we set up the ritual, leaving room to spike the output as soon as I started speaking.

In attendance were people from the house—gardeners, blacksmiths, janitors, soldiers. Hadalce was there, of course, making sure I didn't do any blood magic. And of course Kuril was watching me expectantly. Showtime. I'd had Val and Abby looking over religious texts to come up with a suitably impressive script, and the resulting "spell" took about ten minutes to perform. That should be long enough to seem legitimate without giving people too much time to criticize me.

"Grandmother Kives," I began, streaming the script over my comm. "The child before us has a future yet unfulfilled. The work of a goddess can only be undone by a goddess."

As I paused for effect, Roel yawned.

"My leg hurts," she mumbled.

Cheers went up behind me. Kuril knocked over one of the candles as she dashed to Roel's side, holding her close. I blinked. What just happened?

"Abby's going to have to write you up for prayer," Markus said jokingly.

"She fucking approved this," I subvocalized.

A hand touched my side.

"Thank you," Delain told me. "I was worried it would come to nothing."

I forced a rictus smile onto my face.

"There was no reason to worry," I said. "All according to plan!"

CHAPTER FORTY-TWO

The Oathkeepers

The miraculous awakening led into an impromptu, if short-lived, party. Roel didn't remember the coma, obviously, only that she'd been sitting in the library with Kuril and was suddenly waking up with a giant gash in her leg. The wound still looked pretty brutal. I'd been forbidden from messing with it—miraculous healing wasn't a big part of Therian mythology. The graced allegedly had a closer connection to their ancestor gods than the normal population, so I'd kinda gotten away with my ritual, but Kives wasn't a healer. She was the goddess of time and consequence. The wound that cripples was as much her purview as the body's lengthy process of compensating for it.

A prayer that the wound would eventually heal would pass. A prayer that it would *immediately* heal would not. And if the wound *did* immediately heal, people would look for alternate explanations, and they'd be looking directly at me. The commander had ruled that to be an unacceptable breach of operational security.

So instead I got to watch Hadalce give her the root of some plant—for pain relief, although with a prescientific folk medicine culture, there was no guarantee it'd really help—and let Roel unhappily chew. She was still in obvious pain. After the attention started to overwhelm Roel, Hadalce shooed everyone out. Kuril got to stay. I almost didn't, until a look from Kuril had the vengeful doctor backing off.

"You're back with us," Kuril said, but what she meant was "I love you."

Roel gave her a weak hug. "I don't remember anything."

"Ajarel saved you," said Kuril.

"I heard," said Roel. "I'm so tired."

"Maybe we should let her rest," I said.

Kuril nodded. "Rest well, mouse." Roel gave her a small smile.

"Do you want a book?" I asked.

"She's supposed to rest," said Kuril.

I smirked. "Books are restful."

"*The Alcebiad*, please," said Roel.

"Ah," I said. "Light reading." She made a face at me.

Kuril sighed. "I'll have them bring it to you."

We shut the door behind us, leaving her to her recuperation. Kuril took my hand. I gave it a squeeze.

"Now comes the hard part," said Kuril. "When we were young, our first father fell ill for three *thessim*. He was bedridden for most of that time and could barely walk. He was never the same afterward. Hadalce tried to help him regain his strength, but he slept so much it was impossible to make progress."

Sounded like chronic fatigue to my modern ear. A friend of mine in college had to drop out because she couldn't manage hers. I never found out whether she got better.

"Roel will be a little stiff, but three days shouldn't be enough for serious atrophy," I said.

"Have you ever seen a leg wound like that?" Kuril reached down, tracing her thigh muscle. "The flesh that animates your leg is right here. With a deep enough injury, the leg fails to move at all. It will be hard for her to regain her strength if she can't walk."

"That's . . . not good," I said.

"No."

We looked at Roel's closed door. Kuril squeezed my hand and let go.

"Well," she said. "Worry achieves nothing."

"Actually, it keeps you motivated to solve problems," I said.

Kuril smiled ironically. "In the Vitares family, it tends to trap you in your office."

I gave her a hug. "We'll figure it out."

"Of course," she said. "I'll call for the priest of Gamal. And I suppose the Oathkeepers will want to speak with us now that Roel's awake. Have you had a chance to copy those documents from the Hetalos project?"

We both knew the answer was I hadn't.

"I'll get right on it," I said. "Anything to help the house."

"Thank you," Kuril whispered, and whether it was to me or a prayer to the gods I couldn't say.

I'd avoided the Oathkeepers last time they came around, taking an errand that got me off the premises as soon as the surveillance equipment told us they were coming. Kuril had spoken to them alone. Now I had a battle plan.

The Oathkeepers—and with my nerd brain it was *so* tempting to think of them as paladins—had a hierarchy of initiation, and once they were fully initiated, Javei blessed them with the ability to detect deceit. It wasn't, like, *illegal* to lie to an Oathkeeper, but it was pretty fucking suspicious. Fortunately for me, I had an advantage over the rest of Vitareas, which was that I'd watched my share of cop dramas, and I knew everyone had something to hide. So if I looked guilty that was probably normal for them. No use stressing about that. It just meant I could keep a cooler head when it came to hiding the really bad stuff, like the fact that I was here to kill their gods and uproot their religions like a bunch of weeds.

The dude they sent was on the younger side of middle-aged, with dark-brown hair and a braided beard that hung over his armor, which was of the leather variety. It wasn't like a leather jacket—the way ancient civilizations did this was by curing the leather to make it stiff enough to take a hit from a sharp object wielded by the angry son of a neighboring town. Everything was painted with a pearlescent-white lacquer that kinda made the armor look like mithril, if you didn't see the parts where the friction of normal movement had taken the lacquer off.

There was also a wiry dude with a wax tablet and a stylus, who followed the older dude with obvious deference. He was laden with multiple leather bags, straps crisscrossing over his shoulders. No obvious armor. No nonobvious armor, either, judging by the lack of clattering when he moved. We were pretty sure that going out in armor was a mark of initiation, like the junior Oathkeepers weren't supposed to be getting in fights without Javei's blessing or something.

The older guy introduced himself as Oathkeeper Falerior with a polite smile. His assistant, Initiate Ekoula, courteously avoided eye contact. I'd asked one of the attendants to sit with me—Mesales, who had nominally been assigned to me while I was an honored guest, but whose assistance I had heretofore avoided. Didn't want to be a burden, I guess. Apparently, to the Estheni, what I was actually doing was saying we had nothing to offer each other.

We'd checked on Roel and found her asleep, so it was just me today.

"Roel said she didn't remember anything about the attack," I said by way of greeting. "Given that she was unconscious when I got there, that seems likely."

"We'll get to that momentarily," said Falerior, nodding reassuringly. "I have no desire to disturb her rest. If you'll indulge me . . ."

He motioned to Ekoula, who withdrew a rod from one of his carrying bags. It was dark, topped with a sigil representing an eye, and seemed heavy in Ekoula's hands—although Falerior handled it with no apparent trouble.

"That your testimony can be trusted, I ask that you place your hand on the scepter."

A quick comm scan revealed a divine signature on the object. Three guesses who, first two don't count.

"It's not, like, gonna bite me or anything, right?" I asked.

"Not in my experience," Falerior said pleasantly. His patient gaze rested on me.

"Sure," I said with a shrug. It was probably some kind of scan for my intentions. Fuck that noise. I activated my cloak—not too much, the blessing wasn't that strong— and rested my hand on the eye sigil. Falerior just watched.

"I see," he said. "Well, thank you for that, Lady Ajarel."

"Of course," I said. "So how can I help?"

"Can you tell us about your previous encounters with the whisper known as Lirian?" Falerior asked. Ekoula held his tablet in the crook of his arm, stylus at the ready.

"Sure," I said, leaning forward. "We met for the first time at the arena. My friend Thala wants to reach the Kabidiad, so we were attempting to enroll him here. Lirian showed up and basically warned me not to do that or else bad things would happen."

"What kind of bad things?" Falerior asked. His face was totally open, the very model of polite attention.

"Nothing specific," I said. "Actually, I told her that if she was going to threaten me she should just do it directly, and she said no."

"So she didn't make any explicit threats," said Falerior. I didn't like his tone.

"Just give me a second," I said, trying to pull up the recording of that day. "She said don't enroll him in the Renathion because there are competitions and there are *competitions.*"

"And you interpreted that as a threat?"

"Yes!" I insisted. "She was very threatening!"

"I believe you," he said. The openness on his face hadn't changed at all. He was definitely lying.

"Okay, so, uh, next time, I went to a ball, and she tried to throw me out of it."

"Did she threaten you then?"

"Not exactly, but Roel got attacked. And she sponsored Thala, and Lirian doesn't want that for some reason."

Now, the exact words were true, but I was still kind of edging my way around the fact that Lirian didn't have anything to do with the attack. That was fine. We'd run through the possible scenarios and decided a blessing that detected deception would probably look for something in a narrow range of signatures, and I had the countersignals for all of them preprogrammed into my hand amplifier. I'd flicked it on when I started lying.

"I heard there was a challenge at the Jeneretti's Starlight Ball," said Falerior. "Was that between Lirian and you?"

"Yeah," I said. "She, like, tracked me down. Lady Obol even tried to get her to stop it, but she wouldn't."

"I see. She must have arrived very late, then? I heard the ball ended soon after."

"Uh, no," I said. "I was hiding from her. For, like, a couple of hours."

"You hid from an alleged whisper for a couple of hours." There was not an ounce of suspicion in his voice.

"Um, yes. Also, she's going around calling herself Lirian of Silence. I don't think anyone's contesting that she's a whisper."

"Not much of one, is she?"

"That's what I said!" I waved my hands irritably.

Falerior smiled politely. He was kinda getting on my nerves.

"Is there anything else you'd like to share?"

I wasn't sure whether to mention the first *real* attack, since it would be all sorts of sketchy. I decided to stall for time. "Mesales? Can you bring us some wine, please?"

"Of course, Lady Ajarel."

Falerior turned to me expectantly as she left the room. Okay, that was a horrible way to stall. You know what, fuck it, Kuril had probably mentioned that I'd been attacked already.

"Uh, before this attack, Lirian tried to stab me in an alleyway. It was during a Renathion. My food was drugged to make me go to the bathroom, then she jumped me when I left the arena."

"You've made a truly remarkable recovery."

I'd kept the hand amplifier off for that, so he should *know* I wasn't making up any of that. But he was still sitting there with that dumb attentive look on his face while Ekoula took notes.

"It wasn't that bad," I said. "Relatively speaking."

"Evidently," he said, nodding. What did he *want*?

"Uh, then there was the attack a couple nights ago."

He continued staring at me for a long time. I just stared back, getting increasingly uncomfortable. When it was clear I wasn't going to say anything else, he shifted and spoke up again.

"I've had the pleasure of speaking with many from the house," he said pleasantly. "I'm glad I finally had the chance to get your version of events. I've heard you sounded the alarm on that night. How did you know to do so?"

"Uh, there's a trick from back home," I said, sticking with the story I gave Lirian. "It lets me know if she's around."

"Mmm. I see. Can you demonstrate it for me?"

I glanced around the room as if inspiration would just be waiting on the wall or something. No dice. Eventually I just gave up and told the truth. "Uh, no."

"Pity," he said in apparent *infuriating* sincerity. "How fortunate that you were prepared for her."

"She *did* stab me."

"It was quite rational to be prepared, yes. I didn't mean to imply otherwise."

Like hell, I thought, but I didn't say anything.

"So, you raised the alarm, and then . . . ?"

"Uh, I grabbed a decorative sword from the hallway and ran after her. Roel and Kuril were unconscious in the library, and Lirian had a knife to Roel's throat. She wanted to ask me some questions."

"How thick was your sword's blade?"

I blinked. "What?"

"The width," said Falerior. "From edge to edge."

"Uh," I stammered, holding out my thumb and forefinger. "Like this big?"

He nodded. "Pardon my interruption."

"Why do you want to know that?" I asked. "Wait, you think *I* stabbed Roel?"

"Did you?" Falerior seemed genuinely curious and not at all like he was accusing me of stabbing my almost aunt.

"No!" I yelled. "Why would you even think that?"

"You're the only one who saw her that night," he replied, as if discussing the weather. "Whispers get blamed for all sorts of things."

"I saw her," I said. "She was here. I'm telling the truth."

"No one said otherwise." He smiled. His face looked very punchable. "What did Lirian ask you about?"

"She wanted to know how I knew where she was. I didn't tell her much, just that it was a trick from home."

"It's never good to give information to an enemy," said Falerior.

"Exactly," I said. "But I had to keep her talking so she didn't hurt Roel."

"Keep her talking until when?"

I switched the hand amplifier to not-lies again. "Until I could figure something out."

Falerior nodded again. What an agreeable fucking man.

"How did she escape?"

"I fucked up," I said. "She asked where I was really from. She thought I wasn't really from Salaphi. I, uh, got cheeky, I guess. I was really stressed out and wasn't thinking clearly. She did this thing where she spat on her knife, then cut herself, then stabbed Roel. We're still not really sure what that was supposed to do. She escaped in the confusion."

"That is what whispers do best," said the Oathkeeper in a reassuring tone of voice. "I had heard you came from Salaphi. Is that not true?"

"Kind of," I said, thumbing my hand amplifier. "I've moved around a lot."

"My condolences," said Falerior. "News of what happened there has even reached out here."

"What happened exactly?" I asked, playing innocent with technological assistance.

He looked slightly surprised for a moment.

"I'm sorry to be the one to tell you," he said. "Lady Ajarel, Salaphi was destroyed. Alcebios took them all."

"What?!" I asked. "How—"

I wasn't sure what to say, but I had to be convincingly upset about this—well, actually, I *was* upset about this, but how did I communicate that to the smiling bastard across from me? I would have liked to sink slowly back into my seat, but I hadn't had the presence of mind to jump out of it in shock.

Mesales saved me from my dilemma by returning with the wine.

"The hospitality of your house is great," said the Oathkeeper in a formal tone of voice, before switching to the pleasant tone he'd been using for this whole interrogation. "However, perhaps it would be best if we resumed this later."

"Of course," I said, somewhat shaken.

I watched them leave the house. Remotely, from the safety of my bedroom. Were Oathkeepers like Lirian? Would they notice the cameras?

"What did you think of Lady Ajarel?" Falerior asked his aide.

"Nervous," said Ekoula, eyes flicking as he recalled. "Shockingly informal. She didn't trust you. She gave a lot of incomplete answers."

"Remember that attitude," said Falerior. "You just met your first whisper."

Fuck.

CHAPTER FORTY-THREE

Salaphi's End

I couldn't sleep the night after my interview with Falerior. Instead, I scrolled through camera footage of the village I'd gotten killed.

We'd fled Salaphi after killing that ancestor god—Tarangor, I think?—and exfiltrated before Kives could sic her angels on the ship. We'd left a cloaked orbital relay so we could keep in contact with the surveillance equipment we'd left behind, but as far as I knew none of us had actually looked through the footage. So I'd gone back to see what the hell the Oathkeeper was talking about.

Present-day Salaphi was a ghost town.

Several buildings had burned down, including the chapel in the center. I remembered being in there—a lot, actually; it featured in some of my nightmares. The carvings were so intricate. Hundreds if not thousands of man hours must have gone into those. That was a significant loss.

Nothing moved in the town but wild animals. Smaller ones, scavengers for the most part. I recognized a few from Earth, where our evolutionary histories overlapped, and the others were small enough they probably filled the same ecological niches. There's a word for this in Velean: *veidikori*, which translates literally to "scavenger ground" and dynamically to "the desolation after a battle." Somehow I got that feeling even before I saw the wolf trotting past one of our cameras with a human arm in its mouth. But the wolf was the moment I decided to find the battle.

Falerior said, "Alcebios took them all"—it seemed like a metaphor, but I knew from my comm that he meant it almost literally. But Alcebios was an ascendant god. If they were moved to manifest, it wouldn't be for a dinky little village in the middle of nowhere. Those were more equivalent to mass-harvest events, and they resulted in legends, not rumors: the missing island of Atlantis, the plagues of Egypt, the annihilation of Pompeii. I considered that she might have gone after the Kives tree, but it was still hanging out in the forest, semiotically intact. It was actually pretty cool, you could see it from low orbit when the sky was clear.

Alcebios's frequencies were death, discord, and a progressive aspect of battle. There were legends that she sometimes appeared to people moments before their deaths, in the form of a naked but cloaked woman bearing their own mortal wounds on her body. If it was an etheric event it might have shown up on our recording equipment, but I didn't see anything like that. I felt confident dismissing the theory after I scanned the record for divine emanations on Alcebios's signature and didn't find anything.

So I went backward in the record. It'd been months since we left, and apparently weeks since whatever disaster had hit. I searched alone—the others were asleep. That felt correct, for some reason. I don't know if I would have asked them to help if they were awake. Weeks of nothing scrolled by, until I saw my first glimpse of a survivor. A lone man, dragging a rundown cart with his belongings, leaving the village behind. The cameras automatically tagged him with his designation—M-43—leftover analytical baggage from our intensive study of the social dynamics. I watched in reverse as M-43 spent his last few days in the town digging graves. The dead had been violently killed, large gashes memorializing their last moments as their bodies bloated in the tropical sun. As I continued to rewind, their faces grew less mottled and distorted by death, and one by one the archive's facial recognition system identified them as members of the village. The last to be revealed was F-53; the archive dutifully reported that she was married to M-43. I wouldn't have known otherwise. M-43's face was as emotionless as the archive. He worked mechanically. The only sign of his grief was the dead look in his eyes.

I skipped past him retrieving the bodies, skipped past their deaths, looking for the cause. I found them all gathered together—well, gathered in two groups, brandishing weapons at one another. Not professional weapons—scythes and axes and shovels. Farmer's tools. A pit formed in my gut. I was expecting bandits, or a monster, or maybe a demigod of Alcebios. Not the last survivors of the town doing one another in.

I didn't watch them slaughter one another. I skipped backward, looking for something else. A group of five had left the town; two women emerged as corpses from homes they'd entered earlier and never left. One of them had seen regular visits from others—probably an illness. The other had entered healthy, hours before they pulled her body out. Could have been a stroke, but I suspected it was suicide.

A week earlier the town's population numbered in the low thirties. The disaster had clearly already happened. People were packing up to leave; you could see the weight on their shoulders as they trudged through their tasks. No one smiled. The chapel and a couple of buildings around it were burned-out husks. Wait, that wasn't my fault, right? I thought I remembered setting Tarangor's body on fire before I left. I could have jumped forward again to double-check what happened to the ten or so people who weren't there later, but honestly I didn't want to know.

I skipped back a month this time, checking to see if the chapel was still burned down. It was. There were more faces in Salaphi, fifty or so by my estimate. The oppression that would be present a month later was still evident here. Maybe worse. I saw fights in the streets. People yelled at one another; others pretended their neighbors didn't exist. No one made eye contact, and I was willing to bet that wasn't just for Estheni social reasons.

No one had obvious wounds. There was a weight on my chest and shoulders whose presence was becoming more obvious as I continued to watch the village implode on itself. I skipped backward a couple of days, but on some level I knew. I knew. I just didn't want to see.

I navigated to the day we killed Tarangor. I watched myself lead Arguel to the chapel. We had no cameras inside, but I didn't need cameras to remember what happened next—

—the blade biting into her neck, the spray of blood, the shock in her eyes, warm wetness on my face—

I shuddered.

Somewhere beyond the cameras' field of view, I was lying catatonic in the med bay. But the people of Salaphi were still there. The ruined wall was just barely visible from the angle of the one good camera we had aimed at that area. No one approached the chapel, which it turned out I hadn't burned down after all. No one except Arguel's husband. Mila, I think. He carried her out with their children. When they got near, they became hunched and anxious, as if expecting a predator to spring out at them at any moment. The etheric stain we'd left on the village had lingered, and everyone under its shadow was becoming fearful and paranoid.

Two days later they set fire to the chapel. It didn't help.

My doomscrolling—doomstreaming?—was interrupted by Abby's voice cutting through my rumination.

"Lilith? The medical translator was activated, and your cloak is on. Is everything okay?"

"Oh, uh, yeah," I said. "I used the translator to clear my head."

Did you know that sleepiness is the result of waste products building up in your brain? Did you know that you can just translate those out of your brain?

"And the cloak?"

"Practice," I lied, shutting it off. The flood of guilt and self-loathing immediately came back.

"Lilith," Abby said warningly.

"Commander," I replied. "I reviewed our intelligence on the aftereffects of the Salaphi op. We can retrieve our equipment now."

There was a pause. She had to know that wasn't everything, but with my recent graduation to adult, at least in Velean terms, we were assuming that I knew she knew and was making the decision not to tell her. Or at least I think that's what was happening.

"Thank you for your efforts," she said. *"You should sleep."*

"Oh yeah, why are you up?"

"Because it is morning, Lilith."

I pulled my awareness back to my physical body and opened my eyes. The Estheni blocked their windows with rolling wooden shutters, and the sun was peeking through the seams in mine.

"Ah," I said. "But I'm not sleepy."

"The medical translator could fix that, if that's your concern."

I chuckled. "Lots to do today. I'll just rough it."

"What's bothering you?"

What was the Velean-adult thing to do here? No one fucking explained anything to me, and I'd never seen the others be emotionally vulnerable like this with one another. But Abby had always been there for me, and she'd understand if I didn't get everything right. A culture full of people who lived for centuries probably wouldn't expect me to become an expert in a couple of days, no matter how much it felt like I had to be.

"The village is gone," I said. "We were supposed to help them, but instead we wrecked their home. Now they're all going to end up in other villages with their own ancestor gods. Did we actually help anyone?"

"*You used the knowledge from that encounter to help the Vitares family,*" said Abby. "*Deicide missions are difficult. It's not a weight just anyone can bear. It helps to take your victories where you can, until we go for the kill. These questions will become less pressing once we've killed a god or two.*"

"Just like that?" I asked.

"*Just like that,*" said Abby. "*You'll have saved billions.*"

"For some other god to snack on," I said. "When does it end?"

"*When we've killed them all and the planet is safe. But you knew that.*"

I sighed. "I did. I need to go check on Roel."

"*Of course. But Lilith?*"

"Yeah?"

"*I know it's hard. But you've performed above and beyond what was expected of you. We're all incredibly proud.*"

I walked into Roel's room with a smile on my face. She was awake already, chewing that root they used for pain relief. She was going through a lot of that stuff.

"Hey, mouse," I said, trying out Kuril's pet name for her.

"Don't," she said sharply.

"Uh, sorry," I said. "Can I call you 'hamster'?"

"Mouse is what my mother called me," Roel said softly.

"Oh," I murmured. "Oh, I'm so sorry, I didn't mean to—"

"It's fine," she said, rolling over in bed.

I sat down in a chair next to her bed, first picking up *The Alcebiad* so I didn't have to sit on it. I thumbed through a couple of pages to see if I could read any of it. The little I caught seemed pretty neutral, but my vocabulary was limited.

After a couple minutes, Roel shifted so she could see me again.

"What's a hamster?" she asked.

I hid a smile. Even making her sad wasn't enough to suppress her curiosity. "It's a rodent. Little bigger than a mouse. Back home, we'd keep them as pets. You put this little wheel in their cage, and they just run on it to get exercise."

Roel's brow furrowed. "How big was the cage? Wouldn't they have trouble turning?"

I blinked. "No, you just keep them oiled. They turn just fine."

Roel giggled a little. "I don't believe you. Why would oiling your wheels help a rodent learn to steer them?"

"Ohhhh!" I laughed. "No, the axle is connected to the cage. Like—here, where's your drawing desk?"

"On my desk," said Roel.

"That seems redundant," I said, getting another giggle out of her. "Okay, look, so you've got the wheel, right?"

I drew a picture of a hamster wheel for her. Roel decided that she wanted to design a better one. One that the hamster could *steer*. We passed the morning laughing at each other's increasingly silly designs.

The empty village and the burned-out chapel weighed heavily in my thoughts, but I kept a smile on my face. I'd caused a disaster for Salaphi, and I'd brought disaster to Roel, too. The least I could do was help her deal with it.

CHAPTER FORTY-FOUR

Shopping for Boys

The morning sun beat down on the oiled muscles of a hundred Therian himbos. Markus and Cades were among them. Markus's fame had waned over the past couple weeks, with the crowd's attention moving to whoever had pulled off something flashy the last competition or two. He was standing some distance from Cades, who seemed like he was avoiding our favorite muscle head.

"*What's the deal with him?*" I subvocalized.

"*He won't say,*" Markus said, a touch heavily.

"*We gotta figure that out,*" I said. "*Abby, think you could tail him?*"

"*Your old hairstylist could tail him. He doesn't pay attention.*"

I snorted.

"What is it?" Kuril asked from next to me.

I scrabbled for an explanation. "I mean, just look at them all. Clumsy, lumbering muscle brains."

"That's why we're here," she said. "I thought we agreed it'd be good to expand the house."

"Well, yeah," I said. "I thought you meant, uh, just you."

"Behold, the fruit of Kabiades," Kuril said with a bit of a leer. "There's enough for both of us."

"I'm not having an orgy with my mom!" I waved my hands frantically. "Adopted or not!"

The adoption ceremony had ended up being a simple thing, with me swearing to Gamal to take the Vitares family as my own and Kuril and Roel swearing to accept me as part of the family. There were a lot of smiles among the rest of the house. Some of them didn't even look forced! I was slowly but steadily clawing my way back from the absolute pit of social capital I'd dug myself into by ignoring them all in the beginning.

My new status as Ajarel Vitares seemed to have lit some kind of fire in Kuril, though, because she'd decided to go shopping for consorts while Markus did his thing. Roel was at home recuperating; even apart from her lack of energy, her leg made it impossible to walk.

"He's reached the fourth round every time so far," she'd said. "We won't miss anything."

That was certainly true for me—I had Markus's feed up on my comm. Barked orders from the presiding priest had the contenders all pairing off in preparation for the wrestling event. Markus had taken a couple moments to pick out his buddies from the first day here, but mostly he was looking at Cades, who was looking anywhere but at him. His refusal to seek out another sponsor was extremely fishy; the Voranetti *had* to have some kind of dirt on him. I could almost feel Markus making the decision to win this event just so that Cades would have to deal with him.

Kuril dragged me out to the stalls where young men in eligibility wreaths were aggressively demonstrating their domestic potential. I was expecting us to peruse the selections more, but she walked up to the very first stall. He was a wiry type, brown hair and golden eyes, and he was weaving rope out of a pile of filament larger than he was. I had no idea how he'd carted it in here.

"Godsmile," said the prospect. Kuril looked him up and down.

"Hm," she said, glancing at me to gauge my reaction. "No. How about you?"

"He's standing *right there*," I said. He was looking pretty rattled at Kuril's brutal rejection. "Are you just dismissing him based on looks? You don't even know his name!"

"I'm looking for a consort, not a husband," she said, as if it was the most obvious thing in the world. "Even if he's clearly skilled with those fingers, his brothers obviously stole his portion at the table. We must be decisive. There are thirty-eight occupied stalls; we must assess ten per round if we want to watch Thala. Now, yes or no?"

"Uh, sorry," I told the guy. "Not today."

"Decisive," Kuril said approvingly. "We'll check this side of the path and get the others on the way back."

Markus had paired off with a dude whose name I didn't know yet, but who I recognized as one of the weaker competitors. There was a whole art to this. You couldn't *obviously* avoid people who you knew were going to wipe the floor with you because then you were failing to exercise the manly virtue of courage. But you *could* maneuver around in between bouts such that you ended up next to someone who wasn't one of those people. At the same time, however, those people knew they would win against you, and they'd be trying to close the distance.

Importantly, all of this had to happen under the guise of conversation and general mingling because otherwise it wrapped back around to obvious avoidance and marked you as a coward. That might not matter for the results of the wrestling competition, but you'd get crushed in the passion events with their subjective judging. So even in the strength events, social skills got you further. And Markus probably had more social skills than any two of the others put together.

"How about this one?" Kuril asked.

I refocused on my immediate surroundings. "This one" was a hairy dude who was grilling strips of meat with a suggestive expression. I was not at all sure what was supposed to be suggestive about this, but I dislike people who make that face at me on general principle.

"Pass," I said, making direct eye contact with the dude. It felt great, like I was telling off every overconfident guy who'd made an unwelcome pass at me over the years. His face crumpled.

"The chest hair is nice," Kuril said, tapping a thumb on her chin. His face uncrumpled. "Hm. No."

Kuril was apparently picky about her men. I suppose technically speaking so was I, given that I'd rejected everyone we ran into. But I just—wasn't going to do that, okay?

A couple rejects later we ran into a bare-chested dude with pinpoint burn scars all over his arms and a downright luxurious beard. Kuril stopped to appreciate the view.

"What's your name?" she asked him.

"I am Bofa," he said. "A blacksmith by trade."

I barely held back a snicker. Kuril shot me a questioning glance.

"Nothing," I said quickly, fighting the smirk that wanted to take over my face. "It's nothing."

"As long as you have no objections," she said. "Godsmile, Bofa. From your presence here, I infer you're in need of work."

"Godsmile. My hands have found less to occupy them than I prefer," he said, risking eye contact. Kuril favored him with a smile.

"I would like to hire you to demonstrate your skills at the Vitares estate," she said. "I shall instruct the forge mistress to prepare you a suitable task—tomorrow afternoon? With refreshment and entertainment after your successful showing."

"I would be honored," said Bofa.

We walked away, Kuril with a look of satisfaction on her face.

"*Lilith, are you okay?*" Markus asked, already having pinned his first-round opponent in the minute after the round started.

"No one on this planet can understand my pain."

Twentyish stalls and two invitations (both Kuril's) later, Markus and Cades both advanced to the fourth round. We were a little behind on our schedule—the bouts were, like, six minutes, so at ten stalls per bout, that was, like . . . thirty seconds per stall? Ish?—but Kuril seemed happy. She hadn't pushed me too hard to pick out a guy for myself, which was fine by me. My newly developing Velean senses gave me the feeling that I was mostly along for moral support.

Markus and Cades ended up close to each other during the prebout shuffle, which might have turned out badly for their reputations if Cades hadn't called out Peloman the Cartwright instead. From my experience watching practice bouts, that fight could go either way, with maybe 60 percent odds in Cades's favor. You had to pick on guys your own size if possible, otherwise you weren't being honorable. Peloman was the size of a tiny mountain. No one would doubt Cades's honor today.

This wasn't normal, though. Usually Cades and Markus sought each other out at this point to see who'd win the right to go for the finals.

"*He's definitely avoiding you,*" said Abby.

"It could be for competitive reasons," Markus said. He didn't believe it, either.

"We need to infiltrate the Voranetti," I subvocalized. *"They definitely have something on him. Give me some cameras and I'll have them bugged by tonight."*

"Aren't you keeping Roel company tonight?" Abby said.

"I can do it afterward," I said.

"You haven't slept. You need to rest."

"Okay, I'll do it tomorrow," I subvocalized huffily. *"Get off my case."*

Markus spoke up. *"Lilith, we should chat about—"*

He was cut off by a shout from the priest. His opponent charged him, hoping to gain an advantage by striking first. Markus moved to a crouch and lunged into his opponent's onrush at the last moment, flipping him over his well-oiled back. The poor guy hit the ground with a thump that knocked the wind out of him. I winced sympathetically, then pretended I'd been paying attention to what Kuril was saying. Fortunately, after dozens of men, I was starting to get a sense of her tastes.

"The forearms, though," I told her. She made a nonverbal noise that meant, "Good point." The enterprising street chef in our latest stall—who Kuril had yet to address directly—subtly tried to emphasize the forearms in question.

"What's your name?" asked my ruthless adoptive mother.

"Godsmile!" he said, relieved at finally being acknowledged. "I am called Peioripedes."

"I have no need of a cook. Do you have other skills?"

"Uh—why, yes, of course. I am a painter of some success—"

"Very good. May the goddesses smile on your business." With that, she swept off.

"We're in a hurry," I explained to the crestfallen man as I scurried after her.

"It wasn't for competitive reasons," Markus said with finality.

"What?" I subvocalized. *"You mean Cades avoiding you? Why's that?"*

"It was subtle enough that the audience won't notice, but Cades just threw his fight."

Markus won laurels for wrestling. Cades had already earned his in the racing event earlier. Now the Renathion was shifting to passion events. For once, Markus wasn't heading to the private exhibition area for the massage contest. Kuril had to—she was one of the judges—but we'd agreed I should stay to support Markus. The competitions for singing and dancing had a different slate of judges, appointed by a council reporting to the Visionary, who did their best to appear impartial but always managed to select the Jeneretti's favorite candidates.

Fair was fair. We had a resonator and every intention of changing their minds.

As bare-chested Kabiadesian acolytes swept the arena grounds to clear out the wrestling circles, Markus lined up with the other competitors for song. A dais was assembled from prebuilt sections of beautifully painted wood, including a curved roof that seemed designed to grasp at the laws of acoustics. With Kuril out of sight, it was my turn to step up.

I disappeared.

The judges' seats were placed at the center of the arena seating, the part where it curved around at the far end of the competition ground. The Vitares box was more to the side. This was ostensibly because it was the same box they'd occupied since the city's founding, but there had been renovations to the arena, and the other big houses had boxes close to the center. I headed straight for them. People *saw* me, so they didn't bump into me, but the cloak ensured they would never *understand* that they'd seen me. I threw myself into a presence meditation, focusing on the fact that I existed, forcing my noetic faculties to aim through the fog I was generating around myself.

I made it to the bottom row of benches without incident. I was preparing to jump the small railing to the arena proper when I heard the clattery sound of people running in armor. I looked up at the source of the noise. Three Oathkeepers, led by Falerior the Smug, rounded the corner of the arena, slowing to a more measured pace once they were in public view. Falerior was holding that rod with the eye sigil on it, and it was pointing in my direction.

I immediately pinged an *observe and support* request to Abby and sent a command to my eyes to zoom in on the Oathkeepers' faces, where my comm picked up the meaning of their moving lips.

"—in this direction, but we'll never find her in the crowd," Falerior was saying.

"There are two exits in the back," said one of his buddies, an old woman wearing the same style of armor. "We can block them for now."

"*I'm on your feed*," said Abby.

"You want to stand watch for invisible whispers?" asked Falerior, whose expression communicated long-suffering patience.

"We should prevent everyone from leaving, brother. Smoke her out—" My vision was blocked as Falerior turned to look at her, getting his dumb head in the way.

"*Get moving*," said Abby. "*Do you need a distraction?*"

"Use your best judgment," I said. "I'm going to split them up."

My original plan had just been to cross the grounds and climb up to where the judges were, but with Falerior and his Magic Wand of Bullshit, that was probably just going to turn into a *Tom and Jerry* chase sequence and get Markus's performance suspended. So instead I made my way through all the people pressed up against the railing, wishing I'd taken the high path instead, or maybe ducked into the tunnels beneath the stadium. The next staircase was about a hundred feet away.

I saw the Oathkeepers part ways behind me—a lucky glimpse between egregiously expansive hairstyles and cheering women pressed up against the railing. Falerior was walking sedately along the side of the arena, making surprisingly good time for all that he wasn't in any obvious hurry. I lost sight of his buddies, but if their plan was just to block the exits, I wasn't worried. I had my pulser on me.

I threw myself into presence meditation, keeping the awareness of my soul fixed firmly in my noetic faculties despite the etheric fog I was spewing all over it. The necessity of pushing past people without knocking them over meant that Falerior was gaining on me. I decided to push forward. It's not like he could do anything if he caught up to me, right? The height difference was, like, eight feet, and he was a middle-aged man wearing twenty pounds of armor, if I recalled the chain-shirt stats correctly.

"*Is he tracking your cloak?*" Abby said.

"It's the cloak, or it's just me," I said. "I'm not taking that risk. Move, please."

The lowborn merchant woman—when had I started thinking of merchant-class people in those terms?—didn't hear me. I took a deep breath and shoved my way past her, which she blamed on the lady next to her. The sound of the resulting argument faded into the noise of the crowd as I kept moving. Sorry, gals. It's for the greater good.

"*He can't be tracking you. The cloak should block that.*"

"How am I supposed to know what fuckery these guys throw at us next? Maybe it's, like, a Wand of Track That Cloaked Fucker, and it just magically bypasses everything."

"*That's— Lilith, what would it even track? Your signal is obfuscated.*"

"Bullshit," I said, trying to squeeze behind someone who needed to bathe more. "It would track fucking bullshit."

"*He's almost on you. You need to turn off the cloak.*"

"He'll find me!" I said.

"*I'll walk you through the infiltration if you need it. You can do this.*"

I swore and turned off the cloak. I was careful enough to do it in that order. Falerior didn't stop.

"Shit shit shit he's still coming," I hissed. I was trying to make more progress, but it was harder to move now that I was visible. "Markus isn't on first, right?"

"*You've got ten minutes or so.*"

"That's doable if I don't get arrested," I said. "Fuck, Kuril's gonna kill me."

"*You haven't been—*"

"Thank you, I am *aware!*"

Falerior was almost on top of me, but the staircase was *right there*. I'd be a sitting duck for Falerior to spot if I took the stairs up, but there was a ground-access ramp right next to them. If I could get down there, I'd be out of his line of sight. Maybe he'd pass me by.

I took a risk and dove over the railing. The ramp was made of concrete, and that did *not* make for a comfortable landing. My hands and elbows got scraped up, and I tumbled into a pile of clothing and blunt-force trauma.

"Fuck, ow," I said, rolling to a standing position and rubbing my forehead.

"Damn, that was a tumble," said an elderly voice.

I looked up. My eyes widened as they met the eyes of the Oathkeeper slowly walking up the ramp. It was the older woman who'd suggested covering the exits. Steel gray ringlets hung down from under her helmet and matched her all-too-perceptive eyes.

"Oathkeeper Vanerel," she introduced herself.

"G-godsmile," I said.

"Just wonderin'," she said with a knowing smile, "but have you seen an invisible girl runnin' around?"

CHAPTER FORTY-FIVE

The Case Is Afoot

I was all set to protest my innocence to Oathkeeper Vanerel, but there was only one response to being asked if I'd seen an invisible girl, so all that prep work got thrown out.

"What? That's a contradiction in terms," I said. "If I could see an invisible girl, she wouldn't be invisible."

Vanerel blinked, then bullied onward. "I think we both know that's not the real reason you haven't seen one. Lady Ajarel of Salaphi, correct?"

"Um," I said.

Was I? I was and I wasn't, and either answer could read as a lie depending on how her truth-detection blessing functioned. There were too many unknowns here.

I frantically went over what I knew about Oathkeepers. They were supposedly able to detect deceit, but we hadn't done an etheric analysis of how that worked. *Theoretically* Falerior shouldn't have been able to tell when I was lying, but apparently the Bullshit Rod of Detect Lilith was specifically an antiwhisper countermeasure and not like putting your hand on a Bible before testifying in court—which, while we're on the topic, *how the fuck was I supposed to know that?* So if he'd known I was dodgy from the get-go, maybe using the hand amplifier to cancel out my deception had just forced him to conclude nothing I said could be trusted.

"It's not a difficult question," said Vanerel, taking a step toward me.

Fuck it. If you're going to fall, fall forward.

"Okay, look, lady," I said, glaring at her. "I know you all profiled me, and I probably look suspicious as hell. Fine. So be it. Forgive me if I don't want to say anything incriminating. But also, you know what? I don't know what fucking *counts* as far as your lie-detection thingy goes. As of this morning I'm Lady Ajarel Vitares. So I think that means I'm not Ajarel of Salaphi anymore? Or at least it's not as true as the current name? But, like, I don't know, do I really belong in the family? Like, come on, they've only known me for a couple mo—*thessim*, and, like, I know there's the whole life-debt thing, but I don't even know if they really like me! Roel's just lonely because none of the other kids in her peer group have the same interests, and I'm pretty sure Kuril doesn't even approve of me, but she's desperate, and she's stuck with me anyway, so might as well, right? I mean, fuck, *am* I Lady Ajarel Vitares? I don't know. You tell me. You're the one with the fucking truth vision."

Vanerel whistled. "Sounds like you've got some thinking to do."

"Not helpful, lady," I said, but honestly it was kind of a weight off my shoulders to say all of that to someone, so my tone was grateful.

She closed the distance and grabbed my arm. "How 'bout we chat about it on the way back to the Javeiron."

"Whoa whoa whoa," I said. "You can't fucking abduct me in broad daylight! I'm graced!"

"They always say that," said Vanerel. "Funny thing about that is you ain't got the arm strength to stop me."

"Maybe that means you should stop yourself," I said, pressing my hand amplifier to the wrist that was holding me. I flicked it to one of my presets, a cocktail of overwhelming shame and remorse, with top notes of self-loathing and misery. I called it the Mom Special. Even from the secondhand blowback, I was cringing at how corny that clapback was.

"Girl, I have a job to do," she said. "I'll stop myself when I'm good and ready. And get that thing off my arm. I don't know which fortune teller you bought it from, but she stole your money."

Oh, for fuck's sake. "You don't feel bad about what you do?" I prodded as she dragged me down the ramp.

"I serve the god of justice, girl."

I subvocalized a warning to the rest of the team. *"Hey, uh, quick update, hand amps don't work on Oathkeepers."* I shoved the hand amp back in its hidden pocket and fished around for my pulser.

"So what's all this about not feelin' like you belong? The priest said you were a Vitares, didn't he?"

"You're literally dragging me off for an interrogation," I said, slipping the pulser into my hand. We were almost out of the arena now. "Why are you helping me with my personal issues?"

"It's no reason not to be kind," she said.

"Fair enough," I said, and pulsed her. Then I pulsed her again.

"How many of those things have you got?" Vanerel asked. "Goddesses, Ajarel."

"Fucking *bullshit*," I spat. My hand tightened around the pulser grip.

Vanerel laughed. "How long have you been carrying those arou—"

I snapped. The pulser was accelerating toward her face before I even noticed I'd thrown it. It caught her right under the eye. She gave a throaty shout and released my arm on reflex, hands moving to protect her face.

Fuck the fancy sci-fi weapons. *I* was a weapon.

I followed my Academy training, pivoting to the side and shoving her while my ankle hooked around her load-bearing foot. It was the best option here that didn't cause permanent damage. Vanerel went straight to the ground.

She'd probably had decades of experience on me, but I was younger, and I had the element of surprise, and in a fight that can make all the difference. She wasn't armed, but I wasn't about to get into a fistfight with a hard-boiled old lady in chain mail.

This would be the part where the action-movie heroes of my childhood would go for a knockout blow to the head, but all the mooks in those movies probably ended up with brain damage, and the Oathkeepers were definitely going to hit me with a round of police brutality if I did that. So instead I just yelled at her.

"I'm not a whisper!" I shouted while she scrambled upright. "I didn't hurt Roel! Leave me *alone!*"

I activated my cloak. I snagged my pulser where it was lying on the ground—having picked up a few scrapes the commander would *not* be happy about—and ran for the judges' podium. The Oathkeepers might have a bullshit wand to detect me, but the lady who was close enough to be a problem had no way to talk to the guy who was holding it. Later, suckers.

"*Update,*" I subvocalized. "*Pulsers don't work on them, either. Or at least on this one.*"

"*It looked like it worked from what I saw.*" Markus laughed. He must be watching my feed.

"*Abby—*" Val started.

"*Already on it,*" she replied. "*I have eyes on Falerior. I can get you a deep scan.*"

Val treated us all to the etheric impression of a throaty chuckle. Normally when he laughed like that, someone was about to die.

"Who are we murking?" I said.

"*Much has been made of the corrupting madness of Alcebios,*" he said. "*But given the number of antiwhisper countermeasures they have available, who else might that blessing be effective against?*"

"Ha! Fuck them!"

Val's voice was inquisitive. "*Them?*"

"Uh," I said. "You know. What's-his-face."

"*She means,*" said Abby. "*Hm. Val, there's an antimemetic effect active in the area. Our Merisite opponent is on-site.*"

"Let's fucking go," I snarled. "I don't remember who they are, but I hate them so much."

"*Negative, Lilith, Markus is almost up. Get that relay to the judge's podium.*"

"Yes'm. My MDO is clear," I said. "Abby? Markus?"

"*Clear,*" said Abby.

"*Lilith,*" Markus said in the very patient tones of someone who was waiting for me to remember he was currently naked except for a glorified loincloth and had nowhere to hide an infrared camera.

"It's been a long day."

"*It's not even noon.*"

"It's been a really long day."

"*There's two people ahead of me,*" Markus said. "*Can you make it in time?*"

"We're gonna find out," I said. I booked it.

The cloak got me close to the podium with a minute to spare. On to the next obstacle: the eye rod was pointing directly toward me, and if I approached the podium while cloaked, the Oathkeepers would guess I'd messed with it somehow. They might guess anyway, but so far all they had on me was that I'd assaulted one of them arresting me for a crime I didn't commit. Which, uh, would have been pretty bad back on Earth, but also grabbing me without a formal warrant or anything was all sorts of out of line if we were using Earth rules. I could probably deal with it.

I quickly stripped off several of my more expensive accessories and my reversible shawl. The accessories went into a pouch inside my skirt, the shawl went back on with the darker-shaded inside facing out. I let out the large ringlets in my hairdo and hastily tied it into a small ponytail on top of the existing mess of braids; it wouldn't look pretty, but it *would* look different.

I decloaked slowly, letting the people around me acclimate to my presence instead of suddenly appearing out of nowhere. Out came the amplifier relay, a clay mug we'd stolen from the arena grounds and synced to the resonator back at the *Ragnar*.

"Hey, you," I said, grabbing an attendant. "Top me off." I handed him three *drobol*, which was overkill, but I was in a hurry. He nodded obsequiously and reached for one of the wineskins slung over his back.

"The good one," I corrected him.

He paused, then reached for a different wineskin. One happy consequence from Isseret's tutelage: I knew how to identify the good booze at stadiums. Only the best for our esteemed judges.

I saw Falerior patrolling along the edge of the arena grounds. He was holding the Bullshit Wand loosely at his side, but his attention was on the stands, sweeping over the audience. I tried to pull up Abby's lessons on posture and bearing, letting myself blend in with the crowd. Don't let yourself be too stiff. Don't look around suspiciously. Move with purpose but not so aggressively that you draw attention.

Falerior's eyes passed over me. I breathed a sigh of relief.

Mug of wine in hand, I approached the judges' podium as they listened to some well-toned naked dude sing about some battle I'd never heard of. Gritting my teeth against my comm's attempt to contort "spears joining like clashing teeth" into three syllables, I set the mug down next to the nearest judge.

"A gift," I told her, then withdrew before she could ask any awkward questions like, "Why?" or "From whom?"

"Mission accomplished," I said, vanishing back into the crowd. "Markus, Val, it's all your show now."

"*Want to watch?*" said Val.

"I gotta look for, uh, the fucking person." I hopped on his feed, anyway.

"*I'm blocked here, too,*" said Markus. "*Have these competitions been directly disrupted yet?*"

"*No,*" said Val.

"I'll wrap things up with the Oathkeepers, then," I said. "Maybe we can pivot them against her."

"*I'll move to support,*" said Abby.

It was time. Markus was up on stage.

"O proud daughters of Vitareas!" he bellowed. "Today I will sing for you 'The Lay of Kirigiel'!"

That got a decent reaction from the crowd; we'd picked something well-known enough that obscurity wouldn't be a problem. But our real hidden ace was miles away, cracking his fingers in front of the now fully assembled notion organ. Its console was halfway between an organ and an arcade game: three rows of twelve keys each on the right, and on the left a plunge grip designed to accept your whole forearm for maximum maneuverability or something. A digital display showed a three-dimensional representation of the waveforms being produced at Markus's location.

"*We got this, buddy. They fall,*" Markus said.

"*They die,*" Val replied.

Val pressed the first key as Markus let his first note fly, and the effect was *beautiful*. Literally, that was the key Val was pressing, while modulating the undertones with the left-hand grip. The entire arena was spellbound—even Falerior, distracted from his pursuit by the transcendent majesty of Markus's song.

Then the song began in earnest. Markus was passable on musical skill—certainly in the top half of the randos in this competition—but with the addition of the notion organ, the song was grander than anything Theria had ever heard.

With lightning-fast twitches of his arm, Val shunted etheric tones onto different channels of the notion organ, expanding them or drawing them in. The keyboard wasn't laid out like an Earth piano (the keys had equal sizes), and Val didn't play it like one, either. Every key was quickly and skillfully depressed in sequence, each time like he was setting some switch on a nuclear-launch console, until another twitch of his arm loaded the frequency into the chamber and fired it on another etheric channel.

The story of Kirigiel took shape more viscerally than any other story I'd heard— her common origins as the daughter of an unjustly disgraced blacksmith (with a mere twist of inflection, Markus seemingly impressed on us the shame and squalor of her upbringing), her desire to bring the truth to light, her initiation as an Oathkeeper, and the mystery she solved that no one else could.

I was enraptured, and so was everyone else. (Channel seven on Val's notion organ was outputting a sense of *fascination*.) Feelings swelled and receded with Markus's voice as we experienced every emotional beat of the song. We were swept along with Kirigiel as she followed her destiny and saved the empress from a deadly plot.

And through it all, a clay mug on the judges' podium broadcast the feeling that this, surely, was excellence worthy of recognition. Sorry, kids. We've got a god to kill. You can feel your own feelings some other time.

Markus won laurels right there. That was his second pair; one more and we were set for the Kabidiad. Now all I had to do was stay out of jail until then.

"I've got a plan for the Oathkeepers," I said. "Abby, you got eyes on Falerior?"

"*He's below the podium. Move to the right and you'll see him.*"

I activated my cloak again, restoring my outfit to the state I'd walked in with. Then I strolled to the bottom level of the arena seats, slowly pulsing my cloak on and off. By the time I reached the railing, Falerior was waiting for me.

"So," I said, looking down at him with every ounce of self-possession I could muster.

"So," he echoed, expression just as open and neutral as the day of my interrogation.

"I want to make a deal." I was suave, I was confident, I had value to trade here.

"And what deal would that be?"

"I know you want the truth of what happened to Roel," I said.

"That is, of course, my divine duty."

"I know you've come to some conclusions about me," I said dismissively, "but I'm here to tell you that here at this very Rethanion, there is a, a, um."

Falerior raised his eyebrows. "There's a what?"

"A . . . You know, that thing?"

"I'm afraid I don't."

"The thing! The invisible thing! Their name is . . . Fuck, I can't think the name."

"I don't follow."

I grimaced. "Motherfucker!"

"There's a motherfucker?"

"Yes!" I jabbed a finger at him. "Oathkeeper Falerior, there is an invisible motherfucker in this very arena, and with your help, I swear by all the gods that we will *catch* this motherfucker."

CHAPTER FORTY-SIX

CSI: Vitareas

Falerior didn't respond immediately to my offer to team up. He watched me, very calmly, assessing the situation. Behind him, another contestant stood up nervously, voice trembling a bit as he announced his song to the crowd. Whoever had to follow Markus's performance was always going to have a bad time, and I felt a little sorry for the dude.

"So you would like me to believe this . . . ne'er-do-well is in the vicinity," he said. "The one who you claim injured Roel?"

Was that the same person? "Uh, the person who injured Roel was . . ." I tried. "They were a . . . Fuck, what was I talking about?"

"Is this the same person who injured Roel?" Falerior asked.

"*Lilith, I'm on your feed*," said Val. "*I'm outside the range of the effect, so you can trust me to be accurate. The answer to Falerior's question is yes.*"

"Yes, it's the same person."

"Is this person a whisper?"

"What did you say?" I asked. "I didn't quite catch that."

To my left, I spotted an unobtrusively dressed woman making her way through the benches. If I wasn't looking for her specific shade of blue, I'd have missed her. Abby was carrying an amphora, inside of which lay a higher-powered etheric scanning device. "*One minute*," she said. "*Keep him talking*."

Falerior nodded, satisfied. "Never mind. You've convinced me there's another person of interest here. I can't say you've convinced me you'll be valuable in finding them."

"I have something you don't," I said. "I can find invisible people."

"I don't see a *skios* on you, and I'm not convinced you had an opportunity to attune one."

Thank you for the valuable information, Mr. Oathkeeper. Trust the servants of a god of revelations to offer helpful information about their capabilities. I smiled. Abby was almost here.

"I found out she was in the library," I said. "And I didn't know ahead of time. Your truth vision picking all that up?"

Falerior considered.

"The truth belongs to Javei," he said. "All is known, and all shall be known."

I tilted my head expectantly, a kind of "Okay, go on?" gesture. "So . . ."

"What would you ask in return?" Falerior asked. "I cannot give you this *skios*."

Great. So the paladins were always gonna know my location. "Can you, like, reset it? I don't like being tracked like that."

"All is known—"

"Okay, fine, you can't. Can you at least stop bothering me?" A flash of inspiration struck me. "Uh, it's interfering with my ability to keep to my oaths."

This seemed to get a small reaction out of him. At this distance, with my original eyes, I would have missed it. But my Eifni-issued cybernetic replacements automatically blew up the image of his face to note a slight widening of the eyes, the lips loosening—maybe because he wanted to ask about it?—even as the muscular tension in his cheeks indicated he was actively maintaining that fucking neutral expression.

I struck first, before he was able to finish adjusting. "I can't be a good daughter to the Vitaressi if you disrupt my place in the household. And I genuinely want that."

"This investigation must be concluded," said Falerior. "But if what you say is true, finding this other whisper will do so. We'll honor your place in the Vitares household."

"Sweet," I said. "I'll meet you out back. Follow the *skios*."

Falerior nodded, then strode off. Abby came to a stop next to me.

"Good timing," I said.

"I'm set," she said. "Do it."

I drew my pulser, using my shawl to hide it from the crowd, and fired three times into Falerior's back. Like Vanerel, he made no indication that he'd noticed. I switched to my hand amplifier. He was nearing the edge of its range, so I didn't have time to play around with the settings too much. I nailed him once with the last frequency used, the Mom Special, and then he was out.

"Val?" Abby asked.

"I've recorded the blessing. Do you need me on ops?"

Abby shot me a knowing smile. Val probably wanted to get working on that immediately.

"We'd appreciate oversight, if you can spare the time," she said. "Good work, team. This op has been extremely profitable. Lilith, are you actually working with the Oathkeepers?"

"I planned on it," I said. "Are you saying I should change my mind?"

The commander smiled, wrapping me in a side hug. "You're showing great initiative."

I leaned into the hug, but it didn't escape me that the commander's nonanswer was also an answer in the weird Velean implicit-communication layer: *"You made the call, so you're responsible for it."* My shoulders hunched in a little bit. Abby definitely noticed—she glanced at my body language as she released me from the hug—but she made eye contact and didn't say anything. That, too, was a message.

"So what's the plan?" Abby said.

"Let's assume Lirian's cloak effect is roughly circular," I said. "She's staying out of MDO range, but we can triangulate her by reaching the edge of her range and saying her name."

"Lirian's name," said Abby.

"Yeah," I said. "Wait. Fuck."

"We'd better run," said Abby. "I'll go north."

"I'll meet up with the Oathkeepers," I said. She nodded and moved back in the direction she'd come from. "Markus, can you say Lirian's name?"

"Sorry, I must not have been paying attention, can you repeat that?"

"Lirian," I said.

There was a pause on his end.

"Markus?"

"Team, I'm under an antimemetic effect," said Markus. *"Enemy operative at or near my position."*

I looked over to where Markus and the other athletes were gathered. Behind them was the building where the massage competition was being held.

"She might be going after Kuril," I said. "What does your MDO say?"

"I don't have one, remember?" said Markus. *"I'm flying in style."*

"Shit!"

"Lilith, get to the Oathkeepers if you're still deputizing them," said Abby. *"I'll clear Markus's area."*

"On it." I ran.

I rounded the corner invisibly and almost ran into Oathkeeper Vanerel, who was standing there with the other two. I jumped back and quickly decloaked so no one ran into me.

"Well," Vanerel snapped.

"I'm sorry, I'm sorry, we can work this out later," I said breathlessly. "Kuril might be in trouble. *Please.* I need your help."

Vanerel's expression softened.

"I've spoken with my brother and sister," said Falerior. There was a wide age range between them, and none of them looked related, so he clearly didn't mean they were genetic siblings. "We've agreed to restrict our investigation should your lead play out."

"Okay great, but *we need to go*," I said. "This way! The massage building!"

"Slow down, girl," said the third Oathkeeper, a dude who was either late twenties or early thirties, with a look that said he thought he was smarter than everyone else in the room. "What evidence do we have to believe—"

Go for the throat.

"We can talk on the way," I interrupted. "Move!"

I started running for the administrative building where the massage contest was taking place. My heart was already pounding from the stress of the situation, imagining Lirian holding a knife to Kuril's throat, but my stomach dropped as the Oathkeepers failed to follow me. The *fuckers*. Falerior promised! We'd made a deal! Fine! Fuck them. I could deal with Lirian myse—

The clatter of armor behind me had me almost collapsing with relief. I really didn't want to go head-to-head with Lirian by myself again. Having backup would be great.

Backup, I belatedly realized, that was immune to pulser fire. An almost snarl passed over my face. I was gonna get her this time.

"Her name is Lirian!" I shouted as we ran. "If you can't think that name anymore, that's how you know if she's close! I can tell you more precisely where she is if I get within a stone's throw of her." No precise numbers; comm translation had trouble with those, since it didn't automatically convert the quantity to the local distance units. "Less if it's crowded. Can you grab her if you know where she is?"

"I am confident that we can," said Falerior, voice strained with exertion.

"There's four entrances!" I turned my head over my shoulder and was surprised to see Vanerel had almost overtaken me. Not bad for an old lady. "Let's split up and each take one! I'll try to push her toward you, but otherwise just collapse in on the massage competition!"

"Why are you so sure she's at the massage competition?" asked the third Oathkeeper, jogging along with no apparent effort. Something about his face rubbed me the wrong way.

"That's what happened last time! She, uh. Lost my train of thought, what was the question again?"

"Brother Tiresia asked why you thought Lirian would be at the massage competition," said Falerior.

"I don't know who that is."

"*Now that's interesting*," said Val.

"*We all heard you predict this*," said Abby. "*No need to preen on the ops channel.*"

"*Are you saying you doubted me, commander?*"

I ignored the byplay. "Okay, you two head right, Falerior comes with me. Let's get this motherfucker."

"Sister Vanerel goes with you," said Falerior. "I have the *skios*. We'll use it to find you."

"Whatever." It was better than Tiresia, I guess.

I didn't wait for her, skidding through the nearest doorway and taking the stairs two at a time. My MDO read nothing. The opponent wasn't here. I booked it for the massage room.

"*Lilith?*" Abby asked.

"What is it?" I asked.

"*Did you hear me?*"

"You didn't say anything," I said.

"*The opposing agent is still in your area. Do you feel comfortable performing absence meditation in the field?*"

"Fuck it, why not," I said. "Airplane mode, activate."

"*What? Are you asking for air support?*"

"Shh. Gotta focus."

I slowed to a halt, focusing on the light of my soul. It sputtered and pulsated, throwing streamers of different colors across etherspace. That still confused and worried me during practice because my confidence had gone way up since the inquiry, and I was sure the change would be reflected in my soul. Maybe that was just how your soul looked until you were geriatric like the rest of the team. Until then, though, it was making my job easier.

"Is this the work of a unified self?" I muttered to myself.

I forced myself to remember Abby's hug from earlier, Markus laughing at one of my jokes, Val telling me I did a good job. I remembered the guilt of sitting by Roel's bedside, knowing I was responsible. The way that Kuril seemed to have about fifty pounds less on her shoulders this morning. Everyone thanking me after the ritual that Kives interrupted.

All of it was me. None of it was coherent. I just had to find the cracks in my sense of self and pull them open.

I did.

"Lirian," I said, just to test the waters. Good.

My eyes opened. The path to the massage-competition room was a familiar memory, and I let it guide my feet. A wandering acolyte of Kabiades passed me.

"Can I help you, my lady?" he asked, avoiding eye contact.

My feet stopped.

"I need a sword."

They were stomping their feet for Cades when I walked in, sword sheathed on my belt. My emotions were present, but what I *felt* was the shift of my clothes against me, the shift of the sword as I walked, the changing pressure of my feet against the soles of my sandals.

Vanerel had caught up to me at that point. In my altered state of mind, I could still see the results of cold social calculation in my head and entered the room in front of her to make it look like I was in charge. That could change so very fast, but as long as I kept holding the reins, I could steer.

"Lirian's not in the room," I told Vanerel. "I've bypassed the cloaking effect on myself, so let's check if it's affecting the people in here."

Vanerel nodded, frowning at me.

Kuril saw me, but I waved at her to keep doing what she was doing. I marched straight to the nearest familiar face, which just so happened to be Alceoi Voranetes.

"Godsmile," I said when she didn't acknowledge me. I was helped in this by Oathkeeper Vanerel trying to move up closer to avoid looking like a subordinate. Alceoi turned to look at us with a bright smile, as if she hadn't been ignoring me on purpose.

"Oathkeeper," she said. "Lady Ajarel."

Addressing us in that order implied that Oathkeeper Vanerel was my social superior, which probably wasn't the case, but my thoughts were too crystallized to focus on that.

"Does the name Lirian mean anything to you?" I asked.

"You'll need to speak up," she said. "I can't hear you."

"Might be she's not in the building," said Vanerel, an ironic look in her eyes. "Course, you seemed *so* certain."

"You're one to talk, harassing innocent graced at a public event."

"Ha!"

Alceoi looked at us with a calculating expression.

"There are tunnels beneath this building," she said. "They lead back to the arena. It's how the priests move people around without disrupting the flow of the crowds too much."

I exchanged a look with the Oathkeeper.

"Let's check," I said.

"Signal Falerior. We can head down together."

We left the massage competition behind us. The priest was doing the ritual of threatening a buff dude with a sword. The audience was watching us leave instead. It meant nothing. I was mere blood and flesh.

We grabbed one of the acolytes waiting at the door and got him to direct us. Down the stairs to the ground floor, then down more stairs to a wine cellar. This must be where they stored it. The acolyte directed us to a door on the far end of the wine cellar. I drew my sword. Vanerel scoffed.

"She's just a whisper," she said. "They're assassins, not soldiers."

"You don't have a weapon?" I asked.

"I don't fight," she said.

Look where that got you, I did not say.

"No hard feelings, right?" I asked. "About earlier?"

"All debts come paid in the end," she said cryptically.

I thought about my student loans, abandoned back on Earth with my forever-unexplained disappearance. "Sure. Let's go with that."

I reached to open the door, then paused.

"Uh, Vanerel?" I said. "If I signal Falerior, I have to drop the state of mind that stops Lirian's cloak from affecting me. Can you guard me while I do that?"

"From a whisper?" Vanerel snorted. "You just tell me if she's in here."

She pushed open the door and strode into the tunnel.

"Wait, Vanerel—" I called, running through the door after her.

I was still an operative of the Eifni Organization. I checked my damn corners. It's the only reason I saw Lirian jumping at me with a knife in her hand.

CHAPTER FORTY-SEVEN

Cornered

I had never been so happy to see that smug bitch. Lirian was a lot of things—insufferable, snooty, hateful, know-it-all, arrogant, child stabber, without moral compunctions or human decency of any kind—I could go on, but I won't. Oh, and way less classy than she thinks she is. But the most important thing as she lunged to stab me in that murky, ghostlit tunnel was that *she didn't know how to fight*.

Years of data-driven Eifni combat training had me instantly analyzing her form, her center of balance, the path the knife was going to take, and finding it wanting.

"*Ha!*" I half laughed, half yelled as my reflexes took over and I pivoted out of the arc of her strike, grabbing her wrist with my open hand to throw her on top of her own knife.

The rush of joy knocked me out of my absence meditation. And I felt a sudden, vertiginous shift of perception as I forgot what was going on.

"What was that?" asked Vanerel, turning back to look at me.

There was an *irritating* itch just ahead, on the ground. My brain stuttered erratically as the impulse to scratch something not physically part of my body kept running aground on the black hole in my thoughts. I turned to her, helpless to articulate what was going on.

"Ajarel?" Vanerel's eyes narrowed, and she stepped into what looked like a wrestling stance.

"Fuck," I said, finally putting two and two together. "Enemy presence! I'm cloaking!"

The itch rose from the ground.

"Don't get stabbed!" Leaving Vanerel with that sage advice, I reached for my cloak—and had to abort because the itch was rushing me. I dove out of the way, dropping my sword in the process to avoid impaling myself.

"Where is it?" Vanerel asked.

"Fuck fuck fuck, it's on my ass!"

"Tell me where it is!" said Vanerel.

"I *can't*! Fuck this! I need you to hold it off for me so I can cloak!"

"*I don't know where it is!*" Vanerel shouted.

I let out a little screech of frustration and charged directly at Vanerel, whose eyes widened. She shifted her stance, one leg slightly behind, arms up with the palms out at shoulder height.

Wait, she was preparing to stop *me!*

"No no no, not like that!" She didn't understand. I had to abort. Moments before impact, I rolled to the side and felt the itch slow in front of Vanerel.

"Face!" was the only warning I had time to call.

Fortunately, Vanerel understood because she pulled her arms in front of the vulnerable opening on the front of her helmet. The sound of clattering rings mixed with the rasp of a dagger scattering across them. Vanerel countered with a full-body shove, keeping those arms in front of her face. But the itch had already moved away, and she overextended. Now it was coming for me again. Vanerel was pivoting around as if she could see where the enemy was.

I sprinted toward my dropped sword, feeling that itch on my back and letting the adrenaline pump my legs harder. It felt almost like some kind of magnetic repulsion as my body shoved me away from the dangerous thing. I reached the blade, picking it up and pivoting. I was fighting something with a knife, the reach would help.

"Fuck! Off!" I swung wildly at the presence, trying to deny it an opening. It started to back up. "Vanerel! Here!"

She inched toward me cautiously. Rather than get caught between us, the itch started to circle around toward Vanerel.

A single breath of concentration was all I needed. I dropped into the fullness of my soul, burning its essence into my mind's eye as I prepared to go invisible.

"Night night, motherfucker!" I called, and cloaked.

The itch stopped advancing for a moment. Poor Vanerel was moving to put her back to a wall, probably couldn't see either of the people in this fight. The itch closed in on her.

Oh, it was great to be the one with information supremacy again. Maneuver time was over. I hefted my sword and charged the fucking cockroach two-handed. It was still moving on Vanerel, blissfully unaware of my presence, unprepared for me to raise the sword and cut it the fuck in half—

It dodged the strike.

"What the fuck?!" Then, realizing that no one could hear me, I decloaked. "Seriously, what the fuck!"

The itch disappeared, and in its place was Lirian. The smugness was gone, and she was panting and glaring at me.

"What the fuck yourself!" Lirian snapped. "Who *are* you?!"

"I'm not fucking starting with that again," I said. "How'd you dodge the sword? I was fucking invisible!"

She boggled at me. "It was a *secret*. Are you *stupid?*"

"Why are you even *here?*"

She threw all the contempt she could onto her face. "It's a secret. Are you stupid?"

We'd been so focused on each other that neither of us noticed Vanerel edging closer to Lirian. Vanerel leaped now, securing Lirian's left hand—the one with the knife—and pushing her down to the ground with the arm behind her.

"Let go of me!"

"Yeah!" I said, stomping my foot victoriously. "Get fucked!"

"I'll take it from here," said Vanerel. "Falerior and Tiresia should be here soon. Hey, you. Are you the one they're callin' Lirian of Silence?"

"You win," said Lirian. She was looking at me. "Get me out of here and I'll concede defeat."

"Don't talk to her, talk to me," said Vanerel.

"Is she telling the truth?" I asked Vanerel.

"Not the time! You want a statement witnessed, you come by the Javeiron, and you pay the fee like everyone else!"

"Ajarel," said Lirian, lying calmly on the floor. "Get her off me. Hands find their way."

"That fucking phrase again," I said. "You gonna find more kids to stab?"

"I can destroy your eye-truths with a handful of sentences," said Lirian. "Get her off me and I'll leave."

"Don't you dare, girl," Vanerel said to me.

I looked uncertainly between them. Was she threatening my cover? What did she have on me? She hadn't been in a position to learn anything truly compromising after we'd installed the MDOs everywhere.

"Last chance," said Lirian.

So I could either help Lirian and fuck myself over with the Oathkeepers, or I could keep my deal and Lirian would fuck me over with the Oathkeepers, anyway. Fucking typical.

I was so sick of the cloak-and-dagger bullshit. I was so sick of hidden meanings and information warfare and *invisible fucking knife girls*. And I was sick of ending up in these situations. I'll be the first to admit I'm maybe not the best at them. I'm a soldier, not a spy. So maybe it was time to turn this into a soldier situation.

"Alright, look," I said, and Vanerel looked at me warningly. I shook my head a little to keep her off guard. "Give me a moment to think, yeah?"

"The moment your backup arrives, I destroy your life," said Lirian. "Let the Oathkeeper witness the truth of my words."

"I keep telling everyone, pay the damn fee." Vanerel's face didn't give anything away, but even that was telling. If Lirian was lying, Vanerel would have told me.

"Just—stop talking," I said, and cloaked myself.

"Stay away!" said Vanerel. "You made a promise before an Oathkeeper!"

Maybe that would have swayed a normal Therian. Maybe not. It didn't stop me in any case. I walked toward my downed enemy, hefting my sword. There wasn't really a clean angle to strike. I considered, shrugged, and tossed the sword aside. Both of them flinched at the clatter as it hit the cobblestones next to them. In the opening that provided, I pulled my leg back and kicked Lirian in the face.

I'd have preferred to be wearing steel-toed boots for this, but the local fashion was sandals, so instead I went for the soccer kick, like I was trying to knock her head off. Lirian screamed; there was a *pop* as Vanerel's grip on her arm dislocated her shoulder. Lirian's knife fell to the ground.

I decloaked, trying to shift directly to absence meditation and failing. I was too caught up in the anger.

"Fuck you," I said, kicking her in the head again. The point of impact was right on the buckle of my sandals. That was going to bruise tomorrow, but there was a nice bruise forming on her forehead now.

"That's *enough*, Ajarel," said Vanerel. "You'll kill her."

I went for another kick, but she grabbed me.

"Feet find their way, asshole," I said as she yanked me out of kicking range.

Lirian's eyes were unfocused, but she was clumsily trying to get to her feet. Vanerel shoved me back, moving to reclaim her prisoner. She kicked the knife away as she did so.

"Ajarel, you do *anything* else to harm her and the deal is off, understand?" she said.

"I understand," I said through gritted teeth. Hopefully I'd given her a bad concussion and she'd die from internal bleeding or something. They thought the brain was an organ for cooling blood around here, there's no way they could save her. But she was pretty solid for that slim frame. Maybe she was more durable than that.

I heard the clink of chain mail behind me. The cavalry had arrived. Falerior took in the situation with a glance and nodded to us both.

"Excellent work, Sister Vanerel," he said. "You, as well, Lady Ajarel."

"All yours, guys," I said. "Ignore anything she says about me. I'm sure she believes it, but she's full of shit. Oh, and Lirian?" She looked blearily at me, tears pooling in her eyes. I flipped her off with both hands.

"See ya soon," I said to the Oathkeepers, leaning over to pick up my dropped sword. "Or, you know, hopefully not."

The adrenaline high was definitely fading by this point. I strode past Tiresia, ignoring the skeptical glance he sent my way, and patted Falerior on the shoulder. Bemused, he returned the gesture.

A ragged voice spoke up from behind me.

"She knows what happened to Salaphi!"

Falerior's hand on my shoulder tightened.

I drew in a sharp breath. For a fleeting moment, I felt the bite of my knife into flesh and saw Arguel's dying expression. I looked up at Falerior, knowing that he'd seen, that he *knew*.

I finally understood the meaning of that stupid look on his face. It was the look of a man who knew that everything was connected, that all he had to do was pay attention and the truth would come to him. It was the patience of a spider who'd finally trapped me in his web.

Falerior didn't let go. He lifted an eyebrow. He was giving me a chance to explain myself.

"None of your business," I tried.

"Oh, Lady Ajarel," he said, that look of affable interest drilling into me, "I think we both know that's not true."

CHAPTER FORTY-EIGHT

Justice

It was cool in the service tunnel of the Kabiadesian arena. The use of ghostlights to light the tunnels meant you didn't get any of the ambient heat from torches, and the cobblestones in the road above us insulated the tunnel from this universe's version of the Mediterranean sun. My eyes traced the arches holding up the ceiling rather than look directly at Falerior and the information vacuum that lived in his smug mug. His eyes didn't leave my face. I was finding the attempted eye contact weirdly uncomfortable with the Estheni social senses I was starting to develop, and also uncomfortable for the normal reasons it's creepy when people stare at you.

"Let go of me," I ordered.

"Of course," he said. "Forgive me. Tiresia, there's no need for you to stand there. I'm sure Lady Ajarel is perfectly willing to cooperate."

There was no way in hell I was about to turn my back on Falerior, so I shifted slightly to the side to catch Tiresia turning to help Vanerel tie up Lirian. She was barely paying attention to the process, reacting only by grunting in pain when they jostled her dislocated arm. Those dark eyes were fixed intently on me.

"You have more secrets than anyone I've ever met," she'd told me during her first assassination attempt. I'd gotten inconclusive evidence whether Meris's or Javei's blessing was stronger today, but something told me Lirian was fine with getting captured if it meant learning more about me. Whatever fuzziness I'd inflicted with those kicks to the head was gone. I really should have found a way to stab her earlier.

"What am I cooperating with, exactly?" I asked Falerior.

"All we ask is that you come to the Javeiron and answer some questions. About the fate of Salaphi and your business here."

Right, sure, the temple to Javei with all the high-powered etheric surveillance that implied. We didn't even know how to counter the Oathkeepers' normal blessings, much less the heavy-duty stuff waiting on Javei's holy ground. They'd rip my cover story to shreds in minutes. I raised Val on the comms.

"Val, I need that blessing analyzed like yesterday."

"I'm afraid that window has passed, but I'll work on it."

"Do it!" I hissed subvocally, then addressed Falerior out loud. "And if I don't comply?"

Falerior gave me a resigned sort of smile. "I am not threatening you."

"But? There's a 'but' in that sentence."

"It would make it harder for me to vouch for your honesty the next time you need a contract witnessed." His tone was regretful. Dude was probably the kind of lame woobie who just wished everyone could get along.

"Yeah, okay, you're threatening me. Well guess what? Maybe I'm gonna have second thoughts about vouching for *your* honesty," I shot back, exhaling sharply through my nose. "You said you were gonna be mindful of my position in the house, but now you're dragging me off to the station like some common criminal?"

"I did not lie to you—"

"You sure?" I interrupted. "Seems like it from—"

He didn't stop talking, rolling right over my interruption.

"—But you declared the situation urgent and moved before we could clarify what that meant. And this new information changes things."

I bristled, throwing a hand toward the incarceration party on my left. "*Vanerel* said we had a deal!"

"You were goin' to kill her!" she shouted. "Who'd argue technicalities with blades out?"

"Oh, wow, let's make this my fault. Fuck you guys. I'm out. If that means you can't witness my contracts, I guess Kuril will have to do them. Or Roel, not that you *actually give a fuck*." My voice rose to a screech by the end of the sentence.

"She did this to me, too," Lirian remarked, as though she were just hanging out with us rather than restrained and tied to Vanerel. "Using outrage to deflect from questions she didn't want answered."

"You think I'm faking this?!"

"Lady Ajarel, either calm yourself or put the sword down," said Falerior.

"Like hell," I said, but took a deep breath, anyway. Keep your head in the game, Lilith. They were playing it smart, pitting me and Lirian against each other. Could I throw a wrench in that maneuver?

"Alright, first off," I said, glancing back and forth between Falerior and the other Oathkeepers, "I'm not answering questions where Buttface can hear the answers. This is why she stabbed Roel in the first place, we shouldn't reward that by—"

"Lady Ajarel," Falerior interrupted, "The Vitaressi have requested the Oathkeepers' justice in this matter, and it is the Oathkeepers' justice that will be executed here. I hope we can understand each other."

I gripped my sword until my knuckles creaked, then let off on the pressure. "Fine."

"If you'd prefer to speak in private," he continued leadingly, nodding to the west.

"I'd prefer not to speak at all," I said. "I'm finally having nights where I don't wake up screaming, and now you want to dredge that all up again?"

The conversation paused as I, and presumably Falerior, digested the realization that I was being honest.

"You're so *soft*," Lirian marveled. "Was everyone in Salaphi a coward, or just you?"

The Oathkeepers collectively took a step back from me. I laughed. "There's, like, three of you. Chill."

"I must insist," said Falerior. "None of us want House Vitares barred from trade in the city of her ancestor."

"Wait, it's not just me personally?" I asked. "Isn't that a little too much escalation?"

"You know the truth about a great calamity," Falerior said, meeting my eyes with a look of conviction. I suppressed a flinch at the *C*-word, letting myself relax after double-checking that the comm said he hadn't meant capital-*C* Calamity like the angels were naming us. "The rumors are that Alcebios herself descended on the village. Every temple of Kives has proclaimed a warning to stay away! The sheer number of questions we've had, Lady Ajarel! Now I have the answers in my city, if you'd only just—"

A voice cut through the dim tunnel. "*Your* city?"

Falerior startled at the sound, turning to watch Kuril approach down the hallway with a hulking muscle dude two steps behind her.

"Godsmile, councilwoman," he said hurriedly.

"Ah, good, Lady Ajarel," Kuril said. "I'm glad to have found you. One worries when one's prospective sash bearer charges off after a whisper and fails to reappear. But I see these Oathkeepers have defended my house, *as they were hired to do*."

Falerior didn't say anything.

"W-wait, sash bearer?" I asked. "Isn't that, like, for when you're pregnant?"

"Obviously not yet," said Kuril. "Keep up, Ajarel. Is this Lady Lirian? I haven't had the pleasure, which I assume will continue to be the case."

"Blessings of Meris upon you," Lirian said in the most threatening pleasant tone I've ever heard.

"Quite," said Kuril. She drew near to the captive whisper, followed by the lumbering dude in the competition loincloth. "Explain what you did to my sister."

"Nothing." Lirian smirked.

Kuril looked expectantly at Vanerel. Vanerel stared mutely back.

"*The power dynamic here is convoluted*," said Markus. "*Commander, can I be an Oathkeeper next op?*"

"Well?" said Kuril. "The truth belongs to Javei, does it not? You were paid well for this investigation."

Vanerel sighed. "You're askin' a real deep secret. With whispers, that's supposed to mean Cult business. You won't get that out of her."

"Mmm," said Kuril. "I wouldn't pretend to understand. The Sisterhood has no secrets—our laws are taught publicly. Surely you haven't skulked around this city— the city of *my* ancestor"—with a pointed look at Falerior—"without learning the Law of Opposing Force. Genoma?"

She held out a hand. Genoma's brow furrowed for a moment, then enlightenment dawned and he drew the dagger at his side. In Kuril's hand, it looked considerably larger.

Kuril wasn't a trained combatant: her stab wasn't elegant or precise. But it was quick, it was vicious, and neither Vanerel nor Tiresia were in position to stop her before it plunged into Lirian's leg. She screamed once, then bit her lip to keep from calling out again. Kuril pulled the blade out as Tiresia hurriedly tore strips of bandage off a roll on his hip.

"Lady Kuril! That's enough!" Falerior snapped. "You paid for the *Oathkeepers'* justice."

"Then may it be," said Kuril. "Vitaressi justice has already been served."

"*Damn*," said Markus approvingly.

None of the Oathkeepers dared to speak up; Lirian was in obvious pain and kept her eyes closed. Tears were trickling down her cheeks. I never thought I'd see her cry— it was pretty great, let me tell you. I didn't let myself enjoy it for too long, though.

"So, uh," I said, breaking the awkward silence. "We good then?"

Kuril nodded matter-of-factly. "Let's exit this way. I estimate we'll be late for the next event if we retrace our steps."

"Lady Kuril," Falerior spoke up, "there is still the matter of Salaphi."

She regarded him coldly. "You did not name yourself Falerior of Salaphi when I hired you."

"I did not," he agreed.

"Are we *in* Salaphi?"

"You stand beneath Vitareas."

"Does Salaphi pay for the upkeep of the Javeiron?"

"It does not, but—"

"Then let the Oathkeepers of Salaphi tend to Salaphi. You are far beyond the scope of your investigation, Falerior."

His face gave no evidence of whatever analysis was running behind that polite blankness. Eventually he nodded.

"Then we will complete our investigation as contracted," he said.

"I cut her hair!" Lirian yelled suddenly. "I crippled her legs! Now it's like nothing happened!"

"Shut up," said Kuril.

"They all know I'm speaking the truth," Lirian said.

"I don't recall paying for that information," said Kuril. Her gaze fixed on Falerior. "Punish her. Ajarel, we're late."

I made mocking eye contact with Lirian as we passed, feeling a little like a second grader sticking her tongue out from behind the teacher, but whatever.

"Hands find their way, Ajarel," said Lirian. "Hands find their way."

"Tell it to the judge," I said, following my adoptive mother as she power walked toward the arena.

"I've always wanted to say that," I confessed when I caught up.

"I don't understand what judges have to do with this," said Kuril. "Did you mean magistrate?"

I sighed. Genius is never appreciated in its own time.

CHAPTER FORTY-NINE

Interlude: Suspicion

Everyone around me has gone completely insane.

Roel was in pain.

That was normal now. The throbbing stab wound in her leg was variably salient but never gone. And she'd adjusted to it, partially. Pain had tutored the unthinking movements of the first days of her injury into habitual caution. There were rules for how she was allowed to use her body now, rules like *make no sudden movements* and *you must not scratch the wound when it itches* and *you will never run again.*

The pain was worst in the evenings. She would lie in bed for hours, trying to distract herself until the door quietly opened and everything went blank. Another secret Ajarel was keeping from her, as if there were someone else in the house who could send people to sleep so they woke up with fresh bandages and diminished pain.

One night, *like an idiot*, she'd given up the pretense of sleep and waited up reading with a ghostlight. To confront Ajarel? To banish the ambiguity? Roel wasn't sure. It didn't matter; the door never opened. She got no sleep that night, and the next day her wound burned like Lirian had left her knife in the forge, then stuck it back in. She learned a new rule: *you must pretend to sleep.*

So she did, ruminating until the softest creak of the door announced that merciful unconsciousness had come. Like a rose petal circling the drain, her thoughts spiraled until they arrived at the inevitable conclusion: *you've made a terrible mistake.*

She never should have sponsored Thala. She never should have engaged Ajarel at that ball. In fact, she should have braved Kuril's wrath and stayed home in the first place. She spent hours fruitlessly reliving the chain of events leading up to the library, reading one moment and waking up the next with burning iron in her leg. But there was never a clear decision point, no moment she should have known to say, "Enough."

Everything flowed relentlessly from the moment Ajarel had sat down at her table and named her something—intelligent, isolated, outcast—with a word she'd never heard before but intimately understood. A word that even now she couldn't remember. That was the moment she'd known Ajarel had the *exciting* kind of secrets, just like in her tales, and *needed* to learn more. Like an *idiot.*

She'd forgotten what happened to people in that kind of tale. Secrets came at a price she hadn't been ready to pay.

"You doing okay?" asked Ajarel. They were in Roel's room, both of them pretending to read. Roel couldn't focus on the book in her hands, her thoughts always returning to the one hidden under her pillow. Ajarel spent too long on each page, constantly looking up to monitor Roel. Her eyes were glazed over half the times Roel looked. Every so often, Ajarel would almost guiltily turn the page, like she'd been caught. As long as Roel didn't react, Ajarel would relax, like she'd gotten away with it.

"Roel?" Ajarel prodded.

No, I am not doing okay, Roel thought. *I invited danger into my home. I can no longer walk under my own power. My niece is lying to me, and my sister has relegated me to a goddesses-damned line item in her fifteen-year plan. Everyone around me has gone completely insane.*

"I'm just tired," she said.

"Recovery is tough," said Ajarel. Roel scoffed. "I mean it. Your body's trying to fix the wound, so it's using resources that the rest of your body needs."

"You're very confident that I'll recover from this. Hadalce says the pain might last the rest of my life."

"Hadalce's a *fake/doctor/(informal)*," Ajarel said. Roel took note—both of the strange self-communicating word, as she always did when these little slips happened, and also of Ajarel's strange disdain for the knowledge of a doctor bearing the sapphire of mastery. Was it just the egotism of a magician for the mundane? That seemed in character for Ajarel, but years of reading whisper stories had taught Roel that such personas were usually fake.

"I think I would like to be alone," said Roel. "Could you send Alouren up here with some food?"

"Of course," said Ajarel. "Whatever you need, kid. I'm here for you."

You let me suffer that night, Roel wanted to scream.

"Thank you," she said.

"Welcome." Ajarel put the book down—without noting the page—and left with a worried glance at Roel. The worry hurt. Not as bad as the leg, but still intolerable. But her whisper stories had prepared her for how to handle pain. You were supposed to press on despite it in a desperate quest for the truth.

Roel's hand slid under her pillow and found the small leather-bound journal that had appeared there the night of the attack. She hesitated, looking up at the door as if Ajarel was about to pop back in, having "forgotten" something. She did that infrequently. Was it normal forgetfulness, or did Ajarel know what was hidden under her pillow?

Did Ajarel have another knife waiting for her when the secret was finally revealed?

She invoked her courage with a breath and withdrew the unnamed journal. She opened it, as she always did, to the note on the top of the first page:

"Now you know. Whether the price was fair, only the Whisperer knows."

It was unsigned, which was signature enough.

Further down the page, in letters more confident and more smudged from usage, Lirian had written:

"Archivist: The one styled as 'Lady Ajarel of Salaphi' carries stolen secrets. In the name of the goddess I have sought them."

Roel turned the now-familiar pages, scanning endless lines of data in a tightly spaced script of elegant yet efficient sweeps and curls. Dozens of pages of observational data, complete with sketches of outfits Ajarel had worn, analysis of individual fabrics or stylistic decisions. On the fourth page, there was a fabric sample, with notes indicating it'd been taken on the day of the Renathion where Lirian attacked Ajarel.

"The weave is extraordinarily fine. The thread is stained with a dye derived (E.T.)"—it had taken Roel an embarrassing *thessim* and a half to realize this abbreviation meant "truth of the eyes"—"from turquoise brightflower or equivalent combination. The stitching style is similar to that found in the material culture of Martok (E.T.), but the coloration pattern and the lack of the distinctive cross-hatching pattern at the seams indicates that it's something else. In any case, the major Martokou trade routes are overland to the western reaches of the Imperial Coalition; no one within approx. three hundred *teloi* of Salaphi should own such a garment.

"Addendum, Thephes next: no weaver in Vitareas can identify the thread."

Every entry followed this pattern. After the outfit data followed multiple *thessim* of observation: behavioral tendencies, tallies of eye contact—Ajarel was surprisingly lewd—food preferences, graces displayed, graces not displayed. A section with every sentence spoken in Lirian's hearing, with an unassuming note at the top that had hammered Roel to the ground when she first read it: "Her lips do not follow her voice."

Lirian undertook the same journey in each case: trails leading all over the Imperial Coalition, or outside of it, and then into nothingness. Knowledge she shouldn't have, figures of speech she should never have learned. Contradictions upon contradictions, as if the woman herself were a fiction and not just the character she played.

At the first mention of otherworldly eyes, Lirian seemed almost ready to give in to despair. Roel could barely make sense of the pages containing Lirian's experimental notes, rife with the vain secrecy typical to worship of Meris—Cult jargon, abbreviations, metaphors, and other nonsense to keep away the uninitiated. But Lirian made no effort to hide her final discovery.

"I should have begun with this," she wrote. "I have spoken to several merchants whose routes take them near Salaphi. No one there claims or has claimed the grace of the gods [explaining (E.T.) lack of formal rhetorical instruction, see previous]. But Ajarel's obvious reaction of guilt when Salaphi is mentioned (E.T.) indicates she has personal knowledge of the town and the disaster that is said to have occurred there. Given the rumors that Alcebios herself descended upon the town, the logical inference is that I stumbled into the truth, and that Ajarel is in fact graced—with conflict."

Roel pressed thumb and forefinger to her heart to ward off madness but was interrupted as the door opened. She shoved the journal under the history of the Second Phrecian War in her lap. It was only Alouren, carrying a tray of *setoi* and a mug of lemon wine. Roel gave her a relieved smile, but the lightning of the surprise was still painful in her veins—Horcutio's gifts were ever double-edged.

"Goddesses, it's just you," she breathed. "Come in, scoundrel."

"I brought your favorite," Alouren giggled.

"You might as well announce it to the entire house." Roel sighed and dropped back against the pillow. The motion was too violent: her leg throbbed. *Remember the rules.* "Did you at least make them with lamb?"

"Lamb," Alouren agreed, shoving one of the pastries in her mouth. "Could'm gen 'way wi' beef." She swallowed. "Tajel knows you hate it."

"That's a mercy. Give me some of the wine at least."

Alouren passed her the mug. She took a deep drink, fighting the lightning that wanted to pucker her cheeks. Horcutio must have been especially angry when Kives fucked lemons out of him.

"So," she said, working her jaw to get the sting out, "what'd she say?"

Alouren shrugged. "She said I shouldn't be asking about the soul because it would give me tools to hurt myself. Then she said I should talk to a priest of Gamal again."

"Do you remember her exact words?" Roel knew the answer already. Alouren had never mastered that skill in all their years of pretending to be whispers together.

"Sorry." She looked sheepish every time, which was funny. Roel was in too much pain to laugh.

Roel settled for Alouren's exact words instead, jotting them down on one of the journal's blank pages. Above her stylus lay dozens of lines of observation about Ajarel's occult knowledge. The details she let slip, the secrets she implied she had.

That writing was hers, not Lirian's. She knew she was being an idiot: the gifts of a whisper were always poisonous. The wise decision was to give up the journal—or better yet, burn it.

But she'd lost a leg to these secrets. If she did the wise thing, it would be for nothing.

"Next," said Roel. "I need you to run a secret mission for me."

"I'm ready," said Alouren, practically bouncing.

"Did Falerior leave a message in the dead drop?"

"I haven't had time to check," Alouren said guiltily.

"I need you to do it tonight," said Roel. "And I need you to leave another letter while you're at it. Here." She'd already had it prepared—a passable copy of Lirian's sketch of the knock-out device, instructions on how to deliver it to Roel, and a draft of three hundred *drobol*. Alouren secreted it under her shawl with a smile that Roel didn't return.

"You don't seem like you're having fun," said Alouren, sitting down on the bed with Roel—carefully, not jostling her leg. Roel offered her the mug. Alouren took a sizable gulp; her face puckered instantly.

"I just need a distraction," said Roel. "My heart's not in it."

"We said no lies," said Alouren, bopping her on the nose with a finger. "If this were a cart and the horses died, you'd take the yoke yourself."

Roel looked significantly at her crippled leg.

"Even so," said Alouren.

She'd always known what to do here. In whisper stories, you kept dangerous truths to yourself, even as it drove you away from the people who loved. Sometimes that was enough to keep them safe. Sometimes it wasn't. But it was supposed to be the safest road—for Merisites and their self-destructive secrecy.

Roel was a Maker. There was no such thing as a dangerous truth, only people who misused the truth. She never should have needed to make that choice. They'd promised each other that, back when this was just a game.

But now she couldn't walk.

"Roel?" Alouren looked concerned.

Roel burst into tears. She felt Alouren's arms around her, but the hug didn't reach her heart. There was a wall there now.

"Please don't make me answer that," she begged. "It'll break."

"What will break?" Alouren said. "Roel, you're not making sense."

She wailed into Alouren's shoulder.

"I'm so sorry about your leg," Alouren tried. Roel responded with a squeeze, hating herself, hoping Alouren would accept that explanation and stop digging. Alouren squeezed her back.

"Do you want to talk to Kuril? I don't think she has anything scheduled right now."

Meaning she's not having sex. Roel shoved her off. "No."

Alouren looked helpless. "She's worried about you. Everyone is."

"She's—" Roel bit off the rest of the sentence. *She's trying to have kids instead of taking care of her sister, and her chosen sash bearer is a scion of Alcebios. She heard I'll recover, and she stopped caring that I'm crippled now. She schedules! Her time with me! Like a customer!*

"I don't want to see her," she said instead. "Leave me alone."

Alouren looked anxious. "Um. Kuril said someone always needs to be with you."

Roel looked at her blankly. "She made a schedule and everything, didn't she?"

"She made a schedule and everything," Alouren admitted.

"Why?!"

"That priest of Gamal—uh, Father Demedes? He said it's a good idea," said Alouren. "For, uh, people who get hurt."

"Cripples," said Roel.

"You're going to get better," Alouren protested.

"I'm a cripple," said Roel. "Get out. Go tell Kuril if you want."

Alouren fled, leaving Roel alone with the daylight slowly fading out of her room. She carefully returned the journal to its hiding place under the pillow, then collapsed. She wiped the remaining tears off her face and lay there, numb. She could tell she wanted to cry more, but she was stuck, like a gear that someone had forgotten to oil.

Her leg hurt.

The door opened a third time. She didn't turn to see who it was.

"Lady Roel," said Bofa. One of her sister's new consorts. "I was asked to sit with you awhile."

Roel screwed her face up. "I'm not talking."

"You won't even know I'm here," said Bofa, sitting down in the corner of the room. The couch, by the sound of it.

"Yes I will," she said. "You walked in and announced yourself. I'm not going to forget."

"As my lady says," he said.

They sat in silence for a bit.

"You know, Lady Ajarel laughs at you behind your back," she said.

"To my face, too," he said. There was a gentle smile in his voice. Roel wasn't expecting that, and it left her floundering for some other way to attack him.

"I think I hate you," she said.

"That's okay."

He didn't sound defensive or anything. She rolled over in bed to stare at him incredulously. He was sitting with his arms folded and his eyes closed, but at her movement he cracked an eye open to look at her.

"It's not okay," she said. "I'm Roel Vitares. You're new to the house. I'm more important, so you can't have me hate you. It would ruin your life."

Bofa listened and gave a ponderous nod.

"Better you hate me than yourself," he said seriously.

She glared at him. "I told you I'm not talking to you."

He nodded, closing his eyes again. "There is also healing in silence."

"Then be quiet." She considered. "You can be quiet over here, though."

Bofa wordlessly moved to the chair next to her. He was a big man—Roel was mildly surprised the chair held his bulk—but he made no complaint.

Roel curled up into a ball under the covers. They sat in silence.

CHAPTER FIFTY

Betrayal

I pushed the last stack of paper toward Kuril.

"And done," I said. "I cannot believe you were doing all of this by yourself."

"It's easier on the days when I'm not responsible for anyone who punched an Oathkeeper." She was smiling, but her eyes were sharp. "Nevertheless, I'm glad you resisted."

"Sentences you don't hear back home," I said. "What would have happened if I'd let her drag me back?"

"It depends," said Kuril. "The most likely outcome is that they would have held on to you until they extracted whatever you're not telling us about your past."

"Uh, yeah," I said. "That."

"This is twice, Ajarel," she said. "Lirian was bad enough, but now the Oathkeepers? I've never seen Falerior stray so far from his duty before. What does he have on you?"

"You, uh, know him?" I asked.

"Professionally," said Kuril. "You do know I'm the treasurer for Vitareas, correct? It's a family holding the Voranetti have yet to pry from us."

"Oh, so that's why they were all so scared of you," I said.

"They were under contract," said Kuril. "Falerior is the best of their hounds; it's why I hired his team. Which makes it important that we are *all* prepared for what happens when he comes back with someone else's *drobol* in his pockets."

"Right," I said.

"Before the sun rises, Ajarel. What does he have on you?"

I sighed.

"I . . ." What did I even say here? "It's not blood magic, at least. I promise. You kinda took me by surprise here."

"If I did not, you would continue to put the discussion off." Kuril watched me intently, tapping her charcoal pencil against the nearest stack of papers. "We're family now. This stays between us."

"Right," I said, avoiding her eyes. "I guess . . . It's about Salaphi."

"Lirian announced as much," said Kuril. "Will my own daughter show less loyalty?"

I closed my eyes. "Wow. That's a lot."

Kuril didn't respond. I had to get control of this.

I took a moment to pull myself into that Velean role-playing space, letting myself transcend the persona I currently occupied, letting myself become the person that communicated what I needed. I was not Ajarel, I was Lilith *playing* Ajarel. This wasn't Lilith's shame, it was Ajarel's, and Ajarel needed to disclose it so Kuril would stop digging.

"Okay," I said. I opened my eyes, looked at her. "Okay, you have to promise not to hate me."

"Where's your courage, girl?" Kuril looked unimpressed. "Out with it."

"I was there," I said. "When it happened."

"I take it the rumors are wrong, then, and Alcebios did not descend in person."

"As far as I can tell," I said. "Just . . . the normal human tendency to turn on one another."

"Oh, the Stranger gets her due one way or another," said Kuril. "How much of it was your fault?"

My eyes snapped back to her face.

"You're clearly ashamed of what happened there," she said. "The inference is trivial. Falerior will have seen the same. I know him well enough to know that."

"The tree is kind of my fault," I said. "It's, uh, because I was running. Running away, I mean."

The silence extended out. I knew this tactic, they'd taught us in the Academy to use silence to get the other person talking. All you have to do to resist it is stand your ground, maybe make some eye contact to let the other person know you're not submitting.

But that wasn't the image I was trying to present here. People trust information they've won more than they trust information freely given to them by an interested party. I let the silence draw words out of me, as if they were a shield against the pressure.

"Lady Arguel summoned a monster," I said. "I tried to bring it down. The method was, uh. It was awful. You're better off not knowing."

"Hm," said Kuril. "You weren't born in Salaphi."

"No."

Kuril was silent for a long time. This was a delicate moment; I couldn't afford to disrupt it by saying the wrong thing. She looked up at me.

"How long do I have you?" she asked softly.

"What?" I sat upright in surprise.

"Kives," she sighed, and I couldn't tell if it was a curse or a prayer. "I should have known. A wanderer, living a life of happenstance, stumbling on events at just the right time. I should have known from the start. Lirian is dealt with—how long do I have before she takes you away from me?"

"I want to stay," I said—as Ajarel, as Lilith? "Please. I don't want to go."

"Good," she said. "Then we'll go to the temple of Kives tomorrow and make sacrifices. Hm. Actually, it's Thephes the day after tomorrow. She'll be more receptive on her holy day. I suppose I'll need to adjust some plans."

Oh *fuck.* "I, uh, hope you won't need to adjust anything. And we really don't need to go to the temple. I mean, it should be fine, I left of my own volition all the other places I've been, but this time I'm not going to. I was adopted and everything."

"You're coming anyway. House Vitares leaves nothing to chance. Hm. The monster? Is it dead?"

"Yes," I said with vicious certainty.

"Any other unfinished business from your travels that might drive you out of Vitareas?"

I shook my head. "Best I've got is that Eloi Voranetes hates my guts."

"Right," said Kuril. "That. You said Alceoi was friendly to you. Would that help?"

"Actually, um," I said. "I think she might have been the one who poisoned me. I've been thinking about it. She was the one who told us to check the service tunnels, and Lirian was waiting when we went down there."

Kuril's jaw clenched. "I see."

"Could we—" I started, then second-guessed myself. "Never mind."

"Humor me," said Kuril.

"You said we would have issues if Falerior was on someone else's payroll," I said. "I don't know how much—"

"Excellent idea." Kuril jotted a note on one of six pieces of paper whose organization and significance I couldn't interpret. "I'll hire him immediately. Investigating Alceoi should keep him away from you."

"I won't have to talk to him, right?" I asked.

"I'm sure he'll squirm his way into a conversation or two. It's what makes him a good Oathkeeper. It's better than the alternative."

"Cool," I said. "Um, I'm going to go to bed, if that's okay."

Kuril waved me out. I left her with my lies.

Roel was pretending to be asleep again. My comm lit up with the pain radiating from her leg, intermixing with the emotional pain that almost drowned it out. The poor girl. She'd closed herself off so much since the attack. I'd tried to reach out, but she wasn't ready to talk. She probably just needed space to process or something.

I crept closer to her in the darkened room, pulling up a chair to sit next to her. There was a spike of fear as I approached.

"Hey," I whispered. "It's just me."

She didn't respond. The fear response slowly started to drop.

"I fucked up," I whispered, leaning back against the chair. "I fucked up. I'm so sorry. I tried to keep you out of danger, and it came home, anyway."

Something else was bubbling under her cocktail of pain. Something between betrayal and hatred. It left me feeling distant, like there was a burning wall between me and whatever feelings I should be feeling. Gut pain and exhaustion; like my cloak, but ragged and sharp.

"I can't fix your leg," I said. "I know—I know you blame me for it. I'm sorry. I didn't want this."

Roel lay still, maintaining the pretense of sleep. I almost questioned whether the comm was accurate, but I knew from previous nights that the pain was too much for her to fall asleep.

"Fuck it." I shut down my comm to nonemergency traffic. I sent it a command to reboot its recording function.

It would take about ten seconds to come back online. Until then, I would have true privacy in my head for the first time in years. I didn't waste a second.

"Your muscles are too damaged to move your leg," I said quickly. "Use a machine. This conversation never happened."

I reset my comm settings and sat silently for a while.

"Fuck it," I said again, as if I'd been mulling something over. "Sleep well, Roel."

I stood up, lingering by the bed. Pulsing someone usually blanked the latest fifteen to thirty seconds of their memory, and I wanted to give her time for the idea to sink in. I probably wouldn't be able to get away with this again, so I wanted to give her the best chance I could. If she didn't remember tomorrow, well, maybe it'd be something to ask from Kives when I—

I stopped in my tracks.

So that was her plan. *Hell* no. Nope nope nope. Fuck this, I'm out.

I pulsed Roel and snuck out of her room, breaking into a sprint once I got onto the walkway that ringed the inside of the estate. I don't know if anyone saw me, I just ran. Ran back to my room, shut the door, shoved my fingers into my hair and squeezed.

"Fuck!"

"Are you okay, Lils?"

The unexpected voice took me off guard, and I yelled, pivoting to face the threat, pulser drawn—

Markus looked bemused as his comm shields fuzzed the pulser fire to harmless etheric noise. "Just me."

"You fucking *goon*," I said, throwing a punch at his biceps. He reflexively slapped it aside before it made contact.

"I just thought it'd be funny to surprise you," he said. "Seriously, Lilith, are you okay?"

"Don't fucking call me that here," I hissed. "We have no idea who's listening."

He gave me a patient look.

"And *no* I am *not* okay, I am *not* okay, I might *never* be okay, fuck, fuck—aw fuck, the commander's going to kill me. She's going to fucking cut me open. With, like, a spoon."

Large hands grabbed my shoulders.

"Let's calm down," Markus said. "Tell me what's going on."

Weakly, I pointed at the ceiling.

"I'm—" I said, tears starting to form in my eyes. "I fucked up, Markus. I'm compromised. Fuck me, I'm compromised."

"Let's sit down," he said. "I'll scan you, alright?"

I nodded shakily, sitting down on my bed.

"Your comm shield is fine," he said. "I'm going to pull your comm log from the ship."

"There's," I said, but couldn't finish the sentence. Oh god, I'd really just committed treason. I couldn't bring myself to admit it to Markus.

"I'm seeing a small blip about two minutes ago," he said. "Did you put your comm in privacy mode?"

I looked away. "Yes."

"It's okay, Lilith. We all do it. Looks like your comm shield's fine. No breach was recorded."

"She might have covered it up," I said.

"I just scanned you for indoctrination, and the comm didn't come up with anything."

"She could have interfered with the scan!"

"Lilith," Markus said, holding my shoulders again. "Why do you think you were compromised?"

"Because—" I took a deep breath, released it. "Kuril's dragging me to the temple of Kives the day after tomorrow. To make sacrifices. And I thought about asking her to help Roel."

"Asking Kives?" Markus didn't look angry or concerned or anything.

I nodded slowly. Markus breathed out slowly.

"You're fine, Lils," he said. "You're not compromised. You're just worried about Roel, and your brain was looking for options."

There was a sob in my throat that wanted to make its way out. I couldn't speak or it would usurp whatever I was trying to say. The tears were still flowing. I closed my eyes, restricting my world to just the down mattress under me and the painful lump in my chest.

"I need to pull out," I said. "I can't handle this. I'm going to get sucked in because I finally have a family that doesn't hate me, and *Kives is going to use that, Markus*, I am *weak*. I'm vulnerable. Lirian already used that against me, and she's a half-rate operative. Kives is a *god*. We need to scrap the op. Just leave me out next time."

"Deep breaths," said Markus. "There you go. You're going to be okay."

"I'm fucking compromised," I said.

"Deep breaths. The commander and Val are out on recreation right now." Meaning Abby was out having sex, and Val was doing whatever Val did. "Let's not make any hasty decisions until they're back online."

I fell back on the bed. "She's going to use this time to let us talk ourselves into the wrong choice. We need to get out, now."

"And then what?" Markus asked. "Every time you form an attachment, we call off the op?"

"She has me thinking about sacrificing to her!"

"There's a big difference between thinking it and doing it," said Markus. "There's a standard procedure for fake sacrifices. We'll get you through this."

"It's such a fucking trap."

"We're Eifni, Lilith. We break traps. This isn't the first oracle we've killed. They're not invincible."

I slammed a fist on the bed.

"I know! She's just really going to hurt us before she dies!"

Markus sat down on the bed next to me. "You know I love Cades."

"Eugh," I said, pinching the bridge of my nose. "Yes, I got a blast of that."

"Let's say I jumped ship right now," said Markus. "Cades isn't going to outlive me. It'll end eventually. And even if it didn't, who knows? They've studied centennial drift back on Veles. In most cases, you eventually change too much to have the same relationship. It's always temporary one way or another."

"So what, I just shouldn't care?" I asked. "I do care. That's not something I can control. Roel's just like me. I care about what happens to her, and now I care about the fact that I got her injured."

"You can choose not to care with the proper exercises," said Markus. "But that's not what I'm saying. I'm saying let yourself care—but always remember that there's an end to it. For every relationship you have, there's a point where you'll talk to that person for the last time. Even on this team. Care while you're here. But one day you'll need to move on."

"That's fucking depressing," I said.

"It's the truth," said Markus. "Our infiltrator before you was named Petra. We loved him as much as we love you. And he's gone now, but we'll always carry him with us."

"Are you going to carry Cades with you when we go?" I asked.

"Yes," said Markus.

I thought about leaving the Vitares family behind, leaving an Ajarel-shaped hole in their lives and ruining all Kuril's plans to rebuild the family.

"I can't carry that many people," I admitted.

Markus smiled, patting my arm. "It's always hardest the first time."

"I'm going to fix everything for them," I said. "I'm going to help them rebuild. At least I won't ruin them when I leave. That'll make it easier. That's not too disloyal, right? It's what my cover is supposed to do."

"Maybe we should take on the Voranetti," Markus said. "That should help them reclaim some standing."

He kept a perfectly straight face, but a significant look in his eye reminded me that we were both Velean.

Markus wanted to free Cades from the Voranetti.

The dominoes began to fall. Comments the commander had made about the job being emotionally taxing. The multiyear, sometimes multidecade deployment windows. The team's strange lack of oversight on my growing closeness with Roel and Kuril.

Godslayers were still human, in the end. The team was *expecting* that I'd seek out human contact. After all, they were doing it, too.

All I had to do was walk away when the time came.

I offered my hand to Markus. "Deal."

We shook on it.

CHAPTER FIFTY-ONE

The Old Ways

The following day, Roel didn't give any sign that my idea for mechanized prosthetics had sunk in. If anything, she was more distant and subdued; the finer etheric hints I might otherwise have relied on were getting lost in the maelstrom of negative emotions that was slowly becoming her new normal.

If we were on Earth or Veles, I'd have pulled every lever available to get her to a psychologist so she could process the trauma, but the closest equivalent on Theria were the clergy of their various cults. I'm sure there were good people in the cults, but I was pretty goddamn skeptical about letting a cult use Roel's trauma to drag her deeper in. The Sisterhood of the Wheel seemed pretty chill, so I asked Kuril if they had any resources for this kind of thing, but apparently they left it all to the Gamalites.

I thought about planting a camera in Roel's room so I could see if she was sketching a design or something but ended up not following through. It felt wrong—a breach of the shaky compartmentalization I was starting to build between my mission as an Eifni operative and the life I was building with the Vitaressi. I'd navigate this without requisitioning ethertech to solve my personal problems.

I closed the door to her bedroom, secreting my pulser in one of the many hidden pockets in my dress. It was really convenient that the Estheni preferred flowy clothing. If their fashion tended toward tightness—or, Darwin forbid, nudity—it'd be a lot harder to carry around the tools of the trade.

I breathed deeply: in, out; in, out. I tried to shelve my worry for Roel and my uncertainty about living tenuously in two worlds. Time to do my nightly meditation practice—I realized with pride that it was a nightly habit in truth now, rather than aspirationally—and hit the sack.

"Operative Lilith, you are hereby ordered to report to the Ragnar *for a tactical assessment."*

Or not.

"Seriously? Abby, it's, like, ten o'clock."

"I am authorizing the use of medical translation for exhaustion tonight. Extract from the Vitares estate unseen. Practice not using your cloak. With Lirian incapacitated, there should be no further threats of her caliber."

"Shit." I guess she meant business, whatever this was. Her tone was extremely formal. "On my way."

The only real struggle would be climbing the exterior wall; Kuril had relaxed security with Lirian's capture. Part of me wondered whether Lirian had allowed herself to be captured for exactly that reason; she'd been remarkably calm for someone who was about to get dragged off to Javei Central. Come to think of it, I didn't actually know what they did to people in there, but given that Kuril had ordered them to punish her, it probably wasn't a five-star-resort experience.

I slipped into a darker set of clothes—the shawl I was in had been dyed with brightflower. I made sure to pick up the small bag that was waiting in an unobtrusive corner of my room before I left. Now ready to go, I located an open window and checked for estate security.

The guards all had shuttered red ghostlights. The shutters made them harder to spot in the darkness; the red light stopped their night vision from getting ruined. Pretty effective against your run-of-the-mill thief.

Unfortunately for them, I had cybernetic eyes with built-in night vision. Sucks to suck! Better luck in the next millennium!

From my vantage on the second story, I saw one of the guards rounding the corner. I shifted to the side to minimize my profile in the window—there was a ghostlight in the hallway behind me, it'd make me stand out—and let him pass me by. He was in no hurry. I was, but with stealth work you gotta wait for your moment. Eventually I judged he was far enough away that I could make a break for it. I hoisted myself out of the window, twisting to face away from the building, and sighted my drop. The cobblestone pathway would make for a bad fall, but there was a planter—there!

I landed with a muffled thump, collapsing into a roll rather than letting my feet take the whole impact. Still had my bag? Yep, all good! I kicked some dirt back to disguise the divot from my initial impact and set off to the outer wall.

"And no one was the wiser," I murmured, popping a grin in the darkness. It felt good to be back in my element. Next op, I was going to request a role that only involved parkour and hitting people. That's all a girl really needs.

I looked up at the wall and grimaced. It was free-climbing this or sneaking past the main entrance, which I knew was both well lit and manned at all hours. Well, commander said to get out unseen, so that meant free-climbing time. I looped the bag through my belt, left side, and set off for one of the thicker pillars that partitioned the wall into segments. There was enough room for me to wedge myself into the corner and push myself up with my legs. Kinda like a wall sit, but your legs are walking up the adjacent wall while you scrape your back all the way up. Not pleasant, not comfortable, but I managed it. This shawl was toast, though.

I lugged my aching body over the top of the wall, pausing to take a breather and admire the view. City was quiet this time of night. Your noble types could afford ghostlights if they needed to work at this hour, but most people had to make do with candles. Man, I probably would have done way better in college if staying up late had cost me money.

The night air was cool, the moon was full, and I had some kind of weird training exercise to get to. I dropped off the wall and made my way to the hidden door to the *Ragnar*'s cavern. After a quick scan to check for observers, I sent a command over comms to open the door.

Abby was waiting on the lift.

"Yo," I said.

"Evening," she said. "We're meeting in the lounge."

"Tactical assessment, huh?" I said. "You gonna tell me what's up?"

"You'll be briefed when we start," she replied. She started the lift and took us down.

She'd never pulled something like this on me before, and I suspected it had something to do with my breach of operational security. But I wasn't getting *anything* off her. Etheric, body language, whatever—Abby was perfectly controlled. Surely she'd need to do an inquiry if she were doing an official discipline thing, right?

Fucking Veles, man. Everything was a test, and all the questions had trick answers.

I didn't forget all the social maneuvering I'd been doing the past couple weeks, though. I kept all my defensiveness out of my body language, forcing myself to stay relaxed. Would Abby pick it up, anyway? Would she know what it meant? It wasn't lost on me that the Veleans' whole implicit-communication thing probably meant a multi-centenarian like the commander wouldn't have any issues seeing through the facade of a less-skilled person. She'd had more practice at this than I had practice breathing.

My furious mental calculations came to a halt. We'd reached the lounge.

"After you," Abby said, her lips quirking.

I stepped through the door.

"Oh, you *utter bastards*!" I shouted in delight.

Markus burst out laughing from his seat at the central table. Val merely smirked, steepling his fingers behind *my fucking DM screen*. They'd brought out my RPG books, and my dice were all over the table.

"Tactical assessment, my ass!" I threw my arms around Abby. "What the— Why on earth?"

"Surprise!" Abby chuckled. "Your birthday's in a week. Between that and the occasion of Lirian's defeat, we decided to throw you a surprise party."

"I designed a character for you," said Val. "You can fill in the personality details."

"I'm sure it's minmaxed to hell and back!" I said happily, skipping over to give Markus a hug, too. "Hey, big guy. Is Slinky the Rogue coming back?"

"I decided to branch out," said Markus. "I'm playing a wizard now."

The drawing on his character sheet looked exactly like Slinky the Rogue: a shirtless, overly muscled dude striking a pose. The only difference was the hasty addition of a wizard hat.

"You big lunkhead."

"Waif," he replied.

"Oh yeah, Val," I said. "I got a present for you."

"Isn't that the inverse of your native birthday customs?"

"Smart-ass." I reached into my bag and retrieved the sandals I'd been wearing the day I'd fought Lirian—still stained with splatters of her blood where I kicked her. "Can you do something with this?"

His smirk stretched into something more predatory. "Happy birthday, Lilith."

"Well done!" Abby said, grabbing my shoulder.

"Eyyy!" Markus fist bumped me. "I knew you had this."

"Abby," Val said. "Would you say this means she *vanquished* Lirian?"

He put a weird inflection on the word. I had my comm replay it in Velean—I didn't recognize the word, but the overtones were ancient. Like, someone randomly dropping into *Beowulf*-style Anglo-Saxon English in the middle of a vernacular sentence, kind of ancient.

Abby hummed. "I suppose it would. Will you retrieve it for me?"

Val nodded, rising from his seat at the head of the table and exiting the room.

"What's all this about?" I asked.

Abby stared off into the middle distance.

"There is an ancient code," she said. "Some say older than the Eifni Organization. Those of us who follow it call it the Old Ways; no other name for it has survived. It is a code for those of us who find themselves drawn to war as an art rather than as a career. Before you ask—no, it's no more religious than doing meditations or practicing your katas. Eifni has extensively vetted it for religious contamination and found nothing. It's merely a way to shape your growth as a warrior."

"Hell *yes*," I said. "Is that the thing you do with the amplifier? And you're all like, 'Surrender now because I'm not giving you another chance,' and then you kick everyone's asses?"

Abby snorted. "Yes, that thing. But it's more than that. I am offering to teach you. I am considered a master of the Old Ways, which means I am permitted to take an apprentice—provided you have proven yourself by *vanquishing* a foe in hand-to-hand combat. An utter defeat, such as what you visited upon Lirian."

I stared at her.

"I get to be a motherfucking padawan?" I said. "*Fuck. Yes.*"

Abby beamed. "We're all so proud of you, Lilith. I have to admit, I had a feeling you might accept. So I took the liberty of requesting Val's expertise on the next step."

I narrowed my eyes suspiciously. "Wait a second, is it a math test? Is that why you're buttering me up here?"

"No, you're gonna like this," said Markus. "I think he's almost back."

Val returned, carrying—

"*Holy shit it's a motherfucking sword!*" I squealed.

"Your powers of observation are truly without peer," he said. "Their custom is for the sword to be bestowed by the master to the apprentice, so you'll have to survive an additional few moments without touching it."

"Holy shit holy shit holy shit."

Val gently flipped the blade around, presenting it to Abby, who bowed before taking it from his hands. He made a soft, derisive noise.

"I know we say this every time we hand you a deadly weapon, but this is not a toy," he said.

"Uh huh yeah sure of course absolutely."

"Lilith," he said. "This is a translated weapon with etheric components. If you aren't careful with it, you could cut your soul."

I squealed again. "*It cuts souls?!*"

Val glanced obviously in Abby's direction and sat back down. I picked up the hidden meaning—this was important to Abby, so I needed to not make a fool of myself. That was probably fair. I steadied myself.

"Okay," I told her, grinning madly. "What do I do?"

"I am a warrior of the Old Ways," said Abby. "My road has been long. If you would walk it, then take up my sword."

She offered the sword to me, hilt first. I drew it reverently.

It was perfect. The entire weapon etherically reeked of swordness, which just made all the little touches look just right. The leather wrap around the handle! The curves along the hilt! The ridge down the blade! Damn, I was really going to need to learn some sword terminology so I could gush more.

"Your apprenticeship formally begins when you name it," said Abby. "If you name it wrong, you can try again. Some people take several years of contemplation to fully understand the nature of their sword. Once you've discovered its name, you'll train until I say your apprenticeship has concluded, and you'll be given a spear as a symbol of your mastery."

I could see my reflection in the sword. It was *so shiny*.

"Okay, that's easy," I said. "It's named Lilith."

Markus burst out laughing. The unexpected one was Val, who was full-on doubled over and guffawing from his gut. Abby's face radiated utter *shock*.

"I— Are you joking?" she stammered.

"It's what they taught us in the Academy," I said. "Swords are just swords. The real weapon is me. It's named Lilith."

Val wheezed out, "I told you."

Abby sighed. "Congratulations, apprentice."

CHAPTER FIFTY-TWO

Sacrifice

The temple quarter of Vitareas lay in the center of the city. Eleven buildings in a ring, with the most expensive decoration I'd seen on any Therian building save the estates of the graced. Stepping through the gate, I was bowled over by the amount of color and sheen radiating from each of the edifices.

The temple of Varas was the most prominent—directly across from the temple-quarter gate, sweeping architectural lines and towers making it seem more like a cathedral than the others. Androdaima's was smaller but clearly given the most love of any of them, walls covered with gilded carvings of gears and hammers and pulleys. It was placed next to Varas's temple in what I remembered was the place of honor. Made sense, this was supposed to be her city. There was a whole system to how you were allowed to position the temples, but I didn't remember it.

Kives's temple was off on the right. She was always supposed to be next to Horcutio, who I assumed got the one with the waves on it. But Kives's temple was unmistakable. Kuril practically dragged me toward it.

The building was similar in construction to the Vitaressi estate, with basically a square of building around a central courtyard, which in this case contained a tree— specifically a *fetoulia* tree, which was sacred to Kives. They were known for growing pretty big. I'd heard that after a couple hundred years, the priestesses would build a chapel up in the branches for their holiest ceremonies. They clearly weren't there yet. If our mission succeeded, they never would be.

We'd burn it down, like Eifni burned the sacred groves eight thousand years ago.

The commander's voice reached me through etherspace. *"Are you ready, Lilith?"*

"They fall," I subvocalized.

"They die," she replied. *"Remember what I taught you."*

It was an old trick—maybe even the oldest trick, invented by Eifni himself. It had been the foundation of the mysticism that would eventually be replaced by etherphysics, the noetic breakthrough that eventually let humankind claw their way into reality and drag the gods from their thrones.

Eifni had been neither warrior nor statesman before deciding to raise his spear against the gods. What he had was rage, a rage that had drawn others to his banner and swept through kingdom after kingdom, destroying temples and making the names of the gods into curses.

But you can't kill the god of war—may its name remain unspoken—with a war.

Veleans always acted like this was all part of a big master plan, but in *The Road of Spears* he said ending up in this situation was the worst strategic blunder of the entire campaign. Apparently once he realized the problem, he stalled out for a couple years. How do you fight a war without it being a war?

If Eifni had had military training, he might have gone on to invent guerilla warfare, and the god of war would have lived. But he was ignorant, so his innovation was philosophical rather than military.

Eifni did not go to war. Instead, he very intentionally became himself.

Which just so happened to involve murdering his way through the armies of the war god.

The technical term for this technique was "existential proxy." It was primarily a state of mind based on totally, authentically owning your every thought and action. If I fully mastered this technique, I could punch someone in the face, and instead of committing violence I would be *being Lilith* really hard.

Apparently, to be a master of the Old Ways, you had to do this *all the time*.

Kuril and I entered the temple of Kives. Kuril was here to make sacrifices. I was here—in the tradition of the venerable Mr. Rogers—to be myself.

"Ajarel," Kuril said sharply.

I looked at her, then followed her gaze. There was a sign on the wall, which was simply labeled "Counsel." Below the sign was an empty space in which someone had written two names. I stopped short as I recognized one of them was "Lady Ajarel."

My stomach dropped. The second name, written phonetically in Estheni characters, was "Lilith."

"Lilith," Kuril said, trying out the name. "Unusual name. Sounds Tuman, doesn't it? Maybe she came in on a caravan."

"I could see that," I said, struggling to keep my voice even. "Uh, sounds like I should go in?"

"I can wait," said Kuril. "We can make the sacrifice after your counsel."

"This way," said a woman's voice. I turned to see a priestess in green robes, hair woven under a crown of branches. She smiled compassionately at me. "Godsmile, Lady Ajarel. The goddess told me you'd be here today."

"So she did," I said, waiting for my brain to catch up with the situation. "Uh, godsmile."

"I am Fisher," she said.

"Fisher. Godsmile. So I'll just, uh, follow you?"

Fisher smiled and slowly lifted an arm to indicate the hallway I should take. With an uncertain glance at Kuril, I did.

I was led to a private room, festooned with cushions and soothingly colored drapery. A wineskin, two mugs, and a plate of fruit sat on a table in the middle of the room. Two chairs offered me the choice of sitting with my back to the exit or letting the priestess sit between me and my escape route. That had to be on purpose.

Fisher didn't look like a fighter. I'd take my chances going through her if the need arose.

After we'd sat down, Fisher poured me some wine.

"Lilith," she started, not reacting as I tensed up, "your secrets are safe with me. No, no, not like that. Mother Kives did not reveal all. I only know what was necessary to help you."

"Help me, huh?"

Fisher smiled. "She warned me you would have doubts. This is a safe space, Lilith. Kuril will never learn of your assumed identity, at least from me. You may tell me anything at all, and no word of it will escape these chambers."

But it *would* go straight to Kives, so nice try, jackass.

"Fine," I said. "Message received. What's she want to tell me?"

"That she will heal your deepest wounds," said Fisher. "She has told me how. First, your barren womb can be restored."

"My *what*?!"

"Take but one fig from the sacred *fetoulia* tree," she said. "Then journey north to the spring of Vourel, and bathe there in the moonlight for twelve nights. On the twelfth night, partake of the fig, and Kives will restore your womb."

"Uh," I said. "You know what? Fuck it. I don't want kids. I'm not going back to having periods. Why the hell did she think that was my deepest wound? Get your god out of my uterus!"

Fisher stammered. "But—wait, there's more!"

"*More?!* What else is she offering?"

"She knows your pain!" Fisher tried. "Of not seeing the erotic beauty in those you love!"

"Erotic— *I was fifteen!*" I yelled. "Asexuality is a valid orientation!"

"But she said—" Fisher's mouth moved wordlessly. Then a long-suffering expression replaced the compassionate therapist-type one, and she slumped back. I recognized that look immediately.

"Oh my god," I said. "She trolls you, too?"

Fisher sighed and nodded.

"Her *own priests*?"

"The Greatmother has lessons for us all," Fisher grumbled piously.

"Wow," I said. "That's . . . really something. I'm gonna be honest, I was expecting this to be more about me when I walked in."

"Maybe that's her lesson for you," said Fisher, putting a hand over her eyes. "I'm so sorry about this."

"Psh." I sympathetically poured her some wine. "You good?"

"Thanks," she said, taking a swig. "Oh *come on*, this vintage? Really?"

On the one hand, I had no idea what was going on there. On the other hand, I knew exactly what was going on there, and it was funny not being on the receiving end for once. I snickered a little bit.

"Oh, go on," said Fisher, waving me out. "Go deprive your children of their futures. Apparently it's none of my business."

"Have fun wrestling with your biases," I said cheerfully, standing up to leave. I clapped her on the shoulder on the way to the door. She sighed, taking a sip of wine. I left her there.

"*You get all that?*" I asked the team subvocally.

"*Very interesting,*" said the commander. "*Val, this is your area. Any insights?*"

"*Lilith was very easy to provoke.*"

"Great insight," I shot back.

Val pinged a smile over the comm. "*Kives also didn't use that against her. We can likely consider this to be her confirmation of the truce, or at least an assurance that Kives will not act against us when she uses us in her causal chains.*"

"*There's no way she's telling the truth about that,*" I said.

"*Or that's what she wants you to think!*" said Markus.

"*Markus!*" I complained.

"*We're not in a position to go after her either way,*" said the commander. "*We'll prepare for betrayal, of course.*"

I nodded.

I found Kuril in the antechamber to the main courtyard. In my absence, she had acquired a sacrificial pig, which was wandering around as far as her rope would let it. I suppressed a grimace and met Kuril's eyes.

"Did she answer us?" asked Kuril.

It took me a moment to figure out what she was asking. "Oh, yeah. Yeah, we're good. We just have to sacrifice today and ensure the legacy of House Vitares is strong." A spark of guilt flared up in my chest. "But, uh, you should be careful about all the sex. Your kids will have better futures if you have them after the Kabidiad."

"Hm," Kuril said, her brow furrowing. "That's strange. I've only lain with Bofa twice."

"Wait, what?" I asked. "He's in your office all the time."

"Well, yes," she said. "He gives excellent massages, and my shoulders get sore when I sit at my desk all day. He's also very knowledgeable about the ironmongers of Vitareas. It's been a godsend for sourcing new supplies for the workshop."

"Oh," I said. "Uh . . . Yeah, so it turns out everyone in the house thinks you've been screwing him when he's in there."

"What, on my *desk*? Where would the paperwork go?"

"I don't know! It's not like I was imagining it!"

Kuril folded her arms. "And I suppose that's why it's been nearly impossible to find an attending lady during working hours."

"Can you blame them?" I asked. "*I* certainly wouldn't want to walk in on my boss like that."

"That's why I have sex in my bedchambers!" Kuril said. "They're designed for it!"

I really didn't need to know that last bit, but the Estheni were a lot more open about that kind of thing than Americans, so I kept my mouth shut about it. Kuril wasn't observant enough to notice my discomfort. I hustled her through to get the damn sacrifices over with.

The first thing you were probably supposed to notice was the tree, rising up into the heavens.

The thing I actually noticed was some dude's bare ass hanging out while he— jerked off? For real? What kind of weird-ass kinky stuff was Kives into?

"*You gotta be kidding me,*" I subvocalized.

"*It's not unexpected,*" said Abby. "*She's a goddess of fertility. Considering the etheric resonances, semen would be an appropriate—*"

"Nope nope nope not talking about this," I cut her off.

"Over here," said Kuril, pointing to the altar. I followed her, focusing on my existential proxy. I would participate in this ceremony because I was being Lilith, and to be Lilith in this situation was to blend in with my cover.

It wasn't like the meditative exercises I'd been doing. I wasn't exactly meditating—I was actively interpreting myself *as* myself, moment to moment. Walking as Lilithly as I could. Thinking as Lilithly as I could. Taking the pig's rope from Kuril in the most Lilith way possible.

"Custom says I lead, as your matriarch," she said. "Did Kives instruct differently?"

Trying, as Lilith does, not to be responsible for killing a pig. "Nope. Do your thing."

"Good." Kuril handed me a knife. *Fuck.*

Holding the pig on the altar. Regretting, like Lilith would. Following Kuril's prayers distantly. Watching the shrine keeper bring a bucket to the altar. Looking at the bucket and not the pig. Trying to see if there was blood inside from the last sacrifice. Holding on as the pig struggled. Distantly responding to the shrine keeper's cues. Hefting the knife, all reluctance hidden. Slitting Arguel's throat. Watching the blood drain into the bucket.

Doing what had to be done.

As Lilith does.

CHAPTER FIFTY-THREE

Economic Warfare

With Kives dealt with to Kuril's satisfaction—my brain was still replaying the pig's dying squeal—we adjourned to Kuril's office to plan our next steps. We were joined by Roel and by Bofa, who was pushing her chair. I couldn't see her legs under her skirt, so I had no idea if her muscles had atrophied significantly. Then I realized I was thinking like a primitive and checked the etheric resonance of her legs. According to the significance of the wound, the nerve damage to her leg wasn't going to get better, but the muscles were still in relatively good condition—aside from the stab wound, of course, which was going to take a while for her body to fix.

Or, you know, about fifteen minutes with a medical translator.

The guilt must have shown on my face. Roel caught me looking and scowled at me. I flashed her an apologetic smile and took a seat.

Kuril also sat down. She gave the desk a considering look, glancing up at Bofa for a moment. She frowned and shook her head slightly.

"Well, then," she said. "It's about time I got everyone up to speed. I apologize that I have been so busy recently—by the way, Roel, Ajarel informed me how everyone interpreted the long hours in my office, and I just want to clarify that I've only been having sex with Bofa during the evenings."

Roel tilted her head, then slowly nodded. The new information didn't make her any less miserable.

"The reasons I've been in effective seclusion are quite complicated, but the short version is that we are all doomed unless we can change a lot of things very quickly."

"Doomed?" I asked, giving voice to the worry and surprise on Roel's face. "It's, uh, not like you to be so hyperbolic."

"It's simple mathematics," said Kuril. "The price of iron has been increasing for several years, and it's impacting our ability to do business. I have determined that our financial situation is increasingly fragile. The house will be vulnerable to collapse and ruin within two years."

"I thought we were untouchable!" Roel burst out. "We're invested in the city itself."

"We have been outmaneuvered," said Kuril. "I thought I had the complete picture, and I did not. For your benefit, Ajarel: we still have substantial holdings in the city, but most of our income is earned through commissions—self-locking doors, water valves, counterweight pulleys, and so on. Our earnings have been stable, if not on the rise, for several years. What's troubling me are the numbers from the craft guilds."

Kuril spread out several sheets of paper, each with columns of precisely annotated data.

"These are the bellwether guilds of economic activity in Vitareas. Delve reports a slight increase in business over the last three years. Loam shows an increase of earnings, roughly of proportion eight parts to the hundred per year. Tree, meanwhile, has lost nine parts to the hundred over the same time frame, and Quarry has fallen to *seventeen* from their position three years ago. Do you understand the significance of these indicators?"

"Uh . . . No."

"Economic decline," Kuril said immediately. "Delve and Loam are the most stable of the guilds. Delve because the Jeneretti have skillfully curated the city's industry to require a constant supply of metal, and Loam because the city will require food no matter the circumstances."

Roel looked like she knew all of this already. I tried to make sure I was getting everything so as not to give her more reasons to be upset at me.

"On the other hand, Tree and Quarry," Kuril continued, "are more beholden to the city's fortunes. Quarry has it the worst—when the wealthy stop building, Quarry has to rely on city projects for income, and since the completion of the second aqueduct, we've had nothing but the usual maintenance projects for them. Tree is in the same situation—a laborer struggling to buy bread has little business for a carpenter. As the treasurer of Vitareas, I use these as indicators of the financial stability of the rich and poor, respectively."

"So the farmers are charging more for food, and people aren't buying as many nonessentials," I summarized.

"That's the apparent conclusion," said Kuril. "As for our doom, I was discussing iron prices with Bofa, and we started to have some troubling disagreements."

Bofa nodded solemnly.

Discussing iron prices! I tried not to smirk. He was truly the perfect man for her: they were both incredibly boring.

"These records," she said, moving another pile to the center of the table, "are the earnings reports for Hammer and Wheel. We tend to follow Tree, whereas Hammer is relatively insulated from economic effects; however, they've experienced a loss of nine parts to the hundred. That's the first thing that didn't make sense—Hammer comprises most of Delve's business, so they shouldn't be moving in different directions like these numbers imply."

"How bad are we doing?" I asked. House Vitares did business through the Wheel guild, but I hadn't heard anything about business being tough.

"We aren't," said Kuril. "In the past three years, Wheel has seen an increase of thirteen parts to the hundred. And that tells me that something is wrong with the numbers."

"Not gonna lie, economics isn't my strong suit. How are we doomed?"

Roel glared at me. Sorry, kid, I never got the chance to take Macroeconomics.

Kuril pointed to the Delve sheet. "Iron, copper, and silver are produced in normal quantities." She pointed to the Hammer sheet. "But the main consumer for these materials isn't able to purchase them at quantity. Wheel's metal consumption is a fraction of Hammer's; we can't account for a gap this large. So someone else is purchasing them, and it's not in my records."

"Another house," said Roel. Kuril nodded to her.

"Meanwhile, the citizens of Vitareas are hoarding food and refraining from furniture purchases, but they're hiring engineers as if the aqueduct were pouring silver instead of water. Either the records are wrong, or someone is paying citizens to buy from us."

"You think it's the same house?" I asked. "Why would they do that?"

"Think about it," said Kuril. "What happens if they continue for a year or two, then stop?"

Roel gasped. "At this rate, we'd lose a third of our income. We'd be ruined."

"Not just us," said Kuril. "Delve would suffer, though not crumble, I think. And House Voranetes would have a stockpile of materials to sell to anyone in Hammer who can't balance their account books. Perhaps with loans."

"You sound pretty sure about that," I said.

"Did you suspect that perhaps the *Henadim* were conspiring to create an economic crisis aimed at the political rivals of the Voranetti?" Kuril snapped.

"They know you're the treasurer," I argued. "It was only a matter of time before you found out. Why would they be so blatant?"

"They're not," said Kuril. "We buy from the Jeneretti at fixed rates, per ancient compact. I never would have noticed, had I not decided to take on this particular consort." She gave Bofa a very warm look. He smiled; I scrunched up my nose. "Another sacrifice to Kives is in order, I think."

"It doesn't matter either way," said Roel. "Even knowing their plan, what can we do? It's their grace-given wealth. They can do what they please with it."

I took a deep breath, letting myself half sink into the calm of meditation.

My interaction with Fisher this morning had seemingly developed another layer of communication. It wasn't lost on me that Kuril would never have met Bofa if I hadn't been around for her to delegate work to in the first place. This, too, it seemed, was Kives's will.

It made sense, I supposed. I'd just happened to fall in with a house whose legacy was being threatened. Kives's people went pretty big on the having-kids thing—fair enough, given that fertility was one of her frequencies—but as she'd reminded Fisher today, you didn't need children to have a legacy. My objectives dovetailed very nicely with hers for the moment.

Kives was probably trying to build up some credit with me and/or the team for when the final confrontation went down. Too bad it didn't work like that. No mercy for soul eaters. No quarter for aspiring universe devourers.

But today, I'd play along.

"Okay," I said. "Okay, this is fine."

"Is that so," Roel said acidly.

"Oh yeah," I said, grinning. "We've got 'em good. They won't know what hit 'em."

Roel humphed. "I suppose you have some brilliant plan where you go out and I stay home."

Bofa put a gentle hand on her shoulder. I wasn't able to hide a wince.

"It's . . . not exactly like that," I said. Roel fixed me with an unimpressed look. "Yes, I think you should stay home—let me finish! You need to be here because we're bringing *them* to *us*. I propose we host a ball."

"A ball," said Roel.

"You wanted to find out the truth?" I asked. "This is your chance."

She examined me carefully. Slowly, uncertainly, she nodded.

The commander approved the op.

That wasn't to say that my original proposal was flawless, or that she didn't rewrite big parts of it with me before giving the okay, but by Galileo it was *my* op, and she approved it. I felt like I could fly, or fistfight Cades, or drop-kick that fishy pirate guy off his own ship. You know, the big guy with the stupid forehead from the Kives op. I forget his name. Whatever. Point is, I felt really, really good.

It had nothing to do with getting Markus that third laurel, I knew. She said it was for my education. Nothing was said about my attachment to House Vitares, or the real consequence that this would enable them to survive my departure. She had to know what was going on, though. The one part of the plan the commander seemingly had no problems with was the part that just so happened to get Markus closer to Cades.

I didn't ask, and she didn't tell.

I spent most of a day holed up in Kuril's office while she explained the various trade compacts between the big houses of Vitareas. I took notes, trying to keep my brain from seeping out of my ears while I built up a picture of all the major players. Kuril knew this stuff like the back of her hand. Together, we built a proposal our targets would accept.

Falerior was summoned to the estate. Kuril explained the job to him, with Bofa silently on her right and me on the left, mirroring Falerior's assistant, Ekoula, as we both took notes. Roel sat in on the meeting, staying as quiet as Bofa.

I amused myself during the proceedings by making Ekoula uncomfortable with periodic challenging glares. He always averted eye contact like it burned.

When the negotiations were completed, Falerior adopted a more formal tone, looking Kuril directly in the eyes.

"I understand what you ask of me," he said. "Do I have your oath that this charge is made in good faith, and that you will accept the result of my judgment regardless of its conformance to your preferred outcome?"

Kuril's tone was equally formal. "In the name of Vitares Steelsinger, you have my oath."

"Witnessed, for House Vitares, by the ladies Roel and Ajarel, of the grace of the Vitaressi," Ekoula rattled off. "Notarized by Oathkeeper Ekoula, of the grace of the gods."

"Let justice be done," Falerior concluded the rite.

"I'll have payment sent directly," said Kuril. "Thank you for coming."

"I am at your service," said Falerior, giving no hint of his thoughts. "My lady Roel."

"Oathkeeper," she said, a hint of warning in her voice. I felt a little warm at that. She might be mad at me right now, but at least she was on my side. Falerior nodded to her.

"Lady Ajarel," he said, turning my way.

"How's Lirian?" I asked. "Have you pulled out all her fingernails yet?"

A look of confusion clouded his perpetually bland expression. "Why would we do that?"

"Huh," I said. "Is that not something you do?"

"If you'd like to learn, you're welcome to come visit."

"Definitely," I lied. "Some other time."

"Naturally," he said, his polite smile returning. "Godsmile, ladies."

I exchanged looks with the girls after he left. We were almost ready. All that remained was baiting the trap.

"Decision point," I said. "Are we ready to, uh, release the bowstring?"

"Apt," said Kuril, looking at Roel. "You're the expert. Do you think the plan will succeed?"

Roel frowned. "To be honest, it's normally a bad sign for the whisper if the play-wright lets you know all the details before the plan is attempted."

"And in real life?"

Roel considered. "I don't see how anything could go wrong."

The invites went out that evening.

CHAPTER FIFTY-FOUR

Brightsteel

Every good con needs bait.

That's the secret behind any manipulation, really. If you need the target to act, you gotta give them a reason to. And if the Voranetti had demonstrated anything about their motivations in the time I'd known them, it was that they were hungry. That, the girls informed me, was the mark of the more vicious strain of Varasite houses.

Mercantilists like the Jeneretti might elbow you into an unfavorable trade deal if you let them, but they'd never plot your destruction. Their philosophy was rule through coin. The Voranetti, on the other hand, practiced *conquest* through coin. They were trying to eat us—which you weren't supposed to do, as a house of grace, but when have nobility ever followed the rules?

We could use that. It would really be unfortunate, I'd observed, if the Oathkeepers caught them breaking those rules.

"No, that would be extremely convenient," Kuril had said.

"Irony, sister," Roel had groaned.

Our primary objective was to prepare the house against the economic shock that we were now certain was coming. That was mostly Kuril's work: decreasing costs wherever possible, building up the treasury, sending out feelers to investigate how many of our customers would stick around after House Voranetes stopped subsidizing commerce at the Guild of Wheels. But institutions don't turn on a dime, and our opponents had two years' head start on us. If they pulled the trigger next year, we'd suffer— recoverably, perhaps, with the unfavorable sale of Vitares assets to a newly prosperous House Voranetes. Kuril had declared that an unacceptable stain on Vitaressi pride.

So instead we were going to give them something else to chew on.

Roel and I took a ride out of the city to an ancient Vitares property. Peres came with us. Normally taciturn on anything not craft related, she decided that today was the day she was going to start my initiation into the Sisterhood of the Wheel, the local cult of Androdaima. Which, it turned out, was basically ancient OSHA with flowery prayer language thrown in.

"The Goddess of Delight is fickle," she was saying. "You must work prayerfully and intentionally, every movement in synchrony. An arm carelessly employed may anger the goddess, and she may seek recompense."

"What kind of recompense?" I asked.

Peres looked at me like I was an idiot. "The arm."

"Gotcha. Keep your arms and legs inside the vehicle at all times."

Peres gave the carriage a confused look before deciding to ignore me. "Now, on the subject of fire—"

I breathed deeply.

We arrived after *too long* to a breathtaking sight: a field of brightflowers. Farmers walked carefully among them, each wearing a white shawl—which, in the noonday sun, brilliantly reflected the many colors of the flowers around them.

There was no rhyme or reason to them. No organization, no color wheel, no hue map—just a thousand shades of the rainbow scattered amid one another like a child had gone a little overboard on the cupcake sprinkles. A structure of white stone, also shimmering in reflected light, occupied the center of the field, while smaller wooden huts stood at the edges.

"For processing them," said Peres, nodding to the white building. "Paints, dyes, ghostlight hearts. By compact, the city is supposed to cover the expense, but somehow we always manage to run a loss."

"Aren't ghostlights, like, superexpensive?" I asked. "Why are we worried about money if we've got all of this?"

Peres glowered at me. "The gifts of the goddess are for all."

"Practically speaking, all the major families have fields like these," said Roel. "The ghostlights are the only brightflower craft with a significant margin, and even if we're the only ones who can make them, the other families don't buy them that often. It's not enough to sustain the house. Besides, the point of brightflowers is to create for creation's sake. Androdaima would be cross."

"Sacred flowers. Got it." I leaned down to investigate one. It was so *blue*. So brightly blue that I had a hard time believing it wasn't secretly hiding behind an Instagram filter or something. On a hunch, I had my comm scan the flower.

"*Check this out,*" I subvocalized.

"*Fascinating blessing,*" Val said. "*I have to admit some respect. Commander, look at the radiant braiding on this.*"

"*No idea what that means,*" I subvocalized glibly.

"*It's really, really blue,*" said Markus. "*But Androdaima used a fancy way to do it, so Val's having a moment.*"

"*I am not.*"

"*You totally are.*"

"*It's respect for a fellow craftsman, Markus. You would understand that if you'd ever learned respect.*"

"*Says who? I get respect all the time.*"

The commander's derisive snort interrupted them. "*Clear the comms, both of you.*"

"*Will it work?*" I asked.

Val hummed. *"Further study is required, obviously. I don't see any fatal issues at a cursory glance."*

I sighed in relief, then belatedly realized I'd left Peres and Roel waiting.

"Can I pick this one?" I asked.

"It's yours now," Roel said, not entirely keeping the bitterness out of her voice. "Niece."

I bit back a grimace and took the flower. "You got the ingots?"

In response, Peres hefted a rucksack onto her shoulders. There must have been fifty pounds of iron in there. She didn't even look strained.

A pair of servants brought Roel's chair out to the carriage door. With their help, she levered herself down into it, relying on her good leg and wincing every time she put too much weight on the other one.

"Remember," I began.

"It just has to look convincing," Roel interrupted. "We remember, Ajarel."

I shut up. We entered the white building.

"Godsmile, Lady Erephine," I echoed Kuril, bowing to the head of the Kessim. "And thank you for meeting with us."

"Godsmile," she replied. "Lady Councilwoman. Lady Ajarel."

Erephine Kess was a big woman, probably taller than Markus and Cades even if they had her beat in muscle mass. Her eyes were the now-familiar shade of Estheni gray, and her hair was tied back in an increasingly fractal series of braids, cascading down to her hips. Her expression was warm, every inch the welcoming host. Behind the affectionate smile, my comm picked up signals of rapid calculation and assessment. I noted them briefly but kept my attention on the feedback from the broader scan.

"My gratitude for inviting us to meet with you," said Kuril. "House Vitares has always respected and depended on your house to feed the city. I've often felt that role has gone overlooked in the operation of the city."

"The Divine Husband teaches us to accept our place," said Erephine, "but we have our pride."

Good, that meant she was interested.

"Justly," Kuril agreed. "I am a Maker, Lady Kess. When an engine is out of alignment, I fix it. I have a proposal for you."

"The ingenuity of House Vitares is well-known." She was playing coy—we weren't in the best political situation, so showing too much enthusiasm here would be bad for her house. This was probably the best we could expect.

Kuril smiled. "At our upcoming ball, we will reveal a great work, something we have developed in secret. I ask for your partnership in its manufacture. We will train your smiths and give you—besides us—exclusive right of sale, in compact witnessed by the Oathkeepers."

"Gamal teaches generosity," said Erephine, "but there are limits to what I can offer for such an unknown."

"I understand," said Kuril. "Lady Ajarel?"

I stepped forward, lifting the cloth-covered object I'd been holding and pulling the cloth away. There were gasps from the attendants as the shining bar of metal in my hands tinted the room slightly blue.

"Vitares Steelsinger was renowned for the invention of brightsteel, whose secrets were lost generations ago," I said, still slightly entranced by the shimmering hue as it played over the walls and the furniture. "By the grace of Androdaima"—*and a lot of slapdash improvisation with various lacquers,* I mentally added—"we have recreated this storied and beautiful alloy, with which we will revitalize the city. We hope to produce ten thousand ingots in the next year."

"Praise the goddess," Erephine murmured, eyes fixed on the blue bar. Then they sharpened, fixing on Kuril. "Ten thousand ingots? Has the Dancer stolen Varas's crown again and left it in your chambers?"

"The generosity of the Kessim is well-known," said Kuril, repeating Erephine's phrase from earlier.

Erephine smiled in acknowledgment. "Ten thousand ingots. The old compact gives you three thousand, if I recall? Will you build your crafts from brightsteel?"

"Not yet, unfortunately," said Kuril. "Not until its material properties are better understood."

"Your ambition is worthy of a Varasite," said Erephine. "Why not offer this bargain to a Jeneretes?"

"I would not speak ill of such a noble house," said Kuril. Erephine's smile took on the quality of a smirk, and she gave a nod of understanding. I didn't know what exactly was being implied there, but Kuril knew what she was doing. Erephine took a long, regretful look at the fake—er, I mean *prototype*—brightsteel, then sighed.

"These are hard times," she said eventually. "I will live to regret this, but we are on intimate terms with neither Hammer nor Quarry. Three thousand I could do, I think, and it would be a reckless gamble when children go hungry in the street. Two thousand would be justifiable. But I see from your expression that won't be enough."

"As you say," Kuril said apologetically, "these are hard times. I cannot go lower than five thousand."

"Could we invite another house to this deal?" Erephine's tone was casual, but the read I was getting from her was very much a probe.

Kuril smiled humorlessly. "Whom would we ask?"

Erephine considered her. "I see. If I might offer some advice, Lady Councilwoman?"

"Of course," said Kuril.

"Vitares Steelsinger is long dead," she said, her smile vanishing. "Your house's rivalry with the Jeneretti weakens the city at a time when we cannot afford infighting. We both know they're the only ones who can accept this offer of yours. Frankly, I'm surprised you even bothered. You're the treasurer—surely you know our normal consumption barely approaches the volume of material you're asking for."

My comm nudged me, and I zeroed in on the signal. I held back a smile. *Check.*

Kuril caught the significant look I threw her. Mission accomplished—time to go. "The houses of the graced are not my purview," she replied stiffly. "The honor of the Kessim is well-known. You were worthy of the offer even if its demands were too great."

"Come back if you can invent a more flexible set of demands," said Erephine.

They smiled daggers at each other. I initiated the closing formalities and dragged Kuril out of there before she alienated a potential ally.

"Did it work?"

"One of the attendants had a *very* calculating look on his face," I lied—hopefully I could get away with letting her think I was just very perceptive. "You'd think they'd hire better spies. In any case, the Voranetti will know by nightfall."

Kuril nodded. "Ajarel?"

"Yeah?"

"No magic," she said, looking me in the eyes. "No spells. Nothing that can result in disaster like Salaphi. Promise me this."

"I promise," I said. It was an easy promise. I had something better than magic—technology!

Kuril held eye contact for a moment. She nodded.

Roel wasn't in her room when we got back. Kuril sent someone to fetch her and immediately set to fretting over the contract we'd prepared.

"This is a risk," she said. "We're flirting with ruin."

"In the worst possible case, sure," I said. "It's not going to come to that."

"The secret of brightsteel was *lost*," said Kuril. "This is not true brightsteel. If the contract is enforced—"

"Then something went horribly wrong, and we're screwed, anyway," I said. "Blame it on me if you have to. I can stab a couple of them on the way out."

"*Ajarel!*" Kuril snapped. "Don't you *dare* joke about that."

"Sorry, sorry," I said.

I wasn't joking.

"Oh, there you are," said Kuril. "Godsmile, both of you. Where were you?"

I turned around to see Bofa pushing Roel's chair through the doors of Kuril's office.

Bofa opened his mouth, but Roel interrupted him.

"I asked him to walk me around the courtyard," she said, a touch too fast. I tilted my head questioningly at her, but she ignored me. Kuril didn't seem to notice Roel was lying to her, despite having walked past the courtyard with me ten minutes earlier. "Did it work?"

"It worked," I said. "We'll probably hear from them in a couple days."

I was wrong. Their envoys came that night. By the time they left, we had a morning appointment and the first real step toward victory.

CHAPTER FIFTY-FIVE

Training

I followed Bofa and Roel as they left the meeting. At a distance, of course. I walked casually, greeting the staff as I passed them but staying out of sight of my quarry. Eifni had these sick ether-linked goggles that could show you where your target's attention was pointed, but I didn't have any on me, so I was just falling back on my Academy training for this. It was pretty easy mode—Bofa was blocking Roel's line of sight, and Roel was commanding his attention. They weren't in a hurry, so every so often I started a brief conversation to give myself a plausibly deniable reason for not overtaking them. *Not* with Alouren, who passed me and tried to get my attention. She would definitely keep me there all night.

"Godsmile, Alouren," I said. "Sleep well."

"Actually, I was thinking about what happens to the soul during sleep," she said quickly. "What are dreams?"

"They're— Look, I don't know, kid. Can't you ask a priestess about this stuff?"

"They don't know anything," she said, apparently oblivious to the irony. "You know all sorts of stuff. I thought you might know."

I tried to watch Bofa out of the corner of my eye while wracking my brain for ways to end the conversation. "Well, I don't. Maybe next time."

I managed one step down the hall before Alouren squeezed past me to stand in my way.

"Wait! I have another question!" she said.

I looked at her, then looked down the hall.

"Are you *stalling* me?" I asked.

"No," Alouren said uncomfortably.

"You suck at lying," I said, crossing my arms. "Why are you stalling me? Did Roel put you up to this?"

"I, uh," she said, glazing wildly around the hallway as though inspiration were hiding right behind my shoulder or something. "I'm not?"

"Sure, whatever," I said. "I'm going that way. Please move."

"You can't!" she said.

I nodded slowly, sizing her up. She was shorter than me—bit of a waif, really. No way she topped a hundred thirty pounds. I could bench her no problem.

"Okay," I said.

I reached under her armpits and lifted her up. She squeaked in surprise. I turned ninety degrees and set her down.

"Good night, Alouren," I said. I set off at a brisk walk. Alouren didn't follow.

"I'll tell her you're spying on her," she called after me.

I turned. She looked almost frightened.

"Dude," I said. "My bedroom is this way. Are we cool?"

"I—" She frowned. "I'm not a man."

"Dude is— Actually, forget it. Are we going to avoid unnecessary drama, or do I need to tell the head cook that you're shirking cleanup duties?"

"But I'm not—"

I leaned in. "You make shit up, I make shit up. Understand?"

She looked pretty unhappy at that. A cool evening breeze filtered through the hallway, bringing the scents of the sleeping city to our noses. I know that sounds kind of nice, but actually it didn't smell that great.

"Fine," she said. "Don't hurt Roel. Okay? If you're going to—I don't know, just don't hurt her, okay?"

"I really don't know where this is coming from," I said. "Good night, Alouren."

She watched me turn the corner to the hallway where my room was located, then ran off somewhere else. I rolled my eyes, cloaked, and went after Roel again.

"How many freaking wannabe spies do I have to deal with?" I whined over the comms as I made my way to the edge of the second-floor balcony.

"*What happened?*" Val's voice came to me.

"Well, Roel's clearly up to something, and now she's got Alouren running interference," I said.

"*If you're struggling to outmaneuver untrained teenagers, I've heard tell of an ancient technique called subtlety.*"

"Yeah, but have you *used* it?"

Val's scoff rippled through the etheric channel. "*I am the very soul of subtlety.*"

"I feel like I would have noticed."

"*Quite.*"

I snorted. "Touché."

For whatever reason, losing the verbal spar didn't carry the bite it normally did. That was nice. Felt like I'd beaten something.

"*What's the provenance of the word you just used?*" Val asked. "*It felt martial.*" Undercurrents of approval ran through the question. He thought I'd done something right, too.

In proper Velean fashion, I left all that unsaid and answered the literal question.

"It's French," I said. "There's this sport, fencing, where people fight with rapiers. Uh, thin, wobbly kind of sword."

"*A show weapon?*"

"I mean, it's a sport weapon, so it's blunted. We can't come back if we get killed. But they're meant for stabbing. Someone stabs you, you're supposed to yell, 'Touché.'"

"Mmm. The closest equivalent in Velean is 'Good strike.' I appreciate that you have a single word for it."

"The French do, anyway." I scanned the courtyard to see if Bofa and Roel were down there. Literally—I set my eyes to thermal vision. The ghostlights along the inner balcony showed up as tiny pinpoints, but the only human-sized heat signatures were the wrong shape to be my target. I leaned on the balcony railing and sighed. Alouren might not have been subtle, but she'd managed to slow me down.

Nice try, kid. Eifni cheats.

I pulled up the surveillance-camera feed and flipped through until I found Roel. It was a lot less fun this way. Both of them—or *Bofa them, eyyyy got 'em*—were hanging out in the workshop. Peres was asleep by now, but it looked like Bofa was doing Roel's bidding instead. They'd come a long way from Roel's initial frostiness toward Kuril's boy toy.

"What motivation does she have to build in secret?" Val asked. He must have been tracking my comm activity. I pursed my lips at the thought.

The sucking emptiness of the cloak pressed in around me, insistently tugging on my soul like the last bit of pool water draining out of your ear. I focused on my presence meditation, trying to keep my heart rate from spiking.

"Look at the sketches on the table," I said, as if the designs there were new to me. "I guess she's got trust issues."

"A mobility device," said Val. *"I see."*

I didn't respond. I could only pretend ignorance for so long before the two-hundred-year-old Velean caught some tonal cue or microexpression and figured me out.

"Trust issues," he said thoughtfully. *"But she trusts you, surely."*

There was no etheric content to his tone, as was often the case when he was totally making fun of me. I shoved my annoyance aside and acted like it didn't bother me. Or—wait, if I didn't react, did that make it look like he got one past me without me noticing? Ugh, Velean social fencing was obnoxious sometimes.

"If you've concluded your reconnaissance, the commander requested you back on the ship."

"Is that so," I said, pushing down a spike of anxiety. "She knows I'm running an op here, right?"

"It's training," Val said dismissively. *"As long as your skills improve, the outcome doesn't matter."*

I breathed out sharply. "There's real people here, man. They matter."

"Real, yes. But not enduring. In a hundred years, they'll all be smeared across etherspace—unless we fail, in which case they'll be god fodder—and all that will remain of this operation will be the perfection of your art."

A pair of dogs was having some kind of squabble a couple streets away. My fists bounced leisurely on the balcony railing. It drifted in and out of focus as I kept my attention on the flame of my soul, forcing myself to remember I was here.

"You're a cold motherfucker," I said. "You know that?"

"*Fires die.*"

"Whatever, edgelord."

Val laughed. "*That would be the commander. Come on back.*"

"Turn off your comm," Abby said when I entered the exercise room. The lights were dimmed. She was kneeling in perfect stillness in the center of the mat, hands on her knees. Her eyes didn't open as she addressed me.

"What part of *active operation* is not getting through to you people?!"

Now her eyes did open, considering me in absolute blankness. She'd set her irises to a piercing, luminescent green. They glowed harshly in the shadows.

"Markus has performed in his role for longer than you've been alive," Abby said. "He'll survive the night. Tonight, you will be learning a secret of the Old Ways, passed down from master to apprentice for nearly ten thousand years. So turn off your comm. We will speak in Velean. You will *think* in Velean. We will speak mind to mind, preserving the ambiguities and the struggle of intent that marked human relationships before the invention of facilitated communication."

"Alright, alright." I knelt across from her, telling my comm to shut down nonessential functions as I closed my eyes. I considered leaving my etheric translator running, but something told me that was a horrible idea. "Are we meditating?"

"As you think necessary," said Abby.

"Okay," I said in Velean. "Battle ready."

"Follow as best you can," said Abby. "What will you be when you die?"

"Uh, reincarnated?" I said.

"I meant between bodies."

"A soul only," I said.

"What will you carry with you?"

"I have no ideas," I said honestly. "It worries me about that."

"You've shared your worries before," said Abby. "And they're not baseless. The brain isn't a mere physical reflection of the soul. Even with the *Ragnar*'s stored images of your neural connections, you will lose memories and skills. Parts of your past life will become dreamlike, insubstantial."

"Why would you ever flash, if that's so?" I asked.

"Because I am no longer a child," said Abby. "You will suffer the same personality degradation if you live a hundred years—likely worse, in fact, especially if you develop a neurodegenerative disorder. We haven't eradicated those on Veles, you know. Elective reincarnation is culturally normative and cheaper besides. One way or another, your life will be shorn away."

I sighed. "That's big depress."

"It's a challenge," she said. "The blade lords of the Old Ways apprehended this truth long before Eifni Org mastered reincarnation: we are built up and torn down every day. If you allow yourself weakness, the universe will grind you to nothing. But if your will is strong, then the blade of your self will cut heaven and earth."

"Fuck yes," I said. "Therefore uh . . . How do I do that?"

"We begin with the self. Velean psychology draws a distinction between the self and the identity. The Old Ways do not. They are a unified system of action and belief, termed the 'blade of the mind.' You think of yourself as a fighter because you were in the top of your close-combat class. You think of yourself as intelligent because you outperformed your peers during your childhood. And so on."

"Why is that a blade?"

Abby made a noise of approval at the question. "Have you noticed that when Val makes you feel stupid, you strike at him?"

"That's just . . . me being insecure, I think."

"No," said Abby. "It's lack of experience. When that edge of your self is perfected, your strike will land decisively. As Val's strikes do, when you try to make him feel stupid."

I perked up. "I have made him feel stupid?"

"I said *try.*"

My shoulders slumped. "Oh."

"You must be aware of two truths in order to hone your self," said Abby. "The first is that it is zero-sum. To be fast or strong, you require someone else to be slow or weak. And the reverse is true: I am faster and stronger, so you are slower and weaker. You may find this uncomfortable—I heard you take a breath to interrupt, Lilith, I'm not letting you pretend that you're not. Understand that the ambition behind that discomfort is something to be embraced, but you will always be a child until you can control that act of comparison."

I wanted to say something, but then I'd be proving her right about finding it uncomfortable that I was weaker than her or something, and I wasn't. Also, she kept beating me in spars because she had, like, centuries of practice, not because she was, like, *actually* faster, so I could totally still be faster than her. Which I didn't actually care about, I didn't go around thinking, *Yaaaay I'm superfast,* it's just I *could* have been faster than her, you know?

But in the end I didn't say anything, so Abby never heard my explanation of why she was wrong.

"The second truth is that the self carries the danger of any weapon: you will always be tempted to use it when it is not required. The self warps our thinking and drives us to react without strategy. It will manipulate your memories and sabotage your estimation of your opponents in order to confirm itself. So, as with any weapon, the first and most important consideration is maintaining control of it. If you can do that, death will be nothing to you."

"Because it will preserve me through the process of flashing?"

"Understand this, Lilith. The language of my native culture was called Xhepotre. I wrote poetry in that tongue. I used it to propose to my wife and teach my children— but all I remember of it now is the name. I left the rest behind a hundred years ago. It was no loss. Do you know why?"

I opened my eyes in shock. Abby sat in perfect stillness, those neon-green eyes fixed on mine. The question hung between us in a long silence.

"No," I admitted. "I can't imagine."

"Because I had no further need for it." She said it matter-of-factly, no regret, no wistfulness, eyes betraying nothing but placid attention. "I am I. That which is I, I will carry with me even if this body is destroyed and no other awaits. And with that blade, I will cut heaven and earth."

CHAPTER FIFTY-SIX

A Friend to Wolves

gotta admit, I got goose bumps when Abby dropped that line about cutting heaven and earth. I released a slow breath.

"The skill you will learn tonight is called Growing the Mountain from the Roots," Abby said. In Velean it was only three syllables, "*ak ha var.*" "It is an extension of the blade lords' discoveries about the self. It is applicable both to honing your true self and to enlivening the cover identities that we adopt in our line of work. Going forward, I want you to integrate it into your presence meditations."

"Understood."

"We will begin with the simple case. The first step is to select an aspect of your identity to strengthen. It is traditional for apprentices to spend many days in meditation at this step so that they can settle on the identity they want to build. You will begin that process later—tonight, you will pick thoughtlessly. Be prepared to resist the pressure of that commitment when you begin the real work."

I nodded. "I can do that."

"I know you can." Mild green light highlighted the contours of Abby's eye sockets as they relaxed into a smile. "Now, before you make your choice. I have told you that this skill allows you to build an identity. By implication, it allows you to become anyone you wish."

"Okay," I said.

Abby watched me silently. I sighed. That meant this was another dumb Velean thing, and I had no idea what was being asked.

"Are . . . you asking what I'll use it for?"

The combination of dim lighting and Abby's glowing eyes made it hard to make out if there were any shifts in expression. Although, to be honest, I probably wouldn't have had much of a chance in optimal conditions. Abby didn't give signals she didn't want to.

I was supposed to infer a question here, but there was nothing to prompt me on the question I was supposed to have. Abby refusing to respond to me conveyed *some* information at least, which is to say I was supposed to figure it out myself. So that meant she thought I had all the information I needed. Val was much more of a sink-or-swim kind of teacher; Abby never let me flounder for too long.

Definitely still floundering, though. I had no idea what she was thinking here. Was that the test? Was I supposed to intuitively grow from the roots myself into someone who knew the answer? Because I had no idea how to do that.

"Fucking how do I make myself someone who knows?"

Abby snorted. "I wondered what was happening over there. That's my fault, I'm using a traditional technique and thought you'd figure it out."

"Fuck," I said.

"Some information can't be inferred from context," said Abby. "Don't judge your-self. In this case, the custom is that the master presents a statement of fact, and the apprentice accepts or rejects it after some consideration. The master does not give guidance, as the foundational task of a student is to learn to guide themselves. 'You are the first and last of your foes.'"

"Uh, hold fast," I said. "Is that why everyone in my cohort perpetually argued with the instructors?"

"I'm sure it was one of the reasons," Abby laughed. "Let's try that again."

"It was annoying," I muttered. "You said some information can't be inferred. So you can't mountain yourself into knowing things you don't know."

"Grow yourself," Abby corrected me. "Good answer. But it turns out that's not entirely true. If you build a new self, that self will see things differently and come to conclusions you would not have otherwise reached. That said, you're generally correct: growing a new identity doesn't convey skills or knowledge. Within that boundary, *ak ha var* allows you to become whomever you want."

"Big," I said.

Abby didn't respond.

"Oh—fuck you, that thing again?"

Abby didn't respond.

I huffed. "I am confident there's nothing I can *var* to stop the annoy."

"Good! If accidental." Abby did the Velean head-tilt thing they used instead of winking. "Why?"

"Because it's annoying." She definitely wanted more than that. "And it's not my culture."

"It would be closer to the mark to say that the annoyance comes from experiences you've had," Abby said. "The body remembers. The soul remembers. Both carry your past, and the past returns as your present behavior. *Ak ha var* means taking com-mand of that process, but only warm blood taints a frozen pool. Without mastery and repetition, your underlying self will remain as it froze, so to speak. Do you understand?"

I nodded eagerly.

Abby's face crinkled affectionately. "Begin with the identity you want. Don't be discouraged if you don't have a worthy one—again, it's traditional to spend days refin-ing a concept before beginning this discipline. You will do the same in time, but for now, just pick something salient."

I nodded slowly. "Give me some time."

Couple days of meditation? I could do it faster than that. Abby would be super impressed if I got it now. Her slow incline of the head communicated that my request was granted.

Who did I want to be?

My mind automatically supplied the memory of my time running the ops console and its vision of our souls. Markus's welcoming warmth. Val's scalpel precision. Abby's perfect serenity. And my own soul, a limping, color-saturated mess.

I hated that. I really did. Like, I knew who I was: I was a kick-ass operative of the Eifni Organization. Literally. I have kicked so many asses. I was top of my class in close combat. Uh, almost; Veigo only won that last bout on a technicality and Gana basically doesn't count because they were so far ahead of everyone else. When they deployed us to that elimination action for graduation, I was the only person on my team still alive by the end of the mission. I knew who I was: I was a badass.

"I know who I am," I said. "Why does the console disagree?"

Abby blinked. "Well, someone's into the woods. The console is representing something else. Come back, Lilith. This is just practice, no need to overthink it."

"You said people think about this for *days*," I said.

"Not for practice, they don't," Abby said. A slight smile played around her eyes.

"Fine," I said. "I want to be . . ." *Not that*, not the console's image of my soul, but I didn't know how to articulate that, and it didn't seem like what Abby wanted besides. So try something—cool, someone who could handle anything . . . *I want to be you* was the next thought, but I couldn't make myself say the words. I got stuck on that for a few adrenaline-heavy moments.

Abby interrupted me. "Not 'want to.' Something that you *are*."

"Oh, that's big easier," I said, frantically trying to come up with a Velean phrase for what I wanted. Abby watched me patiently. *Ah.* I had it.

"I," I said, "am a friend to wolves."

She gave me an approving smile. "That'll work."

I sighed with satisfied relief.

"'Friend to wolves' is the mountain," said Abby. "Its roots are the things you've done. Bring one to mind."

I remembered the first match I'd won against Gana.

"Now focus. Burn it into your senses until it drowns out the world."

"So it's like presence meditation," I said. "I'm just focusing on a memory instead of my soul."

"Be silent. But yes, you're correct. Now *focus*."

The rebuke stung a little, but I didn't regret being clever. I focused on the memory, trying to make myself visualize it. I wanted to be like those people who would go like, "I had every movement of the fight engraved in my brain," but, uh, I didn't. I did remember the end of the match, though. Gana'd made a mistake, positioning their knee block wrong and overbalancing as they took the kick. They knew immediately they were in trouble. We made eye contact, and I moved.

It was perfect. I have no other way to describe it. Like I'd woken up in *The Matrix* and knew exactly where to hit. I went for the legs first, forced them to fix that or fall over. The momentum from my stomp kick landing got channeled into my hips as I threw a flawless punch—and they went for the guard, of course they did, Gana always knew how to react to my aggression—but it wasn't fast enough. Solid hit to the armpit, right in the nerve cluster.

Like dominoes, like music, every step laid out in front of me as I slid my foot forward and ripped it back at their knee. Hammer hand to the throat—they caught it on their forearm, but their leg was already folding under them—grinning like a madwoman, looking down at the anger in their eyes—and the *sound* when they hit the mat, *thump-thump*, flat on their back—seven more wins and I'd be able to even the score.

This was how it started, this would be how I scaled the combat ranks and topped the class despite my useless Earth upbringing. *I won.*

Embarrassment that I hadn't actually topped the class threatened to distract me from the glory of that moment. From that flow state I'd never managed to recapture. I tried to push it aside to focus. To remember the soreness from the hits I'd blocked, the hits I'd landed. The smell of the close-combat classroom, plastic mats and rough fabric and sweating students and Gana's sweet acidic cologne mingling with the taste of my own blood. The cheering—no one else had managed to take Gana down. "Lilith *barak*, Lilith *barak*!" Three of us would manage it before graduation, but I was first. I won first.

"Be present with the memory." Abby's voice was gentle, floating, infiltrating my attention without wrenching it away from the scene. "It is part of you—more than part, as long as you remain. Let it be all of you. This is who you are."

"I mean, I can't do this *all* the—"

"Be silent. Focus. In this moment, you embodied the identity you're building. Don't try to force it; that's why you're having contrary thoughts. Be the self in that memory. Let its shadow rest on your soul and displace those thoughts. If you fight them, they'll sink deeper into you. Focus on the memory instead."

I tried, but now that the doubts were present it was hard to just ignore them. I'd never managed that flow state again. I beat Gana twice more before graduation, but they beat me six more times. It felt like more of a fluke, if I was honest with myself. I shifted the weight on my legs.

"You will experience a temptation to dismiss the experience," Abby said, as if guessing my thoughts. "The mind is efficient. It abstracts collections of experiences into monolithic images and discards what does not fit them. Persuade it to desist: your memory is true, and your actions were yours."

"What if—"

"Be sil—"

"What if," I said, talking over her, "the circumstances aren't repeatable? Legitimate question."

She looked at me pointedly. After a beat, she relented. "Why does it matter if they're not repeatable?"

"I, uh." I huffed, trying to figure out how to word the idea. "If I can't do it when I want to, it's not a real identity."

"When you have mastered this first step of *ak ha var*, you will practice visualizing false memories to serve as building blocks for assumed identities. The statistical likeliness of the memory is irrelevant, only its connotations for the identity you're reinforcing. Remember that when you retrieve the memory you've stopped focusing on."

Fuck. She was right. It was gone.

"That will be all for tonight," said Abby. "I'm opening my comm."

I did the same, grateful to be back in English. "So you want me to do this during my meditations now?"

"The mental action is the same," Abby said. "But don't start yet. We'll wait until you can spend an uninterrupted period honing your identity. Most likely that will be after your diversion with the Vitaressi."

"Speaking of which," I said, glaring at her, "I should probably get back to my *diversion*."

Abby closed her eyes, her posture relaxing just a bit. "I know it's important to you. I also know that you haven't forgotten our objective on this planet."

"That's not at all what I was saying," I said quickly.

"No, you were saying that you want respect." She opened her eyes again, meeting my eyes with no trace of emotion. "I'm proud of you for taking the initiative on this. But I am Velean, as are you. If you have to demand respect, you don't deserve it. Show me glory in victory or resourcefulness in defeat—I'll be the first to shout, 'Lilith triumphs.' But show me."

"Fine," I said, seething. "But I've got a meeting with Sael Voranetes in the morning. If you keep pulling me away the night before critical parts of my op, there's gonna be a lot more resourcefulness in defeat to go around."

Abby nodded. "And what are you going to do about that?"

"Go home and sleep, I guess," I said, standing up. "Probably ask you next time if it's important."

"Oh, very much so," said Abby. "Mission critical."

"Oh, fuck off," I said, standing up. "Gimme a hug."

Abby gave really good hugs. Something else she'd accidentally mastered in her half-millennium of existence, I guess. I squeezed back.

"But seriously," I said, not letting go of her. "This is my big-girl grown-up mission. Don't fuck me up."

"I wouldn't," she said. We released each other. "Sleep deprivation won't stop you. You could do this *in* your sleep."

"Lilith *barak*," I replied, grinning like a madwoman.

Abby laughed. "You're not supposed to say it about yourself!"

"I guess I'll wait for you to say it." I patted her on the shoulder. "Okay, I'm off for real."

"Go be a friend to wolves," Abby said. "We'll cover your back."

I set off for the Vitares estate, the wind warm and the moon high in the sky. Time to get some rest. Tomorrow, I was having breakfast with sharks.

CHAPTER FIFTY-SEVEN

House Voranetes

You know how some rich people just, like, don't live in fancy houses? Which, you know, kinda makes sense. Houses are freaking expensive. I always thought if *I* got rich someday, I'd live in a normal house and save a bunch of money.

Anyway, the Voranetti were not that kind of rich people. They were the other kind, whose builders had wandered past the intersection of Extravagant and Loaded to settle on Wealthier Than You Boulevard. I didn't even wanna *think* about how much they were spending to upkeep this architectural monster.

The typical Estheni estate plan was kind of like a big square around a central courtyard. People messed around with it, particularly if they were rich and/or graced. The Vitares compound, for example, was what you'd get if you put four of the normal estates together and knocked out most of the inner edges, leaving the work-shops as their own thing in the middle of the courtyard.

You generally saw the wealthy throwing around decorations to make the courtyard look better—like that Jeneretti mansion with its ghostlights and artificial ceiling—to impress their customers and political allies as they entered through the gate. House Voranetes had apparently decided to skip that step. There were no rooms in the front of the compound, which the architect had compensated for by stacking the compound's rear wing twice as high. I don't know how the fuck they even managed that without rebar and tower cranes; you're supposed to need those to get past three stories or some-thing. Obviously they'd figured it out, though, and the result left them presenting sixty to eighty feet of concrete walls to the street.

Those walls were covered in stained glass. It must have been made with brightflowers because it didn't look like any stained glass I'd ever seen before—it was practically glow-ing at us. Transparent glass windows set into the front wall of the compound ensured that everyone walking past got a full blast of their ridiculously ostentatious display.

They'd whitewashed the inner courtyard with some kind of pearly lacquer that reflected the light from the window display. My breath caught in my throat as we approached.

"Holy shit," I whispered.

"Indeed, even the greatest of our works fails to compare to the excrement of the goddesses," Kuril quipped. Her tone darkened. "Vitares Steelsinger built this palace as a gift for the lady Voranetes, her loyal ally. To summon us here under the circumstances is a cruel repayment of that generosity."

"Small-dick energy," I agreed.

Kuril eyed me sidelong. "I suppose it's true that the men of House Voranetes are quite reserved, but I don't get your meaning."

"Uh, I just meant they're throwing their weight around," I said—then rescued myself, quickly adding, "In an underhanded kind of way." Good one, Lilith.

Kuril let it drop with a noncommittal humph. We lapsed into silence as our clockwork carriage rolled through the gates of House Voranetes.

Socially speaking, I was technically on the same level as Eloi Voranetes. But the technicalities of Estheni social customs had a habit of giving way to practicalities, like—to give a completely random example—if you were a financially insecure house doing hostile business negotiations with your friendly neighborhood business sharks. Or whatever the equivalent was around here. Why didn't they have sharks? They're, like, an evolutionary constant. Heterocausality is supposed to have limits. Did Kives kill off all the sharks just to annoy me?

"Godsmile, Lady Kuril," said Eloi Voranetes in her withered rasp. The pale, slender specter of a woman turned her baleful eyes on me.

Her black hair was starched back into a sleek arch that looked like something H. R. Giger might have sketched at some point. I would worry she might accidentally poke someone's eye out if she weren't nearly seven feet tall.

She wore thin robes of midnight black, woven with silver threads that sparkled in the ghostlight whenever she moved. A winter-blue sash swept over her hips, denoting her authority as Lady Sael's number two. I imagined it was doing its sash-y best to intimidate the sunflower-yellow sash slung across my hips.

"Godsmile, Lady Sael," I replied to the woman sitting behind Eloi.

Sael Voranetes herself was set up on a platform in the back of the room. The first thing you noticed about the Voranetes family head was that she was heavily pregnant, courtesy of a deep-blue dress whose patterns and fit drew the eye to her swelling stomach. That was the second-weirdest thing about the dress; the first was that she had a ruby sewn on either breast. Those were *clearly* supposed to be nipples. It would have been obscene on an Earth dress, but somehow the message it sent was more "expecting mother" than "this is sexy." Something about the cut of the dress, or the dress's evident agnosticism about her cleavage?

"House Voranetes welcomes its ancient allies," said Eloi without a trace of irony. I refocused on the task at hand. "Thank you for coming. Please accept our hospitality."

The Voranetti sash bearer skewered our bench with intent eyes, and somehow it was immediately clear to everyone that Kuril and I had been invited to sit down. We didn't.

After a moment—*almost* too long to be polite—Eloi seated herself. Only then did we sit.

Having concluded the formalities, Eloi peered at my sash, then at my face. She leaned back, satisfied.

"Lady Sael extends her congratulations," said Eloi, wearing the blank face of someone performing a rote action. "Greatmother's blessings upon you and your daughter."

"Greatmother's blessings upon you and your daughter," I replied.

It was going to be like this the whole negotiation—sash bearers were the Estheni version of maternity leave, dedicated assistants for important pregnant women to delegate to. That meant as long as we were wearing the sashes, we didn't personally exist: we were just mouthpieces for our family heads. It also meant the family heads couldn't speak for themselves without making themselves look dumb—contradicting your own sash bearer meant you couldn't find someone else who better understood your goals.

That was, of course, the entire reason we were pretending Kuril was pregnant—she was going to do that a couple of times to make us look vulnerable. Estheni indirection was kind of annoying, but honestly it was nothing compared to Velean social fencing.

I might not be the best at it, but at least the skill I wasn't best at could still beat *their* skill with one hand tied behind its back.

"Your news comes late to this house," said Eloi, who knew for a fact I wasn't wearing a sash when we visited House Kess yesterday. "Our regrets."

"The news is recent, but we're of course honored to inform you in person," I said. "Divine serendipity, perhaps."

Eloi didn't react to the oblique invocation of Kives, but she did give off a pulse of attention. "Then we will not keep you from your festivities. Our purpose here is simple. We have learned of your house's"—she paused—"*other* recent triumph. You need a business partner."

I exchanged a choreographed glance with Kuril. "What have you heard?"

Eloi gestured to an attendant at the door. "Enough."

The attendant returned with a set of scrolls, which he set respectfully on the table. Eloi carefully selected one with spindly fingers, unrolling it in front of us.

"The honorable treasurer of Vitares may of course correct any mistakes made by our analysts," she said. "We doubted the numbers ourselves—you would not be this *stupid.*"

"*What* did you say?!" Kuril growled.

"Shhh!" I told her.

Sael's mouth curled into a smirk, dark eyes considering us from above. Eloi pointedly ignored us, which somehow did a better job of highlighting the faux pas than pointing it out directly.

"You asked Erephine Kess for ten thousand ingots," she said. "A ruinous expense, whose refusal did not surprise you. Treasurer." Her articulation was perfect, making the title into an insult. "But you did not ask the Jeneretti. Is the legacy of your ancestor worth so little?"

"This is incredibly presumptuous," I said, glaring. "Lady Kuril demands an apology."

"Let her first demand our calculations," said Eloi. "You don't have the capacity to produce ten thousand ingots of brightsteel."

"Our process is proprietary—"

"Your process is divine intervention, or it does not exist," said Eloi. "That is, unless your house intends to abandon its ancient duty to the city. But we would not dare accuse the honorable treasurer of that."

"You dare to insinuate it just fine," I said.

Eloi stared at me long enough that I started to feel uncomfortable about the informal language at the end. It was just a power move, I told myself. I endured worse from Val over breakfast.

"There is one way to forge ten thousand ingots of brightsteel," said Eloi. "Vitares Steelsinger, with all her house, could forge no more than two in a day. But those were ancient days. The city is larger, your house with it. Yes, even in its current decline. You could meet your ridiculous quota, *if*"—she stabbed a finger at the scroll—"you reassigned your guildswomen and commandeered their forges. The guildswomen who execute your house's ancient promise to supply the city with devices."

"Total speculation," I shot back.

"What should we think?" Eloi countered. "Your envy of the Jeneretti is known. Eschewing their aid is transparently political. If that is worth more to you than your house's only remaining purpose, then you do not deserve to be here. But perhaps we are wrong."

She turned her attention to Kuril directly.

"Perhaps I should inform the Oathkeepers that our treasurer gave contract in bad faith. There are witnesses; they will speak. So—are you liars or oath breakers?"

"Some hospitality this is," I said.

"Ah," said Eloi. "Of course. We have not offered refreshment. Pirineia?"

The attendant nodded. A moment later he returned with three other men, all carrying baskets. They hastily assembled the food on the table and withdrew, leaving us with the sight of several bowls of dipping sauce and bread. It was fucking *dvoli*, that super-spicy thing that Eloi had gotten me with at the ball. There were no drinks.

Not today, fuckers.

"*Val*," I subvocalized. "*I need you to turn off my spice receptors.*"

The only response I got was approving laughter and a ping in the affirmative. I took a piece of bread and slathered it in the murderous hot sauce, making eye contact with Eloi. I took a calm bite and didn't break eye contact. Her brow furrowed slightly.

"What do you want?" I asked. "I assume you haven't gone to the Oathkeepers already."

"Justice," she totally fucking lied.

"As do I!" Kuril broke in. "If our craftwork is suspended for a year or two, what does it matter? This city is *named for our ancestor*! Let the Jeneretti found their own city. This one *isn't theirs*."

"So you admit it," Eloi said in a low tone.

I eyed Kuril. That was a little too convincing to be an act. But that was all she had to do. Now it was my turn.

Go for the throat.

"We've admitted nothing," I said, taking another bite of *dvoli*. "Are you done threatening us? What was the point of this?"

Eloi looked at me. "Resign the treasury to us. Contract with us to produce brightsteel."

"You did just threaten to destroy our house," I pointed out.

"Is that not enough motivation for you?"

"Okay," I said. "Okay. You know what? I think you know you overstepped."

Eloi tilted her head. "What?"

"The craft subsidies?" I asked. "The price of iron? You trusted someone you shouldn't have."

"If you think this nonsense—"

"We think someone in this city is buying up iron," I said. "The Henadim don't have the resources. There's no reason for the Jeneretti to cause this kind of trouble, it makes them look terrible. And thanks to our contract offer, the Kessim just confirmed it wasn't them. The brightsteel is real. But think it through." I gestured dismissively to the scrolls. "Tell me what happens to the demand for iron if we start production. Tell me what the treasurer should do about that."

Eloi tapped thin fingers on the table, her bread untouched.

"We went looking," I said. "We found you. What was your phrase? There are witnesses; they will speak."

"Is that so."

"Not necessarily," I said. I took another bite of molten death, blissfully ignorant of its attempted destruction of my mouth. "Huh. This stuff is actually pretty good. Anyway, you've got a point about the ten thousand ingots. We don't want to get into any problematic areas with our oaths. After all, it'll make it hard for us and our *business partners* to challenge the Jeneretti."

Eloi's eyes narrowed. Sael leaned forward in her seat.

"You're bluffing," Eloi said.

"Of course not," I said, chewing. "You've met me before. You've seen me afraid. Do I look afraid, Eloi?"

She watched me silently, her expression frigid. "Courage comes easily when there's nothing left to lose."

"Tell you what," I said. "We'll show you the brightsteel. You knock it off with the market manipulation. You get rich, we restore the prosperity of the city, and both of us get the Jeneretti out of the picture. If your craftswomen think the brightsteel is legitimate, we'll negotiate terms. We can slip away during the ball and sign the contract. Deal?"

Every good con needs bait.

"We will, of course, give this proposal the consideration it deserves," Eloi said. Sael said nothing.

But the comm said they were hooked.

CHAPTER FIFTY-EIGHT

Performance

The Estheni didn't just have business meetings and leave. That would be rude! It would imply they cared about business but not about neighborliness, and what self-respecting graced would honor Varas but reject Gamal?

It wasn't like we were all pretending business wasn't the point of the visit—although I could see Veleans pulling something like that—but you couldn't let it be the *only* point, or you were a bad host. So we adjourned from the meeting room to a private courtyard on the second story, where the Voranetti had set up a picnic around an open area. I noted several locations on the roof that seemed like they'd make good firing positions while affording cover from shooters in the kill box. The corner pillars were broad enough that I'd feel safe covering there in the event of a firefight.

In the exposed center of this kill box, the other half of my plan was unfolding: Markus and Cades were setting up to entertain us with an exhibition match. It was a friendly match, which in this context meant when they finished singing we would both politely agree that it was a tie. Theoretically, the Voranetti could—if they really felt like flattering us—give us the win. But that wasn't going to happen, so instead we'd just have to listen to Markus and Cades take turns singing.

Markus was devastated, I'm sure.

I had my comm scan whatever it could pick off Cades. Cades was nervous—not like competition-jitters nervous, more like someone had a gun to his head. The Voranetti were definitely blackmailing him. None of it showed, unless you happened to notice the way he was looking anywhere but at Markus. I did. The Voranetti were all looking at Markus. Kuril wasn't even looking at the competitors, instead exchanging pleasantries with Sael. Now that the business part of the visit was over, us sash bearers were merely important family members and not literal proxies.

It was all logistics for our upcoming ball—which foods would be served, which invites Sael could convince us to cancel, a thousand little questions of influence and favoritism about random event shit I'd never even considered. But I guess that's why everyone was terrified of Sael.

"Your competitor is a fine specimen," said a withered rasp from what had to be a calculated distance just outside my line of sight.

"Uh, yours, too," I said. "Shame it didn't work out that first night."

"A shame I'm certain a woman of your experience can manage," said Eloi. "You've befriended my grandniece Alceoi, if I recall? An insightful decision."

I mean, the way I remember it, this bitch ordered Alceoi to make friends with me, so she was straight-up complimenting herself here, and I couldn't say anything without making us both look bad.

I almost said something, anyway, but then I realized I could get out of this by making Alceoi look bad instead.

"As luck would have it, I haven't seen much of her," I said. "To be honest, I thought she'd forgotten me."

"Allow me to put my thumb on the scale," Eloi said. "Alceoi! Come here, girl."

Shit. I probably should have seen that coming. In fairness to me, I'd been paying more attention to the tactical elements of the environment than seeing whether I recognized anyone here. Alceoi still ranked below the possibility of getting shot in terms of overall priority. Don't give me that look. They have bows and arrows here.

"Long time no see," I greeted her.

"Godsmile, Lady Ajarel," she replied. There was a minor tremor in her voice, small enough I would have missed it if I didn't have my comm to spell these things out for me. She was nervous. Not about Eloi—about *me*. She made a slight deferential nod.

"This one has eaten half a bowl of *dvoli*," Eloi told her. "You remain alone in your hatred of it."

The Voranetti sash bearer stalked away, leaving the two of us watching Markus.

"Is . . . your mouth . . . okay?"

Was that supposed to be innuendo? That was the problem with all this inferential communication. It only works if the recipient knows what the message is. Velean communication is all about playing roles, adopting attitudes and behaviors almost as a kind of reference—"This is what someone might say here, this what they might do"— to push the communicator's intentions behind an additional layer of obfuscation.

Or maybe Alceoi just didn't like spicy food. Fuck, I needed some friends who didn't habitually play mind games.

"I'll live," I said.

Alceoi made a reverse sniff of a laugh, a little amused puff of air through the nose. "I used to think Eloi's obsession with *dvoli* was a power game. But I'm starting to think she might actually like it."

"The taste is good once you get past the horrible spiciness," I said.

"So everyone tells her," said Alceoi. "But they have to. My cousins and my sister did. I was the only one who wouldn't."

"I'm not just saying it. I meant it."

"You're not doubled over and wheezing." Alceoi gave me a resigned smile. "You must have practiced, right? We all saw what happened to you at the ball a few *thessim* ago. So either you learned to like it or you did it despite the pain and the taste. I think under the circumstances you have to learn to like it."

No, I wasn't being paranoid, there was definitely some innuendo there. The comm said she felt—guilty? I wasn't expecting that. Did she feel bad about getting me to walk into Lirian's ambush back during the Renathion?

"You have to do what it takes to survive," I said softly.

She looked at me searchingly. Apparently satisfied, she returned her attention to the competitors. "I suppose you're right."

"You knew."

She didn't look back at me. "Knew what?"

The comm said it was a deflection. I wanted to push her for a more explicit answer, but I didn't want to disrupt our purpose here.

"Never mind," I told her. "I think they're about to start."

Markus had mounted the podium. Shirtless, of course. He probably would have gone with just the competition thong if we hadn't needed a scrap of clothing somewhere to hide the amplifier. I hurriedly switched my comm to Estheni to avoid the normal headache of listening to music in the wrong language.

Something about his posture shifted, commanding the attention of the room. The chatter died down. I *had* to learn how to do that. He took a breath. I smiled. He'd asked his tutor for a very specific kind of song.

"Draw away from me," he sang, "as the tide recedes, to return.

"Let your memory be a promise that the gods keep.

"The walls of Aeschios rise before me,

"Your will held firm within my heart,

"That this city may be the price to bring you home."

There were appreciative murmurs from the audience as he continued. It was a weird-ass kind of love song that probably made more sense if you grew up in a culture where women sent their suitors on dangerous military expeditions to prove themselves.

This one, Markus had told me, was referencing a famous love story about a general named Phosocres. He was having an affair with his queen, but she couldn't marry him openly because it would put him in a problematic social position with the family whose *primora* was the presumptive first husband. So she kept having him fight riskier and riskier battles so that he'd either die and end their ambiguous relationship or accrue so much glory that she could snub the other guy.

Inferential communication only works if the recipient knows what the message is. Cades understood. I could see it on his face. He was holding it together, but I guess you can only exercise so much self-control when you hear your socially problematic crush promising to take self-destructive risks so you can be together.

"Brothers! Stand side by my side," Cades opened his song.

"They come! Raise your shields!

"We will stand; we will not move

"We will show them the strength of men

"The strength of fire in our breasts

"The goddesses have made us for battle

"Forged our legs of bronze,

"Forged our arms of steel,

"So raise your shields and hold the line

"The goddesses have placed us here."

There were more verses, alternating between exhortations to manly bravery and philosophizing about the masculine virtues. Each ending with that line: *The goddesses have placed us here.*

Cades was every bit the boisterous soldier singing a rousing battle cry—singing to everyone, singing to a hypothetical shield wall, decidedly *not* singing to Markus. He steadfastly resisted looking at him, except on that last line. *The goddesses have placed us here.* This is our lot, he seemed to be saying. This is where we belong.

Huh. I'd kind of written Cades off as a dumb jock when I met him. This was actually pretty socially intelligent.

Cades sat down to stomping from the Voranetti ladies. I stomped along with them—I'd stand out otherwise.

Markus took the stand again, preparing for his second song. He was at a disadvantage in this little musical conversation: its medium was a shared context that he didn't actually share. Cades could pull out any song he wanted, but Markus only had the few he'd prepared.

But what Markus lacked in cultural background, he made up for in decades of people skills experience. The resistance was coming, he'd told me. He couldn't respond to the particulars of it, but he could go back on the offensive.

"How beautiful the arm,

"How bright the eye,

"How light your touch upon my face," Markus sang. He didn't need to look at Cades. Cades knew.

"As your arm moves, let me move

"And let me see as you see

"Let us be one, our hearts be one

"I will build in your wisdom

"I will make your will my duty

"And I will fill your bed when the sun sets."

Markus was an excellent singer, but the thing that was really impressing me was how he could pledge to a bunch of *gross* in front of a crowd of strangers. I wrinkled my nose in disgust for a moment. Alceoi noticed.

"Why?" she asked, looking between me and him. "I thought you'd had him?"

"What?!" I spluttered. "No! Why does everyone think that?"

"You must have traveled together for weeks. He's a man. It would have been simple." She made a dismissive hand gesture, then lowered her voice. "So what's wrong with him?" she asked curiously, looking him up and down. "I was thinking about it, but if you know something I don't . . ."

"We're not like that," I said quickly. "I'm sure there's nothing wrong with him. Go for it."

"Maybe I will," Alceoi said with a smirk. She examined me. "You're not offering to share, are you? I've heard of some strange provincial customs."

"No! I'm not fucking Thala! He's like my brother!"

"I'm just saying, you wouldn't have lasted long in House Voranetes if you made a habit of passing up opportunities like that."

"Oh look, Cades is up," I said with finality.

Cades looked pensive as he mounted the podium. He took a breath and almost started to sing—then coughed. He glanced at Markus. He paused, seemingly considering something. Then he sang:

"They sailed upon the waters dark as wine

"Beset by tempests' wrath and scorn divine

"Oh goddesses, give power to my voice

"As I recall the flight of Cesseros!"

I blinked. "What is that song?"

Alceoi replied without looking as Cades continued singing. "'The Flight of Cesseros'? You know, the one about the famous ship captain and her crew of traitors?"

"What does it *mean*?" I asked.

"It's just a story," said Alceoi. "All the tragedy happened because she gave too much homage to Alcebios, so I suppose you could say that's the message."

"*Markus?*" I subvocalized.

"*It means nothing,*" Markus replied. He couldn't quite keep the disappointment out of his voice. "*He doesn't know what to say.*"

I sighed.

"*Time for the fallback plan,*" he said because a godslayer can adapt to any contingency. "*Val, do it.*"

A sense of beauty and fascination filled the arena as Cades sang. The same sense, in fact, that permeated the arena when Markus sang during Renathions.

But somehow we could all tell it was centered on Markus. Somehow *Markus* was what made the song beautiful.

Cades finished his song to the sound of enthusiastic stomping. One of the Voranetti stood up—Gamourin, according to a mental note on my comm. She was one of the women the Voranetti sent to judge Renathions.

"What an incredible display of talent," she said. "It would be an insult to declare one of you superior to the other. And might I say, you have such a—*connection!*"

Cades very carefully did not react.

"Like . . . housemates! It would be a blessing to hear you both in a duet."

Sael Voranetes never missed an opportunity, apparently. "With the Vitares ball approaching, there is a need for entertainment."

"Absolutely!" I called out. "Let's have them do a set together!"

Sael smiled. "Send Thala to us. Let's say . . . six times? That should be sufficient for performers of their skill."

Cades was an etheric bonfire of conflicting emotions. Happiness fighting fear, hope crushed under shame, and grief suffusing the lot. He seemed to really like Markus, but was someone that emotionally screwed up even capable of consent?

"*Thank you,*" said Markus.

"*You be good now,*" I subvocalized. "*I'll expect you back at ten o'clock sharp, or no thong privileges. Don't do anything gross.*"

"*Don't say that, Lilith. I know you were joking, but that's what they've done to him. Cades thinks he's gross. He'll need care and support from all of us to recover.*"

"*Okay, okay, you don't have to lecture me.*"

"A fine gift," said Alceoi, staring at Markus's ass. "My thanks, Lady Ajarel."

"Uh, yeah," I said. "Good luck with that."

CHAPTER FIFTY-NINE

Road to Nowhere

I was going to pulse Roel in a minute. Honest. It had just been a long day.

Running my own op was emotionally exhausting. When I was following the commander's orders, I could just focus on doing my job, but being in charge of *every-thing* was a whole different ball game.

Back home I would have dealt with all this . . . thisness by putting in some head-phones and rocking some Billie Eilish. But, uh, for some reason it hadn't felt like a good idea to bring my phone on a preindustrial deep-cover mission.

"Hey, Val," I said softly. "You awake?"

After a pause, I received a very diplomatic *yes.* I might have woken him up.

"Didn't mean to bother you. A while back you mentioned playing a song," I said. "It was . . . something dramatic. I forget the name."

"*Road to Nowhere,*" he chuckled. "*I suppose it is a little dramatic. What about it?*"

"I was just wondering if I could get you to play it for me."

A brief pause. "*What, now? Over comms?*"

"I guess you're right." I sighed. "Eh, don't worry about it."

"*That was not a refusal. It was just an unexpected request. The commander would never ask for a remote performance, for example.*"

"Well, as everyone likes reminding me, I'm not the commander."

"*I can't remember even one instance of someone reminding you. I'm at the organ now. Pay attention. I will not be background noise.*"

I laughed. "I'll pay attention."

He didn't respond, but I could imagine the thin smile on his face. "*I'm synced. The others have been notified, so we won't be interrupted. This is an adaptation of a very old song, maybe two hundred years before the widespread adaptation of reincarnation technology.*"

"How do you know?"

"*The best analyses use patterns in the text; additionally, the mode of this song was popu-lar in that period. There are old Veleans who claim to remember it being sung up to a thousand years before, but old Veleans always lie.*"

"Of course they do." If you went back as far as the dawn of reincarnation, why not pretend you went back ever further? Masters of the Old Ways were supposed to have mastered reincarnation before Eifni Org.

"I checked, regardless. There are statistical methods to vet the reliability of those claims based on scatter patterns, and in this case our elders are frauds. So our estimate remains twenty-nine centuries after Eifni—still quite ancient. That the song has endured proves its significance. Now, rewritten for the notion organ, that significance can be expressed directly. And . . . we begin."

I still wasn't used to the experience of the notion organ. All the art I'd grown up with had some kind of medium—it was an inescapable prerequisite. I just didn't have the experiential context for ideas and meanings getting beamed into my head. Like I was being told a story, but without the telling, just a story unfolding in my mind. And it started with—

Fire and death.

They found each other in the ruins, each reeling from tragedy. The craftsman's family slain; the mayor's family turned against him.

I felt their bitter grief deep in my chest. The howling loss.

What redress could there be? Who can restore the dead? Who can take up arms against his own family?

I was the mayor, exiled because I would not become a kin slayer. I was the craftsman, returning to beloved dead and a burning home because I was not there to defend them.

I had failed, and the price was fire and death.

They were merely known to each other before calamity struck them down. Now they were brothers in loss.

Together they dragged the bodies from the fire and set them on poles. They left them for the crows, that their spirits would live forever on the wing.

The mayor warned the craftsman that he was pursued. For your service to the beloved dead, the craftsman vowed, I will die to hold off those that hunt you.

I felt his desperation, the dark need to escape twisted into the shape of gratitude and devotion. The noetic tones of the notion organ made the vow ring hopeless and hollow.

The mayor refused.

Let the dead serve us as we have served them, he said.

So they waited, and the hunters came. The brothers had no bows of war—even the craftsman's boar spear had broken in the hands of his eldest son. But with a hunting bow and the night, they slew the mayor's pursuers as they investigated the funeral poles.

I was the craftsman, picking off silhouettes in front of the embers of my home. I was the mayor, driving a broken boar spear through an oath breaker's lungs.

I took my vengeance, a price of fire and death.

They left the dead to the wolves, consigned to the frozen earth. Now the future held nothing: no peril, but no hope. Empty like heaven. Empty like loss.

My family have slain yours, said the mayor. Turn your wrath on me next.

But the craftsman laughed. Hypocrite! If I must endure, then so will you.

I have no grave-price for your beloved dead, said the mayor.

But the craftsman laughed again. The wolves will eat your grave-price tonight.

There was no road for the brothers. No home to return to, no beloved to give warmth against the eternal frost. There were no gods to curse for this fate, only the indifference of men.

Then aid me, said the mayor. Kill them all.

I was the craftsman, with no purpose but collecting arrows to pierce more skulls.
I was the mayor, who no longer needed to become a kin slayer to take revenge.

I *was fire and death.*

The notion organ stilled, returning me to the real world. My heart was racing, and my jaw was clenched. Both of us were silent for a long time.

"Holy shit."

"What did you think?"

"It was great," I said. "Like, actually. I really liked it. Actually, interesting thing about that."

"What?"

"There was this emotion kind of underpinning the main thing. Like, you're sad, but you're kind of angry? I used to feel that all the time back in college. I was in kind of a dark place and just hating everything. When it got really bad . . . Actually, never mind, you're going to make fun of me."

"You're safe. I'm curious."

I sighed. "I used to pretend I was an angel. Like I had a flaming sword and wings of fire and everything, so I could just burn down the campus and then fly away. Wouldn't have to deal with anything, I'd just burn it all down. I don't know why I thought that would make things better, but it felt like it would."

"You were scared," Val said. *"You were imagining what it would be like to be more powerful than the things that were hurting you."*

"I guess. I also felt betrayed. And maybe people wouldn't do the shit they did to me if I could set them on fire."

"Ha! No, I suppose not."

He'd said this was his favorite song. There was a question on the tip of my tongue, and I couldn't bring myself to ask it—he'd tear me apart. But something had clicked, and I had to know.

Well, if you're going to fall, fall forward.

"Who betrayed you?" I asked.

There was a long pause. My adrenaline spiked, sharpness in my cheeks and neck, waiting for the blow to come.

He chuckled.

"I suppose there's little point in dissembling. It was my parents."

I took a deep breath to steady myself. "What did they do?"

"For future reference, you should never ask such a question back on Veles. It will read as a transparent probe for weakness, and the obviousness of the attempt will connote extreme disrespect for the target's social abilities."

"Oh."

Well, that was that, then. I was too rattled to try to figure out what was being said on the Velean-inference layer of the conversation, but that was a closed door if I'd ever heard one.

"Velean medicine considers sexual fetishes to be disordered calcifications of the human arousal system," said Val.

What.

"Arousal is a stimulus-response system, so a human being at optimal levels of function should have the ability to self-determine their arousal response. It's a mere quirk of neural structure—simple to treat with reincarnation technology. Allowing fetishes to go untreated allows for the possibility of sexual incompatibility between otherwise willing partners, decreasing the overall happiness of a society."

"That's, uh, not really how we treat it at home."

"Your former culture doesn't have a choice. Ours does, and we chose to eliminate fetish formation from human neural expression. But this has not eliminated them from Veles. Some Veleans have allowed their fetishes to imprint on their identity—sometimes immigrants, but more often older Veleans whose existences predate the public health measures. The same demographic, as it happens, with the luxury credits to spend on shortsighted waste like reproductively viable bodies."

"Um," I said, "I'm not sure wanting kids is a fetish."

"I do not know my father," said Val, ignoring me. *"I was told that was the point. My mother preferred not to know who had impregnated her. Once the body had served its purpose enhancing her sexual encounters, it would be remanded to the institution that produced it for her in exchange for a fresh one."*

"Holy shit. In late pregnancy? Did they get the kid out first?"

"No. I assume they gave the abortion-ethics guidelines no more than a cursory glance. We are not discussing the kind of institution that cares about the Velean Medical Standards Board."

Val gave a short, humorless laugh. *"I am fortunate that the board did not return their disregard. I was born prematurely. When my mother went into labor, it triggered her comm's emergency medical alert. The witless fool hadn't modified her default settings; the emergency workers who picked her up were from the nearest medical center, rather than her illicit reincarnation center.*

"There are services for cases such as mine. I was preserved. My mother's case was pursued and then dropped. This is common among old Veleans. They have thousands of years of accrued favors and influence; no system of law conceivable can overcome that. So that is the reason why I am one of the only native Veleans."

"Holy shit," I said again. "At least you get to be a native Velean? I kind of wish I'd been born there."

"We are pariahs," Val spat. *"For each of us that exists, there's a story like mine. We are the shame of an entire planet."*

"That's— I don't know what to say. I'm sorry, Val," I said. Quick, think of something sympathetic to say! "Did you get revenge on your mom?"

"I'm merely a world-class moirologist. I can't touch an old Velean. But perhaps in a thousand years I will be able to ruin her."

"Fire and death," I said. "And until then, you're slaying gods?"

"Burning this world will have to suffice until I can burn my own."

Alarming sentiment at first, but it felt—right. I'd felt so often that life had fucked me over. All that stuff could go die in a fucking fire. And I hadn't been able to burn it myself—I mean, how can you burn fucking depression?—but if I *could*, then I would. And it'd be right. Because abuse, depression, hopelessness, poverty, oppression, all that shit *shouldn't exist*. Evil shouldn't exist.

Evil shouldn't exist. That was why I was here. Evil shouldn't exist.

"Let me know if you need me to raise any funeral poles," I said.

CHAPTER SIXTY

Name Your Enemy

The Renathion had come and gone. Markus won his third set of laurels, our improvised alliance with the Voranetti finally pushing him past his sudden unpopularity. We were all politely ignoring that they'd been the cause of that in the first place, but that was the price you paid for being of grace in the Estheni empire.

Unless you were Kuril, of course. My adoptive mom was holding it together in public, but in private she really let it fly whenever the Voranetti came up.

"Roel says it was their mom's fault," Alouren said when I asked her.

Roel's wannabe spy was way too talkative to play the games she was playing, and I wondered if Roel had already stopped sharing sensitive intel with her. My gut said no; Roel wasn't ready for the big leagues yet. I let her keep distracting me while Roel worked in the forge with Bofa.

"Our house has been in decline for about four generations," she continued when I prompted her. "The past is the seed of the future and everything. The last Vitaressi Visionary was Kuril's great-great-grandmother, before she died in battle against the Phrecians. The Jeneretti managed to come out on top in the confusion, but it was House Voranetes who really sliced us up in the years afterward. At least, that was Lady Kerial's belief, and Kuril grew up hearing it every day."

"Not Roel?"

Alouren looked confused for a moment, then something clicked in her expression. "I forget you're an outsider sometimes! They're about ten years apart. Lady Kerial was always too busy to get pregnant, or so they say. Kuril's a lot like her. Honestly, I don't get it. Bofa looks really good, and she's got you and Roel to lean on. Do you know why she doesn't have a kid yet?"

"Uh uh, no, no, hard pass," I said. "I am not having this conversation with you under any possible circumstances."

Alouren casually shrugged me off. "If you say so. Then maybe we can talk about something else, like spells . . . ?"

"Come on, kid," I said. My tone was exasperated, but there was an undercurrent of affection. The kid wasn't smooth, but hell if she wasn't endearing.

"Just one," she insisted. "Or you could tell me a story instead? You must have so many from your travels."

"Well, there was one about a boy called, uh, Haria Poteres," I said. "His family didn't want him to use magic, but he left and went to a school for magicians."

"There are schools for magicians where you come from?" Alouren looked so excited.

I gave her an apologetic grin. "No, it's just a story."

"So what happened? Magic school would be incredible!"

"Honestly, I don't know," I said. "When I grew up, my parents wouldn't let me read it because it had magic in it. Then when I left, my friends didn't want me to read it because it was"—shit, the Estheni had no concept of transphobia—"uh, it was morally corrupt."

"Oh, like those Dancer stories that mock the graced and valorize ass-lancers?"

I choked back a guffaw. The comm said it was a slur for gay people, but— *ass-lancers?* Really?

Alouren mistook my humor and lowered her voice. "I'm sorry, I should be more proper."

"No apologies needed here," I said, smiling. "Maybe watch your language around Lady Kuril, though. Excuse me, that's Cades, I need to find Thala."

I'd volunteered to be the vocal coach for today's singing practice. I know nothing about music, but it was a great excuse to get us all in an isolated location. The quality of the practice didn't matter, anyway—we'd have full control of the performance location and could deploy whatever amplifier tech we felt like.

"I'm just not feeling it," I told them both. "You're just not in sync. Here, let's try having you both take turns with it. I want you to really *express* yourselves while you're singing, okay? Whoever's not singing can watch their partner and really internalize those feelings. I want to feel like I'm hearing two mouths and one soul."

Markus shot me a warning look. "*You're pushing him too hard,*" he subvocalized. I shot Cades a glance. The poor man was radiating so much pain and confusion that it was etherically staining the walls. Yeah, okay, that was probably too much.

"I'm just kidding," I backtracked quickly. "Just a joke. It was fine. We can move on."

Cades let out a slow breath.

"Everything okay, buddy?" I asked him.

"Your family has heaped honor upon me," said Cades. "I could have no complaint."

Dude was locked down like Fort Knox. I had no idea what to say here. "Honor's pretty cool," I verbally flailed.

"Ajarel, maybe you should take a break," Markus said gently.

"And leave you two handsome lads unsupervised?" I joked.

Cades *froze.* Like, he stopped breathing for a couple of seconds. I thought I'd accidentally broken him. Markus looked at me, and my brain shut down as I realized I'd never seen him *furious* before.

"Shit shit shit, I'm sorry, I'm sorry, I'm so sorry," I babbled. "I'm gonna go, I'm sorry, man, please be okay. Uh, Cades? Are you okay?"

"I need to leave," he managed.

"Uh—"

"*Ajarel,*" Markus snapped. "You need to go. I'll handle this."

"No, I'll go," Cades said.

"Stay," Markus ordered him. "Sit down. Take deep breaths. *Ajarel, if you don't—*"

"Sorry sorry sorry—"

I fled the room, slamming the door closed and pressing my hands to my face until I saw stars. I slid down to a sitting position. I'd just fucked up my op. Holy shit, I fucked it up *hard.* Markus was going to straight-up kill me.

Thinking about him drew my attention back to his channel.

"*This is a battle,*" Markus was telling him. "*I've seen your scars. You've stood in a shield wall. You have the courage to face this.*"

"*Face what?*" Cades asked bitterly. "*Go on. Say it.*"

"*You have the courage to face the lash,*" Markus replied. "*The fear and self-hatred in your thoughts that makes you serve them.*"

"*If you intend to make me a slave, I will kill you.*"

"*Never,*" Markus said gently. "*But I'll stand in the shield wall beside you.*"

"*Men should speak directly instead of whatever this is. Talking in riddles, giving orders to women—of grace! This is shameful, Thala.*"

"*As you wish,*" Markus said. "*I think you've been subjected to a kind of violence whose name is hidden. I think you've been kept in your place with pain. I know your character, and I think the only thing between you and freedom is the name of your enemy.*"

"*That's enough, Thala,*" Cades said softly. "*Please. Don't say it. I may be a coward, but I have enough honor left that I will not see you harmed.*"

"*We're safe here,*" Markus said.

"*No. They can hear it spoken.*"

"*They . . . What?*"

Yeah, I also had no idea what was going on there. I'd been pretty sure Markus was talking about, like, internalized queerphobia.

"*Be safe, Thala,*" said Cades. "*Protect yourself. Please. For my sake. Don't lose yourself delving into dangerous secrets.*"

Secrets.

That did it. Everything clicked into place. I stood up, brushed myself off, and knocked on the door, cutting off whatever Markus was about to say. I entered without waiting for permission.

Markus and Cades both watched me carefully as I closed the door and walked deliberately to my chair.

"*Lilith, what are you doing?*" Markus subvocalized.

I raised my eyebrows at him and casually took my seat. I looked Cades dead in the eyes.

"Meris," I announced. "Meris, Meris, Merismerismeris. Meris! How am I doing?"

Cades's face was ashen.

"Fantastic," I smiled. "Look, man, Thala wanted to be sensitive to what you're going through, but the fact is we already know your secret. I don't fucking care. It's not a big deal where we come from, and we definitely don't want you to get hurt for it. But I know there's some people who do, and I have *beef* with them. *Comprende?*"

Cades blinked. "Was that—Tercadian?"

"Probably," I said. I was flying high. I felt good. I felt invulnerable. "So here's the deal: no one hears what happens in this room but me. You can trust me on that, or we can fall back on the fact that I've already made this as bad as it's gonna get. Meris, by the way. Anyone wants to scrap with me over this, I'm gonna fucking scrap with them."

Cades's expression was wary. "That's . . . Forgive me, Lady Ajarel, but I didn't think you liked me that much."

"Dude," I said, "when I met you, I thought you were trying to get in my skirt. If you wanna get in Thala's skirt instead, that's fine by me."

Cades's cheeks colored an impressive red.

"But at least buy him dinner first," I said to Markus, then froze. His expression was extremely cold. "Thala, you okay?"

He took a deep breath, not breaking eye contact. When he spoke, his tone was flatly polite. "Next time you take a stupid gamble, I need you to make sure that your life is the only one on the line. Can you do that for me next time? If it's not too much trouble, of course."

I opened my mouth, but nothing came out. Rage boiled in my chest with no outlet. Cades stared wildly between us.

"Sure, buddy," I said with poisonous cheer. "Happy to do you a favor. It worked, if you didn't notice."

Cades shifted uncomfortably. "I should be—"

"Sit down!" Markus and I yelled in unison without breaking eye contact with each other.

Markus spoke first. "I would like to handle this from here. Please leave."

"Yeah, that was going super well!"

"*Stop* being reactive! Please!" Markus said. "You need to stop and think before someone gets hurt."

He continued subvocally: "*Did you even check what protections they might have put on him before you risked his life?*"

"I didn't—" I said, then realized I didn't have much of a case. "Okay, fine! I basically did it all for you, anyway. Bye!"

I stormed out again, this time in a very different mood. "Supposed to be my op," I muttered, knowing my comm would pick it up.

The hallway was empty. I paced restlessly, eyes passing over the wall murals without taking anything in. Lirian was in prison, and Cades was our best lead on what the Merisites were up to. There shouldn't be a problem now. Besides, we would have noticed if there were some kind of etheric trace on Cades. Darwin knows we'd scanned him enough.

"A good commander respects her soldiers' initiative in the field," Abby's voice came to me.

"Screw that. Good soldiers should follow the commander's lead," I shot back.

"Should soldiers emulate the kind of leadership you're demonstrating?"

"I made the right call, dammit."

"We don't know that," said Abby. *"We don't know if there are other Merisite operatives in the field. We don't know if the Oathkeepers are involved or are otherwise contributing their abilities to the equation. We don't know whether Cades is correct about the Merisites being able to hear her name spoken, or what other information is collected if they do. We simply don't know what the consequences are."*

"It worked," I said.

"It's easier to say that than admit that you didn't consider the consequences." Abby's voice softened. *"You hurt Markus, Lilith."*

I didn't want to think about that.

The mural across the hall from me depicted a dude fighting a giant octopus with a spear. The dude was, predictably, naked, and the sheen on his butt shone a little differently in the ghostlight than the tiles around it. I guess that meant they had octopi here.

The commander was right. Markus was right. Val hadn't said anything, but I *knew* he was thinking it, and *he* was right, too. I'd made a snap decision, and now people might get hurt.

Again.

"Why do you put up with me?" I whispered. "I shouldn't be here."

"We put up with you because you're a child," said Abby.

"I'm twenty-four."

"You could be a hundred and four, but you'll be a child until you grow up. And until you do, it's the duty of the adults around you to show you the way. If we can't, it's because our own wisdom falls short."

"I wouldn't want to put up with me. I don't know what I was thinking. Fuck, I'm going to get you all killed."

"Do you remember what Markus told Cades?" Abby asked.

"Which part?"

"Name your enemy."

"I don't know, the part where every time I make a snap decision, it's the wrong one?"

I kicked the wall. It was made of rock. I was wearing sandals. Smart, Lilith. Real smart.

Abby didn't respond.

"I'm getting the sense that was the wrong answer. Just tell me."

"I can't tell you, Lilith. I don't know, either."

There's no way that was true, but Veleans had a thousand ways to tell you to figure it out yourself. I almost called her on it, but what was the point? It wasn't like she'd just humor me if I gave up. That wasn't who I was supposed to be.

"Look," I said, "I don't want to lean too much on the self-loathing here, but I'm pretty sure the problem is just me. I know there's, like, Lirian and Alceoi and Obol in my way, but it's not their fault I suck."

"*I know you've read* The Road of Spears," Abby said. "*'You are the first and last of your foes.' Striking at your confidence is the enemy's work, is it not?*"

"Okay, okay," I said. "Very wise. Not helpful."

"*No advice is helpful if you shrug it off. Tell me how you would fight this enemy.*"

"Uh, I should just be smarter and not do the things that hurt me," I said. "I know that already."

"*Very wise. Not helpful.*"

A chuckle escaped my lips.

"*You don't have the option to totally control the behavior of any other opponent. Pretend that's not an option here. Take a minute and actually think about it. You have an enemy who presents you with tempting mistakes at regular intervals. How should you fight that enemy?*"

I reached for the stability of meditative calm and tried to make her proud, starting with admitting to myself that I had no idea how to solve this absurd thought experiment. I was my enemy because I kept not being good enough. Obviously the only way to fix that was to do better. I just . . . couldn't. I was never good enough, for reasons I could never see coming. Like—obviously, if I could see them coming, I'd avoid them. I'm not an idiot.

"I'm not sure how to just prevent myself from making mistakes," I said. "They always seem like good ideas at the time."

"*Good! You're thinking,*" Abby said. "*But keep going. There is a difference between a mistake and self-sabotage.*"

Good was good, I guessed. "Look, sometimes I need to make a call, and it's the wrong call. It's not like I know better. I *know* I don't know better, but I still have to make a call!"

"*Why don't you know better?*"

"I don't know! I can't predict the future!"

"*Did you try?*"

I closed my eyes and rested against the wall. My toes hurt.

"*A mistake, Lilith, is a lesson the world is trying to teach you. Self-sabotage is a lesson you refuse to learn.*"

She let me stew on that for a bit. The problem with sitting on concrete floors is they just suck all the heat out of your ass. It was uncomfortable, but I was too emotionally drained to move. Eventually the scales would tip and I'd stand up, but we hadn't hit that point yet.

"I'm not thinking about consequences," I said. "With Cades, I found the solution to the puzzle, and I tried to use it as soon as possible. I only thought about winning. But Markus was thinking about losing, and I let him down."

Abby sent a nonverbal burst of warmth over the comm, and I managed a sad smile.

"So you're telling me that all the times you guys yelled at me to think things through, you were telling me to think things through?"

"*I know this probably comes as a shock.*"

"Fuck," I laughed. "It really does."

"*Laughter is good. Let it out,*" Abby said. I could hear a smile in her voice. "*Are you ready to apply your newfound wisdom?*"

"Yeah. I'll go apologize to Markus," I said. "How's he handling things in there?"

"*Not Markus, although I agree with that course of action,*" said Abby. "*I'm talking about Roel. She entered Kuril's office five minutes ago, and they're talking about you.*"

CHAPTER SIXTY-ONE

Interlude: Severance

Kuril was in a bad mood, and Roel almost regretted that she was about to make it worse. Almost. But the blade was descending, and they had precious little time to get out of the way.

"I'm busy," Kuril said without looking up from her desk.

Bofa stopped pushing Roel. "If it's not a good time—"

"No," Roel said with finality. "Kuril, we need to talk now."

"We can talk at dinner. The Jeneretti—"

"Can wait. Ajarel is occupied with Thala and Cades. We need to talk *now*."

The urgency in her voice finally earned Kuril's attention. The disheveled matriarch of House Vitares had forgone the morning's appointment with the house stylist, and her hair fell embarrassingly down her back in a tangled mess. Roel was far past giving a shit. Her sister's gaze slowly focused on her as her mind broke away from whatever task she'd been so absorbed in.

"Ajarel?" she said.

"She's a whisper," said Roel. "And she needs to go."

"She's your family now," said Kuril. "Don't let your jealousy overcome you."

Roel nearly screamed at her but forced herself to focus on the pain in her leg. She let it drown out the unfairness of it all, the mountain of idiocy she was struggling against. She could do this.

"For what it's worth," she said, "yes, I think you should have made me sash bearer as soon as I became a woman. Maybe then we wouldn't be in this situation, and you wouldn't be so desperate that Ajarel could sneak her way into the heart of our house. Of course I'm jealous, Kuril. But what matters is this: you've staked the *survival of our house* on the trust of a woman whose name you didn't know last year. And I don't think we can trust her."

"This isn't one of your children's stories," Kuril snapped. "The Voranetti are sharpening their stakes. Ajarel's plan is a risk, but the survival of our house is in question either way. Would you rather trust Sael Voranetes?"

"Yes," Roel said simply. For a brief moment she enjoyed the sight of Kuril coming up short.

"You're just saying that," her sister sighed. "You haven't been the same since your injury. Do you think Lirian injured your mind with that strike?"

"Horcutio's bouncing testicles, Kuril!" Roel yelled. "Listen to me!"

Kuril's shocked expression was priceless. "You need to maintain decorum," she managed.

"*Decorum?*" Roel seethed. "Which of us is flaunting their hair like a drunkard?"

Kuril blinked, looked at Bofa, and hastily wrapped her hair in a messy knot. Roel inwardly winced. That was going to be painful to undo later. Then her leg throbbed, and the sympathy turned to cold satisfaction.

"Are you happy now?" Kuril asked, glaring at her. "I suppose not. You still have too many sisters."

"I loved her," Roel said. The admission choked up her voice, but she wouldn't let herself cry. "She didn't love me. Maybe she wanted to—but in the end, I was useful until I wasn't. You're still useful, Kuril. You haven't seen it yet. She doesn't talk to me anymore. She doesn't care. I would *love* to wait until you experience this yourself. It would be *just*. But if that happens, House Vitares will die. The Voranetti claim our assets, the Oathkeepers bar us from commerce in the city, *something*."

Kuril's displeased stare found another target. "Bofa, where is she getting these ideas? Why haven't you discouraged her?"

Bofa shifted behind her. "Roel, perhaps it would help to share the evidence you've collected."

Roel turned in her chair to glare at him. She didn't want to do that.

Why didn't she want to do that?

The answer came quickly. Because then it wouldn't be *her* investigation anymore. Because then she'd just be the useless crippled girl staying at home while the others did the important work.

But this was about the future of the house. She steeled herself.

"I've been in communication with Oathkeeper Falerior," she admitted. "We've been using the Voranetes investigation as cover to continue investigating Ajarel."

"That *terrier* and his thrice-cursed rigidity—" Kuril started.

"Let me *finish*," Roel said, then sighed. "Please."

"No, you're right," Kuril said, leaning back in her chair. "Open eyes."

Are the blessing of Androdaima, Roel automatically completed the phrase in her head. "Thank you, sister."

She took a moment to organize her thoughts. "I . . . didn't want to think I was just collateral damage. Lirian didn't have to—cripple me."

"The doctor says—"

"I *can't walk*," Roel said plaintively. "Have the courage to name it!"

A look of pain darkened Kuril's face, but she said nothing.

"She didn't have to *cripple* me," Roel said again with a challenging look. "There had to be a point. And of course the obvious conclusion is it forces you to lean more on Ajarel, which is—yes, I know, it's a conjecture, don't make that face. So I had Falerior investigate her other alleged victims. The so-called stain on Cades's honor, the accidents and disappearances plaguing any man who would outshine him. Bofa?"

Roel had designed her chair with an integrated vertical shelf, spaced wide enough to hold the thickest volume of Harimenedes's *Annals*—the obvious benchmark; the only longer book she was likely to read was the collected tragedies of Aenel, which were only properly enjoyed in the southeast corner of the library. But she'd cleared the shelf for this (*Parmilion* didn't count) and filled it with documents, one of which Bofa withdrew at her prompt.

She turned a page.

"Gedia: thought to be an itinerant laborer, drowned in an apparent accident. Miner. Efra: bond bearer to House Jeneretes, tripped over a table and crushed his hand, which had to be amputated. Miner. Deirocedes: bond bearer to House Jeneretes, caught an affliction of the lungs after drinking tainted beer. Mine foreman."

Kuril blinked rapidly as she assimilated the information and churned her way toward its implications. "Enough. I know you've run the numbers. How many?"

"It's impossible to say," said Roel. "A thousand people die in this city every year, and the Oathkeepers weren't able to get access to most house records, where those records even existed in the first place. The Jeneretti refused access to their records, by the way; remember that for later."

"They would have done that regardless," said Kuril.

"Sixty deaths," said Roel. "Twice that in disabling injuries."

"That can't be right," said Kuril. "That's more than the number of competitors in the Renathion."

"Exactly," said Roel. "The Renathion cases were the starting place, but when we sent initiates out to gather more information, they came back with more stories than we expected. Mining accidents, drunken brawls, equipment failing. Every report I read mentioned boarding houses *plastered* with wards against Alcebios. Every miner in Vitares knows someone crippled or killed in the last two years. They think they're cursed, but the Jeneretti punish anyone caught talking about it."

"You think this has to do with Salaphi," Kuril said softly.

"Falerior does because he's a terrier," Roel said. "I think it's too targeted. This is goal-driven behavior. A missing foreman replaced with an idiot or a tyrant. The sole veteran on an inexperienced team gets drunk and drowns in the baths. This is a campaign of fear, and Kuril, it's affecting the output of the mines."

"It's not a significant decrease—"

"The Jeneretti are lying on their reports," said Roel. "At least, according to rumor. The metal isn't being bought up, Kuril, it never existed in the first place."

Kuril shot up from her desk. "Then Ajarel's plan—"

"Has no chance of working," said Roel. "When the Oathkeepers inspect their holdings to validate the agreement, they'll find no stockpile, and so we'll have no evidence. But after we willingly open an investigation into market manipulation in Vitareas, what happens? House Jeneretes will be exposed, we'll be censured for bad faith business practices—even if the Oathkeepers won't, the other houses will have a hard time trusting us again after the brightmetal scam—and who's left to fill in the power vacuum?"

Kuril started to pace, and Roel let out a relieved breath. Her sister was thinking, *really* thinking, and that meant everything was going to be okay.

"I find it hard to believe that the Voranetti engaged in such a convoluted scheme to outmaneuver us," Kuril admitted. "It's like something out of your stories. To be blunt, I'm less surprised you uncovered it than I am that you have evidence for it."

"I'm just a crippled girl, forgotten in my chambers, spending my days reading letters about expeditions I'll never experience firsthand," Roel said. "But I've drawn a map from what I was given, and it shows that Ajarel pushed us straight into a hole. We can't trust her."

Roel had never seen her sister look so vulnerable. Her pacing slowed to a stop, eyes moistening, shoulders slumping. For the first time in ages, Roel saw how *tired* her sister was, the weight of the house bearing down on her. This might have been the gale that snapped her mast.

"We should talk to her," Kuril said wearily. "It could have been an earnest mistake."

Roel doubted that, but she could see her sister needed hope.

"It could," she gently lied. "But I'm your family, too, Kuril. Lirian only got my leg. My mind is more than capable."

Kuril approached and knelt very precisely next to her good leg. She wrapped her arms around Roel.

"Open eyes indeed," she murmured. "The goddess may see us through after all. Thank you, Roel."

"Thank you for listening," Roel whispered into her shoulder.

There was a rustle of clothing, then Bofa's muscular arms wrapped around them both. They acknowledged him with simultaneous *mmm* noises. Maybe everything would be okay in the end.

The door to Kuril's office lurched noisily open and energetic footsteps dashed in.

"Guys! Guys!" Lady Ajarel shouted. "Big news! The— Shit, hold on."

She turned around to push the door close. Roel thought she saw her wipe her face on her shawl, but Ajarel was moving too quickly to be sure. By the time she was facing them again, the group hug had broken up.

"We got Cades to talk," said Ajarel. "The Voranetti aren't descended from Varas. They're descended from *Meris*."

CHAPTER SIXTY-TWO

The Price

Merisites? You're sure?"

Roel's face was intent. My comm easily picked up the skepticism she couldn't keep off her face—classic conduit theory, embodied ether reacts more strongly. Kuril was in obvious pain; Bofa was inwardly uncertain, but outwardly presented the reserve that Estheni men were supposed to cultivate.

"I'm sure that Cades is sure," I said. "We'll have to make a call on what that means."

"A truth of the eyes," Roel muttered. "No, it makes sense. More sense than any of this."

I had to play dumb about the *this* even if it was a knife in my fucking throat. "This?"

Kuril opened her mouth but stopped herself with a look at Roel, letting her take the lead. Roel noticed, relaxing an inch at her sister's trust. I looked between them, letting Roel know I'd noticed, too.

"The Voranetes plan doesn't make sense," said Roel. "Buying up metal to starve out the economy—just to disrupt us? Too many uncontrollable factors. Almost a scheme for the sake of scheming. That it even had a chance of working is due to our house's precarious position, not any brilliance on their part. This puts things into perspective."

"Merisites like being mysterious, huh?" I said, remembering Lirian's showboating.

"It's the weakness of the breed," Roel said, as if she'd met more than one. "The sacred mystery: you'll never learn, but they'll make sure you know there was something to find out."

"Take it from the expert," I said with a bit too much irony. The looks I got were cold. Alright, guys. Alright.

For just a moment, I saw it clear as day. If I let out the lump in my throat, I'd cry. I could tell them I'd been hiding things, let them hug the tears away. I could get my family back before they cut ties with me completely. In time they might even understand why I was here, what I had to do—

My comm blared an etheric warning. I snapped out of the vision with a start, cycling my ether shields with reflexes they'd nailed into us at the Academy.

"*Lilith, your comm reported divine contact,*" Val snapped. "*Code four. Countersign. Now.*"

"*They fall. They die,*" I fired back subvocally.

Was this it? Had I just been compromised? Was the commander going to crypt me and I'd wake up back on Veles facing a—

"*She's clear,*" said Val. "*I'm not reading any indoctrination.*"

"*Which god?*" I asked, already knowing the answer.

"*Kives.*"

"Ajarel?" Kuril said. "What's going on? You look . . . feral."

"I *hate* this," I said. "Just . . . Fuck this. Fuck everything. I . . . I'm not gonna say I can't do this. But everything sucks."

"That's why I've been saying we need to bring in House Jeneretes," said Roel. If she had, it'd been while Kives was distracting me. "I have an idea on something we can sell them. *Not* the brightsteel. Something real. And we need to do it *now*. We have two days before we're all signing papers in front of the Oathkeepers."

"Wasn't the whole point of this to keep them out of the loop so our house could keep all the glory?" I asked. We all looked to Kuril.

"I have reconsidered," she said. She didn't look too happy about it, but there was no hesitation in her voice. "If we are to be leaders in Vitareas, it would behoove us to prioritize the good of the city over personal glory."

I couldn't help it. I choked up. It made a small noise that drew everyone's attention back to me.

"Are you okay?" Roel asked, less kindly than she could have.

I walked toward Kuril, trying to ignore the way Bofa unconsciously shifted his footing to a defensive stance as I approached. I knelt down and awkwardly hugged Kuril, who hesitantly hugged me back.

"Ajarel?" she asked.

"You're going to do so well." I sniffled into her shoulder. "You've got this."

Her arms around me tightened, the hug becoming more genuine.

"Have you been drinking?" Roel asked.

"Hugs for you, too!" I said, releasing Kuril and scooting over to her wheelchair.

"Mind the leg."

I nodded, kneeling next to the unstabbed leg and being more careful about it. Roel's hug etherically stank of regret.

"What's going on?" she whispered.

"I just have a lot of emotions right now, okay?"

"You're such a tomboy," Roel said with a forced laugh. I let go.

The tears were real, but my performance hadn't moved my wannabe spymaster of an aunt. Kuril seemed a little more swayed. Bofa was reserving judgment.

"Can I help at all?" I asked. "I could run over to the main Jeneretes estate with a letter or something."

"Good idea," said Kuril. "Just . . . compose yourself first."

"Take an entourage with you," Roel said, glancing aside as she performed some mental calculation. "We wouldn't want you turned aside at the door for lack of fanfare. Bofa, would you accompany her?"

She didn't trust me with the letter, I realized.

"I live to serve," Bofa said. "I can gather some attendants after I bring you back to the library."

"I'll bring her back," Kuril said. "I'd like to spend some time with my sister."

I sniffled loudly. The warmth on Roel's face drained noticeably as she looked from her real family to me.

"I love you," I told them.

I held it together until I left Kuril's office, Bofa in tow. The blacksmith didn't say anything, but he did lay a comforting hand on my shoulder.

"Meet you at the gate in half an hour," I said. "Thanks, man."

"It will pass," he said with a gentle smile. "All life is cycles within cycles. Dark days give way to warm nights."

"Okay, big guy," I sob-laughed. "I'll be fine, go do your thing."

I watched his retreating back.

"*You know,*" I commented subvocally, "*I'm really not going to be able to take him seriously if he marries Kuril.*"

"*Why's that?*" Abby asked.

"*Because he'll be the matriarch's husband,*" I said. "*So he'll have to use the elder suffix.*"

"*Bofades?*"

I started snickering, but it hurt, and the pain gave way to anger as I thought about what a *coincidence* it was that such a nice dude happened to have such a *stupid* name and *fuck this.*

"*Are you ready to talk about what happened in there?*"

"No," I said, drawing in a shaky breath. "Later. I think I know what Kives wants. I want it, too. But I can't— I can't— have it. Can't let her have it. So . . ."

Abby finished for me as I trailed off. "*So you said goodbye.*"

Oh, great. The lump in my throat was back. Fantastic, just fantastic. I tried the tiniest nod and got away with it.

"*You asked why we put up with you,*" said Abby. "*Next time you have that thought, I want you to remember this. You have what it takes, Lilith. That's why we picked you for this team. A mistake here or there doesn't change that.*"

"Thanks," I whispered.

"*Yes, good job,*" said Val. "*Now get back to your room. We need to scan you for divine contamination, and you're leaving in twenty-six minutes.*"

Roel handed me a letter for the Jeneretti that they'd just so happened to seal before I got there. Probably the correct move, given that the letter blamed me for the state of the Jeneretes mines as the bait to entice them into negotiating. I asked about the contents because not being curious would be suspicious, and I politely zoned out while Roel lied to me about the technical specifications of mining equipment.

Did she know I knew? Past a certain point, it didn't matter. I'd deliver the letter as requested, Bofa would report back that I hadn't pulled anything, and then we'd pray the Voranetti didn't have their own last-minute twist at the ball.

I'd accepted the offer of a carriage—I used to think American streets were filthy, but some of the streets here were basically just mud and shit. Four of House Vitares's buffest bondsmen hung from slings inside our kick-ass steampunk horses as they pulled us along, clanking, gilded filigree splattering with street goop. I sat next to Bofa on top of the carriage.

"The cushions would suit your station better," he rumbled. "It wouldn't do to greet the Jeneretti with mud on your shawl."

"They'll live," I said lightly. "I want to see the city."

Whatever he thought of that, he kept it to himself. I spent the ride watching people go about their lives—pedestrians on their way to the market or the temples or the theater, men and women weaving textiles on looms of varying complexity, a yard full of men and women drilling with swords.

I did a double take. There were a lot of Oathkeepers in that yard. Was that—

"Lady Ajarel," called a pleasant voice from the other side of the carriage. "Godsmile."

"Oathkeeper Falerior," I replied before I saw him. He was walking down the street, accompanied by the old lady who'd been with him when I got Lirian arrested. I asked my comm for the old lady's name. "Ah, and Oathkeeper Vanerel. Godsmile to you, too."

"Evenin'," she drawled. "Come to make that statement?"

"Unfortunately, I'm on urgent business," I said with a polite smile. Inwardly I panicked. Had I just landed myself at the Javeiron? Was this Kives again?

"Give our report to the warden," Falerior told Vanerel, patting her on the shoulder. "I'd like to speak with her."

She nodded and split off toward the training field.

"We can't stop," I tried.

"I wouldn't dream of inconveniencing you," he said, settling into a quick stroll that matched the pace of the carriage. "I'd hoped to meet you in passing at your home, but the goddess saw fit that you were always out on some errand or other. At last she relents."

"Thala's training schedule is intense," I said, as if we hadn't deliberately scheduled those sessions to overlap Falerior's visits.

"It must be," he agreed. "I heard he won his third set of laurels?"

"That he did. He's a very skilled man."

"All Vitareas sings his praises. It's breathed some life into the Kabiadesians, you know. A year ago, no one would dare to say anything—for fear of attracting Alcebios's attention, you understand."

I made a noncommittal noise.

"It's good to see the curse broken," he continued, watching for my reaction. I didn't give him one.

"Funny how all the accidents stopped once you locked Lirian away," I said. "How's she doing, anyway?"

"That's the thing about accidents," Falerior observed. "They never completely stop, do they?"

"As long as the accidents aren't invested in Renathion winners, that's fine by me. How's Lirian?" I asked again. "Did you get her talking?"

Falerior smiled his bland little smile. "I would not, of course, presume to air privileged information in public."

"What happened to all that noise about 'all is known, and all shall be known'?"

Falerior raised an eyebrow. "Philosophically, I'd observe that *someone* knows it."

I hated myself for snorting at that because the man was obnoxious, and I didn't want to let him score any points.

"Alright, look, man," I said. "You know I'm not going to give you anything. I got you your big score, and I've toed the line since then. Why are you really here?"

He nodded thoughtfully. "I'm . . . curious, I think. A question I'm posing to myself. If you'll indulge me?"

"Sure, why not."

He lapsed into silence, and for a few moments there was only the sound of the city, the metallic clatter of his armor, and the ratcheting of steampunk horses as they tramped across the cobblestones.

"The Merisites speak of two truths," he said. "''Truth of the eyes' is an oxymoron, but sometimes I wonder if there might not also be a 'truth of the coin.' The Oathkeepers have little jokes about that. Javei guides but does not provide. Bread is true, but truth is not bread."

"The money has to come from somewhere," I agreed.

"And how fitting it is that the graced have the money to feed our order of justiciars," Falerior said without a trace of irony. "The Oathkeepers' justice will find them, too, if it must, but more often they settle their affairs themselves. Common men ought not accuse their betters of lacking grace. Would you trust such a cynic with upholding the order of a city?"

My developing Velean instincts effortlessly read between the lines: The Oathkeepers couldn't afford to piss off their graced donors. There were probably times when they had to, but it sounded like they scapegoated whoever made the arrest.

"Are there a lot of cynics in Javei's service?" I asked.

"Not as Oathkeepers," Falerior said lightly. "One hears stories about itinerants now and then. Righteous beggars serving the villages too poor to hire Oathkeepers of their own."

"Long way to fall," I said. "That must take a lot of courage."

"It's a fall born of necessity," said Falerior. "Or the stories say. One wonders how necessary the decision seemed beforehand."

"Philosophically," I said, mimicking his tone from earlier, "I'd observe that there's only one future, so *everything* is necessary."

"Curious belief," said Falerior. "It doesn't seem to save us from the need to make decisions, does it?"

"I don't think you ever mentioned what decision you were making."

"No, I suppose not," said Falerior. "Godsmile, Lady Ajarel. Thank you for the conversation."

The fucker peeled off and walked back toward the training ground, leaving me too annoyed to be properly relieved he'd gone.

"Good luck, you rat bastard," I called after him.

I was already cranky when we walked in the door, and my mood only worsened when I discovered they'd stuck me with Obol Jeneretes.

"Lady Ajarel!" she smiled. "The Vitaressi have you using their personal stylist, I see! Lovely woman. Eleban, wasn't it? My second tailor's daughter had *designs* on her son for nearly a summer before she moved on, oh, two years ago? It was the longest anyone had held her attention to date, although of course now she's hanging around that *scoundrel* of a stable boy—Iula, I think, for his father, just a *wonderful* man before the accident—did you know he lost the use of his left side? Such a bizarre injury, and of course now his poor wife has to take care of the children on top of managing the bunkhouse—but Eleban, how is she?"

"Godsmile," I managed. "Uh, she's doing okay."

"But of course, of course, she must be, she's done such a good job on your hair. Darker hair than one usually sees—it must be very difficult to show off your depth, isn't it? But those curves are so graceful. You've truly kept it in good condition—you simply *must* share your secrets with me, Lady Ajarel, ha ha! I jest, of course, it's just the jealousy of the old for the young"—here she leaned in conspiratorially—"would you believe that my hair was as dark as yours in my youth? I had young men positively *swarming* me— moth to flame!—and between you and me, some of them found themselves with burns."

I had considerable doubts about anything that came out of that woman's mouth staying between her and me, but I just put on my best Falerior smile and nodded politely.

"I have no idea what that means," I said in an agreeable tone. May she find it as annoying as I did.

Obol laughed as if I'd make a joke. "I'm sure, with hair like yours. And you haven't introduced your man! Excellent specimen. What's his name?"

"This is Bofa," I said. "Kuril's consort, here with me on a *task of some urgency.*" Hint hint.

"Oh, but of course, we mustn't keep you waiting. Your house is hosting that ball soon—is it three days already?"

"It's tw—"

"Time just flies these days, you know. Why, I was supposed to sample Lady Heles's new vintage a *thessim* ago, but first I had something come up, so I needed to reschedule—which she was quite happy to do, you know Lady Heles, sharp as a blade but limp as a willow, so to speak—well, come the day, *she* needed to reschedule—the upwelling gall!—I jest, I jest, we're old friends—where was I? Right, she needed to reschedule, so she told me that she was so terribly sorry, and if it happened again she'd lend me her husband as a peace offering. Now, between you and me, Gebora and I made a great study of the rushes in our day—so to speak—so I was half hoping that she *would* miss our appointment—he's such a strapping fellow even now, you know—"

"Lady Obol," I interrupted. "I'm sorry, but this can't wait."

It wasn't like she'd been ignoring me the whole time, but at the interruption she stopped and seemed to really *look* at me. Bofa was next, her eyes sweeping nonlecherously over bearing and posture and finally examining his face as he decorously avoided eye contact.

"No longer the country bumpkin, are you," she murmured. "Well, more's the pity, but it happens to the best of us. No one's got the time to listen to an old woman these days. It would have saved us both getting our hands dirty."

She seemed genuinely put out about it, too. But I didn't have the emotional capacity to worry about breaking another heart.

"This letter," I said, "is from Lady Kuril and concerns information about a proposed business deal. I highly recommend you read it and pass it on to someone in your house with the authority to make decisions."

"Oh, very well. Letter delivered, off you go."

"Are you— Lady Obol, this is serious."

"Of course," she said. "So serious that she sends her consort instead of accompanying you herself."

I stopped myself from sighing. "I think they believed the contents of the letter would speak for themselves."

"Of course they did." Obol did not stop herself from sighing. "Makers don't understand politics. There's a reason my adoptive house runs this city and your adoptive house is a vestigial estate peddling tinker's wares. Councilwoman Kuril, goddesses grace her, never bothers to observe the formalities. She gets away with it because she's the last of House Vitares, but she has won herself no allies here. That's why they sent me to waste your time, and that's why no one is going to read your letter."

I stared at her, tapping my fingers.

"Oh, don't look at me like that," said Lady Obol. "Why did you think we'd do business with a woman who wants us out of power?"

"Because we've convinced her to chill out," I said.

"And Rucks has taken an oath of silence," Lady Obol countered.

"Lady Roel has a number of ideas to improve the efficiency of your mining equipment."

"Lady Roel is confined to a chair and has nothing better to do than think."

I blinked. "Uh, sure. And her ideas are valuable."

"We have Makers, too," said Lady Obol. "More than House Vitares, brilliant though your aunt may be. We do not need you."

"Okay," I said with a sigh. "Fine. I realize that there's some history here, and now we have to feud like backwoods clans. This is stupid. We know about the mines, Obol."

"Congratulations," Obol said drily. "The Jeneretes mines are renowned across the Imperial Coalition."

"We know about the curse," I said.

"Curse?" Obol said. "You mean the superstitious mutterings of drunken miners? I thought you kept better company, Ajarel. Perhaps that challenge wasn't so baseless after all."

"They said what happened in Salaphi was superstitious muttering, too," I said. "Have you heard the news?"

"Dreadful business," said Obol. "*Entirely unrelated* dreadful business."

"Oathkeeper Falerior doesn't seem to think so," I said. "I'm sure the stewards of our city see the wisdom in investigating. Just in case."

"Nothing was found, and nothing will be found again. Your mother's attack dog can't turn up what doesn't exist."

"And when they check your financial records?" I asked. "With the treasurer's seal as their authority?"

Obol glowered at me. "You're a vicious little brat, aren't you? I don't know what I saw in you."

"I go for the throat," I said cheerfully. "Read the damn letter, Obol. Get it to someone who can make decisions. We convinced Kuril to cooperate for now, but if you guys leave us hanging, everything burns down, and she will absolutely take you down with us. And you know who that leaves in charge."

"Don't make me say it," said Obol. "There's not enough wine here to wash the taste out afterward. Well! I'll make sure the letter gets in the right hands, Ajarel. My word, and may you choke on it. The rest is out of my hands."

"That's all I can ask," I said, standing. "For what it's worth . . . Thank you, Lady Obol. You reached out to me when I first came here. That meant something to me."

"You found your own way well enough," Obol said with wounded pride. "But it's good that the next generation has *some* respect."

"Just us country bumpkins," I said. "Godsmile, Lady Obol."

"Go to hell," she said.

Bofa didn't say anything on the ride home, but he didn't need to. The set of his posture, the furrowing of his brow—they were physical realities reflecting etheric realities, the conduits of meaning that the human soul evolved to discern.

"I wasn't supposed to know about the mines," I said.

"It was always possible that Lady Roel or Lady Kuril told you after I left the room," he said neutrally. "You used the information to achieve their goals."

"We both know they didn't," I said.

The moon was out, the stars brighter than I'd ever seen them on my Earth. The constellations were practically always the same, no matter how differently things played out on the planet's surface. The Eifni Organization had never met aliens. The only life we knew of existed across the countless variations of our planet, a billion variations of if and when and what-could-have-been—and the pantheons that ate them.

And here I was under the same old stars, making my tiny mark on one among countless others.

"Don't tell them," I said at last. "Please. I'm sorry to put you in this situation, but they can't know. Wait until after the ball."

"Lady Ajarel, at the ball—"

"I know," I said, looking up at the stars. They started to blur, like the ones I grew up with. "It's okay, Bofa. It was never going to last. Take care of them for me."

A tear rolled down to the tip of my nose and hung there annoyingly. I sniffed and wiped it off.

The strong arm that wrapped around me was unexpected but nice. Eight out of ten—not as good as Markus's hugs, and I'm not talking about the ten. I cried silently into Bofa's shawl.

"Communication is easier than we expect," said Bofa, "if harder than we think."

It's not too late, he left unsaid. I imagined Kives sitting behind us, smirking and nodding enthusiastically at me. Don't give up your family for the mission—let them heal you first, let them learn what you do and maybe they'll understand.

I won't lie. I wanted it so badly my heart ached. But gods are simple creatures, and the trap was obvious. Worship isn't what you perform, it's what you do. Kives was asking the only price she knew.

But I was a warrior of Veles. Worship is the one price we will not pay.

"There's something I have to do for everyone," I told Bofa. "I can't do it if I stay. I'm sorry, but it has to be this way."

"Then go," he said. "I know you'll succeed. When you do, come back to us."

"I will," I lied.

CHAPTER SIXTY-THREE

Loose Ends

Morning dawned on judgment day. The Vitares estate was boiling over with activity, the staff—bondsmen, I corrected myself—scurrying every which way, carrying supplies and decorations. I imagined the Jeneretes estate must have looked the same way in the hours preceding the Starlight Ball my first night on the town.

We'd decided to show off the virtues of our house another way. An ornate fountain had been assembled in the middle of the courtyard; they were currently hooking it up by way of a gear shaft to a human-powered engine in the workshop. Come nightfall, they'd dump a stupidly wasteful amount of spiced wine in there.

They were hanging one of those steampunk horses above the entrance, this one outfitted with wings. No gear shaft for this one; some poor sap was going to be stuck up there all night, keeping the clockwork pegasus in motion.

Abby's disguise was flawless. The bald head and threadbare shawl proclaimed her a slave, but they were just props. What really sold it was her attitude and posture, the weight behind her steps, the dull eyes of a person locked behind a shell of trauma.

"Just these, mistress?" she asked.

"That's everything," I said.

Val's disguise was almost flawless, but something in his eyes promised vengeance if I made fun of him for this. I fought back a giggle. They took up positions on either side of the crate, lifting it effortlessly with their enhanced physiology.

The estate was bare now. No surveillance cameras, no MDOs, no ether sensors. My room was empty, too, the hidden tac gear and the emergency medical kit tossed in the crate with the rest of the stuff that wasn't supposed to exist in this world. When they searched my room, all they'd find was that the Eifni Organization was one step ahead of them.

Val and Abby walked my secrets right out the front door. All that remained was me.

For now.

Every culture has its rituals, and Veles is no exception. As a warrior arms themselves for battle, it's customary for them to acknowledge each piece of gear with the service it's expected to perform in the coming violence. The violence I was about to encounter

was social violence, but tonight it felt correct. I'd stumbled over the traditional forms
Abby taught me before deciding to make it my own.

I held up a sleek black skirt, facetiously checking it over as if it were armor.

"Good," I told it. "Alright, your job is to let me move fast and not get caught on
anything. You see these shorts? If you get uppity, I can and will leave you behind. Don't
get any ideas. Otherwise, I need you to be menacing and dangerous. Perfect, like that.

"Shawl, you're the statement piece. We're not wearing a lot of color today, so all
eyes are gonna be on you. Don't flap around too much if we need to book it. You were
specifically chosen for this mission for your form factor. But I still need you to cover
my holsters, understood? Great. Good, uh, article of clothing. Now, as for *you.*"

I checked the function and charge level of the pulser with reflexive ease. Its internal monitor reported no functional problems. I aimed it at the wall, letting my hand
melt into its perfectly molded grip.

"One day," I said, "you and I are going to knock out an entire room of bad guys.
But hopefully that's not tonight. I just want to know you've got my back in a pinch."

The pulser didn't respond as I slipped it under the shawl.

"You, on the other hand, need to be ready to go," I said to my hand amplifier.
"We're going to have a small window to make an *impression,* and I need you at your
best. There isn't any room for failure."

I secreted the hand amplifier away and left to find Eleban for my hair. I asked her
to give me something ominous—and despite the uncertain expression on her face, she
delivered. I checked my expression in the studio's bronze mirror and smiled.

Years ago, I'd played a sorceress in an all-evil RPG campaign. If I'd known how
to draw back then, I would have illustrated Lady Raven just like this. And they say
dreams don't come true.

"*That's it, then,*" I subvocalized. "*We're ready to go.*"

"*Are you sure you want to do this alone?*" Abby tested me. "*We'll happily give you
backup.*"

"*I'm sure.*"

"*Attagirl. They fall.*"

"They die," I whispered.

It was time for my last scene.

I announced myself to the courtyard: "I arrive: Lady Ajarel Vitares!"

The graced of Vitareas were positively sparkling, illuminated by ghostlight and a full
moon. A thousand hues of Androdaima's fire twinkled within shining filigree everywhere you looked. Laughter and conversation carried through the air, underscoring a
soaring duet by Vitareas's two most eligible bachelors. Markus and Cades sang in perfect harmony—I frowned, adjusted my comm settings, and listened harder. Yeah, that
wasn't an amplifier, they were just really on the same wavelength. I guess they'd worked
out whatever argument they'd been having the day my house of cards came down.

I was in a weird place, emotionally. I was holding it together, but I swear to Darwin,
if someone tried to engage me in another fucking conversation full of innuendo I was

going to punch them in the nose and then drown them in the wine fountain. For the good of all, I'd elected to lurk around the edges of the party, avoiding anyone directly involved in tonight's drama. It was surprisingly difficult—I spotted Alceoi trying to catch my eye, and the Jeneretti were so all over the place you could barely find a conversation without one.

All the ducking and hiding reminded me of playing secret agents in the mall with my brothers. Some of the clothing stores had these circular thingies where you could slip between the dresses and hide from external view. My parents hated it—one of us would inevitably hide too well.

All that had changed was now all the dresses had Estheni nobility inside them, and I was too tall to hide the way a kindergartener would.

I eventually maneuvered myself to Markus and Cades, using the bulk of their platform to reduce my visual exposure. I'd had the good luck to find a neutral conversation partner: Sela Kess, who I hadn't seen since the Starlight Ball all those months ago. I'd mostly used the opportunity to practice my small talk.

"How is Lady Roel's recovery?" he asked.

I sighed. "Kind of you to ask. I didn't get the sense that anyone cared about her, even before the attack."

His expression fell at that. "It's not my place to comment. I'm sorry about her accident."

"Thanks, man. But don't worry about her, she's the strongest kid I know. How have you been?"

"I can't complain," he said slightly too earnestly. The comm said—

You know what? Fuck it, I was done with all the shadowboxing and done with all the fucking secrets. Whatever he was hiding, he could fucking keep it hidden.

"That's great," I said. "How's your family?"

"Striving for the goddesses' grace," he said. "Recent events have made our position more difficult, as I'm sure you're aware."

"Honestly?" I said. "No. I don't know anything."

Sela's eyes widened at something behind me. "Forget I said anything."

Alceoi's voice cut in. "Moron. If you don't want to be remembered, don't say memorable things."

The Voranetes girl was dressed in a layered dress of brilliant red, with ghostlights sewn into the fabric in a way that emphasized its depth and complexity. She inserted herself into our circle like she owned it, shooing Sela off with a glare. He made himself scarce as quickly as formality allowed.

"So," she said, looking at me. "I hear there's a big deal getting negotiated tonight."

"What do you want?" I asked her.

"Aunt Eloi wanted to know why the Jeneretti brought their negotiators," Alceoi said. "I figured I could just ask you."

"You'll find out sooner or later," I said. "Actually, you know what? Fuck it. Let's get it all started. I'm so tired."

Alceoi smiled sympathetically at me. "You're not cut out for this."

"What, and you are?" I asked. "You hate it, too. You've been miserable every time I've seen you."

She shrugged. "It is what it is. All the sneaking around comes with the wealth and power. Can't have one without the other."

"And it's fucking miserable."

"For you, maybe. And okay, maybe me, too. But the others? Lady Sael, Aunt Eloi, my sister? They swim in it, Ajarel. The only way out is for the honest women to come together and leave the secrets to the whispers. I was hoping you'd see the value in that."

She looked at me earnestly. The comm said she wasn't trying to trick me, but we were so, so far beyond that mattering now. Sorry, Alceoi, the window's closed.

I turned down the implicit request by changing the subject. "You have a sister? You've never mentioned her."

Alceoi sighed but accepted my response.

"She doesn't like to be mentioned," she said. "Growing up . . . I'm sorry, can you repeat the question?"

"I can't remember," I said, heart hammering for some reason. "I just had some thought, it's on the tip of my tongue."

"I hate it when that happens," Alceoi said. "Well, time to tell Aunt Eloi you gave me the runaround. My offer's open."

"Good luck," I told her.

I took my seat at the negotiation table next to Roel, who greeted me with perfect courtesy despite the boiling fountain of emotions steaming off her. She had an open book on the blanket keeping her legs warm, but she was staring off into space instead of reading it.

She was wearing a sash tonight. I wasn't. None of us said anything about it.

Representing House Jeneretes were three women I didn't know. One of them was evidently on the city council with Kurll; I learned her name was Phaeres.

In the Voranetti corner, it was just Sael and Eloi, but being outnumbered didn't make the two schemers any less of a threat.

Lounging against the wall, on no side but his own, Oathkeeper Falerior observed the proceedings with an expression of bland attention. When we were all seated, he pushed himself off the wall and walked to the table.

"By my authority as an Oathkeeper, I hereby submit these negotiations to the eyes of Lord Javei," he said. "Speak in good faith. Earn glory for yourself and the goddesses."

He touched two fingers to the table, metal on wood, then stepped back into a parade rest. That was the cue to start. Eloi beat us all to the punch, rising from the bench she shared with Sael.

"We will be leaving," she said. "There was no mention of the Jeneretti in your promises."

"The brightmetal was a lie," said Roel.

Eloi and Sael stopped in their tracks. Eloi peered quizzically at Roel, then at Falerior. He smiled politely back at her.

"That was an admission of fraud," Eloi prodded him.

"We approved it with the Oathkeepers beforehand," said Kuril. "It was a necessary deception to get to the heart of an issue plaguing this city. The heart of our economy, the Jeneretes mines, have been under attack."

Phaeres glanced at Falerior—who was watching Kuril with mild curiosity—before speaking. "House Jeneretes applauds the initiative of our devoted treasurer. Your lineage shines through tonight."

She couldn't say anything substantial, and all of us knew it. If she tried to blow smoke, Falerior would notice she was lying; if she came clean, she might direct Falerior's attention to the falsified records.

The smart move for her was to scram and leave us with the hot potato, but there was the matter of the letter I'd delivered two days ago. Phaeres made no move to stand.

"This is a business negotiation, not a court," said Eloi, who apparently couldn't be bothered to give a fuck. "Have we been called here for sacred trade, or was that a ruse, as well?"

"The brightmetal was a lie," said Roel, "but the offer was not. The mines are struggling because so many who work there are crippled. We have a solution, a device that will make them useful again. We'd like your assistance funding it, for the glory of your house."

Eloi's mouth quirked in contempt.

"I cannot think of a messenger less suited to that message."

Roel met her gaze evenly. She slowly closed the book in her lap, handing it to Bofa. Then she stood up from her chair.

The blanket fell aside, revealing a lattice of filigree cocooning her injured leg. An intricate system of gears and levers shifted and clicked as she shifted her weight, a grimace momentarily flashing over her face. She pushed her chair back from the table, taking a few hesitant steps before settling into a limp.

"I'll admit it's not perfect," she said to the other houses. "This is only a prototype. But it represents the chance to return the men to work and break the alleged curse on the mines. Lady Phaeres, what's your opinion?"

"Its beauty befits a lady of grace," she said. "I'd like to see it stand up to the conditions inside the mines."

"Good thinking," said Roel. "You're right—this model won't work in rough conditions. But I have others, which I'll happily demonstrate at a later time."

"I wish you luck," Eloi said. "But if you want us involved, you'll need a better offer than glory."

"Take the glory," Roel ordered the withered spite witch like she had a death wish or something. "Vitareas should know that House Voranetes was instrumental in ending the curse—or should I say, the whisper?"

"Should they," Eloi said dangerously. "Think carefully before you give yourself reason to regret."

Roel smiled. "After all," she continued as if she hadn't heard, "it was the actions of House Voranetes that unmasked the enemy in our midst, was it not? Our savior in the shadows, preparing to fight the curse before it spread from Salaphi."

Eloi's brow furrowed. "I have no idea what you're talking about."

"Oh, sorry," said Lirian, who was suddenly lounging against the wall. "That one's on me."

CHAPTER SIXTY-FOUR

Swan Song

Lirian's appearance made everyone jump—one of the Jeneretes negotiators actually screamed. From the smirk on her face, she'd absolutely intended it that way.

Her time in the Oathkeepers' custody clearly hadn't been too hard on her; her dress was a pristine number on par with anything sported by the guests in the next room, and not one hair was out of place. There was a brief pause as we all oriented to her dramatic entrance. She pushed off the wall, flicking back a lock of hair as she effortlessly stole everyone's attention. She favored me with a particularly smug look.

"Did you miss me?"

"I don't miss," I said, and pulsed her.

It was a textbook-perfect quick draw, fingers brushing the safety and trigger contacts in perfect order the moment the weapon cleared the holster. The etheric blast hit her just as the smugness on her face melted to shock, perfectly framing the way her eyes rolled back into her head as she collapsed to the floor.

But that was only the first shock of the evening because the next thing that happened was the legendarily unflappable Sael Voranetes emitting an unearthly scream and rushing to the fallen whisper.

"Oh my girl, my sweet girl," she moaned. "What did you do to her?!"

"Hey, Falerior," I said, ignoring her. "You might want to tell your buddies they're missing a prisoner."

"Two of them," Roel said from behind me. I turned to see her raising her arm, and *shit* where did she get a pulser—

My field of view was suddenly obscured as Bofa launched himself in front of me. He didn't get the angle right—I had to dive to the side as he flew past me and hit the floor hard. He rolled to a stop, unconscious.

Roel and Kuril stared at him, confused.

"Huh," I said. "Did none of us tell him what these do?"

"I . . . suppose not," said Kuril.

"What does it do?!" Sael demanded. "Tell me this instant!"

Roel grimly sighted her pulser at my face. "This."

She fired. The blast splashed harmlessly off my comm shielding. What, you thought Eifni operatives would bring a weapon into the field if it could be used against us?

"She's just unconscious," I told the hysterical matriarch as Roel fired at me twice more. "Okay, seriously, Roel—cut it out. You had your moment."

She glared at me, then huffed in frustration. "It doesn't matter," she said. "The doors are locked. We've authorized your arrest. You're not getting away this time."

I smartly stepped away from Falerior the instant before he grabbed me. The motion caught him by surprise, and he tried to turn the momentum into a lunge, which I sidestepped. That brought me within range of Roel, who grabbed my wrist.

"Stop," she ordered me. I rolled my eyes; she had no idea what she was doing. I flicked my wrist to lever her fingers apart, winding up with a hold on her wrist that I used to throw her into the way of the incoming Oathkeeper. They collided with a grunt from him and a pained shout from her, but that didn't stop the armored man from coming at me. I jumped into the air and hit him full-on in the chest with a double-footed kick, propelling myself back first onto the negotiation table with an *oof.* I did a kip-up, feet snagging the hem of my skirt and tearing it right off me.

I must have looked incredibly strange to my Estheni audience, with thigh-length tac shorts below the waist and high-class party attire above. It didn't matter now. The game was over; there was only one role left to play.

"So you guys sold me out to the Oathkeepers, huh?" I said, breathing heavily. "How's that work?"

Falerior grunted as he pushed himself up.

"I suppose now's as good a time as any," he said. He made a fist with his right hand, brought it to his lips for a kiss, then touched it to his forehead. The semiotic radiation coming off him began to shine with divinity.

"In the name of Javei," he pronounced, "I shall now reveal what was hidden. The stranger Ajarel has made many claims, but two are of note. When she appeared, she claimed that she came from Salaphi. But she came to our city around the time the seeds of madness were sown there. Even traveling at the fastest speeds, it's impossible that she could have been present when the curse began."

Had it been long enough? I signaled my ears to increase volume and noise filtering, but all I got was Kuril helping Roel pull herself up. Roel was breathing in sharp, pained gasps. I warily maintained my defensive stance on the table, watching for sudden moves from Falerior.

"The second claim was made in confidence to Councilwoman Kuril, which I will now reveal to you all. The councilwoman has averred under oath that Ajarel claimed to be graced by descent from Kives and had performed a ritual in Salaphi to avert its destruction. If this were true, it would mean that she performed the ritual at least three *thessim* before the corruption began to spread."

"I'm very forward-thinking," I said, eliciting a scornful guffaw from Roel. I still wasn't hearing it.

"It would seem so," said Falerior, gazing at me amiably. "The survivors claim the source of the blight was a faceless that clawed its way back from the shadowlands, citing an otherworldly cry on the night of the calamity. It is known that such rituals are shared among the scions of Alcebios, but our histories record no counterrituals among the workings of the Kivim."

"If you'd really been graced by Kives," said Roel, now back in her wheelchair, "you'd have claimed you tried to unite two lovers or something to stop it."

"Just so," said Falerior.

I tilted my head. "Yeah, that's fair."

"And so we reach the crux of things," said the Oathkeeper. "Here we are guided by the insights of the whisper Lirian, who discovered the truth of you—or at least its silhouette. A secretive woman, embroiled in conflict, with knowledge she should not have, claiming events that couldn't have happened. This is a matter too serious for complacency, and the evidence strikes too deep. Lady Ajarel Vitares, despite your station, I must arrest you."

Kuril spoke up from her position behind Roel's chair. "I will not allow you or anyone to bring this family to ruin."

"The resolve of House Vitares has been aptly demonstrated," said Eloi. "We would be honored to support your contract."

"Nice one, Eloi," I said, not taking my eyes off Falerior. "Great job capitalizing on the moment."

"House Jeneretes likewise recognizes your contributions to the well-being of the city," Phaeres hastily added. "We welcome your innovations in healing the damage done by this despicable Ajarel."

"Roel spoke the truth," Falerior said gently. "The doors are locked; you can't escape. Come with me. It's over."

I slowly shifted around the table, letting Falerior follow my positioning.

The movement let me observe the audience to this little scene. Eloi's expression was more unsettled than I'd ever seen her. Phaeres was clearly in uncharted waters, and her cronies were practically hiding behind her. Sael glared at me with a deep and vicious hatred as she cradled Lirian's unconscious body.

Kuril was pained but resolute. I gave her an apologetic half smile, and her expression hardened.

Roel—Roel looked tired but triumphant.

"You did good, kid," I said. "But you need to trust your family more. And cool it on the one-liners, okay? They make you look dumb if you screw up afterward."

"She's stalling for time," Roel said, furrowing her brow. I winked at her.

Falerior took a step forward, and I slipped back into my defensive stance.

"It's over, Falerior!" I smirked. "I have the high ground."

"I don't need to fight you," he said politely. "Unless you have the keys, you're locked in here."

"Then I guess it's a stalemate. Hey, do you all want to keep negotiating? I can, like, shuffle back toward the wall so you can see each other."

"Do something!" Sael snapped. "Punish her!"

"No!" Roel yelled. "Block the door! She's had an ally this whole time!"

And then I heard the sound I'd been waiting for—the beautiful, beautiful sound of a key turning in the lock. In my ears, it was a thunderous clunk, but with the commotion in the room, the singing and the conversation outside? Did they know?

Before Falerior—eternally unhurried—had decided to move, the door pulled away, revealing Alouren with a tray of pies.

"Roel, I have that food you—" was as far as she got before the tableau registered inside. Her eyes widened as every woman in the room started screaming at her.

I'd been forewarned, thanks to the magic of Eifni cybernetic advancements. I was diving off the table before anyone else even understood what was going on. I hit the ground with a roll and came up sprinting, ducking under Falerior's arm as he tried to snag me.

Roel hadn't kept Alouren in the loop—which was how I'd gotten away with this—but she had enough situational awareness to try to shut the door before I barreled into it, knocking her and the pies to the ground. I didn't have enough time to lock Falerior in there with the rest of them, so I just jumped over Alouren and collided with a group of graced who'd probably been hoping to hear the news before anyone else. They went down like a bunch of garishly dressed bowling bins, and I lost a few precious seconds extricating myself from the pile.

Falerior had apparently decided that moving fast was okay after all, coming after me like a truth-seeking armored boulder on Indiana Jones's heels. I booked it.

"Stop her!" bellowed the Oathkeeper.

"You'll never catch me alive, copper!" I laughed, running with everything I had. The bystanders didn't know what to make of the situation until I shoulder-checked a lady into the wine fountain because she didn't get out of the way fast enough. That seemed to convince the rest that getting out of my way was the smart option.

A proud-looking woman forewent the wisdom of the crowd, standing her ground with an outstretched hand.

"I invoke the Right of Challen—"

I punched her in the face and kept going.

The exit was in front of me, but there were armed guards in the way, and apparently they'd decided to do their jobs. Fine. I stepped wide, throwing all my weight into it to redirect my momentum toward a refreshment table. Dashing past a group of teenagers who barely got out of the way in time, I grabbed a bowl, praying I'd gotten the right one, and went back for the entrance.

Falerior had done the smart thing and headed straight for the entrance, so my detour was going to cost me. I didn't have time to think and stuck to the plan. I sprinted for the main gate, spilled sauce searing my hand, and charged the guards.

The commander always said to control the flow of a fight. They reflexively took a defensive stance at the onslaught, which held them in place, which made them easy targets. I swung the bowl at the nearest one and—*yes*, I'd grabbed the right one—hot *dvoli* splashed in his eyes. He went down screaming, dropping his sword. I threw the bowl at the second guard's face, trusting his reflexes to pin him down for the moments I needed to reach for the first guard's sword.

Falerior flew at me out of nowhere, forcing me to abandon the sword and throw myself into a dive. We both ended up on the ground, but Falerior snagged my ankle. The guard who wasn't writhing on the ground in pain recovered, coming over but pausing in shock as he recognized me.

"Help me, uh—" Fuck, why hadn't I bothered to learn everyone's names again? "Help me!"

"She's dangerous!" Falerior shouted. From my prone position, I managed the worst axe kick of my life, slamming my heel into his arm.

His armored arm. *Fuck*, that hurt. But the impact released his grip and allowed me to roll away. I pulled myself up, bringing me face-to-face with the poor bondsman who was trying to figure out whether to listen to the Oathkeeper or his master.

"Tell them," I started, then looked at Falerior, who was struggling to his feet.

House Vitares had been my family. They still were; I'd carry that forever. Even though I had to leave, I wanted so badly to let them know, in some secret way, that I'd always love them.

But Falerior was right there. I couldn't tell the truth. If I did, he'd know, and the whole scheme would unravel. I'd managed, against all odds, to find a way to save them from the Voranetti trap, and it wouldn't work unless I played the part of the evil whisper, out to ruin everything.

If I said anything, I'd give everything away.

Falerior was on his feet now. I was out of time.

"I promised Alouren a magic trick," I told the guy whose name I'd never learn. "Now you see me—"

CHAPTER SIXTY-FIVE

Farewell

They'd only posted one Oathkeeper tonight. She was hanging out on the south wall, right next to Roel's bedroom. I could handle one Oathkeeper. If I saved the cloak until I got close, it'd limit the time they had to respond with their stupid little dowsing rod.

Think things through.

It wouldn't work, would it?

They definitely had the Lilith detector on the premises. That meant it was either with the lady outside of Roel's window, or they had a second person inside. If the window guard had it, that meant a fight, and Roel would book it. If the window guard *didn't* have it, I could sneak past her.

But the guy on the inside would detect the cloak. Then they'd raise the alarm. I'd be stuck inside Roel's room before I had a chance to . . .

She wasn't going to hear me out, was she?

I slumped against the alley wall. The tactical situation didn't matter. I'd already fucked up the strategic situation.

"Commander," I said. My voice was rough. "I'm . . . not going to make the attempt."

"*Understood,*" she said, as if receiving a routine report.

It was a kind of compassion, as Veleans understood it. Some weaknesses you probed; others you made a point of ignoring. That, too, was a message. It meant they were treating me as an adult; it meant they trusted me to deal with my wounds without help. It meant respect. It meant I was one of them.

It was hard to care right now.

"Returning to base."

The shower didn't feel weird anymore. I'd been doing baths for *thessi*—for months, but the old routines were coming unstuck from the rust. I let the hot water wash off the sweat from the humid nighttime air.

My psych professor said people who felt a lot of guilt took longer showers. It was supposed to be this symbolic thing, washing away your sins or something. I guess that kind of made sense, but my comm didn't pick up any symbolism when I scanned for it. After about fifteen minutes, I got restless and sent the command to shut the shower down.

The *Ragnar*'s translation engines sucked the wetness from the room and pumped it back as temperature, leaving the air perfectly warm. That included the water in my hair, but I still ended up looking for a towel until the lack of dampness registered. I let my hair fall down my back, the sensation somehow making me feel more naked than my current lack of clothes.

I'd changed.

How had the commander put it? "We are built up and torn down every day." I had become Ajarel Vitares; I had put her to death.

It wasn't even the first time I'd done this, I realized. I'd been Morgan, years ago, before I'd taken the name Lilith. Morgan was dead now. I'd left her back on Earth so I could become . . . I wanted to say Lilith, but that didn't seem right. That was probably going to take some meditation to figure out.

I pulled on a T-shirt and a pair of sweats. The fit was at once familiar and strange. I felt an urge to at least put my hair in a ponytail, but I held myself back. I wasn't Ajarel anymore. Let the weird Estheni hair norms die with her.

When I entered the lounge, Abby was waiting for me. Oh, she had plausible deniability. There was a movie playing on the wall screen, and it was just a coincidence that the good couch seated more than one.

"Liar," I murmured affectionately.

She was too still. There was no way she was actually watching the movie—she was fucking meditating.

I accepted the implicit offer, dropping heavily on the couch and snuggling up against her. Her arm lazily snaked around me, tracing her thumb in circles on the base of my scalp.

"Lilith *barak*," she whispered to me.

My breath caught in my throat, but I shoved the reaction down. "Your eyes aren't even on."

She chuckled softly at my deflection. "I'm practicing an ancient technique, handed down over generations."

"You've seen the movie before."

"Oh good, you've heard of it."

I laughed despite myself.

We both fell silent, but the conversation didn't stop. It was the words I didn't say, the questions she didn't ask me. It was the way she held me anyway, the warmth of it, the fingers combing through my hair. It was the way she ignored the tears that fell on her jumpsuit.

She grieved with me until the tears had run their course. Neither of us said anything to gainsay the fiction we Veleans needed to perform: that my dalliance with the Vitares family was simply part of the mission. A matter of honor, at most—my gift to those who had helped me accomplish my goals.

I was a warrior of Veles. War was my creed, victory my birthright. It was time to leave childish things behind.

The Kabidiad would be held in Bulcephine, the capital city of the Imperial Coalition. Markus—Darwin knows how he talked his way out of suspicion—would be hitching a ride on the same caravan as Cades and two of the other qualifiers.

Apparently there had been a third, but his wife had forbidden him from competing. That would have been the end of it for him, given the whole obedience thing that formed the backbone of Kabiadesian honor. I guess some people just didn't like sharing with the empress.

"You're not going," Abby told me as we briefed for the next stage of our divine wet work. "You've been burned, and if anyone recognizes your face it could lead to further blowback for Markus. I want you on the *Ragnar* practicing *ak ha var*. We may not have another opportunity once we reach the capital."

"No argument here," I said. "Who's backing up Markus?"

"*Markus can back up himself,*" Markus quipped.

"I'll go," Val said, not looking up from his screen. "Abby can stay to pass on her antiquated hobby."

"Spoken like a man who lost his last sparring bout," Abby said.

"I'm positive the Old Ways have something to say about gloating over empty victories."

"Yeah," I cut in with a smirk. "'Glory lieth in the claiming.'"

Val's baleful green stare promised vengeance as Abby proudly squeezed my shoulder.

"*Oh great,*" Markus said. "*Now there are two of them.*"

"It's good to be back," I said.

Even Val smiled. "Welcome back, Lilith. I assume you remember your name."

A joking insult on the surface, a jab at my loyalties hidden below. The me of a year ago would have tried to spit out a comeback and answered him on one level at most.

The me of now merely rolled her eyes. I could tell he approved.

Estheni nobility at war were nothing compared to the rigors of Velean friendship. It was familiar now, even comfortable. My heart still ached to hell, but there was also pride in there. Pride at what I'd accomplished, who I was becoming.

"The mission's not done," said the commander. "We've got about a month to prepare. Most of that will be travel time. Markus, I'll need you to continue your association with Cades. Your primary objective will be to investigate any experience he has with previous Kabidiads. Secondly, anything you can get on his encounters with the Cult of Silence will be useful when we move on Meris."

"Speaking of which," I said. "Val, did you ever end up using the blood sample I got from Lirian? That seems useful now that she's out of jail."

He gave me a thin smile. "I have a direct connection through the *Ragnar*, which we can access as long as she's in signal range. The process proved to be more complicated than I anticipated; Meris protected her *very* well." The smile twisted into a smirk. "Unfortunately for Meris, gods can't adapt, and *I can*."

"Now who's gloating over unworthy foes?" the commander laughed.

Whatever mood had possessed Val receded. "Operationally, I recommend using the connection sparingly. She tends to instinctively activate her cloak when her soul is manipulated, and the structure of Meris's blessing indicates that it makes her aware of outside attention, which would seem to include us. Overusing the connection might reduce its effectiveness."

"So," I said, "she constantly feels like she's being watched?"

"Presumably."

"Awesome! Fuck her! Let's do it in shifts. I call the middle of the night."

They laughed at that. I laughed along, like I was joking.

I wasn't joking.

"Lilith, you'll be on ops," said the commander. "Bulcephine is reported to have a higher level of divine activity, so we don't know what security measures are waiting for us. Without knowing the nature of the enemy's defenses, we have to assume your stint as Ajarel will increase your exposure risk."

"Understood. I can handle ops."

The commander nodded. "The rest of us will need to gather information *quickly*. To that end, we'll reposition the *Ragnar* as soon as Markus and Val leave Vitareas. This is a death blow. I am authorizing any and all measures to secure the influence we need to put Markus on that podium."

"*What about Kives?*" Markus said. "*There was that contact with Lilith during the Voranetes op.*"

The commander turned silver eyes on me. "Lilith, give me your analysis."

"Kives wants me to grow up," I reported matter-of-factly. "In her way. Over the course of the op, she made multiple attempts to exploit my family trauma, with the apparent objective of creating an emotional commitment to House Vitares. The incident where she railroaded me into sacrificing to her may have been an attempt to get me to bargain with her. I can't speculate on her objectives, but maybe Val has some ideas."

"A few—and all of them conjecture." Val synced his touch pad to the wall screen, displaying a bunch of equations he *had* to know I couldn't read. "She would see you as the weak link of the team. The rest of us have already become who we are."

"*Although some philosophers say that we eternally become who we are.*"

Val scoffed. "Those philosophers have never solved a Valdleif system. The strategic objective for targeting Lilith is either full indoctrination or an attempt to steer her off course from a pivotal moment." He turned to me. "You'll need to be prepared to resist when the moment comes. Remember that you have a choice."

"That's not super comforting," I said. "Back on Earth, there's a story about this dude named Oedipus who did everything he could to avoid a prophecy but ended up fulfilling it anyway. That's kind of how it goes. If you tell me I have a choice against a goddess of fate, I'm going to assume every choice I make plays into her hands."

"Fate will mold you like butter if you let her," said Abby. "But you choose who you become. Fate only rules the unthinking."

"Huh," I said. "Is that why we're doing the *ak ha var* stuff and everything?"

"Lilith," Val chided me. "You're a Velean. We were fighting fate long before we learned it had a stomach."

There was something of a feral cast to his face. Behind my answering smile, there was a snarl rising in my throat. A distant memory of cataclysm and triumph.

"They fall," I said.

My team answered me. "They die."

I manned the guns for the duration of the *Ragnar*'s flight to Bulcephine. Part of me hoped for an angel attack or something, but our enemy didn't send so much as a *gvodim* after us, even when we dropped a relay satellite to maintain contact with the boys.

The capital was larger than Vitareas by at least an order of magnitude, massive stone edifices standing guard over endless miles of farmland. Bulcephine was a coastal city, concrete dams stretching into the ocean to protect its harbor.

Bulcephine's guards were more active than the slackers in Vitareas. With the full moon shining, a *Ragnar*-sized hole in a wheat field might be visible from the walls. The ship was projecting absence; they wouldn't see a ship vanishing into a hole in the earth, they'd see nothing vanishing into a hole in the earth. That was still a problem for us. After some brainstorming, Abby took us to the coast.

We quickly determined that there wasn't enough room to set down inside the harbor, and Abby vetoed the plan where we tunneled under the seawall sheltering it from Horcutio's domain. We were limited by the translation engines; we'd need to submerge the ship about a mile away and slowly tunnel under the farmland.

"*Holding position,*" Abby said.

"Copy," I said, punching out of my console and hoisting Val's moirascope over my shoulder. "Gunnery controls are yours. Pop the hatch in twenty."

"*Understood.*"

I lugged the device down the hall to the starboard air lock. The door opened right as I reached it. I plonked the tripod down first, securing it to the floor emplacement before sliding the moirascope on top. I grabbed two safety lines out of paranoia, clipping one to my belt and the other to the moirascope. Satisfied with my preparations, I slammed my fist on the cycle button.

Warm, salty ocean air washed over me as the exterior door opened.

"Scanning now," I said.

It's harder to detect dyadic entanglements in an area than with a specific object. Sure, for some momentous events—"This is the street where JFK got shot!"—you might end up with an etheric connection, but on a random patch of ocean? It'd have to be pretty big.

Fortunately, this was one of those cases where a moirascope caused the good kind of self-fulfilling prophecies. Anything big enough to show up on a moirascope was big enough that we weren't going to mess with it. So, in a convoluted kind of way, scanning the area for unwanted events directly prevented them from happening.

I flipped through the filter settings. I didn't pick up any disasters or miracles. No one made a world-altering discovery here or faced a momentous enemy. I tried Val's patchwork approximation of the Estheni Calamity construct and didn't get anything, although he'd been careful to hedge his bets on the accuracy for that one.

Most importantly, there weren't going to be any ships destroyed here.

"All clear," I said, cycling the air lock again.

Abby waited until I was back on the gunnery controls to take us in. We slipped into the water nose first, guns at the ready. Just because the moirascope had eliminated the obvious possibilities didn't mean Kives didn't have a nonobvious one lined up for us.

"*I'm starting translation on the tunnel,*" said Abby. "*It's going to be a long night. I'm authorizing exhaustion blockers.*"

"Copy," I said, flipping between the various sensors I had available. "Huh. Commander, can you double-check thermal for me? The area seems warm."

"*I'm getting the same readings,*" said Abby. "*Translation is proceeding on schedule.*"

"So, Val's not here," I said leadingly.

Abby laughed. "*Authorized.*"

The ship *was* picking up signs of life all around us, but that's kind of what you expect on an ocean coast. I scanned for divine blessings and got a couple hits, but they were all in the direction of the city. Nothing like Lobsterzilla.

I checked night vision, but the translation process was kicking up a lot of silt, and visibility was shit.

"Do you think we can risk the floodlights?" I asked.

The commander weighed it for a moment. "*Briefly,*" she concluded.

"Here goes," I said, flipping a switch. Four floodlights—two on the bow, one on each of the side batteries—blazed into the chthonic darkness, illuminating a sandbar and not much else.

The sandbar opened its eyes.

"Holy *shit!*" I yelled, scrabbling for the joystick.

The eyes blinked once, gelatinous flesh shifting as a leviathan shifted its tentacles, sand-white skin becoming mottled brown. Even that shift sent shock waves through the water that jostled the *Ragnar* against the will of her stabilizers. My mind boggled at the sheer scale of this thing.

The biggest goddamn fucking octopus I'd ever imagined opened a beak that could fit entire ships and whipped its tentacles toward the *Ragnar*.

My finger found the trigger.

Thud-thud-thud-thud.

The fusion cannons' roar was muted, the sound carrying differently through the water. Seawater instantly heated to plasma. Even underwater, the glare of the fusion rounds whited out my display.

The *Ragnar* rocked back with the shock wave as the high-energy rounds annihilated the stretch of ocean between us and the Gigantopus. They sank into its body and released the last of their energy. For the first and last time, I had the extremely specific experience of listening to thousands of tons of flesh explosively tear itself apart underwater.

It was kind of a giant *blorpschlrp*, in case you're curious.

"*Target neutralized,*" Abby said with a tinge of irony.

"This," I declared, "is the happiest day of my life."

CHAPTER SIXTY-SIX

The Mountain

We were definitely gonna need Val to program a moirascope filter for "giant sea monster ambush" when he got here. If this happened a third time, the commander might turn the car around and go home as a matter of honor.

Our immediate situation wasn't great. We'd just exploded enough octopus meat to stock every sushi restaurant in Japan for about eight years, and they probably heard the boom all the way back in Vitareas. There's no way they missed that over in Bulcephine. We were about to make a lot of friends, very quickly.

On the other hand, it was an open question whether those friends would find us, given that we were hidden under a mountain of seafood and camouflaged by a lake's worth of blood.

"What's the plan?" I asked.

"*Unchanged,*" said the commander. "*You can pull back the guns now. We can tunnel faster with a smaller profile.*"

I glanced at the display. Yeah, she had a point. Thermal, visual, even etheric— everything was gummed up with leviathan smoothie. No point keeping the guns deployed if I couldn't see what I was shooting at.

"So this was a prank," I said. "Kives is pranking us. Is she secretly a trickster god or something?"

"*No, there's a distinct trickster god,*" said Abby. "*Rucks. If it's really a prank, it could mean she's trying to eat* pronoun/him/her."

I blinked as my comm failed to translate the Velean bigender pronoun, then told it to output "they."

"What happens then?" I asked.

"*Normally gods avoid that kind of contest. It's messy. Even with progressive monophase against monophase, it's a toss-up who walks away. If she weren't in a progressive phase, I'd say it was to absorb one of their aspects, but there's no such thing as a double progressive phase.*"

"Unless she's preparing for after she hits biphase," I said, stomach sinking.

"*We started from the assumption that this is a prank,*" said Abby. "*It's just an assumption. I'll have Val run the numbers when he gets here.*"

"I feel like we should be worried about this."

"We should be worried about the Bulcephine insertion," said Abby. *"If this is all intended to help Kives reach triphase, we'll have years to react. There's always the strike fleet."*

I frowned. "Yeah. That's what worries me."

The guys reestablished contact while Abby and I were eating breakfast—*jadisk,* a Velean fish jerky served with sweet vinegar. Abby was taking hers with a side of fruit. I'd just put it on bread and slathered the vinegar over the whole thing like a weird-ass PB&J. Six out of ten.

"Good morning," Markus said. *"End of the* thessim *and we're making good time. Nothing to report. Holler back if you can hear me."*

"Eyyy!" I said. "How's it going, buddy?"

"He just told you," Val said.

"I missed you, too," I said happily.

Abby ripped a chunk of fish off with her teeth. "How's your cover holding up?"

"We're with the Voranetes delegation," said Markus. *"They cozied up to the Vitaressi pretty fast after you left. Falerior tried to get involved, but they fired him a day after he made it clear he wasn't going to let it drop. You could tell everyone knew it was going to end that way, but no one backed down."*

"Shit," I said. "The dude was obnoxious, but he didn't deserve that."

"Tell him yourself," said Markus. *"He's traveling with us."*

"Fuck no," I said. "Make Val tell him."

Val chuckled dismissively.

"Fine," I said. "Then I guess he gets to feel bad."

"Is he still investigating you?" Abby said.

"Not seriously," said Markus. *"I think he's still adjusting to the change. The man lost his entire career."*

"He's waiting for Markus to get in contact with Lilith," said Val. *"He could have been much more vicious during the initial interrogation."*

"He told me Oathkeepers get fired when they go after nobles," I said. "I guess he'll be gunning for me when he gets here."

"One more reason to have you stay on ops," Abby said. "How's Cades adjusting?"

"The Voranetti's representatives are keeping an eye on him. We can't move freely, but we managed to sneak some time the other night."

"Any new intel?" I asked.

There was a pause. *"No,"* Markus said wryly.

"Oh. *Oh.*" I wrinkled my nose. "Congratulations?"

"Congratulations on developing a high-value asset," said Abby, shooting a blank look at me.

"He's been a consistent source of high-quality information," Markus said, as though we hadn't just collectively decided his relationship didn't exist. *"He was leaned on enough that he picked up a bunch of the secrets. The social deviance of his sexuality was deemed enough leverage to keep him in line."*

"That was a really weird way to phrase that," I said.

Val's smirk was audible. "*Did you know that agent-exclusive language doesn't trigger certain kinds of memetic defenses?*"

"Oh god . . . fire," I said, hastily correcting myself at a glare from Abby. "Is it her?"

"*Who?*" Val said pleasantly. "*I'm afraid I can't confirm the identity of who or whatever is triggering our mixed-detector overlays.*"

For all that he was being stalked by an invisible assassin, he sounded remarkably like a spider attending to the vibrations of his web.

"*It's possible we're being shadowed,*" said Markus. "*But we're headed for the capital. Operatives have to report in eventually. This might give us some leads on a certain cult.*"

"Good work," said the commander. "There was a significant Dancer contingent traveling with the caravan, yes?"

"*Yeah,*" said Markus. "*I think they've figured out Cades's situation. The girls have been flirting up a storm whenever they see him.*"

"He was pretty flirty when he met me," I said. "I think that's just how he masks."

"*Yeah, and they've picked up on it,*" said Markus. "*It's all show on both ends. No one's escalating. I was expecting some code-switching when we learned that Rucks's faith welcomed marginalized sexualities, but this is high-level stuff.*"

"*They'd do well on Veles,*" said Val. "*If this sample isn't an outlier, we should recommend preserving some aspects of the culture during uplift.*"

"Duly noted," said the commander.

"Aren't the Voranetes observers going to figure it out?" I asked.

"*No,*" said Markus. "*Bears can't read wolfsign.*"

It was a Velean figure of speech about social structures, reflecting the weird animal associations of their culture. Veleans think of wolves as battlefield scavengers, opportunistically feeding on the remains of human conflict. The botched experiment that led to Earth inventing the idea of the pack alpha never happened on Veles; instead, wolf packs are seen as these highly coordinated social groups where individuals instinctively pick up on the thoughts of others. According to Velean folklore, that even extends to leaving notes for other packs: wolf sign.

Bears, on the other hand, are seen as gluttonous loners who don't need cunning because they can take whatever they want with brute strength. Calling someone a bear on Veles is basically saying they're an ignorant dumbass who thinks they're winning at life when they're actually sowing the seeds of their own destruction. So bears can't read wolf sign because they aren't looking for it.

Their ecology might have been suspect, but the ancient Veleans were apparently just as sociologically attuned as the modern ones. Every culture comes with power structures, and the higher you go, the more of a bear you become. It's the ones on the bottom who need the wolf sign—the references, the figures of speech, clothing, bearing, and attitude; the loaded glances, shared rebellion in silent eye rolls and things not said to each other's parents; all the little details that say, "I'm one of you and we can trust each other"—to survive.

Over the course of a week—taking every precaution—we managed to tunnel the *Ragnar* in a broad quarter circle to the foundation of the city walls. No farther; that was just begging to get us noticed, either by triggering some etheric defense or accidentally undermining the wall. We'd filled the earth in behind us as we tunneled, but the immediate area had been translated into the idea of *solidity*, which we dispensed back into realspace as structural supports for a tunnel underneath the wall.

Eight thousand years of technological progress, reshaping the cosmos like gods, and we used it to build a bunch of arches. The Romans always got the last laugh.

I say "we" on all of this, but there wasn't a lot for me to do, so Abby ordered me to start my meditations for the *ak ha var* process.

I'd initially thought that Growing the Mountain from the Roots was just a flowery name for the meditation technique, but it ended up being mostly literal.

"The body remembers. The soul remembers," Abby told me again and again. "Both carry your past, and the past returns as your present. This is the mountain. It is what you are and what you must become."

The body remembers.

I spent a day remembering pain and enjoyment. The time I broke my arm when my brother pushed me out of the tree house. Blizzards from Dairy Queen after soccer practice. Hot chocolate in the winter. Group hugs in college. Period cramps I'd never suffer again. Soreness after a workout. Knuckles impacting bone, sparring bruises, the knife that sliced my side open during the destruction of Aguin. The agony rending my entire existence that last visit in Pastor Barnes's office.

The soul remembers.

I spent a day remembering isolation and belonging. The weathered wooden sign in the backyard, "Boys Only." Patricia inviting the whole team to her birthday except for me. Losing a snowball fight five to one. Kevin Ellis cornering me in seventh grade until I gave him a kiss; Dad's lecture about modesty when I told him. Finally fitting in with my roommate's friends; the fights when Trent started dating Brian and I reacted badly. Mom and Dad telling me to get over my depression. The uncertainty of the Academy and the bonds I forged there. Refusing to stay down in that last spar. Meeting Markus and Val and Abby for the first time. Saying goodbye to Kuril and Roel.

Become the mountain.

I spent a day finding the shape of it. The walls I'd built against expected violence, the holes I'd put in them to let people in. The way each hurt prepared me to fight the next one. The way I'd been made a victim, the anger that had carried me through. The full meaning of a sword in my hand, the experiences that built those meanings, their meanings in turn, and so on. Every moment, every thought, every experience the peak of its own mountain, overlapping to become *I*.

"Is this the work of a unified self?" Val's voice asked me.

I stood at the peak and answered, "Yes."

"Veleans do not bow to fate," Abby said. "All your life, you have *let* yourself become. That is death—the creeping oblivion of time, dragging you piece by piece into the dark until a stranger inherits your past. From this moment on, seize control. Slay yourself and rise again."

I spent a day slashing it down. I tunneled through anger and grief and pain and bewilderment, wielding my will as a weapon. I found the selves I'd been—the runt of the litter who never fit in, the awkward high schooler hunted by male gazes, the lonely self-sabotaging young adult—and I cut them down.

I followed the threads that wove them and found the mountain's heart: the world was sharp, and I needed to be sharper.

I spent a day deciding who I should be. Not who I wanted to be because my wants were the wants of the girls I'd been—the past returning as the present. Who did I *need* to be to take on eternity?

I needed openness without vulnerability. I needed strength without destruction. I needed resolve without rigidity.

If I tried to measure my blade against the world's, the world would grind me down. I needed to become something else: I needed to become a fire. Warm to my friends, deadly to my enemies. Let the slings and arrows of outrageous fortune pass through me; I'd burn them all.

Slay yourself and rise again.

I spent a day finding the roots of the mountain I would become. Moments I'd stood up to my family. Moments where I'd adapted to succeed. Friendships I'd built. Enemies I'd beaten. My pride in my team and theirs in me.

The glowing embers of a fire that would burn Heaven, as Eifni did millennia ago.

We reached our destination that evening. On the seventh day, I rested.

CHAPTER SIXTY-SEVEN

Parent

The benefit of taking it slow over the last week was that the commander had thoroughly probed the city's defenses—etheric and otherwise—with the ship's sensors. We had a good idea of what we'd be facing from this end, but the walls represented enough of a barrier that our intel on the other side was limited.

The etheric defenses themselves were grand and intricate; no human had wrought these. There couldn't be any ambiguity about that; pre-ethertech civilizations only had access to the blind fumbling of clap-your-hands-if-you-believe placebomancy—weak, unreliable shit like the energy-manifestation people back home. A human working would have looked like an indecisive cloud of protectiveness, faith in the walls shifting the ether and reflecting back to realspace as a meager 2 percent increase to tensile strength or something.

In contrast, the gods' workings were intricate, imposing, and vicious. Varas's signature was all over them—as expected, the capital was her holy city—with select subsections reflecting the contributions of other deities. Meris had built a mechanism to draw the guards' attention to sneaky infiltrators, while Alcebios—despite her mythological reputation as an antagonist to the rest of the pantheon—had woven a curse that would stick to enemies of the city and bring ruin on them.

There was even a thread from Kives promising that the space within the walls would be unshakable and that all who schemed to thwart that stability would fail.

My wariness must have shown on my face when the commander explained that one because she smiled.

"Don't be intimidated," she said. "It's a machine, not a real enemy. They weren't built to penetrate military-grade comm shields."

"There we go, then," I said.

Abby didn't continue the explanation, watching me instead. An unspoken question hung in the air.

"It just feels weird to be able to shrug off the working of a god," I admitted.

"You were built to feel that way," Abby said. "It's deep in our nature—almost too deep to remove. What does the word 'sublimity' mean in your native language?"

"Something that's perfect," I said, then frowned. "No, that's not the definition you're talking about, I knew that was wrong as soon as I said it. It's the feeling when you encounter something, like, *big*. Something that makes you realize you're really small in the grand scheme of things."

"Every culture comes to understand that idea," Abby said. "They might not have a word for it, but it emerges from evolution as a logical necessity. What's the evolutionary origin of superstitious and religious behavior?"

I blinked at being suddenly put on the spot, then recited the Academy answer. "Uh, past a certain intelligence threshold, organisms develop pattern recognition to increase their fitness, and superstition is when the perceived cause-effect relationship doesn't reflect an underlying reality. Religion is the combination of superstitious behavior, pareidolia, and social-cultural group-unification behaviors. Gods manipulate religious superstition to cultivate a food source."

"Textbook answer," Abby said. It wasn't a compliment. "Why does this system emerge on every planet we've visited?"

"The *why* is that you need pattern recognition to increase evolutionary fitness, and people just don't know better how the world works," I said.

"You're not winning any grants with an answer like that."

"I signed up to kill gods, not study them."

"'There is no weapon more deadly than the truth,'" Abby quoted from *The Road of Spears*. "But I'll spare you more guesses, for time's sake. The evolution of cognition enables the development of a more sophisticated soul, which spurs the development of more advanced cognition, and so on. The more sophisticated the soul, the more ancient humans began to realize that they had a *self*, that there was an *I* behind their experiences, that this *I* was distinct, in an important way, from everything else."

"So that's where you get religion," I said, putting the pieces together. "People want to feel like the everything else is friendly to them."

"No." The commander's expression was distant. "You're a child of kindness, Lilith. There are peoples who suffer much more than yours. Veles was one of them, and our ancient religions were as harsh and hungry as the winter that culled our ancestors every year. They were too steeped in death to dream of the peace we know now, but they still made the appropriate sacrifices. Not for kindness. Religions exist so that the grandness of the world can be controlled."

"Huh," I said, thinking of my parents. "Yeah, that makes sense. Why were we talking about this again?"

"Because you've let yourself believe the oldest lie." Abby's tone was pleasant, and a fond smile ghosted over her face. "You think a god can crush you because you think the world can crush you."

"I don't think that's irrational, given what Horcutio did to the ship. You literally died."

"What of it?" Abby's smile wasn't a ghost anymore. "Do I look crushed?"

"I mean yes, you got better, but you still lost," I argued. "I know you're trying to say I should meditate myself into believing I can fight the whole world and win, but that's just delusional. Uh, sorry, that came out a little harsh."

"That idea didn't offend you last time I mentioned it."

"You weren't talking about fighting the whole world at once back then. Just cutting it. I don't know, it doesn't sound realistic at all this way."

"Retreat is useful as a strategy," the commander pushed me. "Not as a habit."

I rolled my eyes. "Sorry for saying sorry, then."

"And now you retreat from retreating."

"I— What do you want me to say?"

The commander's face darkened. "Lilith, you *coward*!"

I stepped back, my eyes wide. The commander had never lost her composure in the time I'd known her. Another apology rushed to my lips, but I held myself back. Panic in my chest. Why was she reacting like this? How did I make it stop?

"Godfire," the commander hissed. "You meditated for a *week*, Lilith. Were you daydreaming the whole time?"

"No, I—"

The commander fixed me with a glare that shut me up immediately.

It was as if a switch flipped—all the emotions drained away, leaving distant remnants of themselves. The panic was locked in my stomach, I *had to fix this*, but I was free again. The commander's glare turned to disgust, which made the panic swell on the other side of whatever glass wall was keeping it from my consciousness.

"Commander," I spoke evenly, "I don't know what I did, but I apologize for offending you."

"You didn't offend me," she said in a more neutral tone. "You offended whoever taught you that panic response."

I froze up. The panic response warped awkwardly as my system tried to figure out what the fuck was going on.

"You don't want to be a child anymore," said the commander. "So get rid of your parents. It was them, wasn't it?"

I gaped at her. "That's— Look, commander, you have to know how bad that sounds."

"According to whom?" said the commander. "Should I be afraid of them? Go meditate on your trauma response. We have time. My master would hunt me down if she found out I let you calcify this into your new foundation."

That was a dismissal, and I ignored it. Anger rose up in me like a fire licking my insides, but I controlled it.

"Never do that again," I said in a low tone.

"Notice how you only drew your blade after I sheathed mine," the commander said.

"I don't care. Never do that again."

"If I don't, Kives will." Something relaxed in her posture. "It's not fair that you're in this position, but I can't be the mother you needed. Not while a fertility goddess has you in her sights. You need to move past this."

My emotions stalled again, then apparently decided to give up completely.

"This is a strategic priority," the commander said again. "Go meditate. That is an order in my capacity as commander of this team."

Motherfucking goddamn *Veleans.*

I'd started the meditation by wondering what I'd done to provoke Abby's reaction, and after I found my thoughts anxiously spiraling the second time, I tried a different approach.

It took me about two minutes to realize I was an idiot. I'd only been thinking about myself. When I tried to place myself in Abby's shoes, the answer was immediately apparent: she'd just learned that Kives had put a target on us, and she'd attacked our relationship rather than risk the failure of the mission.

And with that blade, I will cut heaven and earth, she'd said.

It had sounded so cool when she told me that. I hadn't considered it meant cutting *me.*

And . . . Yeah, okay, maybe Abby was kind of a mothering figure. She knew it, I knew it, but it was okay, right? People needed not to be alone, and I was an orphan for all practical purposes. My parents were still alive, I think, but I wasn't going to be worldjumping to good old planet Earth anytime soon.

All I had left was an immortal ninja fairy godmother. And now that was gone. It didn't change anything that I knew why she'd done it; something was broken that I couldn't fix. She'd hurt me *deliberately,* and even knowing why she'd done it didn't change the fact that she'd been willing and able to.

She hadn't even told me what she was doing. She just did it. If she'd just talked to me—

I'd lost my replacement mother before I'd really appreciated that I had one.

Caught up in the grief of that was another grief, an older one, wondering why I had to get stuck with the shitty excuse for parents that I had. Abby had real kids. If I've been one of them, would I still have whatever panic response she'd triggered in me?

I wanted to tell someone, but the thought of saying any of this to the commander left me feeling hollow. The commander had ordered me to meditate, but fuck that, I needed another human being right now, and she wasn't available.

I pinged Markus first and got an I'm-busy ping in reply. The other option was . . .

Fuck it. I pinged Val, using the signal for *I need backup.*

"Lilith?" he asked.

"I need to get some shit off my chest," I said. "Got time?"

"Ah," he said, as though he'd inferred the entire situation. Maybe he had. I was too drained to care. *"I have some time."*

"Just shut up and listen, okay?" I said. "I don't need any fatherly advice."

"I have not been described as fatherly in over two hundred years of existence."

"Perfect. Now shut the hell up. Here's the deal—"

I finished my briefing with the commander, maintaining perfect professionalism the whole time. She did the same, letting the occasional awkward pause communicate that this had hurt her, too. I wasn't sure if it was genuine communication or if she was rubbing salt in the wound to make sure Kives had nothing to hold on to.

At one point I interrupted to point out that Kives was clearly capable of using parental trauma without an active familial relationship, but Abby flatly replied that it was my job to handle the trauma. After that, I kept my mouth shut, and she didn't signal any awkwardness.

When night fell, I was on ops as the commander suited up for infiltration. Objective: locate an egress point inside the city, past the etheric barriers that prevented us from scanning with deeper clarity.

We were a fair distance from the city gates, so the travelers and merchants camped outside didn't see her as she pushed open the hatch we'd translated into the ground.

I was the commander's gaze as she looked up at the wall, the tension in her body as she prepared to climb it. I was her ears, tuned and filtering for enemies. I was her eyes, cycling from infrared to night vision and back. I was the light exosuit synced to her comm, moving with her biological limbs as if she'd been born with it.

I wasn't her pseudodaughter, but I could be her backup.

The commander fixed her intent on a slight ridge about fifteen feet off the ground, then leaped. The exosuit's pistons flung her into the air with enough precision that the apex of the jump put her right at the target. She almost lazily reached out and snagged it with her fingertips, pressing her boots to the wall below.

"*Contact,*" she subvocalized. I was the inaudible vibration of her throat. "*Do a sweep.*"

"Copy," I said, bringing up the ship's sensors. "No response to contact."

"*Am I inside the barrier?*" she asked.

"No."

"*Acknowledged,*" she said. This was the probable case—etherically, she wasn't *inside* the city—but it would have allowed us to test comm tunneling more safely. She began her climb without hesitation, her boots and gloves fixing her to the wall when she put weight on them.

I could feel the exertion of the climb, but the commander didn't stop until she found an arrow slit. She peered inside, seeing only an empty room, and shifted three feet to the side.

In one minute and forty-three seconds, she reached the top of the wall. This close to the top, a uniform red glow could be seen.

"Ghostlights," I said.

"*Clever. They're preserving their night vision.*"

Night vision still required line of sight, however. The commander carefully pressed herself close to the wall and waited.

Guards passed once, twice. Armored, from the sound of it, and the rhythm of their footsteps revealed they were patrolling in pairs. I noted the timestamps as the commander's ears picked out a third patrol.

"Close to regular," I calculated. "Your absolute window is forty seconds. That's if you move right behind them when they pass. They might hear the noise."

"My adhesive gear is silenced."

"Your clothes aren't."

"True." She sounded unconcerned.

The third group passed, and she carefully followed them until she found a point where the red glow was weakest. She waited just below the edge of the wall until a fourth group approached. One black-gloved hand detached from the wall. Her attention focused on the back of her palm for a moment, then a cover slid open to reveal a camera. She cautiously poked it over the wall.

I was now watching a live stream of the commander's experience of a live stream of her hand camera. Eifni's tech really was the best: the fidelity was perfect.

The wall wasn't crenellated, but it was up to shoulder height of the average guard patrolling along the top. A short step at the edge would allow them more leeway to fire at invaders. Red ghostlights were set into the wall at regular intervals, illuminating a platform about ten feet wide. At the other end was a wooden railing.

The commander turned her camera down the railing until she found a gap about a hundred feet from her position. She examined it for a moment, then pulled back.

"That's my entrance," she said.

"Hell of a climb."

She didn't respond. She just got to it.

I could tell she was tired, even with the exosuit carrying a lot of her body weight. Climbing is super strenuous. But there wasn't any weariness to the exhaustion. In fact, her body was almost getting more excited at the prospect of the challenge.

The commander was really something. *My* body would have been looking forward to a nap or something.

"The light is pretty strong here," I said. "Are you sure?"

"I've been doing this for three hundred years," she said.

"Fair enough."

"Mark me."

Another group of guards was approaching. I waited until they passed. "Okay, mark. You've got forty."

She crawled up and got her fingers over the edge. She shimmied her boots up until she was almost in a runner's pose, except on a vertical surface.

"Thirty."

Her legs tensed, and I felt the exosuit shift to maximize output as *holy shit*—

The commander flung herself into the air in a graceful flip, using her immovable fingers as a pivot until the momentum pointed where she wanted to go. She corkscrewed as she flew, getting a glimpse of the guards, then landed perfectly on the other edge of the wall.

Her boots made no sound as they adhered to the top of the wall. Before her momentum dissipated, she backflipped into the city, pivoting on her toes this time. She caught the wall before it impacted her face, then released her feet, finishing in a Spider-Man kind of pose about ten feet from the top of the wall.

"Yes, I'm sure," she said, full of satisfaction.

"Twenty," I said, refusing to acknowledge her.

"Oh, be quiet. Am I inside the barrier?"

"Yeah. Go ahead."

The commander triggered her comm's etheric-tunneling protocol, the procedure that would tether her soul to the *Ragnar*'s crypt if she died. I waited for a tense moment, then got the signal.

"I have your signal," I said. "You're free to fight the whole city, you madwoman."

"Maybe later," said the commander. *"Let's finish the mission first."*

CHAPTER SIXTY-EIGHT

No Mercy

Abby raced through the midnight streets of Bulcephine like a ghost. Her ethertech boots made no sound as she swept over the cobblestones, translating the noise into conceptual energy and storing it in the force batteries that powered her exosuit.

She wasn't conceptually undetectable—the technology to completely obscure your presence had to be built into your actual soul, like mine was—but centuries of infiltration experience made up for that. It was the art of moving where people don't look, of choosing darker paths and skirting peripheral vision, even leaping onto the walls of buildings when it presented the path of least resistance.

She'd started on roofs, leaping from one flat-roofed building to another, but the roofing style changed as she went deeper into the city. A second ring of walls towered over the one- and two-story buildings that were common farther in, and unlike the larger buildings at the city limits they tended more toward arched roofs. The streets grew wider, too, to the point that an exosuit-boosted leap powerful enough to clear the distance might damage the buildings. So she'd dropped to street level, using skill rather than elevation to escape notice.

Abby's insertion point was near Merchants' Road, so named because it was the path by which most overland trade would enter the city. We saw snatches of it far to her left whenever a cross street intersected it; it was illuminated with ghostlight and tiled in brightly colored mosaic. A display of wealth and power to those who had come to enrich the empire's heart.

But this area was less important, or poorer, anyway—which was often the same thing from a city planning perspective—and there was no illumination to be had. That didn't stop the occasional midnight drunk or nefarious prowler from going about their business, but they had to make do with torches. Abby encountered several fellow night owls, all of whom noticed a brief wind at most.

Her target was a watchtower, which was affixed to some larger structure about two miles out from her position. The streets seemed to narrow in that direction, darkening the ambient moonlight and giving everything more of an ominous feeling. Abby didn't hesitate, her eyes efficiently tracing out possible paths of traversal as she moved to the vantage point.

"Crappy part of town," I commented.

The commander replied with a neutral ping.

There was a young couple on the road in front of her. They were inconveniently positioned to sneak past unnoticed. The commander frowned slightly, then spiked the exosuit's output power. It felt like kicking off a trampoline as she flung herself into the air, clearing the civilians' heads with something like five feet to spare.

She looked down as the boy leaned in and bit the girl's nose off, then landed, and wait what the *fuck*—

The commander kept running.

"Did you see that?!" I shouted.

The commander pivoted into an alley, ascertaining it was empty, and crouched in a shadow.

"*See what?*" she subvocalized.

"That dude, he just— Is he a fucking zombie or something?"

The commander pulled up the memory on her comm. I watched as the boy leaned in and kissed the girl, then they passed out of the commander's field of vision.

"That's not what I saw," I said. "Is that what you saw?"

"*Yes,*" said the commander. "*What did you see?*"

"He . . . bit off her nose. There was a lot of blood. What the hell's going on?"

"*Let me confirm the situation.*"

The commander leaned around the corner, increasing the zoom on her eyes. The couple was still standing there with their arms around each other. That . . . was not the kind of face eating I thought I'd seen. No evidence of blood.

"*Situation normal. How's it look on your end?*"

"Negative over here."

"*Check the contamination filters,*" said the commander. "*I'm going to keep going. Let me know if it happens again.*"

Then she was off again, threading her way through the wind of her own passing. The cobblestones flew underneath her, the exosuit cradling her body and pushing it faster than evolution had ever dreamed we upstart apes could go.

"The hallucination is stable in the ops recording," I said. "That has to be some kind of interference, right?"

"*The tunneling on the ops console is rated for anything up to progressive biphase.*" The commander paused to run up a wall, her boots silently fixing her to the brick. "*Alcebios is the only god here with the passive output to interfere with the connection.*"

"I thought Alcebios hates the other gods. What's she doing in Varas's holy city?"

"*That's the mythology. Never forget the character of Alcebios is a fiction created by the true entity to guide souls back to her. Remember, she helped design the wall. Whatever mask she wears in this culture, what she truly wants is to feed on the etheric energy filtered out by her aspects. There's a lot of death and conflict in a city like this, and if she ever gets out of progressive biphase, she could find scraps for her battle aspect when the soldiers come home.*"

"But then we'd have bigger problems."

"*Much bigger.*" The commander darted down a side street to avoid a party of drunk women, hopping from wall to wall like she was fucking Mario or something. She ended up on a rooftop—flat in this case, and being used to dry laundry—and took a moment to survey the area.

"What actually happens if Alcebios hits triphase? Like, I know she's not stable enough, but what if?"

"*We don't have empirics,*" said the commander. "*But we have well-tested mathematical models for conceptual bleed, and at triphase it would be strong enough to drown out everything else. The interference you experienced would become physical reality across the world. The best case is that the other gods would fight her and win, but they would be starving, and she would be nearly omnipotent.*"

"How would she sustain that level of power expenditure?"

"*She wouldn't,*" said the commander. "*She'd burn through the population in a matter of hours. Then she'd need to expand to other worlds, and each expansion would increase her metabolism.*"

"Shit," I said. "There's gotta be a point where she can't eat fast enough to hold herself together, right?"

"*Some researchers think so,*" said the commander. "*But we're so deep into conjecture by that point that even a slight difference in initial assumptions drastically affects the end result. The question is academic. The only way to ensure Veles doesn't lie in the blast radius is to prevent the scenario from happening. So here we are.*"

It wasn't clear if she was referring to the deicide mission itself or to the watchtower that was now looming above her. It was a long climb. The commander took a deep breath and settled her heart rate with a thought.

"*According to my comm scan, this place is sacred to Javei,*" she said. "*I'd like it recorded in the mission log that I'm attempting a temple breach, given a subjective assessment of minimal risk.*"

"Noted," I said. "You're clear on ops."

That didn't mean anything in this case because I didn't have access to any sensors that she didn't, but you had to say it, anyway.

The commander stepped onto the blessed ground. It felt just like any other ground.

There were sentries posted, but their attention was elsewhere as the commander flitted across the open plaza. She reached the concrete base of the tower and began to climb.

It was like climbing a ladder, but the rungs were a sheer face that her boots and gloves clung to with the implacability of thought. She kept her weight on her boots; the gloves adhered to her hands with the same stubbornness as the walls, but your skin isn't quite that strong. The worst case there was pretty bad.

As I thought that, the commander's hand slipped, and a wet ripping noise accompanied a tearing pain—

"Ow fuck!" I yelled, grabbing my arm in sympathetic pain.

"*Lilith?*" the commander asked. "*Are you okay?*"

"Mm-hmm," I said, not trusting myself to open my mouth. The commander's hand was still in its glove. Her arm was covered in sleeve, rather than finger bones poking through glistening, bloody muscle. She was fine. Everything was fine.

"*What happened?*"

"Interference," I managed. "The glove skinned you."

"*The ops console should have blocked the pain signal,*" said the commander. "*Was that 'ow fuck' just reflexive?*"

"No, I felt it," I said. "I don't know if it was dampened or not. Uh, no comparable experience."

"*It might have been dampened,*" the commander said, confident tone belying a touch of concern in the underlying emotions. She had to know I knew. "*I'll abort if the problem gets worse.*"

"Just get your vantage point and get out."

The tower's face became brick, then wood as she hit the fourth story. She didn't climb all the way to the top—although her glances at it had an evaluative feel to them—but stayed a couple feet below where the sentries were watching. They talked in soft voices as the commander surveilled the city.

From here, she could see over the city's inner walls. Despite the imperfect vantage point, the variable elevation of the inner city exposed a lot of it. The commander was able to mark out several important-looking buildings, one of which we were pretty sure was the imperial palace.

Then she switched to etheric-spectrum analysis and braced herself in shock.

The protections on the palace were even brighter than the ones on the walls. Abby's comm tagged divine signatures from every god in the pantheon. I boggled at the readings—the output was spiking at a hundred eleven *tetrons*; the *Ragnar*'s engines only ran on eighty.

A single spike of radiance towered over the city, ascending into the heavens until it left the range of Abby's comm. The signature was fainter, and there were fewer divine signatures, but we'd seen that frequency before.

"*Lilith—*"

"It's a match," I confirmed, having run the comparison already. "The palace is connected to Kives's orbital shield."

"*So that's what they're protecting in there,*" said the commander. "*Cracking that target is now our top strategic priority, but let's finish the strike first.*"

With one last look at the palace, she began her descent.

"*Good morning,*" Markus called. "*We're about a day from the city, according to the caravan folks.*"

"Morning, big guy," I said. "What's up? How's it going?"

"*Oh, just checking in,*" Markus said. "*We've been missing you guys.*"

"*We have actionable intelligence,*" Val cut in.

"Good morning to you, too." I laughed. "The commander's building our entrance into the city right now. Commander, are you online?"

"*Listening,*" Abby replied. "*I'm occupied. Report.*"

"*Cades and Thala aren't the only contenders here,*" Val said. "*There are five other athletes in the caravan, representing three other towns, and there have been some concerning implications.*"

"Like what?" I asked.

"*Cades wasn't the only athlete with a Merisite shadow,*" Markus said. "*The men themselves won't say anything, but the attendants gossip.*"

"So they *all* had individual whispers assigned to them?"

"*The athletes from Heirou have come the farthest; it seems unlikely that a singular operative was traveling from there to the other towns.*"

"Oh, Darwin," I said. "What the hell do they *want?*"

Abby's voice answered. "*There's only one game in town right now.*"

"*Quite,*" said Val. "*Meris is after the same conduit event that we are.*"

"I thought we were done with whisper bullshit," I groaned. "So what, the Cult of Silence is messing with every athlete in the Kabidiad? What does that even get her?"

"*Meris seems to traffic in open secrets,*" said Val. "*If everyone knows that the man who wins the Kabidiad is a Merisite plant, then Meris can edge Kabiades out of the conduit event. That allows* her *to symbolically marry Varas and reap the rewards of worship.*"

"Fuck."

"*On the bright side,*" Markus said cheerfully, "*it means we would have run into a whisper wherever we went. So Kives didn't set that up for us specifically.*"

It wasn't lost on me that if we succeeded, it prevented Meris from grabbing a hefty power-up. Was that something Kives could time? How deep did that fucker's plans go?

"*It should go without saying,*" said the commander, "*but we can't allow Meris's operation to succeed. We're going for the throat on this one.*"

"Yes, commander," I answered along with the guys.

"*Markus, I need you networking. Identify the competitors who don't have Merisite associations so we can get them in a position to win if you can't.*"

"*I will,*" he said.

"*Your other job is influence. Val, this will be your primary objective. We don't have time to do this the safe way. I need direct-level influence on every noble involved with decision-making. Get me blood.*"

"*By your command,*" Val said, deadpan.

"*Lilith, once the access tunnel is complete, let's see if we can get you into the city.*"

"I thought I wasn't going into the city."

"*We're still keeping you off social infiltration, but I'll need a second knife. I want every whisper in the city killed or compromised before the opening ceremony.*"

"I think my birthday just came early," I said.

"*This is it, team. We have a god in the crosshairs. No mistakes. No mercy. They fall!*"

"They die!"

CHAPTER SIXTY-NINE

Extermination

By midmorning the next day, the boys caught sight of the city walls. The commander had suited up in formal military dress, which was her custom when preparing for a deicide strike. I'd never seen her do it myself—that little op in Salaphi didn't count—but Markus had told me before.

The Eifni Organization's formal uniform was multilayered, a tunic-like long belted shirt over slacks. Over all that was a *hakmir*, a sleeved ankle-length outer garment halfway between a cape and a trench coat. As a field operative, Abby wore a uniform sewn in dark greens and blacks, with her rank indicated by a strip of white cloth running along the inside of her collar. The ceremonial scabbard belted around her *hakmir* was empty for symbolic reasons—less "I am unarmed" and more "my blade will never be sheathed."

Full dress regulations required that the soldier's medals be worn on the left breast of the *hakmir*, but for relaxed formal dress, we were permitted to commission a *hakmir* with the equivalent patches instead. A three-hundred-year veteran, Abby had only opted for the vertical red bar representing the Red Dagger, the medal awarded for personally pulling the trigger on a pantheon-level god.

She had eleven of those: two millimeter-perfect rows of five and one calmly biding its time as the beginning of a third.

I showed up in my own formals. Nothing much to speak of, just a Liberation Star for participating in a planetside action during my probation mission with the team. Abby probably had a pile of those in a drawer somewhere. My collar bar was black to her white, and I'd worn Lilith instead of an empty scabbard.

Abby threw me a *look* when I walked in, which I met evenly. There were layers to the act of—right after she told me to stop treating her like a mother—showing up dressed exactly like her. But I was still her apprentice, and I was explicitly walking in her footsteps. This was me saying I was still committed to that, not out of maternal trauma or anything, but because I knew where the road led, and I was willing to walk it.

The commander came to some private decision and moved on without commenting.

"Step one is getting Val and Markus into position."

The boys were greeted at the city gates by the sound of sizzling and the smell of grilled seafood. From my position manning the ops console, I smelled it through two different noses. It should have been overwhelming—especially given both of the noses I was borrowing had their own take on it—but the console did the lion's share of the work, synthesizing those experiences into something my solitary mind could process.

The caravan pulled off Merchants' Road into one of the designated unloading areas. The caravan master ordered everyone to remain with the wagons while she and a handful of guards went to negotiate lodgings. From the way the caravanners had already sprawled out, preparing to kill time, this was probably standard procedure. Some of the Dancers looked uncomfortable; between the caravan master's guards and the suspiciously defensive positioning of the wagons, I wondered whether there was a history of violence there.

"The fishermen of Bulcephine have earned their honor today!" Cades laughed as Markus and Val joined him at one of the stalls.

There was a twinge of sadness from Markus at that, which I didn't pry into.

"The honor belongs to the All-Mother," the vendor said, smiling as they approached her. "A *thessim* ago, she drew one of Horcutio's brood from the deep and slaughtered it to feed the city."

That *bitch*. "That was *my* kill!"

"You're selling *thessim*-old meat?" asked Val.

"Much of it was miraculously preserved," said the vendor, smiling. "Entirely undecayed, untouched by rot! The sweetest octopus flesh I've ever tasted—for you, five *drobol*."

"Please tell me it's not radioactive."

Val scanned the meat with his comm and shook his head slightly.

"The harbor must be clogged with fishermen," Cades said, furrowing his brow.

"Like my father-in-law's sphincter," the vendor laughed.

"Will they finish before the pentathlon?"

The vendor eyed his build and gave him a knowing look. "The sea is still frothing red, friend. Horcutio's other children came for their due. Anyone who falls in never makes it out. We've got some time before the Kabidiad, but they might need to cancel the swimming portion."

"I hate Kives so much," I groaned. "What the fuck is she up to now?"

"Disappointing." Cades laughed. "I've been waiting years to show the men of Vitareas a real pentathlon. Fate had other plans, it seemed."

Markus felt sad again.

"Dude, what gives?" I asked him.

"*This isn't him,*" he subvocalized, looking at his boyfriend with a heavy heart. "*This is what they made him.*"

"Baby steps," I said reassuringly. "He'll get there."

Markus sighed. *"Sometimes the moment comes too late."*

"We'll have Markus with the other competitors in the Course of Honor," Abby continued the briefing. "We don't know if the Merisites will attempt a strike, so Val will be on bodyguard duty. Keep up the mercenary cover. Mixed-detector overlays active at all times."

"Am I the one who needs that reminder?" Val drawled.

"I know where you sleep," I said.

"I don't know what you think I was implying," he said without any trace of the smugness that was 100 fucking percent there.

"I'm just saying keep your MDO active at all times," I said with a smile, absently tracing a finger over the pommel of my sword. "Right, commander?"

Abby threw me an amused look and continued. "Val, we've got reason to believe that your targets will be active around the Course of Honor in the days leading up to the Kabidiad. I need you to compromise as many as you can. You have discretion of method."

The Course of Honor rose above the surrounding buildings. Stadiums are the same in every universe—they're all built to maximize the number of people who can see the race. There's only so many ways to solve that problem. I'd been expecting something like the Colosseum back on Earth, but while I'd been right on the arches, I wasn't expecting the whole thing to be made from colorful brickwork. Yellows and greens in flowing patterns made the whole thing look like an art installation, rather than the imminent site of the last Himbo Olympics.

The three guys stopped for a moment to admire the construction. Their invisible tail stopped, too.

"MDO picking up a signature on your right," I said.

"I've got it," Val subvocalized. *"Always a hair out of striking distance, that one."*

"We could nudge her closer," I offered.

"Stick to the plan," the commander interjected.

"Yeah, yeah."

Markus and Cades were processed by shirtless priests of Kabiades while Val leaned against the wall and observed the proceedings with a detached air. I'd always found it interesting how the commander vanished into any role you gave her while Val was always somehow himself. Something to meditate on the next time I worked on my *ak ha var*.

Three priests scurried across the hallways, followed by the sound of a feminine voice issuing rapid-fire commands. The voice drew closer, then an obviously upper-class woman rounded the corner.

"Agoura," she said curtly. "How many this morning?"

"Three dozen and four," the priest handling Markus replied.

"Dutiful," she complimented him.

She looked up at Val, who met her stare with the same bemused detachment he'd used on everything else.

"Insolent man. Watch your eyes."

Val tilted his head ever so slightly to the side in challenge.

"I'm a free blade. If you want to give me orders, pay my fee."

He smirked.

The noblewoman eyed him up and down.

She smirked back.

"You're not going to have me on ops while he's seducing people, are you?" I pleaded with Abby.

"*Don't tell me you've never wondered what it feels like to have an erection,*" Markus said.

"Why the fuck would I wonder about that kind of shit?"

"*I did,*" Markus said with a verbal shrug.

"There's a privacy filter. Use it," Abby said. "Moving on to information ops. Markus, get Cades to help you spread the story that you're the only noncompromised candidates in the tournament. The Merisites will be trying to counter you, so Lilith and I will get ahead of them."

"*There's no way we beat out the cult of sneaking at a rumor game on their home turf,*" Markus said. "*This is a risk.*"

"You can only lie so much before you have to deal with the real world," said the commander. "In their terms, truth of the hand beats truth of the eyes. And it just so happens that we have the hand available."

"See that Oathkeeper?" Abby slurred to her new drinking buddy. "He's from Vitareas."

"With the gears?" her buddy said.

"Yeah," Abby said. "And the . . . the lights."

"Ghostlights."

"Yeah." Abby raised a finger, as if about to articulate an important thought. "Bright there." She deflated, the finger dropping.

"Mmm," her buddy said.

"Cult of Silence has been running *rings* around everyone, you know," said Abby. "They're gonna get away with it."

"It?"

"It," Abby nodded. "But that Oathkeeper Falerior? Not him. He stopped them. Only one who did."

"Wow," her buddy said, looking over at the ex-policeman.

Falerior had clearly seen better days, but he was still the affable asshole I'd spent all my time avoiding. Abby had her comm filtering his voice out to keep track of his conversations, and while he'd started out asking about Salaphi, the rumors about Merisite interference with the Kabidiad had clearly caught his attention.

"I think," Abby said self-importantly. "I think everyone needs to know."

The commander pretended not to notice as a man behind her stood up, settled his tab, and casually made his way to the door. He was my responsibility now.

The sound of strumming announced that the inn's bard was about to perform. Abby listened with interest to the opening notes of the song.

She'd paid him to write it.

Abby took a drink and I choked at the taste of thick, warm, syrupy blood clogging up her throat.

"What the fuck are you drinking?" I gagged.

"*Passable beer*," Abby subvocalized. "*Why?*"

"Does it taste like blood to you?"

"*No.*"

"What the fucking fuck," I said. "I need a fucking breath mint. I feel sick."

"*More conceptual bleed.*" The commander eyed her beer warily. "*You shouldn't be gagging. The ops console doesn't do that.*"

"Not for baseline conceptual bleed," Val commented. The privacy filter blocked most of his physical feedback, which was a mercy. "Even at progressive biphase, the effect is too great. Alcebios has turned her attention on Bulcephine."

My stomach sank. "Is that bad?"

"We're about to kill a god," Val said. "Would you prefer the goddess of death find us boring?"

"*But more importantly,*" said the commander. "*We are Eifni operatives. Beating the enemy on their own turf is what we train to do. Lilith, if we can get you into the city, I'm assigning you to be Lirian's handler.*"

I didn't bother hiding my vicious satisfaction at seeing the smile wiped off Lirian's fucking face.

"Forget I'm here," I ordered her. "Forget who I am. I am no one. I am the voice of the gods in your ear. You will follow these instructions, and then you will forget."

She was struggling against the blood contagion. You could see it on her face—she knew something was wrong with her, she could feel Val's hooks in her soul. Her eyes struggled in and out of focus, and she kept almost becoming part of the background. One minute she was standing there and the next she was just part of the scenery. Your eyes glazed over when you looked at her.

But the first order I'd given her was not to disappear.

"You *are* somebody," I'd said with a grin. Now every time she failed to disappear, there was a delicious look of frustration in her eyes as she glared at me.

"Take this necklace," I said. "Can you touch your cult buddies and make it seem natural?"

Lirian nodded stiffly, as if she was trying to force herself not to.

"Great," I said happily. "Touch the pendent on the necklace, then touch them. Everyone you can. Make it natural. Forget you did it. Forget you're doing it on purpose. Do it without noticing. Is this sinking in?"

Lirian nodded painfully again.

"I like you better this way," I said. "I was never here. Stay here for a minute, then forget this whole conversation."

I turned to walk away, stopped, and turned back.

"Before I go," I said, considering. "You know what? Stick with the classics. Punch yourself in the face."

"I hope you can use your newfound power responsibly," Abby said drily.

"I am the very soul of responsibility," I lied.

"We can try to force her to give up her secrets later," said the commander. "We can always get another whisper. For now, we minimize our interference with her behavior and focus on mapping the whole network. *Do not* access the data until we're ready. We don't know how many of them can tell when they're being observed. If they realize Lirian is compromised, they can react."

"Okay, but what about after she's gotten a bunch?" I asked.

Abby looked at me blankly.

"No more games. Kill them."

The man from the inn turned the corner and hurried down an alley. I sighed, disconnected from the ops console, and stretched a bit. The shack I was squatting in smelled of old, musty liquor, and I didn't care for it. Time to get some fresh air.

I secured my sword belt as I stepped outside, right as the man approached my shack.

"Yo," I said.

"Godsmile," he said, trying to get around me.

I stepped to the side, blocking his path.

"Excuse me, miss," he said, averting his eyes.

"Have you heard the good news of our lord and savior Meris?" I asked brightly.

He looked up at me in surprise. "What news?"

"Dunno. It's probably a fucking secret like everything else."

My fist caught him in the solar plexus, driving his breath out. He wheezed, doubling over as I grabbed his head and smashed it down into my kneepad. He cried out, and something crunched. It wasn't the kneepad.

I stepped to the side and threw him to the ground, drawing Lilith from her scabbard. The man was scrabbling to get up, but I stomped on his ankle and levered him onto his back with my foot.

"You've got five seconds to rat out your buddies before I kill you," I said, the tip of my sword hovering under his throat. "What's your plan? Give me something I can work with here."

"Hands find their way! Hands find their way!" the dude moaned, squirming in pain.

"Not this bullshit again," I said. "Two seconds. I'm being super generous here."

"Why?" he asked, holding his ruined nose.

"Time's up," I said.

Could I actually kill this dude? He was . . . pathetic. He'd barely put up a fight at all.

On the other hand, Lirian *had* put up a fight, and look where that had gotten me.

He must have seen the decision in my eyes. "No no no *no*—"

I cut.

Lilith sliced through his throat like paper. His arm was in the way, and she cut through that too.

CHAPTER SEVENTY

The Kabidiad

Twas the night before Sportsmas, and all through the house, not a creature was stirring except for—

"You motherfucking silence cultists, I swear to Darwin," I said, waving Lilith at the fuzzy blur that my MDO said was an enemy. "What did you think was going to happen here?"

The blur didn't move.

"I can't fucking hear you." I sighed. "Come on. Is it a knife? Are you holding a knife? I've got reach on you, hiding isn't going to help. Drop the cloak."

The blur slowly retreated one step.

"Get the *fuck* away from those doors!"

I lunged forward, bringing my sword up for a strike. The blur stopped moving. Then it faded, and I noticed there was a woman standing there. Not Lirian. Phrecian, not Estheni—they tended to have lighter hair, and she had the face tattoos that none of the Estheni understood how to decipher. My comm read them as an identifier, probably a clan marking.

"Peace," the woman said. "I am not your enemy."

"Lady, it's three in the fucking morning, and the fact that you showed up means me sitting here bored out of my skull all night was *your fault,* so don't try my fucking patience," I said. "Either you were trying to get caught or you weren't, and whispers don't get fucking caught. You were here to stab someone, right?"

"The lady's secrets are not mine to share," the woman said with an odd little smile. "But I see you have her gifts, as well. Am I to take this clumsy questioning at face value, or is it merely a truth of the eyes?"

"Ask me how patient I am. Go ahead. Fucking ask."

"Does it matter?" the woman said. "Everyone will have heard a woman's voice shouting about whispers in the athletes' housing where she did not belong. It's done. Whatever your branch cult has planned, your eye-truth has perished. The supposedly incorruptible Vitarean contenders are no longer above suspicion."

I stared at her blankly.

"I keep telling you people about the fucking monologues," I said. "You really weren't ready for this, were you?"

She arched an eyebrow. "Ready for wh—"

Lilith impaled her between the ribs, puncturing her lung and punching out the other side, pinning her to the door. The immediate collapse of air pressure cut off her speech. Her mouth opened and closed, but only a gurgling rasp escaped as her eyes dulled and she went into shock. A final, sticky cough expelled a gush of blood down my sword, then she fell unconscious, slumping against the door.

My comm could read her now. The etheric weapon had cut through her blessing. Not dead yet, but no one was going to save her.

She was right that everyone probably heard that, but the Cult of Silence was fundamentally unprepared to play the game against Veleans. All their strategies were designed for other whispers—and you didn't just *kill* other whispers; you left them alive to play their part somewhere else.

These idiots didn't know how to react to an outside-context problem who actually wanted to win.

The Amazing Lungless Wonder over here had failed to anticipate the strategy that would have been obvious to any Academy graduate: knifing the other dude and controlling the narrative over his dead body.

My sword jerked out of my hand as the door swung open, revealing an adorably bedraggled Cades with a sword of his own.

"Ajarel?" he said with surprise, glancing at the bloody sword tip poking through his door. "Gods above, what have you done?"

"Officially, that was you now," I said. "Nice to see you, too, by the way. Put the sword away, you're borrowing mine for a bit. *For a bit.* I want it back."

Cades ignored me, stepping gingerly around the door to look at the corpse.

"Why?" he whispered.

"She was trying to stab you," I said. "C'mon, dude, you know what Lirian did back in Vitareas. These guys are terrible."

Cades gave the body a long look. "I thank the gods I was born a man," he said at last. "I do not have your strength."

I left out a sharp, frustrated breath. "Dude," I said. "Seriously? That's where you're going with this?"

He didn't respond, continuing to look at the body.

"Alright, look," I said. "I've got a kind of, uh, silencing spell on this hallway. I'm gonna drop it after I explain the plan, but first, we *have* to talk about this, man."

"Is now really the best time?" Cades asked.

"Yes. Shut up. Okay, so, where I come from, they think you guys have it all backward. We think women are these weak, emotional creatures who need men to make all the hard choices."

"That's absurd," said Cades.

"Your mom's absurd," I said. I rolled over him before he could respond to that. "They're both wrong. People are just people, dude. We did, uh, really good philosophy on it, and it turns out that whether you're a man or a woman doesn't affect things that much. The strongest woman is gonna be stronger than like ninety-nine percent of guys."

"Surely not stronger than me," Cades said with a brief, pained smile. His face fell. "I didn't mean that kind of strength. I'm a—"

He fell silent. *Coward,* the unspoken word hung between us.

Like, literally. Military-grade comms are cheating, and I was never, ever giving mine up.

"C'mon, man," I said. "Weren't you, like, a soldier? That takes a ton of courage."

"I wasn't killing . . . women," said Cades, looking at the corpse. "It was on a battlefield."

"You think this is any less of a fucking battlefield 'cause they're not wearing armor?" I asked. "She was going to stab you."

"Maybe she should have," said Cades.

"Charles fucking Darwin," I groaned. "Okay, this is above my pay grade. This is officially a Thala problem. Go cuddle up with him or something. Doctor's orders."

Cades reddened. "You show me more patience than I deserve."

"No!" I pinched the bridge of my nose. "Listen to me, you muscle-brained moron, it's *not your fault*! None of this is your fault! They taught you that you were gross and weird, and you *let* them, and now you think it's true! You think Thala is a bad judge of character?"

"I— No—"

"I believe you can stab as many people as you want," I said, patting him on the shoulder. "Men, women, and—well, anyone who tries to stab you, anyway. You told me you'd stab me if I tried to make you a slave, remember?"

"That was in the heat of the moment," Cades said quickly.

"These fucks?" I said, pointing to the corpse. "They made you their slave. All of you. So in a moment, I'm going to drop the sonic—I mean, the silencing spell, and I need you to tell everyone that she was a Merisite and you killed her because she was trying to cripple you. I was never here, okay?"

"I . . ." Cades started, looking extremely overwhelmed.

"For fuck's sake," I muttered, storming over to the door next to Cades's. I kicked it a couple times. "*Markus, wake the fuck up. Your boyfriend is having an existential crisis.*"

"*What did you do to him?*" came the immediate reply.

"*Wow, that's your first response? This is fucking persecution.*"

Markus emerged almost immediately.

"Cades," he said soothingly, moving toward him. "My little soldier."

Cades turned bright red at that. I coughed, looking anywhere but at Markus, who apparently slept naked and had not bothered to put anything on. I was so embarrassed, I wished I could vanish.

After a moment's reflection, I decided to do just that.

"Baton fucking passed," I said, and disappeared.

It doesn't take that much damage to cripple an organization. Knock out one in ten people and you can bring everything crashing to a halt. The Cult of Silence was smart about that, at least: they kept their people compartmentalized, each whisper reporting to a superior and otherwise remaining ignorant of the others.

But here, like so many other ways, they weren't prepared to face the Eifni Organization. The Cult of Silence still held religious services. We'd given Lirian a device that was functionally etheric paint. She might not have known who attended those midnight rituals with her, but a brush of the fingers was all it took to mark them for death.

Secrecy should have been their defense, but we'd weaponized it against them. News traveled slowly among Merisite channels, so even though I'd killed about thirty whispers over the last week, only a few of them had known their lives were in danger. Those ones put up more of a fight, which made me feel better about putting them down.

Now the Kabidiad was here. They'd been working the rumor mill pretty hard, but we'd made Falerior into a folk hero, and the affable ex-Oathkeeper had played his part perfectly. The counterrumors the Merisites had spread only lasted until they reached someone who'd met the man. Here, too, they'd played themselves: the religiously mandated showboating about their operations made it too easy for people to side with the humble truth seeker against the whispers trying to delegitimize him.

They probably would have figured it out eventually. It wouldn't have helped; we'd been scraping Lirian's mind every night to counter their plans. There are tools to beat that kind of information advantage, but the Merisites didn't know them.

We'd successfully run out the clock. The athletes were assembling before the Pallastine Gates, clad in nothing but their competition thongs and six flower garlands—two on each arm, two around the neck. Markus and Cades stood next to each other, not holding hands. They might as well have been, for all the etheric radiation they were throwing off.

A chorus of horns sounded, a warlike drone that was taken up all over the city. The crowd cheered as though trying to drown out the horns. With a rumbling noise, the Pallastine Gates opened.

Behind them, the Course of Honor awaited.

The athletes began a song about being like Kabiades, marching in time to the beat.

"We men of honor, / children of the Striver, / battle mates of the Lancer, / lovers in-the-idiom-of the Divine Consort," they sang. I grimaced as my comm forced the English translation into the wrong number of syllables.

The athletes marched through the gates, three abreast. They were a diverse group—mostly Estheni, but seemingly every ethnicity in the Imperial Coalition had at least token representation. Their body types ranged from leaner twinks to muscle heads like our boys. Markus and Cades weren't even the biggest dudes there—that honor went to a seven-foot goliath in the first rank of the parade who was giving off a divine signature. A demigod of Kabiades, or maybe a really weak godseed. Comm wasn't freaking out enough for that.

"Commander," I said.

"*I see him,*" came the reply. "*We'll deal with him later.*"

I took my hand off my disruptor pistol.

I gave Markus and Cades a thumbs-up as they passed. They ignored me, probably because I was invisible. Whatever, it's the thought that counts.

Readjusting the straps of the duffel bag on my back, I strolled through the gates with the athletes. There were side doors to the arena's interior, and I slipped through the one on the right.

My comm laid out my path. Val and the commander had done the necessary recon, calculating the optimal locations to place the amplifiers that would kill Kabiades. I followed their directions, dodging priests and slaves going about their duties as I made my way to an auxiliary storeroom in the corner of the building.

According to my comm, the commander had prepared an empty barrel in the corner. She'd used a translation device to drain all the wine, then slipped a stealth device inside.

My eyes slid over it a couple of times before I sighed and realized I'd need to drop my cloak so I could use absence meditation. Hopefully no one barged in while I was working.

I pulled a crowbar and a mallet out of the duffel, then dropped the cloak. Sinking into absence meditation took a few nerve-racking moments, but eventually I dulled my noetic senses enough that I could notice the damn thing. I pried off the top of the barrel with the crowbar, dropped the whole duffel in—gently, of course; Val would kill me if I damaged one of his amplifiers—and hammered the top back on.

I slapped an MDO over the door on my way out.

"Five down, three to go," I reported.

"*I'm nearly done here,*" said the commander. "*Val, do you have signal?*"

"*Confirmed,*" said Val. "*I need the receiver on the empress until the opening ceremony is over, then you can move it back on the judges.*"

"*Got it. How's that?*"

"*Perfect.*" I could imagine the look on Val's face as he reclined back in the command center. Once he got the empress's signature, he would need to solve the conversion equations that would make her a perfect symbol of Varas in the eyes of the amplifiers. He'd be monitoring several soul links at the same time. None of us had any doubt he could pull it off.

For my part, I had to lug three more amplifiers inside. Invisibility was really a curse when you thought about it.

I sat down heavily in the noble's box the commander had secured, dropping the cloak as I did so.

"Annnnd that's all of th— *Holy shit,*" I said, recoiling from the sword the commander had pressed to my throat.

"Language," Abby said mildly. "Do we need to have another chat about surprising your allies in the field?"

"I'm gonna be honest, I didn't see the sword," I said, gingerly nudging the blade away from my throat.

"That is when you should be most wary of the sword."

Abby tucked the weapon back into a niche next to her seat. Okay, c'mon, how was I supposed to see that? It was completely out of sight to anyone walking in the door!

I glanced at the woman on Abby's left. She appeared to be paying attention to the opening ceremony, but the stiffness in her posture and the way she seemed completely oblivious to us belied the soul link that was controlling her behavior. A platter of assorted cheeses and fruits sat untouched next to her.

"How's the lady Yotharios?" I asked.

"The compulsions are holding," said Abby. "Worst case, she dies ahead of schedule."

I stared at her a little more. "It's kinda creepy when you don't hate their guts. Shouldn't we just put her out of her misery?"

"She needs to be seen up here," said Abby. "The more windows we give Kives, the more chances she has to engineer an interruption."

"She could have interrupted me during any of the amplifiers," I said. "She might seriously be letting us do this."

"Do you see Kives's sword?" Abby asked.

I sighed. Point taken.

"Looks like the empress is up," I said instead of answering.

The chief priest of Kabiades—I guess he was like their pope? Muscle Pope?—was concluding his remarks about honor and striving for glory and all that. He commanded all present to bow before the empress and relinquished his podium.

The empress stood up, walking to an elevated section of her viewing box. She wore a golden headdress and three colorful layers of shawls, each designed to allow the others below it to peek through. She had a commanding presence and an echoing voice, which I didn't pay attention to because of all the alarms my comm was throwing off.

"Oh fuck," I said. "I guess we found her sword."

"The target is a godseed," the commander said. "Repeat, target is a godseed. Markus, you're authorized to abort."

Markus didn't respond immediately.

"Let me shoot her," I said, looking the commander in the eyes. "We've got the rifle up here."

"*If* Markus calls the mission abort," said the commander. "Markus?"

"*Not yet,*" he said slowly.

"This one's strong enough to do permanent soul damage," said the commander. "We don't know its abilities, but you're not fast enough to land a strike on it."

"*You're welcome to switch,*" Markus said.

"Don't get yourself killed," Abby said softly.

"*I'll figure something out,*" said Markus. "*Trust me.*"

Abby and I exchanged a look. She left out a slow breath through her nose.

"Let the record show that Eifni operative C3-32-3204, self-designation Markus, social officer, has consented to direct contact with a hostile godseed. Stop that, Lilith."

Under Abby's glare, I noticed myself sinking into the cloak. Sheepishly, I shut it off.

"It's just an enemy," she said. "You know how to deal with them."

"Thanks, Mom."

She pelted me with a grape.

Abby turned to a tripod-mounted device she'd set up behind a decorative tapestry. The tapestry blocked people outside the box from seeing it, but this was a military-grade etheric scanner. It would have no trouble punching through the weak semiotic interference the tapestry presented.

"I've got the target on the scanner," said the commander. "How's it look, Val?"

The only response that came through was laughter.

"Val?"

"*It's a godseed of Varas,*" Val said. "*I don't even need to do the conversion equations. She's already the perfect asset for this strike.*"

I frowned, glancing at the commander. "This has to be a trap. It's too perfect."

"*It's Markus's decision,*" said Val.

"*And I said you should trust me,*" Markus said. "*Let's get through the passion events as though we're committing. We don't need to abort until the end. I can throw a race or two if I have to.*"

"As long as I get to shoot her when you do," I said.

The demigod I noticed earlier had empowerments in a lot of areas, and apparently one of them was massage. We learned his name was Pereges shortly before learning that he was a Problem.

"*I'm running semantic-feedback analysis on some of the judges,*" Val said. "*According to these results, they've been instructed that Pereges is supposed to win.*"

Unlike with Lirian and Lady Yotharios, we hadn't escalated to direct control with our compromised judges. Yet. Forcing them to vote for Markus didn't automatically make him win; we had to avoid obvious behavioral weirdness that would undermine confidence in our judges. Especially since Val hadn't "compromised"—ugh—all the sixtysomething women involved with judging the Kabidiad.

But what Val *could* do was introduce particular concepts via the soul link and see how the targets responded. They'd experience them as nothing more than passing thoughts, unaware that our technical officer was harvesting all the semantic associations that those thoughts dislodged in their minds.

"I could shoot him," I offered. "That would solve a lot of problems, really."

"It would put the Cult of Silence back in the running," Abby said with a frown. "If our candidate wins after his competition suffers a mysterious injury, everyone knows what that means."

"Fucking eye-truths," I muttered. "How about I poke them all in the eyes, huh? See how they like it then?"

"*That would be a hand-truth,*" Val said, like a traitor.

"We don't have time for this," the commander said. "These massages aren't long. Val. Burn one of your assets. She resents the order and wants to take Pereges down. Let her rationalize the reasoning."

"*On it.*"

"Markus, introduce a little dissonance with the hand amplifier. Don't push it if the divine blessing interferes at all."

"We only had three out of five of those judges, right?" I asked. "We might lose our majority."

"We have the tech advantage," Abby said. "All we need is the plausible deniability to use it. We didn't need soul links to win in Vitareas."

"It's gotta be the empress who ordered this, right?" I asked. "If I had to get married to whoever won this thing, I'd make some fucking decisions about it."

"We'll see how hard she fights Val on it," Abby said.

I pulled up Markus's feed, watching as one of the judges directed a question to the giant demigod.

"Is she the one we're spending?" I asked.

"*Yes,*" Markus said.

The other judges looked surprised and concerned. The look on Pereges's face made it clear that he wasn't happy about it. The awkwardness was thick enough that you could feel it—courtesy of the hand amplifier in Markus's thong. He wasn't *just* happy to see you.

"I may have misheard," the demigod said slowly in Markus's feed.

"I asked, is it abominable for a woman to direct her husbands to have sex with each other, as it would be if they had no wife?"

"Wait, isn't that what they asked you?" I asked.

"*Word for word,*" Markus subvocalized. "*It must be a quote from something.*"

"*Not a Kabiadesian source,*" Val said. "*Gamalite, perhaps.*"

The big dude's face spoke volumes, and all the pages of those volumes were covered in variations of, "What the fuck, this is not supposed to be happening right now."

"I . . ." he said, "would not presume to judge a woman's actions as abominable."

"Even if she orders the abominable?"

"Well, that's not to say— I mean, it is abominable. Everyone knows that."

"So you condemn the wife's decision for her husbands."

"I— No."

From the looks our lady was getting, she had just torpedoed her political career. But that didn't matter; the damage was done. Even if it was an unfair question, the dude had gone down in flames. Markus had already done spectacularly; we had our shot. If he helped Cades out we might even be able to bump Pereges down to third.

"*If this doesn't work, there's always the physical events,*" Markus said. He sounded subdued.

"We have more control here," said the commander. "This opponent has divine enhancements, and they're clearly not for his brain. I'm not trusting all of this to a physical contest."

"*Just a thought,*" said Markus. "*Val, I need a favor.*"

"*Now?*"

"*Push Cades through, too. Ahead of me.*"

"*Hm.*"

Abby tapped her fingers on the armrest of her seat. "Is this part of your secret plan?"

"*Something like that.*"

The commander considered.

"Fine," she said. "I trust you. Val, do it. Lilith, you and I get to figure out how to stop a demigod."

I grinned. "I have an excellent track record there."

"Without shooting him in the face."

"Oh. That's a lot harder."

We fell into silence. My face brightened, and I lifted a finger.

"What about—"

"No shooting him anywhere else, either."

CHAPTER SEVENTY-ONE

They Fall, They Die

The problem with the pentathlon events was that it was really annoying to cheat.

An Eifni deicide team is a precision instrument designed for slow insinuation into a culture. We are the boiling pot, introducing change so slowly you don't notice before it's too late. You don't know you've been visited by godslayers until you wake up three hundred years later and no one believes in the old religions anymore.

Even the heaviest ship will turn if given a slight push over decades. The Eifni Organization has optimized to create that push by utilizing social influence, soft power, and an absolute information advantage.

Turns out, none of that is useful when it comes to rigging a contest about running really fast.

The five events of the Estheni pentathlon were wrestling, sword fighting, javelin throwing, distance running, and swimming. Cades and Markus were certainly going to do well, but they had to do better than Pereges. Otherwise we'd end up with a conduit event involving a godseed of Varas and a demigod of Kabiades, and instead of killing Kabiades we'd have to watch as both of them grew stronger.

It would have been great if we could just drown Pereges during the swimming event, but it was canceled this year. The water was still unsafe, even though the blood was mostly gone from the harbor. The empress had decreed that they weren't gonna fuck with Horcutio's wrath—I'm paraphrasing here—and knocked it down to a quadrathlon.

Convenient for our boys, who hadn't gotten a lot of swimming lessons over the last year. But suspiciously convenient for Pereges, who was now much harder to get rid of. Given who was ultimately behind the harbor closure in the first place, it raised some worrying questions.

This wasn't like Elsinat, where Kives had trolled us over passengers for our fake pilgrimage. There was no humor to it. She'd managed to arrange things so that this op collided with a Merisite operation years in the making, then set up an obstacle in the form of Pereges that would punish us if we pulled out.

She'd maneuvered us to a position where we had to thread a very narrow path, and that path ended with Markus within bite range of a godseed. Most concerningly, she'd passed up every opportunity to stop us.

From a Velean perspective, the implicit offer was clear. We could cooperate, or she could force a trade. And Kives had more pieces to spend.

"I don't like the idea of a demigod hooking up with a godseed," I said. "Depending on what happens in that relationship, Pereges might develop into a godseed, too. Then all of this becomes worse than pointless."

"*Kabiades can't immediately rebirth himself in that case,*" Val said. "*We'd have to assume that Kives can pick the best possible timing to restore him from the godseed, but a successful strike on Kabiades would leave a lasting wound in etherspace. He would have a shadow of his former power.*"

"None of that matters against someone who can call her shots this well," I argued. "I think Markus should focus on knocking Pereges out of the contest, even if he loses, too."

"*I'd be willing,*" said Markus. "*But let's not give up hope of winning yet.*"

"That's how Kives hooks us!" I said.

"We'll consider it a last resort," said the commander. "For now, let's wait and see."

"*Hold on, they're briefing us on the pentathlon,*" Markus told us. "*Sounds like we're running a lap around the city instead of swimming down the coast and running back.*"

I steepled my fingers. "That'll take them near the ship."

"*Oh— Grandfather of an octopus,*" Markus swore, a phrase from his culture of origin. I'd never dared ask what it meant; the etheric overtones were heavily sexual. "*You know how the top-ranked performers in the passion events get to go first? Pereges is in our group.*"

"He shouldn't be," said Abby.

"*Someone put their thumb on the scales,*" Markus said. "*Well, we tried.*"

"Are we sure you can't outrun him?" I asked.

"*With all those blessings? I don't know what all of them do, but I'm not arrogant enough to think I can outperform that much etheric power just because my muscles are made from extra-spicy meat.*"

Abby tapped her fingers on her chair. "If we can't speed you up, we can slow him down. Val, rig the translation engines for carbon dioxide."

"*Clever,*" Val said. "*I should be able to walk the output in front of him. Markus, make sure you stay out of the affected area.*"

"*I'll need to keep Cades out of the way,*" Markus subvocalized. "*Let me go talk to him.*"

"Tell him I said he's allowed to stab people," I said.

"*I will not.*"

Pereges jogged right through the oxygen-free zone like it wasn't there.

"*Uh, Val?*" Markus said.

"*Give me a moment,*" Val snapped.

Watching through Markus's feed, I saw him glance back at some runners following behind the giant demigod. The effects were diminished, as Val was targeting Pereges, but several of them started wheezing, and one had to stop and gasp for air.

"*Wasteful clown of a god,*" Val seethed. "*I can't believe this.*"

"I'm pretty sure the clown god is Rucks," I said.

Val ignored me. "*Kabiades put individual blessings on* each muscle. *And—why would you ever* do that to his lungs? *Who in their right mind uses reflexive translation for godflaming* oxygen?"

"So the god of himbos also gives you dumb himbo blessings?" I asked.

"*Seems so,*" Markus said. "*I don't think Cades and I can catch him, but we won't fall too behind.*"

I looked at Abby. "Let me know if you want me to shoot him."

"Keep a level head," she ordered me. "Val, enough. We have more chances at this."

"That's what Kives wants us to think," I said gloomily.

"This isn't my first kill," the commander said. "Stay focused. I will not allow us to get lost in a metastrategic game of subverted expectations. Kives does *not* control us."

"Yes'm," I sighed.

"Let's prep for the next attempt," said the commander. "It's the javelin toss after this. The utility translator is in the corner."

"Where?"

"There."

"I'm not seeing— God damnit, commander."

"Glad to see you're keeping up with your absence meditations. Try not to get skewered."

I waited until I was invisible to flip her off.

The Kabidiad was not the Olympics. There was that beauty pageant element to it, and a lot more emphasis on what we'd consider the fine arts back on Earth, but it wasn't a sports tournament.

It was training for war.

There wasn't a break. After completing their jog—some of them more oxygenated than others—the athletes were immediately handed javelins. They had one minute to paint symbols on the tips. Then they had to hurl them at a cluster of wooden shields on the other end of the Course of Honor. The competitors who punctured shields would score well—if it was farther back, even better.

The weak point of this system was the lack of instant replay cameras, like we had back on Earth. If the symbol on a winning spear were to suddenly change, who could prove it?

I grinned, invisibly hefted the utility translator, and stepped out into the arena.

Markus and Cades came in together, right on Pereges's heels.

"*Make sure you get a look at the beefcake's autograph,*" I subvocalized to Markus.

"*On it.*"

I pulled up Markus's feed. The priests of Kabiades were hastily ordering the athletes into groups of twelve, and our favorite muscle heads had just missed the cutoff for the first group. Markus craned his head, zooming in with his eyes to catch a glimpse of the demigod's symbol.

The first group finished painting. Rather than let them catch their breath, the Muscle Pope led them all in a hymn to the Lancer while the paint dried. That was a common trick for the clockless Estheni—the length of the hymn served as a timer.

"Val, can you calculate the traveling arc on those things or something so I don't get impaled?" I asked. "That would be such a dumb way to die."

"That's doable if the commander keeps them in her field of view," he said.

"On it," the commander said.

Through Markus's feed, I heard the Muscle Pope bellow the order to launch. Twelve javelins hurled through the air, following dotted lines that my comm projected in augmented reality. Val had been kind enough to make Pereges's line a different color.

I lurched forward invisibly, lugging the translator with me. Out of the corner of my eye, I watched Markus and Cades prepare their own lances on Markus's comm feed. I had to hurry.

"What did you write on yours?" Cades asked Markus.

Markus looked at him warmly. "Honor."

Cades returned the look with an expression so tender I thought they were going to start making out on the spot. But instead, Cades showed Markus his own spear.

"Courage," it read in Estheni.

"I'm so proud of you," Markus said softly.

"We'll make it to the end," Cades said. "Together."

"Together."

They stepped forward as Muscle Pope began the next round of hymns.

Meanwhile, I'd just reached the shields, feeling my stomach sink like a rock.

The shields were all set in these little frames that tilted them toward the sky. The idea was clearly that a lance that punctured a shield would fall back, tilting the shield off the frame and preventing future javelins from hitting the same shield until the ranks of slaves on the sidelines could retrieve them.

The problem was that someone—or more likely a whole sweatshop full of someones—had needed to produce hundreds of these, and they looked kinda cheap up close. They weren't all that sturdy.

And Pereges's spear had hit the shield so hard it broke the stand. It was super obvious which one was his. The crowd was chanting his name.

"Oh, come *on*," I said.

"Lilith! Get out of the way!"

I looked down at a dotted line traveling from my stomach into the ground.

"Oh, fuck me."

I leaped to the side. The javelin embedded itself in the sand of the arena, spraying grit everywhere. A loud wooden *thud* sounded somewhere to my right.

"You've got attendants moving in," the commander said. *"Do the swap and get out."*

"There's no point in swapping Pereges's symbol," I said. "It would just tell everyone we're messing with him. Looks like Cades missed the mark, though. I'll swap him instead. I'm telling you, Kives has us over a fucking barrel."

"That's enough about Kives."

"Yeah, yeah."

As a horde of bald people descended on my position, I used a highly sophisticated military device, channeling energies that were once the sole purview of angels and gods, as a glorified spray painter. As far as the priests of Kabiades were concerned, Cades hit the damn target.

I hadn't expected the Estheni to figure out tournament seeding, but apparently I should have known better. The athletes were grouped by how far they'd thrown their javelins, then distributed sequentially in wrestling rings around the arena. Those who had hit the farthest targets—including Markus, Cades, and our demigod friend—wouldn't face one another until the upper brackets of the wrestling event.

The goal was to hit the top sixteen because apparently the sword-fighting event worked differently at the Kabidiad. Rather than duke it out in a bunch of 1v1s, they were splitting everyone up into small armies of about twenty. The wrestling champions would each get command of one, and the event would culminate in a giant sixteen-way battle.

But first they'd need to make it through the wrestling event, which meant Markus and Cades finally had to split up and head to their assigned areas of the arena. I kept Markus's feed up as I lugged the utility translator back to the box that Abby had commandeered.

"Fight with honor," Markus said, resting his hand on Cades's shoulder. "If they want to give us glory, we'll take it gladly."

Cades puffed himself up. "Even the gods could not stop me from—"

"Cades," Markus said softly.

"Thala?"

Markus gave him a sad smile. "Don't hide. I know your heart."

Cades slowly breathed out. A wry smile crept over his face.

"I'm a half man," he said quietly. "I have the strength to cross the shadowlands, but my passion is diseased. Kabiades would never sponsor an ass-lancer into the Blessed Vale. The Kabidiad changes nothing."

Markus shifted his grip to the back of Cades's neck and pressed their foreheads together. I instinctively looked around to make they'd gone unobserved before I remembered the Estheni considered this normal behavior between comrades in arms.

"My ass is excellent," he said matter-of-factly. Cades nearly guffawed. "But I know that's not all this is to you. You treasure my heart, as my heart treasures you."

"I do," Cades whispered.

"Don't give up," Markus murmured. "We'll have time to sort out the rest later." He released Cades, smiling and returning to normal volume. "But for now, we have glory to reap!"

Cades returned the smile. Not a mask, just a smile. "I'll see you in the victor's bracket."

"Should I even be surprised at this point?" I said, popping a grape in my mouth. "Pereges has been hanging out under that choke hold for a while now."

"*It helps when your hack job of an etheric enhancement suite obviates the need for breath.*"

"And that's the match," the commander said. "Val, your intel says the captains get private changing rooms, right?"

"*It does.*"

The commander pursed her lips. "Then I suppose it's my turn. Hold the position, Lilith."

I popped another grape in my mouth and threw her a thumbs-up.

The commander slipped outside—seemingly, nothing more than an orderly of the lady Yotharios on a private errand. I pulled up her feed as she passed through crowds without attracting so much as a second glance.

Snatching a serving tray, she located Pereges's room and stepped inside. To the left of the door, an armor stand held a helmet, a skirt, and a back-heavy shawl that basically looked like a cape. A wooden sword and shield waited next to it. The fabrics were light green—almost certainly brightflower-based dye—and a priest of Kabiades was painting Pereges's symbol on the shield in the same color.

"Godsmile," Abby said politely.

The priest greeted her in return, finished his work, and left. It was far from uncommon for athletes in the Kabidiad to receive propositions from the nobility.

Abby waited a few moments to ensure no one else was coming in. She began stripping.

"Don't tell me you're— Oh no," I said.

"*Complain on your own time, Lilith. We need to use every available weapon. If he gets caught being unfaithful to the empress during the Kabidiad, that's it for him. One of us had to try this.*"

The commander pulled out her hand amplifier, set it to a combination of breathtaking beauty and unrestrainable lust, and hid it inside her growing pile of clothes.

"That's—" I said. "Okay. Okay. We're godslaying. Gotta do icky things sometimes. Right."

I closed her feed regardless.

A few minutes passed before Abby pinged for enemy contact.

"*Godsmile, big man,*" she said seductively. "*I liked what I saw on the field.*"

There was a long pause where I tried not to think about what was going on down there.

"*Impressive,*" she said. "*Pity. Well, I'm falling back to safe house two.*"

"What happened?"

"*He had enough self-control to run screaming for the guards. I've been made. The good news is they probably don't think I'm a whisper.*"

I leaned back and stared at the sky. "Oh yeah?"

"*I left my clothes behind. They will certainly remember that they saw me.*"

I kept staring at the sky. Somehow, I got the feeling that Abby running naked through the operations area was actually a prank on *me*.

"I hate Kives. I hate Kives. Fuck it, I'm just beating him to death."

Val snorted. *"Just like that?"*

"It's a battle. Lots of things happen in a battle. Fuck it! Fuck it, we're doing this."

Did Kives set out to troll me? Or was this her revenge when she looked into the future and saw me blaming her for everything that was going to go down?

There's no such thing as alternate futures. There is, was, and only will be one future: causally closed, the sum consequence of every decision made by every agent. Oracles might have more impactful decisions than most other agents, and Kives more so than other oracles, but knowledge is *not* power. Sometimes you see the muzzle flash too late to get to cover. Sometimes there's nowhere to hide from the oncoming train.

I was going to teach Kives the difference between knowledge and power.

I picked up one of those wooden swords the boys were using. They were heavier than they looked; it felt like there was metal inside. The wood itself was light and porous, and each army had been provided with long, thin containers of dye to dip their swords in.

The Estheni had invented medieval paintball, and that was cute, but a heavy club is a heavy club.

By the time I hit the field—cloaked, of course; precisely enough that people would avoid me without noticing me—Markus and Cades had already formed an alliance with one of the men from their caravan, who'd made it to the wrestling finals.

Two of them had ganged up on a lone army while a third screened the skirmish from opportunists—namely the opposing coalition that was forming around Pereges. Light green, pastel yellow, pearlescent off-white, and some hellish shade of maroon were the colors of the dark lord as he advanced on our heroes in blue and teal. The unaffiliated groups maneuvered out of the way, waiting for an opportunity.

Was Kives baiting me into a trap? What would happen if I failed?

Well . . . Pereges didn't get his head smashed in, I guess. Either he survived and took the victory, or he got injured, everyone blamed it on whispers, and we rolled the dice on whether the legend of Oathkeeper Falerior was enough to keep Meris at bay.

I reflected ruefully that the commander had probably made a cost-benefit analysis just like this one before Kives had sent her packing. Or not packing, if you catch my drift.

I dipped the sword in a container of maroon and sprinted for the battle.

Men were leaving the melee in droves, bearing pigment-covered bruises in the shapes of death blows. A ring of Kabiadesian priests dutifully tallied the fallen so that the captains could be appropriately scored at the end. Blade in one hand, hand amplifier in the other, I set phasers to "foul betrayal!" and struck one of the green-skirted dudes from behind.

Honor is such a fragile thing. Pereges's coalition dissolved immediately in a flurry of shouts and imprecations, each side thinking the other started it. Pereges tried to rally everyone, but the damage was done. Markus's teal regiment slammed into their flank, and a stream of teal-streaked casualties began to separate out from the battle.

I walked through it all like a shadow. I holstered the amplifier and drew my pulser, closing in on the demigod, who stood head and shoulders above the crowd. Markus was trying to carve a path toward him, but I pinged him to back off.

This target was mine.

A gap appeared in the fighting, and I saw my chance. I raised my pulser and fired. Pereges slumped but didn't fall.

"*Don't tell me he has fucking pulser shielding,*" I subvocalized.

"*Those asinine blessings release a lot of radiant energy,*" Val groaned.

"*These are some of the best useless blessings I've ever seen,*" Markus said.

I grit my teeth. Kives could only react. If the reaction wasn't good enough, she lost.

I fired again. And again. The blessing disrupted most of the pulser blast, but his consciousness *had* to be feeling fuzzy now. I squeezed the trigger twenty, thirty times, then holstered the weapon with a snarl and swung my maroon paint saber at the side of his head.

It connected with a *clang*. Slowly, momentously, the demigod fell.

"*So Markus,*" I subvocalized, sprawling invisibly against the arena wall. "*I think we're gonna win at this rate.*"

"*I think you might be right,*" he said. He didn't sound happy about it.

"*It's getting close to now or never, man,*" I said. "*Are you really going to go up there and stab a godseed?*"

The sun was setting, and the Course of Honor was lit up with a thousand ghost-lights. A circle of lights, shielded so as not to disrupt the competitors' vision, had been set up in the middle. The Kabidiad would end with 1v1 exhibition matches after all, featuring the four greatest warriors in the Imperial Coalition.

With my timely intervention, our boys' boys had amassed more kills than any other army. That, according to Kabidiad logic, meant they were the greatest warriors in the land. The other two were random dudes I didn't know; Pereges was supposed to get one of their spots, but no one could wake him up.

Cades wearily disarmed his opponent and pantomimed a strike at his throat. Equally weary, the other dude bowed out of the ring. I really felt it. It'd been a superlong day.

I heard Markus sigh over the comm.

"*Cades won,*" he said with a mixture of relief and fatigue. "*That decides it, then.*"

"*Okay, great, so there's an exit by your rooms—*"

"*No. I'm not aborting. Let's see this through.*"

Abby's voice had undertones of sympathy. "*I am updating the record. Eifni operative C3-32-3204, self-designation Markus, social officer, has waived an offer to abort the mission.*"

Val simply murmured, "*My friend.*" My comm registered nothing; what emotional depths lay behind Val's words, I had no idea.

Markus exchanged a few words with Cades, and the two men embraced each other. Then he stepped into the ring, lifting up a blunted exhibition sword.

His opponent was a lean man, whipping his sword around in the light. They saluted each other, then began circling.

"Markus, you don't have to fight the godseed," I said.

"*I'm not.*"

Before I had a chance to process what that meant, Markus struck.

Kabiadesian dueling techniques are built for show. Eifni operatives don't train that way. He never stood a chance.

The blow shattered the man's femur, crippling him. Markus immediately threw his sword away, crouching as if to help the downed man, but the priests descended on him and pulled him away.

"Thala!" Cades shouted after him.

"Courage!" Markus shouted back, then they dragged him past me into the arena.

Cades looked after him, dumbfounded. So did I.

Inflicting a crippling injury was grounds for disqualification in the Kabidiad. In one stroke, Markus had eliminated both of Cades's opponents.

Cades had won the Kabidiad.

The first lesson I learned about Velean adulthood was that everything they say is a lie. Performative half-truths, exaggerated misstatements, misleading implications; every act, every word a performance to convey the proper image.

There were other lessons sprinkled over the course of the Kabiades op. They were important in their way. But the last lesson was that the lies—weren't lies.

Let me tell you how it happened.

There's a subfield of paraphysics called conduit theory that talks about how to bridge the gap between etherspace and realspace. If you just want to muddle people's judgments for a bit, you can use a hand amplifier to bootstrap a frequency from etheric background noise.

But if you want to build an antenna straight to God, you need to start with something significant. You need to conjure the idea of God so strongly you can practically smell him. And then, if you're in the godslaying business, you need to break him.

The empress was a walking symbol of the Imperial Coalition. She wore a golden headdress, carved with the sword-and-scales of the Varasite faith. The many-colored layers of shawl spoke of disparate elements of society, united with gold and cowed with the sword. When she stood, she was statuesque—powerful, important, larger than life. When she walked, it was the inexorable march of military prowess and market pressure.

Standing across from her, Cades stood like the Divine Himbo himself. He was wearing the widest shawl I'd ever seen on a man, standing before a marble stand with a smaller silver crown. His muscles gleamed in the ghostlight. Slinky the Rogue would have been proud.

Completing the trifecta, the Muscle Pope stood before both of them, expositing on the Kabiadesian values of who the fuck cares, it's an oppressive sexist matriarchy. But the audience was just lapping it up—and from a conduit-theory perspective, that's what matters. Ten thousand pairs of eyes, staring down at the image of their gods and only seeing . . . their gods.

Real shame if something were to happen to them.

The priests that took that boyfriend-endangering fuckhead away were unarmed, and the commander had a spear. Getting him out of the room they'd stashed him in was simple enough that it was almost beneath notice.

That heartless fucking bastard didn't take up a weapon of his own. The commander, wrapped in a combat exoskeleton, stayed hidden in the shadows of the entrance. When she shifted, the matte reflection of ghostlight played over the smoke-darkened steel of her spear.

He walked out onto the sand. Calmly. The empress's guards moved to intercept him, and he stopped, showing no fear.

Why should that two-faced backstabber show fear in the face of violence? What does death mean to a Velean? We've slain it. Death is just another role, to be picked up and discarded when we feel like it.

Cades saw him out there.

Markus smiled, and he told one of those Velean lies that also happened to be true.

"Cades," he called. "I love you. You don't need to hide."

It was *true*. He *did* love Cades. He *did* want Cades to be free of all this shit. But only a motherfucking sociopath puts their boyfriend in front of a soul-eating monster for the greater good.

But Cades had no idea that he was a means to an end. It was as if some great weight had been lifted from his shoulders. Cades stood taller, and he smiled almost disbelievingly, as if he couldn't believe the situation he'd found himself in.

"Enough," he said clearly. "Enough. I am a man of honor. Enough. Hear me: I am Cades, son of Calades. I am a lover of men, and I will not live a lie. I cannot marry the empress."

For a moment, the world stood still, as if everyone were frozen in time. The shocked silence stretched out into a timeless moment, as if the Imperial Coalition itself were processing what Cades had said.

Val's laughter rang in our ears.

"*Got you.*"

The world—*cracked*.

Cades's transgressive moment swelled and bulged, bouncing between the hidden amplifiers in the arena, choking out all meaning except this one instant, this *one* idea: *the champion of Kabiades has refused the hand of the daughter of Varas.*

The champion of Kabiades is a lover of men.

The champion of Kabiades is an abomination.

It grew deeper, stronger, until the air was thick with it, until you could *taste* it. The amplifiers poured hundreds, *thousands* of *tetrons* into the growing mass of blasphemy, condensing it as Val used the barriers of Kabiades's own temple as a focusing lens for the weapon that would kill him.

The shock, the violation, the *wrongness* built up, so strong that my comm warned me about conceptual bleed.

I felt the pressure even through my comm shielding. Most weren't so lucky.

I watched people collapse all over the arena, their souls crushed by the sheer weight of it. Others would be lucky to escape with permanent changes where their souls didn't align with the conduit event. We'd probably just single-handedly turned an entire generation of athletes gay.

"*Amplifier six burned out,*" Val said. "*Compensating.*"

"*Burn them all if you have to!*" the commander ordered. "*Kill it!*"

"*They* die," Val snarled.

The world *cracked* again, deeper this time, spiderwebbing in some ineffable way through the heart of everything, and then the pressure was gone.

I *had* to know, but I couldn't move. I didn't dare speak.

Abby had no such compunctions. "*Val. Status.*"

The pause before he spoke was the longest of my life.

"*Kill confirmed,*" Val said. "*Kabiades is dead.*"

The scene descended into violence almost immediately, but it wasn't my concern.

I was emotionally numb, completely exhausted, and I had just watched a god die. But I had one last loose end to take care of.

"*MDO is showing activity at amplifier six,*" Val said. "*I need you to investigate.*"

I pinged him in the affirmative, wrapped myself in the floating warmth of my cloak, and went to kill the target.

I knew who it was. Somehow, deep in my soul, I knew. Kives had thrown Lirian in my path one too many times, so I was going to take her fucking toy away.

"*It's Lirian,*" Val said.

"I know."

"*Do you want me to freeze her?*"

"No."

"*Suit yourself. Don't take too long.*"

"I won't drag it out. She needs to die."

I wondered if it was also that I needed to kill something, but the thought of cutting her down didn't shift the emptiness I was feeling. If anything, it just felt like—checking off a to-do list item. Fold laundry, get groceries, take out the fucking trash.

I said nothing and knew that Val heard everything.

I rounded a corner, dodging between screaming civilians, and headed for the supply room where amplifier six was located. The door was open, and there was wine and spilled food everywhere inside.

I drew Lilith, dropping the cloak and sinking into absence meditation.

She was there in front of me, and she was a complete mess.

Her hair was frizzy and unkempt. The normal smirk was gone, her face instead dominated by bloodshot eyes rimmed with dark bags. She staggered out of the doorframe of the ruined storeroom.

"What have you *done* to me?!" she screamed at me. "Eyes all the time! In my sleep! What just happened out there?! *Who are you?!*"

I contentedly observed my pounding heart and what felt like a deep-seated muscular need to rip her limbs off. I would settle for the sword. I strode forward.

"Tell me," Lirian sobbed, falling to her knees. "Tell me, tell me *please*."

I noticed that she was in extreme emotional distress. The sword would fix that. I kicked her—not really even a proper kick, just a shove with my foot. She was just crying now.

"I can't believe that *this* is how you're going to die," I said. "I always thought it'd be more climactic."

I raised Lilith for a strike but was interrupted by every alarm in my comm going off at once.

Just behind Lirian stood—me, but *not*. Not whatsoever. She was naked and bloodstained—and I'd seen that body enough in the mirror to know it was definitely *mine*—except for a hooded cloak, which covered all her face above a mouthful of sharp teeth. That mouth was smiling now, slicing its gums with its own teeth, causing little driblets of blood to trickle down its chin into a gaping neck wound. Blood poured freely out of her throat.

Messages scrolled frantically past my eyes as my comm practically began to implode.

Warning: Divine manifestation!

Warning: Etheric-shield degradation!

Warning: Error establishing etheric tunnel!

Warning: Scanner suite offline!

Warning: Etheric shield critical!

I couldn't move. The cloaked woman rasped, but no words emerged, only blood gurgling from her mouth and the gash in her neck.

Lirian looked up at the manifestation, sighed, and fell unconscious.

A strong hand grabbed my hair from behind, yanking my head back, and then someone dragged a knife through my throat.

It hurt. Getting stabbed hurts really bad. But my thoughts were mostly on trying to save the arterial blood that was now spraying everywhere from my ruined trachea.

I collapsed to the floor, choking on the warm blood filling my throat, pressing uselessly against the fountain of blood. It was getting dark.

I needed to leave this body.

Warning: Error establishing etheric tunnel!

But I couldn't. I tried again and got another error.

"So this was our killer," said the man who'd killed me. "Amateur."

Warning: Error establishing etheric tunnel!

As the last light left my consciousness, reaching desperately for anything that could help, my oxygen-starved mind slipped into a meditative mindset.

I felt the etheric tunnel connect. With a sigh of relief, I died.

CHAPTER SEVENTY-TWO

Interlude: Wake

The world *cracked.*

Cades had seen a broken pane of glass once. The craftworkers of Vitareas were ingenious and thorough; the glass had been coated in translucent lacquer to prevent total fragmentation. It was like a spiderweb, but the clean lines of the world became jagged and disjointed in its cracks, and if it met your skin, you bled.

The weight of his sins had driven him to his knees. He stared up at his empress, who had withstood the spiritual pressure without flinching. Her eyes had glazed over, and her expression was one of horror.

Cades felt that same horror inside of him. There had been a warmth inside his heart, so familiar he'd never noticed it until it was gone, replaced by shattered glass.

The truth, *his* truth, still echoed in the Course of Honor. Whatever great power had seized it and seeded it upon the wind had been so mighty that the great arena itself had cracked. Some had perished, but Cades couldn't bring himself to think of that. Not now.

He had finally thrown away the mask. And the price had been—everything.

"You." Empress Kovaliel was trembling, staring at him with hatred and disgust. "What have you done?"

"I'm the one you want," a gentle voice said.

Thala, like the empress, had not been crushed by that baleful weight. His demeanor wasn't proud as he faced the empress, but neither was it humble. He looked her in the eyes, and somehow it was clear that there wasn't any lust behind it. It was a challenge.

"Kill them both," Kovaliel ordered, and strode away.

All around them, the empress's guards were recovering—those who had survived the doom. Cades picked up a sword from a fallen man and edged toward Thala, who didn't even have a weapon. Thala looked wearily at the enemies surrounding them.

"Together to the end," Cades murmured to him. "I'll meet you in the shadowlands, my love."

Thala didn't answer him. Cades knew that meant his lover disagreed.

"You never speak of the gods," Cades said. "Are you faithless?"

Thala breathed a sigh of relief.

"Everything will be fine, my little soldier," Thala said. "Let's talk about that later, okay?"

His lover's sweet lies washed over him as the royal guards charged.

"Please, commander."

The commander idly twirled her spear, considering the situation. A godslayer must never forget that her spear aims for heaven.

Markus stood implacable among foes, begging for his lover's life. His earnestness bothered her, but even Veleans struggled with proper dissemblance in the face of romantic entanglements. She'd forgotten the phenomenology of it—her last was over four hundred years ago—but the patterns were carved into her like a river through sandstone.

A hundred calculations fired through her mind—impact on morale, the demands of honor, the ever-present shadow of the oracle who was their ultimate enemy. It was too early in the campaign to gamble on far-reaching decisions.

"We have no use for auxiliaries at this stage," the commander said in the tone reserved for deflection.

"He's eligible for the Red Dagger," Markus said, ignoring her move. *"He's performed greater service than most of Eifni."*

The haft of her spear met her palm with a pleasant smack, and Abby allowed herself a micromoment of savor before tossing it back to the other hand.

The trouble with Markus, in the final accounting of things, was that his general disinterest in Velean social propriety belied a cutting instinct for manipulation. He always knew where to strike her, sometimes even better than Val. If she allowed the manipulation, her decision became a forced choice, and Kives would certainly gain a foothold of some kind.

Abby cleared her mind with an old meditation technique. She looked down at the spear in her hand.

They had slain a god today. Blood ought to be honored with blood.

"Hold position," she told him calmly.

Markus sighed with relief. *"Thank you."*

Abby engaged her exoskeleton and launched herself into the air.

She slammed into the dais that Markus and Cades were standing on. Cades swung wildly on reflex, a blow she effortlessly parried.

The empress's guards paused their attack, sizing up the new arrival who had seemingly fallen from the sky.

The commander spun her spear once, reading victory from the battlefield like it was a book. She determined with satisfaction that she had time for the full-length Challenge.

"Hail to you. I am a warrior of the Old Ways," she announced, setting her hand amplifier to battle pride. "I walk the road of spears, battle song on my lips. Hear my challenge: by blade lore and bloodshed, I am wolf friend, I am death friend. I am war, and war is my companion."

She settled into seventh form, meeting the eyes of her enemies.

"I give you this chance to surrender the field. There will not be another."

Behind her, Markus shifted.

"*Go,*" she ordered him. "*Safe house three is civilian proofed.*"

She didn't spare him a second thought. Thirty armored men charged at her position.

The world *cracked.*

Bofa paused midmassage. Kuril made a small, disappointed noise, then a more inquisitive one as Bofa sat down heavily on the bed.

When a response did not seem to be forthcoming, she rolled over to take a look at him. His expression was clouded, almost pained.

"What's wrong?" she asked gently.

Bofa stared at his hands. "I'm not sure."

Kuril extracted herself from the sheets, pressing herself up against his back. The warmth of his skin was pleasant. Very pleasant. She wrapped her arms around him to get more of the sensation.

"You are such a pillar for this family," she murmured in his ear.

That was evidently the wrong thing to say because he shifted away from her. She let her arms drop as he scooted to more of a conversational distance.

"I confess, I have felt . . . burdened," he said. "Between you and Roel and—well, for you two, things have been difficult."

Kuril had a decent guess which name he'd avoided speaking but made no acknowledgment. Ajarel was never coming back, no matter what she'd told Kuril's overly trusting consort.

"I'm sorry to hear that," she said. "I will call for a priest of Gamal. I can also select another suitor or two if you'd like to split your household duties. Roel's invention has generated enough budget that the expenditure would be painless."

"Kuril, I don't need an immediate solution—"

"Why not? Problems should be solved before they worsen—"

"I don't want to be *solved,*" Bofa said.

Kuril's brow furrowed, and she blinked once or twice. "I don't understand men."

"Neither do I," Bofa said. "I'm sorry, Kuril. Maybe you should send for the priest."

"You are forgiven," Kuril said. "We *are* grateful, you know. There's just something about you that makes it hard to remember that things can bother you, too."

Bofa looked up at her. "That was why I sat down."

"Hmm?"

"I call it my hearth," said Bofa. "It's what warms me when I act as I should. But just now, it felt like something broke. I can't feel my hearth right now."

Kuril stared at him with concern. Then she crawled over the blankets, snuggling into his lap. She wrapped her arms around him, scratching the back of his neck the way he liked. He was very warm.

"I'm sorry about your hearth. Everything will be okay," she told him. "The priest will make it better."

He squeezed her tight. His arms were warm, too, which made her happy. Her brow furrowed.

"Am I warm to you?" she asked.

"Very much so," Bofa said contently.

"That doesn't make sense, given what philosophy says of heat exchange. Do you think our senses are deceiving us?"

"You sound like you want to do the math."

". . . Yes," Kuril admitted. "But the desk is over there."

"Do you want me to let you go?" Bofa asked with a chuckle.

Kuril considered. "No."

She snuggled into him further. He could nearly hear the gears churning in her head.

"However, if you could pull the desk over here—"

The world *cracked*.

The man in servant's robes paused elegantly as Councilman Laoh shot to his feet.

"Do you hear thunder?" asked the councilman.

"The councilman has strong ears."

"I think it's coming closer," the councilman said, shortly before the ground began shaking. "Earthquake!"

The councilman's teapot fell off the table, shattering on the tiles. The man in servant's robes gave it a frustrated glance. Smuggling the poison past palace security had been effortful.

The councilman looked up with concern. "Heaven's grace, man, the tomb!"

"The heavens will most certainly secure your ancestor's tomb," said the man in servant's robes, moments before the distant sound of snapping wood heralded an absolute cacophony of collapsing stone and soil.

It seemed the heavens had not, in fact, secured the councilman's ancestor's tomb. The man stared into the middle distance with a philosophical sort of air.

"Godfire!" he shouted.

"What a strange expr—" was all the councilman was able to get out before the other man brushed a hand past his neck. The councilman blinked experimentally, then his head fell off. The rest of him collapsed in the same instant, blood mingling with poison tea on the ground.

"The mission's a bust," said the man, who was stripping out of the servant's robes as fast as possible. "Is Aldr okay?"

"*Banu Mi timed the earthquake too well,*" said a voice on the other end. "*They were crushed instantly. We can pull them out of the crypt once we exfiltrate you.*"

Something wasn't adding up here.

"Kriamin," the man said. "Can you confirm that was a pantheon-level kill?"

"*Confirmed,*" said Dr. Kriamin. "*They killed Bunsin.*"

"Bunsin?" The man froze. "*Bunsin?!* What moronic throwback okayed a first strike on Bunsin? He's the most useless god they have! We had Eishi in the *godflaming* crosshairs, and they fucked us for *Bunsin!*"

"*If I had to guess, Banu Mi's playing games with them, too. Rade, you're standing around at the scene of a murder. Let's move. We can have the Skolfr at one of the pickup spots in three minutes once you generate the random selection.*"

Rade sighed. "Just a second. Something really isn't adding up." He looked around the room. From his inner robes, he retrieved a small case with a spinner, activating the etheric scrubber with a flick of his thumb.

"*You can do math problems on the ship. Get out of there.*"

"Got it. It's the poison tea." Rade nudged a pottery shard with his foot. "I killed this sucker a minute after I served him the tea. Following?"

"*Against my better judgment.*"

"Charmer. So there shouldn't be any dyadic entanglements on the tea. It didn't do anything except piss me off. Unless Banu Mi can target an event just from the annoyance caused by her intervention."

"*I don't think she can do that.*"

"You don't *think*? Godfire, you *knew* there was an oracle, why didn't you brush up on your moirology?"

"*Be glad I didn't. Without exception, moirologists are smug assholes. The entire breed.*"

"You're already a smug asshole. It's not like my situation would get worse."

Kriamin evidently decided not to contest the point. "*Have you got a number for me?*"

Rade looked at the spinning wheel as it stopped. "Site four. Anyway, how did Banu Mi know to mess with the poison tea?"

"*It was an earthquake. It would be hard not to mess with the tea.*"

"Right when I poured it, though," Rade argued. "That was Banu Mi. Don't fight me on this. You *know* what her work looks like."

"*It has to be coincidence because the alternative hypothesis is that random number generation isn't actually effective against her and she's only been playing along.*"

"Godfire!" Rade yelled, kicking the headless corpse of Councilman Laoh. "Godfire! What the *fuck* is wrong with this planet?!"

Forget physical exfiltration. He wasn't going to sit around waiting for whatever comedic response Banu Mi had planned. He knocked over a few oil lamps and called it good when he saw smoke.

By the time his comm warned him about the angels, his soul was safely en route to the *Skolfr*.

Not today, bitch.

Roel leaned against the wall, the same way Lirian liked to stand when she appeared out of nowhere. Unlike the whisper, Roel did it because it let her put all her weight on her good leg. The wound was well on its way to recovery, but it seemed like the pain got worse every day, no matter how much *golos* bark she chewed.

Alouren was pacing while they waited.

"You should sit down," Alouren told her. "We don't know how long she'll be."

"I need to be standing when she comes in."

"She could be here already. She does that all the damn time."

Roel's eyes flicked to Alouren's face. Ajarel wasn't the only person who swore that way, but until recently, Alouren hadn't been one of them.

"That's not how it works," Roel said, keeping her thoughts hidden. "We can't talk about her when she's here."

"Well, your leg needs a rest," Alouren said irritably.

"It's fine," Roel lied.

Alouren shot her a look that said she knew the truth, but she'd learned to stop pressing her best friend about it.

The inner door opened, revealing an old man in black robes. Roel's eyes widened slightly. Behind him, oily torchlight illuminated the halls of the catacombs of Bulcephine.

"The viewing room is prepared," he intoned. "Know that you tread upon ancient paths. Each step is an echo of stories lost in ages. Tread carefully, lest you be lost in them. Welcome, outsiders, to the Lost Road."

Roel bowed her head in respect, then risked her guess. "Thank you, Archivist. Lead the way."

He met her eyes, smiling slightly, but didn't confirm or deny it. "This way."

Roel's first step on the black stone of the Lost Road was with her crippled leg. Pain shot through her thigh. She tried to tell herself she was beyond caring, like the heroes of her stories, but pain was actually very hard to ignore.

She'd taken a tincture to stop the tears before meeting with the Cult of Silence. Her eyes itched from dryness now, and when no one was looking, she soothed the discomfort by pressing a wet cloth to her face.

Clamped around her waist, the assistive device swiveled with each step, using the motion of her good leg to push the crippled leg where it needed to go.

Your muscles are too damaged to move your leg. Use a machine. This conversation never happened.

Roel had done all the work, but the idea was Ajarel's. Not something she'd come up with on the spot—something she'd already known and wasn't supposed to say.

No wonder Lirian was obsessed with her. What else had she known?

As always with Ajarel, the questions came too late. Lirian's message had been hesitant, wary of overconfidence, but ultimately out of alternate explanations: Ajarel was dead.

Her secrets propelled Roel along the Lost Road toward her final resting place.

The catacombs were covered floor to ceiling with shelves for the dead. Many were empty, others occupied by anonymous skeletons with tarnished keepsakes. Their names belonged to Meris now. The path intersected identical corridors apparently at random, the monotony broken only by the occasional door of black stone.

Roel walked at a pace that kept the pain to a minimum and wasn't entirely surprised that the old man remained exactly three paces ahead of her.

The old man took turns at random—as far as Roel could tell, having given up on memorizing their path a handful of turns ago—leading them deeper into the heart of Bulcephine. They never saw another person, but sound carried far in those corridors: occasionally the Lost Road brought them the distant noise of footsteps and whispered voices.

Intellectually, Roel knew those sounds came from real people, but it was easy to believe they were the echoes of moments lost to time.

The door to the viewing room was carved from unmarked black stone like all the others. The old man pushed it open and motioned them through with a smile.

The room was cold and somewhat cramped. There was a matching door on the other side, which for all Roel knew was just another entrance to the Lost Road. In the center of the room, a shroud-covered body rested on a table. Roel avoided looking at it.

Lirian was lounging against the wall, the usual smirk absent from her face. She tore her eyes from the body as they entered, acknowledging them with a humorless quirk of the lips.

"Lirian," Roel said, painfully making her way to the whisper. They grasped hands briefly, Roel allowing herself to lean against the wall. She didn't quite manage to keep the relief off her face.

"Godsmile," Alouren greeted Lirian, tone somewhere between nervousness and excitement.

Roel kept her face blank but sighed inwardly. At some point, she was going to have to take her idiot best friend aside and have a conversation about hiding her attraction. Lirian wasn't the first woman she'd favored with this behavior—and thank the goddesses no one had noticed, or there would be trouble—but she was certainly the most dangerous.

Well, depending on whether you counted the body on the table.

Lirian slipped into character with a twist of effort that Alouren missed and Roel didn't, returning the greeting with a warm smile. "How was the journey?"

Roel shot her a warning look. Lirian tilted her head apologetically and turned down the warmth about half.

"It was about as painless as it could have been," Alouren said.

"You look better," Roel said before Alouren could give them any real information.

Lirian did look better. Last time Roel had seen her, Lirian's face had been covered in makeup to hide the bags under her eyes, and there were obvious cracks in that sense of perfect poise and control she liked to project. She wasn't quite back at her full potential, but she lacked that sense of *being hunted* that had started to manifest over her last few *thessim* in Vitareas.

"I can sleep again," Lirian said. "You have no idea what it was like. I actually thought I was going to die. Every time my eyes closed, I'd feel her looking at me."

"Bad dreams?" Roel asked.

"More than dreams," Lirian said with a shudder. "We can feel eyes on us. I know when I'm perceived. The stronger the perception, the stronger the response. And this—it was horrible. And it stopped when she died."

Roel forced herself to look at the figure under the sheet.

"Show them," Lirian said.

The old man nodded, then pulled back the sheet.

The body had been preserved with a process that had shrunken its flesh. Roel braced herself for the smell of rot, but what she actually experienced was the acrid stench of the embalming chemicals.

Her throat had been cut, and the shrinking effect of the preservatives had pulled the wound open to the point that you could see the back of her throat. The face was almost skeletal, the skin pulled taut around bone—with the exception of the eyes, which almost bugged out of her shrunken face.

"It's not her," Roel said immediately. "Ajarel had brown eyes."

"No one has violet eyes," said Lirian.

"Clearly at least one person did."

Lirian's lips thinned. "The hand-truth of the body was recorded by an acolyte when it was added to the Archive. Show her."

The old man nodded, producing a leather-bound rectangle about the length of a forearm and half as wide. He opened it, revealing an astonishingly lifelike sketch of a face, sealed in transparent wax.

Roel's breath caught. The face was Ajarel's. Her eyes were closed in the picture.

"Was Ajarel a faceless?" Alouren asked.

Lirian shook her head. "Feel her eyes."

Roel reached out, hesitating, then touched one. The surface was smooth, unnaturally so.

"I'm no expert on how eyes feel," Roel said. "But it feels very different than rubbing my eyes from sleep."

"Eyes are gelatinous sacs filled with a fluid," Lirian said. "The embalming process usually deflates them. Those are not eyes."

Roel breathed in sharply.

Your muscles are too damaged to move your leg. Use a machine.

"They're not eyes," Roel said quietly. "They're machines."

Lirian glanced at Roel's leg. Roel didn't react; she couldn't prevent Lirian from making inferences, but she could avoid giving her more information.

"That's impossible," said Alouren with a glance at Lirian. "You can't see with a machine."

Roel exchanged a look with Lirian. Alouren didn't know about the sleepers. She still thought the unnatural sleep was a purely magical phenomenon. But if Ajarel had one impossible device, why not two?

"The conclusion seems impossible, but everything points to it," Roel said. "Those eyes aren't natural. They were a replacement."

"Then how did she lose her natural eyes?" Alouren countered. "There's no scarring."

"Maybe she was faceless *and* she had impossible machines," Lirian said. Roel could tell that even she wasn't convinced.

"No," Roel said. "There's no explanation for any of this. Too much of this is impossible. If we keep chasing answers that make sense to us, we'll be wasting our time."

Lirian made a noncommittal noise.

"Loradian Saga, book three," Roel said. "I don't have the exact quote memorized, but something like, 'The boundary of the world is the boundary of understanding, and thereby the end of understanding shall ever be the end of the world.'"

Everyone looked at her.

"Loradian Saga?" Lirian said doubtfully. "You think Ajarel was the Calamity? She's—dead."

"Where's Thala? No one has seen him since the Kabidiad, among the living or dead. Who made the sleepers? It can't have been Ajarel—they bore no toolmarks. She wasn't alone in her mission."

"Sleepers?" Alouren asked. Roel waved her off, mouthing, "Later." That seemed to satisfy Alouren enough to keep going. "It didn't *feel* like Ajarel was the Calamity. Maybe she was a god?"

"What kind of god can be killed with a knife?" Lirian asked. "Roel is right. We're wasting our time looking for explanations we can understand."

Alouren grew pale. Lirian only looked weary; Roel supposed she'd had more experience with their enemy than the rest of them. Even the old man looked unsettled.

"I will search the Archives for lore," he said. "There may be answers to be found."

"There are no answers," Lirian said. "Not for the Calamity."

"We've answered at least one," he said with determination. "Godsmile, ladies. Lirian will guide you back."

Then he was gone, as if he'd never been there. Neither door had opened.

"I'd like to talk with Lirian privately for a moment," Roel said. "Alouren, can you wait outside?"

Alouren looked at her curiously, then nodded and left.

"What is it?" Lirian asked when they were alone.

Roel cut straight to the point. "I want the Seal of Meris."

Lirian snorted. "You've read too many books."

"I know a lot about the Lost Road."

"From books."

"I want to keep my memories," Roel said. "This is too important. The world is ending."

"You don't understand," Lirian said. "All of that is made up. The Seal, losing your memories? People invent ancient memory-stealing magics because they don't understand that secret keeping is an act of discipline and devotion."

"I understand that very well," said Roel. "And then I watched you let Alouren into this room, so now I *know* there's an ancient memory-stealing magic."

Roel stared at her challengingly. For a few seconds, neither woman looked away.

"*Fine*," Lirian said. "You're like a puppy or something. In the name of Meris, keeper of all truths and so on, do you swear to safeguard that which is hidden?"

"Yes," Roel said instantly.

Lirian leaned over and kissed her on the forehead. "There. Sealed. If you talk about this with someone who doesn't know about it, it'll melt your soul."

"Noted," Roel said.

"I'm not lying. It happened to one of my brother acolytes."

"What was his name?" Roel probed.

"Olonia," Lirian said instantly.

"And should I change the name when it's my turn to lie about it?"

"There are no lies." Lirian smirked. "Only eye-truths. Welcome to the Cult of Silence, Roel."

CHAPTER SEVENTY-THREE

Epilogue

I dreamed about the gods again as my comm ferried my soul back to the *Ragnar*.

This much I remembered. They were ragged, bleeding, hungry. I saw a rabid fox with rotting teeth—a vengeful warrior with a broken sword—a hollow-eyed girl, bleeding from a gash in her neck—a spider—a leper—and above them all, a matriarch: contemptuous, sadistic, and furious.

I surveyed them all, and I knew that they could die. Everything dies.

Ageless columns of stone stretched down the audience chamber, from my position at the entrance, to the dais where they all stood. On each of those pillars and on the stones beneath our feet, ancient carvings recorded an endless history of godly deeds, sacrifices made and boons given. Blood dripped from the red stars above, trickling down the carvings.

Then we tried to speak. The matriarch opened her mouth, the words coming out as unintelligible rasps and gurgles as the blood bubbled out of her slit throat. I was contemptuous, with no throat. My body wouldn't move.

One of the pillars near me smiled with a mouthful of sharp teeth. The stars above began to shift into a bloody constellation of a wound.

Then the cataclysm struck: a flash of purifying fire, cracking heaven itself, immolating the gods. The apocalypse descended around me, but I felt nothing. They blazed and were torn, falling to earth in a shower of flaming meat.

The gods died; Alcebios laughed. Her talons reached for me.

The neural cradle crackled around the back of my head. Just like that, I was alive.

Lungs full of stinging fluid, I coughed and hacked. My throat was raw; my arms stung from the touch of a dozen needles, removed before they'd restarted my brain.

I opened my eyes, and light seared them closed again. I retched; my stomach tried to dump its contents, but it had never been used. Instead, bile squirted up my throat, burning the back of my esophagus. I tried to push myself up to vomit, but my arms didn't respond right, and I hit my head on the side of the resurrection pod.

"*Hrol din nagar eigerlein,*" Abby snapped. "*Lilithkar leit!*"

I inhaled raggedly, crying out as I coughed harder.

"*Vanas, Markus! Vanas!*"

I was in the med bay.

That was the first thing I noticed. The second thing I noticed was that the lights were too bright, and opening my eyes had been a painful mistake. I closed them immediately.

"Ow," I said. I expected my throat to hurt—last I'd noticed, it'd felt like someone had shoved a handful of glass down the back of my esophagus—but it was fine now. I coughed experimentally.

"The pain is psychosomatic," Val said. "You'll live."

"I don't believe you," I said. "What the fuck did you do to my brain?"

"Your brain is fine," he said.

I caught the deflection. "*Val.*"

"The headache," Val admitted, "is because this body can process a wider range of visual spectra than your soul is used to, and the closest experiential analogue to that discomfort is a migraine."

I bore stoically the news that they'd fucked with my brain. Too late to do anything about it now.

"How long," I sighed.

"The adjustment period should be less than a week. If you take your time, closer to two."

"I bet I can do it in three days."

"Not with your eyes closed, you won't."

I forced my eyes open and turned my head to glare at him.

Val was lounging in a folding chair, reading from a tablet. Next to him, a half-eaten salad sat on one of the pull-out table surfaces the Eifni shipwrights had scattered around the *Ragnar*. He lifted his fork and took a precise bite, not lifting his eyes from whatever had occupied his attention.

He didn't acknowledge me. My head was splitting, but I couldn't close my eyes again after making such a big deal about it.

"Level with me," I said, trying to lever myself into a sitting position. "What else is in this body?"

"Lungs, evidently," Val said. "We're still waiting on evidence of cognitive function."

"I fucking died, man," I said. "Can you lay off for one fucking minute?"

Val paused, then set the tablet down, meeting my eyes—I guess for the first time, technically speaking.

"The scientific literature," he said, indicating the tablet with a minute shift of his head, "recommends creating an atmosphere of familiarity to minimize the psychological impact of your first flash. Maintaining a sense of continuity reduces the chance that you develop some kind of dysmorphic disorder."

All that shit was a transparent excuse for him to bully me. Which was, of course, exactly the kind of familiar atmosphere Velean scientists recommended for someone in my position.

I tried to hold back a smirk, but I failed. It became a smile, then a full-on laugh.

"You asshole," I wheezed, blinking back tears. "You glorious, perfect asshole."

Goddamn Veleans. It was a fucking mistake for the universe to invent us, and we were going to spend the rest of eternity teaching it regret.

Val cracked a smile. In a moment, he was laughing, too.

I laughed away my death. I laughed away my fear of flashing—*I survived my own death*, what could possibly matter more? I laughed off the pain and stress of the last couple months, the insecurities, the family I'd found and lost. I laughed off Lirian. I'd kill her someday, or maybe I'd just wait for her to die of old age. What was she to me? *I was immortal.*

I was a warrior of Veles. I was a fire transcending time. They could kill me as many times as they wanted, but they would never stop me from burning their world clean.

"Lilith?" I heard Abby call.

"I'm awake!" I shouted back.

A few moments later, the commander's head poked through the door frame. "Good morning, apprentice."

I tried to pull myself up again. "Okay, seriously, why can't I move?"

"Resurrection sickness," Abby said. "There's nothing wrong with your body, but your soul needs to acclimate to the connection. You know the beds are comm controllable, right?"

"I can't move my fucking arms," I said, flopping one demonstratively. "The bed is not my concern right now, okay?"

Also, I'd forgotten. Shut up.

I remote piloted myself to a sitting position, looking at Abby's smiling face. I gave her a half-hearted smile back.

"Speaking of apprenticeship," I said. "Did you guys get my sword back?"

A brief shadow of a frown passed through Abby's expression. "No. The body and the sword were gone when I got there. From the fact that we were unable to locate them, we've concluded that the Cult of Silence took possession."

"Fuck." I closed my eyes in frustration, letting the migraine abate. "Let's go after Meris next. We've compromised most of the agents in the city."

"We'll decide our next steps once you're field ready," the commander said. "For now, your objective is to recover from resurrection and acclimate to your new body."

"I don't get like a bad grade in the Old Ways for losing my weapon?"

"It's just a sword," Abby said. "Pick up a stick and call that Lilith. I don't care."

"But—" *It was a gift*, I wanted to say. I guess that was less of an Old Ways thing and more of a me thing. I didn't finish the sentence.

"I can replicate the sword," Val offered.

I pursed my lips. "No. It wouldn't be the same."

Val turned accusing eyes on Abby, like this was somehow her fault. Abby smirked back. He shrugged, as if to say it was my decision.

"It's good to see you're functional," Val said. "There was a concern that the etheric tunnel would collapse midtransit."

"I think it almost did," I said. "Do you guys get the dreams when you translate?"

"Everyone does." Val's tone of voice indicated that he was going to continue, but he made us wait while he took another bite of salad.

Abby didn't wait for him to finish chewing. "Not everyone."

Val waved her off, swallowing. "Those statistics rely on self-report. The best explanation is agitation of the conceptual centers via etheric noise. The mechanism was confirmed in laboratory testing. The people who claimed not to remember have either failed to remember or intentionally deceived the researchers."

Abby allowed herself a slight smile, directing an aside at me. "The dreams tend to carry a sense of destiny. You can imagine how a sample of Veleans would respond."

Something about her tone and bearing communicated another layer of meaning: *You can lie about this if you want to.*

"Oh, that's cool," I said. "In that case, my destiny is killing a bunch of gods at once. Anyway, I brought it up because Alcebios was definitely bleeding through my translation dream. Emphasis on the bleeding."

Val and Abbey winced at the pun and the resulting comm feedback.

"Sorry."

"You are forgiven this once," Abby declared. "Rest well, Lilith."

"Please no," I said. "I'm bored already. Please save me before I die again."

Markus chose that moment to barrel through the door, apparently fresh out of the shower. At least he'd put some clothes on first.

Right. Yeah. Markus. For a moment, I'd forgotten.

"Lilith!" he said, coming in for the hug.

I couldn't really move, but Markus was perceptive enough that he noticed me shying away.

The joy drained out of his face. "Oh."

I avoided eye contact. "Hi, Markus."

Val and Abby somehow managed, through that Velean command of body language, to recede without moving away. It was just me and Markus until we worked this out.

"You're upset about Cades," he said.

I stared at the wall. I didn't trust myself to say anything.

In my peripheral vision, I saw Markus sit down on the bed next to mine. "Cades is fine, Lilith. He's lying low with that Dancer caravan we came in with. He said he wanted some time to himself."

"Good."

Markus sighed. "It's not fair. But it was necessary."

I whirled my face toward him.

"The empress could have *eaten his soul*! You sent him up there! You said you loved him, and you sent him up there!"

My eyes were wet. I tried to wipe the tears away but only succeeded in flopping my arm into my lap. Fuck it. Let 'em roll. I stared Markus in the face, fake migraine blaring in my skull.

There was a hint of pain in Markus's face, but who the fuck knew with Veleans. I did not know this man. He'd always seemed friendly and approachable, and he hadn't batted a *fucking eyelid* while he sent Cades to his death.

"I knew you were going to take this hard," Markus said softly. "I know what you've been through and what godseeds mean to you. And I'm sorry for hiding it from you during the operation."

"You don't—you don't *hide* things like that. Fucking hell, Markus. Fuck. Fuck."

Abby stirred ever so slightly. "Deep breaths, Lilith."

Oh. I was hyperventilating. Sure enough.

I coughed and tried to get control of my breathing.

"Remember what Kabiades was," Markus said. "Beyond the persona and the cultural baggage. He was a god of athletics. Cades's sexuality doesn't impact that. In a few decades, he would have been eaten."

"And that makes it okay to stab him in the fucking back?"

"Of course not," Markus said. "But as a means to save the souls of every athlete in that arena and beyond? I'm sure Val can show you the equations."

"I don't care about the *fucking* equations!"

Markus nodded, looking compassionately at me. "What do you care about?"

That just made the anger blaze hotter.

"I know this script," I said. "Poor baby Lilith, she's too fragile to make the hard choices. She'll understand in a hundred years. Fuck that. I'm not doing it. From now on, you fucking tell me if you're gonna pull shit like this."

Markus closed his eyes for a moment, then opened them again.

"We don't have to follow that script," he said. "I don't need to hide things from you. But then you can't react like this when I do. If you'd had this reaction during the operation, it would have jeopardized the mission."

I clenched my jaw. "Okay. I have to admit that's fair. But, counterpoint, fuck you."

Markus cracked a grin. "For what it's worth, I was confident the empress wouldn't attack him directly. Well, Val was."

I turned my glare on Val, who met it with a look of amusement.

"It was certainly more difficult to calculate the behavioral distribution," Val said. "The divine component of the godseed behaves according to the same rules as the god itself, but the human soul adds a significant degree of randomness. In this case, however, both its human and divine natures were in alignment: Empress Kovaliel would never take an action she could order someone else to do."

I focused on slowing my heart down. "You can't convince me he was safe."

"Of course not. Statistics mean nothing with Kives in play," Val said. "She will bait us into forming attachments again and again, and losing them will cause us significant emotional pain. She cannot kill our bodies, so she will target our minds. Then she'll use that pain to turn us against one another, as you nearly turned on Markus."

"She definitely killed my body," I said, sniffling. "I mean, I got better, but still. How long was I out, by the way?"

"Two weeks," Abby said.

"And in those two weeks, you missed the chance to say goodbye to Cades," Markus said. "She might have killed you just to deny you closure on that."

"Or that's what she wants you to think," I said, smirking.

"I'm sorry," Markus said. "I'll make sure to tell you next time I throw someone at a godseed."

"Fuck, I'll volunteer," I said. "Dibs on killing the empress."

"Breaching the palace is an important objective," Abby said. "But that will come later. We'll let you rest."

"Group hug first," I demanded.

I couldn't move my arms, but Markus lifted my right arm around his shoulders. Everyone crowded in, even Val.

"We got one," I said.

"We did," Abby said. "Eleven to go."

I spent a couple weeks in the spiritual equivalent of physical therapy.

A lot of the activities were the same: repetitive physical movements, various ways to practice moving slowly and deliberately, rebuilding my muscle memory from the faint spiritual echoes I'd carried over from my last body.

The others had dropped comments here and there; reading between the lines, they'd known it was only a matter of time before I died, and they'd tried to soften the blow by packing my new body with every enhancement that would fit.

Darwin help me, but I loved it.

My ear implants were state-of-the-art. A slight modification to my neural tissues had left me with perfect pitch. The machinery that replaced my eardrums could pick out a whisper in a room packed with rowdy drunks. I could hear the highest squeaks and the lowest rumbles. I could differentiate between a hundred thousand subtle variations of vocal tone.

I could see colors that didn't exist. My default range of vision extended from infrared—I almost didn't need the thermal cameras in my ocular implants—to ultraviolet. I nearly cried the first time I looked at a black-feathered bird and realized the black was hiding brilliant patterns outside of the human-visible spectrum. The visual precision was so fine I could see the stars move.

My body was stronger than I'd ever dreamed I could be. Ether-reinforced skeletal plating rendered me immune to anything short of a charging elephant. They'd layered pylons in my muscles so I could control them remotely. In my second week of rehabilitation, I bent a steel bar with my bare hands.

My thoughts moved like blades over ice. Val put me through a battery of cognitive tests; I blazed through them, scoring a 20 percent improvement over my previous records. My working memory had been expanded to ludicrous levels, and I spent a couple weeks holding eleven different numbers in my head *just because I could.*

But what does it profit a girl to gain a kick-ass new body at the cost of her soul?

The scans said I'd sustained some damage. Alcebios had burned me, and while some of the damage would heal, my soul might end up with some scarring. My death hadn't exactly been easy, either. Between the fallout of the Kabiades hit and the weird jumble of emotions that had been my last encounter with Lirian, I'd gotten pretty messed up.

There were days when I didn't leave my room and days when I was furious with everyone for no reason. One time, I punched Markus in the face and then cried for four hours. I also tried to hit Val with a chessboard, but that one doesn't count. I maintain that anyone would have done the same, soul damage or not.

I couldn't stand the taste of mac and cheese anymore. It'd been my comfort meal, an easy bowl of junky nostalgia on my worst days. The nostalgia was gone—either because it'd never imprinted on my soul or because Alcebios had burned that away—and the flavors were subtly different on my new tongue. I gave up on it after my third try.

But the team was patient with me. Love and compassion go a long way toward healing spiritual injury. I got better, if slowly. By the third week, I'd reached the point where I almost felt like myself again.

That was when Val decided to knock on my door.

"I would like to ensure this never happens again," he said, and his eyes were like knives.

The commander had not approved.

Val had shown her the math.

The commander had grudgingly approved.

I took in the nighttime air of the tiny coastal town as we strolled up the hill. Ahead of us, a *fetoulia* tree rose hundreds of feet in the air above the temple of Kives. My eyes effortlessly picked out the small shrine hidden in its branches, and for a moment I visualized it crashing down.

Val kept pace beside me, carrying a small box. He'd refused to tell me what was inside.

We passed onto the temple grounds beneath an archway. There was no watch, no guards to defend the temple from thieves. Anyone who stole from the Mother of Destiny was asking for it.

The atrium was dark, but that didn't matter to my implants. I swept the room once, looking for an ambush, but found only the list labeled "Counsel." Last time I'd set foot in a temple of Kives, it'd been my names—both of them—on there.

Now there was only one, written in English.

"Murderers," I translated for Val.

"You had much better insults available to you," Val said to the empty air. "The message is received."

The air didn't respond.

"So, in here?" I asked.

"The tree," Val replied. "We have an offering to make."

I glanced at the box in his hands and didn't ask.

The temple's inner sanctum smelled of sweet flowers and perfume and incense, mostly covering up the faint smell of rotting organic matter. The *fetoulia* tree rose into the Mediterranean night, spreading its branches over the town like the sheltering mother goddess who held it sacred. Val and I came to a stop.

"Would you like to say a few words?" Val's tone was ironic.

"Yo, Kives," I said. "We had a truce, and you killed me. Not cool. Your turn, Val."

Val nodded imperceptibly. "It occurred to me that there are only two ways for you to learn about the contingencies of this situation. Either they occur, in which case they cannot be avoided, or they are explained to you. In light of your breach of this farce of a truce, we're here to explain."

Val opened the box and pulled out—a rock. Volcanic, by the looks of it. My comm didn't detect anything special about it. He absently ran his thumb over the rock as he spoke.

"The world was called Fregeja," he began. "They had no oracle, as your world does. It was rather a god of pathways, reaching his tendrils out to other worlds. He could not be permitted to continue, and lesser efforts to eliminate him had failed. I deployed there with the Sixth Extermination Fleet aboard the battleship *Tjoras*."

The moonlight gave Val's face a cruel cast as he told his story in the heart of Kives's temple.

"Your kind need a functioning biosphere to survive. When all else has failed— when you've averted every other death we could bring—we take that away from you. You've seen our ships. They are among the weakest the Eifni Organization is able to deploy. The *Tjoras* was armed with twenty antimatter cannons, ludicrously more powerful than the weapon we used against Horcutio's monsters. She was one of fifty battleships, each with an escort. We scoured Fregeja to the very stone."

He held up the rock, as if demonstrating.

"I was only a scholar at the time," he said, "investigating whether etheric dyads— the phenomena your primitive theology calls 'destiny'—could form across different realities. I was able to secure permission to fire the *Tjoras*'s weaponry, selecting a small city as my target. Call me murderer if you wish. When the operation had concluded, I visited the impact site and selected a particular stone. Perhaps, I thought, it might have a destiny."

Val tossed the rock carelessly onto the roots.

"Or perhaps not. My offering to you."

He bared his teeth.

"We will kill you, Kives. But I've read your behavioral distribution. I know what motivates you. So—here's Lilith. You killed her, but she still lives. That is the future that Eifni will bring to your planet, for everyone under your care. Give them to us, and we will ensure an endless future of cause and effect. Or—you can attempt to kill us, as I assume you've killed our allies. When the last Eifni signal fades from Theria, you will face the extermination fleet, and that will be your final legacy."

Val closed the box with finality.

"Godsmile, Greatmother. I'm sure we'll learn your answer soon enough."

I snorted. "She's probably going to ambush us the minute we leave the temple."

Val tilted his head. "Too optimistic."

I focused my hearing and picked up the sound of running footsteps heading our direction.

"Should we get out of here or something?" I asked.

"If she wants us to hear her answer, it will find us wherever we go," Val replied. He didn't move.

The footsteps drew closer. One set of footsteps was closer, with several others behind. Val and I turned our backs on the tree to wait for Kives's messenger.

We didn't need to wait too long. He burst into the inner sanctum, a weather-beaten sailor type with a chest under one arm and a nasty wound on the other side.

He staggered to a halt in front of the tree, looking at us in panic.

"Help," he wheezed, then collapsed on the floor. The chest slipped out from under his arm, breaking on a conveniently placed stone.

My comm said he was dying, but the chest had fallen close to me. Was this Kives's message, then? I leaned over and gingerly nudged it over, revealing a folded sheet of parchment.

"Did she write us a letter?" I asked. "Weird-ass delivery method if so."

I slowly unfolded the parchment, then gasped in utter delight.

I blinked, just to make sure I wasn't imagining things. The parchment in my hands remained the same.

"You know what, Kives?" I said. "I'm not mad about getting killed anymore."

"Lilith," Val said resignedly.

"Don't worry, I'm still gonna kill her," I said. "But she got me a treasure map! We get to hunt real-life pirate treasure!"

Val narrowed his eyes. "A bribe of some kind?"

"Maybe these other guys will know."

The people chasing the wounded pirate had just entered the temple. I grudgingly lowered the treasure map. There would be time to obsess over it later.

Around the corner came a familiar figure carrying a torch and wearing a tricorn hat. As far as I knew, there was only one tricorn hat on this entire planet, and I had not parted with its new owner on the greatest of terms.

"Alright, Scumhorn, you've reached the end of the—" she said, then stopped dead when she saw me. "*Danou?!*"

I slowly raised the treasure map, blocking her view of my face. "Uh, who's that?"

The ring of a sword leaving a scabbard was her only answer.

Thinking quickly—quicker than ever, thanks to my new mental enhancements—I folded the map back, leaned down, and picked up a stick, which I brandished menacingly.

"Godsmile, Erid," I greeted the old sea captain. "Please don't kill me? We might get blood on the map."

"That's— You're—" she spluttered. "Why? Goddesses, I hate you *so much*."

"We can probably consider that Kives's revenge," Val said, emerging into the torchlight. "Godsmile, Captain Erid. Why were you pursuing this map?"

Erid stared at him suspiciously. "It's supposed to show the way to the sacred islands of Horcutio. They're chock-full of pirates these days, and it's my job to clear them out."

"Is that so." Val grinned in the torchlight.

I chuckled. "What a . . . *coincidence*."

About the Author

T. R. More is the author of the Godslayers series, originally released on Royal Road. Their passion for writing stems from the traumatizing memory of Professor Dan's dance moves in Philosophy 201. More previously worked with screaming children and now works with screaming computer programs. They live in Richland, Washington.

Podium

DISCOVER MORE

STORIES UNBOUND

PodiumEntertainment.com